Theft of Decks

Book Four

Lars Machmüller

CONTENTS

<u>DEDICATION</u>

When I was a kid, I used to get beat up for being a nerd. Heh. No surprise there. I was a pale, weird-ass shut-in, who preferred the company of his Commodore 64 and bike rides to the local library over "proper" hobbies like soccer and *checks notes* hanging out near the convenience store.

Today's a different world. There's a lot more to deal with. Information overload, so much division. Yet, one detail, I've found has changed entirely for the better.

Nerds stand up straight. Rightfully so. We have become numerous enough that we can no longer be dismissed. Instead, we can celebrate our obsessions openly and proudly. And no-where is this as obvious as in LitRPG.

For that, I thank you all. All you fellow nerds and weirdos in LitRPG? Don't ever change! You're the best. Together, we'll take over the world, any day now!

<u>HOW DID WE GET HERE?</u>

This is a question I ask myself often. My answer to date: it must be a mixture of misfortune, violence, and a refusal to quit. Oh, and a spattering of good luck. If that particular blend sounds illogical, well, so is our ascension to our current position.

For a while, our small group of four seemed destined to a fate of obscurity, poverty, and an early death on the Waves in Isarn. Then Chase came up with a "good" idea on how to earn a home for ourselves, a real life, and power. Things...spiraled downward from there. Entirely out of control. We found ourselves enslaved amidst the ranks of the armies of Light, promised violent deaths with no sign of reprieve. We planned to evade said fate, but, if I am to be honest, our odds were not promising.

Then our world view was turned upside down.

Chase met Arnault Cavinian. When I say "met," I should really say "was almost killed by." Even now, months and months after the incident, I fail to understand exactly what went down on that fateful day. A few details do stand out.

- The army we were attached to—a full Lightborn army—was slaughtered to the man.
- The one exception to that cause, one uncarded noble Lightborn healer, attached herself to our group.
- We earned a Deck of Darkness. Yes. The vaunted Deck of Darkness, thought lost for the ages. It granted us power, cards no one's seen for centuries, and one giant target on our backs.

Following that day, our journey has been one of momentous highs, life-threatening lows, and constant growth in strength, versatility, and the cards at our disposal. Although I realize that the list of our actions might seem slightly insane in hindsight, I swear, they seemed logical at the time.

First, we infiltrated the cathedral in Isarn and stole a Deck of Light. We also slew an inquisitor and made a few additional enemies. The latter part of this was unintentional.

Then we decided that the Elemental towers in Earth's Ward would become our home. Why not? They have excellent teachers, wonderful defenses, and loathe the Lightborn about as much as we do. Also, they have the Library of Earth's Ward! Imagine, the collected knowledge of Ordei, at our disposal.

Alas, it was not to be. We did earn our place, managed to clear the high bar of acceptance. Yet again, our string of good and bad luck collided impressively, as we uncovered a Lightborn conspiracy aiming for the theft of the Elemental Decks harbored within the towers. Quoting Kith, "We had to put them down. Stealing decks is *our* thing." Yet, while we did avert the heist, we also managed to out our own presence in the process.

For political reasons, that meant that we lost any chance at staying. Yet, the Elementalists didn't just kick us out of their home. No, they had higher hopes for us, and put us on our current path.

Earth's Ward. I miss it already. The schedules. The scholars. The *minds!* Someday, I shall return.

Yet, first, we needed to earn the support of the Furyborn. That part did not come easily. We were, in no particular order, derailed, ambushed, detained, tested, spied upon, nearly eaten, made to strip naked, tested again, spied upon again, and forced to stand up to a plain behemoth. That last one, frankly, should not be something anybody ever should have to experience. Yet, somehow, we muddled through and made it to the holiest of Furyborn places, Heart Halls. There, through another series of grueling tests and struggles, we earned the trust of their elders. And eventually, their support as well.

The path laid out by the High Elementalist is ambitious and, quite frankly, I did not like our odds at first. Yet, now, it looks like the end is just in sight.

While the Furyborn and the Elementals stand up to the Lightborn, we are going to create the real solution against their stranglehold on power in Ordei. We are going to build an *alternative!* We are going to found a home, open to anybody who does not care to stay under the steel-capped boots of Lightborn nobility.

With every single deck we amass, we improve the foundation of the Wellspring we will be able to erect. As of this moment, we have gathered four of all five decks. Our Wellspring, at this point, will already grant better bonuses and stronger Guardians than any existing Wellspring on Ordei. With the final one on board, we will be able to build a home that can stand the test of time. That can *last!*

One deck is still missing. The nigh-on mythical Liberty deck. We *need* it for our collection to be complete. For the gains and increases to match those that are currently only spoken of in stories. Finally—and I loathe that I need to add this detail— we need it for the Elementals and the Furyborn to officially throw their lot in with ours. As if we hadn't proved ourselves already.

For all that I complain, it does make sense. For the two powers to throw their full support our way, they need more than just proof of our capabilities. They need proof that our chosen path is actually viable. That we will be able to deliver.

For myself? I find the idea that a bunch of nobodies like ourselves might carve out the foundation for a new world order ridiculous, outlandish, and...utterly enticing. I will do anything to make it happen. Though, I will never admit as much to the others. Somebody needs to be the voice of reason here, at least on paper.

CARD REFRESHER FROM BOOK THREE CAN BE RE-VIEWED AT THE BACK OF THIS BOOK.

CHAPTER 1

I have complained. Too much. That was my hubris. Early today, my nemesis arrived. Wrapped in waxed paper, it was a gift from the Elemental towers. Their compiled "knowledge" on the lands of Liberty and its people. It is, in a word, horrifying. An assembled hodgepodge of information, notes, speculation, and smatterings of actual knowledge. I'm supposed to make sense of this? Before I am done with it, I will kill somebody.

They escaped like thieves in the night.

Not like actual thieves. They had extensive experience with that part. Getting away from a crime scene was rarely like in the stories, flitting from shadow to shadow, changing clothes and tripping up pursuit. Rather, it was more a question of blending into the crowd, having a safe haven prepared, and, as often as not, tossing a few copper drahms to the right city guard to look away.

No, this was storybook. Something that could have been cooked up by a mother spellbinding her children with fantasies concocted by her over-active imagination. Their group woke up in the middle of the night in Heart Halls, the forest-covered capital of the Furyborn, crept out the back door, and literally blended into the shadows as Chase activated his Circle of Darkness, hiding them from any watching eyes. As a ripple of shadows, they crept out into the night.

They had help. The cozy dwelling they had called home for the past couple of increasingly frustrating weeks, faking a retreat from the public eye, now held a group of Furyborn. Among these was a single Furyborn rogue holding a newly fledged Deck of Darkness. He'd be faking Chase's presence, granting any new wielders Dark cards from behind a curtain, keeping any spies from realizing the birds had left the nest.

Their escape wasn't painless, of course. The duration of Circle of Darkness was short, forcing them to move in stops and starts, locating hiding places along the way. Yet, Kith was there, his Shadow Master card granting him intangible shadow summons who flitted everywhere, alerting him to movement and allowing him to plot out the best possible path.

When Kith first earned his card, he'd earned a nosebleed from having to digest the sensory information stemming from two shadows at the same time. Since then, he had improved, a lot. At this point, with his Twice the Fun card, he'd learned how to call double the number of summons for three other cards *at the same time*. Some summons demanded more presence than others, though. Kith was up to three shadows circling around them all, keeping him fed with visual and auditory information, and claimed that he'd manage four any day now.

The visual of watching Kith practicing amidst a swirl of ghastly specters, and a disconcerting smile on his face, was wholly disturbing. Yet, the practical gains were impressive. At this point, he'd mastered having one shadow hovering far above for an aerial visual, while the two others ranged around their group in a wide circle, keeping them aware of any inbound issues.

Of course, it helped that the Furyborn elders had prepared for their escape as well, aiding them in any way they could. The northeastern path they took saw no roaming Furyborn patrols. Neither were they beset by any of the monstrous amalgamations of trees and wielders who strode the forest at all times, ready to inflict pain on any intruders.

Even so, when they finally reached the tall grasses demarcating the border between the bloodied grounds and the Lightborn lands, they released collective sighs, letting heavy burdens slip from their shoulders.

They'd made it away safely. Sinking into the tender, luscious grasses, they groaned, soft laughter and sighs being the only sound apart from the ever-present hum of nature.

"What's this? Trespassers?" A loud voice broke the silence.

As one, they leapt to their feet, weapons slipping from sheaths and cards shimmering on activation, as they turned on the intruder.

Serafine Valerian, erstwhile noble, now fellow delinquent, slipped into position. She shimmered with brightness as buffs and shields slid into effect, one after the other. A buckler on each arm, ready to deflect any physical attacks. Where usually the open airs and open smile along with the heart-shaped face framed by blonde curls of the Lightborn would make men stand taller, now, there was nothing but cold efficiency in her movements, a promise of death in her eyes.

Liam was on his feet in a second, armed and vigilant. The tall Lightborn, moonlight gleaming from his recently shaved head, looked nothing less than formidable; subtle waves of fiery light moving across the surface of his armor. His shield and truncheon were dead steady, and his eyes cold as his gaze roamed their surroundings.

Cilia, meanwhile, flung herself into position behind Liam. The go-to expression of the lithe, short, mixed-race girl with the dark, blue-tinged skin was a critical frown, as if she expected the world to try to pull a fast one on her. Here, it was turned into an aggressive snarl, as her hands roamed her belts, picking out the right crafted items to fling at the attacker.

Kith was a flurry of movement. A second ago, he'd been lying on his back in the grass. Now, the short, stocky Furyborn; with the wiry, unruly hair was scrambling away, hands grasping for his hand axes. Colors burned in his eyes, even as shapes burst into existence behind and around him, cards summoning life from nothing.

Chase remained in the grass. After months and months of constant training and combat, the lithe, agile Darkborn was in a shape where he'd be able to leave the rest of his group in the dust and be on his feet while the others were still struggling to get up, even if he only had one hand to help him. Apparently, he also had lower expectations than his companions, because he'd foreseen something of the sort. He rubbed his face, wondering whether he should let it all play out. It might be fun. However, the odds of somebody getting hurt were...well, not small. Speaking up at the top of his voice, he announced, "Nordon. You're an ass!"

At that name, the group froze. Kith started to curse under his breath, followed by Liam.

Cilia growled coldly, "Two seconds. I was *two seconds* from sending a droplet of fire your way. It would have melted the flesh off your bones, leaving you a charred mess. It would also have given our presence away. *Why*, Brewer Nordon, did you think this was a good idea?"

Entirely unrepentant, the culprit stood up from a nearby clump of grasses, dusting off his clothes. Nordon looked nothing like a person who'd even be *able* to hide. Rather, the full-length leather apron on top of a frame built for both frontline fighting and competitive eating looked like he might attack, and cackle while he did so. The fabulous dark waves of his hair and oiled beard announced that he could make a crazed attack look good, too. "I figured it'd be funny. I was wrong, though. It was *hilarious*!" He guffawed. "Besides, I had a new potion to test out. I wanted to see if it would obscure my presence from any roaming eyes. Looks like it worked." His grin didn't fade in the least from their collective glares. "Now, are you going to laze about forever, or do you want to get going?"

Eventually, despite his ribbing, Nordon was the one who took the longest to get going. He had, at a safe distance, his entire life's work packed away on two massive carts, each dragged by a caarnath, with an additional pack animal lumbering behind. The contents of the carts were a huge mess of crates and sacks in one cart, and, beneath a burlap covering, an absolute mess of glass, brass, and bronze that was the entirety of his brewing and distilling apparatus pulled apart and put into protective crates to protect them from the rigors of traveling.

As they journeyed, they did it at a caarnath's pace. To be fair, the large reptilian beasts were fast for their sort. Waggling his brows, Nordon intimated some sort of "secret feed" that made the trio disregard the usually languid and lumbering pace of their race. Together, their group rolled across the rolling plains in a meandering route to avoid the worst potholes and challenges of the terrain.

"I'll be honest," Kith said. "I don't get it. No offense, Nordon." He waved at the taller man. "But we could go twice as fast without you. Also, we're better able to hide than Stinky, Chewy, and Messy there." He gave a sideways at the caarnaths.

Cilia scoffed. "We've been planning this for almost a month. The fact that you haven't paid any attention is entirely on you. Nordon, I fully understand if you *are* offended. We can still dump Kith and move forward without him."

Ignoring the sputtering outburst from Kith, Nordon waved away the notion. "No offense taken," he said amiably. "He is right, of course. You'd be able to move a lot faster without me. Only…even if you ignore my questioning your scouting capabilities—"

"Please! You only spotted us because you knew we were coming." Kith scoffed.

Nordon ignored him. "I will claim that speed is not all. Most often, tactics and know-how beat speed. Over years, I have built up an expertise and network that—"

"He is a smuggler." Sera's tone did not hide her disdain for the profession. "He knows other criminals, who to bribe and who to avoid."

"That's…a rather harsh depiction of my qualities, Ms. Valerian." Nordon then chuckled. "Not entirely incorrect, but I do find that you're selling my talents short."

"Sorry, mate." Chase slid his arm around Sera's midriff. "You'd think that, after this long living with low-life scum like ourselves, Sera would have lowered her standards, but no. She's a work in progress."

Sera slapped his hand away. "*I* am a work in progress? At one point, we will have to compare notes, see who has come the furthest. But yes, I am being unduly harsh, Brewer Nordon.

Apologies. My disdain for your profession should not be taken out on you as a person."

"Especially when he's one of maybe a handful of persons on Ordei who actually know how to get us safely into Liberty territory," Cilia added drily.

"Thank you, Cilia," Nordon said. "That might be inflating my rarity slightly. A number of traders have connections with the Liberators, but your point is well-made. Liberty society is one of strict control, lots of rules and supervision—meaning, of course, that the black markets are alive and thriving. Also, learning how to meet up with their traders outside the border is one thing. Actually gaining access to their lands is something entirely different. I do hope you'll find that the slower rate of travel makes up for what I can bring to the table."

Cilia nodded, eyes blazing. "Oh, it will. Rest assured, once we hit Liberty lands, I'll have milked you *dry* of information. We will know things you didn't even realize you knew!"

Blinking, Nordon donned a stilted smile. "Should I be intrigued or afraid by that?"

In unison, Chase and Kith said, "Yes."

***

Despite the initial shock, and their precarious position right between the much-beset capital of the Furyborn and the troop-covered western edge of Lightborn lands, that first nighttime stretch of travel proved tense, but uneventful. According to Nordon, that wholly matched expectations. Yes, the Lightborn were clearly ramping up their military activities in response to the taunts of the Furyborn and their—very—public announcement that they now held Dark cards. However, the stretch of no-man's-land between the two territories extended for miles upon miles, most of which was rarely, if ever, patrolled. Besides that, they'd carefully calculated the date of their departure, aiming to leave before any larger troop movements would start to arrive.

Most of the march that first night was spent in slowly decreasing tension. Yet, as the sun emerged from beneath the horizon and throngs of Lightborn military failed to come forth, they slowly started focusing less on stressing about their situation and more about what had happened in between their last discussion and now.

"I'm aware that we haven't been able to talk properly about everything," Nordon mused, as he patted the neck of his caarnath. "Us sitting down in public to discuss eloping would rather ruin the surprise. It's also why I left Heart Halls three days ago, to hide any hint that we left together. So, could you maybe update me on anything that's happened since the elders told me about the plan?"

"I...will handle this one," Sera hurried out. "Otherwise, Kith will spend the entire time attempting to assuage his hurt feelings over you getting the drop on him."

"Lies!" Kith spat. "I don't even know what that ass-thing means!"

Sighing, she ignored him. "Before we talk about this, however, we will need to gather for a moment. Cilia? If you would?"

Cilia engaged her Heart card and they pulled in closer, allowing them to talk without the risk of any sound emerging for Nordon to hear. The carts rumbled on ahead of them, while they followed in a tight semicircle, shut off from the myriad natural sounds of the outside.

"Thank you," Sera said. "This is simply to reiterate the exact level of trust we have in Nordon and agree on how much to share and what not to share."

Kith snorted. "Trust? What's that?"

"It's what gets rubes killed." Chase smirked. "To be honest, I think he's on the level. And by that, I mean that the man is entirely in this for his own winnings, and to learn as much as he possibly can. That means we can trust him to be fully on our side for at least as long as he's got something to earn from us."

Cilia raised a finger. "Point. He is also a fellow scholar. He clearly values knowledge. Hence, anything we've learned from Arnault, we can hint at to keep him intrigued."

Liam added, frowning, "What does that mean, though? He knows we have the deck. That's enough to land us in trouble."

Sera nodded. "It means that, despite the fact that I would prefer to be open and upfront about our plans, we should limit how much we share with him. If, Light reveal him, he betrays us, we should keep everything involving the High Elementalist, Gunnha, and the exact scope of our future plans from him."

"That's easy, though. Because we don't really *have* any elaborate plans at the moment beyond snatching a Liberty deck." Liam shrugged. "I mean, that *was* the last thing they told us, right? The Elementals don't have the power to move directly against the Lightborn and support us out in the open—nothing new there. And Gunnha's hiding and making sure she and the other Dark wielders don't get caught."

"Liam, dear." Sera took a few long steps to rest her hand on his shoulders as they walked. "I know you like to compartmentalize." She met his eyes and winced. "To simplify situations. Sometimes, however, you would do good by thinking more about the larger issues. Because, yes, judging from the correspondence we managed to exchange with Gunnha before leaving, she and her fellow wielders are still avoiding notice. Yet, they are also expanding throughout Lightborn territory, granting more impoverished people cards, sending wielders to other villages where they are likely to escape attention from any inquisitors."

Liam ducked his head, looking like he felt a headache incoming. "See? This is why I try to keep things simple. *Don't...*" He turned toward Cilia, then shrugged sheepishly when he saw she wasn't about to do anything. "Please don't scold me. It's just...it gets so big. What does it mean to us?"

"A wide gamut of complications," Sera said softly, patting his shoulder. "Some negative, such as the fact that there are more people at risk of discovery. A growing web, with additional strands that can unravel and reveal the burgeoning increase of Dark wielders everywhere. However, there are also positive aspects in that the power of our allies grows...and we will have more friends to call upon and bring in, should we get that far."

"Okay, yeah. That makes sense," Liam admitted. "But what does it mean *right now*?"

Sera blinked. "I guess...well, nothing right this very moment. It is just something to keep in mind."

Liam huffed and turned his face away from Sera. "See? So much thinking for little gain. This is why I'm not a fan of capitalization!"

She halted in her tracks, staring at Liam's wide back as he kept striding away. "That is *not* what I said at all."

The others, who were treated to Liam's all-too-knowing wide smile, broke out in laughter.

Cilia waggled a finger at Liam. "Mean! Also, she's right. You should think more about the larger picture. Mostly because, when you do it, you occasionally come up with good ideas. You sell yourself short, when you shouldn't. Moving on. The same situation more or less applies to the Elementals. Yes, they are still stuck in the towers. However, they are also in that same strange pact of near-but-not-true-war with the Lightborn that still allows them to travel the lands mostly freely, trade and move about. Meaning, they *are* in a position where they'd be able to help somewhat, in the right situation. We just need to come up with what that could be and stay on top of it."

Grimacing, Liam nodded. "Okay. I get the point. We're not on our own anymore. Except, right now we are—and we've got Nordon to worry about."

Chase blew a raspberry. "We've already covered the basics. Don't tell him more than he needs to know. Lead him on with knowledge. Oh, and we make sure that he doesn't get his main prize until we're actually successful. That way, he's got every incentive to ensure that we get out alive. Anything else?"

When everybody else had answered in the negative, Cilia dropped the effect of her Heart card, letting the outside sounds back in. They caught up to Nordon, who was trudging alongside his cart backward, watching them all with a slight smile.

Before any of them spoke up, he held up a hand. "Just wanted to say something quickly. I mean, you guys seem like you've grown in power a bit. But...sometimes, you shouldn't rely too much on your cards. Because there's such a thing as lip-reading."

For a full minute, the only sound was the low-pitched grunting of the caarnath.

Nordon broke the silence with a full-bellied guffaw. "Aw. You should see your faces. I can't actually read lips. It's still a good point. Wise up, kids. Don't get yourselves cheated. So—you were talking about me? What was the verdict?"

they resolved the discussion amiably. nordon really was easygoing and didn't push the point. the anticipation of receiving dark cards, when they made it back out from liberty territory safely, was enough for him to promise any help he could deliver. also, they had one additional offer to make him to tide him over until they'd be able to give him the final payment for his assistance.

CHAPTER 2

"Lightborn Guardians. Estimated mid to mid-high diffi-culty. Low defense, medium speed. Allocate twelve ranged mass, two ranged hands, four melee mass. No hopefuls. Fifteen to twenty minutes effect, at most." What. The. Pits? There are more like these. Fifteen of the scraps of vellum, bundled up into one stack, clearly of a kind. The High Elementalist (or her scholars) figured *this* would be helpful to us? Why?

"Why? I mean, thank you. From the bottom of my heart. But *why?*" Nordon's voice was cracked and confused, for once bereft of the smooth layer of self-confidence.

Behind them, the caarnaths had been released from their burdens. The placid beasts chomped on the long grasses in the distance, looking entirely pleased with life. In the background, the sun baked down on a never-ending sea of grass, with them at the center. The promise of darkness and a relief from the constant heat of the day was still a few hours away.

"It's quite simple, really." Chase grinned, lounging inside the thirty-foot circle of grass they'd had the caarnaths stamp down for them. "You're about to get Furyborn cards. It's a bribe. A good one, too. You're delivering a lot. Or, at least you claim that you can deliver a lot, and we choose to believe you. So, here's a taste of what *you* are getting. Not the real thing, but...real enough to make a difference. So, go on. Hold out your hand."

"But...won't the Furyborn be upset? They're very selective about who earns cards in their lands."

Chase scoffed. "They gave us this deck with the clear understanding that we were aiming to *use* it, not just gather dust in my...okay, that analogy doesn't really make sense when the deck resides inside me. Even so, they knew I was going to use it, and use it I shall. So, take my hand, or I'm taking back the offer!"

Nordon leapt forward, face distorted in a panicked grimace. Then he grasped Chase's hand and held on tight.

After half a minute, Chase spoke up. "Now, I'm not afraid of familiarity, but I think you're making my girlfriend jealous."

Sera chortled. "No. No, I find all of this almost too amusing. Can we all hold your hand as we choose our cards from here on out? It looks comforting."

Chase smirked. "Not to me, it isn't. Big guy here has a stronger grasp than you'd think. I think he's a bit needy."

Dropping his shoulders like leaning into a punch, Nordon took two steps backward, gasping. "Whew. That never gets any less intense. Also, even though my mind was stuck in decision limbo, I *could* hear everything you say."

"Good. That was the intention." Chase beamed. "Get anything good?"

"Anything good?" Nordon boomed. "Some people are willing to spend *years* risking their lives to earn Furyborn cards. You offer them to me as a...tiny bonus, and you ask if I got anything good?" He shook his head in disbelief. "Yes! It's amazing! And I feel like, for some reason, I should be upset about it!"

In passing, Liam punched his shoulder, making him cry out. "Get used to it. That's life with Chase for you. Even when he's nice, he'll make you mad."

Nordon's eyes were still far away. Eventually, he cleared his throat. His musing voice gained in power and volume as he spoke. "Yes. I got something good. Exactly what, I will not be able to show you until we arrive and I can put up my still. But expect to be overwhelmed!"

"There you go, making a promise sound like a threat." Chase snapped his fingers. "You'll fit right in. Now. We've promised Cilia and Sera some very exhaustive and detailed testing of some of our new cards—"

"There will be calculations, and lots of them." Sera smirked, to widespread groans.

"Fortunately," Chase continued, "we've got other details to go over first—the plans for the coming...how long do we expect this journey to take, Nordon?"

"Depending on how many detours we need to take and the speed of our beasts, anything from three to five weeks."

"Okay. We can work with that. Three to five weeks. Obviously, we need to have guard duty overnight."

Nordon held up his hands. "I actually have a few crafted items—traps, really—that can alert us to anything creeping within range."

"Huh. That sounds pretty amazing. What's the range?"

"Six hundred feet, give or take. I need to place the trap tokens in a circle first, though, which is a bit of a pain."

Sera nodded. "I can see that. It's nearly a full mile of walking."

"We were *not* doing math, yet," Kith scolded. "But I love it. It means I won't have to stay up for all of us."

"Sure. I still say we need to keep one guard at all times to catch anything at range," Chase said.

Kith, Liam, and, surprisingly, Nordon all groaned in concert.

Chase scolded, "Don't make me be the responsible one. I'm not cut out for it. But we've been ambushed enough times that we definitely want the added security."

"How often? Why?" Nordon asked, clearly at unease.

Chase started to count on his fingers, but ran out. "Yes. I think the answer is yes. For many different reasons."

Shooting sidelong glances at the others, Nordon eventually hazarded, "Is it too late to ask for a raise?"

Chase rolled his eyes. "Guards at night. Apart from that, we take turns with chores, obviously."

"Also, *somebody* is no longer exempt from cooking," Kith added drily.

With a flourish, Chase activated Clothed in Living Light, giving him two thumbs-up in response, one shining brilliantly. "Fair's fair. Though I expect it'll be a while before anybody enjoys my cooking, since I never learned in the first place. That, however, leaves us with the question of what we're doing along the way."

"We're...traveling?" Nordon said. "It's not like we'll have plenty of downtime. What little time we don't use for traveling, we'll use for chores, gathering stuff to add to the rations, which are *not* that interesting, or maintaining our gear."

"There are many ways I could say this. I'll just start with 'no.' First off, you don't know Cil, if you think we're going to spend a full month traveling without training and retaining our edge."

Cilia gave a perfunctory nod. "There's a reason we're still alive. I am that reason. Nobody shirks."

"What she said," Chase intoned with a half-bow. "Second. Like I mentioned earlier, we have new cards that we need to incorporate into our routine. Power is worth nothing if we don't know how to use it properly and efficiently. Finally." He concentrated and lifted his shirt a bit, displaying a Light card fading away, replaced by the thorny frameset of a Fury card on his stomach. "I got myself *this*."

[**Home Turf Advantage**
Epic, Fury rogue
Tier three
Passive, permanent
Any successful rogue is a distrustful rogue. They need to be alert, awake, perceptive, and cautious, ready to catch any

danger to themselves and their kin. Yet, nobody can live their life in constant alertness without losing their edge.

This card, when activated, allows the rogue, and anybody in their group, added benefits while resting. They will recuperate easier, their wounds close faster, and they will need less sleep to stay sharp. Also, any food and drink consumed will be more nourishing.

"It's like I said. Food just doesn't taste the same when you're away from home."]

"But...that's ridiculous."

"Ridiculously helpful, perhaps." Chase grinned. "Point being, we have at least a couple of extra hours a day, quite often in near dark, where we can do what we want. What are we doing? For me, I have found myself struggling to keep up fully with my increased attributes in protracted battles. Mentally, that is. Apart from our team practice, I'll probably resign myself to hours of self-torture through mental exercises, attempting to catch up."

"I will focus on planning and overseeing our training, like you said." Cilia nodded at Chase. "We all need to get used to our new cards, and decide which approaches work best. For me, I also have a backpack filled with, so far, unhelpful information about the Liberty lands to pick apart for useful knowledge, Nordon to question, and a couple of new cards that will absolutely take some getting used to." She closed her eyes and grimaced.

The others shared questioning looks. Liam was about to ask something, when the soil beneath Cilia started to rise. Within fifteen seconds, the loose earth solidified into something resembling clay, eventually rising into a large earthen seat, still with a solid covering of grass on top.

Cilia sat down in a regal motion, ignoring the sweat on her brow. She tapped her right leg, then recited the details.

[**Touch Grass**
Uncommon, Fury crafter
Tier four
Active, medium duration
In many instances, the crafting itself isn't what matters, but the circumstances surrounding it. An item crafted in wind and rain with a rotting tree stump for a table will inevitably be worse quality than one made in a warm house. This card allows you to sense, shape, and direct the soil and plants around you with a speed and efficacy depending on your Mental Power.
Long cooldown
"No crafting bench, dear? Ah, but nature provides. It always does."]

"Like this. We all have full complements of droplets ready, and the elders gifted me with a complete set of leatherworking tools to add to what I got from Master Benneth. Once I know best how to make use of the cards at my disposal, I shall see if I am able to come up with something else on our journeys that can make a *real* difference, or I'll have to wait for a proper setup and better materials to work on adding to our equipment."

Liam grunted. "Sounds good. It'll be hard work for me—and a lot of help from Cil. Most of my new cards are passives, so that's just getting used to when to use them. But some of them will definitely need a good deal of practice. Like how to use Helping Step in a fight. Kith. Punch Chase, please."

Chase yelled in protest, while Kith leapt to the task, eager to help.

In the blink of an eye, Liam disappeared, reappearing right next to Chase in time to fend off Kith's fist.

[Helping Step
Rare, Light fighter
Tier four
Active, very short duration
Being of the Light means being there for those in need. This card, when activated, lets you move to anybody in your group currently engaged in a fight in the blink of an eye. It will, at most, let you travel forty-five feet.
"Surrender, Darkspawn. There is no point on this battle-field I do not command."]

"Will you please stop that? I'm not a target dummy!" Chase protested.

Kith smirked. "Yeah. He's a regular dummy. Now, for me, it will also be hard training. But I will also have to spend quite a bit of time on my new acquisitions." His mouth quirked up minutely as he looked at Nordon.

Nordon blinked, then started glancing around himself. "You planning something? You really don't have to show off on my account. It's— *What's that damn thing?*" That last part he shouted at the edge of their cleared circle of grass, where a small, tooth-filled head poked out of the grasses.

"Shush, you," Kith said with a good deal of satisfaction. "Don't you scare poor Spike."

"Spike? Was that the best you could come up with?" Liam smirked.

"He likes it!" Kith shrugged. "Besides. It suits him. Doesn't it?"

There was no denying that. Regardless what else you could come up with, the animal was spiky. In fact, that was the one dominant factor about the beast. About six feet long, the brownish beast stood no more than a foot tall and managed to look entirely unthreatening, even with long spikes bristling from his entire body. The short, soft blend between a hedgehog and a giant squirrel carefully snuffled at Kith's hand, accepting a piece of fruit from him.

"Wait a minute. Is that a bonded beast? You actually got the elders to grant you a bonded Guardian?" Nordon knelt to look closer at him. "What can he do? I mean, what, or how does it work?"

"That's part of what I need to figure out. The card's fairly simple."

[Ties That Bind
Rare, Fury summoner
Tier two
Passive, permanent
Most summons are temporary, restricted to when the card is active. Yet, with the right choices for a Wellspring, any summoner earning new cards may choose a card like this. With permission from the owner of the Wellspring, you will be able to bond with any resident Guardian. This Guardian will then be permanently attached to you like a regular summon, until the Ænima powering it runs out. The effect of this card will remain active, regardless whether you switch to another Tier two card.

In addition to the Guardian's own attributes, it will be awarded a permanent increase to its Agility, with one point for each three points of your own Agility.

"What do you mean, I cannot summon this again if it dies? Go away, you ridiculous little man." The summoner of Naz has an ugly eye-opener.]

"Meaning, Spike here's going to be a hell of a lot harder to catch than regular dozing rodents. Also, yes. Dozing rodents are their official name, not my fault. It comes from the soapy... Urgh, Cil, help me here. That sleepy effect?"

"Soporific."

"Yes, thank you. Soporific poison in his spikes. Also, he can do *this.*"

The gentle beast looked straight at Nordon, then unhinged its jaw, enlarging its mouth to three times the size.

Nordon scrambled back in shock. "Gah. Stop it. Why are you *like* this?"

Sera sniffed. "It is a rite of passage. I am so sorry. Or, I would be. Rather, I am delighted that I am not the target anymore."

With no sign of shame whatsoever, Kith beamed at the larger man. "Yep. That's it. I'm definitely not getting back at you for catching me off guard earlier. That would just be childish."

Chase cleared his throat. "Speaking of childish, didn't you—"

A shape slammed soundlessly down to the ground in front of Nordon.

Nordon reeled back, uncommonly high-pitched voice blurting, "Die in a fire!"

The new arrival looked small and ragged around the edges. It grew more impressive as it stretched, expanding its wings and tilting its head. The shape of the hunting bird seemed to solidify, showing a proud, streamlined form nearly four feet tall, a gleaming plumage of brown and orange tones and a deadly-looking beak. It cawed softly, its tone questioning, as the four-inch-long talons kept it perfectly balanced.

"And *now* we're even," Kith announced merrily. "Meet Radine. My second bonded Guardian."

"We're *not* even," Nordon sputtered. Then his lips quirked up in an unpleasant grimace. "But let's move on and let's all forget this happened...*for now*." That last part, he murmured just loud enough for everybody to hear.

Awkwardly, Chase cleared his throat. "You know what I find disconcerting?" he asked nobody in particular.

"I'll go with everything that just happened," Liam said drily.

"Yes, but no. The disturbing part is that this is the first ever normal name Kith's ever used for any of his summons. Remember the Tainted Earth? It's been named Bulky, Stacks, and...Lumpster, unless I remember wrong. Why, all of a sudden, would he name something with an entirely common girl's name?"

"Well, I seem to remember somebody named Radine back in Isarn," Liam mused.

"What can I do?" Kith beamed happily. "It just fit so well. Radine, just like her namesake, looks beautiful and proud, but is really dangerous, and has some secrets that..." He coughed into his hand. "Will surprise you."

"I also seem to recall that she left you with a couple of ugly scars," Liam added.

"True. Let's hope it's not entirely too prophetic, shall we?" He grinned. "Anyway, I have these two beauties and a few new cards to get used to. Both when I'm off on my own, and while I'm playing with you. That will keep me busy for a good long while."

"That leaves just Nordon and myself, then." Sera tapped her leg contemplatively, a tight frown building. "As before, I find myself falling behind in Steps. I am only on the nineteenth Step."

Nordon made a strangled noise in his throat.

"You will get used to it, if you stay near us for long. I never truly expected to hit Tier two, yet here we are," she told him with an understanding smile, before turning back to the others. "There is only one new card that will take some real getting used to." Her left arm flashed under her shirt, and she focused on the empty spot of soil right at the center of their messy half-circle.

On the ground, the downtrodden stalks of grass started to slither and move, being swiftly subsumed by a growth emerging from below. Before ten seconds had passed, a two-foot-tall, near-perfect cone of a wiry, hardy growth, filled with three-inch-long thorns had emerged into their midst. Then she outlined the details.

[**Nature's Shield**
Uncommon, Fury healer
Tier two
Instant, medium duration
Part of a healer's job is taking care of damage. Yet, an even better approach is ensuring that the damage never happens in the first place. Some healers weaken enemies or shield their allies to ensure the damaging blows can never land. Yet, ensuring that the enemy never arrives in the first place is surely preferable to either approach. Upon activation of this card, the wielder calls upon nature to raise, shape, and place a few lengths of thorny underbrush. The height and toughness of the raised plants depend on the Mental Power of the healer.

"Oh, you're stuck? How sad. Maybe you shouldn't have tried to kill my friends!"]

Liam whistled softly, and stepped forward, wincing as a tiny drop of blood started to trickle from the prick of the thorn. He grabbed onto the bush and pulled hard, grunting quietly before he managed to tear one of the long, vine-like growths in two. "Sturdy."

"They are?" Sera beamed at him. "Wonderful. I can only imagine what they would do to somebody who is *not* specialized in Strength and Toughness. Regardless, this will be my main project for myself and in group training, properly incorporating the thorns into our defenses. Apart from that, I will be the one in charge of crunching the numbers for our cards, figuring out what works best and what doesn't."

"Thank you," Chase mouthed silently at her.

"I...think I've heard enough." Nordon wore an inscrutable expression. "You are telling me, that, looking at a situation where you'll be going off into the unknown, in a stressful position, you look at the chance to get a bit of downtime and instead say, 'No. I'll work even harder.'"

Chase shrugged. "I'll be honest, man. If we hadn't been mostly living like that, we'd be dead already. Constantly improving and bitching over Cil as a mean taskmaster is what's kept us going so far."

Cilia nodded darkly. "And don't you forget it!"

Nordon flung his hands up in the air. "All right. Screw it. Count me in!"

Liam looked at the tall crafter. Then at his bulk, which, although impressive, definitely veered more toward somebody who enjoyed his own ales than any sort of fighter. "You're going to start training with us?"

He started to laugh. Deep peals of laughter that led to a wheezing, coughing fit as he bent in two. Holding up a hand, he eventually managed a hoarse, "Darkness hide my sins, *no*. Not in a million lifetimes. But, I will use the spare time that card of Chase's gives us for something else than snoozing. Maybe I'll be trying to create some new recipes, for teas and...some horrible ideas I'd dropped for being too ridiculous. I might not be able to keep up with you crazies...but perhaps I can help stir the pot a bit."

Upper lip quirking up in a half-smile, Kith whispered to Chase, "What have we done?"

Chase chuckled, ignoring him. "Glad to have you on board. Give it your all. And if that requires you getting back at Kith for taking a bit of teasing too far? Go right ahead."

"Oh, come on now!"

CHAPTER 3

"Lightborn conscripts. Twenty hopefuls, twenty melee mass, only one hand. No ranged. Estimated low difficulty. Low defense, medium speed. Allocate six ranged hands, plus an equal number of hopefuls. At least thirty minutes effect. Casualties will be taken out of your hide, Hand Borenious." Okay. I think I'm starting to see the point here. That last part about the casualties is obviously a personal addition. But the rest revolves around the Liberty defenses. The Liberty line is attacked, or approached, by forty Lightborn people. Twenty of those are uncarded, twenty Tier-ones and one Tier-two. My question is then: which "effect" is insane enough that six ranged fighters and six "hopefuls" are able to stand against forty damn Lightborn? That of the fog clouds?

"**K**ith. It's time we had the talk," Cilia announced loudly, following an underwhelming evening meal, where they discovered exactly which level of luxury Nordon had afforded for himself and the rest in provisions and quality of food. The answer was "little to nothing."

Kith snorted, shooting a lopsided grin back at her. "All right, Cil. I'll tell you all about it. You see, when a girl and boy are bored and possibly drunk, they—"

"Stop." She held up a hand. Her eyes were serious and challenging. She called out to Nordon. "Apologies for this, but this is personal." A brief flash on her heart indicated that she'd hidden them all behind the muting effect of her Heart card.

Nordon, to his credit, shrugged and started to gather the bowls to clean them.

"All right, Cil. If it's serious, it's serious. What's the rub?" Kith scratched his head, causing his unruly hairdo to stand up even further. Colors blazed agitatedly in his sclera.

Cilia led them in silence until they were well out of sight of Nordon. She turned around, and said, softly, but directly, "You are going to explain exactly what your Heart card does. And you are going to leave nothing out."

Kith blinked, then sniffed. "I— Nah. That's not happening, Cil. I told you. It's personal and my *own* issue! Besides, it sucks."

Chase spoke up, unease and confusion written clearly on his face. "Cil! This isn't us. If Kith doesn't want to tell, he doesn't have to."

"He does. *Because he's lying to us!*" Her snapped words broke any hint of joviality that might have been left in the air. "Look at him."

Kith glared at her defiantly, but he didn't outright gainsay her.

Cilia's voice proceeded, softer and more intimate than her usual manners. "You saved my life when I was just a little girl. That was the first time, but it was far from the last. You're *family*. You think that I am going to just let this lie, Kith?" When he didn't say anything, she continued, scowling. "Be like that. I will tell you all what I've concluded so far, and then, Kith, you are going to tell me, to my face, that I am right."

Ignoring his disdainful snort, she stabbed a finger at him, as if it were a weapon. "On several occasions over the years, Kith, you've outdone yourself. Managed to succeed in situations that should really have seen you caught, beaten, or killed. When that prig of a guardsman, Hebitus, caught hold of you back near the harbor. That day where Grinning Harriet went looking for us all on the Waves, and you said you'd lead her away. When we fought the gaborn. On other occasions, too. Situations, where you managed to not only survive, but excel against all odds."

Liam spoke up softly. "Cil. We've *all* succeeded against all odds. That's what surviving on the Waves is!"

Chase, meanwhile, looked troubled, mouth turning downward, eyes flickering as if he were coming to a conclusion, and didn't much like it.

Cilia shook her head. "That was what I thought at first. I don't know when I started noticing, really. After our fight with the inquisitor in the cathedral of Isarn, perhaps. You matched Chase for speed and Liam for staying power, keeping up in a battle that should've seen you outmatched. And afterward? You were *tired*."

"We were *all* drained after that fight, Cil," Liam insisted.

"No." Chase looked as though he wanted to shout, or cry, or kill somebody. "I remember. The backlash was bad for me, when my buffs stopped working all at once. But Kith wasn't just tired, like he'd worked hard. He looked dead on his feet. Older."

"Please don't," Kith said. "Just stop." He sounded fragile.

Chase pressed on. "It's only gotten worse since. When Instructor Boneridge set that huge salamander on us in the towers. After the battle with the behemoth on the carved plains. Regular battles are okay. But you've looked more and more drained on these occasions. And it hasn't left you afterward."

"When we went up against all those Lightborn who were going to drag us all away into slavery," Cilia said softly, "you matched Chase for speed. I saw it. You kept up with him, in control, speed, and staying power, even when he was running on the highest possible boosts and should, by all rights, leave *all* of us behind. And afterward...you were left with your first grey hairs."

Kith's hand flew to his head.

"There are only a few. But they weren't there before the fight. And this is why I'm not letting it go. There is a cost, right? One which you are paying to keep us all alive?" Her voice broke at the end.

Kith looked at the ground. He closed his eyes and didn't say anything for a long while. Eventually, with a huff, he laughed. "This is exactly why I didn't tell you, you know. Because you're going to tell me to stop using it. Then, I'm going to ignore you, and we're going to have a nice, big fight about it. Can't we just skip the entire thing and move on to acting like there's nothing to talk about?"

Sera spoke up for the first time. "Not if this is something that affects all of us. Which it will, if the cost is going to have an effect on you. Tell us, Kith. They are—I am—your family. Please."

Kith shook his head sadly. "That's the entire problem, you bloody idiots."

The insult was so bereft of emotion, nobody even reacted.

"You *are* family. That's the Fire-scoured point!" He did look tired now. Like he was about to keel over and sleep for a month. He squatted and put his head between his hands. He started speaking in low tones, dully at first, but with increasing emotion. "You know how some claim that Heart cards are not random? That's true for me. Right from the start, I knew this fit me perfectly. Too well! I was never strong enough like Liam, fast enough like Chase, or clever enough like you, Cil. So, when I needed to, I made do. Because I *will* do my part."

"You actually think any of us believe you're not pulling your weight?" Chase asked incredulously.

"Not the point. Point is, you've all kept my ass alive so far, and I'm not backing down. I'm keeping you safe, whatever the cost. At some point in the future, I might be strong enough that I'll be able to stand on my own, and do what's needed, without this aid. For now, I won't refrain to use it, if I think it's needed."

Cilia took a few steps forward, knelt and looked him straight in the eye. "This is where you tell us, Kith."

He hesitated, then asked, "Mind using your card, Sera? The one that improves our Heart cards."

"Done."

He took a deep breath, and started to recite.

[Cost of Life
Heart card

Medium duration

At what cost, power? This is a question many ask themselves. You do not need to. You know the price. Whenever you need to, you have power, right at your fingertips. Upon activation of this card, your attributes are doubled for the full duration of the card, with no instant detrimental effects afterward. The only detraction? Every activation will cost you a year of your life force.

Cost of Life will now also increase the rarity of all your cards by one for the full duration.

Long cooldown

"It whispers, does it not? That pulse, that promise, of strength and power, right at your disposal. You need only reach out."]

"A year? Light scour my soul. A year? *Kith, you stupid little rat! I—*" Liam pushed his fist into his mouth and bit down hard.

"How many times have you used it, Kith?" Sera asked softly.

"Ten, I think. No. Eleven." He snorted. "I think I'm starting to get ahead of the game, though. Remember what Instructor Boneridge said about Tiering up and lifespan? If I hit Tier five, that should earn me another fifty years to work with. If it works like that, of course." He shrugged, still squatting, talking at the ground. "There you have it, Cil. Happy now?"

"You know I'm not, you dolt. But…I *am* glad that you finally told us. Also, at least now I know what we are aiming for."

"Huh?" Kith frowned.

"You said it yourself. You need to get stronger, to the point where you'll never have to use the card again. That, I guess, will be the plan for the near future. Then, getting us all to Tier five, for starters, so those wasted years won't have that much of an impact."

"But—"

"But nothing. You are an inconsiderate, stubborn ass, you have a horrible sense of humor, your taste in girls is beyond questionable, and you could do with better personal hygiene. Even so, you remain family, and I'm not letting you waste away, when a little extra work would have made a difference."

"Seriously? That's all you're saying?" He looked from Cilia to the others. They in turn either nodded or shrugged. He gaped, then announced loudly, if hoarsely, "Well, Fury rend you all! I do *not* smell! Whew. Okay, maybe a little." He went silent, then continued, voice cracking. "Radine spotted a stream back here. I'll…I think I'll go scrub up a bit."

As one, they pretended not to notice the tears streaming down his face.

The next few days faded away to nothing, caught in an emergent pattern of marching, practice, and (mostly) self-imposed masochism. Chase's card meant that they woke up with the sun, much-used muscles feeling rested even when they damn well knew they should still be sore. Then, they spent a short while preparing for the day's march, feeding the caarnaths and eating.

The marching was, with rare few exceptions, dull, wearying, and uneventful. They marched the endless eddies of the green sea, constantly on the lookout, but rarely in an actual state of alarm.

Their scouts helped. Kith's recent additions to his menagerie were, in his own words, not the same as his summons. Where his shades were entirely subservient to him and integrated into his mind as additional layers of his own impressions and senses, the bound Guardians were more personalities of their own, linked with him and holding entire conversations inside his mind, though with elaborate emotional messages rather than actual words.

Spike, it turned out, was curious, constantly on the move, eternally alert, and surprisingly affectionate. He'd tramp down elaborate paths in the grasslands and look out for predators, always circling back for pets, affection, and affirmation that he was doing a good job.

Meanwhile, Radine was aloft, floating on the winds high enough above them that they often had trouble seeing her. She'd send Kith mental images of the best routes, of any potential trouble or threats and bad terrain. One important detail they learned was that there were actually large bodies of Lightborn on the move, but they were mostly far to the south.

They learned two additional things about her, which only led to Kith doubling down on the name being a perfect fit. One, she was actually an innate illusionist. Although she was unable to truly control or alter the illusionary copy, her actual, invisible body was about a dozen feet from the illusion. Two, she was a tease. If she wasn't leading them through the occasional muddy pit, she loved surprising them, diving to rip her illusionary body right through them, or hitting them with the breeze from her actual body passing them in near-misses.

Even with them cursing Radine on a constant basis, the two Guardians added to the blend of their scouting capabilities in a way that allowed them to travel faster and safer. They'd stop for a quick rest about noon and then be off again for an interminable march until early evening. Then, they'd spend a short while foraging and performing whatever small repairs were needed.

In the evening, they embarked on the actual work. At first, they spent most of their time by themselves, as they tried to master the specifics of their new cards. Then, once they had the basics down, they expanded to teams of two or more, changing their compositions to get the most amount of experience and familiarity. They trained, experimented, and honed their existing skills and new cards.

Sera challenged Liam to see how well her thorns would hold up as a last-second recourse against a charging enemy. The answer was "not good." The vines needed precious seconds to settle before they were truly bothersome. Then, she linked together with Cilia instead, seeing how well they'd be able to combine their cards to shape the terrain into something difficult for enemies to approach. That experiment was almost scarily efficient. Within a limited space, their combined efforts could remodel a decent area with potholes, trenches, and layers of thorny vines that would be hard to pierce for anything smaller than a gaborn, all handled in short seconds. Of course, then Chase had to go and show off, using his new One with the Soil card.

[**One with the Soil**
Epic, Fury rogue
Tier four
Instant, long duration
The stories all tell us about the massive fireballs, the summoned swarms of locusts, and ground-breaking attack cards. Yet, they neglect to remember one thing: that is not how most fights are won or lost. The slip of a foot. A patch of gravel or slippery mud. These are the small things that spell the end for a huge number of fighters. With this card, you and your group will retain perfect balance, regardless of footing and weather.
"Dear Lord Baluz. It takes more than a punch to the chin, a muddy slope, a dozen summoned simians, and an Agility debuff to throw me off my feet. Admittedly, not that much more. Call it a tie?"]

By itself, it granted their entire group excellent balance, even up against mud or bumpy terrain. Combined with his high Agility, it gave Chase insane control of his movement, allowing him to slither through their combined defenses like they weren't even there.

They got creative after that.

Kith tried to work alone in an attempt to figure out how best to arrange his menagerie against imaginary enemies. That was a constant series of stops and starts and quite a bit of cursing, as he had to come up with efficient ways to summon and mentally command all his summons and Guardians in the proper order. He barely even used his other cards at first, instead working on formations and optimal summoning to ensure he'd be able to react properly. Cilia, true to her word, was all over him, pushing him to work harder and smarter.

Chase, when he wasn't annoying Sera and Cilia, kept to his self-prescribed mental training, toiling through every mental exercise they'd amassed at this point, only pausing for some rare stretches and physical exercises to reset his mindset. Because he didn't need to activate Home Turf Advantage until they had to sleep, he was able to keep Spoils of the Undeserving active during the entire day. Before the third day was over, he earned the first point to Mental Power, showing that the card was still worth gold.

Cilia, when she wasn't joining forces with Sera or harassing Kith, spent her entire time trying to learn how to abuse the Touch Grass card to improve her crafting capabilities while away from an actual workstation. She quickly found that she was able to raise, smooth, and harden a surprisingly high-quality worktable, create effective drying racks, even harden clay to the point where they could work as containers to hold solutions needing to be applied to leather. It would not help her create some truly high-quality items, but she concluded that it would be sufficient to allow her to experiment—especially once Kith had Spike start to hunt nearby animals for their skins.

Liam, meanwhile, was chomping at the bit for them to finish their initial exercises so they could get deep into the team practices where he'd be able to properly use and fine-tune his new cards. He practiced the use of his Helping Step card endlessly, but concluded rather fast that he would need the added stress of movement and conflict, even if fake, to adjust properly. Until then, he paired up where he could, or simply resigned himself to endlessly pushing himself with physical exercise. He managed to land a single increase to Agility during this and counted himself lucky.

Nordon, meanwhile, cooked. That was it. Most of his brewing paraphernalia he kept tidied away and protected. Instead, he unpacked four differently sized cookpots—one a massive cauldron that had to weigh at least a hundred pounds—and a handful of knives, mortars, and other smaller items, and went to work. At first, he didn't even explain anything he was doing. He just cut, boiled, mashed and mixed, tasted, sniffed and cursed. Sometimes, he poured an entire pot onto the ground as they left, while at other times, he'd pour the contents into another container. After three days, he did ask for Kith to have Spike drag in a live beast, if possible. For taste testing. This, of course, didn't comfort anybody.

Just before noon on the third day of travels, the cart exploded.

They were traveling at a rather sedate pace. In the early morning, Radine had lured them into a sinkhole, which trapped one of the carts for half an hour. Kith had spent the rest of the time looking like a thundercloud as he kept explaining to his new Guardian that, no, it was neither funny nor acceptable.

They were sweaty and covered in mud. By unspoken agreement, they'd decided that they would allow themselves a slower pace. Kith had just earned a series of approving groans with the announcement that they'd reach a small stream within the next half hour, and a few smiles emerged here and there, when a loud, ringing clang erupted from the hindmost cart, followed by a caustic mess bursting into being.

As one, they grasped for weapons as cards flashed everywhere and they went into combat mode, looking about for attackers. The caarnath reacted more animalistically, emitting a deep, unsettled hiss, pulling down its head and starting to run off to one side as fast as it could, with the cart still attached, bumping across the uneven plains.

"Stop the cart!" Nordon cried. "It's not an attack!"

Liam wavered for a second, then flung himself after the stampeding beast. He grasped onto the beast's harness and tried to set his feet. Instead, he was dragged after the beast as it roamed out of control. Yet, after less than a hundred feet with Liam still dragging its heavy head down, it slowed down and eventually stopped.

Nordon ran after him along with the others, panting, holding one hand up. "Wait. I can explain. Just let me—"

"Shut it," Kith snapped, flinging both hands out to grasp his hand axes. He closed his eyes, then snarled, and his Tainted Earth started to ooze into being on the soil. "Whatever happened, it's pissed off some nearby Guardians. We're about to be under attack!"

Chase cursed, looking at the single cart behind them and the other one way ahead of them. He made a snap decision. "Kith. Move up to Liam, dig in, get your eyes out and tell us what's coming. We all move up to you, defend there."

The following minute was a tense, anxious affair as Chase, Nordon, Sera, and Cilia escorted the other caarnaths and the second cart to where the first panicked beast was about to run off again. All around them, snarls and high-pitched whines emerged, promising an incoming avalanche of bestial attackers.

When the attack came, it was entirely underwhelming. In a near-laughing voice filled with incredulity, Kith shouted, "Pigs! It's just pigs!"

In actuality, they were boars. A sounder of boars, nearly two dozen of them. Most were female, with a few of the young ones having long, glowing tusks. All of them were large and fast. Emerging and disappearing back into the tall grasses like phantoms, they were by no means "just pigs" and should have been a disconcerting match-up for anybody.

In practice, they ended up being ridiculously easy to handle. The Tainted Earth Kith summoned stood at the center of their chosen defensive spot. Its widespread, malformed shape kept solid under their feet while grasping at, slowing, or outright stopping any offensive piggy.

Kith stood farther back, in constant contact with Spike and Radine, calling out when beasts moved against them.

Any boar that managed to fight past the Tainted Earth was met by Liam. His Become the Clay card on top of his Draining Ward sapped their Agility and increased his defense to where even a well-placed bite barely scratched him.

Sera was constantly circling to keep an active view of the battlefield, ready to fend off any attackers with her twin bucklers, every buff up and aiding, while her Cry for Blood card was at her beck and call, ready to call magical shields into being the moment it was needed.

Meanwhile, Cilia crawled on top of the cart, readying droplets for attack.

Below her, Nordon huddled, having gathered the caarnaths together, trying to keep them calm.

Yet, a single young boar managed to make it past the grasping soil of the Tainted Earth and Liam to attack Sera. Only, instead of getting bowled over by the beast, Sera managed to land a ringing blow to its head with her buckler, flinging it to the ground.

Chase called out in triumph. "Don't kill them! They're weak! Kith, have Spike knock out any boar he sees. The rest of you, knock them down if you can." Then he dove out into the grasses to add chaos among the massing boars.

They sent uncertain glances after him in response, but did as he asked. Shortly, they realized that, yes, the animals were actually rather weak. Whether it was due to their own inflated attributes or their numerous overlapping buffs and training, the animals presented no real challenge. They knocked them down, allowing for the Tainted Earth to grasp the weakened beasts.

Finally, they were left staring off into the sea of grass, looking at path after path of downtrodden grasses, trying to ignore the piteous mewling from the surviving downed boars.

"I have at least five piggies sleeping out in the grasses." Kith panted. "Spike's been a *good* boy! Now, *why* the Pits did you want to make our life harder for us, Chase?"

Wiping sweat off his brow, Chase grinned weakly. "It was a split-second thought. You remember how we once talked about that, at some point in the future, we'd be strong enough to control the battlefield and make sure that we could have those who need the Ænima make the kills? This is it! We're strong enough! And what do you know? We have a healer who's right at the cusp of hitting her fourth Tier!"

Kith opened and shut his mouth. "I'd complain, but...Fire boil my blood, you're right." He closed his eyes and nodded to himself. "I'll drag the last ones here. Wait. Do we even know that they're Guardians? If they're regular beasts, there'll be no Ænima for Sera."

Cilia was carefully packing her droplets back into the belts crisscrossing her jacket. "They are Lightborn Guardians. Look at those glowing tusks. Now, Sera, you had better get your hands dirty. Meanwhile, we are going to have a tiny chat with Nordon about just what the Pits happened here. Care to explain yourself, Nordon?"

The first time they'd seen Nordon, he'd been, if not an intimidating sight, then at the very least an eminently composed one. Behind his bar, at the center of his distilling apparatus, he had been entirely in control, the master in his element.

Now, he was gasping like a fish out of water, eyes darting from them to the more than fifteen boars downed around them. He shook his head as if trying to clear it of intoxication, then blushed furiously. "That was my fault. I am *so* sorry! I am. Are we— Are we okay to talk now? Shouldn't we take care of this?"

"Explain," Cilia insisted. Behind her, a boar squealed piteously as it bled out.

Nordon hung his head. "I don't brew as I travel. One main rule I have. I like control. The better temperature control you have, the less you move your mixtures, the better you're able to define the result you will end up with. But with the fervor of you kids, you got me to thinking what I *could* do."

"And that was the end result?" Chase struggled to keep a smile from his lips as he pointed back at where the cart had exploded.

"No!" Nordon exclaimed indignantly. "I figured, well, the initial parts of brewing are simple. You just boil water with a lot of grains or barley or whatever you're messing around with and that gets you mash. You can actually induce magic already at this point. I'll try not to be too technical—"

"Too late! What went wrong, man?"

Nordon sighed. "At first, nothing. I was going to use the spent grains for, well, let's call them biscuits. Small bites, you could carry in a wrapper and eat for a small boost before a fight. It wouldn't be as good as my *good* brews, and the taste and texture would be questionable, but I thought it might net you a few added temporary points to Toughness."

Liam spared a moment from his vigilance to look over his shoulder. "Questionable taste? I've eaten seafood from Lake Isarn. For two points to Toughness?" He scoffed and rolled his eyes. "I'd eat that glowing pig right there. In fact, I think I will."

Nordon burst out in laughter, then winced. "In that case, I might have something functional for you in a day or so. A starter, at least. Anyway, my first attempts were going so well, I decided to experiment a little. See what I could make work while we were on the move. I scrounged up a little something that would work for wild yeast and got creative, thinking I could come up with something fun." He lowered his head. "That was my mistake, and I should have known. The whole process became a mess, basically. The motion of the cart interfered with the fermentation and the temperature fluctuated. And even if you are lucky to get good yeast that can handle all that, you need to allow the mixture to breathe somewhat. I thought I had it under control."

"I'm not following. What went wrong?" Liam asked.

"His beer exploded." Kith snorted.

"My beer did not explode!" Nordon protested. "Also, it was more of a wild ale, with notes of—"

"What was the ringing sound?" Kith interrupted, with the smug expression of somebody who'd already divined the answer.

"That was...erm. That's to say, the lid must have been too tight. With the magic added to the brew and the natural fermentation process, pressure built until, well..." Nordon's voice faded.

"Until your beer exploded."

"I think we're getting off track here," Cilia concluded. "Kith. Were we spotted?"

Kith didn't answer, just let his wide, incredulous gaze glance over the setting, dead and dying boars studding the landscape with piteous squeals and grunts, where Sera moved between them, calmly slitting their throats with merciful efficiency.

"Were we spotted by humans? Water wash away my fading patience, I'm surrounded by imbeciles!"

Kith beamed an insouciant and absolutely unapologetic grin at her. "No, Cil. Radine's circling right now, and she's not seeing anything. Though, I'll admit, I was rather distracted for a bit. Y'know, when the beer exploded."

Nordon spoke up softly, hanging his head. "I am so sorry for this. I will limit my experiments from here on out. There will be no more surprises."

"Perish the thought." Sera's voice intruded from beyond. She was a sight to behold. The sun-kissed Lightborn had tied her bountiful curls back in a tight ponytail and rolled up the sleeves of her sensible, white healer's robe. Even so, the robe was covered in darker streaks and her arms were dipped in blood nearly to her elbows, with a gory spatter straight across the front. Her eyes burned bright, and she looked like a blend between a human sacrifice and a maddened killer. "I have learned a lot from staying with my new family over the past months. There is one main lesson I have taken to heart. If it worked, it was no failure."

Chase leapt up to her and embraced her, gore and all. He leaned back. "So, it did?"

Her fiery expression nearly made him back away. "Two Steps. I am officially a Tier four healer."

CHAPTER 4

"Two gaborns. One adult, one juvenile. Estimated high difficulty. High defense, high speed. Estimated little effect from Prism. Two minutes or less. Do not engage. Repeat. Do not engage. Fall back through C-6, F-7, and H-8, hopefuls and mass run first. If attacked, hands apply any canceling and slowing cards to defend. Ranged backup incoming, all hands or stronger." The more of these I read, the more they are starting to make sense to me. The Prism has to be whatever effect works on those entering their lands. Mental effects, stronger the weaker the intruder is? Must ask Nordon. Anyway, hopefuls, mass, and hands...I keep seeing those. Should be Tiers? Looks like there's a progression of sorts. It all looks rather organized, too. I approve.

"I am not ready for this," Sera murmured.

They'd spent a good while with their kills. They debated what they wanted to do, before loading six of the largest beasts onto the cart and finishing the rest of the march to the nearby stream. There, Cilia got to work with the precious skinning tools she'd been awarded by her teacher, Master Benneth. Carefully making incisions, she skinned the beasts for their pelts. Afterward, they butchered two of the carcasses for the meat, which would keep them for the rest of their journey. Also, Nordon kept a large portion of the fat and blood for himself, for reasons unknown to them.

Sera went out of sight of the others, thoroughly washing after her kills. When she returned, she'd been by herself a bit, kneeling in a meditative pose, looking deep in thought while the others worked, rested, or checked over their equipment and pack beasts after the skirmish.

"Anything you want to share?" Chase asked softly.

She looked up and slowly exhaled, her expression softening. Her brow creased, and she brushed a couple of curls behind her ear as she tried to gather her thoughts. "This. I am not ready for this."

Chase chuckled and sat down, putting his hand on top of hers. "You know how we men can be a bit slow? Well, that goes twice for me. But even so, I think I need a bit more to go on than that. Is it the whole part where we're infiltrating Liberty? Because none of us are ready for that, I think."

Sera huffed in silent laughter and shook her head. She gestured in a southeastern direction. "Back in Isarn? I was looking forward to 'earning' my first Tier as a healer as a reward for completing my tour with the army. Do you know how that would happen? My parents would *purchase* a handful of Guardians for me to kill, with a crossbow or similar. I was never going to go into direct conflict. So unfit for a *lady*." She imbued the word with scorn, then snorted. "Oh, and as for my prospects? Once I was back, I would be properly married off to improve our family's lot. Depending on the match, that would be it for my growth. A generous husband might see me to the second Tier eventually."

"Ah," Chase said. "It's the power of it?"

She nodded. "Did you know that the lord of Isarn was only a Tier-four? Whenever we do settle down, we are never going to be nobodies. Somewhere between Isarn and here, we have *become* the powerhouses that people talk about at soirees and banquets and...that cannot be. The Serafine in my head is not ready for that."

Chase nodded thoughtfully. "I get it."

"You do?" she asked. "How do you handle it?"

"I don't." He laughed. Then, with a lopsided grin, he got up and waved at the rest of their merry band. "Honestly, that's the point I'm getting at, I think. If you haven't noticed, *none* of us are in any way prepared for any of this. But that, if anything, is what's allowed us to make it this far."

"We are so unprepared we are triumphing? Is that the point you are trying to make? I am so glad I picked you for your looks!" Her teasing smirk took the barb from her words.

"In case you hadn't noticed, I approve of your looks as well. Ardently." His eyes bored into hers until she coughed and looked away. "And no. That is not my point, woman! My point is that we are making our own way. We adapt. We figure out how the world works, and then we find a way to make that work for us! In truth, that's why I can even sleep at night. If I were to try to come up with ideas for how I'd try to make myself fit inside the thousand rules of the Lightborn upper crust or try to accommodate the insane ideas the Furyborn hold?" He scoffed. "I'd go crazy. But, just like you've noticed, we *are* growing strong. To the point where our collective group is a force that people can't just walk over."

"You say that like it is something natural. How do you *deal* with that?" Her words were soft, but insistent.

"By knowing that whatever's going to happen, we'll be the ones making the calls. That's the entire point. Sure, we have *no* clue what the future will look like, and there will be others who have opinions and influence. But the ones whose opinions I care about, and who I'm going to really listen to? They're the ones right here in the dirt with me."

Sera looked up at him for several long seconds. Wordlessly, she stretched out a hand.

He helped her up, and she let herself be pulled straight into his embrace. Grasping his head softly between her hands, she whispered, "You know, I would not mind getting dirty—"

"Are you ever going to pick your cards or *what*, woman?" Kith shouted from his seat on top of a caarnath. The animal looked resigned to its fate.

Chase closed his eyes. "Sometimes..."

"I agree." She tapped him on the nose. Then she grasped his arm and pulled him along. "All right. Let us do this! Gather up."

Nordon, hands filled with feeding bags for the caarnath, blinked. "What are we doing?"

"New Tiers. We always discuss the proper direction and what we need, to ensure that our cards work, both solo and with the group as a whole," Sera explained matter-of-factly.

"Oh. I feel like I should be writing this down. Can I even listen in on this? I'm not part of the group."

Chase snorted. "Just because we're keeping a few secrets, we're not going to walk around in silence for a damn month. You already know which decks we have. Anything beyond that's just filler. So. Direction!" He bowed, ceding the scene to Sera.

She nodded. "My attributes are as follows."

Personal Info:
Name: Serafine
Title: Dark/Elemental/Light/Fury healer
Step: 21 (Tier 4)
Strength: 15 (+1 Tier bonus) = 16
Agility: 18 (+1 Tier bonus) = 19
Toughness: 19 (+1 Tier bonus) = 20
Mental Power: 35 (+13 Tier bonus) = 48
Potential: 12 (+1 Tier bonus) = 13
Points available: 2

Nordon sputtered at the mention of her Mental Power, eyes bulging.

"Same as yourselves, I received another one-time bonus to my class attribute, Mental Power, from the latest time the Deck of Darkness hit a limit and spawned a new deck. A nice bonus, but not one we can expect to repeat any time soon. I also managed a single increase to Toughness from our training and marching."

"Nicely done," Liam said admiringly.

"Thank you." Her brow furrowed and lips tightened. "That leaves me with a tiny bit of a quandary. My distribution is becoming increasingly lopsided, purposely so. My Mental Power allows me amazing impact from my cards and wonderfully rapid perception and reaction time. Yet, when it comes to my personal defense, I am starting to feel like I need to invest in Agility and possibly Toughness."

Liam frowned. "That's not just because you're unused to your bucklers?"

"No. They will take some additional getting used to, but they do their job. I can manage keeping an eye on my surroundings and still deflect anything coming at me from a distance. Also, the bucklers are light, so they do not slow me down. It is more a question of my body not being fast enough to keep up with my mind."

"Ah. Like Kith, but in reverse." Liam nodded and laughed. "It's a good idea, honestly. Listen to your body. Increase your Agility to where your actions feel natural and smooth, your Toughness to where you don't feel fragile, then you can get back to aiming for the highest Mental Power on Ordei again."

"Yesss. Give me a chance to get ahead of you in Mental Power again!" Cilia said.

Laughing, Sera waved her off. "As to cards: There is one detail in particular I aim to choose. A stronger healing card. The ones I have are Tier one and two. They have served us well, but the stronger enemies we face, the greater the risk that somebody manages to cause horrid instant damage. That is something I cannot heal straight away at this moment. Anything else?"

Cilia nodded and stepped forward. "Good idea. I have two thoughts. First is that you do have a dispel against effects of enemy cards, but it's weak. A stronger version would help. Also, anything to help us control enemies would be a great idea. Sleep, stun, distraction like Kith's bees...something along that line. Anybody else?" she asked the others.

Liam shook his head. "Your shields and that card of yours that drains incoming damage and dumps it back on an attacker have saved me, again and again. I love stuff like that. No other ideas."

Kith nodded in agreement with Liam's comment, shrugging.

Chase spoke up. "Treat yourself. I mean, we're not in a bad spot. If you can choose something that will make life good for us when we settle down in the future? I say go for it."

The others murmured agreement, right until Nordon cleared his throat. "Erm. Can I say something?"

"Certainly sounds like it." Kith smirked. "Go on. Don't be all prim and proper. We like our princesses straightforward."

"Ignore him," Cilia added, deadpan. "We all do."

"Well. What I meant to add, so you make the right choice for you, is that...well, Liberty has a certain *style* for its cards, if you know what I mean."

Cilia perked up. "Do go on. This is like Light often being boosting, blinding, bright, and explosive and Fury focusing on nature, yourself, and wildlife?"

"Just so. Well, the thing with Liberty? I am no scholar, but from what I've seen and learned? Their style is focused on making life easier for yourself by stopping everything that could come against you."

"Uh. Come again?" Liam frowned.

"I'm with Liam here. What does that mean?" Chase said.

"Well. Since we're talking about healers. Sure, there are normal healing cards. Yet, where a Light healer card might net you a nice Toughness buff for your group, a Liberty card could just as easily cancel any enemy buffs, or make them work in the reverse."

"What? Reverse healing? No! That would be...bloody frustrating!" Kith groaned. "What would that even look like for summoners?"

"Like I said, I am no scholar, and I avoid direct conflict. Yet, I have heard about summoned creatures that repress other summons, that slow, dazzle, or confuse those caught in their range. Fighters can often cancel other martial cards, have them backfire or be repelled; casters can countermand the effect of other cards. Obviously, Liberty crafters are famous for their shield effects." Nordon grimaced. "That's about all I know. But anything that could possibly defend from such effects could probably be a good idea for your near future."

Sera inclined her head. "I...*we* truly appreciate that."

"Yeah. It's almost enough to make up for trying to blow us all up." Kith snorted. "You know. When your beer exploded."

Sera closed her eyes and silence fell over them all. Within seconds, she opened her eyes, smiling.

"The Tier four upgrade first." She exhaled. "I did it. I increased Blessing of the Night to Legendary."

[Blessing of the Night
Legendary, Dark healer
Tier one
Passive, long duration
Once tapped, any attribute increases on you and group members in range are boosted to a high degree. Any active Light card effects of nearby hostiles are reduced to a third, except for Tier-one and -two wielders, which have theirs entirely quelled.

Long cooldown. *"You dare come into this, my domain, and challenge my superiority?"* The king of Fury is brought low.]

"That's insanity!" Cilia burst out. "The vast majority of Lightborn hostiles will be Tier-one or -two. And those who aren't will still have theirs reduced in efficacy! Also, the wording for the boosts will mean higher buffs."

"I love increased buffs," Liam added, feeling his biceps. "I can already sense the effect."

"I do not have it engaged right now. Dolt," Sera said with a fond smile. "This was all I hoped for. Any future clashes with Lightborn will see us much better positioned. Now...this might be awhile."

It was a while. They looked at one another awkwardly, waiting for Sera to finish the process that, once initiated, couldn't be paused. Kith started to whistle tunelessly at some point.

Liam raised an eyebrow. "Any bets on whether this will be a new record?"

"That's a trap. I'm not betting against Sera!" Chase countered.

It took less than five minutes. "Whoo." Sera shuddered and fell to her knees, panting. "That was powerful. Tier five will be *insane*." She accepted Chase's hand and got back to her feet. Then she faced them all anxiously. "I...did not get my heal. There were some close approximations, but nothing really good. Even so, the Dark card was promising, even if Uncommon."

[**Poison Paradise**
Uncommon, Dark healer
Tier four
Active, instant
You may select a group member or yourself. Any active negative infliction on them, be it debuff, poison, or sickness, is forcibly extracted from them. The force of the infliction is converted into a temporary short-duration boost to Mental Power for the inflicted. The power of the boost is dependent on the power of the infliction.
Short cooldown
"I took a sip from my devil's cup. Slowly, it's taking over me."]

Cilia squinted, mouthing the wording to herself. "Yes. That is *way* more powerful than it could appear at first glance. It won't apply to every situation, obviously, and the Mental Power boost is just a bonus. But the fact that it can remove *anything*, including sickness? That alone could land you a job like...favored healer to all the damn nobles of the realm."

"I think I prefer the present company." Sera smiled. "Yet, those were my thoughts too. Though, I *am* looking forward to learning which kind of Mental Power increase a Tier four debuff will grant us." Inclining her head toward Nordon, she continued. "I believe I did get something that applies to what you were mentioning about Liberty."

[**Shimmering Sanctuary**
Uncommon, Light healer
Tier four
Passive, long duration
Upon activation, this card creates a warm, bright sun above yourself. Wherever the sun shines, it protects the integrity of your group members. No hostile debuffs or counters will be able to take effect within the sun's radius. Any hostile effect repelled in this manner causes the sun to shrink until it fades to nothing.
Medium cooldown
"Feel this, friend. The warmth of life. Enjoy it, for soon, it shall be lost." In death, the Benign Blade defeats the Legion.]

She activated it, and a dozen feet above her head, a compact, golden miniature sun shimmered into existence, shining a warm light down upon them.

"Beautiful." Liam sighed. "Even if it never activates, I will feel better going into battle under its protection."

Cilia grimaced. "This one, in turn, is a bit *less* overwhelming than we could hope for. The effect sounds wonderful, yet the medium cooldown is a long time once it fades away, and we'll have to crowd within...fifty feet of Sera? Even so, it's better than no protection, and you'll just have to upgrade it when you hit Tier five."

"When, not if?" Sera coughed. "No pressure, huh?" Shaking her head with a soft smile, she moved on.

[**Shroud of the Elements**
Uncommon, Elemental healer
Tier four
Passive, long duration
Beyond all else, the mission of the healer is to protect. However, in order to be able to do that, they need to be able to concentrate on their task; whether it be healing, boosting, or protecting. When unleashed, the Shroud of the Elements provides a whirling combination of the four elements to jolt, distract, and knock enemies off-balance, allowing the healer to focus on their job.

"Flectere si nequeo superos, Acheronta movebimus." The Shroud is unleashed. The healer stands tall.]

Kith made a dismissive sound deep in his throat. "Sure. That's not unfair at all. I get to play with air. The healer gets to unleash *all the damn elements!*"

"Please." Sera rolled her eyes. "First off, you do not play with air. You have *feet tornadoes!*"

Kith crossed his arms over his chest with an impressively fake scowl. It didn't help his argument that, after a few seconds, the area below his feet started to churn up air, and he bounced up and down.

"Second..." Sera trailed off. "No. There is no second part here. I believe this one is going to be eminently useful. I will be honest regarding my final choice, however. The wording has me ambiguous on the efficacy."

[**Balance in All Things**
Uncommon, Furyborn healer
Tier four
Passive, medium duration
Furyborn, above any other, know about balance. If your compact with Ordei is out of alignment, everything will reflect on you accordingly. Upon activation, this card activates the manifestation of said balance, centered upon the healer. Balance *will* be enforced.
Long cooldown
"When a man is flawed, that which he touches is flawed. Become unflawed."]

One after the other, they looked around, none of them attempting to speak. Eventually, their gazes slid toward Cilia, who stood there, frowning.

After nearly a minute, where her frown grew increasingly pronounced, Cilia flung up her hands in frustration. "How the Pits would I know? That's frustratingly vague. Balance how? How far? To which degree? How do you affect it?"

Sera nodded. "I know. There was an all-attributes boost I should have picked instead."

"*No!*" Cilia said. "Of course you shouldn't! If I got this choice, I'd have picked it myself. Not knowing what it does would have consumed me! Besides, it looks like it's something you can activate and not think about, just like two of the other three. If you don't need the elements to defend yourself, or the light to defend us all from debuffs, you can...do whatever this does. Also, it sounds like it could possibly be..." Cilia frowned, then giggled, an uncommonly girlish sound from her. "We'll need to learn exactly what it does soon, or I'll wring my mind, thinking in circles."

That evening, they learned it. Sera did attempt activating it during the march, but nothing happened. However, once they'd finished the day's chores, and they had the chance to properly test it out, they set to figuring out what, if anything, triggered the card, and what its actual effects were.

Late evening, they sat on six grassy chairs raised by Cilia in a circle as the setting sun painted the sky with vivid colors. Chase nursed a burgeoning bruise around his eye with a slab of meat cut from one of the boars.

Sera refused to meet Chase's eyes.

Liam cleared his throat. "What have we learned then?"

Kith spoke up, laughter in his voice, while he cradled Spike's head in his lap, scratching his neck. "That that is the strangest card I've ever seen."

Chase glared at him with the one good eye, which just made him smile even harder.

Cilia ticked off on her fingers. "One. We have learned that the card does exactly what it says. It enforces balance. Two, we have learned that this balance is centered on Sera *and* anybody physically with her, within a radius of...about a hundred feet, wouldn't you say?" She grunted in answer to their nods. "Thank you. Three, we have learned that the enforcement of said balance comes in the form of what you might expect from a Furyborn card—namely, nature. Examples?"

Liam mused, "Slipping on the grass, unexpected potholes, unexpected muddy patches."

Kith joined in. "Strong gusts of wind. Once, a cloud of dust half-blinded me too. Oh, and there was this one thing that I might have spotted, too. What was it? A rock?"

Chase snarled at him. "Yes. It was a rock. A Fury-torn rock. I flung it near Sera as a test. Instead, it collided with another rock on the ground and somehow bounced back to hit me right in the eye."

Cilia looked as if she were struggling to not laugh herself. "Thank you. Yes. Nature itself seems to wake up and act in small measures against whoever goes against the wielder. Four, it only counts actual actions, and there are degrees to this. If you merely walk or run at Sera, yell, threaten, anything not directly hostile? Nothing's going to happen. If, say, you push her, smaller reactions will ensue. But if you try to kill her or do something that could cause serious damage, the balance will turn downright hostile, with something not directly hostile like debuffs somewhere in the middle. Does that sound about right? Any additions?"

They agreed to the explanations.

Cilia sighed and smiled. "In that case, I'll have to congratulate you, once again, on your choice. As an isolated card, it might seem subpar. But if we find ourselves at the center of a battlefield again, with tons of attacks and cards flying every which way? This is the type of card which could turn the tide, simply by making a large number of smaller actions turn against the perpetrators."

"One thing to add," Chase finally said.

Sera blushed.

"That damn effect lingers, too, overriding any attempts at healing," he growled. "It's been twenty minutes, and it's still not letting Sera heal my bruises."

"I'm *sorry*!" she said. "I think as long as the card's still active, I can't do anything about it, and I switched from another Tier four card earlier, so I can't switch back yet. I'll heal you as soon as I can!"

With grudging grace, Chase finally relented and split into a grin. "I'll admit, this would've been damn funny if it happened to Kith!"

***

"This is the indebted who insisted on talking to me, Awakened Venis?" The speaker was tall, handsome, with huge arms. The tresses of his long, blond hair glowed in the morning sun to the point where it was nearly blinding. He was currently seated in front of his tent, running a whetstone over his elaborate longsword. It would be easy to dismiss him as a strong goon, were it not for the casual grace with which he wore his heavy armor, and the outlines of the two cards barely visible under the bright white tunic.

The soldier arrayed in front of the speaker looked uneasy about the situation, but nodded decisively. "Yes, sir. Refused to lay out the details to me, even when I...prompted her."

The tall man smirked at the look of the welts emerging from the short sleeves of the indebted. "Dismissed, Awakened Venis. Wait near the training grounds, until I have had a little chat with her."

Relieved, the soldier saluted, performed a turnabout, and marched away.

The tall man stood and cracked his neck, sighing in relief. He sheathed his longsword and smirked at the indebted before him. Leisurely and languidly taking his time to stroll around her, all the while looking at her. He took in everything. The clear definition of muscle on the low-set woman. The dirty bandage clumsily wrapped several times around her head. The row of fresh scars along one sunburned thigh that looked slightly inflamed. The hair, hacked down to an uneven mess, which had clearly been done by anything but scissors. The single dirt-colored card on one arm, ringed by the characteristic Elemental frame. Finally, the gritted teeth, the steel-set look in her eyes. There was determination here, he decided, and backbone. "Do you know who I am?" he asked softly.

A curt nod. "Armsmaster Tehol. Undisputed leader of this scouting regiment. Near worshipped among your troops for your even-handedness, fairness, and capability in planning."

The smile increased to a smirk. "Flattery. Interesting choice. In this situation, I would also have accepted 'the one who holds my life in his hands' or 'as a god before me.'" His voice grew cold. "What I am *not* accustomed to is having my time wasted by indebted." She tried to protest, but he spoke over her. "I know who you were. But I also know that you are slow to catch up. You believe that, because you used to be a Protector in your precious towers, that grants you any sort of clemency as an indebted. Well, it doesn't. It makes you a tool that is slightly less likely to break, but a tool nonetheless. And tools that do not fill their purpose are discarded. *Do I make myself clear?*"

"Perfectly, Armsmaster Tehol." Her voice was properly subdued, but she couldn't hide the tension in her shoulders.

"Good. Then talk. What was so important that you found it necessary to incur the displeasure of Awakened Venis?"

The strong Elemental kept her eyes firmly fixed on the ground. "A short while ago, you issued an order to everybody. It was aimed at your troops, but it was mid-training, and I was present for arms practice along with other indebted." She hesitated, then continued, choosing her words carefully. "You gave orders to keep an eye out for a specific mixed group on the plains."

Tehol froze. His gaze shot in every direction around him, before reassuring himself that nobody was looking or listening in. He fixed on her again. "You have my attention."

She affected not to notice. "Sometimes, we're sent into the plains instead of Lightborn scouts, when there are rumors of threats—ambush predators, stronger Guardians and the like. As often as not, we find nothing. When we do...well, it's easier to risk a single indebted than somebody with actual training." The disdain in her voice was hard to miss. "I was supposed to look for a group of blitz boars—and I found them, as they were being effortlessly slaughtered...by that very same group of people."

"How can you be sure? And were you spotted?"

She scoffed. "I might be indebted, but it's not like Darkness has stolen my eyesight. We had a slight, curly-haired Lightborn girl, a one-handed Darkborn, a bloody Furyborn, and one mixed bag of a girl. That, and a disgustingly handsome

Lightborn man? It's a mix you don't see often." She snorted. "As to whether I was spotted?" Her arm flashed once.

Armsmaster Tehol's arm shot for the hilt of his longsword, before freezing in place. Before him, the Elemental's form slowly grew hazy and undefined, as the soil moved to cover her. Within five seconds, she looked like nothing more than an ill-defined, lumpy clay statue.

Her voice emerged as if nothing had happened, though. "When I lie down and activate my card? Even your scouts would be hard-pressed to spot me. And given that they took down a dozen blitz boars in five minutes, you'd best believe I stayed right there, unmoving."

A wide gamut of emotions ran across Tehol's face, until settling on pinprick focus. "This is a gamble for you," he mused aloud. "You're hoping that this will lead to your freedom."

She nodded, not trying to dissemble in the least. "Exactly. From what I understood, this could be worth quite a deal. You have a reputation for being honorable. I am betting everything on it, in order to make it back home." She took a deep breath, then blurted the rest. "They were about a mile east of here, and continued north-northeast."

Tehol narrowed his eyes. Then, he put on a genteel smile, tapping his lips. He started to circle her again, mulling over her offer. Mid-step, he wheeled on her from behind, forcing a hand-kerchief between her lips. Ignoring her muffled complaints and struggling, he drew his longsword, pointing the tip at her.

Looking cross-eyed at the threatening tip of the elaborate, ornate weapon, she stopped struggling. Sweat started to run from her brow.

"I must admit, I'm disappointed. I expected more, when I received an Elemental Protector to add to my indebted. Your kind were supposed to be these vaunted masters of defense, lay-ing claim to perfection in both diplomacy, combat, tactics, and whatnot." With a flourish of his hand, the sword flashed out.

She winced, and, through gritted teeth, watched the band-age trailing off, falling from her head. A trickle of blood ran from her scalp.

"Turn your back on me," he commanded.

She did so.

Slowly, deliberately, he tied the bandage back in place, this time sealing the handkerchief inside her mouth. Then he circled around to face her, with a gleam in his eyes. "You are, of course, right in your assessment of me. I *am* honorable. I do care about the thoughts of my own troops. Yet, you have made one mistake. This? It's the sort of secret that is only worth anything as long as it remains a secret. And your training should have prepared you for the only way to properly keep a secret." He squinted for a moment, then sliced the edge of the longsword across his forearm, hissing slightly at the blood welling up from the cut. Even through the pain, however, his smile was wide. "You were right in one thing, though. Somebody is definitely getting rewarded for this. I'm just sad to say it won't be you."

The indebted sank to her feet as his words rang out. "At arms, Awakened Venis! Your indebted tried to attack me. Prepare her immediate execution. I believe the indebted are growing rebellious!"

CHAPTER 5

"Five Elemental Guardians. Spark bulls. Two adults, three juveniles. Estimated low difficulty for killing, high for capture. High Toughness, low speed, high offensive. Estimated reduced effect from Prism. Three minutes at most. Do not engage; repeat, do not engage. We attempt capture. Fall back through G-1, then E-1. Backup will be arranged at E-1 with grouped slowing and subdual."

Nordon was little use when it came to enlightening us on how the Prism worked, because he was blindfolded each time he crossed. But comparing these notes with his comments has allowed me to determine a number of conclusions on their vaunted defense.

1. The Prism applies for anything entering their lands.

2. It is some sort of mental effect, but, most likely, works depending on the power of enemies.

3. I adore their defenses. So organized!

For a full two weeks, they continued their pace with solid progress. They debated the topic and decided that there was no reason to press hard on their speed. As long as they weren't spotted, they would rather move ahead at an even rate, allowing them time to train, practice, and learn. According to Nordon, they had already made it north of any of the main access points from the Lightborn lands to Furyborn lands, so the odds of their getting caught in the midst of any large troop movements were low.

Hence, the group slowly plodding northeast across the grass-covered plains went into a cycle of repetition and experimentation that filled their entire day from sunup to sundown.

They traveled, they talked, they trained, and they fought. Well, mock-fought, though their clashes were savage enough. Everything they did was with the purpose of either strengthening the capabilities of one of them or their combined strength. They tested card combinations between people, compared attributes and impacts, changed cards and tried again.

At first, Cilia and Sera spent an inordinate amount of time between the two, practicing their terrain manipulation cards in tandem. Eventually, they perfected three different setups between them. One was a static defense they'd erect each evening.

It was a combined creation inspired by the Lightborn camps, encircling their camp, allowing them to create full defenses for all within just twenty minutes. The arrangement was simplistic, but should hold up to anything but the largest Guardians or fliers—a circular trench, immediately followed by a steep earthen bank heavily infested with thorny vines. Because they could open the encirclement at a moment's notice, they kept it fully closed for added security.

Then came an ambush scheme. A setup they could use for any situation where they had the time to prepare in advance of a fight. They manipulated the terrain, conjoined with slowly encroaching walls of vines, to funnel enemies straight into an uneven, pothole-filled surface that'd eventually make enemies hit a lowered area filled with vines that couldn't be seen from a distance. It took maybe an hour to set up properly, but looked promising for safe takedowns.

Finally, they practiced what they termed the "panic defense." Something they'd be able to fling up within two minutes, if they were caught unawares, before switching to their combat cards. Mostly, it was a question of combining a thick mass of vines with a ton of potholes to make a head-on charge dangerous, combined with a few hardened and partly shielded positions where summons, Kith, or Liam could stand tall even against larger numbers of attackers.

The evenings became filled with math. In between drastic re-arrangement of the local soil, they spent an inordinate amount of time testing card combinations and trying to quantify their effects. They had, of course, already practiced their old cards. Yet, with their new Furyborn and Tier four cards in tow, they went all-in on trying to expand their knowledge beyond just what they felt and thought, to measurable differences.

This resulted in them all creating and rearranging sets of cards, go-to combinations they could use for specific situations. Adopting Sera and Cilia's approach, they went with three separate sets: for defense, for attacking, and for ambushing.

For instance, if they fought a defensive battle, Liam would go with Become the Clay for personal defense, Draining Ward or Escalating Defenses (which summoned personal shields for every effective attack of his) depending on the enemy, Convince the Unbeliever for the self-heal and Agility boost and either Tribune of Retribution, Blindness to blind enemies or Helping Step if he needed mobility.

Or, if they were ambushing, Sera would opt for Blessing of the Night for attribute boosts, Spark of Divinity for further Agility boosts, Heart of Hearts to boost all their Heart cards and either Shimmering Sanctuary or Balance in All Things, depending on the type of enemy they were up against.

Their training did reveal a few flaws along the way. It also exposed how certain cards proved to be either so situational they would rarely ever be used, to outright bad choices. A few of these revelations were surprising. Others, not so much.

For instance, Liam had both Unleash the Elements and All Out on Tier three. Both focused on offense, with All Out working on *every* kind of offense, and Unleash the Elements granting Elemental damage. In theory, both good, depending on the enemy. Only, Liam had chosen another Elemental card for Tier four, Tempest of the Land, which was vastly more powerful. He *could* apply both Elemental cards, but the effect was nowhere near as pronounced as going with All Out on top of Tempest of the Land.

Others suffered from having solitary cards that were so good the others in the Tier couldn't measure up. Chase, for instance, had never even used Unending Decay for Tier one. In theory, the damage increasing per strike was great for taking down tough enemies. In practice, the chance for permanent attribute increases from Sticky Fingers or added mobility from Steps of Brilliance were just too good alternatives.

Kith was ecstatic to conclude that his new Tier four card, Pillars of Air, was both surprisingly effective *and* versatile. Once activated, it created twin funnels of air under his feet that helped him move at absolutely ridiculous speeds. Not only that, he could perform truly astounding leaps that helped him outmaneuver his adversaries and gave him utterly ridiculous agility in combat. The downside was that the card was active, meaning that any break in his concentration could have the funnels cutting out mid-sprint. He managed a few rather spectacular wipeouts before he found the proper state of mind. It did see his active control over his summons lessen in combat, but most often, the added versatility and speed made up for it.

Following her increased ability to alter the battlefield, Cilia decided to further experiment with her crafting, but this time focusing on finding non-combat additions to their arsenal.

Their attributes did not skyrocket. They did not manage to gain some sudden influx of understanding or unbeatable new techniques. However, with every additional day, they managed to improve on the already impressive cohesion of their group, add to their inherent understanding of one another's capabilities, choices, and mindset.

That was not to say they didn't improve. Sera managed an increase to Agility on top of what she'd already selected. Cilia's strenuous crafting on top of the physical training landed her a point to Toughness. Kith, with his constant, draining abuse of his new Pillars of Air also earned a point to Toughness. Liam was pleased to gain another lovely boost to Agility. And Chase, with his training card, managed to increase both Strength and Mental Power again.

Of course, they didn't work themselves to the bone every damn minute. They spent nearly as much time goofing around as they did training. Sera and Chase often left the remainder of the group for some much-needed privacy. Liam started performing experiments with their cooking ingredients, often to outrageous results. Cilia pestered Nordon with innumerable questions, to the point where he started wincing when she cleared her throat. Kith returned to his old-time campaign of horror, trying to see who was most susceptible to scares from his shadows, and now, from Radine as well.

This evening, Nordon was gathering up the bowls from their quick evening meal—soup, rendered from boar fat, with plenty of local vegetables added to the mix. Spike was muffling about near his feet, begging for scraps.

They were ready to split up and start the training, when Cilia spoke up. "Before we start training, I would like to show you something."

Eyes gleaming with interest, they instantly drew near. Nordon unceremoniously dropped all the bowls to the grass, making it there before anybody else. Behind him, Spike unleashed a high-pitched squeal of joy and dug in.

"I prefer to keep to myself when it comes to crafting," Cilia started. "I will ask for advice when needed, but I prefer privacy once I know what I'm doing and where I'm going."

"You can say that again," Kith said. "The infiltrators in the towers could learn a bit about secrecy from you."

She rolled her eyes. "I decided that it was time to try something new. Rather than trying to improve our arsenal for combat, I figured we could do with something that would aid in the time in between. With that in mind, I have something for each of you." She turned to one of the carts and ducked under the tarp, extracting one bundle after the other, sharing them out, until every single one of them, including Nordon, stood with a soft, rolled-up bundle. "These are some of the boar hides, obviously," Cilia mused as she unfurled hers. "I failed to make the fur as soft as I would have liked. Yet, nonetheless, I would like all of you to try to sleep on them tonight."

"Count me in." Liam snorted. "Extra comfort? I'll take it! Why all the mystery, though? You're acting like Chase."

One side of her mouth quirked up. "One part of Furyborn magic is the thought that there is power in the land, and a balance between that and yourself. Unless I'm wrong, I've managed to make that power stick within each skin. With a good night's sleep, if I did it correctly...parts of that power should circle back into you."

"You're saying, if I cuddle this piggy, I'll earn part of its Strength?" Liam gawked at the fur and hugged it tight.

"No. I tried something new here, keeping the exact attribute undefined. But you *should* temporarily absorb some of their attributes."

They carried on loudly, asking questions over one another.

Cilia waved them all away. "I don't know how much. Neither do I know how long the boost will last during the day, and if it'll slowly fade away. But it should work." She held up a hand, triumphantly exclaiming, "And I believe that the effect of one of them...that one"—she pointed to the one Kith held—"actually worked well enough to become permanent."

The clamoring following *that* proclamation was a lot louder and lasted for longer. Eventually, they simmered down, and Cilia, blushing from their praise, looked at her feet. "I...can't say exactly why it worked this well. It might be something about the skin belonging to a Guardian and retaining some power."

Nordon mused, "I have some thoughts there and I'd like to talk about it with you later. And...am I really allowed to keep this? Do you have any idea what you could sell this for?" He indicated his own sleeping skin, reverently carried in his arms like a slumbering baby.

"Actually—"

"Stow it, Kith. Yes, you are allowed, Nordon. Are you with us here or not?" Cilia nodded firmly. "Now, we are going to talk about the specific effects later, but I do have one other creation to share." She walked back to the cart and returned with six other rolled-up hides.

Chase unfurled his, then blinked at the sight of the preserved facial features of the boar's head still affixed to the skin. "Wow. That's uncanny."

She caressed her own hide thoughtfully. "For these, I went with a different tack." She unfurled her own hide and wrapped it over her own slight frame. The boar's head, ears and all, created a sort of animalistic hood, letting it shadow her face. "You guys remember that evening and night back in Heath, when we were waiting forever, while Kith tried to locate the deck for us?"

"I remember Heath's miller." Kith chuckled. "Such a hero!"

Ignoring him, Sera asked incredulously, "Remember it? It was the most wet and unpleasant night of my life I have ever spent inactive."

"Exactly. And there was no doubt that being that wet and miserable made us cold...and slow. So, I figured that I might be able to do something about it."

Chase had donned his own, hood included. He now looked more like the quintessential image of a Furyborn, animalistic and scary. His voice, however, filled with awe. "It's *warm!*" he blurted.

"You're wearing fur in the Light-blinded *sun.*" Kith laughed. "What did you expect?"

"This," Cilia snapped. "This is what I have to deal with." She rounded on Kith. "Kith. *It's warm, because it's imbued with fire.* It will keep you warm on cold nights, and, I believe, is actually water-resistant enough to fend off nearly all rain."

"Oh," Kith said. "Why didn't you say so right away?"

She glared at him. "None of these, unfortunately, became permanent. They should last for a month or two, but no more. It didn't feel close either, even with Sera's cards boosting my attributes, and with my Ritual of Fire and Chosen Focus: Fire both improving the process. Likely because the blend of the fur and fire are not a natural mix. I have *thoughts* on that."

Chase chuckled. "I'm sure you do. And I'm sure somebody else, who *isn't* me, can actually contribute to that. Anyway, *are you out of your Fury-rent mind?* This is insanity, Cil! Look at what you've managed! You think, for one moment, that any of the carded crafters in Isarn were able to create permanent enchantments?"

"They were not," Sera stated.

"They absolutely were not," Nordon added. He cleared his throat. "If you don't mind, I have something to say, and to discuss." He glanced around at them in turn, looking nervous before eventually blurting, "I...have been observing you, quite a bit, on this trip."

"Creepy much?" Kith said.

"No. I mean, obviously, I didn't know what to expect from you, going into this. I hoped that I'd be able to guide you across the Liberty borders, let you loose on the other side and earn my reward. Maybe learn a few useful secrets in the process."

"That is very candid of you," Sera said with a guarded expression.

"A fair exchange, I figured." Nordon nodded, scratching his neck. "Only, I think we need to take a proper, hard look at the plan. Because what I've seen on this trip is way too interesting for me to pass up on. And especially you, Cilia, changed my mind." He sighed. "In short, it's time we sat down and had a good long talk about what we're going into, and how to prepare for it. Because, otherwise, you might as well just surrender your lives right at the border."

They agreed to skip training for the evening, and cleaned off the bowls and utensils before getting ready for a planning session. Meanwhile, Nordon brought out a waterskin that definitely didn't contain water. *"To get in the proper spirit of things.*" Now, he took a long drag of the skin and passed it around.

Liam took an enthusiastic gulp, then hesitated, lowering the waterskin with a hiss. "That was...weird. Is that thyme and apples? It's very strong."

"It's something new." Nordon grunted. "My own concoction. It's strange, but bearable, and it makes you wonder who'd come up with something like that."

"And why." Liam took another experimental mouthful, sloshing it around in his mouth.

"Exactly. Yet, it's not horrible enough that you can't get used to it." He winked. "Which has pretty much been my experience with Liberty so far. They're weird and hard to understand, but to a degree where it's not wholly unbearable. Now, if you don't mind, could you inform me what you already know about Liberty? That should allow me to add what I know."

Everybody looked at Cilia, who rolled her eyes and spoke up. "It's a short tale. We know about as much as the average layman. Liberty used to be part of Ordei alongside all other powers, before the schism between Light and Dark. Only, where the Darkborn got themselves trounced and wiped off the face of Ordei, the Furyborn eventually decided it was worth going to war over, and the Elementals landed with their strange 'not really a ceasefire, but not a war either' with the Lightborn. Meanwhile, Liberty decided to just...fade away."

"That's not inaccurate," Nordon mused. "Except for the part where you think the average person knows this much. People are *stupid*! Also, don't worry, Kith. You're not getting any lengthy history lessons today."

"Praise the Light!" Kith groaned. "Cil can get...enthusiastic about these things."

"Suffice it to say, yes, they slowly receded from being a major part of the power balance on Ordei. Then, about four decades ago, they decided to create their external defenses—and that was it. Nobody's heard from Liberty as a state since them. One day, they were a functional government, ruled by the leaders of their guilds; the next, they were a tale to tell your kids about, hidden away behind a layer of roiling fog banks."

"The Prism?" Cilia asked.

He nodded. "Just knowing that name shows you're a step ahead of regular laymen." He scratched his neck. "Pits, it's a weird place. The way I learned about it in the first place was a tip. Liberty, according to official sources, is entirely closed. Yet, Earth's Ward and the occasional fortunate Lightborn city still see sporadic visits by Liberty traders.

"That's where I came in. One of my informants said they'd spotted a band of Liberty travelers approaching a city near me, and I hurried to meet them. I traded with them, made a bunch of borderline horrible deals, and in exchange…he told me when their next caravan would arrive." Nordon smirked. "Some people believe that, to be a successful trader, you need to make a killing, push as hard as you can, in every single trade. Fortunately, those idiots go quickly out of business. *Contacts!* It's all about contacts. Who do you know? Who can you call upon? Who can you bribe to make problems go away?"

"Who will warn you that Soil is about to get invaded and allow you to get away in time with all your money and goods?" Cilia added drily.

Nordon cleared his throat. "Yes. That too. No hard feelings, I hope? Regardless, for a few years, I invested a lot of time, money, and effort into learning about the black-market traders arriving from Liberty lands, getting to know them, and eventually, weaseling my way into their trades. And last year, I managed, for the first time, to get myself invited into their lands with my own wares, and to craft for them upon request."

"That is going to be our ticket in, then?" Sera asked. "Masquerading as your hired help?"

"Just so. Also as guards. Chase there will not pass muster as a brewer, I'm afraid. He is not handy enough."

Chase glared silent death at him.

Nordon chuckled and waggled his eyebrows. "Now, before we get into the practical aspects of our little trip, you need to learn about them first. You need to learn about the Savior of Liberty."

Kith folded his legs up under him on his seat, groaning. "I thought you said this wasn't going to be a dull history lesson."

"And it isn't. This is real, and it's now." He raised an admonishing finger. "First thing you need to understand. The Savior lies at the heart of Liberty society. He is the one and all, their protector and their warden. Worshipped and feared." He continued, ignoring their confused looks. "The change was absolute and sudden. One day they were led by their main guild representatives. The next, the Savior was in place. Nobody's been able to tell me about the details of the takeover process, but I doubt it was peaceful. With him as a leader? Things changed. The Prism went into effect, they retreated from official interaction with the outside world entirely, and their society was rebuilt."

"Rebuilt how?" Cilia frowned.

Nordon hesitated. "You'll have to understand that I don't know that much. I've been transported into their capital exactly once. Most of the time, I've been hidden away, kept by myself with limited access to the populace. Also, the people I've talked to are working illegally. Not exactly the kind of people who enjoy answering in-depth questions about their lives and history. But, the way I understand it, *everything* was torn down and built anew. Government functions, their trades, their schools, *the integrity of the Deck of Liberty.* The Savior took everything and remodeled it according to his plan and whims."

"Hold on," Chase spluttered. "You can do that? Rearrange how a specific deck works?"

"Not easily. And not bloodlessly, either. Which, as I understand it, is a good description of those days. He tore down every existing Wellspring and erected them anew in the capital. The Reclaiming, they call it. True believers, at least, or those I'd call fanatics. Those who dislike the Savior are more graphic about it. Long story short is that everything changed, the Savior was left holding the reins, and nobody cares to, or dares, criticize him."

"So, he is, what? A despot?" Sera asked.

"Never. Ever. Say that! In fact, never say anything even remotely negative about the Savior. Within Liberty lands, He is the living embodiment of all that is good in the world." Nordon waggled his eyebrows. "At least, that's what everybody says out loud, and that's what you'll say too. Because if you don't, you may disappear."

"Oh. It's that kind of place," Chase announced. "Remember when White Wings took over all crime on the Waves?"

"Ah. I get it," Kith said. "The guard nailed White Wings eventually. But for about two weeks, nobody dared criticize him. Not because anybody liked him, but because he had eyes and ears everywhere, and bad things happened to those who spoke up."

Nordon waggled a hand in a "sort of" gesture. "It might have been like that in the start. Now, four decades later? The entire *system* works to ensure that you behave. Kids grow up knowing the Savior to be the only truth. Also, yes, bad things happen to those who speak up."

"Huh." Chase rested his chin in his hand, looking off into the distance. "When we get into it, the Furyborn are pretty dead set about their truths being the only real truths—but at least they don't punish you if you disagree, because it's your right."

"It gets worse," Nordon said. "Liberty folks are still regular people—even those who're born to think of this Savior as a living god—but there is one other, ahem, strange detail about Liberty."

"Weirder than them being cultish and worshipping a living god?" Liam asked incredulously.

"Judge for yourselves," he spat. "Personally, I believe that whoever came up with it deserves a long flight from the top of the towers. The bastards went and weaponized bureaucracy."

Sera looked perplexed. "There is nothing inherently bad about bureaucracy. The Elemental towers themselves have a thriving bureaucracy—"

"Yes, yes." He interrupted. "But they don't try to control who gets to eat."

"What?" Sera asked flatly.

"When you are born, you become part of the system. Growing up, you learn how to follow the process and do what is expected to you. This entitles you to chits that allow you to eat, to gain new clothes, shoes. Decides where you live. Once you are of age, and have walked the Steps to reach the first Tier, you have to gain your Liberty card, which proves your dedication to the cause. Following that, if you survive to reach a higher caste, you are awarded with more responsibilities, but also more rights. You also—"

"Stop. Please." Sera held up a hand, near frozen and brow furrowed. "I have *so* many questions arising already, and I fear that if you continue, I will lose track of half of them."

"Apologies." Nordon bowed. "I am no storyteller." He trailed off. "Perhaps, I could be. I do have one persistent idea in my head. A tale about a talented youngster by the name of Sal, spending years and years at the Elemental Academy before completing his first semester by the twelfth book—"

"Nordon. Focus, please," Sera insisted.

"All right, all right," he grumbled. "Ask your questions."

She huffed and furrowed her brow. "Chits, I understand. Getting locked into poverty and settled in a certain situation by those in power? I can see it. The rest raises questions. First. Does everybody walk the Steps?"

"Oh, yes. I'm not sure about the details. But yes. Every single person."

"And everybody *has* to gain cards, you said?"

"Oh no. *The* card. Once you're of age and have walked the Steps to hit the first Tier, you gain your Liberty card. Shows your devotion to the Savior. Coincidentally, that's what it's called, too. Devotion to Liberty. That's for the lowest Tier, or caste, of course. Any future cards are yours to pick."

"For a second there, I thought it sounded decent, even." Kith's eyes were wide. "Everyone is assured food, clothing, a home? Sounds like heaven. But forcing people to fight? And having to choose a specific card? And what's that about castes?"

"Castes. Yes. Or, rather, as they call them, tiers of dedication."

Liam's head seesawed back and forth between the speakers. "This is so confusing. Why name it something else?"

Nordon smiled sympathetically. "It's Liberty. They do things their way. And you're right. It's confusing as the Pits. When you get used to it, it makes a kind a sense, though. Just think of it as a way to reward those who climb the ranks with rewards, jobs, and responsibility according to their success. Higher Tiers, better caste, better job, more prestige." He made an "ah" sound, holding up a hand. "I know what you're going to say. That's exactly what it's like everywhere. Those with higher Tiers tend to have more prestige, better jobs, everything. Except, here, it's not an option. It's *how it works*. The moment you hit a higher Tier, your caste changes and you are more important. The progression is set in stone and carefully maintained through bureaucracy."

"I guess it will make sense when we see it up close," Liam mused. "Or not. So far, though, it doesn't sound as bad as I'd feared. I mean, I don't think I'd like the pressure, or other people deciding for me. Still, if you put it up against the Furyborn, who've got enemies everywhere, or the Lightborn, where *nobody* is going to help you? Getting training, cards, food, and a place to live sounds positively heavenly. Why would anybody call the Savior a...what's that word you used? Despot?" He shrugged, then his eyebrows rose and he slapped his leg, making Kith next to him jump and glare. "Hah. No! Okay, I think I got it." He pointed to Nordon with a triumphant grin. "What happens to those who don't agree?"

Nordon snorted. "Spot-on. That *is* the issue. Follow the rules, do as you're told, don't mess up? You're set for life. At least, the sort of life you're allowed within the rules. But the moment you do mess up? Get scared, get hurt, disagree with the Savior? Your privileges fade like dew before the sun. Dissenters are not accepted. That's a fact of life. Coincidentally, that dissention is also our way in."

"Ah." Sera nodded in appreciation, while the rest of them looked confused. She smiled. "Simple math. Bureaucracy plus unhappiness equals corruption. We saw it often in Isarn. Those who disagreed with the leaders' positions and still held some degree of power would often abuse that power subtly to suit their own agenda."

"Just so." Nordon nodded. "Also, just because the rules are strict and bureaucracy is rife, doesn't mean that Liberators aren't humans. There is still greed, avarice, and a desire for pomp, decadence, and the *best* alcohol known to man." He smirked. "Those who rise in castes are just as normal as the rest. And they, in general, have more power to bend the rules. My own contact is a hand—that's a Tier-two—who doesn't much care for the Savior, and spends a lot of his bureaucratic power bending the rules for those close to him."

"Ah. And because he can bring in exotic goods, and even have you custom-craft alcohol according to their desires, those who might otherwise turn on him keep quiet or even help him get away with it," Chase said.

"I can see you're going to be wonderful partners for this. That is exactly it. Now. About a week from now, we're meeting my contact, outside of the Prism's effect. There, we'll agree what's going to happen. Last time, I spent three weeks in a decrepit basement in a border village, constantly at work. He promised me, if I were to accept any future jobs like that, he would be able to arrange something better. We will see which sort of agreement we can come up with, but I will, of course, push for as much freedom as possible." With an apologetic smile, he sank back in his seat. "Regardless what happens, once we're in there, you will be on your own when it comes to reaching your goals. I will be kept busy working. I will aid you however much I can, but don't expect a lot."

Cilia squinted. "To sum up, we cannot be sure that we will be allowed to walk free, that we can walk around on the street uncontested, or that we will even be in the right parts of Liberty lands?"

Nordon dipped his head in agreement. "Worst-case scenario, you might even have to leave me behind entirely and make your own way back across the border once you've done the job." He tapped his heart. "I will fend for myself."

For a while, the plains sported only the sound of the wind whistling through the tall grasses. It was interrupted by Chase's barked laughter. "Good."

"Good?" Nordon asked.

"Pits yeah! More than ten years from now, when I'm thirty and old"—he ignored the sputtered indignation from Nordon—"when I sit near our Wellspring and tell the tale of how we stole the final deck...we wouldn't want it to be easy. I'd have to lie as much as Kith does. Nobody wants that."

"I never lie! Anymore. About my Heart card," Kith protested, and was promptly buried in a swell of laughter and jeers.

CHAPTER 6

Not often do the towers introduce a text by exclaiming that it will have inaccuracies. Yet, it is the case for this chorography. We correct when we may, add what we learn. Even so, the fact remains: we have ample correct information about Liberty lands from before they receded from the rest of Ordei. Following their recession, what we have is a collection of hearsay, anecdotes, and evidence gathered from questionable sources. We shall endeavor to preface the relevant pieces accordingly. Who is the author here? *I love them!* I figured the rest of the information from the towers would be as cryptic as the notes. No clue if this thin book will be useful, but their approach is a fresh breeze of air. (Page 1.)

Nordon's Liberty contact had arrived, and he was *not* happy. In fact, he was currently shouting at Nordon, at the top of his lungs. "Six persons. Six! Last time, you had two guards, and they stayed outside the Prism, waiting for you! Now, you want us to somehow find food and rooms for five others?"

Except for Nordon, they all waited at the side, taking in the discussion without commenting or reacting overtly.

The terrain had changed drastically over the past couple of days. What had been a living, thriving sea of grass with an expansive infrastructure of plants and animals had turned, not barren, but...disrupted. There were plants, yes. There were also signs of animal life. Yet everything, from the plant life to the soil itself, looked torn up and half-broken, like the landscape had been subjected to constant disruption for years upon years and finally resigned itself to the present state being normal.

Nobody cared about the landscape. Their eyes were drawn to one thing. One unnatural abomination.

As far as the eye could see, in the northeastern direction, lay the Prism. The vast, roiling bank of low-hanging grey clouds, unnaturally clinging to the ground, churning and roiling in a constant sea of movement. The clouds looked at the same time natural and arcane; like an enigmatic god had taken a naturally occurring phenomenon and magically anchored it in the real world. Deep within, however, half-seen shapes flitted about, hinting at...something.

Their contact was a man, somewhere between thirty and forty years old. He looked *tired*. Even before Nordon told him about the changed circumstances, he looked like somebody who was running on pure obstinacy, constantly dismayed about the state of the world. Physically, he was classic Liberty. His skin had a slightly blue tinge to it, his ears were pointed, and he was below average height. Beyond that, he sported a receding hairline, watery eyes, and a physique that might have been muscular at some point, but was definitely turning soft.

If Chase had seen him on the street in Isarn, he wouldn't have looked at him twice, except for deciding whether he was a possible mark. Having observed him for ten minutes and running, his senses told him no. Not a mark!

Although the man was clearly out of shape, his movements hinted at somebody with hidden reserves. His strange clothes also hinted at something, though Chase was unsure exactly what it meant. He wore loose, azure pants, with a matching loose shirt, all exquisitely tailored. The shirt was asymmetrically cut, letting the sleeve on the left arm run long, while the right arm was exposed.

Chase couldn't look away from the card displayed there. It wasn't merely the fact that it was the first Liberty card he'd ever seen, and the border of spike-filled clouds in shades of blue was both intimidating and intriguing. No. There was a humanoid shape on it...something dark, overpowering, and...drawing power to itself? Scary.

Nordon was the face of patience and understanding as he took the criticism without complaint. "I told you last time, Reen, that next time I would need better accommodations and protection. This is not a matter of me being unreasonable. It is a matter of me being cooped up in a basement without anybody to guard my back if things go badly."

Reen wasn't having it. "I have guards. Eyes on the street. I have also already arranged for better rooms, and the chance to get out of the house every once in a while."

Nordon ceded the point with a gracious nod. "This would all be fair, and acceptable. If they were people loyal to me. As we agreed last time, having somebody entirely at your mercy doesn't lead to increased trust, and I need to have more control in order to be sure that the risk is worth it. Because I *am* risking my life when I enter your lands."

Now Reen had to cede the point, though he did so with little grace. "Where does that leave us, then? Your *friends* here would stand out in the capital, and if I have to risk myself to find additional room for all of them, I'd be out a lot of favors. What's in it for me?"

Nordon slapped him on the back, beaming at the smaller man as he stumbled a step forward. "*Now* you're speaking my language." He beckoned the rest of them with two fingers, and they slowly trooped over. "Show 'em some leg."

Reen looked hopefully at Sera, and entirely failed to show his disappointment, as Chase slowly started to pull up his right pant leg. His features went from dismay to shock in a split second, as his eyes bore down on the Elemental card outlined on Chase's right leg. "M...Minds?" he eventually managed.

"Yup. Tier-fours. Each and every one of 'em," Nordon stated, as if their accomplishments were his personal achievement. "And they're not just muscle either. Well, Liam here, perhaps. Muscle, shield, and the biggest biceps you could ask for, along with a pretty face for the ladies."

"Hey!" Cilia complained.

Liam snorted. "Cil. You think I *mind*? Being gorgeous muscle is what I do best."

Ignoring them as if nobody had spoken, Nordon continued, pointing at Kith. "Kith. Summoner. Adept at scouting and as strong with a weapon as anybody I've served with." He moved on. "Sera. Healer. Excellent healing skills *and* a prodigy at non-magical healing, too. She *will* put her services at your disposal." Another step, another person. "Chase. Rogue. Faster than anybody I've ever met. Really. It's ridiculous. He also sneaks and hides well, and if you need an item liberated, no pun intended, we can probably come to an agreement."

"Sure will. Not for free, though," Chase drawled. They'd already agreed upon this. Additional jobs would likely be the key to how they managed to get out, look around, and find a deck for themselves.

"Last person is the one you'll be the most interested in, though. While the others will help ensure that I can focus entirely on working, without having to fear for my safety, Cilia is a crafter like me. Only, where I focus on alcohol, she is adept at leatherworking. Do you possibly think that you could come up with some ideas for where you could apply the works of a Tier-four crafter with Elemental cards? Because I believe she could theoretically blow your *mind*!"

That was what they'd come up with, so far. They'd only put their Elemental cards on display, unless forced to do otherwise. Being Tier four already made them stand out. If they showed off cards of all four decks, they wouldn't be able to walk in peace anywhere.

Reen's answer sounded like somewhere between a cough and gurgling. He cleared his throat and looked away, but not before they could all see the avarice alight in his eyes. "We...might be able to come to an arrangement. Give me five minutes. I need to do some thinking."

It didn't take five minutes. It took half a day. Reen separated himself from their group, pacing back and forth, deep in thought. He returned awhile later, trying to convince Nordon that only he and Cilia should enter Liberty lands. When that failed, he threw a minor tantrum, threatened to leave, before he actually *did* leave—with the caveat that he'd attempt to get everything handled.

He arrived alone, late in the evening, looking stressed but more collected than earlier. He took one look at them and snarled, "Get moving. We're entering the Prism. Right now! Get those carts rolling!"

"Is everything okay?" Nordon asked.

"Yes! But we have to move *now*. I made a deal, but we don't have much time. We'll need full silence from you for the next while. Not a word! And everybody, hold on to a cart. Hold on tight! You do not want to get lost in the fogs. And, regardless what you experience in there, remember—*it's not real!*" He barked the last part, eyes glancing about almost feverishly.

They hurried, hitching the carts to the caarnaths, and took off immediately. Nordon led the way with Reen at the front of the carts. Weapons out, sharing nervous glances with one another, they followed behind. One by one, they entered the Prism, ready to make their way into another realm, steal a deck, and lay claim to history.

CHAPTER 7

"The following has been reported as coming from an un-carded Liberty escapee. Confirmed by another source, and it fits snippets of other information. It regards Liberty and the use of cards. Apparently, they grant cards to anybody who walks the Steps to hit the first Tier and beyond. Any single person, regardless of affiliation, mental or physical state. As you will soon learn, their society is arranged drastically different from the towers. Even so, do they not see the issues here?"
At least, it is obvious that the writer is an Elemental. Yes, of course, some people might be dangerous to give cards to. But do you know what's even more dangerous? Hoarding the power and creating arbitrary rules for letting others join their fancy club. (Page 3.)

The Prism was a world of its own. A grey world of constantly moving clouds. From one step to the next, the outside world of colors simply faded away. The only thing remaining were the rolling clouds, thick enough that they could barely see. The grey formations assaulted the eyesight, layering itself thicker and thicker. At first, they could see a hundred feet ahead. Then, they could only see to where Reen and Nordon led the march. Within half a minute, the clouds were thick enough on the ground that they could barely see the outline of the cart they held onto.

Then the sensations crept in.

For Chase, they first came as whispers; barely audible voices, right on the edge of his hearing, trying to lay claim on his attention. They wanted him to...what? He could almost hear it. Their suggestions sounded so reasonable, so heartfelt. He just needed to move a bit closer.

Now, there were lights, too. An outline of something—somebody—beckoning to him. They looked almost angelic, like some blessed spirit from out of religious tales.

The air around him pushed him, nudging him like everything in the world agreed that following was the only proper choice. It was getting cold, but something about the intangible presence promised warmth, safety. It made so much sense. Only, if it made so much sense, why was his mind so lethargic? Why was the shape the only visible figure in a sea of fog? With a grunt, and one of the mental exercises Sera kept foisting on them, Chase tried to concentrate.

Every single sensation faded away at once. As if entering a freezing waterfall, the mental stimuli swept the whispers into the background. There was no true warning. One moment, following the figure seemed like a perfectly reasonable idea; the next, he wondered how he'd even let himself consider it, when they'd been warned. His hand tightened in a death grip on the cart slowly rolling forward.

With the mental pressure gone and the ability to truly think recovered, he was able to focus on the physical sensations. The figure had gone. There were no lights. Yet, the hint of warmth in the distance remained, as did the cold surrounding him, and the whispers. Without the mental aspect, however, the whispers were unintelligible rather than promising, murmured voices at the edge of hearing.

Chase marched on, one step after the other, focusing on the sensations, trying to triangulate where they came from. Right when he thought he was getting somewhere, the sensations dropped off. One second to the next, every physical sensation faded away, leaving him with only the roiling fog for company.

A minute later, the cart rolled out into the fading light of an evening sun. They could see again. All were present. Kith looked like he was ready to keel over. Cilia, Liam, and Sera just looked mildly annoyed. Regardless, they'd made it into the lands of Liberty!

There was no reprieve. No pause. Reen rounded on them immediately, speaking at a whisper. "We are *not* in the clear. Follow me, and stay quiet. If we get spotted now, we're all done for."

They kept quiet and followed the carts bumping across the uneven, cracked terrain.

Chase's eyes swiveled about. Before him, Kith moved with his gaze fixed straight ahead, surely deeply embroiled in the sensation of his summons or his bonded Guardians. At the top of a nearby low hillock, he spotted an armored person looking straight down at them, weapon in his hand. For a moment, Chase wondered whether he should attack, or say something. Then, the figure nodded solemnly down in their direction before turning about and walking away.

The minutes stretched on as darkness grew around them. The moon was but a sliver on this unclouded night, granting them limited light to walk by. The oppressive sensation faded little by little, as the lengthening shadows hid them away.

At some point, they encountered a smoother path and turned left. This reduced the noise from their passing and let them move ahead faster. Even in the limited light, Chase recognized the tracks from cart wheels and countless feet in the hardened dirt under their feet. There had to be civilization somewhere nearby.

To their relief, Kith grew increasingly relaxed, granting them the occasional whispered announcement that they weren't currently at risk.

Once, Chase spotted a sliver of moving shadow in the air at the edge of his vision and smiled to himself. Regardless of what their stupid names were now, knowing that the shades and Radine were scouting was a comfort. He didn't glance at the cart where Spike was currently sleeping. His presence had been the topic of yet another fight between Nordon and Reen, but in the end, he'd relented.

Reen himself didn't relax at any point. His gaze constantly swiveled about, and he jumped at the smallest noises. He pressed on, even when it looked like he was about to keel over from the strain. Finally, though, he turned on his heels, beckoning for Nordon to follow him, as he walked back to join their trailing cart.

The caarnath plodded to a standstill, and they crowded around Reen.

They'd been walking uphill for a while. Reen pointed at where they were approaching the crest of the hill. "We're reaching our goal. On the other side of that hill is the village of Hand's Rest. It's where we have our hideout. It'll be cramped, and awkward with this number of people, but we will make do. Now, before we enter the village, you'll need some instructions, so you don't mess up everything. Nordon knows this, but the rest of you don't."

He frowned, gathering his thoughts, before pointing back where they'd came from. "Out there, in the lands of Light, or in Earth's Ward? You can walk around everywhere. Some Lightborn officials might take offense to high-Tiered Elemental wielders walking around unsupervised in their lands, but most places, your particular blends of races won't be an issue. Well, except for the Darkie there." He sniffed at Chase. "Anyway, in here? People do get born who aren't Liberators—and we do have outsiders joining us now and again. You are not unique. You're just rare. As a group, you are noticeable. This makes you stand out, *which is a bad thing.* Why is this a bad thing?"

"Well, because—" Liam started.

Reen raised an admonishing finger, prompting him to silence. "Rhetorical question. You don't know enough to speculate. It's because everything about you screams *outsider.* Your clothes, your cards, your posture. And the moment you open your mouths, you're bound to give everything away. Today, we are going to take care of the worst of those issues, and also get you cleaned. Hygiene is important, you know?"

Sera looked as though she were ready to snap at him, but she swallowed her outburst.

"Once we're done, you should hopefully be less noticeable on our journey. With that said, I still need you to avoid talking to anybody until we reach Salvation—that's our capital, in case you are simple."

"What happens once we reach Salvation? Will we be able to gain a modicum of freedom there?" Sera asked.

"Liberty fend," Reen spat, with the looks of somebody who'd been asked to drink Waves water. "No. But there, at least, I'll be able to hide you all away properly, so we aren't in constant risk of being discovered."

He turned on his heels and started back up the hill, huffing as he marched.

Sera snarled, "I do not think that I like that man much."

Chase gave her a one-armed hug and whispered into her ear. "You don't need to, love. You just need to smile and look lovely...right up to the point where we rob his people blind."

Her nostrils flared. "I can get behind that plan."

They crested the hill and continued onward. There, they were surprised to discover, they were able to walk straight into the village of Hand's Rest.

It was a weird transition. At this point, they'd experienced quite a lot of what the world had to offer. The different races had vastly differing approaches to defense. Yet, Lightborn, Furyborn, and Elementals had one thing in common: the fact that they *had* defenses. Here, the dirt road turned into a paved street at the same time as the first houses started to appear on either side. No walls. No guards in sight. Nothing. Simply a smooth transition from soil to paved roads and houses on either side of the street.

Chase sweated, waiting for an ambush, for guards or hostile Guardians to come pouring out at them. He shared looks with the others, who looked similarly unease Kith especially had trouble containing his nerves, sweating profusely, one hand on the cart to guide his progress while his senses were elsewhere, scouting all around them. Yet, nothing happened. They walked through the dark streets, completely unimpeded by anything or anybody.

Their only indication that anything was happening came when Reen veered to one side of the road. He didn't hesitate, didn't say anything, only grasped a door handle on one house that looked every bit the same as those on either side, opened the door, and gestured them inside.

They found themselves in a foyer, equally dark, with little to guide their way. There were clothes on a rack, sets of footwear, a painting of some angelic figure on one wall, yet no luxuries, nothing to give any hints at where they were or who the place belonged to. Beyond, one door of three stood open, golden light shining out at them.

Reen pointed in that direction and said in a low voice, "Walk right in there. You'll be aided, one after another, and told where to sleep. *Don't* say a word. I'll take care of the carts." Then he walked back out the front entrance.

They shared glances. Kith sneered and opened his mouth, but Nordon slapped a hand over it and glared at him. Then Nordon led the way into the next room.

It was a kitchen. A simple, much-used kitchen with a wooden table, worn to a dull shine, and the look of having fed an army of people, big and small, over decades. The windows were shuttered, however, and dark cloth had been layered on top, to prevent the light from being visible from the street.

A person sat at the table, surrounded by a number of implements, tubes, bottles, and a large bowl filled with water.

Sera squeaked in surprise. She hadn't noticed anything until they moved.

Unspeaking, wearing the same clothes as Reen, only brighter and with a deep hood draped on top, they merely pointed at Nordon, the first person to enter the door. Then, they extended the digit to point out the chair across from themselves. Nordon moved, and the person, still without a single noise, held up a hand, indicating that the rest of them should stay where they were.

The next couple of hours were some of the weirdest and most tense Chase had ever experienced. It didn't truly feel like they were threatened with exposure right at that moment. Even so, the slightest of sounds from any of them was enough to have the person call them out with a gesture, bidding absolute silence as they performed their art.

Because that was apparently why they were there, in a stranger's kitchen. For body paint.

With no explanation, they could only watch on in confusion, as the person grasped Nordon's arm, unfurled his voluminous sleeve, placed the arm carefully on the table, and started *shaving* his lower arm. Then, they patted the arm dry, opened a few of the small bottles next to them, dipped in a brush, and started to paint.

Chase knew that cards were not something you could easily hide. The flash from the activation of a card was easily visible, especially in a dark room. Also, the magic inherent in the cards wasn't something you could just cover. Cards were not properly subject to physics, or they'd just be able to rub a bit of dirt on themselves to blend in.

Whatever paint the hooded person used worked, though. The first layer fully covered Nordon's regular Manipulate Water card. Then, they mixed and applied a layer of plain colors to approximate his real skin tone. Once that was done, they got on with the *real* job. They rolled up their *own* sleeve, revealing the Liberty card standing out there, planted it on the table opposite of Nordon, then got to work replicating it, one to one.

In the following hours, they got a damn good look at the Liberty card. Mostly, because there was nothing else to do. They stood there in a cramped kitchen, awkwardly trying not to stare at one another, avoiding any noise, because even the slightest whisper resulted in a brusque gesture from the painter, commanding them to silence.

Admittedly, the card, which Nordon had introduced as Devotion to Liberty, looked impressive. The color scheme as well as the image itself seemed to draw in the eyes, to keep them fixed on the Savior.

Even with very limited knowledge about Liberty society, they knew this was who they were looking at. The Savior of Liberty, painted in a blue so dark it was nearly black, stood at the center of the image. From all sides, flowing whirls of energy streamed toward him, in a color palette that started light blue and got consistently darker. The Savior himself was portrayed as an imposing figure, stern and hard, eyes closed, yet with eyes disturbingly drawn on top of the eyelids. Elbows out, his hands nearly met in front of his chest, where a blue whorl of energy rotated between the palms, as if he were about to release a blast of magic.

At some point before morning, they were ushered back out of the kitchen door, all of them now affixed with the image of the card, and pointed toward a set of stairs that led downward. There, they found a large basement with a few candles to banish the worst of the darkness. Reen was there already, as were a huge wooden tub filled with water behind a prominent divider, and, blessedly, a pile of their sleeping furs and blankets.

Reen was already asleep, snoring with a thin, whistling sound. It didn't take the rest of them long to follow his example.

The following day, they rose and bathed, leaving the water in the tub looking like the filthy slush from the Waves. Reen instructed them that the painted cards were water resistant, not water proof, and to take care while bathing. They ate a simple, but filling breakfast of bread and fruit that had been set out for them.

Apart from his warnings, Reen ignored them until it was time to go. "Now, remember what I said. Do not talk to anybody.

Do not attract attention. Just follow, and we'll soon get out of the village and get on our way. Once we make it to the trade roads, we'll be able to mingle with workers, produce carts and others, and you will stand out less. Above all, shut the Pits up, and we can get through this without any of us getting caught."

"Question." Kith raised his hand.

Reen glared at him.

Kith ignored the hostility, merrily smiling at the man. "So, obviously, you're pissed that somebody beyond Nordon came along, because it makes your life a lot harder."

The glare became a death stare, and his upper lip trembled in distaste.

He pretended not to notice. "My only question is: Are you going to be a moron about it?"

Sera slapped her forehead.

Reen looked as if he were about to suffer from apoplexy. "You dare call me—"

"Yup. I mean, I could come up with better words, if you want? We could go with fool. Oaf. Dolt. Dullard—"

"Kith. This isn't doing us all any good," Nordon said in a tone that clearly attempted to salvage the situation.

Kith snorted. "Well, neither is his attitude. Now, that painter upstairs wants to keep it a secret who they are, so we can't give away their name or something if we're caught? Sure. I don't even care. But if this prissy piece of work expects us to traipse behind him for the next few weeks in silence until we reach the capital and he can tuck us away silently? He can take that and stuff it up his freedom-loving arse."

Chase leapt to his feet, at the same time as Reen got up, his infuriated blush making his cheeks a deep purple. "That's it. I'm not listening to this anymore," he snapped.

"Yes, you are," Kith snarled. "Because, even if you're beyond furious with us for making your life harder, I think you're not an absolute idiot. And walking out that door would be an idiot move."

Reen got right up in Kith's face. It was a ridiculous look. The two were about the same height, but Kith had spent the past many months bulking up and pushing himself to the brink of exhaustion. The squat Furyborn was reaching a degree of wide muscularity that made his low stature quite unimportant. Reen, on the other hand, looked like somebody whose biggest muscle was his writing hand. "Are you saying that you're going to try to stop me?" he growled.

Kith's answer was a disdainful snort. "If I did, there wouldn't be any trying about it. But no. You're quite free to leave. Only, if you do that, you're right. We'd probably get caught. Eventually, so would you, I guess, because your blessed Savior probably isn't a fan of smugglers. So, how about you sit back down and we talk like normal people instead?"

"You think you're suddenly in charge?" Reen pressed on.

Kith groaned. "Get *off* it, man. You're in charge. But you're being an idiot if you try to make us shut up for however long it takes us all to get to Salvation." He pointed at Cilia and Sera. "You sure didn't look like you minded the idea of making use of Cilia's crafting, or Sera's healing. Well, I'm a damn good scout. But I won't be able to scout properly, if you're not frigging talking to me, telling me what to look for. That goes for all of us, really. And, let's be entirely honest. What is going to look *more* suspicious? Me and the girls"—he waved at the others, including Chase and Liam—"traipsing after you like a pack of baby ducklings? Or us actually talking like living, breathing people, and *learning what we should look out for*?"

Reen's sneer didn't abate. A vein in his forehead pulsed as though it were ready to burst. Eventually, though, he exhaled forcibly. "All right. But I am in charge. And as long as we're in Hand's Rest, my order stays. Complete silence! It would be too easy for somebody to notice your accent or weird behavior, and trace it back to this house."

"You've got it, boss." Kith smiled.

CHAPTER 8

Every single person we talk to admits the following: Liberty card wielders all have to pick the same card at the first Tier. Also, that card, Devotion to Liberty, as something almost unheard of, does not just offer something positive. It also steals from the wielder. Even so, more than half of them refuse to say anything negative about it. We need more knowledge. I'm asking Reen about this. Either the Elementals misunderstand something, or the Liberator society is weirder than we expected. (Page 4.)

Hand's Rest by day was even stranger than it had looked during the night. It was nothing like any village they'd ever seen before.

Villages were simple, both in Lightborn territories and the Furyborn villages they'd seen. Lightborn lands generally saw the village erected with some sort of central leader as a mayor, some noble or other, usually one low in the hierarchy. They would build a central building, that usually dwarfed everything else. Then, everything else would sort of sprout from there, with any actual planning depending on the mayor's whims and desire to control everything. Eventually, everywhere except for the absolute centers of Lightborn territory, would include outer walls and, as often as not, defenses.

Furyborn villages were slightly different, in that they were usually more martially inclined, with a greater focus on defenses due to the ever-present threats. Also, leaders lived alongside everyone else. On top of that, there was even less planning when it came to their streets and orientation. Rather, their cities grew as they desired according to the individuals erecting their homes.

Hand's Rest was nothing like either of those. In fact, it was so unlike anything they knew that the entire situation felt almost oppressive. When they entered the near-deserted street, they realized that they were at the upper part of a slope, with the village stretching out below them, and could get a good look on everything, instead of the vague impressions they had to work with the day before.

At first, there was one thing that sprang to mind. There was no discussion that this was a village, and a small one at that.

The slope had to hold no more than three to four hundred dwellings, at most. Yet, the degree of order, straight lines, and homogeneity in construction put even the noble quarter in Isarn to shame. From this height, they could see not a single off angle. Every house, every street was meticulously arranged, originating from a central square and expanding at right angles in a square grid, equidistant from each other, creating a pattern that looked both supernaturally accurate and extraordinarily easy to navigate.

This was not rich housing. They hadn't magically emerged in some village that housed retired noblemen or anything like that. The constructions were well-made, but not ostentatious. Each and every one of the dwellings were rectangular, built from fired clay bricks, with flat roofs. However contradictory it might sound, it was the similarities in the dwellings that truly made them stand out. Not only were they near-identical in style and size, the only details that made them stand apart even the slightest bit were the tiniest of personal touches—small decorative patterns or potted plants hanging from the overhangs of the roofs. Oh, and each and every one of the houses was painted in a light-blue color.

As they walked, they realized that these weren't the only colors. A few times, in the distance, they spotted a few clumps of larger houses, still identical in construction, only, with a darker blue color. They were, Chase realized, the same colors as their own outfits. Their group all wore loose shirts and pants in the same color as the smaller dwellings, while Reen's robe matched the larger housing. Nordon *had* gone on about the caste system—but at least they didn't differentiate between women and men. Yet, it was one thing to hear about it, and quite another to see, in practice, how upfront they were about it. "Look at this house," it seemed to scream. "Whomever lives here is more important than you, which is why they've earned more space and more status. You may now be suitably deferential."

Chase hated it already.

Following their long trek the day before, they'd been allowed to sleep in. At this time of day, with the sun well up in the sky, the village wasn't deserted. However, neither was it bustling. It would appear that most people were already wherever their day job required them to be, or stayed inside their dwellings. They still met a few people in the streets, all wearing the weird, lopsided shirts that left their card visible on the right arm. The same as they were wearing, helping them blend in. Most carried the light blue of the Tier-one citizens, though they did spot a single darker blue shirt at a distance, with two light-blue people trailing after him.

They followed the streets for about ten minutes before leaving the village. The paved streets were well-made, visually impressive with a fancy, colored pattern, and allowed them to enjoy a rare fast walking pace, as the carts were barely jolted around. To their surprise, they didn't walk in a straight line, instead moving in a zigzag line from the southern end of the village to the northeastern.

From the short walk, they didn't learn anything definite. Still, it looked like that amenities were also planned into the village construction. They spotted a few wells around the village, centrally placed. They spotted no craftsmen, though; no smithies, no traders in the street. It was downright confusing.

Again, they had to gawk as they left the village. One square of the pattern had been completed, with the outside having its own paved street. Yet...that was it. Nothing to demarcate the difference between inside and outside, and not a *single* thing to stop an invader or hostile Guardian from rampaging. Either they had an absolutely insane confidence in the protective capabilities of that Prism of theirs, or there were things they couldn't see.

"Where are the Guardians?" Kith broke the pervasive silence. They'd left the village behind, and, after about ten minutes of marching, had also passed the few locals near the outskirts, with only stolen glances marking any curiosity toward the unfamiliar grouping passing them by. Now, they were alone again, back on the well-kept dirt roads, moving north and east. "I didn't see a single one near the border, and neither Radine nor my...other skills have spotted any. Yet."

Chase blinked. That hadn't been anywhere *near* the first question lining up inside his mind after seeing the unfamiliar setting of Hand's Rest. But now that he thought of it, it was a damn good one. Every society—every *single* society of Ordei— was built around the usage of Guardians. According to the Furyborn elders, defining how you wanted to establish the creation and maintenance of Guardians was a core part of what happened when you established the first Wellspring for a deck. The fact that they hadn't spotted any so far? Just another indicator that something in the lands of Liberty was subtly, entirely off.

Reen just laughed. "We are far away now that we should be safe to speak." He sneered—what seemed to be his default expression—and shook his head. "You wouldn't see them. Our Keepers, or, what outsiders call Guardians, are hidden right in the open."

"It seems to me that the differences in naming terms are very much bound in the mentality in your lands. The same for the Tiers. Could you explain the differences to us?" Sera asked earnestly.

Chase recognized it for what it was. An outstretched hand. An offer to start over, with less animosity.

Reen merely looked at her, then at Nordon. "Have you explained nothing at all to them?"

Nordon smiled. "I have explained everything I knew. Your society is not easy for outsiders to penetrate."

He murmured something under his breath. With a deep exhalation, he barreled into an explanation. "Our Keepers are multi-faceted. They keep the peace, keep watch, and *keep quiet.* Yet, they are in every village, every city, watching, looking out for anything out of the ordinary, anything that is worth sending guards out to investigate." With a half-smirk, he added, "Yet, they also keep *away.*"

"So, they're hidden? Watching over everybody, like spies?" Kith asked. "Was that the reason our path through the village took all those turns?"

Reen gave a grudging nod. "Yes. They rarely, if ever, move, once they've found the best place to stay. In some places in the capital, they've even been integrated into the buildings themselves. Here, they are mostly half-hidden between buildings, on rooftops and the like. But!" He raised an admonishing finger. "*Never* call them spies. Keepers are there to help, to ensure that any issues or traitors are found and reported before they manage to work against the interests of the nation."

Kith snorted. "Sure. Just like the city guard back in Isarn was *totally* there to guard the city, and not to line their own pockets."

Reen frowned, but didn't gainsay Kith. "The important part is knowing where they are, and not acting suspicious. You may not alert them the first time around, but once you attract their attention, you can be sure that guards will follow."

"Duly noted." Kith tapped his forehead in a mocking salute. "Once we're done here, I'm definitely sending Radine to deliver a few updates to the Fury Council. They need to know where we're going."

"I will help you pen the missives." Sera said.

"Appreciated. So, Reen. What about the Tiers? How do they work here?"

Reen didn't answer for a while. For once, however, his demeanor was neither mocking nor distanced. Rather, he looked contemplative. Eventually, he began an explanation. "Nordon was the second outsider I'd ever talked to. There was one Lightborn smuggler before that, but he tried to backstab me and run away with my goods."

They exchanged glances. Was he expecting an answer? A reaction?

"There is no such thing as official interaction with outsiders. But you should know that, in here, you are all reviled as being close to devils. Your collective races, wielders, and Guardians are painted as a united threat, working together to destroy our way of being."

Chase was the first to gain control of his faculty of speech. "Seriously?" he croaked. "You're trying to claim that Lightborn worked together with, say, Furyborn and Darkborn?"

Reen nodded. "You will find that the official attitude on outsiders is *horribly* skewed toward fear and hatred, much of it well-earned. But that is not my point. My point is, I have no clue how little you know, and every time I think I have an idea where to start, I realize that my explanations will probably leave you in need of further explanations."

Liam grinned. "Nothing new there. That's me every time Cilia opens her mouth."

Chase interrupted. "Please ignore him. Also, you're good, man. Just start wherever you'd like. We're not dumb, generally. Ignorant? That one, I'll own to. But we catch up quick."

Reen nodded slowly, a sheen of concentration overriding the general disdain as he walked in front of the others. His voice started out soft, thoughtful. "If there is one thing you need to know about Liberty, it's this: The Savior? The stories might lie. The scripture might be made up in part. But make no mistake. He is a god."

Into the shocked silence, he continued, his cadence picking up as he warmed to the task. "The scripture is simple. The Savior used to be removed from Ordei, like all other gods. Yet, when He saw the corruption inherent in the old system of government, the myriad schisms and power struggles, and the manyfold enemies threatening our way of being from all sides, He would not stand aside, but chose to act." He raised and brought down his arms like flinging something onto the ground. "He destroyed them all. The old leaders. The corrupt, those too far gone to save. Then He rebuilt the system from the ground up, starting with our cards and reworking everything from there.

"Following the scouring of the old, He proceeded to ensure that his work would last forever. He soon realized the main flaw of the old system. Even if his divine powers were enough to complete the task, it would not be enough to maintain it forever. Hence, He reworked the deck to ensure that our collective powers would work to *strengthen* ourselves and keep us safe, instead of pulling us in a thousand different directions."

He looked back and saw their collective confusion. The smirk was back in an instant, but slightly more good-natured. "Don't worry. This time, I won't have to struggle to explain it, because I can use the Savior's own words." His gaze went distant, and he started to recite. It took a moment before they realized he was explaining a card description.

[**Devotion to Liberty**
Uncommon, Liberty fighter
Tier one
Passive, permanent
This card is a compact, between the Savior of Liberty and every wielder in the lands of Liberty. It irrevocably binds the wielder for as long as the card is worn, reinforcing the bond between them and their home. The channel between the two is active and constant as long as the card is equipped.

The Title bonus for any wielder is doubled, both for attribute gains or any other gain. In return, twenty percent of any Ænima earned by the wielder is passed on to the Savior, as the prime defender of the Liberty lands.

No cooldown
"As you become mine, so I am yours. Servants, both. You serve me. I serve Liberty." The Savior of Liberty.]

"What?" The sound of their group's collective shock and outrage interrupted Reen's low, collected voice.

Chase spoke on in sincere disbelief. "Why would anybody ever choose that? You walk the Steps twenty percent slower. For what? A few extra attributes from your Title? That's the crappiest trade-off I've ever heard of."

"First off, it's not like we have a *choice*," Reen said heatedly. "Decks are carefully protected in the city of Salvation, and anybody who hits that first Tier *has* to travel there and choose the card. Second..." His voice drooped, and took on a quality that was more tired than anything else. "Most people believe, in the depths of their hearts, that the exchange is worth it."

He pointed back to where they came from. "It's hard to deny the evidence. Wherever you go, you can see that it works. Cities are maintained. Corruption staved off. Traitors located and executed. And our lands are defended from the raging invaders. Invaders that we all get the chance to see and fight against. All for the low price of a single card, that probably wouldn't be that impressive anyway."

Liam scratched his neck. "I mean...it still sounds like you're the ones paying, and that Savior's the one gaining. But okay. Knowing what most people think helps. Also, for our group, the Title increases would be more than just a few additional stat points. So, probably not the worst boost for a Tier one card. Why's it sound like you're not a believer, though?"

Kith rolled his eyes. "Because he's like us, of course. He's a criminal. He's seen some things, which means that he knows the official lies are just that. Lies. So, what did the trick, my man? What made you go against the good old Savior?"

Reen stopped walking, and, behind him, they were forced to stumble to a halt to avoid walking right into him. "I am going to stop you right there," he said in a cold voice. "You don't know our lives. You don't know our world. You haven't lived our sacrifices. You don't get to come here and tell us what's real and what's not."

Chase suddenly realized something. The belligerence in the man's demeanor. The lashing out, the sneers. Behind that was nothing so much as a sea of pain that threatened to spill out. "He's right, Kith. We have no clue. We don't know what they've lived through—what they still live through. Until we truly understand, we shouldn't be too fast to criticize, and never out in the open." He turned from Kith back to Reen. "Help us understand. Please. At which point did you start doubting the Savior?"

Reen's lip twitched. Eventually he spoke, pain in every word. "I don't. I don't doubt His message, His godhood, the veracity of His claims and needs. I merely saw the *cost*. And I couldn't bring myself to believe that it was worth it." He started to walk again, setting a slow pace, looking entirely lost within his own mind.

A few times, one of them looked as if they were about to speak up, but Chase stopped them. He'd seen the look on Reen's face. It was that of somebody making their way through a difficult transition. Pushing him now wouldn't do any good.

Finally, Reen spoke up in a near whisper. They had to move closer to hear him. "Part of what the Savior did is that He broke us all and reconstructed us as one. We are all part of the cycle. All intended to shape, aid, and toil for the betterment of all. Kids are allowed to be kids. Young, innocent, wonderful, they are...one and all fed, cared for, taught." He pointed with a thumb behind them, at the border they'd left behind. "When you turn fifteen, however, you join the Blessed Hopeful. Named, because you are hopeful that you can make a difference. Hopeful that you can help your kin, that you can pay back what the Savior gifts you. A few others. I forget." He massaged his brow. "Hopefuls are sent to the border, to defend us all."

"At fifteen?" Sera repeated incredulously.

"Yes. This is not something they do on a whim, of course, and the hopeful are by no means sent off unprepared. They are given the best training by many-year veterans, outfitted with good equipment. Also, we have the Prism on our side, aimed and powered by the Savior." He winced. "It is by no means safe. Yet, it is what keeps us safe. And when you have done your duty and earned your card, you may retreat into regular society, find a niche that suits you, and your Title and the earned bonuses from your Steps will make your life easier."

"Wait. I know I'm slow." Liam ducked Cilia's slap. "Slow, not dumb, Cil—don't hit me. But that can't be right. I mean, Cil told us about how those...hopefuls, as you called them...that they didn't fight alone. That they'd have others protecting them."

"She is right," Reen said. "Once you earn your first card, you're no longer a hopeful. You're part of the mass—the Great and Prosperous Mass. The large, powerful force of our people, who are stronger than regular hopefuls, who would be able to take on any uncarded outsider one-on-one and come out victorious. They have received at least a bonus of five to their attributes from walking the Steps, and another two from the card, doubling their Title bonus. They are not weak. Yet, if we only had hopefuls and those of the mass, we would be in trouble against invaders or strong Guardians." He huffed. "When you are of the mass, you will be kept fed, clothed, and housed, forever. You will be safe and sound, and never be let go. You will also be guided toward a job that suits your strengths. But this job will rarely go beyond simple physical labor, or perhaps the most simplistic of administrative tasks. If you want to grow, to spend your life on something more important, be given back more? You need to go back to the front. Fight to become a hand."

"Nordon mentioned that. A hand is when you become Tier-two and receive your next card?" Chase asked.

"Just so. If the Great and Prosperous Mass is what makes the wheels of our society turn, the Hands of Motion are the ones who direct or protect it. We are paid back more for our sacrifice, are given better housing, better jobs, aides, a lot of bonuses. In return, when Devotion to Liberty is upgraded from Common to Uncommon, the share of our Ænima that goes to the Savior increases from ten to twenty percent. Also, the Tier two card, you're allowed to choose for yourself. There are certain cards that...well, mostly, you get to choose exactly what you'd like."

"Was that when you started doubting whether the cost was worth the sacrifice?" Sera asked softly.

Reen didn't answer immediately. He nodded, before clenching his eyes shut. "Eventually, yes. I became an administrator. I'd proved my capabilities along the border, capably aiding the hopeful under my care. I proved my worth twice over, showing that my gifts were better as a quartermaster and a mind than in a formation. So, they sent me back here, to aid the process of ensuring that we had as little spillage as possible between hopeful, mass, and hands."

"Spillage." Liam pronounced the word as though he were chewing on a rotten drumstick.

"Exactly what it sounds like. The more people continue the path toward higher castes, the more Ænima flows toward the Savior, and the better He can protect us all." He grimaced. "I can even agree with the principle, still. But agreeing in theory is one thing. It is quite another to sit face-to-face with a sixteen-year-old hopeful and explain that of course he should continue the fight, just because he lost a hand. That a young widow, who only ever wanted to become a crafter, needs to walk five more Steps and earn her second Tier before she can be allowed to manage detailed craftsmanship." He reached out for the caarnath as he walked, petting it softly.

To Chase, it looked more like he was trying to draw some warmth and closeness from the animal to steady himself. "We appreciate the knowledge, Reen. The more we know, the less chance we mess up horribly. What about the higher castes? I mean, I expect that it'll be more of the same—higher Tiers equal more responsibility, more rights and more prestige? Also, what about yourself? What is it exactly that you do?"

His lip quirked up in something reminiscent of a smile. "In theory? My job is as a card advisor. I exist as an intermediary between what could be and what is." His hands rose in defense, and he laughed softly, self-disparagingly. "I know, I know. That was how I was introduced to my position. As a ranged fighter, I was always better at redistribution than actual fighting, at ensuring that the right people arrived at the right place. If I had more time, I could decide battles beforehand, simply by means of stacking the odds through careful choices. When I became a hand, they told me I would be able to continue that, on a grander scale, by guiding people to their proper places in life, showing them what they would need to do to gain their dreams and find the cards to support that dream." He smiled wistfully, sadly, as he walked, stroking the caarnath at his side. His hand shook a bit.

"The Hands of Motion are many things. We are numerous, capable, have proved ourselves in battle. We represent maybe ten percent of all wielders in the blissful lands. We are also *entirely* subservient to higher castes. That part is not advertised as much," he spat, the look of hostility back on his face. "Soon, I learned that my job was less about ensuring that people obtained their innermost desires and more about pushing them to continue on their path to walking the Steps instead of settling for less. I learned—" His voice broke, and he walked in silence for a while, jaw clenched. When he started to speak again, his tone was tight and cold.

"In order to perform my job properly, I needed information. Details on available positions, on the needs and demands of our society. On *losses*." He spat the word. "Soon, I learned more than I wanted to, and started seeking out additional facts. That was when my faith was first tested. I learned how many die, seeking to obtain higher castes. Yet, that wasn't the real crucible. When all is said and done, people choose it for themselves. *They* decide whether they want to settle or want to reach for more."

Following behind Reen, they shared glances. Yet, nobody commented on the fact that Reen's voice clearly told that he was nowhere *near* as accepting of that part as he claimed.

"Eventually, I learned what happened to those who fail. That broke me. I—another time. I will tell you another time." He shook his head, disrupting his flow and returning to his scholarly explanation.

"The Hearts of Liberty. They are those who have earned their third card. Those who proved that they understand and are willing to pay the price for freedom. They oversee and judge disputes, manage small or middling cities, make large-scale decisions, and are the higher administrators and distributors of wealth everywhere in our society. Less than one in twenty-five of all who earn cards manage to climb this high."

With a wry voice, he interjected, "They are also the reason I reached out to Nordon. Hearts are powerful, and have a good deal of influence...and they are the ones most susceptible to being influenced by outside 'gifts.'" Reen smirked. "If you have what they want, they can make your life a lot easier. Sometimes, what they want is exotic."

"Ah. Corruption." Kith nodded sagely. "Finally, you speak our language."

Ignoring him, Reen continued. "Now, we proceed to hearsay, mostly. The Pristine Minds of Liberty form less than one percent of all those who manage to earn a card. Yet, they are the *real* powers in administration. Those who handle the powerful posts and make the important decisions. They are also well removed from lower castes. Even a hand like myself is rarely allowed to interact with them."

He made an elaborate gesture, somewhere between a half-bow and an introductory wave. "The Pillars of All, then, reside at the pinnacle of all. These are the blessed wielders who are allowed to stand at the side of the Savior, aide him in governing the blissful lands. Their numbers fluctuate, but everybody knows who they are. At the moment, there are three."

Sera looked like she was having trouble with something. Her face was intense, yet confused. "There is something I do not understand, Reen. You say that you, that the society as a whole, incentivizes everybody to keep walking the Steps and striving for more?"

He grunted in agreement.

She rubbed her face. "There is something I am not seeing here. Lightborn society? They differentiate, only allow those they like to earn cards in the first place. There is less impetus to risk your life. Even so, a Tier-five in the Lightborn ranks is powerful, but not legendary. Yet, you say that you only have three Tier-fives all told, and nobody higher? How is that even possible?"

"Oh." Reen's face turned sour. "The cost of our peace, again. Every time you gain a new rank, you are required to increase the rarity of Devotion to Liberty. The boost to your Title improves—and so does the cost in Ænima. If you are of the mass, it only detracts ten percent. As a hand, at Uncommon rarity, it is twenty. Anybody becoming a Pillar will receive fifty percent less Ænima."

For a while, there was silence. Then Kith sputtered, *"Fifty!* That's—that's robbery! But what's that Savior of yours even *do* with the Ænima?"

"What does a living god do with the vast accumulated life force of countless hostile Guardians and wielders trying to invade our lands? Is that an actual question? *I talk to people about cards.* The divine is slightly beyond my reach."

After that, there was silence as they walked the seemingly unending dirt road. Their faces wore wildly varying expressions. Some were lost in melancholy. Others looked like they were perusing a puzzle that was missing a dozen pieces. Some looked affronted, like they needed to stab somebody. At least one person smiled happily, lost in the daydreaming of how to steal the accumulated Ænima of a god.

CHAPTER 9

The Elemental towers rarely, if ever, receive fugitives from the lands of Liberty. Why this is, we cannot say, and sources disagree. Also, those who do arrive are, with few exceptions, cardless. Hence, even the rare few who are open to the possibility of talking cannot prove that they belonged to the so-called blissful lands. This dearth of trustworthy information lies at the core of our challenge. In our coming chapters, we will delve into black-market trade and what these items have taught us. That *is* a conundrum. However, at this point, if we safely return, at least we can help the towers with some information. Nobody leaves, because they'd have to stride through the effect of the Prism, under the eye of a living god. I'd bet that isn't good for your health! (Page 6.)

Their travels over the next couple of weeks were fast, unobstructed, and mostly lonesome.

That was not to say that they were alone on the roads. Not by any means. However, they found that those traveling the Liberty roads were, by and large, not inclined to socialize.

Perhaps, they mused, it had to do with Reen. Any other travelers who would overtake them, or they overtook, he would talk to, alone. His curt, no-nonsense behavior and barely hidden scowl, even from a distance, made no secret of the fact that he was not interested in small talk.

What their travels lacked for in socializing, they made up for in visuals. The blissful lands, as the Liberty areas were apparently called, were a marvel.

At this point, they'd experienced a lot of different landscapes, from the harsh, wind-bitten terrain of the carved plains, over the lush, dense forest of Heart Halls, to the failing, sickened nature near the Prism. Yet, they had never experienced anything that appeared as mild and, for lack of a better word, tame, as the Liberty lands.

Before the first day had passed, they hit the first real trade road: a packed-dirt tributary joining the paved road, clearly crafter-made, one of the trade arteries allowing people and trade to move fast, safe, and unimpeded throughout the lands.

The sun was their constant companion, providing a warm, pleasant backdrop to a green, bountiful countryside. Healthy-looking growths sprawled wild, but rarely reached the roads, as if even nature respected their purpose.

Everywhere they passed, the lands were soft, rolling hills transitioning into gentle rivers, healthy soil offering berry bushes as tribute to the passing travelers.

Constructions aided the ease of traveling as well. For every mile, they passed signs clearly announcing directions and distances. Also, the road was constantly jotted with low-ceilinged, basic shelters, set up with rough fireplaces, simple wells and firewood already prepared.

Reen took it as his due, explaining that one of many jobs available for the mass was that of a road tender, constantly in motion, traveling the roads to ensure that everything was well maintained and commerce could move freely.

There were weird choices, aesthetic and infrastructure-wise, along their travels. Simple things that nonetheless made them wonder.

First off, there were no villages or cities near the main roads. Every single one of those would have their own byroad leading to said city or village and nowhere else. According to Reen, this was just how it was. Traveling was for traveling, and you wouldn't be distracted by passing through a lot of different cities on your way, because you wouldn't stumble upon them.

Also, there were no fields, no farms, no orchards, or obvious places producing food. That part was strange. The climate was amazing, the soil looked healthy, and in the Furyborn lands, solitary farmers would already have been at work preparing their plows. Somebody had to be farming, somewhere, to keep the people fed.

Reen refused to answer that. He clearly knew, but his face closed off and he shut up, ignoring them entirely.

Lack of socialization aside, the roads were decently busy. They were navigated mostly by carts like theirs, moving produce, animals, or crafted items in the direction of the capital. Yet, that was just a part of it. There were solitary travelers, tenders working to maintain the wayside, crafters like Nordon traveling to the villages with their equipment on smaller carts. Several times, Reen pulled them to the side of the road, as larger groups of soldiers marched by in the direction of the border. They had to admit that the soldiers—mostly hopefuls with a few mass and hands interspersed—looked professional, well-equipped, and well-fed. They definitely looked more put together than the Lightborn army they'd been forced to follow.

They talked along the way. Of course they did. Spending several weeks without any planning, any exercise, any real communication wasn't going to work for them. Yet, they did come to an early agreement with Reen. They would stay away from any interactions with other travelers, because their fake cards could be easily discovered up close, and he'd make sure that they weren't interrupted along the way. Also, at times, he would make them march to the next shelter, because he discovered Keepers nearby, surveilling the overnight dwellings. In return, he and Nordon would watch the roads, allowing them some time for training to expend the nervous energy that they stored up through hours without release, letting poor Spike out of the cart to run around and burn some energy.

Despite that restricted training, they spent large parts of their journey inside their own heads, focusing on mental exercises to eke any limited improvement out of the time on the march. Given that everybody, except for Liam, at this point had broken the threshold of twenty in Mental Power, the exercises weren't as effective as they would have hoped for. But Chase, Liam, and Kith managed to gain a solitary increase along the way, getting Kith to twenty-five. Kith also got a single point to Toughness, as did Sera.

Radine returned halfway through their trips, with a small bag of messages tied to her leg, straight from the Furyborn elders. According to them, there were few unexpected developments to report. The Lightborn forces had started to amass near their borders, but had yet to attempt any larger movements. The fresh pack of challengers inside Heart Halls were taking to their brand-new Dark cards with a vengeance, learning and developing new tactics. Of course, it was a work in progress, and expanding on practices and knowledge obtained over years and years was slow going. Here, however, the individuality of the Furyborn was doing them good, with their willingness to carve their own paths and attempt what felt right.

Two additional messages made their way to them alongside the one from the Furyborn. One from Gunnha, the other from the towers.

Gunnha was moving up her plans to include more people to their ranks. They had warned her about the risks, of course. Any inquisitor near a person using Dark cards would be able to sense them and come down upon them with a vengeance. If Gunnha herself was caught, the entire damn scheme could come tumbling down. Yet, according to Gunnha, the risk would be worth it, especially because Lightborn forces were increasingly moving westward, toward Furyborn lands. She traveled the lands of Light, staying outside the larger cities, picking her destinations according to word of mouth. Anybody she granted cards to, or, at least the *option* to gain cards when they hit that first Tier, would know somebody else. Some other family or person, who deserved a chance for personal growth. So, she traveled, constantly staying in motion, not staying in any one place for long enough for suspicion to spread.

The High Elementalist, beyond any of their allies, had her hands tied, what with the situation of the Elementals being what it was. Even if there hadn't been factions inside the towers who disagreed on whether they should even fight the Lightborn in the first place, their situation allowed for little space to maneuver. Yes, their defenses were beyond comparison, solidified and powerful to the point where even the combined Lightborn forces would have trouble cracking them open. But they were also deeply entrenched, with few offensive forces, and little organization outside their lands. She did what she could, with what she had. That boiled down to three approaches: Spies, to ferret out what was going on. Diplomats to nudge the Lightborn in a desired direction. Trade, to aid who they desired to support and deny those who they didn't.

They had already started. Even if their overall decision toward the Lightborn might not end in outright war, the assault by the Lightborn on the towers had been enough to bring out some drastic changes in attitude. Tradesmen delivered weapons and armor to the Furyborn territories, traveling far north and south to avoid Lightborn forces. Meanwhile, the Lightborn were denied. Diplomats strove for concessions, directed to push the Lightborn as hard as possible. They knew full well they were likely to see none. But with every new angle, every unexpected approach, they pressured their diplomatic forces, made it harder for the Lightborn to keep up a coherent facade. Finally, their spies worked harder than ever, delivering reports in large numbers, keeping on top of the myriad developments throughout the lands of Light.

The waves were high. According to them, power was fluctuating among the Lightborn, with a single noble, Thomas Beforant, grasping the reins of power and pulling hard. There were counterforces—of course there were. With a society like the Lightborns', nobles, military, and church always vied for dominance in a constantly changing flow. Yet, this noble, apparently, had the church in his grasp and was doing too well at keeping the other nobles and the military in check. His tendencies were, as of yet, unknown. When he eventually made his move, it could be overpowering. Until then, the spies simply reported the same details that Gunnha had sent, with a lot more detail. In short? The Furyborn were likely to soon become targets. Massively so.

Following their initial talk, Reen closed up. It seemed to them as if, while explaining their new situation, they'd managed to dig into an unhealed wound, and now the pus spilled out. He vacillated between quiet, introspective moods and a sort of sullen resentment toward the world in general. At times, he managed to open up, and even asked a few questions about the rest of Ordei. All told, the short, sullen man walked the world like a man caught up in the specters of his past. That all changed when they reached Salvation.

For the past few hours, the terrain had risen. Now, they'd reached a viewpoint that was clearly meant to show off the resplendence of the capital of the blissful lands. Salvation lay before and below them, like an unending ocean. The beautiful, rhythmic patterns of buildings stretched out, painted in varying shades of blue, aiming for the horizon for miles and miles. The early afternoon sun baked down on the lands, and clouds idly wafted across the massive city, painting darker nuances onto the buildings below.

From here, the layer of buildings looked unending, the perfect angles to the roads extending for as far as the eye could see, granting them an unmarred view of the entire setting. They knew that they were about to enter and be swallowed by this ocean, and, even with the day being sunny and warm, it felt vaguely threatening.

Until they focused on the palace. Then the vagueness faded away, and the threat became all too real.

The palace lay at the center of Salvation. Of course it did. Just like with the rest of Liberty lands, there were no defensive walls near the palace. Not a single fortified tower, entrenched position, or guarded bridge across a moat to be seen. The palace, the midnight blue of its construction so dark it looked like black, did rise several stories above the next highest dwellings. Numerous tower spires stabbed toward the sky like an army holding pikes, with the main tower rising the highest. Somehow, the placement, the size, and the darkness of the palace combined to compensate for the lack of overt military emplacements.

The palace loomed.

Sure, there were spots of dark-blue nuances across the city, entire reaches that were dominated by the azure blue of the hands, with even larger constructions sporting the cobalt or navy blue that alluded to the homes of hearts or minds.

Yet, none of those could compare. In a world of nuances, the palace screamed power, threat, and dominance all at once.

Reen seemed to feel it too. He glowered at the far-off intimidating structure as though it had hurt him personally. Eventually, he pointed, to a section that stood out in no perceptible way. "Down there is where we are going. Sixteen quadrants west of the palace and eight south. Should we, for any reason, be separated, that is where you need to go. My name is on the door."

"Anything we need to be on the lookout for?" Chase asked.

Reen shook his head. "No. Quite the opposite. Keep your head down. Try to not look too much like an outsider. No gawking, no stopping in the middle of the street." He hesitated, before pressing on. "Do not mistake this for a safe situation. There are Keepers everywhere in Salvation, and watchers aplenty to look out for things that might threaten the Savior. Our only real opportunity lies in how many people live here. They cannot keep an eye everywhere at all times. Mind you, if you get caught? You should kill yourself, to avoid giving the rest of us away." He turned on his heels and started to move along the path and down the hill.

They shared shocked glances for a while.

Eventually, Kith commented drily, "If I ever get married? I want him to hold a speech. It'll end in blood and tears, but it definitely won't be boring."

Their first impression of Salvation was rather strange. The entire Liberty civilization, according to Reen, had citizens numbering in the hundreds of thousands. Nearly a hundred thousand of those resided in Salvation alone. Yet, the city actively refused to look the least bit like a capital should.

Their progression was simplicity itself. The decline leading from the viewpoint down to the lower ground level of the capital lent itself to defensive measures. However, the road was wide, softly slanting and easily traversable, with no thought given to defending from incoming forces. The same when it came to the city itself. Just like in Hand's Rest, there were no city walls, no guards who stopped and ransacked the carts. At one point, the city simply started, without fanfare, announcement, or even a simple sign to say "Welcome to Salvation." In fact, a large number of workers were busy constructing the foundations to another quadrant where they entered, expanding the city yet another block southward.

Chase didn't gawk as he walked. He followed the carts as he should, making sure that he looked both tired and uninterested in his surroundings, like an exhausted worker returning home, just one of many. He did pay attention, but he did it surreptitiously.

Inside, he was screaming.

Salvation wasn't horrible. In fact, it was the exact opposite. Yet, everything inside the city pulsed with the sensation of something here being entirely, utterly *wrong*.

It was too clean. Too orderly. It wasn't just the city itself, though that was very much a culprit too.

The buildings they passed were well-kept, created with uniform looks and little wear and tear. Every so often, they saw construction workers or people on maintenance, applying new paint to the buildings, repairing even the slightest decay along the way. Everything was kept up to date, and up to standard. The only differences lay in the degree of luxury and size afforded depending on your caste.

Having spent a long time in Isarn, the towers, and Furyborn territory, the uniformity felt unnatural to Chase, like they were facades hiding the real city underneath. In Isarn, the difference between somebody surviving on the Waves and the nobility lounging in luxury in their walled enclosures was insane. Here, even the lower castes enjoyed a level of comfort and quality that would surpass what most people living in the lower city of Isarn had. Chase knew that, objectively speaking, this had to be way better, but he couldn't bring himself to like it.

The people were strange, too.

There wasn't a single thing that Chase could point to as the defining outlier. An adult Liberator returned from work, toolbelt at his side, lines portraying the exhaustion on his face. A young couple walked hand in hand, heads nearly touching as they discussed something. An old woman pushed along a small hand cart holding scraps of leather. Yet, everything seemed off, fake even. Like nothing here was what it looked like, and the people were all players, following the lines of some horrid script.

Little by little, the details stacked up inside his head, combining to tell him what felt so off.

First—there was no sensation of being a big city here, apart from the number of people in the streets. In fact, there was no noticeable difference between Hand's Rest and Salvation, except for how far the capital stretched. The construction was the same; the buildings were the same. In fact, if Chase wasn't wrong, it was even the same damn pattern in the paving stones on the ground. Sure, they had larger buildings here, when they hit a building or building block belonging to Tier-threes—those Hearts of Liberty—but a hundred feet farther along the street, they could've been right back in the village again.

On top of that, there were no markets. No vendors. No street sharks trying to hustle passersby, no pickpockets eyeing their next marks or...any of the details that marked a *normal* setting.

Some of the things were there, just hidden away. Well, the craftsmen and stores were there, even if the criminals weren't. They passed by a large home that gave off a strong scent of freshly cut wood. The single, unassuming wooden sign hanging next to the entrance door sported the image of a stack of planks. Other buildings hid warehouses, smithies, restaurants, possibly even entertainment venues behind the nondescript facades, judging from the scents, sounds, and images on the signs.

They reached Reen's home well into evening. What had, from afar, seemed like a short journey turned out to be several hours of walking, concentrating to avoid standing out. It was an uneventful trip, but the uncanny nature of the city along with Reen's warning that there could be watchers everywhere had them all on edge. Reen finally stopped in the middle of another unassuming stretch of street and moved on to open a door in an azure building, this one with a simple drawing of a deck of cards below the words "Reen M."

They quickly followed him inside, one after the other. The first room was a decently large entrance hall, and Reen, yawning, started to take off his coat and boots, gesturing for them to follow his example.

"Can we talk here?" Kith asked cautiously.

Reen nodded, rubbing his eyes. "As long as you don't shout."

Kith nodded and took a deep breath. "In that case, I should like to know what the *Pits* is wrong with this place! Where are the kids? Why don't people smile? Why did you just leave the carts in the street? *Why wasn't this door locked?*" That last sentence he exclaimed through gritted teeth, as if he could barely keep himself from yelling it out loud.

Reen raised an eyebrow. "What is wrong with your world that you are afraid to leave something in the street for fear of it being stolen?" He waved him off. "If you worry about your spiked pet, be calm. I have a few workers from the mass around. I'll make sure they bring it in, and feed your beast."

Chase, frowning, wanted to call Reen out on that point about security. Only, the more he considered the situation, the harder it was to find the proper words. Obviously, they'd been brought up in a lawless mess of a place. Still, crime was universal...wasn't it? Sure, the Furyborn might be an exception, what with their social conditioning on doing what aided the community and all that, but there'd always be some who were ready to ignore rules if it meant they'd get a step ahead, right?

But this was different. Given that their living god (and what an insane detail that was to enter into the mix) was the one who defined exactly what you earned and when, were there really any ways to get ahead that didn't go through the official channels? Why would you steal, if everybody had the exact same chances? *Would* you steal? Even to himself, his mental arguments sounded weak, and Chase found himself reeling, doubting everything he thought he knew. What a *nice* introduction to Salvation.

CHAPTER 10

There is a living black-market trade operating with Liberators. Yet, certain facts are undeniable. They do not share secrets. They do not accept any known denominations—only trade. Their numbers ebb and flow, as those in charge come and go. Compared to Elemental, Lightborn, or Furyborn smugglers, however, they appear surprisingly...peaceful? Law-abiding? These are not hardened criminals. That does make you think. Same goes for Reen. He's frustrating, tight-lipped, and hostile. But nothing about him screams violence. He looks like what he is. A clerk gone awry. Yet, why is this? (Page 10.)

The rest of the day disappeared, as Reen did what he could to make the remainder of their arrival to Salvation comfortable. They bathed (making sure not to scrub at the card on their arms), were fed, and were introduced to the two rooms where they'd be for the entire duration of their stay, as well as the rest of his home. Some of the workers had to spend a good while emptying the second, larger room, because they had only expected it to house two persons. Nordon, just as planned, took the second, smaller room.

There was no debating it. Compared to the house they'd stayed in back in Hand's Rest, this was a step up on all accounts. It was larger, at least twice the size from what they could judge, and the quality of the furniture, the decorations, the materials— all were better than what they'd seen back then. It wasn't ostentatious by any means, but everything, from the curtains to the dinnerware, looked like quality, like something even a well-established merchant back in Isarn wouldn't be ashamed to use.

The following day, they slept in, and awoke to the scent of food. They slowly came to, took their time to stretch and talk, before ambling into the dining room to join Reen.

The Liberator looked different in his own home, seated at the end of a long wooden table, packed with foodstuffs. More at ease, if not peaceful. His constant frown was momentarily displaced by a faraway look, as he sat, cradling a steaming clay mug. He nodded absently, as they trailed in and murmured something they chose to take as "Help yourselves."

They dug in, animatedly speaking and joking as they tried the new food that had been prepared for them. Some of it was entirely normal, if good quality, like the spread of fruits before them. Some looked conventional, but had something intangible to set it apart, like the bread, which was savory and chewy, with a lovely, thick crust, but a strange taste that made Chase think it wasn't made from wheat. Other things again...

"What *is* this? It's disgusting!"

"Kith!" Cilia scolded.

"What? It is!" He took a large mouthful of the steaming drink and swished it around in his mouth. "It's bubbly. Also, sweet *and* savory at the same time. It's like tea and soup had a gassy bastard child."

"Komainey," Reen said. "It's a brew concocted from mushrooms and...herbs. I'm not sure which ones. It has a slight restorative effect. Also, I notice you're already on your second mug." He raised an eyebrow.

"I know. It's horrible, and I want more." Kith laughed.

Reen snorted, before pushing his own plate aside, mostly emptied. "Do not worry about cleaning when you are satisfied. As a senior administrator among the hands, I have a few servants from the mass arriving twice a day to aid me. Once you're done here, I'll take you to where you will be crafting over the next weeks. First, though, we should probably talk in detail about what you should create."

"Also, what the rest of us get to do. I mean, we want to make sure we're as safe as can be, even if we're in danger of being caught," Chase said.

That was the approach they'd agreed upon. Nordon had done his part. He'd brought them to the capital, the home of the Liberty decks. They would act as dedicated guards, right up until they figured out exactly how the situation worked. Then, they'd see about sneaking into the city and learning more, questioning others about their possibilities, finding out precisely where the decks were and how they could gain access to them.

Reen nodded. "Rest assured; there's room for you too. I hope that you're prepared for boredom, though. The way I've arranged things, you aren't going to see the outside of the room often. We're minimizing risks, making sure you don't unwittingly expose yourself to a Keeper and give the game away."

Brows furrowing, Chase nodded slowly. "That sounds fair. But we're going to go over it again, once we've had a chance to look at the place. We don't mind boredom, but *we* know about staying safe, even if we don't know the ins and outs of Salvation."

With a shrug, Reen ignored him like there wasn't more to debate on the subject. He turned to Nordon. "You. Last time I had you past the border was more of a test run. We needed to see if you were able to stay hidden, if you could work with the equipment we had prepared for you, and if you could actually deliver what you promised."

Nordon hummed appreciatively. "Exactly. In my opinion, we ended at two for three. Your equipment was, on the whole, badly calibrated, created for large-scale brewing and no finesse, and the material was, to say it delicately, subpar. Which is why I've brought my own equipment this time. Combining your existing gear and mine, we should be able to hit a better effect even at larger quantities. So..." He rubbed his hands. "What are we brewing?" He reached into a belt pouch, extracting a quill and inkpot.

"I was thinking of a two-prong approach," Reen mused. "We have no known brewers in Salvation who are able to infuse substantial attribute increases into their drinks. This means that any such drinks you are able to concoct, I will be able to trade to great effect."

Nordon jotted a few notes. "Preferred attributes?"

"Mental Power," Reen announced. "Most who partake will be hands and above, who have already retired from active battle. Mental Power will make their days more palatable. Following that, you should go with Toughness, Strength, and then Agility. Though...is Potential even possible?"

"No. Not for regular brewers." Nordon smirked. "Good for you that I am not a regular brewer. It depends on my ingredients, though, and their potency. I cannot promise anything, but I have the cards for it."

"I will ensure that you have anything that you need. You will have the best quality ingredients available to hearts and below." He cleared his throat. "On top of that, we have a number of large vats, tuns, and barrels available. You did say at some point that you can only handle a given quantity of magic-infused brewing a day, right?"

Nordon nodded. "Yes. The process is taxing. While I do have some control over quantity versus quality, there is an upper limit to how much I can conceivably add effects to."

"What's that mean?" Liam said. "Quantity versus quality? I mean, I get the words, but in this situation."

Nordon smiled affably. "It's a choice for me. I can bestow my optimal effects on smaller quantities, or create smaller boosts on larger quantities."

Reen mulled it over. "I believe we should do both. A complete gamut of offerings will grant me the best chance at getting what I need. On top of that...I think there is an opportunity here to create something entirely new."

"I'm listening." Nordon leaned forward with folded hands.

"Let us just say that most of my clients will not be partaking in your creations for the taste, but for the effect. To be frank, they just don't care, except for the effect. However, I have confirmed that you are also capable of creating excellent taste experiences. So, to not let that gift go to waste, I believe that we should also have you experiment with brewing larger quantities of drink without any effects...but where you create new and interesting flavors from known ingredients."

Nordon's eyes gleamed. "That does sound like fun. Of course, we never agreed on this. We could run into an issue where I might not have the *time* to do everything, let alone the energy. While your offers of crafted Liberty items in trade have been generous, I'm not sure it would justify me running myself ragged. Especially when we already had an agreement."

The two haggled for a while. Chase was amazed by the rapid back-and-forth, how it seemed that they spoke a different language than he did, where no meant maybe, maybe meant for the right price, and everything was a battle. Eventually, they agreed that Nordon would also, on top of the promised items in trade, be granted striplings, shoots, and seeds of every plant and fruit he worked with, so he would have the chance to bring them all back to Earth's Ward for his own experimentation.

"That brings us to you." Reen turned to Cilia. "You are an unknown. You also represent an entirely different craft, which I know a lot less about. I will have to secure the equipment necessary for you, which will be difficult and possibly dangerous. I will not deny that you being a Tier-four holds certain...promises. But I need to know if you can actually deliver. So, what can you actually do?" His tone was dismissive, even doubtful as he leaned back in his chair, folding his arms across his chest.

"No." Cilia delivered the word with a cold glare and a brisk shake of her head.

"What do you mean, no?"

"Take your pick. No, I am not doing this dance. No, I am not justifying myself to you. No, I do not intend to *haggle*." She snorted. "Among our number, Kith and Chase handle the haggling. Liam, if they're female, pretty, and stupid."

Liam grinned and nodded.

Cilia leaned forward, staring him down, one finger pointing at him. "I have a Mental Power of forty-seven. Using all my boosts, and those of Sera on top, I level out at an effective Mental Power of above a hundred. I have crafted permanent items. *Permanent.*" She waved him off. "It's not a question of whether I can meet your standards. It's a question of whether you will meet my demands."

"Demands?" Reen blurted, wide-eyed from her claims. "We didn't—"

"You will deliver the best ingredients you possibly can. That's in your own interest, of course, because the results will be better. On top of that, for every two items I make, I will create one for our own use, which we will keep."

"Buh." Reen's exclamation was less a word, more a strangled sound.

"Finally, you are not going to pay me in traded items. I do not care for what any amateur craftsman can create. I crave information. Information about crafting, about Salvation and the lands of Liberty in general. You are going to spend at least an hour a day telling me about your world, and you will hold *nothing* back. If you do, I do not intend to work for you."

Hostility flashed on his face. "That— I will not bow to that kind of pressure. Nordon, you insisted that she would help."

Nordon chuckled. "Oh no. I insisted that she *could* make a difference, in theory. I have seen her creations used in practice. They are beyond reproach. Whether or not you can arrange an agreement with her is not up to me."

Cilia leaned forward. "I could spend the entire time here helping to guard Nordon, which is what I was hired for. But I don't mind working. In fact, I expect I'd enjoy getting to work with Liberty materials. Yet, learning is my real interest. So, help me do that, and I will make sure that you earn enough from our visit that you'll be swimming in gold."

Watching from the sidelines, Chase could only shake his head in amazement. For all that she often seemed dismissive of social interactions on the whole, Cilia could be downright devilish at times. Not only had she denied bartering on his terms, she'd also ensured that, if he accepted, they would get all the information that they would need in order to locate the decks and abscond with one.

Reen wavered with indecision. His nostrils flared, and he looked about to flip the table at the thought of being treated like this. Yet, he was practically drooling too, wide-eyed at the thought of what a Tier four crafter could bring to the table.

Chase decided to give him the final nudge. "Hey, Liam. What's the boost to Agility from that armor Cil made for you?"

Liam grinned and knocked on the hardened leather scales underneath his shirt. "Oh, this shoddy old thing? I think it was...seven. Yeah. Seven. That's all right, I guess. But the gloves make up for it, being tough enough to withstand unenchanted strikes."

"Pfah." Reen flung up his hands in disgust. "Cease your theatrics. If that's true, then okay. You have a deal. Cilia, I promise I will indulge your curiosity for an hour a day, and you will help me create items to bring every hand and heart in Salvation to my side."

Cilia and Reen spent awhile talking specifics about what he would prefer to have crafted. She outlined her weaknesses as a leatherworker, making no secret of the fact that she thought herself a novice at many actual techniques, even if her gifts and attributes were impressive. He didn't promise anything, but generously offered to attempt to find any writings on the subject that might help her improve her techniques.

Eventually, Reen stood and waved for them to follow him. "Let's go look at it, then? Give you two the chance to become intimate with the place where you will spend the next three weeks, before we come back here and talk specifics."

"Okay? I thought we were going to spend as little time on the streets as possible?" Chase asked. "You know, decrease the risk of us getting caught."

Reen grinned. For once, there was no snark, no derision in there. Just sheer, boyish enjoyment. They followed him into the foyer and past that into his sleeping chambers, which were painfully clean and orderly. He stepped onto the frame of the bed and reached for the tall chandelier hanging from the ceiling. "You're not wrong. That's why I have *this*." He pulled on the chandelier.

A loud click preceded an entire section of the wall soundlessly sliding open.

He jumped down, preening at their astonished looks. "I did tell you that hands earn a few perks, didn't I?"

That last part was a horrible lie, he admitted. In a city as driven by administration as Salvation was, you'd never get away with creating something as overtly off the books as this was. He had, he explained, over the years, ever so slowly managed to talk the other hands living in the remaining homes in his enormous quadrant to rearrange walls and living spaces in order for him to take over a massive hidden living space, right within the homes themselves. As he guided them into first one corridor, and then another, they observed, and learned.

The internal space might be huge, but it was anything but ostentatious. The hallways were simple, there was not a single window to the outside, and the many doors along the wooden corridors implied that the rooms beyond were likely not the largest.

They weren't alone in there. They heard voices as they walked the long, narrow halls, interspersed with sounds of living or crafting. Judging from the low sounds, whoever was in here was anything but overt about the fact, keeping noise subdued.

After a few twists and turns, they arrived at another corridor with only three doors, set at a greater distance. Reen pointed at the first door. "This will be your room, Cilia. Now, I only expected one crafter, so it isn't fully ready yet. I use it for storage, and have not had everything removed. For now, you can take a look and tell me if you need anything large remodeled or installed. Then, we can spend some time back in my home, talking about your requirements for materials, tools, equipment, and the like."

Cilia nodded. "And with you answering some of my many questions."

"That also," he assented with a grudging nod. He knocked on the next door. "Nordon? This one's for you. I've had your equipment moved here, but you'll have to install it yourself."

"That's fine." Nordon smiled. "I wouldn't trust anybody else to do it, regardless."

"You will find that I've made a few additions to my own equipment since last time. You may find some of it useful. You get yourself comfortable and set up on your own time. Once that's done, start thinking about what you want to create, and the two of us can sit down and talk about possible ingredients and quantities."

"We'll do that. I definitely want to play around with whichever mushrooms you've used for that komainey."

Reen smiled. "I figured as much." He turned to the others. "As for the four of you, you can divide yourselves as you see fit, make whatever arrangements you need. I'll bring food to you myself at set intervals, and you'll be free to go back and forth between here and your rooms back at my house. The door will be locked when there are outsiders in the house, so there is no risk of anybody stumbling on you. Just...try to limit your time in the hallways here. Those who live here prefer privacy. I'd like to keep it that way."

They conferred for a moment. Then Liam and Kith settled in with Nordon, while Chase and Sera followed the others back to Reen's home, for what Chase expected would be a *riveting* discussion about leather and leatherworking materials.

When Sera merrily informed him that was a pun, he glared at her until she skipped away.

CHAPTER 11

"Trading with Liberty smugglers is rather akin to trading with the Furyborn, in many ways. They do not accept our coinage. They have eclectic tastes. And, if you start to understand their desires, you will be able to make some excellent trades. Surprisingly, for a people who disappear anybody who enters their territory, they care not one whit for weapons. Enchanted luxury items and permanent crafted items—they will trade nigh-on anything for those. Also, small protective items are desired." Interesting, but...logical, I suppose. If you're fighting on the front lines, you won't want to explain to the higher-ups how you got yourself an Elemental-crafted sword. Luxury items, though? Hmm. The book may be small, but it could end up granting me some useful insights I can use for Reen. (Page 9.)

"**A**re you ready for this?" Cilia's voice, businesslike and curt, shot out across the room, ripe with challenge.

They were back in their room, joined by Nordon. The empty, undecorated room, which had nothing inside except for Spike and their own equipment. Reen promised he'd find some actual mattresses, but the first night they'd make do with their own bedrolls.

"Do we have to?" Chase wheedled from where he lay on his bedroll. "It's been a long, long day."

Kith smirked and knelt next to Liam. He twirled his hand until Liam awarded them all with a low, growling snore. "Liam agrees with you, mate."

Sera laughed. "Please. Liam would have been able to sleep through Soil getting burned down. Also, I *need* something to distract me. I can already tell that our guise as guards is going to be even more taxing than my purity lessons back in Isarn."

"First off, I'm not going to ask—" Chase said.

"I *absolutely* am!" Kith snorted. "Purity lessons?"

Sera rolled her eyes. "It is a lot duller than your filthy mind thinks. Spiritual purity. Purity of mind, mixed with being the perfect doll to hang off my eventual husband's arm and look elegant."

Chase snorted. "I can see *that* going wonderfully."

"Please stop distracting yourselves and wake him up," Cilia said. "There are quite a few details I learned today that will make our task harder."

Nodding, Kith prodded the big man until, rumbling and complaining, he sat up in mostly coherent fashion.

Nordon was looking from the sidelines. "This is *intriguing*. Is this how you usually handle planning? I am amazed that you have ever gotten anything done."

"Me too," Cilia said drily. Standing straight, she addressed the room. "We have a problem. Not just one, to be fair. We have several problems, and I'm not entirely sure how we should proceed from here."

"Line 'em up, one by one, and let's have a crack at it." Chase shrugged, a motion that looked entirely off with him lying down. "You know how it is. We can come up with plans for pretty much anything, but we need to know what we're dealing with."

She nodded curtly. "Okay. Issues." She frowned, glaring at nothing for a moment before continuing. "Some of these, Reen told me outright. Others, I've started piecing together, and I may need confirmation that they're true. But Reen has been true to his word so far, telling me everything I ask about."

"Does that include what the Pits he's up to here in the city?" Liam yawned. "Who all the people back there are?"

Cilia shook her head. "You saw him back on the road. The moment things got too personal, he shut up and stopped talking. I didn't want to risk that again, so I didn't ask. Once I have all the answers I need, I'll prod him on it—because, you're right, we'll want to know what we're embroiled in here, and if it can lead to further trouble—but for now, I want the larger-scale questions answered first."

"The stage is yours," Liam magnanimously declared with a sweeping bow from where he half sat up.

Huffing, she grimaced, then raised a finger. "Issue. The decks in Salvation are gathered centrally. Like in the Elemental towers. You would think that with them granting cards to every single person hitting that first Tier, they'd make access easier, but no. It has all been built up into some sort of official ceremony mixing administration and official congratulations for aiding Liberty society...it's an entire thing. These card-granting ceremonies are, as often as not, large, well-protected, and *very* official."

"Huh. Okay. That's—" Chase started.

"I have barely begun." Cilia stopped him. "Issue. They do not use any form of currency. Like the Furyborn, there is no coinage, no gold, nothing like this."

Exclamations rose throughout the room. Nordon simply nodded.

"Reen was being entirely serious when he said that the Savior provides for his people. They, very literally, provide for everybody. The hopefuls eat with their troops. Those of the mass eat in large, public kitchens. Hands and above have their food delivered or cooked in their houses by servants. All in its place, and everything under control and within constraints. The only reason that he's been able to arrange for extra food is that he has a contact in the kitchens." She dismissed the issue. "Food isn't important. What *is* important is the fact that we will not simply be able to pay for transactions, or bribe somebody to look the other way. Not easily, at least."

Chase blinked. "That also explains what Reen is doing. He's expanding his influence, having crafted items made to use as bribes, when there is no money."

"Thank you for explaining the obvious," Cilia said. "Issue."

"Is that a thing we're doing now?" Kith interrupted. He sprang to his feet. "Issue. Cilia is being dramatic!"

She glared him down. "Issue." She looked him straight in the eye to see whether he'd say anything. "Surveillance is worse than we feared. Reen does not want us to even leave the house, while we are here. Yet, out here isn't the worst. The thickness of Keepers on the ground—or on rooftops, in alleys or built into the bricks, as it were—increases the closer we get to the palace. They also have mundane guards, of course, but the largest problem here, as I see it, is that they keep attentive eyes on everything.

"A final issue," Cilia said, now sounding disheartened. "I suggested that we should be allowed to leave the house at night when visibility was worse. That won't be possible, because there is a curfew in effect. Always has been. No leaving your home at nighttime, except if you have a reason to, and permissions."

For a while, nobody said anything.

Chase was the first to clear his throat. "Are you done? Please tell me you're done."

She nodded.

Kith held up a hand, stopping Chase in his tracks as he replaced Cilia at the center of the room. "Sorry, brother. But I've been working, too. There was no way I'd be able to spend the full day just sitting around or helping Nordon lug his stuff around the room. No offense, mate."

"None taken." Nordon smiled. "Setting up is the worst part of the process."

"Anyway. Issue." Kith hissed, drawing out the *s* sound. "I've got Radine out, and she's pretty much confirming everything Cil said. The Guardians—erm, Keepers are everywhere. Hidden on roofs, in alleys, on walls. Mundane guards are less spread out, and, from what I can tell, they are different from home."

"Different how?" Liam asked.

"More professional. More polite. More likely to question you in depth and check your documentation than threaten you with a beating. Pits, some of them aren't even armed."

They took a moment to let that sink in.

Liam frowned. "That's...good, though. Isn't it?"

"Yes and no," Kith responded. "Think about the city guards back home. They might be worse opponents when it came to doing a snatch and run. But with what we're planning? Having guards who pay attention to detail, who actually *think*? That's bad."

"Oh."

"Also, the real issue here is *that there is no crime*. Nothing normal, at least. I've been paying attention. How do you pickpocket somebody, when Keepers are watching everywhere? How do you cheat somebody in the market, when there is no Fire-scoured market? *Who steals food when they give you food?*" Kith's voice rose in pitch as he progressed, and he trailed off, looking wild-eyed.

"I'm not..." Liam scowled. "Is this a bad thing?"

"Yes," Chase said without doubt. "It means that our usual tricks won't work as we're used to. They have guards looking for different things, with a different mentality." He hesitated before adding, "Though it might also be a weakness, given that they're not used to regular crime."

"Focus. Good observations," Cilia noted. "Anything further to add, Kith?"

He shook his head. "I will learn more, soon. I've had them all stay close to begin with. The range for my shades is nowhere near good enough that I'd be able to have them enter the palace. And I'm keeping Radine up high to avoid getting spotted."

"Good choice." Chase nodded. "Also, with the way they're running things here, there's probably some magical defenses or something in the palace. Maybe don't try anything, at least for now." He tapped his leg. "Okay. Summing up. We have three weeks now. Twenty-one days, where we are safe, and do not need to think about food, lodging, or anything. We also have a hideout that's likely to keep us safe, given that it's been here for years already. This means that we are set to do as we please and have a lot of freedom to get to work on Cilia's numerous issues."

She glared at him.

With a wink, he continued. "The first challenge, I'd say, would be to earn the chance to go out freely—or as close to freely as you can get in this place. Night or day doesn't matter right now. The important thing is that we find a way. That means either getting permission from Reen, obtaining some better disguises, more realistic fake cards, or some documentation that will stand up to scrutiny. Probably a combination of sorts. Then, we need to decide on the target. Is there some public spectacle where the decks are outside the palace? Or should we attempt to infiltrate the palace itself? Whichever target we go with is going to decide the route we should take afterward and what we'll need to handle.

"Following *that*, we can try to come up with a proper plan. We can investigate, talk to people, get to know what works and what doesn't." He smiled, gesturing in a half-circle at their surroundings. "Salvation is huge. There are people everywhere. As long as we're not likely to be arrested on a whim, we don't stand out much. Individually, I mean. We'll be able to get to work properly, find some weaknesses. Because, mind you, this *is* a job. There won't be any frontal assaults here. We leave the dying to soldiers."

"Poor bastards," Liam muttered.

"Finally, we need to focus on one tiny detail, with which we've had a *lousy* success rate lately."

"Getting away?" Sera asked.

"Getting away safely." He nodded. "Stealing a deck isn't going to help us much, if it leaves us stranded inside enemy territory, with watchers everywhere. Either we need to steal it without alerting anybody—a bit of a hard sell, most likely—or we need to have our exit strategy ready and waiting."

Nordon cleared his throat. "So, what you're saying is that, even if you're entirely out of your element, you don't know what you're up against, and you don't know the rules of this place, you're still going to go ahead?"

Kith snorted. "Please. If we backed down, just because we were out of our depth, we'd *never* get anything done."

Chase pointed at Kith. "Also, we should likely add to the plan that we need to make sure Nordon gets out alive."

"Much appreciated. Though, I will say right now, if we make it out? I think I'll be running off to the far end of the world. You guys bring trouble." Nordon only sounded half-jesting.

"Trouble? We haven't even gotten started yet," Kith said with a disturbing smile.

They started to dig into the specifics of their discussion, trying to find the starting points for how they could get going. For hours, they debated back and forth on how best to convince Reen, how it'd be possible to bribe other locals without gold, and which option would work best to ensure that they'd be able to walk the streets of Salvation without fear of getting made.

Eventually, they dropped off one by one, falling asleep with simplistic plans or vague notions on how to proceed. There was still nothing specific, no realistic openings they could see with what they knew at this point. Hence, the consensus was to spend the energy on learning as much as possible and building from there.

For the next week, that was exactly what they did. Cilia and Nordon spent their time planning and getting started on their crafts, and Cilia spent her hour every day questioning Reen on anything they could come up with that might be useful.

For Cilia especially, their stay was wonderful. In her own words, she learned more about Liberty society in those days than the combined hoarded knowledge of the Furyborn and Elementals. Also, not only was she encouraged, but she was *expected* to craft her best possible creations—and she was given almost anything she might need for it.

She started from scratch, having Reen bring in clean kills. That, she insisted, was the best approach here. Knowing that, with her From Farm to Table card, she'd be able to gain bonuses on top of everything else.

[**From Farm to Table**
Uncommon, Fury crafter
Tier two
Passive, permanent
The vast majority of crafters prioritize. They outsource, purchase goods, ingredients, and materials, purchase semi-finished products. It allows them to trade on the craftsmanship of others and craft a lot faster.

Yet, there is a joy in handling every part of the process, a certainty in knowing, intimately, every tiny item that you include. With this card, throughout the entire gathering and crafting process, you are able to imbue minute quantities of magic into the materials. Hence, the enhanced effects of the final product will be improved, based on how large a part of the process you have handled yourself, up to a maximum increase of sixty percent.

"Get yer filthy hands off me kill. That'll be a coat worthy of a king, it will!"]

On top of that, she and Reen agreed, she and Sera should combine their forces in order to gain as large a bonus to her Mental Power as possible. Yes, there might be a better chance to craft something permanent here, were she to go with her A Hint of Permanence, which did exactly that, but Reen insisted that the chance of obtaining repeat customers were better by crafting items with high bonuses and a limited duration.

As to what she was creating? Relatively simplistic creations. Reen brought examples of local ornamental creations, which she toiled to recreate. Although everybody in Liberty wore the same loose clothes, people did add stylistic choices in the shape of unobtrusive necklaces, earrings and nose rings, and, to Cilia's relief, intricate leather armbands.

For herself, she decided to go with duplicates of the very same. Not just because the idea of having interchangeable armbands that granted you boosts was very attractive, but because Reen himself was adamant about how they were excellent bribes. A bracelet that boosted your Toughness, yet looked like an ordinary, simple adornment? That would be excellent!

Nordon had a lot of fun, too. He spent every waking moment tinkering with his creations. Often, he'd be through the secret door and inside his crafting room before the others had even had breakfast. If he wasn't performing tests on his equipment or the concoctions he began, he was discussing, testing, or combining new ingredients with a focus that bordered on obsession. After a full week, he was crafting at least six brews concurrently, while working on two dozen other starters.

Cilia and Nordon weren't the only ones who truly enjoyed themselves.

Liam was a happy man. He had always been the one person among them who handled inactivity best. With his impressive physique, he'd often taken on simple jobs as an enforcer, which, often enough consisted of hanging around and looking tough. He had a comfortable chair, as many pillows as he dared ask for, and from time to time, Nordon would even invite him to taste-test something. It was rarely alcoholic, at this point, but it was often decently tasty, and the experience was novel.

Kith spent most of his time in his own chair next to Liam, eyes downcast. Reen complained about his lack of professionalism. Yet, Kith was always working. Always elsewhere, investigating, looking, searching. Learning. He spent most of the day looking through either Rabine's eyes, or those of his shades. Although he itched to get out and do something practical, there was a whole new world out there, and it was his for the taking. Salvation might be insane, seen with the viewpoint of somebody coming from Lightborn society. Yet, it was never *dull*.

Sera, at Cilia's side, did enjoy the theory crafting, discussing how to handle the process from dead animal to finished product in order to obtain the best possible boost. Even so, apart from granting Cilia a buff to her Mental Power when crafting, she had little to do. Yet, her long years with dusty tutors and dustier tomes had taught her how to handle long periods of silence and little input. She lost herself in mental exercises and also took to investigating Cilia's book on Liberty, to keep herself busy. That was not to say that she wasn't bored. She just knew how to deal with it.

The same could not be said for Chase, who, at their side, was starting to go stir-crazy. He was not used to sitting still for long, and suddenly they were stuck in the building with little to do except plan, plot, and talk. It was torture. Although he did manage to push himself to stick with the mental exercises for long enough to gain another increase to Mental Power, the experience was taking its toll. He needed air, space, and the chance to run amok.

Every single day, following their evening meal, they'd gather in their larger room, discuss what they'd learned and what progress, if any, they'd experienced.

At this point, their combined efforts had granted them a fuller understanding of what Salvation was and wasn't, and just how everything was run.

They'd put the idea of crashing the card-granting ceremony and stealing a deck out of their heads, for now. It turned out that the decks, at that point, were heavily guarded, both by regular guards and a veritable throng of defenses in the palace. Even if they somehow managed to get away with the deck, they'd have the entire city mobilized and on their tails.

No, they'd have to get into the palace off hours. Somehow. This...proved an issue. Normal people didn't just enter the palace. There were routines. Checks. Documents to be scrutinized and accepted by clerks and guards. Also, the palace was too far away for Kith to investigate without leaving Reen's house.

The same applied to any nightly excursions. The curfew was not anything new. It was the state of life in the blissful lands. *Anywhere* in the blissful lands. Anybody who was out during the night, from nightsoil handler to cleaners, could expect to have their credentials and reasons scrutinized by roaming guard patrols.

That remained the key point. They couldn't leave the house, as long as they didn't have proper disguises and documentation. And they couldn't come up with proper disguises and documentation from within the house.

This evening, with two weeks of their stay remaining, they were settling into what was now swiftly becoming routine.

"I'm leaving and nobody can stop me!" Chase, wild-eyed, paced back and forth. "I'll be back before morning. Then, I'm sure, I'll have a solution for us."

"No, you're not, and yes, we can," Sera said firmly. She put a hand on his shoulder and looked him in the eye. "Nothing's changed, and you know it. As long as we don't have a proper way to get out there safely, you going out to investigate is going to put us all in danger. Do you want to put us all in danger?"

"Yes! No? Argh! Of course I don't. But this is torture. How anybody can get used to something like this is beyond me."

"It's not that bad." Liam smiled. "Just do what I do. If you get bored, have a nap. Or do sit-ups. Or pushups. That'll help with those scrawny arms of yours, too. Hey, maybe we can switch it up a bit, and Chase can be a taste tester."

"We cannot," Nordon said, head bowed over a piece of parchment, busy scribbling something in the margin. "For all that you will eat or drink anything, you have a surprisingly refined palate, Liam. Chase, meanwhile, believes that apples and melted cheese go well together."

"Of course they do." Chase huffed. "Crunchy *and* tasty."

"It's a crime, is what it is. I don't care about your past crimes, but this should be grounds for execution. We are not swapping."

"If we could, for once, stay on topic?" Cilia's eyes had started to show signs of exhaustion from the constant work, physical as well as mental. "The leather for my first batch of armbands is almost ready. The dyes have taken quite well, and I believe that I should be prepared to actually craft them. Do any of you have suggestions on which attributes I should try to enhance? For the ones we are keeping, mind you."

"Mental Power," Chase said, without any hesitation. "Maybe it'll give me the strength to not jump off a roof."

"This is Salvation, man," Liam drawled. "Everything's one or two stories and the roofs are flat. Jumping off a roof won't hurt you." Seeing Chase's venomous look, he held up his hands. "Helping!"

"I am, I believe, starting to get through to Reen," Cilia hazarded. "He gives me anything I want, information-wise. I just can't get too close, or he shuts down entirely. I think, if we could just figure out what his *deal* is, I could actually talk to him, one intellectual to another. If I tell him what our plan is before then...he will do something drastic, I'm afraid."

"I think we might have to chance it, regardless." Chase sighed. When he looked around, he noticed them all staring at him. "What? Don't tell me you're not seeing this. I know, I'm getting antsy, and that has me jumping at shadows and all...but are we really getting anywhere? Kith?"

Kith, sitting on his bedroll with his back against the wall, leaned his head back, while one hand stroked Spike's soft, adoring head. He held an inscrutable expression. "Do you want the simple answer, or the one where I'm the most amazing person on Ordei?"

Chase blinked. "I...that last one? Have you actually found something?"

Kith growled. "I'll be honest here. I should be ashamed that it took me this long. All this caring about others, the greater good and whatnot, has me growing soft."

"You are making *no* sense, mate," Liam said. "Get to it."

"I'm making *all* the sense. We've spent so much time among others, thinking about helping the entire world, saving nations, building homes and futures that we've forgotten what this is about."

Sera frowned. "I would say that you defined our goals rather eloquently, Kith."

He patted Spike's head softly, before slowly climbing to his feet. "That! That right there is what I'm talking about, princess. If, by sheer accident, my actions happen to help somebody along the way? No problem. But I'm not in this for the world. I'm in this for *us!*" He cut off his own argument with the slash of a hand. "Reen out there? That standoffish, defensive, sour prick of a Liberator? He asked us, very nicely, to respect the others living here inside the building. And like a sucker, I listened."

"I—" Sera stammered. "I fail to see the issue."

"We are living with a criminal. Criminals cannot be trusted to act in anybody's interest but their own. Because of that, if you want to work together with others, you *always* need to know what they want and what they're mixed up in." He snarled. "That bastard out there? He's harboring fugitives from the Savior. You wonder why he's so guarded? There's your Darkness-smothered answer! You wonder why he doesn't want to let us go out into the city? It's because he's afraid we'll bring the law down on him." Kith shook his head in disgust. "I'm sorry. I should have learned this on the first day. My instincts are all rusty from misuse."

"Oh." Chase sighed. Then he repeated it, but with more emotion. "Oh. That's excellent, though."

"Right?" Kith grinned, a ferocious glint in his eyes. "Now, we're actually getting somewhere. We've got what it takes to push him to *actually* help us, and not hold us back."

"Kith!" Cilia said, her tone cutting. "We have talked about this before. What are our thoughts on blackmail?"

With an increasingly panicked look, Sera intruded. "That it is a horrible tool? That we are better than this?"

"Sorry, Sera." Kith grinned. "The correct answer is that we need the full details before we blackmail anybody or it may backfire. But." He held up a hand at the sign of her nostrils flaring in anger. "Don't be mad. Blackmail isn't our first option. If there's any other option, we take that, because blackmail tends to back people into corners. Am I right, Cil?"

"Full investigations first. Then we act." Cilia nodded with the expression of a teacher who was proud of her student.

With her fists at her side, Sera glared from one to the other. "I cannot tell what infuriates me more. That this is your take on the entire situation, or that you believe I am mad, *because blackmail might be ineffective*. We are not going through with anything before we have the full picture."

"Exactly what I said." Kith grinned. "We'll find out just what's going on. Locate the best angle. *Then* we blackmail him, and everybody's happy."

After a while, they all agreed that Kith had earned the punch. Even Kith.

CHAPTER 12

"Protective items. These form the majority of our trades. From small trinkets that can annul singular blows over entire armors with defensive properties, to shields able to cancel out cards or protect from the onslaught of casters. Maybe seventy percent of all trades have covered these types of items, with the rest being a wide mix between more esoteric creations, exotic foodstuffs, or, well, trash." Oh. This was what we talked about back on the bloodied grounds. Possibly. The taste, the vibe, the...emotional attachment of the different decks. It could look like the Liberty deck is mostly defensive. That, or their military just makes it easy to "lose" the occasional crafted item that you can then trade away. (Page 12.)

"The jig is up, mate." Chase slid into the chair across the table from Reen, leaning forward to look him straight in the eye.

Behind him, the others slipped into their own seats around the table. Kith decided to remain standing, leaning against a nearby wall.

"You will have to be more specific," Reen drawled. His eyes were still closed, and both hands wrapped around a mug of ko-mainey, as if he were drawing energy straight from it. "Have you been spotted? Is Cilia unable to continue crafting?" His eyes slid open to a slit, and he took them in with nostrils flared. "Or have you decided to backstab me and steal from me? Because then I wish you luck with getting out of our lands again." One eyebrow raised, the sour-faced Liberator smirked at Chase.

"We know what you're doing with the people back there in the building." Chase looked him deep in the eye as he said it.

Reen affected a dismissive snarl at the comment, but he couldn't entirely hide the wince of fear at the remark.

"It took us *ages* to find out what was going on. There are still quite a few details we don't understand. Why do you feel the need to hide and feed at least sixty uncarded Liberators? I mean, we've seen that there's circulation to it. Some leave, others enter, and they're all damned thankful to you. So, we doubt there's anything...what's that word you love to use, Sera?"

"Immoral? Underhanded? Nefarious?"

"Thank you. We doubt there's anything nefarious to it. But why? Why does somebody who counsels others about cards need to hide fugitives?"

Reen looked at the exit, then seemed to deflate. When he spoke again, he sounded a decade older. "Why should I tell you? You've already got enough to see me dead."

"Because we're curious? Because seeing you dead isn't in anybody's interest?" Chase snorted. "Oh, and because my girlfriend insists we should try to be better people. I'm not sure I see the pull, to be honest, but she *is* fairly nice to look at, so I'll try to—*ow*."

"What he is trying to communicate is that our history with bigoted powers has been less than friendly. Meaning, we are more likely to help you than blackmail you. But we need for you to help us too," Sera said. "Make us understand what is going on. Then, we can help each other."

Reen looked like a deer, spooked at a sudden movement and ready to bolt. "You're not guards at all, are you?"

Liam grinned, as if he'd just been served a double platter of meat and gravy. "Now he's getting there. No. Not at all. But we think we might be on your side." His grin dropped. "As long as you tell us which Fire-scoured side that *is* already!"

Reen's face was a vision of emotional surrender. It ran the gamut from panic, over to rage, then to abject despair. At first, his words were nigh inaudible, but his voice grew in strength. "I already told you. I learned the cost of the *Savior's* system." He spat the word. Holding his head with both hands as though it were too heavy for him to bear, he addressed the table. "I became a hand, defending my people behind the Prism. I spent several years on that front line, battling against Guardians and enemy soldiers. I saw people killed or falling by the wayside, being sent on, too wounded to fight on. It wasn't until I earned my promotion and came back here that I learned what really happens."

He spread his hands on the table, palms down. "What do you think happens to those who can't fight? Who *won't* fight, or don't have the mental stamina for it? I never even considered it, merely dismissed the thought." He made a motion with his hands as if sweeping something aside. "Only, when I started working here, I learned, in truth. Part of my duty is to sometimes tour the lands, talking to other villages. Not only did I see the numbers, but I got to see the effect of it all in practice." He snarled. "Nobody in the blissful lands fails to do their duty. If you do not comply with the demands? You are removed from society. And you will be *forced* to aid the Savior. There are...camps. Gigantic fields, with soldiers keeping the failures at work. Cavernous underground terrains where mushrooms are farmed, with poor, uncarded bastards who rarely see the sun.

The food we eat? That bread you like so much, Liam? It's made from the toil of those enslaved by those in charge."

For a while, awkward silence reigned around the table.

Sera said softly, "We guessed. Not that it was this diabolical. But we assumed you were doing your best to help people."

"Not me. I just thought you were a prick." Kith smirked.

Reen barked a laugh filled with incredulity. "I...can't blame you. It's taken a toll on me. But that's me, then. I spend my days trying to find those in need of help, and hoard favors from other hands and hearts that I can spend and trade in order to keep a rare few safe from the weight of the system."

"We understand. And what's more," Cilia cut in, "we expected something along this line. And if there's one thing we don't mind, it's getting in a low blow against any pricks in charge. So, how about we sit down, actually *talk*, and we figure out something that can help both you and us?"

He tapped the table nervously, with increasing strength, until he finally slapped both hands down on the table. "All *right*! Let's do this. Who the Pits are you, really, and how can you help me hide sixty people from outright slavery?"

They didn't tell him everything. They'd gone back and forth over that detail a few times, with both Liam and Sera preferring being outright earnest. Eventually, the others had outvoted them, for one reason. Reen didn't seem like he'd approve of their going up against the Savior directly, when he was doing this much to stay away from notice.

Instead, they'd gone with part of the truth. They told him that they were thieves, that they were here for an amazing score that would allow them to retire back outside of Liberty lands, and they were attempting to make sure that they'd be able to get away with the loot without getting the entirety of the Savior's henchmen on their necks.

Reen actually took that quite a lot easier than they expected. With their high Tiers, he'd already expected that something was off. The fact that Cilia was able to deliver on her crafting promises had come as a bit of a surprise to him, but he just couldn't see four Tier-four persons acting as guards—especially with their personalities being so unprofessional.

Chase and Kith both refused to accept that this was aimed at them, of course.

Reen got past the initial fear of getting caught with surprising ease. It could probably be attributed to the fact that he'd already passed years stressing over the risk of being caught. Putting that past them, they moved on, focusing on finding a combined goal for their forces. That part proved all too easy.

"Hiding inside the blissful lands isn't easy, when you have no cards. As long as you're young, it's possible. But once you start growing up, you will find that your credentials are checked more and more often. If you don't have any details that excuse your presence when you're investigated? You're snapped up and either sent to the front or to the camps." Reen grimaced. "Liberty lands are widespread, and we do have some distant areas where people can hide. I have a few groups who are building new lives in different places. Yet, getting them out there is difficult. Every time I move out with one of their groups, I risk getting caught the same as when I brought you all into Salvation. The bigger the group, the larger the risk of detection. Eventually, somebody's going to discover us, and it will all come tumbling down."

"Huh. So, they basically need the same as us, then?" Chase mused. "Something to hide them in plain sight. To make them fade into the background—at least until they can start building their new lives elsewhere." He hesitated. "You're not trying something large-scale, then?"

Reen snorted. "Please. Go directly up against the Savior?" He rolled his eyes and smirked. "I've come to terms with the fact that I'm an idiot. If I was clever, I'd accept the cost of the Savior's peace and live my own life in peace. But even if I'm stupid, I'm not suicidal. I just want to help who I can."

"In that case, the plan is straightforward," Cilia said. "We sit down, and we find out what it will take to properly fake having Liberty cards, instead of these hand-drawn attempts."

Of course, it wasn't entirely that simple. Anybody with what looked like a proper card, with magical glow, living flow in the edges of the card and everything, could still be called out and demanded to present proper documentation. And depending on who cornered them, the depth needed for that documentation would differ.

But now, with the thought that he might actually have some qualified help who'd try their best to assist him, Reen revisited the situation. By "qualified help," of course was meant "criminals."

Back in Isarn, they'd rarely messed about with forgeries. Not just because half their number couldn't read or write back then. Rather, because Isarn wasn't governed by administrative processes in the same way that they were in Liberty lands.

An unexpected aide came about in the form of Sera. She was in no way accustomed to the art form of forging documents. She was, however, intimately familiar with official writing, with word choices, quality of parchment, stamps, and the like. Being born in Isarn as a daughter to one of the foremost noble families meant that she would have been likely to marry into another powerful family. That title would bring with it, first and foremost, one primary important job—that of being arm candy and prettily agreeing with her eventual husband.

Yet, there was another aspect to it. In Isarn, noble women were often expected to handle larger parts of the administrative tasks of their households. And when it came to the Valerians and capability, they did *not* mess about. Serafine had been taught, and she'd been taught well. Meaning, she and Reen sat down to solve the riddle of being able to create fake copies of personal documents that would convince even the most critical clerk.

Meanwhile, the others tried to figure out the answer to the question that had been plaguing them since they arrived: how would they be able to fake their card better? The task was still tough. Yet, with Reen at their side, it didn't seem surmountable.

Finally, they also agreed with Reen that the initial deadline they'd posed of three weeks was now merely a technicality, and they'd take however damn long it took to get things handled. Now, it was merely a question of getting to work, until they'd finally manage a breakthrough.

***

<u>The Visionary Chapel, Stradeburg</u>

There were many types of congregations. There was the everyday service. That one usually brought in the actual believers. Everyday churchgoers who knew the rituals, knew the hymns, the tenets of the Circle, and actually *listened* to the sermons. Then you had the symbolic, tedious gatherings on holy days. These most often consisted of bored people from all tiers of society who came to maintain an image of piety before escaping to the actual celebrations. There was also his favorite, the official proclamations. The situations where he was able to stand up in front of everybody—commoner and noble alike—and tell them how the world worked, and how the church would act to keep them all safe. Most often, those were on the topics of heresy or misinformation, but they could also be a lot more practical.

The congregation gathered before Archbishop Desahl was not an unusual one. Just like the church needed to show to the world that they were relevant, and would help and aid them, so the senior priests also needed to keep up their internal communications and keep up the same appearances toward their flock. Usually, these were dull affairs, closer to a regular meeting than a service, where he would lead the sermon, outline recent changes, geographically as well as culturally, and any challenges this might bring with them.

Today's service was not going well.

It wasn't the recent developments in the conflict with the Furyborn. The Church of the Circle was used to conflict and knew well how to capitalize on it and present it to the public.

Also, most people, commoner and noble alike, knew by now that the Furyborn as a whole were raving nutcases who'd rather slit open their own throat than talk about peace. The truth, of course, was rather more nuanced than that—but nothing that could be easily presented. That wasn't the reason for him having a bad day.

Said reason was sitting in one of the hindmost pews.

The Visionary Chapel in Stradeburg was one of many local chapels. It was not the most visually impressive, nor was it the largest by any means. It barely measured three hundred feet from end to end, and the arches met less than sixty feet above their heads. However, it was old, first planned and erected by Archbishop Nevalem, the original visionary behind the church's schism with the Church of Darkness. Its centuries-old walls carried murals outlining the wicked practices by the Church of Darkness leading to the schism, as well as the happening itself. They were graphic in nature. Archbishop Desahl found that the place helped form a natural backdrop for these services, reminding them all of the weight of history and their common ground.

Today would have worked out just fine. The service was well-planned, played perfectly into their hands, and the recent trouble with the Dark deck had seemed to fade into obscurity.

That was, until Lord Beforant decided to make an appearance.

The noble looked every bit the preening fool that some sources would paint him as. He was almost ridiculously handsome. At times, if he sat still, the eye could cheat you into believing that he was no mortal, but a marble statue dedicated to celebrating the heights of mortal beauty.

Desahl knew, for a fact, that he was clever and a political powerhouse. He also held Desahl's balls in his grasp, scarred and wizened though they might be. And right this moment, he was letting everybody in the chapel in on that fact. He lounged on a pew, entirely alone. In one hand, he held a large bag of glazed nuts, which he was, loudly and messily, devouring. The other held a bottle of red wine, from which he took healthy swigs.

He didn't comment on the service. Merely chewed, drank, yawned, and tapped his feet. Overtly disrespecting what was supposed to be one of the utmost positions of power in the lands of Light.

Archbishop Desahl gritted his teeth and bore it.

Eventually, the service ground to an end, and he blessed his flock, allowing them to trail out the door, with plenty dark looks at the invader. He held his place at the far end of the chapel, until the door slammed shut behind old High Priest Nultry. Then he hid a sigh and walked toward his visitor. Slowly, as everything he did these days.

"Lord Beforant." He bowed his head deeply. "Was that truly necessary?"

The noble's voice held a measure of deep satisfaction. He didn't bow back, merely extracting another glazed nut and observing it as if it held all the secrets of Ordei. "Oh, indeed it was, Archbishop Desahl." He tossed the nut into the air and caught it. Gorgeously. However that was even possible. "I believe I told you that I am an enthusiast of the arts? Yes, indeed." His perfectly manicured brows furrowed. "There is an art form to what we do. Politics. The manipulation of persons. Weaving human-shaped threads into the most exquisite of carpets."

Desahl bowed his head. "I am afraid I do not follow."

Beforant raised a finger and took a deep pull of the bottle. He let out a deep sigh of satisfaction. "Wonderful. I am aware you do not follow. Even when I have explicitly ordered you to. Yet, instead, I find you here, attempting to *lead*."

Desahl froze. *What did he know?*

"The art form of politics. I am *better* at it than you. Yet, since you decided that you needed to attempt to grasp the reins of power for yourself within the church, I needed to bring power back to where it belonged. Which I did by visibly and overtly disrespecting you at the center of your power *and getting away with it.*"

He bowed deeply, ignoring the pain in his neck. "Lord Beforant. My deepest—"

"Stop. I care not for lies, nor excuses. Attempting to gather power for yourself and testing your limits is a natural reaction. Yet, I inform you now—next time, my lesson will be more overt. You will not enjoy it."

Desahl, sweating and with his heart trying to escape his chest, searched for any useful answers. He ended up with a simple, "I understand, Lord Beforant."

"Good." He clapped. "Then, we can continue with what I actually came here for. We have located our targets."

He blinked, reeling. *Targets. Surely, he could not mean...* "The wielders of the Dark deck?"

"The very same. They were seen en route to, and you're going to love this, the border of Liberty!"

The archbishop sputtered, mind going a mile a minute. "Liberty? But...oh."

"Yes. Oh." Beforant smiled amiably, as if he hadn't just been threatening him a moment earlier. "We already know that they had control over several decks. Elemental. Light. Dark. Now, clearly, they have somehow managed to steal from, convince, or suborn the Furyborn and gain one of *their* decks."

"And they plan to create a Wellspring from an entire set of decks," Desahl hissed. "We *cannot* let that happen!"

The high-pitched giggle looked absolutely out of place on the tall, handsome nobleman. "See? This is why I am going to leave you in place! Because, even if you sometimes step out of line, your heart is in the right place. You know full well that we cannot allow them to hold a full set of decks."

"Exactly. We—"

"Especially when *I* need it." He almost purred.

Desahl's heart stopped. His gaze slowly rose to the smile on the noble's face. The vein standing out on his forehead. The eyes, half glazed over with an expression somewhere between avarice and fervor. It looked...demonic. He considered his options. Telling the man that he couldn't have the Dark deck, that it would be heresy or worse. Suggesting alternatives. Eventually, he settled for a hoarse, "Yes."

"There we go." Beforant leapt to his feet and patted him on his head, like a good dog. He called over his shoulder. "We're not catching them before they enter the fog. This means we need to reroute some of our forces from the Furyborn and the Elementals, and catch them when they come back out. We're dragging in reserves where we can, making sure our web is cast wide enough to catch them and rousing all our pet nobles. You do what you need with your inquisitors!"

"But..." Desahl limped along behind him now. Dignity forgotten, pain forgotten. The only thing that counted was that damn deck. *Liberty?* "We've never broken through that barrier! How do we even know they'll come back out?"

Beforant stopped near the doors. Holding one of the large double doors, he beamed an excited smile back at him. "Just look at what they've managed so far. How could they not?"

CHAPTER 13

Another interesting detail regarding crafted Liberty items. They are impressively uniform. Where the Furyborn focus on aggressively individual crafted items, we at the towers strive for the middle ground. We like the tried-and-true methods, yet adjust our methods and creations to suit the individual Protectors. Items from Liberty? They seem to arrive from the same molds, with the same crafted benefits. Some of them are even permanent, if weak. That's another point in favor of the theory that these are military items, "lost" and off-loaded. But how can you mass-produce crafted items, and with permanent benefits even? Maybe some of the strongest wielders here are crafters? (Page 15.)

"**I**'ve done it! *I've done it!*"

The words slowly pulled Chase out of his trance, from where he was learning how to wriggle his left ear.

Silly as it might look, it was one of Sera's mental exercises, albeit one he'd never managed to properly connect with. It required the user to mentally isolate and engage their body, one muscle at a time, in a fixed rotation. Properly mastered, it helped distance the practitioner from outside distractions or boredom—something that Chase sorely needed in their new home—and eventually helped them improve fine control of their body. He'd attempted the exercise numerous times, but had never been able to distance himself properly to get past the silliness of it. Now, with too much time on his hands, and few distractions, he finally made it—and to his surprise, he'd even gained an increase to Agility from it. Not Mental Power. Agility.

Blinking as the importance of the shouted words finally struck him, he leapt to his feet and stared at Cilia. She sat at her worktable, surrounded by pointy and sharp implements arranged in a meticulous pattern that nevertheless made Chase think of a torture chamber. In her hands, she held something. A leather bracelet, almost simplistic in its creation, with it being nothing but a braided and reinforced pattern of three leather strips looping into one another. Yet, every visible part of the leather strips had also been carved with tiny, near-invisible patterns, adding to the sensation of the leather forming endless loops.

"Are you certain?" Sera hastened over from the other end of the room. She and Chase ended up staring down at Cilia from across her worktable.

For the past while, Sera had kept two of her cards active whenever possible. Knowing that they would stay here for nearly a month, she'd activated Home Defender on top of that, because she could activate that, and then switch over to another card with it still granting its boost.

[**Home Defender**
Rare, Fury healer
Tier three
Passive, permanent
Some people do not care about home. Others will take what they have and defend it to the last. This lets you designate an area with a one-mile radius for yourself, where you will always have the upper hand against any intruders. Inside that area, your attributes, except Potential, and the attributes of those allied with you, will be increased by +3.

The effect of the card will remain active, regardless whether you switch to another Tier three card. Once activated, you cannot establish a new home area for a full month.

"I was unaware the Wind-torn Healer lived here... Lads. I'm sorry. Put those weapons away. We're going home." A sergeant saves his men.]

Spark of Divinity was straightforward, easy to use and a godsend. It granted an increase to whichever attribute you chose—in this case, Mental Power for Cilia's crafting. The boost was not overwhelming in itself—five points.

The real difference here came from Blessing of the Night. At this point, the boost from Blessing of the Night more than doubled any buffs. In this instance, that resulted in a total increase of eighteen points from Spark of Divinity and Home Defender combined. Yet, that paled in comparison to the synergies with Cilia's cards.

Cilia, even without cards, was at forty-seven Mental Power. Ritual of Fire boosted that to above eighty, with Chosen Focus: Fire easing the use of the ritual and reducing the draining effect. Blessing of the Night on top of that improved the boost, shooting her Mental Power to above a hundred and twenty-five—and that was before adding in Spark of Divinity and Home Defender.

All told, the full effect should land her just above a hundred and fifty Mental Power, though the math, according to Sera, became questionable at a certain point, because they had to make up any tests and comparisons themselves, and some effects, like the From Farm to Table card, were not quantifiable.

Chase didn't honestly understand which level they had reached. It wasn't important to him, either. What was important was that he knew them. He knew their strengths, their limitations. Yet, he was no longer certain that the usual limitations, as he knew them, applied to Cilia. She was approaching a level of competence and mental capacity, where they had to constantly readjust their sights and goals upward.

Cilia was often taciturn. Feelings, to her, were not something that needed to be projected every other minute. Her friends knew how she felt about them, so she did not need to spend energy on showing exactly how she felt at every single moment.

Right this moment? She *glowed*. An almost-tangible sensation of self-satisfaction surrounded her, along with the tiniest bit of awe.

"I haven't tried it. But the sensation. It works. I am sure." In an insecure voice very unlike her, she said, "Try it on, Sera."

Sera took one look at her, to see whether she was being serious. Then, slowly and gently, she grasped the bracelet and reverently slid it over her hand. It rested on her wrist, a bit tight on Sera's well-trained wrist, where it would fit perfectly on somebody a bit thinner.

Above the leather bracelet, the painted Devotion to Liberty card on their arms was starting to flake off. Even though the paint clearly held magical ingredients, it was not supposed to last forever. According to Reen, that was expected, and he had somebody else who would re-paint the image before they left. These days, it left them all looking strange, as their real cards started peeking out underneath the covering fakes.

Chase had always loved the image of Blessing of the Night. It depicted Serafine herself, cross-legged in the moonlight, soaking in power and exuding strength simultaneously. It was equal parts peaceful and ferocious. Now, goose bumps traveled up his spine as a shimmer ran up her forearm, ever so slowly covering both the fake image and Blessing of the Night. In its wake remained Devotion to Liberty, yet not the inert, dull image they had carried. This had everything of a real card. The shimmering edge around the card. The ever-present sensation of motion, as if the contents of the card were about to leap out of their constraints. And the Savior at the center of the card looked *real*. Intimidating, present. All-powerful.

"Liberty free me," Chase breathed. Then he snorted as he realized the irony of the outburst.

Sera held out a shaking hand, then caressed the image on her arm. Her hand didn't pass through the illusion. "It hides everything below, and it still looks like my own arm. How does it even do that?"

"That part took me awhile," Cilia admitted hoarsely. Her gaze was transfixed on the image, a single tear running from the corner of her eye. "I have to give credit to Reen. He managed to secure a shipment of shimmer moles. They're these Lightborn Guardians that…you don't care. The point is that their skin takes to illusion magic like nothing else. Now that I know which sensation we need, I can create five or six of these a day, and I believe I will be able to make them permanent, too."

Chase coughed. "Really? I can't wait to see Reen's face when he hears that. The sour-faced bastard is going to pee himself when he realizes that his dream has come true."

"The sour-faced bastard knows how to hold his water." A voice emerged from behind Chase. "He also tends to react when he hears yelling from nearby." Ignoring Chase's mumbled apologies, he strode across to Sera, reached out, and then gingerly retracted his hand. It trembled, ever so softly. His gaze traveled from the bracelet to Cilia and back. "Permanent? Can you really do that?"

"Yes," she simply said.

Reen's eyes met those of Cilia, boring into her with an intensity the sullen Liberator had rarely exhibited. "With this, you are going to save a lot of lives. Mark my words, I *will* repay you properly."

"If you really want to repay us," Chase said, "help get that documentation done so we can get out into the city."

"It will be done by the end of today."

"I…okay. That wasn't the answer I expected. You've clearly been busy. Thank you?"

"No need for false pleasantries. Cilia has already done more than enough to repay me a thousand times over." He bowed deeply to her. "When you decide on any targets for your robberies, do talk to me. I will aid you in making this worth your time, and more."

The interchange preceded a shift in personality that was almost scary. Reen went from being recalcitrant and careful with his information, to answering any question they had—any question whatsoever. Now that he realized he'd actually be able to keep those under his charge safe and start rebuilding *properly* for those who'd found themselves repressed by the system, he didn't hold back.

The city of Salvation opened to them.

A full day later, with Cilia having created a full complement of illusionary bracelets for their group, they took their first proper stroll through the city. Not as a full group—Reen had been very insistent that the makeup of their races would make them stand out too much—but one by one, with Reen striding along, helping them come to terms with how to find their way around, how to act and what to look for.

Chase drank it in and asked for seconds.

It wasn't difficult, really, understanding the intricacies of Salvation, once you started to take in the details. The incredibly widespread capital's low buildings and ever-present, dull facades all looked the same, except for the varying colors of the buildings. Yet, behind the immaculately maintained walls, Reen explained, the people living their lives were as different as everywhere else in the world. A few were true believers, following the words and commands of the Savior with abject devotion. The rest just wanted to find a place to be and live in peace.

Outside of the color schemes, there was no room for nuances in Salvation. Either you were part of the system, lived and breathed within the rules set up to contain you, or you were...well, a living god, really. Because, as Reen explained with several horrendous examples, anybody who deviated from the system was removed.

Everything was set up to enhance that setting. There were few public places where citizens were able to congregate, enjoy themselves, or plot against the state. There were no pubs, no libraries (this, Cilia took as an affront—even the Lightborn empire had libraries, even if they were closed to the public), or, really, places for anybody to form attachments to anybody else. You were part of the system, yet always fully, horribly alone. Even the public kitchens, where those of the mass ate, were created with solitary eating stations, so as to discourage mingling.

The sole standout from the dull, perfect monotony of the city lay in the palace. Everything about it made it stand out at the center of the capital. The tall towers that were visible from anywhere within Salvation. The colors, dark blue that seemed to pulsate and draw the eye. The way it was set apart from the rest of the city by a wide, open plaza of paved stone, also set in a dark-blue color.

That palace told a story. One that even a simple person like Chase could decipher. It explained, in no uncertain terms, the same thing that the walls surrounding the upper city of Isarn did: "We are better than you. We are more important than you. *Know your place, peasant.*" Except, with the Lightborn nobility, there was always the dream of one day being able to earn enough that you'd be able to join their ranks. Sera had been proof of that, knowing from childhood that she'd be gifted cards and a safe place in life. Not so here. The palace was removed from the rest, and the only way to truly become part of that would be through war, risking your life again and again on the front lines, and showering the Savior of Liberty with the well-earned Ænima stemming from your kills.

Chase hadn't been in the city for a full day, and he already wanted to burn the damn thing down.

For the next week, there was nothing for them but dedication to investigation. They walked the streets, learned what they could, and returned to share it with the others. While they did this, Cilia and Nordon kept crafting every day, all day, until even Nordon said that he was getting a bit sick of the taste of his own concoctions.

Little by little, however, they expanded their horizons, and, with Reen's help, learned. They learned how much of the city he knew, how many people were willing or unwilling members of his network. Most were simple members of the mass, people willing to do a little work for a little extra, be it medicine, crafted items, or mere promises of aid, should they need it. Those of the hand were less direct, able to aid with copies of information, slight deviations from the norm in their bureaucracy, omitting a tiny detail to give him an opening where needed. Reen also admitted that he rarely did interact with those of the heart. However, large parts of his energy were dedicated to them, to figuring out who he could safely approach, who was too devoted to the Savior, and who might be able to make some larger-scale changes unheeded, in return for gifts or favors.

They got increasingly familiar with the Liberty Keepers. Spotting them was the hardest part. The Guardians in other nations were wildly varied. Same here—except, they tended to be smaller in size. Also, something had been done to them. Likely some detail handled through the Wellspring. Not only did they have some sort of camouflage making them blend in with the background, they also were, compared to other Guardians, more lifeless and static. The first time Chase spotted one, hidden in plain sight on the roof of a house, he almost leapt from the shock. The squat figure looked more like a burlap sack leaned against the edge of the roof than anything else. Yet, though its body was immobile, the eyes were constantly moving, observing. Following that, they became more and more adept at finding the Keepers.

Once they recognized how to spot them, they learned more details about them. How they rarely reacted if you looked like you were about proper business. How body language, noise, and surprising movements were what ticked them off but they'd ignore most everything that fell within "normal" behavior.

Following an unexpected experience with a cart collapsing from a bad axle and a large, winged shape extricating itself from a rooftop and slamming down in the street moments later, they learned how some Keepers *would* move in person, if they decided there was a reason for it. That experience also showed them that their forged documents *did* indeed hold up to surface scrutiny.

Every evening, they'd round off with two meetings. First, dinner with Reen, where they discussed the discoveries of the day, attempting to ask the right questions and learn more. Then, they'd return to their own rooms to see how much closer they'd gotten to their real target.

"Damn. That's that entire quadrant off the table, then." Chase leaned forward and pointed at Reen over the table with a half-eaten sausage. "Honestly, man, is there anybody left in the southern parts of the city worth robbing who you *haven't* made deals with?"

Reen had undergone something of a transformation over their stay. He laughed more, brooded less, and was less likely to be insulted by any barbs. "I'm sure you can find a few. I do need something to do for the future. Don't want to get bored."

Chase snorted and inclined his head. "I'll drink to that. Or, I would, if Nordon would ever finish some of his *good* stuff!"

"The *good stuff*, as you so correctly name it, is for trading." Nordon smirked. "You'll drink the cheap ale I brewed with Reen's bad equipment and be thankful."

"You're the worst dad!" Chase exclaimed. Then broke into laughter along with the rest. "Honestly, man. Your bad ale is pretty damn good. Also, I thought you couldn't even *brew* ale this fast."

Nordon tapped his left forearm proudly. "You can't."

Shaking his head in amazement, Chase turned back to survey the others.

Kith was gesturing at Cilia, explaining some interaction he'd seen with exaggerated motions. Liam had pulled up his sleeve, and was clearly talking about some combination of cards and their effect, while Sera nodded sagely, brows furrowed in contemplation.

It was as relaxed a gathering as they'd ever had. Chase decided the time was right, and leaned over the table at Reen. "So. Hear me out, mate. You've made it pretty obvious that most Liberators, even the hearts and minds, have...let's say, limited riches. That those who have the most interesting stuff lying about are generally out of our reach, because they're partners in crime with you. Right?"

"I'd agree with you so far. That, of course, is not to say that they have nothing. You have seen the difference between us hands and the mass. The differences between me and the hearts, and the minds again, are every bit as pronounced. The Savior provides for those who aid him the most."

"Right. Right. Only...how do I say this." Chase grimaced, choosing his words carefully to present the lie as convincingly as possible. "We haven't made it as far as we have to make it back with a handful of pretty vases and wall paintings." He leaned forward even farther, whispered, "We're going for some *good* stuff, hear me?" Leaning back, he nonchalantly suggested, "So, how about this. You've got the palace. Huge damn thing. Really, a city to itself."

"No." Reen's voice was ice-cold.

"Nah, hear me out. What I'm saying is, you'll know where your precious Savior is at certain times, right? There's...ceremonies and stuff." Chase grinned. "This means, with the right preparation, a scouting tour or two, with Radine up top to look out for us, we'll know exactly where to hit. And I'm damn sure the palace will have some fun stuff—items the Savior, being a god and all, won't even miss. Goods that will allow us to retire into luxury once we're back out of the blissful lands again. The only thing we'll need is your advice and help, what you can gather about the palace, so we know what we're doing."

"No," Reen repeated. Any hint of relaxed comradery had entirely faded from his expression. He spoke up loudly, interrupting the other conversations. "I am going to say this only once. *Back off* from the palace. Any attention there is going to see us all in camps."

"But—"

"No. If you insist on continuing with this, you will not be staying here. You have given me some wonderful creations, and hope for the future I didn't have just weeks ago. But, mark my words. This will see you dead or trapped, and bring me and all of mine down with you. I will not stand for it."

A while later, they were back in their own rooms, kicking back.

Chase, groaning, tried to fling a blanket over his shoulders. Getting tangled with the fabric, he cursed and his left arm and hand animated with a flash. He pulled the blanket around himself and scowled. "That could've gone better."

"Exaggeration of the year, brother." Liam smiled. "Boy, he did not take that nicely. Why'd you do it again?"

"Liam, we agreed to this." Sera sighed. "If possible, having Reen's information on the palace would make our approach much easier."

"Except I blew it. I should've been much more circumspect about the whole damn thing. Slowly built to it."

"Wouldn't have changed a thing," Kith said. "You saw him. He's pissing himself from the mere thought of going up against their precious Savior. Nothing we say or do is going to change that."

Still scowling, Chase slowly nodded. "Okay. That means we hold the course. Do a small job or two, just to show Reen we mean business. Circle closer to the palace. Then do an investigative run, when?"

"Six days from now, during the day. I've been able to get my shades close enough to the palace to learn a few things." Kith's smug smile lit up the room. "Not only are there no Keepers right inside the palace—none...not a one—but they have a daily tour of the premises. Apparently, it's a once-in-a-lifetime thing for newly married people. Be awed by the splendor of the Savior's palace—that sort of thing." He grinned. "Also, they arrange the written documents, showing who's allowed to visit—in a hand's house outside of the palace. Chase and I can get to those in seconds."

"I'm all yours." Chase perked up, rubbing his real hand against his shining one. "Good. This will be a true test of our skills, and we'll have to assume this can go horribly wrong. Who's going?"

"We all are," Cilia intoned with finality. "This is the first step of where we need to go. If anything goes wrong? We all stay together to deal with the consequences."

Sera nodded. "We are all in this together. For good and for ill."

"Good. In that case? We have six days to learn as much as we possibly can, get prepared, and pull off a smaller heist."

CHAPTER 14

Liberty items, with few exceptions, fall into one of two categories: reactionary and precautionary. This can be something like reacting to a boosting card effect, canceling, countering, or taking over said boost. Or something like an item limiting Light, or, in some cases, non-Liberty effects within its radius. Regardless, their items rarely come with active effects of their own. Interesting. Maybe that ties in to that Devotion to Liberty card—that, with their own Title boosts, as long as they cancel out anything else, they expect to be stronger? Needs looking into. (Page 17.)

The next days slipped away, like Kith at the chance of free booze. They kept touring the city, learning about their surroundings, about Keepers and defenses. Shockingly, the increased knowledge led them to conclude that there *were* no actual defenses in the city. Everything here was handled by means of the surveillance enforced by the Keepers, the guards, and the administrative systems in place. Judging by what they could tell from the outside and the snooping of Kith's shades, the same applied to the palace as well.

They slipped in two smaller burglaries—on a local hand and a heart, both in separate quadrants from their own, and both reportedly faithful believers. The jobs were almost too easy. They'd already checked over the schedules of the residents themselves, as well as the servants who worked with them. In both situations, there were easy gaps in the schedule, allowing them to walk right in.

To Chase's shock, that was the case in both places. They did walk right in. No locks, no defenses, no damn thing to keep them out. They were able to walk right back out with a few items that would fetch very good prices back home—a golden locket, a collection of silver jewelry, and two personal porcelain trinkets that Reen recognized as crafted items that would cool down liquid.

Reen didn't applaud their thefts. He did, however, aid them in finding their targets, and pointed out another few possible targets even farther away.

Finally, they made it to the day of their first intrusion.

Kith, with his shadows, could see exactly when the administrator in charge of the lists went to visit the lavatory.

Chase had already taken notice of the Keepers nearby and their limited angle of vision. He slipped the latch on a side window in the closest alley with a long piece of wire, shimmied inside, and had the rolled-up document in his hand within fifteen seconds. He nearly tripped over a chair, righted himself, and was back outside, handing it over to Sera.

Then, he moved to the mouth of the alley, lounging and keeping up his guard, while Sera added their names to the list, slipping the strip around it to keep it nicely furled up again.

The next few hours, they spent in tense anticipation. Kith hid out in the alley near the administrator's home to make sure he didn't notice their alterations. Thereafter, the real work lay in trying to distract themselves.

Yet, the bored administrator kept to his habits of not making any changes to the list on the day. Right before noon, he marched to the palace, handing the document over to the official in charge and went home, showing absolutely no engagement at any point.

They gathered back in their room following the noon meal. Cilia stood before the others in a last-minute iteration of the rules. "You know what we have to do. Today is *absolutely* just for scouting. We do not engage with anything. Do not touch anything. Do not steal anything, Kith. Do not eat anything unless you're offered, Liam. Do not do anything harebrained, Chase."

"This is hurtful," Chase grumbled. "It feels like she's even meaner than usual."

"She is judging you based on historical evidence. Nothing mean about that," Sera said, a twinkle in her eyes.

"Do not throw a hissy fit because somebody pats you on the behind, Sera," Cilia continued, as if nobody had said anything. Ignoring the explosive huff that erupted from Sera, she continued. "Today, we locate the decks, spot their defenses, and find the exits. *And that is all*. Then, we go back home, plan for next week, or the week after that, when we have the liberty to both craft items in preparation for the heist, and have an effective exit strategy ready for afterward."

"I would prefer the week after," Nordon said softly. "I will be leaving with you, and that way, I would not leave Reen empty-handed."

"Oh. Are you sure?"

Nordon nodded. "I'll cheat myself out of most of the payment he's promised, and he'll never let me back in again. Still, compared to the possibility of getting Dark *and* Liberty cards? That doesn't matter. Especially not when you stop and think about just how furious he'll be."

Nods and groans followed Nordon's statement.

"Anyway, I'm with you. I'm getting out before the fires start. Well, as long as I don't have to be part of the actual theft."

Kith snorted a laugh. "We wouldn't have you even if you offered. Amateurs are bound to make things even worse."

"Harsh, but true. So...when are you leaving?"

The palace stretched out before them. On the edges of the building, it started at a mere two stories, with huge doors everywhere and people strolling in and out as if a visit to the palace were an everyday occurrence. Stretching nearly a mile before reaching the towering heights of the spires, it rose and fell in elevation, like a deity had decided to create a mountain range in the shape of a crown.

Here and now, standing in front of the huge, sprawling edifice, it seemed to have a presence beyond the merely physical. The darkness of the building seemed to draw in the early afternoon sun, adorning the entire structure with a sheen, an aura, that was at the same time ominous and awe-inspiring.

They weren't alone. Two dozen people stood around outside their assigned entrance, talking softly in pairs. Given that they were supposed to be bridal pairs, Liam and Cilia had arrived together, as had Sera and Kith. Chase went armed with an excuse about his spouse being pregnant and the accompanying forged documentation.

There was no fear of their lack of intimacy betraying their pairings being faked. Among the many interesting tidbits Reen was able to tell them about the blissful lands, one particular piece of information had intrigued and horrified them all.

At age eighteen, anybody who had managed to pay their dues to the Savior and join the ranks of the mass were awarded a spouse. They were allowed to arrange for a marriage themselves beforehand, as long as both were mass or above. Yet, if they hadn't? They would be helped along, in enormous ceremonies, presided over by one of the minds, or sometimes even one of the pillars. It was, Reen insisted, a positive day; one imbuing the feeling of reaching a milestone, of completing a duty that society expected of you, as opposed to one of deep emotional impact.

Regardless what the reasoning was, facts were that seeing newlyweds being indifferent or even cold toward each other was nothing weird or outlandish. It was to be expected, after all.

Chase carefully hid the grin that wanted to form on his face. Today's ceremonial tour of the palace was actually supposed to *help* the newlyweds strengthen their bonds, by "bathing in the glow of the divine." If Chase got the chance, he'd be pleased to see the divine light dim a bit.

He wasn't the only solitary figure among their group, either. The duties of the mass were manyfold, and they couldn't all attend at the same time.

"Gather around, everybody." A low-set, mixed-blood—half Furyborn, half Liberator—with the azure clothes of a hand, waved them forward. "My name is Anita, and I will be guiding you in today's journey. Today, you get the chance to see in person a larger part of the palace than during your ceremony. I hope you are prepared, and awake, because, for many of us, this will be the closest we come to actual divinity." Her words sounded only half rehearsed, with a core of sincerity that showed off her awe. "First things first. I need to make sure everybody is here."

Then followed the inevitable checking of the list, as well as the presentation of documentation. Chase started to sweat as Anita called for an administrator. Fortunately, it turned out that somebody else on the list hadn't arrived, a common occurrence, and the newly arrived administrator made a few notes and strode away.

"Before we start, I want to set one thing straight," Anita said with mock severity. "Today—you aren't just allowed to gawk. You're *expected* to. If something is too overwhelming, just say the word, and we will take a short break." She leaned forward and mock whispered, "I fainted during my own tour." Speaking up louder, with a brilliant smile, she waved away her silliness. "There will be no judgment here. You can stare all you like."

She turned around and indicated the entrance into the palace beyond. In truth, it didn't seem too overwhelming. The near black of the building made for an impressive backdrop, sure. Also, the large windows along the outside of the palace were meticulously crafted with stained-glass murals and symbols that likely had important connotations to the Liberators. It was impressive and all, but nowhere near overwhelming to them. The cathedral back in Isarn had been gaudier and shinier, with more impressive murals. The Elemental towers were grander, taller, in defiance of the heavens. The Heart Halls had been vast and *intimidating*, with dangers and wonders hidden everywhere.

Their guide pretended not to notice. She extended one arm, indicating the length of the palace. "You all know the history. The palace was only erected about forty years ago, when the Savior saw our plight and descended to bring us Salvation." Tapping her nose, she continued in a conspiratorial tone. "What you may not know is that the palace wasn't always this large. The original palace had but a single spire, and was about a third of the current size." She pointed at the far end of the huge plaza that separated the splendor of the palace from the regular housing beyond. "In fact, we will be performing another expansion soon. The might of the Savior grows, and his palace along with it."

"The...city expands along with the palace?" a tiny female Liberator with a deep voice asked.

"Exactly. The nearest two quadrants surrounding the palace will be torn down, allowing the palace to grow accordingly. Then, the city will also expand accordingly on the outside." Anita beamed. "There are markers, both in the palace and in the city itself, showing you the years of our expansion. For those who are interested, I can tell you where they are located. Picture that, being able to see for yourself how the might of the Savior has grown over time."

Chase blinked, suddenly reconsidering the scope of the palace. That was...okay, it wasn't that surprising. They did move people about constantly anyway, and considering homes were entirely similar, it likely wasn't perceived as anything out of the ordinary. Still...he started to count the homes along the far edge of the plaza and got to about a hundred before dropping it. The idea of callously displacing hundreds, maybe thousands, of people just like that? It didn't sit well with him. And apparently, that was just how it was, the city and the palace shifting in an ongoing pattern.

They moved inside the palace. At first, there were few signs of this being the home of a divinity. Sure, everything was squeaky clean, even without a cadre of servants in sight, and there was a tile floor, walls, and a stunning ceiling patterned in a tiled mix of the Liberty colors. Yet, it was nothing groundbreaking. Nothing that made you think that you were anywhere special, except for the size and width of the corridor they were traversing, and the mood of their tour guide and the other participants.

Then they entered the map room.

It was a large, circular room, constructed with the same tiled patterns on the floor and ceiling as everything so far. The ceiling stretched upward in a dome, and held numerous windows that allowed the light to stream in. It was also entirely empty, except for four exits and the single construction at the center of the room.

It was a map. A huge, fifteen-foot-wide map of the Liberty lands. It was topographically exact, showing streams, lakes and rivers, mountains and forestland. There were miniature buildings, depicting the placement of cities, the buildings showing their relative size, even the colors of the lands changing according to the different terrain. It must have taken forever to get it to this level of precision.

It also floated in midair.

There was nothing there. No ropes, no mirrors, no strings or carefully hidden mechanics. Chase knew tricks to fool the eye, and he spotted nothing. Just a massive map weighing hundreds of pounds, floating at the center of the room.

To Chase's surprise, his voice was hoarse as he asked, "Can we...can we go close?"

Their guide smiled in delight. "Of course you may. Touching is forbidden, though."

He nodded and moved closer. Still, he saw no hidden tricks. Just the blissful lands. As he stood over the map, recounting the journey they'd made from Hand's Rest to Salvation, he realized the lands were a good deal larger than he'd expected. Judging from the maps, the Liberty lands stretched at least six weeks of a hard march for normal people from end to end. Once again, he had to recalibrate his mental estimates of just how powerful and numerous they were as a race.

Huh. Chase squinted, as he spotted something. A series of smaller, glowing runes set into the floor in several places below the map. Looking up, he thought that he spotted the same up there. *Interesting.*

Their guide, Anita, led them on, introducing them to marvel after marvel, historically important documents, weapons and creations of former Liberty generations, murals, statues...in one situation, even a small rune-covered cube that, when touched, *sang* a chronicle revolving around the evolution of the Liberator defenses and their increasing strength.

Only, Chase realized, this was just like the Church of the Circle telling their story about the evil wielders of Dark. It was carefully curated and told to omit every single detail that might be critical of the Savior and his society, as well as any detail leading up to the retreat from the rest of the world. It was no surprise to him, but it was still overwhelming to grasp that this was all that any Liberator would ever see—this carefully constructed tale that skirted the edges of anything that might not sound like complete and utter victory. Any part that might talk about the history of the Liberators beforehand? Gone, except for the same tale they'd heard before, repeated nearly word for word. Enemies on all sides. Corrupt Liberty leadership. Calling out for salvation. The Savior, answering. After half an hour, Chase fought to keep a sneer off his face. After an hour, he wanted to gag.

Soon, the immense size of the place started to show. Most of the other visitors started to get that glazed look of somebody who was slowly reaching the limits of their endurance, both mental and physical. One wonder after the other, on top of literally miles of walking, with Anita constantly prattling on about the joys that the Savior brought to their lands.

They still stayed attentive, though. Below the obscuring illusions of their bracelets, Sera was running Blessing of the Night, with Spark of Divinity boosting Mental Power on top of that, to keep their minds sharp and active.

Finally, they reached their goal.

It lay at the center of the palace. In a large, open-aired circular room at least a hundred feet across, they could see a staircase circling the inner wall. The staircase—flimsy, bereft of any sort of railing or anything obvious to hold it up—corkscrewed ever up and up, disappearing into a ceiling placed several hundred feet above their heads.

Chase wanted to look into that tower room or whatever was up there so badly. With the creations and expensive items they'd already passed on this tour, could you even picture what would be hiding up there, out of access for normal people? Only, his brain was entirely refusing to speculate. Because now, they were here. Right this moment, they'd reached their target. Against all odds, they were present in the very room they needed to rob, under the nose of a living god. It was perfect.

CHAPTER 15

We have not been able to trade anybody for sufficiently strong Liberty items yet. It would appear that either their crafting is limited, or they only trade their weaker items. Even so, they make for useful ancillary items for the best of our Protectors. Even a single strike averted in a fight can mean the difference between life and death for our trusty defenders. This is why, when they properly perform their job, I adore the towers. They always work to improve their teams, see where they can build on existing synergies, shore up any weaknesses. I'm starting to believe that the perfect system would be a mix of the Elementals and the Furyborn. The tenacity and toil needed to do the legwork and investigate what works best, mixed with the willingness to experiment and tread your own path. Oh, and we absolutely need a few of these basic items as well before we flee. (Page 17.)

The decks were everywhere. Floating freely inside the large open interior of the tower, they hung there, ignoring gravity entirely. The dark-blue covers promised every secret under the night sky, if only you dared reach out.

Chase had to forcibly constrain himself. *They were right there.* He could just reach out and run, and they'd bloody *have* it. As long as they got away safely...

Stick to the plan. That was the deal here. Cilia would kill him otherwise. He plastered on an awed smile—not the hardest thing to accomplish in this situation—and took in the details. Defenses? None. Traps? Possibly, but nothing visible. Access? Well, a few of the decks were nearly within reach from the floor. Guards? He looked around surreptitiously. Not a single one. How Light-blinded weird was *that*?

What else? Ah. Numbers. There were more than eighty decks floating here. That was at least three times more than in the Elemental towers. That sounded about right. It wasn't like they had any accurate numbers. Yet, so far, every new deck required more wielders to burst into being than the one before that, incremental numbers making it impossible for anybody to bring forth an endless number of decks. The Lightborn, so far, were the ones who'd managed to spread the most, with the largest number of decks to show for it.

Anita cleared her throat, awe and joy battling for supremacy across her features. "I entirely understand, my friends. The ceremonies for obtaining your first card, while inspiring, are not as grand as this, being able to take in their full splendor." She went quiet in a theatrical pause, then blurted out, "But there's more!"

The persons on the tour paused as one, blinking. The remainder looked expectant, overwhelmed, and, in one case, about to fall asleep.

Chase and the others, however, nervously stopped and tried not to look too put-upon.

Anita failed to notice in the least. "Today, we have been allowed to grant you the honor of feeling the strength of Liberty with your bare hands. Usually, you only get the one chance, when you are granted your card. Yet, the pillars have granted permission that you may get a second chance to feel for yourself the power of your heritage. That which forms and shapes you." She clapped softly. "So. Form a line. Take your time. And get ready to truly feel that which makes us all who we are. The strength at the heart of Liberty."

Their group slowly shuffled into a line. Slowly, Chase and the others, exchanging nervous looks, followed.

Before them all, Anita made a show of kneeling and beckoning at the decks above.

Chase, who was a fan of good showmanship, was not impressed. Whatever else was going on with their bubbly guide, this part sounded rehearsed, and not even well-rehearsed.

The other people on the tour gasped in appreciation, though, as one of the decks slowly started to trail downward, shimmering as it turned in the air. Eventually, it hit Anita's outstretched hands.

She sighed softly and closed her eyes. "Go on. One at a time. You have been granted permission."

They slowly approached, one after the other; the setting was stunning, but wondrous. They knelt to touch the cover of the deck and gasped, smiled, or, in one case, burst out in tears at the sensation. When they stood back up, their faces were transformed, shock and reverence struggling for supremacy.

Sera was the first of their group to approach. With a nervous smile, she knelt as everybody else did, cautiously stretched out her hand, and touched the deck.

The deck erupted in a flash, a burst of expanding darkness, covering at least ten feet, rising up, with Sera at its center.

Anita cried out, barreling backward, staring at Sera.

Chase watched in horror, as her arm slowly rose, pointing at Sera.

Her mouth opened, and she screamed, "Alarm! Help! Alarm!"

Everything seemed to slow down. Chase watched, simultaneously in shock and entirely unsurprised. Their tour guide scrambled backward, at the same time as thunderous footsteps could be heard in the distance, from the north, along with shouted orders. The deck, left to itself, slowly drifted up into the air again. So did all the other decks, spiraling closer to each other in a harmonious formation.

Fight? Flee? Try to grab a deck? Chase snarled, and made a leap for one of the bottom decks. Mid-air, he struck something and was repelled. He hit the ground hard, gaze fixed on the near-transparent shield growing into being around the dancing formation of cards. He punched the ground and leapt to his feet, coming to an ugly conclusion. "We run for it!" he shouted. Then he activated his Fight Another Day card, allowing them to double their speed, and turned for the southern exit, the one they'd entered through. The others followed, and they sprinted as one, ready to react. Light burst everywhere, as they activated cards, one after the other. Kith's shades emerged, immediately falling behind.

Above them, a sunny cover emerged, protecting them from the effects of hostile cards.

They were, at this point, at the very center of the palace. Getting back out would be tough. However, they were strong, and well-protected. If they could just get away from the first, attentive guards, they could—

"Darkony! Darkie!" Kith cried in alarm.

Above them, the glow faded away, replaced by the ever-present dark blue of the ceiling.

Little by little, Chase grew weaker. Their buffs were being canceled, or drowned out, somehow.

Cilia's arms moved in a blur, several of the droplets that she'd kept hidden on her person flying out. They failed to activate.

Hoarsely, Kith shouted, in a voice that sounded close to tears, "My shades are gone. But I saw Him. He's coming!"

"Who, damn you?" Cilia snapped.

"The Savior."

The words emerged like a punch to the gut, even as they kept running for it.

Chase nearly stopped running at that point. The Savior was coming for them. A living god. A being so powerful that even their own cards and items were turning on them. What could they even do? They were dead. They were done.

From ahead of them, shouted commands rang out as well.

Kith and Liam barreled into a small squad of guards. They were unarmed, but they had momentum and attributes on their side, and managed to hit them just as the guards rounded the corner. Seconds later, both Liam and Kith were armed, slowly forcing back the remaining three conscious guards. Cilia bombarded the guards, precious droplets reduced to powerless irritants, which nevertheless managed to distract and annoy.

Chase grimaced and ran to leap into the fray from the side. The shouts of reinforcements from farther ahead made him reconsider. For once, violence wasn't going to solve all their problems. He closed his eyes for a second, thinking furiously, then sprang into motion.

The Savior might be a god. Yet, He wasn't almighty, or Liberty would've conquered the rest of Ordei already. So, there was a way out of here. There had to be. He just had to find it.

His first step was activating Winds of Change. If he was going to find a loophole through this, he'd need to be able to check out *all* his cards.

Among the Raindrops fluttered and failed, only a small puddle of acidic drops managing to sprout into being. *Damnit.* He switched his Tier two card to Race of Life; then, seeing that the boost failed to take effect, to Nights of Criffhaven.

So, his Winds of Change card *did* work. Yet, all others failed to come into effect or died moments after activation. He switched to Sticky Fingers and grinned in exultant triumph, as his first activation of the card netted him an increase to Toughness. Also…there was something else weird. His Home Defender boosts were still active. There was something there. They could find a way to abuse this.

Liam ran into a wall. He slammed back and fell on his ass, dropping his purloined spear.

Kith, following straight on his heels, managed to put one hand up and slow himself in time.

A dark-blue barricade shimmered into effect, covering the wide corridor from floor to ceiling.

Kith experimentally prodded the barricade. His own spear tip pinged off, as if it had impacted with something crystalline.

The barrier was still growing stronger. The remaining guards beyond, who just seconds ago had been reeling, fighting for their lives, were no longer preparing for a fight. No, they were backing off slightly. Kneeling.

Oh no. Chase had a sinking sensation in his stomach. They were trapped. There was no escape. They'd have to… "Go dark!" he snapped.

"But it doesn't do anything!" Kith shouted back. "My poor shades are *gone.*"

"Just do it! Fully dark!"

A series of brief flashes shot through the corridor. Just in time. Behind them, something—somebody—moved into the corridor, following them. A presence, strolling slowly along as if he had all the time in the world.

They all recognized Him from the card. Devotion to Liberty. The single card uniting every wielder in Liberty lands. Granting Ænima from every single person to...the male shape standing before them. The thought threatened to bring Chase to his knees, even as his eyes hyper-focused on the approaching figure.

The Savior was humanoid in appearance. That much was certain. Yet, *human* would be going too far. He towered above them. At least seven feet tall, He resembled a human, as if He had been carved from the darkest crystal into an inhumanly beautiful form, and then clad in midnight. He shimmered as He walked, wearing the same as everybody else in Liberty...only *more*. His long, dark cloak was a susurrus along the hallway. The voluminous hood covered his face. Around him, the world seemed to adjust itself, details becoming sharper, sound crisper in a wave as He proceeded.

That vision of perfection cemented one detail for them. Sure, Reen had talked about him as a living god. Yet, it had never truly felt like anything but exaggeration, like half-truths. Until this moment.

Five shocked persons in disarray, only two with weapons, faced off against a living god.

Chase saw the inevitable. He knew what needed to happen. They had to surrender.

Cilia flung a droplet at his head.

Kith sprinted ahead at the very moment she did so, stolen spear raised, arm propelled back, ready to throw.

The Savior looked inhuman. Even faced with a surprise attack, He showed no reaction. He ducked unnaturally fast, evading the droplet. Then he held up a long-fingered hand, the other still hidden somewhere within his voluminous cloak. The world froze around them, leaving the Savior untouched.

Chase was caught by an unseen force. It felt almost like a massive, invisible hand had him in its grasp, something with enough strength to clench and squish him to death, should he so choose. His head was frozen as well, but he could see the others were similarly caught.

Behind him, a tinkling, breaking sound announced the crystal wall that blocked their path tumbling to the ground. Loud footsteps foretold the arrival of guards, a seemingly unending stream of them.

Chase barely noticed. His eyes were fixed on the Savior. The tall, superhuman shape, who cocked His head slightly, as if in contemplation. For the first time, they heard His voice.

It was everything you would expect from a deity. Deep, smooth, with an echoing resonance, as if it were slightly out of touch with reality. The proclamation was verdict and fact. "The intruders shall be judged."

They were dragged, ungently, along the corridors. A few minutes later, they were surprised to find themselves back inside the hollow tower, looking up at the decks floating in the air above, now back to their regular, spiraling patterns, as they were forced into a kneeling position.

The Savior stood above them. Perfectly straight-standing, yet entirely inhuman, wielding a scepter, and cradling a deck in His lap.

He took a long time to speak, seeming perfectly content to simply look at them all.

Their paralysis had worn off. Not that it mattered much, considering they'd been cuffed and all had a guard flanking either side of them. Still, Kith squirmed, as if he were about to say something provocative.

Fortunately, the Savior beat him to it. He raised one arm, pointing the scepter at each of them in turn. Cilia's leather bracelets twisted and snapped, and the illusions faded along with them. "Is the Church of Darkness our enemy now?"

Of all the things he could've said, that was one they did not see coming.

Sera spoke softly after a moment of silence. "The Church of Darkness? As far as I know—as anybody knows—they've been destroyed for centuries now."

"Yes." The voice was the sound of a stone lid sliding closed over a tomb. "All Dark cards presumed lost. Explain!"

Chase spoke up. There was something in the air. He couldn't entirely define it, but it felt like...back when they'd faced off against that inquisitor in the cathedral of Isarn, there had been an air of inevitability, of judgement. Like, whatever they did, they were doomed to die. Right now, there was something similar, yet minutely different. A slight sensation of...possibility? An opening in the midst of the oppressive sensation of power pushing down on him.

"I...guess I'd better go with the short version? Well, we were indebted in a Lightborn army, when they clashed with what turned out to be a holder of Dark decks. Most of the army was destroyed, but we managed to get out of there alive, and the holder gave us Dark cards. Ever since then, we've been on the run from inquisitors and...well, all Lightborn, pretty much. Well, we figured that Liberty lands might be the one place they wouldn't be able to catch us, so we ducked in here. Only, you guys are very strict on cards, and we learned that you couldn't just walk around without actual cards, so we found a way to get around that. Except, it likely wouldn't be perfect, so we had to see if we could get away with getting to a deck in here, and getting *real* cards, and then we got caught." Chase finished his explanation breathlessly, looking down at the floor, both to avoid having to look straight at the Savior, and to not have to see the reactions from the others.

"You are not lying," the Savior pronounced. There was a slight undertone of incredulity there. "Yet, you are not telling the entire truth either."

Chase kept his head down. He'd failed. For a second there, he'd thought it might work. One thing he'd learned, in his many confrontations with authority, was that they nearly always underestimated you. If you acted up just how stupid you were, they were likely to believe you, or at least play along, to the point where you'd be able to get away with reasoning that otherwise would be frowned upon.

He'd thought that he might be able to skirt the truth, deliver some sort of half-baked version of what actually happened, and beg for clemency. Except, now, the half-god right in front of them would see them slain and take their decks for himself.

"Did you intend to steal a Deck of Liberty for yourself?" The words were a sword hanging over their necks.

"We did." Chase kept his head bowed. What else could he do at this point?

"Are you innocent otherwise?"

"No?" Chase couldn't quite keep the confusion from his voice. "We are thieves. That's how we became indebted. We've always been thieves, done anything we could to survive. We haven't killed anybody here in your lands, but...no."

"What is it you want?"

The words hit him with such impact, it almost felt like a physical strike to Chase. At least, this question he could answer without hesitation or doubt. "A home. That's all we've ever wanted. Just a home for us all."

There was not a whisper in the large, open space. The silence grew louder and louder by the second.

Eventually, Chase had to look up to see what the Pits was going on. He regretted it immediately, as the Savior's eyes bored straight into his. He noticed, with a sort of detached sense of fear, that His eyes were faceted, like gemstones.

At long last, the living god spoke. The deck in His lap floated through the air, past their vision, and He intoned, with a voice as definite as a high priest quoting scripture, "Induct them."

CHAPTER 16

Of course, we have details about Liberty society from before their borders closed. There are texts ranging back to before the first schism in the Church of the Circle. The children of Liberty used to be like us. With their own idiosyncrasies, preferences, and cultural differences, of course. Yet, they were part of Ordei, were open to negotiations, trade, and politics. Following the schism, however, they grew remote, slowly disengaged from all other races and cut off all but the most necessary trade. Some historians claim that the borders were simply the last in a hundred planned steps, meant to remove Liberty from the conflicts of the outside world. I'm not sure I buy that. At the very least, it doesn't match the stories telling about the violent overturning of the old leaders, or the arrival of the Savior. (Page 20.)

To say that they were confused would be the understatement of their lives. They stayed where they were, kneeling in confusion, as the Savior walked away with large, floating strides.

"Lower your heads." A voice arrived from the side, not unkindly.

Chase turned his head, saw the slicked-back hair and queasy skin of a Water-aspected Elemental as she approached them. Elemental she might be, but her shirt was the dark blue of a third Tier, a Heart of Liberty, and her exposed arm proudly showed the Devotion to Liberty card. In her hands, she reverently cradled the deck that the Savior had passed off.

Blinking, first Sera, then the others, lowered their heads.

The Elemental passed them by, tapping them one by one on their heads with the deck. Then she bowed her head, intoned something silently, and let go of the deck, reverently watching it float back into the formations above. "Do not make any selections yet. Stand, and follow me, and I will explain."

Wordlessly, they obeyed. The guards followed close behind, still armed and alert despite them all being cuffed.

They traveled for a while in silence, the Elemental walking with a soft smile on her lips. Once, Sera started to speak, but a rough shake from her guard disabused her of the notion.

Eventually, they reached the room with the floating map again. The Elemental walked right up to the map, extracted something from within her shirt, and touched it to the map. "Come," she bid them.

They shuffled closer to the map. Chase noticed that the guards stayed back, as if this discussion wasn't for them.

"Outsiders do not understand Liberty. This is a fact, made abundantly clear by how they continuously send their Guardians, their scouts, their slaves and soldiers off to die against our proud defenders."

She waited, a tiny inscrutable smile on her lips, as if waiting for them to deny it.

After a brief, uncomfortable silence, Kith decided to take the bait. "Well, it's kind of hard to understand you lot, when nobody can get in without getting killed. Curiosity kills the sneak thief, and all that."

She laughed. "You *are* just like me. This is why the Savior selected me to induct you, I believe." She slowly slid up the sleeve on her left arm, proudly displaying the wave-covered frame of an Elemental card. "My name is Emilia Swiftstream. I was born in Earth's Ward to poor parents. My childhood was not horrid, but it was not one I would wish on my children either." She furrowed her brows. "You likely are unaware, but the Elemental towers have different forces under their command. They're not all the vaunted Protectors."

Kith made a strained noise, but nodded.

Frowning slightly, she continued. "I couldn't quite make it into the rank of Protectors. So, I was offered the alternative. Join the ranks of the Elemental armies that the Lightborn allow to move about and aid with undesirable work, until I grew strong enough to try joining the Protectors again. They trained us, outfitted us, and set us loose on all the Guardians and beasts that the Lightborn themselves couldn't be bothered to handle. Eventually, they also sent a few of us to investigate the Liberty border."

She shrugged. "I got caught between a pack of spark bulls and the Prism, and soon, I found myself wading through thick fog, hallucinating until I was disarmed by a group of Liberators. That is when I learned the real truth." Her voice became more intent, her gaze piercing. "Liberators don't care who you are. They only care that you do your job. Outside? It's all about connections, birthright, and money. In here, things are simpler. Provide for the Savior, and He will care for you in turn."

"What's that got to do with us, Emilia?" Chase was starting to get an idea of where this was leading.

"Just like me, you have been granted a second chance." She scoffed. "So, you used to be thieves. The Savior cares not. He only cares about the good you can do for his people. Show me your arms and legs, please." Her eyes widened as they slid over their assembled cards. Her voice was slightly hoarse as she continued. "You will be able to do so much, if you so choose. Tier-fours, all of you. His wisdom will set us free." The last part sounded like some sort of litany.

Clearing her throat, she indicated the map. In addition to what they'd seen before, now see-through areas expanded to all sides, showing the known terrain of Ordei. "Lightborn, Elementals, Darkborn, even Furyborn—we are all welcome here. As long as we provide for Liberty in turn."

She bowed before them.

Liam blinked and frowned at the unexpected turn of events.

Then she expanded with her hands in a circle. "As Freedom is given to us, so we shall provide in return. Let us always devote ourselves to Liberty, that we may be treated as we deserve." She touched her heart and forehead. "Devotion to Liberty is a choice. One, which you will take every day, from here on until your eventual demise, many years from now. Yet, the choice begins now, with a single decision. Choose to embrace Liberty, by choosing the right card, or reject the choice and face the consequences." She bowed her head again.

Liam cleared his throat. "Okay. Cil says I'm not supposed to say that I'm stupid. I just like when things are out in the open. So...either we choose the same card as everybody else, or...we're out?"

"Actions have consequences." Her smile was soft, but her eyes were cold. She held the deck forward for them to touch.

[You have located a Liberty Deck. As the holder of a Deck of Darkness, you have the option to accept cards from it or bond with the deck, absorbing it. Which do you choose?]

Chase knew what to expect. It still surprised him, and he had to fight down a giggle at the thought of what would happen, should he choose to absorb the deck. He pushed the desire for mayhem deep down and chose to accept cards.

[You have decided not to bond with the Liberty Deck. Your Wellspring is unchanged. However, adding Liberty to your arsenal improves your Title. As a reward, the first ten card wielders of Darkness are granted an additional bonus to their Title based on their class in addition to the regular Title bonus.

From the Deck of Darkness, you have received +2 to Agility per Tier from the rogue class instead of +1.

From the second Deck, Light, you have received a boost to your health. Detrimental effects to your attributes and mentality last only half as long, and you are much less likely to fall ill.

From the third Deck added, Elemental, you have received a bonus of +1 to all attributes.

From the fourth Deck added, Fury, you have received the power of the soil. Whenever you are in the vicinity of soil blessed with the strength of a Wellspring with which you are aspected, you will gain an additional temporary +5 boost to all attributes.]

Chase fought hard to keep his face straight. He wanted to know what the final effect would be *so badly*. He felt certain it would be extremely overpowered.

He moved on to his card options. Nothing new in the approach. He had five options to choose from. Yet, one of the options was, unsurprisingly, Devotion to Liberty. Chase decided not to linger for too long, considering there was nothing to be gained from it. He knew what he had to pick.

[**Devotion to Liberty**
Common, Liberty rogue
Tier one
Passive, permanent
This card is a compact, between the Savior of Liberty and every wielder in the lands of Liberty. It irrevocably binds the wielder for as long as the card is worn, reinforcing the bond between them and their home. The channel between the two is active and constant as long as the card is equipped.

The Title bonus for any wielder is doubled, both for attribute gains or any other gain. In return, ten percent of any Ænima earned by the wielder is passed on to the Savior, as the prime defender of the Liberty lands.

No cooldown
"As you become mine, so I am yours. Servants, both. You serve me. I serve Liberty." The Savior of Liberty.]

He picked the card with a soft sigh of relief that the regular Potential rules apparently didn't kick in for that card. He'd hate to receive it at Epic, paying forty percent of his Ænima straight out the gate.

Now, he could only hope that the Tier two and above options would make up for being forced to choose an underwhelming Tier one card. However, instead of the expected Tier two selection, he was struck by the buzz of receiving a new Tier one card, and the world faded back into existence.

Around him, the others hissed or cursed as they underwent the same experience.

As the last of them completed their selection, the Elemental stepped back, watching, as their new cards slowly faded into existence on their arm. Finally, she sighed. "A compact has been entered. You have been inducted into our ranks. Welcome to Liberty."

Following an awkward silence, Kith squinted down upon his newly awarded card. "Well, that was lovely. We're free to go now?"

Emilia flung back her head, releasing an unguarded, tinkling laughter. She blinked merrily, held a hand to her chest, and said, with a voice as dry as the nether Pits, "No."

She strode over to Kith, tapping him on the chest. "You attacked the Savior. For some unfathomable reason, He decided that you may do more good working on our side than as a bloody example in the Execution Plaza. *This does not mean you get to go free.*" The hissed snarl was replaced by a brilliant smile. "Quite the opposite. I would love to draw your attention to your new card again. One sentence, in particular. *The channel between the two is active and constant as long as the card is equipped.* Usually, there is no need to go into details about what this does. Most Liberators live their entire lives without having to find out the details. Yet, with you, I will make an exception. Not only—ah." She halted herself and turned to Liam with a blissful smile. "What wonderful timing."

They followed her smiling gaze to the center of their group where Liam stood, twitching, mumbling something as he haltingly flung a hand up, patting his brow, closing his eyes and massaging his eyelids. His voice was near-panicked. "What is— Who? *There's something in my head!*"

"You should be honored." Emilia smiled. "Most people go an entire life without feeling the touch of the Savior. Yet, those of us who teeter on the edge of salvation are more likely to be visited by His splendor."

"*I have a god in my head?*" Liam held his head between his hands, eyes scrunched closed.

"Say rather that He, in his wisdom, may find you as He chooses, wherever in Ordei you try to hide."

"Wait. It's gone now. I'm free!"

"Be respectful," Emilia snapped. She rounded on Liam, nostrils flared. "You—all of you—have been granted a second chance you do not deserve. The same as I was. This does not mean that you get to walk around unchallenged. *As you devote yourselves to Liberty, so He in turn devotes himself to you.* Twice in the first year, I felt His presence touching on mine. Then, as I continually proved myself, it became less. Now, I occasionally walk near His physical form, yet the knowledge of Him being with me, being able to reach out to me and touch my spirit, it warms my heart."

Chase sighed. "Let me be honest here. I might as well, because...you're going to learn, sooner, rather than later...we don't do too well with authority. In fact, some of us tend to be a tiny bit disrespectful at times. Especially Kith. Is that going to be a problem?"

She clasped her hands before her chest, then made a complicated gesture, as of a bird breaking into flight. "The ways of Liberty are many and varied. He does not judge your personality. He does not care about your lack of grace. He only demands that you serve Liberty, as it, in turn, will serve you." She took a deep breath before huffing. "Stop looking at me like that. I will use smaller words. You are not yet free. Until you have proved that you will choose Liberty, I will walk alongside you. Expect the divine to ensure that your presence is working to do exactly what is demanded of you. And *know* that He will be aware, should you attempt to evade his reach, and the consequences will be harsh. Switching away from Devotion to Liberty will be counted as the same as trying to flee. You get *one* chance at Liberty."

Shackles, Chase realized. These were shackles—yet, of the soul, rather than physical ones. He tried to see some way out of it and failed entirely. "How exactly do we prove that we want to choose Liberty?"

"I am glad you asked. Any path toward Liberty starts with a single step. Our journey will start tomorrow. I cannot wait to see you walk your first Steps."

He stared at her, crestfallen. They'd come this far. Walked so many Steps. Yet, now, it felt like they were right back at the start. Trapped. With no future.

***

"Reen is going to be *pissed*," Kith said.

They had been installed in a chamber of their own. It was bare-bones, with bunk beds, simple chests for their possessions, and a single, massive wall hanging depicting the Savior glaring down on them in solemn judgment. Following that, they'd been professionally and impersonally disarmed—had any weapon, crafted item, and armor stripped off and confiscated.

"Kith, you bloody idiot. Why would you mention him? What if *He* chooses to listen in?" Liam asked.

"Well, first off, He *can't* listen to us. Otherwise, Emilia or the card itself would've said as much. Find us? Sure. But there's nothing beyond that. If He could hear me, I'd have a few truths to tell the disgusting, Fury-rent—"

"Kith," Sera interrupted softly. "You are not helping."

"Helping? *Helping?* We just lost our chance at freedom because we decided that robbing a god was a splendid idea. I fail to see how I can make things worse!" His eyes were wild, as he spun in a half-circle.

"For starters, you could get us all killed," Sera snapped. "I was against this entire venture in the first place. At least have the decency to not make it even worse."

"Princess." Kith deflated, and his panic changed into a deep fatigue. "We've sold ourselves into slavery. We're being tracked and any step out of line can see us killed. Once again, how can it possibly get worse?"

"I don't think that's right, mate," Chase mused. He waved a calming hand at Kith. "Yeah, all right, I agree. We've messed up bad. To the point where it's hard to see any bright spots beyond us all still being kept alive. But I don't think you're entirely right." He walked outside the circle of silence from Cilia's active Heart card and knocked on one of the walls. "See? You can't hear me." They looked at each other, as he walked back into the circle, repeating himself. "You couldn't hear me right then. Our cards are back to working again. Whatever they activated in the palace, isn't something they can just turn on and off. Or, so I think. Same goes for the powers of that Savior of theirs. Sure. We just had our asses handed to us. I can't explain half of what they did. That doesn't mean they can do *anything* they want to."

With an exaggerated gesture, Chase pointed with his stump at the Liberty card pulsing softly on his arm. "Whatever else is going on here, it's a card. Same as all other cards we have. Doesn't mean that the Savior can just do anything. And, the channel being open and active, whatever else that might mean...well, Liam, how'd it feel? Like a person?"

Liam shuddered. "No. It was like something emerged that shouldn't be there. Like that time when I was half-asleep and Kith thought it was funny to make one of his shadows rise *through* my chest. One moment there was nothing; the next, I was screaming and clutching my heart."

"You think it can pop up without any of us noticing?"

"It was like an *itch* on my *soul*, Chase. No!"

Chase grunted. "There you have it. He can find us, but we'll know when He does so. Also, it's not like we know exactly how much the card is able to convey—so we veer on the side of safety. My point is, if they jump in, we'll know, and maybe not talk about killing a god for a few minutes."

"Maybe we should not talk about killing a god *while at the center of their power* at all!" Cilia said through gritted teeth. She glared at Chase until he backed down. "But I agree with Chase. Yes, we messed up. Yes, this is bad. But—" She winced, moved her hand in a cutting gesture, even as she turned around, staring at the wall.

"What's going on?" Liam asked.

She repeated the gesture. Chase mimed holding a hand over his mouth. They waited for a few seconds in awkward silence.

Eventually, Cilia exhaled noisily, pinching the bridge of her nose between two fingers. "That was disgusting. Like somebody let their nails trickle along my spine." She showed her teeth. "Yet, it was also educational. I believe Chase guessed it correctly. This presence? I felt no hint of understanding or deeper thought." She tapped her head.

"I agree. Still, you're talking about the difference between a god being able to find us and running through your thoughts. What difference does it make, Cil?" Liam said dejectedly.

She snorted. "Two things. First, we'll know when He checks on us. Second, the *moment* we swap to another card, the connection's gone. That's probably not something we should try in Liberty lands."

"Yeah. That Emilia did say that." Chase rubbed his chin. "I could see that going poorly. We swap our cards, and they'll alert every single Keeper and army out there to our presence. We'd be found and dragged back to who knows which punishment."

"Right. Bad idea. What's the right call, then?" Liam asked.

Chase shrugged. "For now, we play along. Act like true believers, do what they say, until we find out what they want us to do. Then we decide if it's worth it, or if we cut and run. Best situation would be us getting back near the border, where we can slip back out through the Prism before they have a chance to catch us." He shrugged. "Or maybe we convince them we're the best Liberators ever, and we get a real chance at a deck."

"That doesn't sound bloody likely. Also, what about Reen and Nordon?" Kith asked.

"They'll just have to worry. Nothing we can do about it for now. As long as there are no guards kicking in Reen's door, he should probably count himself lucky. We'll have to wait and see. Hopefully, we'll be able to think of something so we can inform them what happened." He sighed. "Anybody have something else that's super important? Otherwise, I'd really like to crawl into bed and forget this day ever happened!"

Liam made a strained noise. He flung his hands up in frustration.

"Use your words. You're a big boy now!" Kith drawled.

Liam glared back at him. "I was trying to find a silver lining in all this mess. Then I thought I found it in the Devotion to Liberty card. Sixteen additional attribute points from Title increases? Not horrible, right? Except, it doesn't work. Not a single bloody point. We're being cheated."

"Oh." Cilia blinked, then squinted. "I suppose it does make sense. Title increases are permanent. Hence, you would only earn the doubled reward from any future Title increases you receive with the card equipped. If—"

"No, Cil. Cheated!"

Chase rolled his eyes. "I'm going to bed."

CHAPTER 17

On one point, all our historians do agree. The schism in the Church of the Circle was part of what caused Liberty to withdraw from the rest of Ordei. The Liberty leadership of that time created an official announcement, that could basically be boiled down to "Fix your messes. We are not going to be part of this conflict." I can relate. If we had the chance to finally withdraw ourselves from the rest of the world, I'd get to work building my own Prism posthaste. (Page 21.)

"We *just* finished traveling the blissful lands. Now, you're telling me that we need to cross them all over again?" Liam's pained words contained all the torment of a hundred combined blisters.

"I am telling you that you earned a second chance. You should probably be a bit more grateful than you are at the moment."

Emilia had woken them up at dawn and led them out of the palace and into the city. She didn't announce what was going on until, hours later, they realized they were approaching the edge of Salvation, leading back west.

"But...we don't have anything with us," Liam said. "No bedrolls. No packs. No snacks."

"You could probably do with cutting down on the snacks, big boy." Kith snorted. "He's got a point, though, Em."

"My name is Emilia." Her face was blank and reserved as she strode ahead of them, talking without turning her head.

"Oh, relax. We're not formal here. And if we're supposed to spend a good deal of time together, I'm sure you'll get used to it."

The Elemental ground to a halt. She turned on her heels and rounded on Kith. "You clearly do not understand," she hissed. "I do not intend to *get used* to your lowly behavior. This is not a question of whether or not you can win me over. It's whether you can live up to the requirements of our Savior and earn your right to move further on your path to Liberty. Personally, I doubt that even all your combined Tiers and whatever strange Dark cards you have are worth the effort." She turned around again and marched away at a rapid pace.

They looked at one another, and the steep incline up ahead that announced their departure from Salvation. "She seems nice," Chase ventured.

Their questions went unanswered for half a day. Emilia maintained a disdainful distance from them all as she marched ahead of them without any attempts at socialization. They, in turn, talked between themselves, without reaching any sort of general idea on how to handle the situation or her.

They weren't pushed to the limit. Nowhere close to it, in fact. Emilia, for all her annoyance, didn't set a tempo that they couldn't follow, nor did she herself eat or drink without offering them any sustenance. Rather, she led the way, expecting them to follow.

It was more than a bit confusing to them. Sure, they'd been deprived of their weapons. Also, there might be Keepers nearby, watching their every move. Yet, Kith had Radine confirm that the area was safe, for miles. There were no nearby guards waiting to ambush them, troops ready to move in formation. They could, right this moment, switch their cards away from the Liberty card, knock Emilia out and...run. Her turning her back on them even looked like it invited them to try. There was something ominous about it, as if she were simply fully convinced there was no way they would be able to go against the will of the Savior.

In the early afternoon, their throats were starting to become rather dry from the dust and marching. Chase had also experienced a contact with his new card, deeming it to be the same experience as when he'd once woken discovering that a lizard decided to bunk down right next to his cheek. The swift sensation of realizing something cold and *wrong* was so very close to him.

Eventually, Kith decided that the best approach to their confusing situation would be the one that usually held true when women were involved.

Sic Liam on 'em!

They'd just slowed down for the second break of the day at one of the pre-constructed shelter spots along the main road. This one, they swiftly realized, held a single Keeper front and center, right out in the open. A large, statuesque beast sat on its haunches at the back of the sheltered area, on top of the low brick wall. Its shape was dust-covered and unmoving, large wingspan extended and providing the rest area with a bit of shelter from the sun. A good number of the bone ridges along its back were adorned with woven cloth, dried flowers, even a copper ring. They looked like offerings of a sort.

Emilia sat right under the Keeper, kneeling.

Liam slowly approached her, while the others tried to act as though they weren't paying attention to them. "Erm, Emilia? Mind if I ask a few questions?"

She didn't look up. Head bent, hands folded ahead of her, she did speak up a bit. "Yes. Six."

Liam blinked. "Six questions? Okay. I guess—"

Her head snapped around. She *growled* at him silently. Then she turned her head back around. "Apologies. Six, yes. Three days. No deviations."

Liam returned to the others, confused, as surprised as the others at this complete lack of any context whatsoever. Soon, their break was over, and they were back to walking, coughing softly from the dust of the road.

That evening, they finally had some of their questions answered. They arrived at a larger shelter, having seen, in the distance, the back of a cart trundling off the main road. Inside the shelter, a small table held a full spread of food and drink arranged for the six of them. Inside the shelter, six bedrolls lay unfurled.

They fell on the food and drink with a vengeance, finding it filling, if a bit bland.

Afterward, Emilia faced them all down as if ready to deliver a ruling. "I hope that this will make you take me more seriously. When I say that the Savior provides? I mean it. The Savior knows what we need. He will ensure that we will be fed and sheltered on our way to our destination. When you believe, you do not need to think about the details."

"You're saying that we can expect for this to happen everywhere from here and until we reach our goal?" Cilia asked.

She gave a curt nod. "Put your trust in the Savior. He will not let you down."

Cilia evaded the comment. "Can we be told what we will be doing? Also, when and where? We've always preferred to spend our days preparing properly for what we need to do."

"You may ask. Only, I have not been told yet. The Savior will inform us when it is pertinent." Emilia softened a bit. "As to preparing yourself, that is proper behavior. Judging from your tempo today, I am the one with the lowest Toughness attribute among us, so we will set our speed based on my shortcomings and need for recuperation. We will leave at dawn. What you do with your time until then is your choice."

For a while, that was the only concession to their curiosity, however grudgingly it was given. Liam tried to talk to her twice, and both times was shut down and sent back reeling with curt dismissals.

They talked between themselves for a while, opting to keep Cilia's Heart card concealed rather than displaying it out in the open. Hence, they steered away from anything secret. Without weapons, they also felt like any weapons training would be ridiculous. Eventually, they decided that they would still work on dueling, using only the Dark cards they currently had on display. Of course, it would lead to ineffective results, given that they wouldn't be able to bring the full gamut of their powers to bear, but they might get used to working with the cards that the Liberators *thought* they had.

They couldn't find it in them to throw their full energy at the task, however. The recent developments had been too much, too fast, and they were still reeling. After Chase managed to get himself caught by Kith's Tainted Earth for the third time, he fell into a dark mood and refused to train any longer. The others, without any deep discussion, agreed to use that as an excuse to end any further activities.

The following day, Chase awoke to the sound of soft footsteps.

He faked being asleep, and, through slitted eyes, observed his surroundings, noting the hint of light in the horizon promising dawn would arrive soon. He'd always slept light. It was a habit, beaten into him by dozens of close calls on the Waves. Across the tiny shelter, he noted Kith tensed up, while Cilia, who usually slept on her back, lay on her side, facing the exit. Apparently, he wasn't the only one who kept up his light sleeping habits. Of course, Liam was snoring enough to make the table shake.

The footsteps approached. Soon, they solidified into the presence of a young man in the light-blue outfits of the mass, with a large rucksack. His singular card glimmered softly on his arm. He looked apprehensive, but not nervous, and his leggings and sandals were covered with dust as if he'd been on the move for a while already. The young Liberator stood stock-still for a moment while he observed them, then slowly slid off his rucksack and started to remove items from the inside, placing them on the ground before him. That done, he nodded to himself and started donning the rucksack again.

Chase made a quick decision. He slid out of his bedroll, still in his underpants, and approached the young man. "Morning."

At first, the young man only nodded amiably. Then, as his eyes slid over Chase's body, he gasped. He bowed deeply, almost looking as if he wanted to prostrate himself. "Honored Pristine Mind."

Chase chuckled. "Not me. Or...rather, say, it's a work in progress. Nothing pristine about my mind, that's for sure." He took in the young man's reaction. No. The kid, he decided. There was an uncertainty, an innocence to him that Chase himself had lost at an early age. Even so, they were likely not that far apart in years. "That's breakfast?" he asked.

The kid's smile was a frozen rictus of uncertainty, paired with that nervous tension you got when you knew you were dealing with somebody who could mess up your day. "Yes, sir. Breakfast and water for six. I'm supposed to wait around and clean up after you when you leave, take the bedrolls back home."

"That's good of you. You've been up early, too. Very impressive work ethic." Chase nodded to the side, encouraging the kid to follow him away from the opening to the shelter. He smelled an option to pump somebody for information who didn't cling as tightly to it as Emilia. Once they were around the corner, he sighed. "Now we can talk a bit without risking waking up the others. You don't mind, do you?"

In response, he squirmed ever so slightly in that way that said beyond a doubt that he was incredibly uncomfortable and would rather be elsewhere. His facial features were controlled as he bowed, though. "Of course not, Honored Mind."

Chase decided to let it go. "I appreciate that. And please, cut down on the honorifics. I'm not used to that. What's your name?"

"Elmen, Hon—sir." Even if he managed to avoid the title, Elmen couldn't quite bring himself to meet Chase's eyes.

"Elmen. Good, honest name. Now, Elmen. Our guide back there? Emilia? She's rather tight-lipped. And since this is our first real, official trip to work for the Savior, I've got so many unanswered questions. Being curious with nobody to answer your questions is the *worst.* Can you help explain how your system works? How did you know that we were going to be here?"

Elmen blinked, then looked relieved, when he realized that this was something within his powers to answer. "Oh. It's the Keepers, sir." He pointed back to their shelter. "The blissful lands are wide. If anybody has to cross three days of travel from here, they'll need food, water, shelter, firewood for the winter—all sorts of stuff. Of course, they could carry that with themselves, and sometimes they need to, if they're big groups, right? But small groups like yours? They just talk to the Keepers, tell 'em where they're going and what they need. I also talk to 'em on a daily basis, and they tell me what needs doing, or I mention if we have something pressing on our end."

Chase reeled for a moment, while his mind caught up. So *that* was what Emilia had been doing when she was "praying" in front of that Keeper. She was informing people of their progress, telling them which provisions they'd need. "Oh. You're from a local village then? Who handles all this stuff?"

"Yup. I am. I'm the runner for Shore of the Mass. My village." Elmen pointed with a thumb behind him. He was warmed up to the subject now. "We're not big, but we have *three* hands. One of them manages all this stuff, makes sure anything from or to the Keepers is forwarded to the right people. Old Hannah is fastidious, but Liberty free me if I know what we'd do without her."

Damn. That was insane. Not only did they have a network of lookouts across Liberty lands but, they also had people who actively listened in, and forwarded orders and information to select cities and villages. This meant... Chase couldn't entirely grasp the enormity of that. But now it made more sense that the Savior and his ilk were unafraid that they would do something stupid. They'd be able to forward notices to everywhere, gather forces to throw against them at no notice. They'd be able to mobilize all cities against them within hours, if that's what they wanted. "That's nice. How do you like the job?"

Elmen shrugged. "Sometimes, it's a lot of work. But I like the freedom of it. I get my orders, and I need to keep the shelters pristine. Apart from that, I'm on my own, and decide when to do what. On top of that, sometimes, I see important people." He trailed off, and didn't *quite* look at Chase's cards.

They chatted for a while more, before Chase said goodbye and ambled back to the others. He was deep in thought as he slipped under the bedroll, nodding to Kith and Cilia.

Reen had said something along the line of this, hadn't he? That Liberty was ruled by bureaucracy. Well, this just cemented it. It also underlined the difference in potential between, say, the Furyborn and Liberators. The Furyborn were always wary of attackers, always looking out for people potentially encroaching on their borders. Yet, the best they could do were flying messenger Guardians, like Radine, who was currently asleep in a tree behind them. Useful and fast, yet nothing compared to a system like this. And the way Elmen had talked about things...usually, their aid was limited to food and provisions. Yet, when the need was there, they were ready to grab weapons and get on the move. Everybody. The idea of a world where even the simplest of villagers were ready to grab a shovel and move on the warpath at a moment's notice? It was scary.

Their day started not long after dawn. Either Emilia was a sadist, or she just loved serving the Savior so much that she couldn't wait to get started. Regardless, she got up, went and "prayed" to the Keeper, before waking them all up to eat and get started on the day's march.

To their relief, Elmen's delivery included minor provisions for their journey, including small leather water flasks for everybody and some hardtack for the trip, which turned out to be surprisingly tasty, so they wouldn't have to go all day without food.

The day passed by at a glacial pace, with the mood taking a slow turn for the worse, as Emilia refused to elaborate on their task, their goal, or even Liberty as a whole. Chase sharing the story about the ever-present Keepers with the others didn't help the mood at all.

It eventually turned out to be Sera who managed to force the first crack into Emilia's standoffish facade. Under the pretense of wanting to learn more about the Savior, she approached her armed with knowledge about the Church of the Circle atop her regular curiosity.

It wasn't the curiosity that did the job. Rather, it was the idea of correcting Sera's preconceptions about divinity. For the rest of the day, Emilia walked with Sera, elucidating the joys of the Savior and how he was clearly superior to the Church of the Circle or any other divinity out there.

"She is entirely unable to shut up about it," Sera complained, a deep, unhappy blush on her cheeks as she gestured animatedly. "The Savior this. The Savior that. I am not sure exactly what happened to her, but she has grasped onto the idea of the Savior as her own *personal* salvation to the point of obsession."

"Shouldn't you wait until Cilia has her Heart card active?" Kith pointed at Emilia striding along alone on the road ahead of them.

Sera gasped before whirling on her feet to look at Cilia, who met her gaze with an eyeroll and a tap over her heart. "That was *low*, even for you, Kith!" she snapped.

Kith sniggered, right until Liam put him in a headlock, whistling as he continued his march with the struggling, groaning Kith unable to escape.

Chase smirked at their antics. It was good to see them have some fun, on an otherwise grim and mirthless journey. "Is there anything worth listening to there? Or is it sheer fanaticism? It might be fun to set her up with an inquisitor, see if they would kill each other or fall in love."

Sera blinked. "Mm-hm. That could be...explosive. As for value? Yes. I am learning. One important detail, which you should *all* hear." She waited for Liam and Kith to disentangle themselves from each other before continuing. "You have learned a certain insouciance from back on the Waves."

"That can't be right. Not if I don't know what it means, I haven't," Liam said.

She smiled warmly. "A casual level of disrespect, as it were. You care not for the importance of authoritative figures, status, or titles. With time, I have decided that this is a point in your favor, because you judge people on their personality, not status. However, in this exact situation, it will do you no good. In fact, any hint of disrespect toward the system, the Savior, or established protocol will be seen as an attack."

"Whoa. Touchy much?" Kith said.

"Very. Emilia is not stupid. She will see the lack of sincerity, should you all suddenly claim to love the Savior. Yet, being upfront about your—our—dislike is a bad choice. It puts her on the instantly on the defense."

"No more Savior jokes. Got it." Liam nodded.

"As to what I have learned...a few useful details, beyond the confirmation about how their system utilizes the Keepers." She pushed a few curls behind her ear. "She is a true believer. Entirely integrated in Liberty. Even if she has only been here for about a decade, she believes her life here is better, *worth* more than the mercenary struggle for survival outside of Liberty. She has no desire to ever leave again. *In that, she is not alone.*" Sera held up a finger for emphasis. "The average Liberator, according to her, has no desire ever to leave this place. She admits that the stories they are taught about the outside are not entirely accurate—a bit of an underexaggeration, if I am any judge—yet that does not change that she is *very* certain that, even should the Savior open all Liberty borders, most people would stay right at home, where they are safe."

"You really think that's true? I mean, aren't people curious about what's out there?" Chase asked.

"I honestly cannot tell. It would seem that they are fed with lies, told that there is nothing good out there. If they are not taught history, do not learn about other cultures...she may be right."

"So, the normal people...those of the mass, I mean, and the hopefuls, whatever they call all those poor suckers at the bottom...they just believe anything they're told?" Chase didn't bother to hide his anger.

She shook her head. "No. She was open about that. Not everybody in the populace takes to the teachings of the Savior. Yet, she presented it as a point in His favor. That even if you do not truly believe, you will still be allowed to partake in the glories of His splendor, as long as you do your part."

"*Serafine Valerian.* Is that sarcasm I hear in your voice?"

Sera shuddered. "It very much is. I did, once, mention that I had heard a rumor about the camps Reen told us about. She said it was *just*, if somebody refused to work for the good of society, that they should be made to do so. Who *thinks* like that?"

"Erm. Your parents, probably?" Kith grinned.

She narrowed her eyes. "I am ignoring you now." With a huff, she turned to the others. "I will say this for Emilia. Even if she is intense about the Savior, she is honest about the system itself. She is a heart. That means she is supposedly one of those at the core of the system, who understands the price of Liberty and is willing to pay the price."

"Only, she's really a hypocrite?" Liam raised an eyebrow.

"No, she is a true believer and willing to walk the walk. She is scarily intense at times. Yet, her peers are not. She is open about large parts of their society only paying lip service to the Savior, about people doing what is needed to gain perks, not to fight for Liberty. Also, that when a good deal of these people retire into positions in society, after years of fighting, they are less than adamant in upholding the virtues of their divinity."

"Oh. You mean, like any normal person with a brain would?" Kith snorted. "If you tell me that I need to fight invaders in order to be able to earn a proper life, you best believe I'll reap the benefits afterward."

"Just so. Yet, there it lies. Since so many people think that way, the system, even when it works, has the chance of—she calls them false-faced believers—running roughshod over those lower in the ranks, out of self-interest."

"Oh." Chase blinked. "I think that was what was up with Elmen." He gestured back where they came from. "That runner who brought us our food. At first, he looked damn nervous, but then he relaxed a bit. It was like me talking to a guard back in Isarn, only reversed. He was probably afraid that I was going to do something to him, because I was higher rank than him."

"Yes," Sera agreed. "That is exactly it. In a system where higher rank means being closer to divinity, those of higher ranks are rarely questioned in disputes."

"Suddenly I have an increased respect for Reen," Liam said, and spat. "He might be a pain in the ass, but at least he didn't buy into that crap. Any other *useful* information from our zealot, or was it all religious mumbo-jumbo?"

Sera grimaced. "Even affording her all possible respect, she talks a *lot* about religion. Rites, traditions, theories, and ways to improve your closeness with the Savior beyond fighting. It all turned into a muddied jumble in my head. I might be able to make sense of it in time."

"So, you're actually diving back in?"

"The sacrifices I make for us all." The back of her hand rested theatrically against her forehead.

CHAPTER 18

One interesting aspect regarding Liberty Guardians. Before the first schism, Guardians were not turned on each other. Rather, they were solely used to roam and defeat dangerous unaspected Guardians. This is well-known. Less well-known is the fact that Liberty were the first to turn their Guardians on the other races. Defensively, to be sure, ringing themselves with their Guardians. Yet, they changed the mechanics, paving the path for a world where Guardians could be turned against each other. I think this historian has a different idea of what is and is not "well-known" to non-historians. Guardians used to just defend all of us? That sounds...idyllic? Idealistic? Untenable in the long run, to be sure. (Page 22.)

"The Savior does not differentiate between races." Emilia's eyes roamed from one to the other, earnestly, restlessly. "He differentiates between *people*."

Chase looked at the others. Nearly three full days of hard marching hadn't taken any toll on them. They looked ready, even antsy, for something to happen. Okay, Kith looked more like he was about to roll his eyes at the prospect of Emilia talking about the bloody Savior again. He hid it well, though. At least for Kith. But they were, one and all, ready to find out what they were even supposed to be doing out here.

The day before, they'd turned away from the main road and moved into trackless territory. Their direction took them across rolling hills, through a valley covered in gravel that seemed to actively impede your progress, and around the outskirts of a swathe of living boglands that stretched as far as the eye could see.

Emilia stopped them in the middle of nowhere, waiting at the foot of a single hilltop. The hill, surrounded on all sides by a large vibrant forest, protruded from the surrounding trees like the bald crown of a monk's head sticking up from his robes. There were no shelters, no nearby roads, buildings or other signs of civilization, except for a single plume of smoke on the far side of the hill.

"I have told you this before, using other words," she continued. "But you need to hear it again. I was an Elemental. I had no famous family, no cards, and came from no influential background. Even so, the Savior took me in and made me part of his family. He taught me, showed me the truth, and asked me to prove my dedication to Liberty. So, I did." She expanded her arms with both hands palm down, as if to say, "That was all there was to it."

Marking them all with a stern look, she said, "You could have thrown yourself at the mercy of the Savior. You could have asked for His aid, to become part of his family. Yet, you didn't. You decided to act in bad faith, to *hurt* His faithful. This means that your path toward proving your dedication will be longer and harder." She started to walk up the hill. When she reached the top, she turned around. "Your first step starts right here."

They all followed her up the hill. Then they hid and observed the people on the far side, miles and miles from society.

"Who are they and what are they doing all the way out here?" Liam knelt, half-hidden behind the trunk of a tree that had been struck by lightning, yet somehow eked out a semblance of life, sprouting new shoots from its blackened trunk.

It was a disparate group. Maybe a hundred people, all told, of all ages, genders, and shapes. The one thing that set them apart was that more than half of them wore regular clothes. Rough, dirty leather for the majority, it looked like. Still, after all this time spent among the nuances of blue, the rough shades of brown and black looked dirty, even unnatural.

Their dwellings were not too shabby, all things considered. The small wooden buildings had a ramshackle look to them and were far from uniform. Yet, the mud-covered thatch on the rooftops probably provided them with at least a semblance of dryness. The buildings stood in a half-circle around a clearing, which was filled with several different workstations or wooden contraptions, some of which were sheltered from the weather. All told, the dwellings weren't pretty, but they'd seen worse shelters in the Furyborn village of Cemano. They'd lived in worse, too, both in Soil and on the Waves. Marking it as different from the rest of Liberty was a wooden palisade, clearly demarcating the contours of the village. Outside the palisade, the forest had been cleared for a few hundred feet, creating an open area for any guards to spot intruders.

The inhabitants were currently hard at work, it seemed. Nearly all those present were busy with something. One elderly woman was crafting fletching for arrows, while a young man sat on a stool near a low fire, basting something onto a beast spitted over a fire. A few kids ran around, while others were arriving from the depth of the forest, or looked like they were about to leave.

"They," Emilia said with distaste, "are the lowest of the low. They are the ones who, met with the fact that freedom has a cost, turn to lawlessness."

"Oh." Chase saw it immediately. "They're shirkers?"

"Just so. Those who flee from society into the wilderness try to create an alternative to the Savior, unknowingly attempting to fight His ways." A grim smile made its way onto her lips. "Yet, they miscalculated. They were not aware that He may track all card wielders, if He wishes. They admitted a few of the mass among their numbers."

Trying not to display the emotions surging within him, Chase nodded sagely. "An understandable mistake. I'm guessing most would be hopefuls who couldn't handle all the fighting? Then there'd be a couple of the mass who were unhappy with their lot in life and wanted to get away and do their own thing?"

She waved away his questions. "The reasoning matters little. Facts do. The facts, in this case, should be perspicuous, even to an outsider." She pointed down, first at the woman crafting arrows, then to a rack off to the side that held a handful of wooden spears. "They are crafting weapons." At another two dwellings mid-construction. "Their numbers are growing." A stab at the young man tending to the meal. "They are *stealing* the Savior's resources." Whirling on them, her words were calm, even serene, yet delivered with an inner fire that made no secret of her conviction. "The Savior has known about them for a while. One of these crimes could be ignored. Maybe even two. Combined, they lead to a simple conclusion. Care to tell me what?"

A sour taste filled Chase's mouth. It wasn't like he agreed with her. Yet, he could see what she was aiming at. "You believe that they're going to, at some point, clash with the rest of Liberty. But...they're way out here, away from anything else?" He faced her, trying to somehow connect, to make this stop.

She nodded, cold eyes watching, judging. "I hear you. As a wielder of Dark, you will know about persecution. I sympathize with your emotions." There was no hint of sympathy in her voice or eyes, though. "Yet, the Savior knows. He does not age, cannot die. He has seen dozens, hundreds of iterations of these situations. These are rebels who have arisen in defiance of the word of the Savior. They are following a path that will lead to division, to conflict, to war. They must be dealt with." She was really getting into it. Walking out to the center of the hillock, she held up her arms, closed her eyes, and flung back her head in supplication. "The Savior has revealed the first step of your path to salvation. He has called to you. *Will you answer?*"

A piercing cry came from the distance. A kid stood in the clearing, pointing up at them with a trembling finger. They had been spotted.

"What exactly does your Savior ask us to do?" Kith asked with a dark look.

Chase felt it too. That sinking feeling. He knew what she was going to say.

"The children can be saved. They have been under the influence of people choosing the wrong path, through no fault of their own. With time and gentle guidance, they can be steered back to the right path. Everybody else has had the chance, the freedom, and the upbringing they needed to know that they were free to choose." Emilia's voice grew hard. "They chose death." She took off the rucksack she'd been carrying since the first day, put it on the ground, and opened it. She stepped back and swept a hand at the contents, revealing a cornucopia of weapons. "Time for your choice."

Below them, in the tiny settlement, more voices arose in alarm, in fury and fear.

Kith looked ready to kill. Only, the odds of him killing the *right* person in this instance weren't good.

Sera, meanwhile, was reeling. White as her namesake race, she sputtered, eyes nearly comically wide as she faced Emilia. "But. Surely, you can...they can get a second chance?"

"They had a chance. Several chances. They chose death. Even were we to give them a final chance of working in a camp, now that they have started down the path of opposition, they would bring nothing but division and darkness." She glanced down the hillside. "Also, they are sure to come charging in soon. I will prepare myself whilst you make your own decision."

Chase felt it coming. The sensation of something touching upon his mind. Of an intrusion. Something alien forcing itself into contact with his mind. He nearly groaned at the timing of it. Why now? Wasn't it enough that the bloody Savior wanted them to slaughter an entire group of losers? He wanted to stay around to make sure they didn't run off? With a snarl, he fought it down. Fury rend him, he wasn't just going to take this.

With an effort, he focused, trying to take in the sensation, to block it off—and failed utterly. The sensation in his head was intangible, nothing he could grasp on to or fight down. Yet, it wasn't imperceptible. He could *feel* the contours of it, its limits— the thread of conscience that strained away from it, like an invisible umbilical cord pointing away, back toward the city of Salvation.

The sensation faded, leaving Chase mentally stumbling, with a burgeoning headache. Only to see Liam stepping up behind Emilia and clocking her in the temple with a sweeping hook.

Emilia dropped to the ground, out of commission, like a card on cooldown. For a few seconds, there was nothing but stunned silence on the hilltop. Then the shouting started.

Sera, Cilia, and Kith all yelled over one another, panic warring with fury and outrage. Chase closed his eyes, frantically trying to reassure himself that the sensation in his head wasn't still there.

Liam ignored all of them, face set in an expressionless mask as he knelt to feel Emilia's pulse. Whatever he found, it seemed to satisfy him, because he nodded and stood back up. Then, at the top of his lungs, he shouted, "Listen!"

That worked. Cilia looked as though she were about to stab him, and Sera was in a state of shock. Kith just growled and started to rummage around in the rucksack to equip himself with weapons. He extracted a short sword and dove back in.

With a calm bordering on murderous, Liam growled, "We said that we'd decide when to cut and run. *I* think that this would be a good time. Who's with me?"

His voice tinged with hysteria, Kith laughed shrilly. "You feel you've given us a whole lot of choices here? You just killed her! There'll be Liberty soldiers incoming any moment!"

"She's not dead." Liam shook his head. "We'll have a nice head start. And we can warn the people down there they should probably start running too." With a sarcastic sneer, he pointed down to where a handful of spear-wielders were pointing up at the hilltop, clearly debating whether they should start the climb. "Unless you think slaughtering a few dozen losers who've done nothing wrong except trying to avoid what they mistake for 'freedom' in here is a better choice? We can wake her up and claim somebody just flung a rock at her, then get to killing?" He rolled his eyes. "I didn't think so. Which way are we going?"

"Hold up," Chase said. "You might be onto something."

"What's that now?" Liam asked.

"Just...hear me out." He glanced at the people milling about down below, before pointing at the unconscious Liberator at Liam's feet. "Clearly, poor Emilia was struck in the head by a rock. Those damn rebels throwing stuff, am I right? When she wakes back up, she is going to have a massive headache. Only, it won't really matter, because, one, she'll be alive, and two, the handsome bastards entrusted to her care managed to take care of her tiny rebel problem in the meantime."

"You want to..." Kith mimed stabbing with the short sword he'd picked, confusion and disbelief warring on his face.

"Pits no!" Chase laughed. "I just want to make those poor bastards down there disappear without a trace, convince the bloody Savior we're fully on his side, and get that damn deck we've come all this way for."

That stopped them cold. Sera blinked, looked down on the settlement and back at Chase. Cilia made a sound in her throat that was part laughter, part keening.

"How exactly do you intend to manage *that*?" Kith eventually coughed.

Now, Chase grinned. He felt a fire running within, filling him with restless energy. "Well. Do you trust me?"

"No!" Kith's response was prompt. After a few seconds, he shot him a savage grin. "But they're starting to climb the hill, and everything's already gone to shit anyway. If it fails, we'll be running anyway. Whatever you intend to try, you've made me curious. So...dazzle us?"

Moments later, Chase met the climbing spear-wielders halfway up the slope, with the others a bit farther up-slope. He'd leapt onto a fallen tree trunk and was watching them manage the climb.

They were three women and two men, clearly in decent shape, who moved as if they'd had military training. Even so, they were far from the agile, loping movements that would carry Kith up the hillock in half a minute. Whatever else happened, the spear-wielders were clearly outmatched.

Chase shouted, "Ahoy there, climbers. How about you join us for a little chat?"

It took about a minute to talk them out of outright attacking. Showing them that they were all Tier-fours seemed to do the trick. Explaining to them that they *really* didn't mean any harm, and they absolutely needed to have a discussion about options, took a bit longer.

Shortly, they managed to gather a group of three on top of the hill. The rest of them ran back down to explain to the others in the settlement that there wasn't likely to be any *imminent* danger.

"Run this past me again." A grizzled old man named Toran, with half his right hand missing and the rasping voice of somebody who'd smoked some of Jezabel's cheaper products, pointed down at Emilia, who lay still on the ground between them all. "She's a heart. Charged with ensuring that you lot kill us all?"

"Except for the kids," Kith added helpfully, bouncing on his feet. He seemed to have decided that this was all some sort of hilarious practical joke and was treating it accordingly.

"Right. Except for the kids, of course. Only, you're *not* planning to do that?"

"Pits no," Chase said seriously. "We're new to Liberty, but we're not into wholesale slaughter. In fact, you'll find that people wanting to start over, build a new life is somewhat dear to us."

"Good, good, good." Toran nodded sagely. "Also, you're all minds—sorry, Tier-fours—and have *Dark cards*, because that's a thing now." He gulped. "Except, we're all screwed anyway, because the Savior *can find us through our cards and knows where we are*?" He panted as if he'd run a sprint. His half-mangled hand was touching his arm nervously, as if he could sense the connection from the card. "Does that about cover it?"

Chase nodded amiably. "That sure would seem to be the case. Just putting this out there, by the way. In some situations, it's better to say the quiet parts out loud: Dark doesn't mean evil. We're not going to kill you all and sacrifice your children or anything."

Apparently, that did not help. Toran looked at the other two, before sighing, the sound of somebody who'd been tired for so long that it was the new standard. "I'll be frank with you. I don't know what you want. I don't know what you're planning or why you look like you're in an excellent mood. I just know that, in a bit, I'll have to run for my life with the others of the mass, in order for my new family to hopefully be able to evade pursuit and survive. If you don't plan to hurt us, I intend to leave. Now. Unless you have anything to add?"

Chase grinned. "Actually, I do. How would you like an alternative, where you all can survive and escape together, with the Savior convinced you're dead?"

Toran snorted, exhaustion and disbelief fighting for dominance. "You offering?"

"Indeed I am." Chase leaned forward and touched the man's arm, adding that slight mental nudge to allow the decks to activate and offer him a new choice. A new path.

Toran's eyes screwed up as he took in the new offer. Eventually, he blinked and focused on Chase. Something had changed in his eyes. Before, he'd been sullen, resigned, and low-key furious at the world. Now, there was a frantic desperation there. "Is this real?"

"Sure is. But it does bring with it a few challenges. See, in order to make Emilia here"—he nodded down at the unconscious Elemental; a large bruise was already starting to blossom into being across her temple—"believe our lies and make the rest of them leave you all alone, you won't just need to disappear. You'll also need to *convince* them you've all died. That part, I don't know how to do, yet. And we have until this annoying broad wakes up." Grinning, Chase waggled his eyebrows. "How'd you like to get creative?"

It turned out that holding an offer of new cards in one hand and the threat of imminent destruction in another was an *excellent* way to help people get in touch with their creative side. It also helped them get to work right away.

Oh, it wasn't all constructive. There was a lot of panicking, a good deal of confusion and tears. Yet, with Toran's rough voice outlining the possibilities, they managed to adjust to their new situation in record time.

Liam volunteered to keep an eye on Emilia and try to knock her out again if it felt like she was coming to. All the others went down to help with the arrangements. And there were many.

Having to pack up their entire lives, while the hourglass was running out of sand, had to be a horrible sensation. To their credit, it turned out that the rebels were conscient enough about their precarious situation that they already had preparations in place.

A steady stream of movement was ongoing between the small, unnamed settlement and the deeper forest. People carried provisions, weapons, tools...anything they'd need to reconstruct their lives elsewhere.

Meanwhile, Chase faced twelve people at the center of the clearing. All the carded people of the rebels. There was no common denominator among them. Men and women, young and old, tough and scrawny. Yet, he held their attention in the palm of his hand. "Here's the deal. There is one aspect to your card you haven't been told about. This sentence. *'The channel between the two is active and constant as long as the card is equipped.'* It actually means that, as long as you have the card equipped, that scary-ass Savior of yours can follow you, find your location." He ignored the gasps, cries, and questions. "However, that only applies for as long as the card is active. How do we fix this, you ask? Well, today is your lucky day. In a moment, I am going to walk among you and share my decks. Then, you are going to be offered four new cards each. Dark, Light, Elemental, and Fury."

"Why?" an old woman asked.

"What do you want?" added a scrawny young man in an apron.

Chase held up a hand. "I could answer questions for the next few months. And I honestly wouldn't *mind*, either. But we're running on a schedule here. I'm going to make this short. No, there are no strings attached. We don't have any weird rules or religions for giving you cards. Just make sure, when you switch to another card, that you *never* activate Devotion to Liberty from here on out. My guess is they'll be able to start tracking you again the moment you do that."

With a grimace, he added, "There is one detail for when you choose your cards. For most of you, it won't even be a possibility. But, right up there on the hill, we have a very unconscious Heart of Liberty. We need to convince her that you're all dead. I don't know how. Illusions. Fire. Acid water. But if you have the chance to pick a card that will help her buy into the idea that we've killed you all? I suggest you take it. Also, once you've started accepting the cards, you can't pause the process." He shrugged. "We're doing what we can without cards as well, but any help you can add will, ahem, help," he finished with a weak grin.

CHAPTER 19

Apart from that first defensive gesture, the people of Liberty before the activation of their defenses were the least confrontational power on Ordei. They were ordered, proper, and dependable. You knew when their trade caravans would arrive. They had schedules where you could enter their lands and apply to be granted Liberty cards. We have little information about the specific cards, but know they were viewed as a wonderful, defensive addition to your selection. What changed? What made them switch? Was it solely the change in leadership? We might never know. A bit populistic, but it works. I crave to know. Why? Why the Savior? Why the Prism? Why everything? (Page 22.)

"Emilia! What a relief!" Chase cried out and slowly backed away from her supine form. "We were afraid that their attack might kill you!"

Emilia groaned, curling up with her head in her hands. Through bloodshot eyes, she looked up at him. "What happened?"

"Somebody hit you with a slingshot or something. Then, when we charged them, they pulled back and things got hairy for a while. Cilia stayed with you to protect you, while the rest of us handled matters."

"Handled? What do you mean?"

"Sit up slowly, please. Liam had to use his One Heart, Opened card, sharing his own life force with you. We think maybe you got hit worse than we initially thought, because the big fella is pretty damn weak right now."

"I'd resent that, if it weren't true," Liam snarked. Then he groaned, readjusting himself on the ground.

Out of the entire fabrication, that part was actually true. Sera suspected that Liam's punch had rattled Emilia's brain worse than they thought, because, even after hours, she wasn't coming to on her own. Eventually, Liam had to share quite a bit of his own life force with her to heal her and make her wake up.

She accepted Chase's hand reluctantly; then, groaning, got to her feet. "What happened after that?"

Chase cleared his throat. "Things got a little...out of control. I honestly expected them to talk, to surrender, to do something. Only, they kept attacking, with slings and simple bows. Eventually, we had no resort but to attack."

He guided her to the edge of the hill.

She walked slowly, hunched over from the pain in her head. When they were able to peek down upon the settlement, she gasped and wavered on her feet. "What did you do?"

Fire. Even after several hours, the palisade was still ablaze, as was the single large storehouse. You wouldn't think that a settlement as tiny as this would be able to create a bonfire as large as this, yet the tongues of fire reaching up from the few wooden constructions still standing grasped for the skies. The roar was easily audible even from nearly a mile away.

"Well, they kept retreating, then attacking. We took them down, one by one. Eventually, though, they retreated into that big building at the back." Chase coughed. "I don't know what they did. Either it was a card effect, or a huge, amassed portion of something explosive. What I do know is, that when it looked like they were trapped, they decided to blow themselves up rather than surrender. Bloody lunatics."

It had been an Elemental caster card that formed the basis of their plan. In battle, it'd be close to useless, because it had a truly glacial buildup period, and hitting anything moving would be near impossible. Using it to blow up a single large building, though, was not only feasible, but easy. The result was so effective, it flung burning embers hundreds of feet from the initial impact and left a charred circle where the larger building had once been.

Emilia stared down at the vista before them, her demeanor troubled. "The kids?"

"They were also in there. Nobody got away." Chase looked at the ground to evade her gaze. "I know we failed you, the Savior. There was just...we couldn't see a way to get in there. Do you think we should try to search the woods, see if somebody made it away?"

Frowning, she looked at the endless forest below them. She started to shake her head, then groaned and held a hand to her forehead. "No. If any of the mass made it away alive, we will be able to find them. If a single hopeful or two made it away...we lose a few all the time. That won't make a real difference," she spat. "The forest will reclaim this place within the year." Emilia teetered on her feet and looked like she was about to keel over. "I will need help walking, I'm afraid."

Chase rushed forward, waving at Kith. "We've actually been preparing. We managed to nab a few things from the village before it went up in flames. While you were out, we made a stretcher for you. I'm sure it's horribly uncomfortable, but we can get you back to civilization and some proper healers soon. Dark cards really don't grant proper healing powers."

"I would resent that, except, it is entirely true." Sera smiled. She indicated the furs tied to the long poles. "I *am* a healer, however, even if my Dark cards are better at debuffing or removing poison than actual healing. Speaking as a healer, I recommend you lie down now. We will handle the rest, Emilia."

Emilia let herself be nudged into position on the stretcher and even sighed in relief. "I must admit, for a moment, I feared that we failed. I even thought that you decided to attack *me*. I apologize for my unclean thoughts."

"But we did fail, Emilia." Chase was happy that she was rattled, because he was sure she'd be able to hear the fake notes in his plaintive comment. "We failed to save the children."

"Further proof that you are exactly what Liberty needs. Most people would care more about themselves than some unknown children. Rest assured that I see you did all you could. Now, let us depart, so I can tell the Savior that you succeeded in your quest."

Chase took his place carrying the front end of the stretcher. As they slowly raised Emilia from the ground, he carefully avoided looking back at the still-raging fires. So much effort, and in the end, she hadn't even been suspicious. There were so many details that they'd struggled to prepare, all rebels inducted into a swift setup, creating an elaborate con.

They'd excavated the midden, gathering all the bones they'd been tossing there over time, and dumped them inside the huge building they blew up, so anybody investigating the torched remains would find charred bones. Animal bones, sure, but...it was better than nothing, they reckoned.

They'd sacrificed a lot of items—jewelry, weaponry, and the like—to the same purpose. In order to create an image of having had a lot of people inside.

Not one, but *two* rogues had gotten lucky, receiving cards to help obscure their tracks. A Dark and a Water-aspected Elemental card, respectively. They were currently trailing the fleeing group, working in tandem to ensure that nobody following would be able to notice their path.

Radine was currently tracking the rebels from the skies, with their blessing. Not only to assuage their group's desire to know that they'd gotten away safely, but also in order to be able to find and alert them, should anything change.

Also, Kith kept insisting that having a hundred rebels in his pocket, ready to use, was something he'd always wanted. The others mostly ignored him.

That evening, they camped out in the open again. Only, there was something different. Something changed, that wasn't just the lingering stench of smoke on their clothes.

When Emilia fell asleep, and Cilia used her Heart card for silence, Liam was the one who managed to put it into words. "It's like that time when I saved Daira from the guard who was harassing her."

"Oh. I'd forgotten about Daira. She was the *best* waitress. She gave me a whole loaf of bread once, when Chase was down with some stomach troubles." Kith smiled fondly.

"That demands an explanation," Sera said, as she arranged her bedroll next to Chase's.

"You want to know about Chase's stomach troubles? Kinky!" Kith waggled his eyebrows.

"Beast. You know what I mean. How does aiding a waitress even *remotely* look like what we did today?"

"Oh. I have this one," Liam said, self-confidently. "After I'd helped her, we had easy work for more than a year, until old Sullivan fired her. If we were around, she'd point us at easy marks—rich suckers with a taste for the drink and no cards."

"Okay. Yes. Today's work could make our future work easier. A bit of a stretch, but I can see it."

"Also, we're bound to eat a *whole* lot better than before, now. Especially if that Savior dude makes us full minds and gives each of us our own mansion."

Sera snickered. "Again, you might be right, but I would not get my hopes up. Emilia did say that our path would be long."

"Oh, and one last thing that's just like back then? It just felt good. Right in here, you know?" Liam tapped his heart. "I'm all warm, and I don't even need to activate my card."

Sera got up and hugged Liam. He blushed like the embers of the rebel settlement all the while.

Their trip home was a lot less tense than the outward march.

When Emilia woke back up, Liam used his life share card again, and the final remnants of the damage faded away, along with any resentment she might have harbored toward them.

They never knew what it was…whether it was due to them putting a stop to any disparaging remarks about the Savior, the success of the mission, or them having ostensibly saved her life. Yet, the Emilia who walked with them on the return trip was entirely different companionship.

Sure, she still spent an inordinate amount of time praising the virtues of the Savior. However, she also shared stories from her old life, and told them other details about herself. Apparently, she was very into pottery, and had turned an entire room in her home into a workshop dedicated to clay and painting. It was an "elaborate mess" and she loved it.

On top of that, she let them in on a bit more about her life and education within the borders of Liberty. She readily admitted that the transition hadn't been as flawless as she'd initially alluded to. She had—and still maintained—a number of reservations about how they ran things within the protection of the Prism. Especially when it came to education.

The official stance on the other races outside of Liberty lands was, as she called it, less than nuanced. The other races were presented as warmongering, bloodthirsty, and unthinking, and any hint that outsiders were cultured or held anything worth aspiring to on their own was downplayed. Emilia recognized that the point of this was to push down any desire to leave Liberty, to search for something better elsewhere—but between them, she insisted that Liberty had enough going for it that the truth would be an even better option.

As to her work *for* the Savior, that turned out to be a lot more educational than hearing about His virtues. Apparently, despite her insistence that Liberty welcomed anybody who contributed, regardless of race or past, the actual number of outsiders allowed to stay in their lands was rather limited. The numbers of outsiders who made it past the Prism and surrendered instead of fighting to the death was low to begin with. Following that, their induction into society, into learning to accept their new roles, how to behave and not to behave, was a journey rife with stumbling blocks.

According to her, Emilia had been fortunate that she was young when she first entered the blissful lands. Not only did she not have several decades of being infused with ideas of the supremacy of Elemental society, she also had been, in her own words, mistreated to a degree where she was very open to accepting new ideas.

Most people were not.

Elementals knew about the world. They lived and thrived on collecting knowledge, and knew their place within it. They accepted that they were, to a point, living under the thumb of the Lightborn, but mostly integrated the notion that Elementals would one day see their deserved renaissance. They *wanted* to find their place in the world. Even those who might accept that the Savior had created a skewed worldview often had trouble with the idea of walling themselves off from the remainder of Ordei.

Lightborn had another issue. That of supremacy. Or, at least, illusions of supremacy. Any single Lightborn strong-willed enough to make it through the Prism usually had very strong ideas about where they fit in society. Their definition of that place, impressively irrespective of whether they were currently at the top or bottom of the food chain, tended to be that they belonged at the very top. Although a lot of them, according to Emilia, did adjust well to the idea that they'd become more important the stronger they got, the fact that the Savior would eternally reign supreme did not sit well with them. They were also not fans of the isolation part.

Furyborn were on a whole other level. In fact, there was currently just a few Furyborn walking free and fully inducted into Liberty society. Very few made it past the Prism to begin with—the majority being sole Furyborn wayfarers on their once-in-a-lifetime journey into the world, attempting to earn something important that could benefit Furyborn as a whole. Add to that how deeply ingrained the idea of personal independence was to them as a people, and you had the recipe for trouble.

Emilia was rather frustrated about the whole thing. Enough so, that they ended up taking turns lying to her about how they definitely were starting to see the joys of the Liberty way.

They returned to the official paved roadways of Liberty lands, along with the added comfort that brought, and took the chance to pump Emilia of all the information they possibly could—hopefully without giving her the idea that they might try to steal from the Savior again.

It worked a lot better than it really should have, Chase figured. Sure, the information they received was necessarily wide and varied, but learning from a heart who came equipped with the mindset of an outsider, and traveled a lot, was wildly different from that of her peers who had often never left Salvation, let alone Liberty.

They learned that the Pristine Minds were actually those who most often made public appearances. It would be what they could look forward to, should they eventually be fully accepted. On top of being responsible for larger cities, they often were the ones who traveled and handled bigger ceremonies or explained policy changes or new decisions from the Savior to those a bit lower in the hierarchy.

The Pillars of All were mostly responsible for larger ceremonial occasions in Salvation, on rare instances alongside the Savior himself. Like the huge mass marriage ceremonies, or some of the enormous seasonal feasts. They rarely took part in the day-to-day business of things and were known to mostly stay in the palace, working to interpret the will of the Savior himself and put it into action. What that meant in practice was harder to decipher, because very few people actually *talked* to them. Chase decided that it probably meant the bastards got drunk, ate too much rich food, and lazed about. Obviously, that was what he would do.

Their return to Salvation was unchallenged and easy. Entering the palace this time was a different experience, guided by Emilia, who strode ahead of them like a returning conqueror.

Only when they were finally seated in an elaborate, ornate waiting room and Emilia went ahead to report on their success, did the realization truly kick in. They might meet the Savior again! Their stress levels went through the roof, as they devoured a huge platter of tiny strips of what looked and tasted like fried pancake batter, along with a large bowl of cherries.

Emilia returned, smiling.

They crowded around her, asking her what would happen.

As a response, she asked them to follow her. After a minute's silence, she took it on herself to act like their personal guide, given that she thought the official guides focused too much on what everybody already knew, and too little on the *interesting* details.

"You will find that you can actually tell the difference between the different expansions right here. Not only is there a difference between the arrangement of content—the early expansions still felt the need to add murals to define the Savior, while later ones take that knowledge for granted. Earlier expansions also include the addition into the walls of certain items *of which we do not know the function*! Of course, those of us with the right to walk the palace speculate—a lot—but there is no official description or definition. They could be merely decorative, powerful weaponry, items of divine providence that help Him gather Ænima from his faithful. We will likely never know. Personally, I like the idea that they are defenses. Picture that. Divine creations that were meant to combat anybody audacious enough to go against the Savior, but left to themselves forever, since there was never any need for it."

"That has a certain poetic tilt to it. I like the way you think." Liam smiled. In the past days, he'd managed to reach a slightly better relationship with Emilia.

Chase still thought that he was overcompensating, confused by Emilia looking like she was immune to his charms.

"You know what's even better?" Kith drawled. "Knowing what we're wading into! Are we getting imprisoned? Commended? Sent on another job?"

Liam slapped the back of his head. "Kith!"

Emilia looked equally shocked. For a different reason, it turned out. "Imprisoned? Liberty does not have prisons! That would run counter to everything we stand for!"

There were no pointed gazes exchanged. Nobody rolled their eyes or said something surly along the line of "No, you just send them to camps instead."

Oblivious, she continued as they walked the endless, resplendent hallways. "Also, you have performed commendably. I should probably apologize. I wanted to surprise you with this, but hadn't properly thought through the uncertainty of your situation." She smiled and bowed with a satisfied flush. "Due, in no small part, to my recommendation, one of the pillars accepted my suggestion. You will become a proper part of Liberty!" She beamed, glancing from one of them to the next in anticipation of their reaction.

Sera saved them all. Where they were frozen in different states ranging from "I just need to avoid groaning in mental pain" to "Quick, fake a smile," Sera stepped forward and engulfed Emilia in a large hug. She awkwardly steered her around, until she faced the others and subjected them to a pantomime that, impressively, managed to convey that they'd better act happy right this moment, or there *would* be consequences.

They managed. Decently. Even Chase managed to avoid any sacrilege. After a minute of gratitude, he steered the conversation onto a slightly safer course. "What does that mean then? I mean, in practice. Do we stay in the palace? Are we going to study all day? What's the plan?"

"Ah." Emilia ducked her head. "I'm sorry. I don't know exactly what will happen. You'll have to understand—this is unprecedented. Five persons of your power, finding solace in the Savior, truly becoming part of us? That has never happened before. The usual pathways to being inducted into our ranks—they won't be sufficient in this situation. The Savior will be informed, though, and I am sure he has ideas how you can best serve Liberty."

She reached a large archway before them and turned around. A small smile played on her lips. "There is one thing I have been allowed to inform you about. It is one of the basic principles of Liberty. One which I hope you take to heart. That of reciprocity." Her smile grew wider. "When you serve Liberty, Liberty serves you in turn. Please, enter, and earn your just deserts as newly fledged Hands of Motion."

They slowly followed her, blinking, gradually starting to realize what was happening. They had made it to the center of the palace again. To the hollowed-out tower, the seat of all power of the blissful lands and the home of the Savior.

A Deck of Liberty slowly descended from the ceiling toward them.

CHAPTER 20

What happened to the Guardians? This is one mystery that will likely remain unanswered until the clouds surrounding Liberty finally lift. Theories abound. Yet not a single believable sighting of a Liberty Guardian in the wilds has been confirmed since the clouds descended. This is the best! Even if I fail at everything else, I will be able to return to the towers and become an acclaimed historian and wise woman known throughout Ordei. Of course, the truth of things is rather depressing. Taking the defenders of your realm and turning them on your own people? That's disgusting. (Page 22.)

A bald, male Liberator holding a large tome stepped forward with a smile, gently intercepting the deck before it hit the ground. He bowed deeply to Emilia. "Esteemed Heart. I thank you for delivering the newcomers to my care."

She inclined her head in return.

Cradling the deck as softly in his arm as one would a newborn, the soft-spoken, gaunt man made a curt movement with the hand that held the tome, and a servant came running with an armful of small, soft pillows.

The servants arranged the pillows in a semicircle, before placing a final, more ornate pillow right behind the man and hurrying away again.

With a satisfied sigh, the Liberator sat down cross-legged on his pillow, then gestured for them to join him. "Heidel, Hand of Motion at your service. Do not worry unduly. I will not deprive you of your reward for long." He patted the deck, looking at each of them in turn.

Chase took him in. The man's soft demeanor and warm smile would make it so easy to relax—if it wasn't for his eyes. Those eyes were cold and calculated. A man who'd fleece you for all you had and make you think he was doing you a favor.

They eased onto their pillows, Sera with enough grace to make the Liberator seem like a slouch, while Liam's muscular behind seemed to make his pillow disappear.

"Your group forms a bit of a conundrum, do you not?" Heidel said with a thoughtful smile. "So much power, yet you know so little...of our teachings, of the rules and logic that shapes our lives." He smirked. "I am aware the good Heart has done her best to educate you, yet, in her own words, there is still one major aspect left undefined." He smiled. "Lo and behold. Yet again, I am glad I got up in the morning, because this is what I do!" Clapping his hands together with force, he then spread his arms wide. "I enforce the Savior's wants and wishes when it comes to choosing your cards!"

For a moment, they were silent. Eventually, Liam spoke up. "But I thought it was just for the first card that you were forced to choose a specific card?"

Heidel sighed happily. "And once again, my position is justified. Your claim is entirely true. Yet, at the same time, it also shows that you do not understand. Now, let me ask this. Just because something is not prohibited, does that make it a good choice?"

Chase thought of the "all-hour stew" back on the Waves and shuddered. "Definitely not."

"Exactly. For an outsider, a rogue choosing a scouting or far-sight card might be perfectly logical. Yet, in the Liberty areas, there are no such hidden dangers. No roaming Guardians. No lurking enemies. We know where our foes come from, and spotting them is no issue. *This* is why I am here today. I suggest types of cards that you should avoid, either because they do not belong in the blissful lands, do not match the future for anybody with the status of hand or above, or because they displease the Savior."

Liam, bless his heart, asked the question that pressed on all their minds. "What happens if somebody chooses a card that you'd call unwise or unpleasing?"

Heidel bowed. You'd think it would look silly to bow from a seated position. He managed to pull it off, somehow, the practiced movement conveying both respect and warmth. "Liberty in the choosing is at the core of our society. Even so, actions have consequences."

Chase blinked. He didn't even elaborate. Yet, that had been a clear-cut threat, even if Heidel's smile hadn't wavered at all. Was that something they taught you here in the palace? "Okay, so, you likely have lists of Liberty cards to avoid. That's easy. However, we also have Dark cards that we've already picked."

"Yes, you do. And isn't *that* just a wonder?" He smiled. "Your past decisions have already been made. Once we have made our decisions today, we will spend a few minutes to jot down all your card details—for our records, you understand. We respect the fact that you come from different situations, and could not abide by these rules. Still, that does not mean that you are exempt from consequences, should you choose to abuse your cards." He chuckled and waved affably. "An unnecessary precaution, I am aware. Still, it needed to be said. *For now*, I can inform you about the types of cards that you should avoid as well as naming a few specific Liberty cards to steer away from. It is just a matter of you, dear friends, deciding which of you wants to go first."

"Me! Those buggers always make me choose last, for some reason," Kith said.

"The *reason* is so you can see what the rest of us pick and not make any spur-of-the-moment choices that all of us will regret." Cilia's voice was close to a snarl.

Heidel chuckled. "I see that you are a woman of my own heart. And you were…the crafter, I see. Cilia, was it?" He waited and then nodded in confirmation. "Cilia here is, of course, entirely right. Choosing your cards should only ever be made with the full weight of forethought behind you. And you are the summoner, then. Kith. Yes. Well, Kith, the choices for a summoner are rather easy. In general, you may pick anything you like. The only exception lies with any summoned creatures that spy on people. Also, you should avoid any purely scouting summons, since those are eminently useless."

Kith did a wonderful job of not reacting, not giving away that he already had several cards that focused on just that. "No scouting. No spying. That's easy. Anything else?"

"A moment, please. Please note, at this point, you have earned the honor of becoming a hand. That means, you will be awarded with Tier-two cards. No more. No less. The rest will follow through continued obeisance." He thumbed through the tome, harrumphing as he reached the spot he wanted. With a practiced flick of the wrist, he sent the tome skidding across the polished tiles, turning on its path to land right before Kith. "On top of those general recommendations, we have these. Eight of them in total. Please memorize and avoid them."

Kith grunted and leaned forward. "Seeds of Sorrow sounds fun. Why's that one banned?"

Heidel blinked, slowly. "The summoned seeds burrow into a living target and, if unnoticed, grow to a size where they may make a person *burst from the inside*."

Kith smiled, nodding eagerly.

"Because we've had horrible training accidents with those," he snapped.

"Oh." Kith slumped and returned to reading. After a while, he looked up eagerly. "Ready!"

With a wide smile, Heidel intoned, "As Freedom is given to us, so we shall provide in return. Let us always devote ourselves to Liberty, that we may be treated as we deserve." Then he leaned forward, deck in hand, and touched Kith's arm.

"I love this part." Kith grinned fiercely before closing his eyes. About a minute later, he returned to them, shuddering. "Yes! Just like running naked through the street at night!"

Sera closed her eyes. "I did not need—*nobody* needed that image!"

Kith winked. "What can I say? I'm a giver!" He cleared his throat and turned to Heidel. "I *like* Liberty cards! I went with Mine to Keep."

Heidel frowned and bent to pick up the tome. Then he browsed through the book before locating the spot he was looking for. "Ah. I had to read up on this. Not a common choice for Liberators, given that we aren't often attacked by wielders. Yet, useful in the right time and place." He squinted at the illustration in the tome, then compared it to the shimmering image of the new card on Kith's arm before nodding in satisfaction.

Kith grinned. "Well, we've had our share of clashes. I dare say we could've used it."

[**Mine to Keep**
Rare, Liberty summoner
Tier two
Passive, permanent
Denying your enemy their strength can win half the battle. Making their strength your own can win it all. This card grants any of your summons who hits an enemy a minor chance to remove any active, positive effects on enemies. Any positive effect removed in this way will temporarily be replicated, in a weaker version, on the summoner.

"Tower of Power, you call yourself? Ah, I see. Because you have improved yourself to inhuman strength through your boosts. Whew. This is not *your lucky day."]*

Chase blinked at that. Then he pictured the card combined with Apian God, and immediately coughed. "Yeah. I like it. We might not need it often, but *when* we do..."

"Right?" Kith grinned. "Now. You next, Sera! Try to top that!"

"Oh, that is what we are doing now?" Sera raised an eyebrow. "Challenge accepted. Heidel?"

Smiling widely at their antics, Heidel was already thumbing through the book. "Healers, I admit, have a few additional cards to avoid. We especially do not approve of anything that conflicts with shield effects. We have had bad experiences in the past with a few of those conflicting with the Prism. Otherwise, there are a number of other specifics that we prefer to avoid." He pushed the tome toward her.

Sera took it all in, eyes widening slightly. She read through the section three times. Eventually, she nodded to herself and rubbed her hands together nervously. Two minutes later, she expelled her breath in a slight shudder.

[Bubbles of Blue
Uncommon, Liberty healer
Tier two
Passive, long duration
The effect of this card is twofold. First, it increases the defensive properties of any party member, based on the Mental Power of the wielder. Second, any shields erected by the wielder will be improved accordingly.
"All day and all night. Everything he sees is just blue. Like him. Inside and outside."]

Heidel did a double take. "Ma'am. That card was on the list."

Smiling softly, she shook her head and indicated the tome. "No. Please do not be alarmed. There was a disclaimer on the page."

Blinking, he looked down, letting his finger fly across the page. "Only disallowed for wielders with cards granting shield effects."

She smiled. "Exactly. I have none of these, as you'll see later on. On top of that, Liam, who is our frontline fighter, already has a card that improves the effect of his armor. With this on top, he will be nigh untouchable."

Heidel looked uncomfortable, but relented.

Chase did what he could not to stare at Sera. That had been a bald-faced lie. She totally had a shield card. Cards, even. Cry for Blood could create shields. Oh, and so could Shimmering Sanctuary. Meaning…for some reason she'd gone entirely against the desires of the Liberators.

Cilia must have caught wind of what has happening, because she spoke up. "All right. I'm up next. I'm guessing that I will be offered Manipulate Liberty? I had the option at the first Tier already."

Heidel turned, and smiled as the conversation returned to less controversial topics. "That is exactly what will happen. If you are eventually offered the chance to become a heart and earn another card, we will have more to talk about. Yet, this one is simple for you."

Right enough, Cilia spent less than five seconds making her choice.

[Manipulate Liberty
Common, Liberty crafter

Tier one

Permanent, passive

This card allows you to sense the heart of Liberty, reach out and touch that sense of freedom, of protection, of defending your home and loved ones in the name of freedom. Eventually, you will learn how to add the power to your crafts. Manipulating your aspect will drain your stamina.

"We live in a world of chains. Everywhere they float, as the invisible conductor of a devilish symphony. Now, grasp your power and break the chains." Neira, Pristine Mind, addressing a class of crafters.]

Nothing surprising there. Well, except for the fact that it was still called a Tier one card. Chase mused that it had something to do with the Devotion to Liberty card.

Liam cracked his neck, looking at Chase. "My turn?" He turned to Heidel. "My turn."

"Ah. We don't often see fighters of your, ahem, obvious physical aptitude." He blushed ever so slightly. "There are less restrictions on fighters in general. The same limits upon manipulating shields applies. On top of that, there are a few cards to avoid that deal with recursive effects."

Liam frowned. "What? Why do the others get to speak like they want and I don't? That doesn't sound like freedom to me!"

Heidel's smile slipped, ever so slightly, as he turned to the others. When no help was forthcoming, he asked, "What?"

With a low groan, Sera hid her face. "Liam. I love you. But 'recursive' has nothing to do with cursing. It means something that happens several times in succession."

"Why didn't he just say so?" Liam's face scrunched up in honest confusion. "Also, what's *that* mean, then?"

Chase had to fight down a grin. Liam was the absolute *best*. Some of his attitude and apparent stupidity was plain Liam. Yet, sometimes, it was an act, putting others off-balance and causing them show their true selves.

Face stuck in a glassy-eyes smile, Heidel looked back and forth between Sera and Liam. As he saw that nothing else was forthcoming, he cleared his throat. "Apologies for any lack of clarity on my part. I will rush to add that this limitation applies to rogues as well. The point here is that there are cards aplenty that do not work instantly. They may improve your own attributes or condition with consecutive attacks, or work similarly against your foe. They can also be cards that apply similar effects over time. If there are hard limits to the card, those are fine to choose. Yet, the open-ended ones should not be chosen. Say, a boost increasing your Toughness by ten for a medium duration? Acceptable. But one increasing your Toughness by one each minute? Horrid choice."

"Oh. Those." Liam nodded. "But why?"

"See, we have found in the past, that people who chose that overestimated their own staying power and ended up hurting themselves, because the effects didn't kick in fast enough. It's a simple protective factor, aiming to ensure that our people thrive. Cards with flat increases or activation times are simply better."

Chase's eyes met Cilia's. They shared an unspoken comment. This was such a weird, arbitrary decision that there had to be more to it.

"Hm." Liam grunted. "Okay, I guess." He didn't comment on the fact that they already had a bunch of those card types. "Show me what's not okay, then."

Heidel had already found the relevant pages. He slid the tome toward him.

Liam being Liam, he couldn't stop himself from commenting on the different banned cards.

Heidel's face, as Liam said "Oh, this is cool," and "Man, I want this," to different cards was a study in self-control.

Eventually, though, Liam said, "I got this," and closed the tome.

Silence spread among them as they watched Liam's expressive face go through countless different emotions over the next few minutes. Disgust, doubt, joy, confusion, elation—it was a confounding procession. Eventually, he opened his eyes with a shuddering laugh. "Oh, you're going to love *this*."

[Canceling Strike
Common, Liberty fighter
Tier two
Active, instant
A lot of cards grant the wielder added power or skill. Certain cards, however, *require* a degree of both, before they become useful. This is one of those cards. Any parry by the wielder against an incoming attack will completely annul the momentum from the enemy's attack.
Very short cooldown
"Come on now. I'm bored. You call yourself the Juggernaut. Jog on over here and hit me again."]

"Ah. That is a classic." Heidel nodded. "Of course, if you fail to parry, you are in trouble. Yet, it is an exquisite card against large monsters with more brawn than speed or physical wielders."

"Yes!" Liam said. "I hoped that was how I should read it!"

Chase saw Cilia's nostrils flare at the realization that he hadn't been certain about the card he'd chosen. He decided to save Liam from being scolded. "My turn then. No cards with open-ended recursive effects, you said, and no playing around with shields?"

Heidel smiled. "Just so." His hand twirled in a subtle gesture. "And one other detail. This might be strange to outsiders. Yet, in the blissful lands, we do not tolerate crime. Of any kind. We do not allow rogues to select cards that are aimed directly at crime. Theft, trespassing, invisibility—that sort of thing. The full list is here."

He carefully didn't drop his smile. "That sounds fair." Chase spent a few minutes going over the extensive list, trying carefully not to think about the fact that a lot of his cards were likely to be on the banned list. A few times he had to ask for help to read the words properly, but eventually had it all memorized to a decent degree. One thing confused him, though. A lot of the banned cards were ones that granted a chance at eventual huge attribute increases, either by being recursive, with kill requirements or other specifics that would allow you to reach higher boosts than normal flat increases.

Heidel reached out and touched his arm with a forced smile. The world faded away.

Chase repressed a laugh. The first offered card, right there, was called Liberty to Steal. Unsurprisingly, it had been on the list. With a sinking sensation, he noticed that two of the remaining four options were also banned. He took in the only two options:

[With Bare Hands
Rare, Liberty rogue
Tier two
Active, instant
Any enemy is easier dealt with if they are bare-handed. Any strike by the wielder that hits an enemy's weapon will cause them to be disarmed. Strikes will also cause shields to drop.
Short cooldown
"Anybody else? You were so cocky a moment ago. Now that you...whoa. Put that bow down."]

It wasn't *bad*, per se. It was just that, if he had to think back at how often he'd had to face off against just a single person, where him disarming them could have made a substantial difference—well, there weren't a whole lot of situations coming to mind. Usually they faced off against Guardians, an overwhelming number of enemies, or wielders who had more tricks than simple close combat.

[**Fly Free**
Uncommon, Liberty rogue
Tier two
Active, very short duration
Freedom is an intangible concept. Except for specific cases, like the effect of this card. For a very short period of time after activation, the wielder is entirely free of gravity, allowing them to leap several stories, bound across chasms or cross streams without getting their feet wet. Beware the duration.
Very short cooldown
"I'm free as a bird now." The Thief of Cormick flew high, but fell far.]

Not a horrible choice either. It would allow him to get just about anywhere. Only...Steps of Brilliance already did that, and would allow him to change directions underway. He could think of exceedingly few situations where his Light card wouldn't do the job and do it better.

Chase's temper flared. So, he'd have to choose something subpar, simply because the bastards had some weird arbitrary rules on what you were allowed to do? Why, though? It made no sense. The Liberators already showed they had little regard for human life. Given that they flung all their citizens into mortal danger, regardless of their interests and desires, it wasn't a question of caring for their well-being. Efficiency? No. Not that, either. If they wanted more efficient combatants, there were a lot of options for doing so, outside of just saying "You can't choose these." No. There was more behind this. Except...he couldn't see how to circumvent it.

Frustrated, he ended up picking With Bare Hands. At least that one could be useful in specific circumstances.

Heidel approved. "Ah, yes. That card is rather effective when it comes to hostile melee wielders. And at Rare, even. That addition with it working on enemies wearing shields is rather phenomenal." He clapped and made a complicated gesture at a servant. Within seconds, the servant raced over and took the tome from Heidel, handing off a small journal, ink and quill instead.

Heidel stood up and smiled. He raised the Liberty deck into the air and, with a soft glow, it floated up to rejoin the other decks.

Heidel bowed. "Well chosen, everybody. I will jot down your new choices. Now, the part I have really been looking forward to. Please follow me."

They walked for a few minutes, until they reached a large, square room, bereft of the adornments and luxury otherwise ever-present in the palace. Heidel sighed in pleasure. "Please go through your existing card choices and show me the effects of each one. I look forward to chronicling their details for our records. Also, this is self-explanatory, but I will point it out. This time and this time alone, you are exempt from any punishment for switching away from Devotion to Liberty."

Liam spoke up. "But what if we're about to die and-"

"No. No exceptions. This. Time. Alone."

They looked at one another. There was no escaping this, it was clear.

Kith started out, focusing and explaining the details of his every Dark card, as he summoned them in turn. Shadow Master, Tainted Earth, Coils of Shadow, and Antithesis of Light: each of them spiraled into existence, one by one.

When the dark, oversized-crow-shaped figure of Antithesis of Light faded into nothingness, Heidel harrumphed. "Thank you. Your choices are, on the whole, acceptable, and Tainted Earth could easily have been a Liberty card. As you know, we do not approve of spying summons like those shadows of yours. You are wise not to try to hide anything, however. They were spotted when you first violated the peace of the palace. However, this will not be an issue, since you will never switch away from Devotion to Liberty again. Hence, we elegantly avoid any issues."

Liam went next, laying out his choices in full detail: One Heart, Opened, Draining Ward, Ravenous Shadows, and Tribune of Retribution, Blindness. He showed off each one, using the others for volunteers to display the effects.

"Interesting choices. Personally, I would not encourage defensive tactics like yours that draw out conflicts or encourage getting hit—there is too much that could go wrong. Yet, clearly it has worked this far, and granting yourselves a healer-like ability on top of a regular healer is inspired."

Cilia followed his show-and-tell: Manipulate Darkness, A Hint of Permanence, A Dearth of Materials, and Trail the Mirror's Edge. She manipulated the truth about the latter, obviously, claiming that it only influenced Dark enhancements in crafting, because it would have been a dead giveaway that she had Light cards otherwise.

Heidel did not seem to take heed of her dissembling. He nodded as he wrote. "I look forward to hearing about the results in practice. Tier four crafters are a rare sight for us. You will be granted information on where and how you may craft."

She bowed, hiding her face, which was probably for the best. Cilia wasn't the best at hiding her emotions in the first place, and the implications that she couldn't just craft what and where she wanted to...those would definitely be among the list of comments to set her off.

Seeing her complexion, Sera jumped in to take over. And she lied. A lot. Blessing of the Night was no issue for Heidel, because she lied about it having a cap on boosted attributes. Neither was Cry for Blood, because Sera took care not to tell him about the shield aspect of the card. He seemed to approve of Poison Paradise as well. Heart of Hearts, though?

"I...cannot say that I approve. Now, don't get me wrong. The card would not be on the banned list here. Yet, nobody would ever choose it. We all know that Heart cards are close to useless and do not reflect any proper way to aid the Savior. Actively choosing to strengthen your Heart card instead of choosing a real card—and at Tier three too?" He shook his head.

Now it was Chase's turn to jump in, allowing Sera to hide her indignation. Fortunately, with the others going first, he'd had a bit of time to consider his approach. He knew very well that at least one of his Dark cards would be solidly on the banned list here in Liberty. The fact alone that Sticky Fingers was all about stealing was likely an issue, and the fact that it was both recursive and open-ended went against their weird, arbitrary rules yet again. With that in mind, he carefully rephrased the wording on Sticky Fingers, adding a five-minute limit, and leaving out the chance for permanent gains.

Heidel didn't seem to notice. Rather, he seemed aggravated at the description of Free of Perdition, demanding that Chase repeat the description two times.

[**Free of Perdition**
Rare, Dark rogue
Tier three
Active, medium duration
Activating this card allows you to forcibly swap one of your chosen attributes temporarily with that of another living creature in short range. For a brief while, become as strong as an indomitable rager, as swift as a sky hare. If the target does not resist the effect, they will also see their attribute score temporarily replaced with yours. The effect remains until the cooldown runs out.
Medium cooldown
"How did you do that? Those skinny arms? It cannot be. 'The Beast' Sinclair has been brought low!"]

Heidel seemed extremely agitated, until Chase explained the specifics, how the second part wouldn't work on somebody with higher Mental Power than yourself, and that there was a natural limiter to how much your attributes could increase. That made him relax slightly.

"Well. I must admit, I do not like this one. It forces you to adjust to large attribute changes on short notice. If your tactics revolve around this, and it fails to work? No, I don't like it at all. Also, Circle of Darkness is yet another example of cards for spying and sneaking about that we do not approve of." He sighed, then came to a conclusion. "All told, it could be worse. We suspected that your, ahem, less than lawful past would include some shady choices. We will make a few allowances for you, since none of these are *entirely* at odds with the Liberty credos. With that in mind, allow me to let you in on a few rules that will stay in effect from here on out. First off: as before, you will keep your Devotion to Liberty card active, always. Failure to do so will be viewed as treason. Kith. Your Shadow Master card would be banned, but with Devotion to Liberty applied, there is no issue for you."

"What if—" Kith started.

"No exceptions. Also, Cilia, you are allowed to craft in your spare time, as long as you present any crafted items for verification and registration within the week. Obviously, you will not be allowed to keep all your...droplets, you called them? Should you be called on a mission for the Savior, you might be granted some of them again.

"Liam, Sera? You keep up exactly how you have done so far. Exemplary! Sera, you are allowed to use your—" He squinted at his journal. "Poison Paradise card, should the need arise to help your fellow Liberators."

Rounding on Chase, his eyes narrowed. "Chase. Your journey will be harder, I fear. Your card choices, your class, your past—all put you under increased suspicion. You will have the chance to prove yourself in the years to come."

Raising both his hands to the sky, he intoned, "On behalf of the Savior, I congratulate you on your ascension to hands. May you give as much as you receive." Lowering his hands, he gave them a businesslike smile. "Now, please stay here. In a few minutes, somebody will be along to show you what your future in the blissful lands is going to look like."

With those words, Heidel, comfortable smile plastered back on, bowed to them and backed out the door. The last thing they saw before the door slammed shut was a mass of palace guards saluting and trooping away.

Hoarsely, Kith asked, "Did we just avoid getting ourselves executed?"

CHAPTER 21

For the next chapters, we are going to leave behind the history of Liberty, or any speculation on what has happened in the years after their borders closed. Instead, we will focus on what we know about the fog surrounding their lands, normal wildlife, and cautionary tales regarding their territory. I am going to skim those. That is quite a bit too late for us. (Page 28.)

Heidel's words held true. A few minutes later, a beaming servant came to guide them along, all the while chattering away about what an honor it was for them to be raised so quickly, how happy she was on their behalf, and how bright their future looked.

They shared glances, but Cilia's glares and muted gestures made no secret about them staying silent for now.

They walked for a long time, leaving the palace and striding through the clean, beautiful streets of Salvation. The servant kept prattling on, about their surroundings, their future, what she enjoyed. After what had to be nearly three hours, she stopped in the middle of a street, right next to a door. "This is you."

"What?" Kith said drily. "That's ours?" He pointed at the door.

She giggled. "Of course, silly. You have been raised. That means you've earned a better place to stay, and your names will be added to the door tomorrow." She lowered her voice, adding a conspiratorial grin. "Of course, you're a bit special, aren't you? I've been told that you don't have any positions for now. This means somebody will be along to help you find your proper spot among us. But for the next couple of days, you're free."

"Erm." Liam scratched his ear. "What about food? And are we supposed to stay in here?"

"Oh, silly. Some of the mass will be along to handle the menial work. Hands don't frequent the public kitchens. For now, you can relax, get used to your new home, and enjoy yourselves. I'm sure you'll have fair warning if you're supposed to be doing something. Congratulations again!"

They walked through the house in a shell-shocked state, barely talking, just taking in the last hours, their new situation, their new *house*.

There was nothing surprising there. The house was the same size as Reen's, with a slightly different room layout. Instead of a few larger rooms, they had several smaller rooms. All had a lingering scent of fresh paint, but had been cleared of any signs of whomever had stayed there before. Only a childish poem carved into the back of a chair held any hints as to the old occupants.

They eventually wound up in the kitchen, where a large table set with exactly five chairs waited for them.

Cilia sat down, back straight, and waited for the others to get seated. Then she held up a hand, before a bright light flashed over her heart. "We can speak."

They all started to speak up as one.

Cilia interrupted them. "Wait. Kith. Make sure we don't have any spies."

Kith gulped. "I thought they said not to use my shadows?"

Her snarl was feral. "No shadows. Please talk to Radine. I have checked over the room from the inside. You need to check the outside. We're making sure nobody's spying on us, or listening in."

"You think...? Okay, okay. I'm doing it." Kith interrupted himself.

A tense silence emerged as they all watched Kith's facial expressions shift, his eyes twitching as he went through an internal communication with his bonded Guardian.

He focused back on the room with a shudder. "Whew. Yeah, we're under surveillance. No discussion. Four Keepers that I could see. None of them close enough that they'd be able to see in here, unless they have powers we don't know of."

"We'll have to chance it," Cilia said with a grim look. "We are being lied to."

That didn't have quite the impact she expected. Sera nodded. Chase rolled his eyes. Kith snorted and said, "Ya think?"

Liam blinked. "Wait, what? We're being lied to? About what? This isn't our house?"

"Mind if I take this one?" Chase asked. When nobody complained, he nodded. "The entire thing since they caught us. It's been one huge lie. That part about us being accepted into their society? A lie. About earning their trust. Lie. Those reasons they stated for limiting cards? Lies. Everything we've done since their precious Savior beat us like kids caught pilfering has been one large test, prodding us, checking to see what we would do."

"So, everything with Toran and his people...was that a test as well?" Liam asked, clearly lost.

"Yes. Well, not that Toran and the rest knew anything. They were simple targets. I'm just saying that *we* were being constantly tested. First, if we were going to try to run. Next, if we were willing to do as they said. They rushed us out there, likely because it was such a good target."

"But Chase, they flat out said as much," Liam said.

"They did. *But they never stopped testing us!* Those limitations on cards make no sense to anybody who's had the chance to learn about working on their build. Also, didn't you see those guards outside? They were ready to take us out, if it turned out that we refused to do as they said, were caught in a lie, or wound up having cards they would not be able to tolerate in the long run. Now, Kith, you tell me, have you ever seen four Keepers surround a single home?"

"Not outside of the city center," Kith answered darkly.

"Exactly. We are *still* being tested." Chase sighed. "On what, I can't say. You heard Emilia. She said that she had to take some classes or something, and when she was judged ready, she was fully accepted into their society. Does that feel like what they're doing here?"

"No. It might be because there are five of us," Sera mused. "Or because it is harder to indoctrinate people who are already tightly connected. Only, as you say, I do not believe the normal procedures are going to apply to us."

"Usually, I'd say that's a good thing," Liam grumbled. "Only, that's not in the cards, is it? Oh, and speaking of cards: what do you mean they lied to us about the rules and bans?"

"I can answer that one." Sera got to her feet and paced the room. "Kith, would you please check the outside for us again?"

"You're freaking me out here, princess." Kith closed his eyes, fading back into his connection with Radine. "We're good. Now, can you tell me what's got you so spooked?"

Sera turned toward them. The normally collected woman tended to carry her upbringing with her, including an unwillingness to bend or show weakness even under the worst pressure. Right this moment, however, she looked delicate, fragile even. "The Savior. He is no god. He's human."

"Yes!" Cilia's outburst mixed with the outcries of the others. She spoke up over the rest. "That was what I was missing!" She groaned. "It makes so much more sense!"

The others started to speak all at once.

Sera held up her hands and glared at them. "Relax. I will explain." She waited for them to calm down before continuing. "You may have noticed that I lied about having any shields. At first, that was more of a defensive measure. I noticed that they were trying to avoid us receiving specific powers. Hence, I decided that I could cheat my way to getting those powers, just in case."

"That's my girl." Chase chuckled.

She rested one hand on his forearm and continued. "Once the rest of the rules and banned cards started emerging, however, I noticed the patterns. Yes, there is a focus on shields that I still find slightly confusing. Yet, most of the other banned cards focus on one thing alone: keeping others from growing too strong." She patted Chase's arm. "You noticed something, too. Good job on lying about your cards."

"Ah. Lying. Is there anything it can't solve?" Chase grinned, then turned somber. "You're right. I couldn't tell *what* it was, but I decided to play along. Now it makes sense to me, though. You guys all read the banned cards for your own class. Do you agree?"

Liam squinted, speaking aloud as if figuring it out for himself. "You are telling us that all those banned cards aren't to protect the people of Liberty from making bad choices and protect the Prism—but to keep anybody from reaching heights where they would be able to hurt the Savior?"

"Any summons that would allow people to spy on the palace. Any cards that allow them to grow powerful enough to challenge somebody incredibly strong. Cards that deal with shields, that allow anybody to drain large number of attributes, that cancel large numbers of existing shields and protections," Kith ticked off.

"Oh." Liam perked up. "Yeah. Heidel grew *really* tense when Chase was talking about his Free of Perdition card."

"I honestly think you may be onto something," Kith said. "But does it change anything?"

"What do you mean?" Sera asked. "It changes *everything!*"

Frowning, he made a noncommittal sound. "Does it? Really? Okay. Let's play with the idea a bit. Let's say that the scary fellow in the palace actually used to be a regular person like the lot of us. He rose to power, overturned the leaders, probably killed a lot of people who knew him personally, and installed himself on the throne. All agreed so far?" Kith looked around and nodded to himself. "Then he, what, decided to recreate the Deck of Liberty and base it all around himself as a god, while he closed off the Liberty borders? I wouldn't mind a hundred thousand women worshipping *me*, to be honest."

"Focus," Cilia snapped.

Kith smirked. "Yeah, well. Clearly, he was onto something, because nobody's deposed him yet. Of course, with this damn card," he tapped the Devotion to Liberty card, "he'll have received enough Ænima that he's at an absurdly high Tier by now. We all know that it becomes harder and harder to reach higher Tiers—but half a century of receiving ten percent or more of all Ænima from *all* wielders in Liberty? Let's be honest here. We were up against him—did it truly feel like you were fighting against a person? Or did it feel like we were insects, struggling against an uncaring god? I'll tell you what I think. I think that, once you reach a certain level of power, it doesn't matter if you *are* a god, or if you're merely as strong as a god."

"No. It matters!" Sera insisted. "A god would be able to do anything they wanted. Ignore anything. If you are human and a wielder, you might become close to immortal at higher Tiers, but you are still affected by the rules, by other cards. You cannot be everywhere, understand everything. You can be cheated."

Chase whistled appreciatively. "That *is* a damn fine point. You can't steal a god's deck while he's on the crapper."

"And we're back to toilet humor." Cilia groaned. Grudgingly, she added, "I agree with those two, though. Sure, we aren't going to face off against somebody who's at...what? Tier eight? Ten? But that doesn't mean that they're going to know everything. In fact, everything else adds to that: the setup with the Keepers; their education; the cards; the way their entire damn *society* has been erected to keep people loyal to him and ignorant of what's going on in the world outside. It all speaks of somebody in charge who's desperate to *stay* in charge."

"Okay." Kith nodded begrudgingly. "I'll grant you that. The guy probably isn't all-powerful, all-knowing and all that stuff. Still doesn't change my point. As long as *we* aren't strong enough to dare go up against him, he might as well *be* a god."

Nobody talked for a while. Cilia looked like she wanted to speak up a few times, but stopped herself.

Eventually, Chase slammed the table and half-stood up. "Damn my ass to the Pits. The natural order of nature has been ruined. Kith has managed to come up with an argument to flummox all of us! We might as well give up and become good, faithful worshipers of the Savior! Eh?" He looked at each of them in turn, getting only frowns and growls, especially from Kith. "I'll agree with you so far, Kith. We don't know what we *can* do right now. Also, the odds of cutting our losses and running for the border aren't looking too nice, what with all their Keepers able to send messages everywhere. It'd just take one of them to spot us, before we have an entire army on our backs." A half-smile quirked up at the edge of his mouth. "Leaving us in a bad position, weaker than the opposition, without the knowledge we need to act." He looked expectantly at the others, waiting for a response.

Liam snorted. "What else is new?" he said under his breath. Then he blinked, and repeated the words. "Wait. What else is new?" This time, his tone was thoughtful rather than sarcastic.

"*Exactly!*" Chase breathed. "This is just like what we've done so many times before..." He grinned weakly. "Okay, not *just* like it. Still, we may be out of our depths, but we're not lost. This is where we start, from scratch. We're being tracked, we're being monitored, still don't know what they're planning to do with us. But as of this moment, it looks like we've cleared the worst of their suspicions. That means, as long as we don't get caught, we can start learning, gathering information, creating an actual plan."

For a while, nobody said anything.

Sera spoke up first, doubtfully. "You are saying that, even knowing we have Keepers watching our every move, you want to continue with our original plan?"

"Nah. Something new. Something better. Now, we can actually start acquiring some useful info regarding the palace, learn how to enter the place, to escape properly without triggering all of their armies. Pits, we might be able to earn ourselves a deck even within their weird rules. It's just a matter of figuring out their weaknesses and exploiting them. And once we have an actual plan, we let Cilia run over it a thousand times to spot all the flaws."

Cilia narrowed her eyes. "I've trained you well."

Liam barked with laughter. "Count me in. I've always wanted to outwit a god. Erm. A...you know what I mean!"

Kith warned them that Radine spotted somebody entering their house, and they paused for a while.

It was a servant of the mass, bringing them dinner. He was distant, professional, and, once he spotted one of the cards on Liam's leg, clammed up tight, stuck somewhere between awe and fear, considering he'd clearly expected hands rather than minds. He spent a while cleaning the house as they ate, and took care of the kitchen as well, moving about calmly, as if he'd been with them for decades.

Liam eventually did manage to wheedle a few facts out of him. They would have at least three visits a day, more if the house needed any sort of renovations. The visits would all come at the same times each day, all week. They didn't have to do anything, but the helpers would appreciate it if they pointed out any potential issues. A few hours later, approaching evening, he left.

"This is the weirdest place. He didn't even tell us his name." Liam shook his head in confusion.

"I hate to break it to you." Sera smiled fondly. "But not knowing the name of the hired help is less rare than you would think. I doubt my father knew the names of any of the cleaning staff."

"Well...I hate to break it to you, but *I* doubt your dad's winning any prizes for being a good person." Chase grinned. "Where were we when we were interrupted?"

A light flashed near Cilia's heart. She said drily, "We were planning high treason, stealing a deck, and cheating a god."

"Ah. Sounds like we should be able to finish early, then. Let's get to it."

They spent the next few hours plotting. At this point, it was less about any actual plans than it was about arranging for the approximate directions they'd be taking. Also, given that they had no clue what the Liberators had in the books for them, they half-expected something to come along to interrupt them anyway.

Hence, it was a bit of a surprise when they were actually afforded several days of uninterrupted freedom. They were allowed to come and go as they pleased, walk the beautiful, clean streets of Salvation, enjoy the parks, train, and generally do as they liked.

They kept expecting the other shoe to drop. For some official to come see them, tell them they'd be divided and sent to separate places, for their "education" to start. Yet nothing happened. It was like they were kept in a limbo, without anything pressuring them.

They turned to getting to know their area. They started getting to know people in the neighborhood as well. At first, Salvation had felt like a ghost town. There'd been no bustle, no entrepreneurship, no cackling street kids running away with stolen produce. Yet, that didn't mean that there was no life in the city. It was just very different from what they knew.

People didn't just hang out in groups. When you wanted to enjoy yourself with somebody you knew, it was in smaller groups, and nearly always in areas that were meant for the purpose—the lush, vibrant parks, larger public areas like the plazas or the dedicated class parks.

Sometimes, public spectacles were arranged, word of mouth spreading the news. These, they avoided, after learning that they were often held in the central, aptly named Execution Plaza.

The class parks were a surprise to them, but a positive one. Not only did the Savior expect people to keep physically active, he also encouraged everybody to keep up martial training at all ages, keeping them ready, should the need arise to send them into action again.

Hence, Liberty had large, open-air areas constructed as settings appropriate for the different classes to build and maintain their prowess. Large, sawdust-covered arenas for dueling and weapons practice for fighters. Intricate arrangements for the target practice of ranged fighters, with targets both moving and stationary. Schools and target practice for casters. For every single class, they had elaborate constructions ready and available at all hours. They even had hands with healing powers standing by in case of injuries. Crafters were an exception to the rule, because any crafters in Salvation were expected to work within their expertise and given the equipment and stores to comply with that.

They swiftly agreed that they should all spend some time each day training. Both in order to get to know some of the locals, and to train the effective use of their Liberty and Dark cards, for as long as they couldn't freely use all their other cards.

Above all else, however, they looked for tails, for surveillance, for any sign that they were being actively tracked outside of the Keepers. To their surprise, they saw nothing. Either anybody tracking them was so far out of their range that they wouldn't stand a chance of catching them...or they weren't being followed at all. Nobody sent long looks or even curious glances after them on the streets. It was like a lack of inquisitiveness had been bred into the locals.

On the third day, Kith went to visit Spike. He'd been complaining about being unable to see his bound Guardian all this time, but it was becoming worse. Truth be told, nobody disagreed, and even Cilia felt for the adorable Guardian and wanted to know that it was doing okay. Of course, checking in with Nordon and Reen, learning that they were okay and not about to do something drastic, was also a priority.

They'd argued about it for a while. Given that their Devotion to Liberty cards constantly tracked their presence, they didn't want to give away their very own smuggler or Nordon. Eventually, they agreed that, as long as he and Radine kept an eye out for Keepers and other watchers, Kith quickly dipping in to touch base with them would not be a real risk. Especially considering the—very real—prospect of Spike eventually becoming so agitated by his master not being around, that he'd break out into the streets.

Hence, they all went about their business as usual...training, chatting, getting to know others of their own classes. Cilia left to learn more about how crafting worked for somebody like her, and what she was allowed to do on her own. Sera, to her great pleasure, learned that Liberty healers were all allowed to listen in to lectures that helped them heal better, and was looking forward to a scheduled talk about treating birth defects.

One by one, they finished with their tasks, returning for the evening meal and to talk about the days to come. Only, Kith didn't show up. The evening servant came and went, and they moved out into the foyer, covered by Cilia's Heart card, debating whether they should set out to search for him, when the entrance door slammed open.

Kith stalked in, looking fit to bursting. He started to speak, then caught himself with a visible effort. "Can we...?" He tapped his heart, looking at Cilia for permission.

She nodded as the card flashed behind her shirt. "It's active. You can talk. What's going on? Do we need to move?"

He snarled. "Not right now. I..." Kith kicked the wall, punching it for good measure. "Darkness drain his gods-cursed blood!" He took a deep, shuddering breath. "It's Reen. He was the one who betrayed us!"

CHAPTER 22

I'm taking a break from the tome for a while to jot down my own thoughts. Of course, it helps that the current chapters are all about precautions for those outside Liberty lands and no use to us at all. Still, I struggle to find the mental stability to come up with any preliminary conclusions. The sheer thought that somebody could possibly manipulate a deck in order to propel themselves into false godhood—it's scary. (Pages 29-45.)

Kith talked.

Once they learned that there was no over-arching threat of them being revealed or attacked, and he confirmed that he'd taken care to not be followed as he walked home, they marched him into the kitchen and sat him down to eat.

He ate like a starving bright wolf. In between bites, he told them what had happened. "I knew it, right when I entered his home. I could see it in his eyes. You remember what Liam looked like, back when he *accidently* slept with my girlfriend?"

"I've *said* I was sorry, like a thousand times. I didn't mean to." Liam flung up his hands.

Kith snorted, aiming a smirk at him that didn't reach his eyes. "Oh, I know. I'm just rubbing it in by now. But he had that same look on his face. He knew exactly what he'd done, and he was totally certain I was there to make him pay for it. Didn't even have to say anything."

"But how? *Why?*" Sera asked.

"The how was pretty simple. One of the many times he was out in the city, he simply walked by the palace and informed some of the guards that he'd spotted us in the streets and heard about a plan to steal a deck. Then he told them our descriptions and walked back to us, acting as if nothing had happened."

"That would do it," Liam agreed. "They just leaned back, waiting for us to walk in. No wonder the Savior was right there, along with all those guards. It's like we were just putting on a play for all of them."

Kith nodded sadly. "The why of it is, unfortunately, also rather straightforward. He'd said that we shouldn't try anything. Apparently, he has connections near, or in, the palace. When they told him that we kept snooping around despite all his warnings, he decided that we were likely to get him caught. He might even have caught us manipulating the lists...he didn't go into details. Anyway, he decided that it was us or him, concluded that he'd rather see *us* hang than himself. Of course, he had a ton of justifications, all the people he's responsible for and everything, but that's the long and short of it." Kith frowned. "He didn't even get a reward for it. Moron!"

"And now that we're free again?" Chase asked.

"He asked us to stay the Pits away. Of course, he knows that he has no way of *making* us do anything, and that we can get him in deep trouble, if we say anything." Kith shrugged. "It's not like we want to get Nordon killed either."

"Hrm." Chase tapped a rhythm on the table, deep in thought. "That's a possible opening for the future. Not getting Nordon killed. But nudging Reen to help us."

"In his defense, we did do exactly what we promised not to," Sera said.

"And he ratted us out, setting us up to get killed, and we didn't betray him in return. I'd say that leaves the scales tilted in our favor. Regardless, that's a possibility for tomorrow. I can't come up with anything he can help with right now anyway." Chase shrugged. "So, how were Spike and Nordon doing?"

"Spike was wonderful. He was getting fat, too!" Kith said enthusiastically. "Honestly, if I had the chance, I'd sneak him over to our house. However, there's no true way to hide him over here, and we know things will go south if he's spotted. Fortunately, he and Reen are getting along well, and he can stay there until we leave!"

"And Nordon?" Chase raised an eyebrow.

Kith groaned. "He wouldn't shut *up* about foam stability! It's not like I asked! Anyway, the moment he knew we were okay, he moved on. He is doing what he loves, gets all the ingredients he asks for, and is fed and watered. I doubt he needs anything else."

Sera sighed. "Thank you, Kith. This might not feel like a net gain for us, but I do believe it is."

"Sure, I guess. I mean, having somebody to potentially blackmail is never bad." He frowned.

"That is not what—why would you ever think that was what I would say?" She took a deep breath. "I mean that knowing that our capture was no accident was helpful. It increases the odds of us pulling off a successful theft at a later date."

"Oh. Yeah. That makes sense, I guess. They weren't just magically clever to catch us, but had help. So...for now, we don't do anything with Reen? Regardless what he said, he's feeling guilty. If we ask him for anything that doesn't incriminate him, I'm sure he'll help."

"That sounds like a plan." Chase nodded. "Having some-body in our corner in case we need more knowledge or a helping hand is going to be useful."

"But...he betrayed us. How could we trust him again?" Sera stared around the table in shock.

Cilia chuckled, reaching out to squeeze her shoulder. "Sera. Dear. Trusting him again implies we trusted him in the first place. We were working *around* him, keeping him in the dark about what we were doing." She shrugged. "Besides, now that he knows *we* know, he's not going to risk anything. Now, we can continue our planning. The crafting approach might give us a step up—I need to tell you what went on there." She rubbed her hands together, but ended up with her jaws cracking open in a massive yawn. "But maybe we've had enough excitement for one day."

Kith snorted. "Sure. Crafting. Excitement."

"Better ramp up that excitement, or the next droplets you're getting will be duds!" she snapped.

"Crafting. Yay!"

CHAPTER 23

There is one topic my mind keeps coming back to: deck manipulation. The intricacies available the first time you erect a Wellspring for your type of deck. The Furyborn elders did promise to tell us about it when it became relevant—but these past weeks have made me think. For a good long while, I believed that the only real customization available revolved around choices regarding your Guardians. Yet, now I must conclude that there is more. A lot more. The "Savior" created an entirely new card from scratch. What about the inquisitor cards that help them hunt down Dark wielders? Are those Wellspring choices too?

Cilia did get her chance to talk about crafting. Apparently, yes, it was acceptable (if frowned upon), to become a crafter and not make it the basis of your job. Those who'd made that choice, however, were still expected to participate and pay their dues to society by crafting useful items in one of a handful of smaller crafting locations strewn throughout Salvation. The places themselves were lovely: an arrangement of crafters with stations separated by trade; all tools provided for; all materials granted; welcoming crafters all too willing to share their knowledge.

It was a paradise for any up-and-coming crafter starting out in their trade, with several dozen different crafts represented in each location. Yet, it was also limited, both when it came to the quality of their crafters—not a single one had reached their third Tier—and the quality of their materials. Regardless of how they decided to distribute any rarer crafting materials arriving to Salvation, the crafting stations were so far down in the hierarchy, they never saw any of it.

Still, Cilia would have every chance to practice her workmanship, as well as her practical ability to enhance her materials by means of the manipulation of Darkness. They'd welcomed her profusely, given her a thorough questioning to try to understand the options and limitations concerned with Darkness in leatherworking, and promised her a full list of ideas for crafting next time she'd arrive. This way, Cilia sneered, she would get the chance to aid Liberty society optimally. As she explained, there was no encouraging of anybody to experiment; rather, it was all about the common good.

Still, she might get some new ideas from what they'd come up with. Also, there was a chance of being able to hoard some crafting materials for her own use. Although they did limit the crafting materials you were allowed to use, she could use her A Dearth of Materials card to cut down on material use and sneak some back for personal use.

They eventually shot down that idea. Not only did the palace know about her card and its effects—the risk of being observed was also unnecessary, as long as Reen might deliver materials, should they need them.

Their group was slowly switching gears, starting in on planning the activities of the coming days, when Kith shot to his feet. "Deactivate," he snapped at Cilia, tapping his heart.

Her Heart card deactivated in an instant.

"Here? Hello?" The voice arrived from the foyer, merry and bubbly.

"Emilia? In here!" Kith yelled, causing Liam to punch his shoulder.

Emilia strode into the kitchen, a warm smile fixed on her face. "You *are* here. I was knocking for several minutes."

Chase's mind raced. "Sorry. We were deep in a discussion about our new cards. It got a bit heated, I'm afraid."

"Ooh." She actually clapped, like a little girl with a new toy. "I can easily imagine. The Savior truly favors you, for you to be awarded with second-Tier cards already. And for all the opportunities."

Liam had been stuffing his face with the remnants of the morning meal. Now, he perked up, with a handful of tangerine slices halfway to his mouth. "Opportunities?"

"Yes! We are off for another adventure!"

Whatever controls were still ongoing, it seemed like Emilia at least had softened toward them. This time around, they were afforded the opportunity to switch clothes, scrub their teeth, and handle any last-minute necessities. Still, with virtually all their equipment either confiscated following their failed theft attempt or back at Reen's, it took less than ten minutes before they were walking through the late morning of Salvation, Emilia leading the way.

Eventually, she spoke up beyond superficial information, her voice contrite. "I am aware that I was a bit hard on you last time. I apologize for that. Yet, you never know with newcomers. Most are so...ungrateful! But you proved your dedication beyond a doubt. And you saved my worthless hide, to boot. Now look at yourselves. Hands, one and all, ready to toil, to lift us all in the right direction."

Chase fought down the need to roll his eyes. He couldn't even find it in himself to dislike Emilia. There was no veil there, no filter. She said exactly what she believed, and she very much *believed*. Trying to convince her, to debate her on her positions would be entirely useless. They might as well use her, milk her of all the information she could provide.

Right this moment, the information they needed was rather straightforward. "Where are we off to, Emilia?" he asked.

Her smile paled. "To the border. We have an intrusion. A big one. We need your strength to take them down."

The edge of Salvation lay before them. They could see the new row of houses being painted. A single larger edifice painted in the nuances of the hearts overlooked a long row of the mass. Right this moment, however, the enormity of the expansion, reaching as far as the eye could see, faded at Emilia's statement.

They shared nervous glances. Was it the Lightborn? Had they actually broken through? Would they have to fend off an invasion?

Liam, bless his heart, focused entirely on the task. "What are we looking at?"

Emilia bowed her head. "I am unaware if you are familiar with the term 'stampede'?"

"A sudden, panicked rush of beasts?" Sera asked.

"Yes. That is one meaning of the word. In this situation, however, it has another meaning." Emilia cleared her throat. "Usually, Guardians act in packs or on a singular basis, depending on their nature and their specific temper."

Chase snorted. "Could you perhaps dumb it down a bit? We're all from the slums, and only Sera and Cilia have any sort of book learning."

Emilia smiled, nodding. "It means that, even as Guardians, wolves are likely to stay in packs, usually in smaller groups, but sometimes as many as thirty. Gaborns, however, are solitary animals, as Guardians and animals both, that only come together for mating and raising offspring. When Guardians are created, some things change, but they still retain, or gain, some of those animal instincts, even if they no longer need to procreate or, really, act like animals most of the time. Does that make sense?"

Chase wiped his brow. The sun was out in force today. He looked up at the hour-long incline ahead of them leading them up the heights overlooking Salvation. "I guess it does. So, you're saying that, most often, you'll only ever see smaller groups of Guardians. Except a stampede is something different?"

"Just so. There are certain...directives, perhaps? Certain unknown reasonings for why Guardians do what they do. Are they led by other divinities? By card wielders? Corralled by armies?"

They shared glances. This was one thing that they actually *had* learned. It was part of what the Wellspring decided. Among the Lightborn, the Guardians would gather in a cordon surrounding Lightborn territory, defending the Border against any outside Guardians. If the concentration of Guardians along the Border reached a certain critical mass, some of them would take off, hunting for enemy Guardians, soaking up Ænima to survive, until they'd eventually run out or die in battle.

Among the Furyborn, it was different, as the Guardians were allowed to live alongside Furyborn people until their Ænima was depleting, and they were eventually sent out against their enemies for an honorable death in battle. Elemental Guardians were used as training dummies, allowing for the Protectors to grow and earn Ænima in semi-safe environs.

Emilia would've known this…if she'd actually managed to become a Protector.

Emilia continued, not catching any of the subtext. "No matter the reason, the general lack of overwhelming numbers, along with the effect of our Prism, allows the hopeful the chance to fight on an even basis against the Guardians. Only, on rare occasions, we experience this. A surge, whether it is a natural phenomenon or not, pushing more than one group to range ahead, disregarding species, natural inclinations, and whatnot. Sometimes, they even drag regular animals along with their numbers, although those tend to drop off or die, given their lack of supernatural stamina."

Kith cleared his throat. "I…think we've heard of this before." Also, fought it. On the carved plains in the Furyborn lands, they'd called it a swarm. A naturally occurring phenomenon, leading to life-threatening results. Here, it might be something else. "How many Guardians? And what are the hopefuls doing? Erm. And…what's our task?"

Emilia walked with her head straight, ignoring the gentle incline. She didn't respond to the first part. "The hopefuls and the mass are pulling back, at the moment, at a controlled pace. We have called in what hands and hearts can be expected to aid from nearby villages and towns, yet the stampede has hit a stretch of land that is relatively far from larger settlements."

She smiled brilliantly. "This may seem like a defeat to you. Let me tell you otherwise. Even if stampedes rarely happen, this is entirely normal. Losses among the hopefuls are expected to be entirely within acceptable bounds. The local hands and hearts approaching add a skillset that will help contain and slow the stampede, yet they do not hold the power to defeat them. Left to run amok, they would be able to cause actual damage to our lands—but the Savior provides. He always does. When needed, the hearts and minds step in. On rare occasions, the pillars have even been known to come to the aid. Yet, this time, we are able to let them all use their prodigious powers elsewhere." Her beatific smile lit up her face.

"So that's where we come in," Liam grunted.

"You still haven't said how many Guardians there are. That's making me nervous, Emilia," Kith said.

Emilia continued to smile. "Oh, quite a few. More than two hundred. Yet, that is the wonder of it. With the Savior having just granted you additional access to his powers? I have faith!"

The conversation ground to a halt after that. Emilia didn't yet have access to information on the power, danger, or types of Guardians approaching, but promised that she'd be able to provide that soon. Yet, she *was* able to tell them about their destination. They were aiming straight east, and would be able to use the roads for almost the entire stretch. Depending on their own speed and the efficiency of the hands and hearts slowing down the stampede, they'd be able to hit the enemy about two days from now.

That night, when Emilia was sleeping soundly, they were able to hold a private conversation.

"*Please* tell me I'm allowed to kill her!" Kith pointed at Emilia's sleeping form.

"Please tell *me* that she's outside the range of your Heart card, Cil," Chase commented drily.

"She is," Cilia said. "Why do you think I put my bedroll down all the way over here? Also, why would you want to hurt her?"

"*The hopefuls are within acceptable losses. We will only lose like a hundred or two. We have plenty of spares.*" Kith's mocking, exaggerated tones made no secret of the fury behind the comment. "What a horrible bitch!"

"It is not entirely her fault. She has been indoctrinated to think like this," Sera said. "Even so, that was a horrid comment."

"You think?" Kith snarled. He pinched the bridge of his nose. "Sorry. Not your fault." He waved in the direction they were traveling. "Listen. I'm just throwing this out there. *This place sucks.* The Savior sucks. People suck. And our lives are going to suck, if we stay here. How about we just shoot past that stupid stampede and run for the borders instead? We'll be able to escape and make it back to friendly territory, build a real life somewhere. I can run back and fetch Spike tonight!"

Nobody spoke for nearly a minute. They were deep in thought, caught up in their own mental worlds.

Eventually, Chase cleared his throat. Hesitantly, without any of his usual energy, he said, "If that is what you all want? I'll go along with it. My decision, though, would be that we stay. This might still be us being tested. If we run, a few days away from the border, what are the odds they've still got hundreds of hopefuls and other poor suckers ready to fling at us?" He grimaced. "Honestly, I think we could make it, even if it were a trap. My real reason?" A half-smile emerged. "We come from the same place. We've been in the same literal shit. When we were back there, all I could think about was how we just needed a bit of power, and we could make a life for ourselves. Then we grew stronger, and learned what the world really looked like, and..." He continued at a near whisper. "It's not enough." After a while, he repeated, louder, "Fire burn my eyes, it's not *enough*! I don't want to just find a nice safe spot for the five of us, as we watch the Lightborn ruin Ordei and dominate everybody else."

"Do we really need the bloody Liberty deck for that, though? If we return, right now, we've already got four damn decks, and will be able to create a Wellspring stronger than anything the Elementals, Lightborn, or Furyborn have," Kith asked, colors awhirl in his eyes.

"You know the answer for that as well as I do," Chase said softly. "We've had the same discussions. We've spoken to all those in power. Is it possible that they'll back us, even if we fail? Sure. Is it possible that they're going to, instead, throw all their power at the plots that aim to strengthen their own kind? It's a possibility that they'll back us. *But do we want to take that chance?*"

For a while, the only noise was that of Kith softly pounding his fist down on the plank floor of their shelter. "I really, really hate this place." He sighed. "But I guess we're not in *imminent* danger right now."

"Really." Liam's voice was dry as the preacher's sermons back in the lower market.

Cilia snorted and started to cough. She waved away their attention, wiping tears from her eyes.

"You're such jerks. What I mean is that, once we're finished killing these monsters and...now I see your point." He barked a laugh. "Okay, my mistake. *Once we've defeated hundreds of Guardians* and get back to Salvation, it doesn't feel like we'll be in imminent danger. Besides, the more missions we handle for them, the more I'd say they're likely to loosen our leashes. I guess, what I'm saying is, even if I'd rather torch this place, I guess I'm up for another go."

Chase reached over and patted his back. "How about the rest of you?"

Cilia nodded. "We are in a much better position to plan properly now. Count me in."

"You know me. I'll do what you guys do." Liam flexed. "But I *would* like to show those stupid guards in the palace just how strong I am when their deity daddy isn't around to save them."

"If that's the general gist of it," Kith said, "I'm going to write—well, I'm going to have *Cilia* write—an update to the Furyborn elders, so they can actually read what we're writing. Then I'll send Radine on a long flight with the message, so we can hear how things are going outside the borders of these inbred yokels."

Sera smiled. "I have said so before—but I am proud of you all. Even with you calling them yokels, Kith. Regardless what your reasoning is, the fact remains, if we pull this off, we will be able to save a lot of people from danger. That is worth quite a few risks, in my opinion."

"Pfft. Altruism." Cilia rolled her eyes. "I thought we taught you better."

CHAPTER 24

What then, I ask myself, should be *our* approach to constructing a Wellspring? If we manage to obtain all five decks and are able to create a Wellspring from scratch, with benefits that haven't been seen on Ordei for hundreds of years...what should we do? What should we *do*?

"What's the largest intrusion that's happened while you've been here, Em?" Liam asked.

They were mid-march on the next day, and were starting to run out of "safe" conversation topics. They'd asked Emilia about everything they could come up with, from the topic of education in the blissful lands, over the best way to walk the Steps and to the topic of personal belongings. That last one had been mildly confusing, as the answer was, apparently, that anything you personally owned was yours, right up until it wasn't anymore.

"My name is... Ah, nevermind. The largest? Let's see." Emilia tapped her lips. "Well, I don't know if it was the largest, but I actually watched this one from a distance. It was insane. We had *three* gaborns enter the Prism at the same time." She nodded emphatically. "It must have been during mating season, and the female entered, followed by two males chasing her. I don't mind admitting that I nearly wet myself when I saw them!"

She beamed at them. "That day truly taught me how the Savior provides for us all. The wild beasts, of course, spotted the hopefuls retreating on the far side of the Prism, and found them to be excellent morsels. The huge beasts threatened to run amok over the lands unchallenged. Yet, at the time, one of the pillars was visiting the border—and she stepped in to save them. In the end, she laid down her life for her fellow Liberators, but she managed to hurt them enough that the troops incoming were able to kill the surviving beasts within the day." She breathed deeply with a small smile on her lips. "Truly, that day was when my belief grew from a tiny sprout to a flower in bloom. What are the odds?"

The others didn't comment.

Chase cleared his throat, trying not to display the discomfort he experienced. "It does sound like a miracle," he lied. "There was one thing I was curious about. There are only...four Pillars of Liberty?"

"Three." Emilia smiled. "One gave his life for the Savior last winter."

"Three. Okay, thanks. What I'm a bit curious about is that, well, from what we were told, once you hit the fifth Tier, your natural aging slows down by a *lot*. So, how come we don't have any more pillars?"

"Ah." She nodded softly to herself. "That is a very insightful question, Chase. Part of the answer, of course, lies in the sacrifice inherent in following the Savior. Each of us, and the higher Tiers especially, sacrifices a large part of their Ænima to the greater good. Every time we increase our Tier, we improve our connection to the Savior, and to Liberty itself. We Hearts of Liberty dedicate thirty percent of all Ænima to Liberty. I do not know how much pillars give away, but it is not negligible."

Chase bowed, mostly to hide the shock and disgust he felt. "That is very magma—what's the word, Sera?"

"Magnanimous," Sera said.

"That's the one. Very good of them."

"It truly is. I am envious of their ability to give." Emilia sighed. "I can only hope to aspire to their greatness. I am fortunate enough that I have been allowed to join you in battle this time and do my part. Another sign that the Savior smiles upon you—that He does not feel the need for me to watch out for transgressions on your part."

Chase felt his smile growing increasingly uncomfortable. "Yes. It will be an honor, risking our lives at your side!"

That night, they came to two horrific conclusions. One, that there was no such thing as peaceful retirement for higher-Tier Liberators. If that were the case, there should be a growing number of elderly pillars. Two, that something else was happening in Liberty society. No matter the increased cost in Ænima, a people acclimatized to constant fighting should, by all rights, produce a Tier-six. And, according to Emilia, this had never happened.

The sun peeked over the horizon. In the background, Emilia was visible as a vague outline, half-prostrated before the Keeper above their shelter.

"I'm never going to get used to this," Kith murmured, as he looked at the three large packs that had appeared during the night. "We don't need to prepare for our trip. We just...leave, and this all shows up in the morning, like we'd prayed for it. And tomorrow it'll be gone like it was never here in the first place."

"I am totally getting used to this." Liam rummaged through one of the packs. "Ooh. They've packed cinna berries in here. Who's hungry? Kith? I seem to recall you loving cinna berries?"

"We're not talking about that story!"

"If you're just stuffing yourself, share it around." Cilia yawned. "Otherwise, let's see what's there. According to Emilia, we should hit the beasts around noon today."

Grunting, with a mouth full of berries, Liam started to extract items from the packs, laying out weapons and armor on the ground before them. He choked, then guffawed as he found a truncheon, well-oiled and maintained. "Hey! These are our favorite weapons. How'd they know?"

Emilia's voice crossed the open area. "The Keeper system is efficient, fueled by the power of the Savior. You should have learned not to question His gifts by now."

"Yeah, but..." Liam waved with his hands in several different directions, as if that were explanation enough. "Color me impressed, is all I'm saying." Their own weapons still lay safely back at Reen's, untouched from where they'd left them the first time they entered the palace. He peeked up, with a huge grin. "Hey, Cil. You've even got your droplets back!"

Kith leapt forward, rushing to inspect the edges of the hand axes they'd put in there. Once he was done checking them over, he asked, "Hey, Emilia. Whoever you can send the thanks to, please do so. Working with the kind of weapons that we're used to will make a huge difference. Now, do you have any information what exactly we're up against? It'd be good to plan ahead for this stuff."

"I have learned more," Emilia said. "Not that this is going to help us a lot, I am afraid. We have six different species incoming. Some of them are capable of ranged attacks, one species can rush ahead in a targeted burst, and this frog-like creation has a blinding burst from their eyes. I'm sure that there will be other surprises once we engage them in battle, but those are the ones the hopefuls and other stout fighters have discovered so far."

"Hrm. Numbers? You said a few hundred, right? What can they do?"

She nodded. "A few specimens, injured, or weaker than the average, have fallen behind, allowing hopefuls to sweep in and take them on. Maybe a hundred and eighty Guardians remain. The shock frogs are the most numerous. About eighty of those. Then we have a dozen winged, owl-like creatures, only bigger. Two dozen thunder rats. Smaller beasts that can launch a targeted ranged attack that ruins your hearing and messes with your balance. Three huge, armored snakes, powers unknown. Ten stick stalkers. Man-height bipeds, but with explosive bursts of speed. Finally, we have an entire herd of beautiful, white horses. Soil soarers. More than fifty of them. Very limited control over soil."

Chase grimaced. "That does sound like a mess, all right. Could you...I mean, if you intend to fight, could you explain which cards you have?"

"Oh. Those are easy. I believe, above all, in the Savior, and in the virtue of simplicity. My cards increase Strength and Toughness." She strode over to the backpacks, untied a large bundle strapped to one of them, and stood back up, smiling, as she held up a massive, two-handed axe that looked as if it could chop wood and necks alike with few issues. "I have found, that with enough Strength, enough staying power, my trusty axe and the Savior at my side, few things can stand up to me."

They finished eating and started the day's march. Within the first hour, they started to notice birds on the horizon. As they moved ahead, the sounds of carrion crows mixed with the sounds of beasts, and the setting before them became increasingly clear.

They braved one final incline, a small grass-covered hill leading up to grant them the full vista of what they were facing. There, they were confronted with reality. Hearing that they were up against a few hundred Guardians was one thing. They'd prepared for that. Watching the monsters roam across the gorgeous grasslands, leaving flattened grass and churned-up soil behind them in a stretch hundreds of feet wide was something else. Even the swarm they'd faced inside the canyons of the carved plains in the Furyborn lands had not been as intimidating as this. Watching the beasts striding along as one overpowering collective, out for blood, was scary as hell.

Also, they were not prepared to see the soldiers.

They'd met hopefuls a few times, so far. When they traveled the roads on their way to Salvation, they'd come across them, marching proudly across the stretch, strong and prepared, led by a few powerful, capable members of the mass or hands.

These were not the same.

The few dozen Liberators stumbling ahead of the growling, whinnying, screeching mass of empowered beasts might have been calm and collected at some point. Yet, following what had to be *days* of stumbling ahead of their pursuers, they were reduced to animalistic beings, mindless flight being the only resort left to them.

One of the runners turned around for a moment and stopped, before fleeing once more. Behind him first one, then another of the huge frogs stumbled and fell. The Guardians both got back up and continued their chase, only a bit slower.

That seemed to be the only thing that kept them alive. A few of the higher-Tiered soldiers occasionally used their cards to slow or attack the Guardians, allowing the hopefuls and those of the mass among them a chance to catch their breath, to steal ahead a few feet.

Ugly, broken human bodies marring the landscape here and there behind the stampede showed that their race had not been without cost.

Chase murmured something under his breath. Then he stood up straight, raised his sword above his head. At the top of his lungs, he yelled, "Enough! Dinner's served, you ugly, mis-bred freaks!"

For the sake of theatricality, that should have been enough. By all rights, Chase believed, the Guardian horde should veer toward them, granting the fleeing Liberators a much-needed reprieve. In practice, a few of the fliers swerved slightly toward the sound, before returning their attention to the prey in front of them. The rest of the bloodthirsty beasts did not waver.

He twirled the short sword for emphasis, then shrugged. "Eh. I tried. Kith? Do you mind?"

Kith slammed the heads of his hand axes together with a ringing sound. "Do I mind spreading chaos?" His ensuing laughter was not entirely sane, and his voice rose into a hoarse shout. "You think to stand before me? You think yourselves mighty? Behold my power and weep. *I am legion, for I am many!*" Between the flashes on his body, shapes started to emerge. The ground disgorged the twisted, bubbling shape of the Tainted Earth. Coils of Shadow sent dark vipers slithering in between the grass stalks. Above them all, Antithesis of Light soared, the dark crow-shaped form hovering in defiance of gravity as a dark light started to build within its beak.

Liam turned to Emilia, shaking his shoulders, allowing the shield to settle properly on his arm. "He's *such* a drama queen. I swear, half the reason he became a summoner was to show off."

"I...won't say it's not working," she half-whispered as she saw the numerous creatures emerging before Kith.

In the background, the Liberators were still running, managing to create some distance between the distracted Guardians and themselves.

Cillia snorted. "Listen!" she barked. "You know the drill. I break their momentum. Then we engage. *No* heroics. Liam's the only one who takes them head-on. And Emilia, please, stay with Kith to begin with."

Offended, Emilia shook her head. "Hide behind with the summoner? You believe I am afraid to face the enemy? Death does not scare me."

Chase smiled. "We don't doubt your courage. What we need is for you to understand the way this is going to work. Because we are not going down there to fight. We are going down to *kill*." He smiled at her, mirth not reaching his eyes. "Besides, if you believe sticking with Kith means being safe, you don't know anything. He's not your regular summoner."

The first droplet sailed down among the leaders of the stampede. No heads turned. No Guardians responded to the missile. Then, darkness fell.

From one second to the other, a circle of darkness erupted into being, covering the leading group of soil soarers. On either side of them, similar circles emerged in short succession, swathing the entire breadth of the stampede in darkness. Screams and pain-filled whinnies emerged, as beasts fell to the ground within the shadows.

"All of you! Close your eyes! Breaking them up now!" Cilia shouted. She stood at the front of their group, hands moving lightning quick as she extracted the next set of droplets from within the crossed belts on her midriff.

Liam positioned himself at her side, feet grinding into the soil to get settled. In front of him, the Tainted Earth lowered itself, settling down below the level of the tall grass as it seemed to imitate Liam.

On Liam's left side, Kith slammed his hand axes together again. He leapt from one foot to the other, murmuring under his breath as his eyes flittered back and forth, directing his summons with a wild-eyed grin.

Emilia was glued to Kith's flank, shooting nervous glances at the over-eager summoner.

Chase leapt up and down, windmilling his arm and stump to loosen up, on Liam's right side. His Nights of Criffhaven kicked into effect, granting him the first of fifteen eventual increases to Agility.

Meanwhile, Sera stood at the far back of their group, twin shields readied as her eyes flickered constantly between the patches of shadows…estimating, waiting, as she listened to the chaotic sounds within the darkness.

The first beasts emerged from the far side, blinking to take in the light.

Droplets of lights burst apart; blinding explosions erupted, right as the bubbles of darkness fell away. The sounds of animals screaming erased any chance at normal conversation.

"Sending in the vipers!" Kith yelled at the top of his lungs.

Chase barely heard it over the noise of impact, of bestial pain. He saw the large, owl-like creatures swarm their way, only to be met with a series of dark missiles shooting from the dark crow hovering above them. He bared his teeth in challenge, even as he felt his solidity increase beyond Emilia's buff—a clear sign that the first beasts had died and Sera was using her Cry for Blood card.

Now, they truly had their attention. Like a wounded giant, the horde slowly veered and turned, bloodthirsty cries emerging as they located their new challengers. The equines raced first, with some of the ugly, boil-filled frogs leaping behind them, croaking loudly.

Chase cursed deep within at the need for secrecy. Usually, they could have faced the beasts with a dozen of different strategies. They could have waves of acidic water rushing down upon the incoming stampede, could have Kith and Chase racing among the diving owls on invisible platforms and living boots of air. Instead, they were reduced to Dark and Liberty cards. He snorted and spat. A disarming card. Fat lot of good that was going to do against hundreds of weaponless enemies.

No. They were reduced to the basics. Less than that, even, because they were forced to keep that damn Devotion to Liberty card active at all times. They'd asked. Several times. There were no excuses. Meaning that Sera couldn't even use her Blessing of the Night card, hobbling enemy Light effects and increasing their own buffs. And Chase didn't have Sticky Fingers. This was going to be a long, costly grind.

Good thing that he really, truly needed to work off some frustrations. Besides, grind was what they did best.

The Coils of Shadow were loose among the blinded enemies now, adding to the chaos. Rushing in among the wild Guardians, the vipers bit, depositing their venomous payload and moving on to the next targets.

The leading owls swooped in. Dividing their attention between the Antithesis of Light summon and the six humanoids on the ground, they screeched in unmitigated bloodlust, showing hand-long claws that sparkled in the sun.

"'Ware the claws. There's magic on them!" Liam shouted. Then he settled himself behind his shield and prepared for the first attack.

The owls were clearly ambush predators, not used to being caught out in the open. They dove in from above in dazzling displays, claws-first, for a single, bloody impact. It was feral, and scary. During the night, or against unprepared foes, their dives would be absolutely devastating.

Half of them died in the first attack.

Liam's truncheon struck one, head-on, flinging it back like a broken doll. Simultaneously, his shield swung back and impacted the one that was trying to catch him from behind, leaving it downed and stunned.

Kith met one with both his axes. Then he rolled forward, letting another ambusher strike the ground hard. The squawk of the bird was surprised, as Emilia's heavy axe punished its inattention, cleaving it nearly in two.

Chase danced to avoid the diving claws of yet another bird, slashing it across the wing and leaving it clumsy and wounded.

Meanwhile, Sera fended off first one, then two diving slashes with her shields, letting them flap away unsatisfied.

The problem for the owls became blindingly obvious right away. Although they were nearly the size of regular humans, they had to weigh, at most, a third as much. They had no sort of impact, and, bereft of the downward momentum of a dive or an ambush attack, they truly weren't that dangerous.

They did threaten the Antithesis of Light. A trio of them circled the dark bird, taking turns to dive to the attack. Only, the summoned bird moved in unnaturally fast jolts and dodges, and kept spewing a constant stream of piercing, dark missiles from its beak. Once, an owl nearly managed to slice into the summon, but bounced off a shield, hastily erected by Sera while Emilia was distracted.

It took less than a minute before the last owl fell from the skies, studded with dark spikes. Emilia rushed over to finish it.

"Prepare for the real attack!" Liam shouted.

In front of them, the cacophony increased. The charging horde had rearranged itself. The poor summoned vipers had mostly been stomped into the ground or eaten, and the Guardians were now changing their targets, rushing forward in a massive wave, aiming straight for their position.

It wasn't pretty. A good deal of the leading soil soarers were limping or slowed, poisoned by the vipers, and the positioning of the monsters was off, with the thunder rats rushing ahead underfoot of the larger equines and the three huge snakes just behind the leading row. One soarer stumbled and was instantly caught up and ground down by the man-tall form of a snake. Beyond, the slower shapes of the stick stalkers and the frogs followed.

Cilia yelled, "Chase. Distract. Liam, Kith, Emilia. We hold, make them pay—*then* we pull back."

Emilia looked like she was going to say something about the throng of incoming Guardians, but clenched her grip on the axe instead.

Chase let off an ululating cry, then sprinted straight at the incoming beasts, every single point in Agility boosting his speed to the level where it felt like he was flying.

In response, everything within close range of him started to veer toward him to trample him into the ground, to consume him utterly.

He kept yelling, now reduced to curses and meaningless noises. A few dozen feet before meeting their front line, he veered sharply left, and activated his Circle of Darkness.

Chase would never stop being amazed by his Tier-four Dark card. To him, it barely registered. The light of the sun dimmed slightly, as if he watched the world through a dirty window. Beyond that, though, his vision was absolutely clear and unimpeded. From without, however, it was a source of impenetrable darkness, absolute black with no vision possible, except for those of above thirty in Mental Power.

The swarm of Guardians continued, regardless. Yet, where Chase encroached the path of the leading beasts, they stumbled and slowed down slightly, inviting collisions with the ones right behind them.

Closer, he cut, moving back toward his friends, still moving at an angle. Energy roiled within him, along with a burgeoning joy as he found that he was able to keep up the pace of a damn charging stallion.

Closer. His short sword snipped out, catching a panting stallion across the muzzle. It reared in shock, letting a trailing mare run straight into it and knocking it to the ground. He barked a laugh and struck again, letting his foot shoot out to hit a thunder rat right under its ugly chin.

The momentum of the smaller beast exploded upward, and a burst of force emerged from it, missing Chase, but leaving him reeling as if he were slightly drunk.

He nearly slipped, caught himself, and raced away, putting a little extra distance between him and the edge of the pursuit.

A bit before he reached Kith and Emilia's position, he let the card wink out, leaving him visible once more. He sprinted on, racing past Kith with a wild grin, before he ran back to cover Liam's right side again.

The wave of beasts hit them.

For a moment, it looked like suicide. A whinnying, screeching, croaking onslaught of beasts out for their blood, all aiming for Liam at the front.

Yet, their line was already broken and uneven after Chase's run—and then they hit the Tainted Earth, which grasped at legs, tails, and bodies, draining Toughness from enemies, even as it slowed them down, sometimes even stopping a thunder rat dead in its tracks.

In an impressive display of sudden organization, the lead three soil soarers whinnied, and a burst of energy erupted from their hooves, tearing up grass in straight lines toward Liam.

Liam hunkered behind his shield, a layer of shadows blossoming before him. He took the impact...and didn't budge. In fact, the magic dissipated as it struck the shadows, feeding his Ravenous Shadows card and converting it into Strength for the tall fighter.

Seconds later, the foremost beasts hit him directly, and they pressed on, trying to push right through him. On all sides, Guardians spread out, threatening the same for all the others.

They were instantly at risk of being overwhelmed. Even if it had been broken several times, the momentum of the incoming stampede was near impossible to face.

Impossible or not, Liam faced it. Feet solidly planted, shield grasped tight, truncheon firmly fixed in his grip, he did not give an inch. A hoof struck his shield with a booming impact, and he grunted, truncheon ripping out to force the soarer's head sideways. Draining Ward activated, increasing the efficiency of Liam's armor, even as it drained the enemy's Agility.

Beyond, a massive snake head rose into the air, before slamming down at him.

Liam leapt back, avoiding the head; his truncheon shot out to strike a thunder rat that ran *across* the soarer's flank to leap at him.

Another magical attack was devoured by Ravenous Shadows, adding to Liam's Strength.

"Lights!" Cilia's shrill voice sounded above the din.

A moment later, they watched through squinted eyes, as another droplet of Light exploded at the forefront of the Guardians.

"Disengage. Now!" Cilia shouted.

They fell back, fighting to add some distance between them and the pursuit. It wasn't pretty, or perfect. Emilia was hit dead-on by a burst from one of the thunder rats, leaving her reeling and bleeding. A second later, though, Sera's healing pulse from Cry for Blood struck her, and Kith was able to defend her, striking out left and right to fend off two steeds trying to finish her.

For a few minutes, they simply ran. Behind them, the Guardians once again stretched out according to their natural speed, leaving the soil soarers in front.

"Cooldown's over. I'm ready again!" Chase yelled. He grinned, and the others sounded off with their readiness, one after the other. "Now!" he shouted, before turning on his heels and activating Circle of Darkness again.

They repeated their actions from last time. Chase cut across the line, sowing discord and disarray in their ranks, before they set themselves to face the enemies, allowing Liam to leech enemies of their Agility and absorb magical attacks for Strength. This time, however, the initial clash was different, as the foremost steeds were more wavering and unprecise in their attacks.

Where the first clash had only lasted for about twenty seconds, the second one took almost a minute, allowing the beasts beyond the frontmost rank to start circling around in an attempt to surround them. They managed to escape the closing jaws of the trap, and race ahead of the Guardians, leaving a couple of them behind on the ground, dead or badly hurt.

Kith howled with laughter. "It's working! It's working!"

Emilia, sending confused glances over her shoulder as she ran, yelled, "What's working? Are they drunk?"

"Blinded!" Chase grinned. He ran backward lightly, taking in the pursuit with a self-satisfied smirk. "Liam's card. Every time they hit one of us, their eyesight gets worse. For *all* of them! Do we want another repeat?"

"Nah. Look at them stumbling. We're ready to put the hurt on 'em. Let's circle around, so we can meet back up with my Tainted Earth. Poor thing is way too slow to keep up!"

They did just that, loping ahead in a long swing to meet up with the Tainted Earth, placing it optimally to slow down their attackers. Then they repeated their strategy.

Distraction. Defense and damage. Debuff and disengage. Sera had loved the alliteration for their plan, and was at the core of the execution. Wherever something went wrong, a parry failed or a magical attack made it through, there she was to send a well-timed heal their way, or, when Emilia was distracted, present a shield to fend them off entirely.

And for every time they clashed with the enemies, the Guardians grew more confused, their eyesight more damaged, at the same time as their imprecise attacks helped feed Liam's burgeoning powers.

Their next defensive holdout lasted for a full two minutes and cost the soarers, with nearly two dozen dead or wounded enough that they couldn't keep up pursuit. When they were forced to split, from the overwhelming pressure of the incoming Guardians, the effect of Tribune of Retribution, Blindness was punishing enough that a few of the frogs—apparently not blessed with the sharpest of eyesight in the first place—started to move in the wrong direction.

Emilia, thrilled with the discovery that they were actually holding their own, shouted, "Don't mind the stragglers. The hopefuls will catch them afterward."

Their pure defense turned into punishing strikes, as they were able to abuse the wavering eyesight. That did bring along a few close calls, as they learned that not all the chasing Guardians relied entirely on sight to follow. The enormous snakes were constantly on their trail, relying on smell, and the thunder rats turned out to have excellent senses, to where the card barely worked on them. The stick stalkers were already blind, it turned out.

Even so, the desperate defense slowly turned into a massive grind, a rinse and repeat with devastating effects on the Guardians.

There were some close calls along the way. Before the Tainted Earth finally held the weaker beasts down, a group of thunder rats managed to swarm and nearly overwhelm Kith with their disorienting attacks. Only a succession of swift heals and a single well-timed shield from Sera let him cut his way out.

As the stick stalkers—stick-thin humanoids that looked to be made up of claws, mold-covered bones, and children's nightmares—overtook both the snakes and soil soarers, they attacked as one, showing a scary level of coordination and teamwork. Ignoring everybody else, they exclusively focused on Chase, for some reason, going in for the kill. Unfortunately for them, at this point, his Nights of Criffhaven was already maxed out, on top of his already prodigious attribute increases from Sera's Cry for Blood, Emilia's two cards...even that damn Devotion to Liberty card. He was not just in touch with his body. He was in charge, so much in control that he flung himself through the air, dodging attacks as effortlessly as if he wore Kith's damn tornado boots!

The stick stalkers weren't powerless. They had an ability that let them fling themselves forward at increased speeds for at least fifty feet. Yet, the ability came at the cost of maneuverability, and once he learned to recognize the triggers, Chase evaded them with ease. Meanwhile, Liam and the others punished the rail-thin Guardians for getting distracted.

That clash took less than two minutes. A tense two minutes—but when they pulled back, the last surviving monstrous humanoid had a broken leg.

The frogs were harder work. Not only was their skin tough as hardened leather, but a number of large boils on their skin, when struck, erupted into corrosive bursts of a sticky, acid-like substance. Yet, they were also affected hard by Tribune of Retribution, Blindness, leaving them struggling to see and react to attacks. Kith and Emilia proved to be extraordinarily adept at dispatching them, while the others played distraction. In the end, less than a dozen remained, hopping off in different directions.

They slowly looped around, talking as they jogged. Emilia was breathing hard, but the others ran as though they could do this forever.

"How do we do this?" Kith asked. "The blindness might wear off soon." He shot a glance back at the three huge beasts following them. "Not that it makes a huge difference with those things."

"I say we face them head-on." Liam beamed. "I feel *strong*!"

"Liam. We talked about this. No grandstanding when it's unnecessary," Cilia scolded.

"You *never* let me do anything fun!"

"How are we on droplets?" Sera asked.

"All out. There will be no aid for this." Cilia sighed, leaping over a grassy knoll.

"I can probably do it." Kith smiled, tapping his heart.

"Not necessary." Chase grinned, forestalling the protests from the others. "I saved the best for last. I am going to need some bait, though. Oh, and a bigger weapon."

Both Liam and Kith split into huge grins.

Seconds later, they turned around. Liam and Kith stood, side by side, waiting for the large reptiles to catch up. Chase loped straight at them, rolling his shoulders, as he tried to get used to the weight and awkwardness of wielding Emilia's large axe one-handed.

"They really *are* ugly beasts, aren't they?" Chase heard Kith say, before his entire attention fixed on the incoming Guardians. He had to agree, though. They were exactly like the ordinary snakes you'd see in the wilderness in the Furyborn lands—piddling things, with negligible poison—only, these were stubby specimens, so wide compared to their length that they almost resembled caterpillars. Their scales looked thick and extremely sturdy, and, along their length were bright dots, looking almost like they'd been infused with fist-sized crystals. So far, they'd managed to avoid getting bitten or trampled by the beasts, which was a good thing, considering that their teeth were the length of his forearm. The fact that—regardless of buffs, blindness, and everything—the snakes were able to keep up as well as they did was a testament to their prodigious strength. A fact which Chase was counting on.

He activated Circle of Darkness one final time, racing past the beasts. They all started to turn his way, but as Liam and Kith began to shout and bang their weapons on Liam's shield, two of them veered off, leaving Chase with just a single snake. A single snake nearly as tall as he was, that likely weighed in at around fifteen times what he did. Also, one which, right this moment, wasn't able to see him.

Chase took a deep breath. Then he activated his single remaining Dark card, Free of Perdition, and focused on stealing the Strength of his enemy.

Within a second, he felt the effect. An inhuman surge of power struck him, making him feel invincible, filled to bursting with raw Strength. He grasped the two-handed axe single-handedly, the handle creaking under his grip. Chase bared his teeth at the huge viper, tongue hissing in his direction. A few seconds later, he estimated that the secondary effect of the card should've taken effect, and surged around its stubby length.

The large axe burrowed itself nearly a full foot inside the central body of the beast. The sensation was like trying to row through the Waves. Not entirely liquid, but close.

The secondary effect of the card saved Chase's life. Where the primary effect was guaranteed to work, granting him the same level of the chosen attribute as his target, the secondary one only stepped into effect if his Mental Power beat that of the target. And apparently, the snakes did not have Mental Power as their main stats.

A second after the axe struck, the gem-like studs alongside its length flashed—and erupted into foot-long, sharp shards of glinting bone: jagged, but pointy, and long enough to impale a man fully through the chest. The snake rocked, aiming to roll over him...and rocked back, lacking the monstrous Strength needed to complete the maneuver.

Chase gasped, taking a second to realize just how close he'd come to being flattened and pierced through by the damn thing. Then he shouted at the others to back off, and got to work dismantling the weakened snake.

The rest was merely a matter of time and effort. Once they knew about the ability of the snakes, they were able to tease the spike out and disengage, before closing with them once again. And for as long as Chase's buff was effective, his every strike carved deep grooves into the hard scales of the beasts.

Soon, they simply pulled back, watching as the sluggish movements of the last, fatally injured Guardian slowed and, eventually, stilled entirely.

Emilia stood there for a moment, blinking, shell-shocked. Then she sank onto the ground. "I can't believe it. The Savior has truly provided by bringing you in. I believe even a pillar, with a full guard of soldiers, would have had trouble with these."

Kith smiled, a weak, but not unkind smile. "We're not done yet. Almost, but not entirely."

Two minutes later, they'd circled back to where more than a dozen of the thunder rats were still trapped by the Tainted Earth.

After a short exchange, Sera and Cilia grabbed a hand axe each and got to the grim task of finishing off the rats, by now too drained to use their ranged attack.

Kith, leaning on Emilia's shoulder—which, surprisingly, she didn't object to—said, "That's how it works. Crafters and healers shouldn't be front and center—but we all lose out if they don't walk the Steps. So, we adjust. Unlike Chase, who just hogs all the Ænima to himself."

Chase, sitting in the grass, watched as Cilia butchered the final rat. Then he raised his middle finger at Kith, even as he let himself slump back into the embrace of the soft grass, groaning. Those damn buffs. The rush was insane, but the comedown was the worst!

CHAPTER 25

I keep coming up blank. The circumstances surrounding our eventual Wellspring are easy to decide for me. It should be readily available for anybody, regardless of station, money, or power. It should only be guarded to keep anybody from stealing the deck, and otherwise free to use. But when it comes to the Wellspring itself, to the Guardians it will generate, I am drawing a blank. Should we try to keep it hidden? Dominate our surroundings and build an indomitable army? Try to invade the lands of Light? I...think I need to spend more time with the Liberty book instead. These hypotheticals without clear answers are messing with my mind.

The aftermath of the battle was simple—surprisingly so. Their surroundings were an absolute mess. Bloody carcasses lay everywhere. Human corpses were strewn farther back. A fortune in meat and crafting materials was available for the taking. Yet, Emilia insisted that they would not be required to handle any of it—and also that they would have no say in the use of the crafting materials.

Disappointed, but unsurprised, they aimed straight for the nearest village, where they were treated to the much-needed use of baths, followed by a huge meal.

"This is weird, isn't it?" Liam asked. "It feels weird." He leaned back in the padded chair, hand resting over his bloated stomach. His hand indicated the well-furnished living room they were in, and the dozen plates and platters, some still half-full, on the ornate table before them all.

"What?" Kith sucked the meat off a bone. He was attacking the remaining platters as if his stomach were a direct depository to the Pits. "Nothing weird here. We came. We dominated. Now, we're treated to the, erm, treatment that we totally deserve."

Liam shrugged. "Yeah, but... We've been here a few hours now. This is someone's home. A heart too, judging from the color, not some nobody. And we haven't even met them. What are we doing tonight, Em?"

"We are sleeping here, of course," Emilia said, with an amused smile. "Do you believe we'd have you sleeping in a cramped storage room in some house of the mass? Liberators know gratitude, Liam."

He grimaced. "That's not what I mean at *all*. I just mean...we've had somebody thrown out of their home, and we haven't even had the chance to thank them for it? That feels weird. Rude."

Emilia leaned across the table. The movement made her burp, and she held a hand in front of her mouth before patting Liam's hand with her other hand. "It's a matter of perspective. We—all of us—belong to the Savior. So do our homes, our goods, the very beds we live in. For the heart living here, this is nothing but a minor convenience. Which do you think he prefers? A roaming stampede of Guardians? Or having to sleep in another available house for a night?"

Liam turned his hand and squeezed hers in return. "Put it like that, it does make sense." He leaned back with a satisfied sigh. "What do you all say? Is it time?"

"Time for what?" Emilia glanced from one to the other.

"Not yet." Kith waved a bone in denial. "I barely started."

"Barely started your sixth full plate, you animal," Sera said. "It is time."

Cilia nodded and explained. "Time, Emilia, for the time-honored tradition of sharing our improvements. Where we discuss our future improvements, plot our paths, and...vie for dominance, by showing others that their Mental Power is falling woefully behind!"

Sera raised an eyebrow. "Somebody is feeling *way* too upbeat." She smiled at Emilia. "Also, yes. That is absolutely what we do. Allow me to start." She cleared her throat. "Obviously, my progress here was nowhere near as impressive as it could have been, and I need to get used to receiving less Ænima than usual. Yet, I did gain a single Step from the thunder rats. Also, my latest training, *which I have kept up with, as a matter of fact*," she raised a challenging eyebrow at Cilia, "has granted me another increase to Mental Power. Our fight showed me in no uncertain terms that our tactics are working. Hence, my latest increase will go into Mental Power as well."

"And it's not because you're failing to keep up at all," Cilia teased.

Sera mock glared at her, rattling off her details. She purposefully lied about Dark and Liberty being the only decks contributing to her Title.

Personal Info:
Name: Serafine Valerian
Title: Dark/Liberty healer
Step: 21 (Tier 4)
Strength: 15 (+1 Tier bonus) = 16
Agility: 19 (+1 Tier bonus) = 20
Toughness: 20 (+1 Tier bonus) = 21

Mental Power: 36 (+13 Tier bonus) = 49
Potential: 12 (+1 Tier bonus) = 13

"I, for one, have also been diligent in my training," Cilia said. "Only, like we discussed, I really wanted to spend my time crafting, which has not truly been an option lately. Hence, I have focused on mental exercises, easily handled on the road. The battle, I must admit, was fruitful for me. The fire droplets were rather effective, and I gained two Steps. As discussed, I am sticking with Mental Power. I believe, with the right materials, I *will* be able to regularly unlock the creation of permanent items by now."

Emilia made a choking noise, holding both hands in front of her mouth with a wide-eyed look.

Cilia smiled at her. "I am glad we met you, Emilia. You look like somebody who would be able to keep up. Just like Sera. So far." Her gaze was laden with challenge.

Personal Info:
Name: Cilia
Title: Dark/Liberty crafter
Step: 23 (Tier 4)
Strength: 13 (+1 Tier bonus) = 14
Agility: 21 (+1 Tier bonus) = 22
Toughness: 16 (+1 Tier bonus) = 17
Mental Power: 36 (+13 Tier bonus) = 49
Potential: 11 (+1 Tier bonus) = 12

"Now, *I* have not kept up with my training. At all," Kith said. "Oh, don't give me that look. You know I've kept myself damn busy lately, Cil." His grin widened. "Besides, I'm not allowed to use my poor shadows. *But* I got myself two whole Steps from the fight. Being in the thick of it really helps! Though I decided to go with Strength and Toughness this time around, for added staying power."

Personal info:
Name: Kith
Title: Dark/Liberty summoner
Step: 23 (Tier 4)
Strength: 19 (+1 Tier bonus) = 20
Agility: 23 (+1 Tier bonus) = 24
Toughness: 19 (+1 Tier bonus) = 20
Mental Power: 24 (+1 Tier bonus) = 25
Potential: 11 (+13 Tier bonus) = 24

Chase grimaced. "Normally, I would say so as well. Only…I was sure I'd earn a Step from today with those soarers, and the massive snakes. Except, I didn't. And I don't even have that sensation when you're right at the verge of the next Tier. Perhaps there's an increase to how much Ænima is needed before hitting Tier five?"

Sera patted his shoulder. "I am sorry. Even though my family knew a lot about walking the Steps, those were heights we never aspired to."

Emilia, unexpectedly, broke in. "There is. This is also part of why so few reach the rank of pillars. There is a natural limit right at the edge of the twenty-fifth Step that requires additional Ænima to pass. The Savior pronounces it as the true test of the faithful."

He blinked. "Oh. Ah, well. I'll get there any day now. As for my training lately, it's been acceptable. I've earned a single increase to Toughness."

Name: Chase
Title: Dark/Liberty rogue
Step: 24 (Tier 4)
Strength: 20 (+1 Tier bonus) = 21
Agility: 24 (+13 Tier bonus) = 37
Toughness: 23 (+1 Tier bonus) = 24
Mental Power: 28 (+1 Tier bonus) = 29
Potential: 33 (+1 Tier bonus) = 34

"I feel like I've caught up with Mental Power now, to the point where I can easily keep up mentally, even when my Agility boosts kick in. I intend to keep it balanced like this. Training to ensure I don't fall too far behind in either of the other attributes, even as I spend every point I get on Potential."

"What?" Emilia burst out. "Why would you…who does that?"

Chase grinned. "Me? It's a trade-off, really. I don't grow as strong as Liam, or reach the ridiculous Mental Power of either of those two—but it's been a long while since I got a card below Rare." He waggled his eyebrows. "Now. Are you taking any bets on whether we're likely to get our Tier three Liberty cards soon? Because, with my Potential, I'm betting I might even get an Epic rarity card. How about that?"

Emilia leaned back in her chair, looking as if she'd been punched in the face. "But…"

Liam held her hand. "Take your time, Em. It's not your fault that he's being ridiculous. Which you are, Chase!" he scolded. "That's almost as ridiculous as, say, being in your fourth Tier and earning *three Fury-shorn Steps from a single fight!*"

"Noo!" Kith gasped. "You didn't."

Liam raised an eyebrow. "I didn't? Listen and weep."

Personal Info:
Name: Liam
Title: Dark/Liberty fighter
Step: 23 (Tier 4)
Strength: 19 (+13 Tier bonus) = 32
Agility: 20 (+1 Tier bonus) = 21
Toughness: 30 (+1 Tier bonus) = 31
Mental Power: 15 (+1 Tier bonus) = 16
Potential: 10 (+1 Tier bonus) = 11

He flexed. "I *like* where I'm at. Sometimes, I feel the need to become a bit more in control, a bit more economical with my movements. But honestly, I think this is working."

Emilia looked at his massive biceps. She murmured something under her breath.

"What was that?" Chase asked.

She blinked and blushed.

Chase knew damn well that whatever came out of her mouth next was going to be a lie.

"Oh. I just said that I couldn't possibly share anything here. Compared to you, I am falling far behind. In fact, I haven't heard about *anybody* who works like you do. Planning together. Growing this fast."

"Oh, come on. You've been assigned to us twice now. We like you. Odds are, we'll get teamed up with you again. That means you're going to grow just as fast as us. So spill." Liam's words were warm and spoken with an absolute certainty.

"Oh. Okay, I guess." She cleared her throat.

Name: Emilia Swiftstream
Title: Liberty healer
Step: 19 (Tier 3)
Strength: 14
Agility: 12
Toughness: 15
Mental Power: 13 (+3 Tier bonus) = 16
Potential: 11

"I don't know how you normally do this, but..." She started anew. "I decided to become a healer, not to heal—that's not an approach that feels natural to me—but because I believed that would grant me the chance to gain the best buffs. I don't think fast in battle. I don't have the mind to handle a lot of crazy cards like you have that need me to be aware of everything and any-thing. That's why I wanted buffs, so I could raise myself *and* those next to me. Yet, even if I add my buffs to this, I won't even reach two-thirds of Cilia. And she's a *crafter*! Where do I even go from here?" She looked at them beseechingly, something for-lorn in her expression.

Liam chuckled. "The answer, dear Em, is always 'up!' Al-ways one more Step. And you're damn close to the next Tier, too. With that in mind, and having watched you fight? I'd say your Strength is *just* fine. Your Agility could use some work, but my recommendation would be Toughness. You don't fight like Chase, prancing about like it's some noble's dance."

"Hey!" Chase held a hand to his heart in mock offense.

Liam ignored his outburst. "You take the hits and keep coming. That takes Toughness. Though Sera's going to say that you should add mental exercises to your routine too, for better, quicker decisions. Even with the bonus from your Title, your de-cisions mid-fight could be sharper. But your foundations are good, and you have a *mean* strike. Anything to add?" he asked the others.

Dead silence came at him from all sides.

"What?"

Cilia sniffed. "He's all grown up. So responsible. It's almost too much."

The mood in the house was warm and friendly. They only stayed for a single night. Then they left and went home—for a certain value of "home."

Their journey, this time, was mostly uneventful. There were only two extraordinary happenings along the way.

One belonged to Kith, who tried to convince Emilia that they should be allowed to keep their weapons between missions, for training purposes. He actually managed some leeway at that, in that she asked for permission through the Keepers. Unfortu-nately, the answer was a resounding "no," and they mournfully left the packs with their gear at the nearest shelter.

The other was less of a surprise to them. The first evening, after reaching their shelter for the day, Liam and Emilia went for a walk. Following that innocuous detail, their bedrolls just happened to be next to each other. Liam refused any comment for the rest of the trip, which Kith, of course, took as a challenge. Still, when Emilia finally left them at their home in Salvation to go deliver her final report about their mission, there was no de-bate that they would see her again.

"I am going to sleep for a *week*!" Liam yawned, pouring himself a glass of fruit juice while the others puttered about in the kitchen, arranging for light afternoon snacks.

"You're not going to take a bath first? Emilia's not going to approve of that. Unless she *likes* dirty boys. Does she like dirty boys?" Kith grinned, plopping down on the chair opposite him.

"Okay, I'm going to strangle you. *Then* I'll sleep for a week," Liam growled.

"You'll do no such thing. We all need to talk. Plan." Cilia rapped the table with her knuckles in passing.

Liam and Kith groaned in concert. "Now? Can't we laze about for a bit?" Liam asked piteously.

Kith suddenly went still. Then he stood up and left.

"Now see what you've done?" Liam pointed at Cilia. "You've chased him away with all your threats of work!"

The door slammed in the background.

"Who knows if he's *ever* coming back?" Chase added.

Caught up in the task of slicing some fruit that had been set out for them, Cilia leveled the fruit knife at them. "I *will* stab you. Get to thinking. We need proper plans now. Also, Kith looked properly disturbed. Who's checking up on him?"

Before anybody could do anything, the door in the foyer opened again and Kith strode back into the kitchen. With a furrowed brow, he read a tiny, rolled-up document. "Radine's back. I have the latest news from the elders. I...think, for once, we should probably listen to Cil. We need to talk."

That was enough to change the mood. Within the minute, they were all clustered together at the table and Cilia ensured they wouldn't be overheard by anybody.

Kith cleared his throat and shook the parchment. "This is from the elders only—nothing new from the High Elementalist. The situation along the Furyborn border has changed. And not for the better—or so I believe. The Lightborn have not engaged with them, nothing more than a few probes here and there. Their forces keep amassing, but not to the point where the elders fear for an all-out attack. In fact, their reactions, so far, have been truly underwhelming, considering the challenge the elders flung at the entire Lightborn empire." Before any of them could speculate, he continued. "I know why." A muscle twitched under his eye. "They've come here!"

"What?"

He nodded, expression downcast. "When Radine returned, she saw a huge force gathered near the Liberty border. My conversations with her...well, they aren't quite conversations. But she is able to convey images, emotions. From what I could tell, it wasn't a small force." He wrinkled his nose. "Before you ask, no, I can't get much more from her. No numbers, no proper troop compositions or anything really solid. Sorry."

"Huh." Liam huffed. "Well, if nothing else, at least that confirms that our decision to stay here was the right one."

Chase laughed nervously. "Damn. Yeah. Picture fleeing back out of the Prism with half the Liberators on your ass and stumbling right into a Lightborn army. That would be fun."

"It also clarifies just how important it is that we create a proper plan," Cilia said. "Regardless how many Lightborn there are, we can always leave in a different direction—if we are able to flee without pursuit, at least. Yet, unless we find a way to get to the deck, that is not going to happen."

Pushing the piece of parchment across the table for anybody else to look at, Kith spoke up. "I actually had an idea for that. And it heavily involves you, Cil."

"Listening." Cilia folded her arms, raising an eyebrow.

He smirked. "You all know how I spent forever scouting the area around the palace before we tried to steal the deck?"

Liam huffed. "Yeah. Fine waste of time that was."

"That's what I thought, as well. Only...you all know how I found out about that tour, and about getting checked out near the entrance." He shrugged. "Except, that's the single situation I've seen of people just being admitted with a simple check of their credentials. Everybody else who entered was escorted in, due to some pre-made agreement or something."

Chase grunted. "That sounds annoying. Also, figuring out how the internal mechanisms of how to get an invite work in practice...sounds really, really difficult?"

Kith nodded. "Right on. Right on. But did you know that there was *one* person I saw who didn't have to go through a security check?" He snorted. "Of course you don't. Because I never mentioned it. It was one of the damn pillars."

"I...don't see it," Cilia admitted after a while. "What's that got to do with me?"

Kith leaned forward eagerly. "You managed to craft illusions that fooled their best guards. We just need to get ourselves one of those fancy dark-blue outfits that the pillars have. Then you get a good, long look at one of those Tier-five bastards, craft an illusion to build a replica of their face, and hey, we've got a person right there, inside the palace. And this time, because we'll be looking like an actual pillar, nobody will dare to stop us or question us before we're stuffing the deck in our pockets." He shrugged. "Walk right back out, ditch the illusion, wait for the next mission that takes us close to the border, and then we run for it. So. What do you think?"

"That's..." Cilia shook her head in amazement.

"More filled with holes than those underwears I made Chase discard," Sera said.

"So comfy! They were my favorites." Chase groaned. "Still, I need to agree with Sera here. That's the weakest, most incomplete plan I've ever heard you come up with." Kith started to complain, and Chase spoke right over him. "I also love it."

Now, everybody stared at him.

Chase chuckled. "I know, I know. That made no sense. Just bear with me. *Yes*, every single part of the plan after entering the palace, including the escape, needs work. Also, yes, there's bound to be issues just finding some of their fancy dark-blue outfits. Still, you've all heard Emilia. If there's one thing they do here in the blissful lands, it's blind obedience to those who're higher in rank than yourself—and with the exception of the Savior himself, a pillar's going to be as close to an actual god as you can get, without having the Savior himself before you. Whatever else we'll need to work on, I agree with Kith there. Nobody's going to question a Pillar of Liberty about *anything*. So, for what it's worth, I say, sure, it's a dreadful start. But it's still a start. Let's work with it!"

Cilia blinked. "But...you don't even know what you're asking. The old illusion bracelets only had to portray a still image. A face is...a face!"

"Deep," Liam said.

Cilia's finger stabbed out at him. "Don't! Just don't! Who even knows if I can create a lifelike illusion of a face that doesn't look horribly scary?"

"I have faith," Chase said quietly.

She went back to glaring. Eventually, her glare softened slightly, and she sighed. "Okay. We can try. On several conditions."

"We're listening."

"First, this isn't going to be the only plan we're working on. I don't mind trying to see if it works, but in case it's impossible, we'll still be trying to find alternatives. Second, we'll get in contact with Reen again. If this works, and even if it doesn't, we'll want to get our hands on crafting materials that we won't be able to get by ourselves. Weapons, too. Third...I'll need something to write on. This is going to be extensive."

Hours later, they split...to rest. That was one thing they agreed upon. After the battles they'd survived, they needed a chance to rest properly before even considering any new plans.

CHAPTER 26

The following excerpts are selected from a very small se-ries of tomes, books, and other writing material we have ascer-tained to be likely to be created within Liberty lands after they closed off. Actual verification is still outstanding. Again, I am absolutely in awe with the writers here. There is little padding, and they explain their sources. There should be laws for this. Now, let's see what they have to bring to the table. (Page 46.)

There was a crowd today. In Salvation, that was some-thing out of the ordinary. Yet, to Chase, crowds felt like the most natural thing in the world. Having people around you that you could navigate amongst, use for your own purposes, hide behind or interact with when need be—that was the native state of being. Not this weird civilization, where people stayed in their houses most of the day.

Even so, the crowd they were in felt off. Usually, a proper crowd was in a state of constant movement, hundreds of people, each going their own way; sometimes gravitating toward natural attractors—merchants, entertainers, priests, or the like. Not this one. As one, they had their eyes and attention affixed to the one ongoing spectacle. As if their entire existence depended on it, they gawked at the massive, wooden platform liberally stained with the lifeblood of countless victims, and the stately five-Tier Liberator orating from above.

Chase knew good public speakers when he experienced them. He'd heard the high priest of Isarn nearly churn the public into a riot. Seen the bard of Esenti, as he made every single woman fall in love with him. Watched in horrified fascination, unable to tear his eyes away from the twenty-minute drug-fueled rant of an innkeeper cursing out the entire world, including his parents, his kids, and himself with equal zeal and ardor.

The Pillar of Liberty—and what a horribly stilted title that was—was anything but impassioned. Her speech, ongoing now for at least half an hour, revolved around the meaning of life, and how it was supposedly fully intertwined with serving Lib-erty. Chase wasn't too sure, and it appeared that the pillar wasn't either. He'd stopped paying close attention awhile ago. He did, however, have a bit of fun appreciating the irony of an-ybody preaching about life from the center of Execution Plaza.

The Tier five wielder was impressive enough, he guessed, standing out in a detached and proper way. She looked stern and authoritative, like somebody who could scold you and make you thank her for the experience. She also moved with the calm confidence and control of somebody who was no stranger to the battlefield. Of course, given that she was a Tier-five in the blissful lands, that part was a given. She had to have faced, and survived, thousands of Guardians and enemy combatants over the course of her life.

Yet, there was something Chase was missing here. Some aspect that failed to make sense to him. Why, when the pillar was less inspiring than a preacher who'd sniffed chaosweeds, would these locals all show up, and be as caught up in the speech as they appeared? Was it truly that they were so bereft of entertainment that this was the *good* stuff? No. There was a tenseness to their attention, a fixed focus that somebody easily distracted—like Kith—could only aspire to at the best of times.

Maybe it was less a desire to listen to the sermon—because this was definitely a sermon, the speech having clear ritualistic repetition from the crowd, quotes from the Savior himself, and aspirations for how the mass should behave—and more a need to be *seen* listening attentively to the sermon? Perhaps part of being a Liberator was following the mass and being seen doing what you were supposed to do. Or possibly, Chase was just missing something fundamental.

At least Cilia was getting exactly what she needed from this. She and Chase were the only ones of their group present— Chase to keep an eye on her and the crowd, and Cilia to get the perfect image of what the pillar looked like, to see whether she'd eventually be able to create a lifelike illusion of her. It wasn't like the others didn't want to be present, but they all had work to do.

Liam was touring the fighter training areas of Salvation, making friends. He was still attempting to see whether it was possible to build up connections inside the populace that might help them with their endeavors, though it was looking more and more implausible. Apart from that, he was also simply learning more about the city and its people. That part was going much better.

Kith was spending a *lot* of time with Radine, pushing the limits on what their bond was able to convey. He insisted that they were slowly building an improved common language, a way that they could mentally talk without actual words. Also, he was putting a lot of work into preparing their escape plan. Knowing that the Savior had Keepers snooping on travelers throughout Liberty lands put some natural limitations on free travel—limitations that they'd need to somehow circumvent, if they were to get away unchallenged.

Sera was spending time with Reen. When Kith found out that Reen was the one who'd betrayed them, he'd—impressively, despite the shock—had the wherewithal to set up certain hours where they'd be able to call upon Reen and go for a walk with him in the city to talk, without any watchers likely to spot what was going on. Of course, there was the risk that the Savior was able to notice Reen alongside any of them and spot the connections, but they'd considered it remote enough to risk. Regardless, they'd agreed that they needed the crafting materials, and also, that they needed the information that somebody as familiar with cards as Reen could provide. Sera was adamant that there was more to the banned cards and limitations than they were seeing, and she was going to get to the bottom of it.

"I think it's trailing to a close," Chase murmured close to Cilia's ear. "Praise Liberty. I thought we'd be trapped here forever. I might have dozed off a little."

Cilia pointedly did not smile. But her eyebrows did rise infinitesimally. She nodded. In her hands were several rough sketches of the pillar's features, hair, and ears. They showed an emphasis on her slightly upturned nose, and the prominent scar drawing the left side of her mouth downward. "I have enough for a start, I think."

Around them, the crowd was indeed starting to dissipate, a dispersing of the pattern, as they went each to their own. Chase was torn between several different ideas. He needed to get a better sense of the populace, to learn how not to stand out. For that, he should really try following different Liberators, see how they moved, where they went. That could be key to learning how the locals thought. Then again, did he really *need* that? They were aiming to leave this place. For that, they should really stay focused. And what would really help with that... "Hey. How about we follow that pillar for a while, see where she lives?"

"No. Horrible idea. If that was what we wanted, we should get Kith to follow through Radine. It would be so easy to give away what we're doing."

Chase considered what he'd just been thinking about and grimaced as he recognized the truth of her words. "Does it hurt? Being right all the time?"

This time, she did laugh. "No. It's the only momentary pain relief from all the headaches you guys give me!"

They turned and started to walk back home. Chase flung his arm around Cilia's shoulder. In response, she shrugged it off, glaring at him. They only walked about a hundred feet, when Chase felt something was off. He tapped Cilia's arm and stopped to talk to her, keeping her back toward where they were coming from. Nonchalantly, he glanced out of the corner of his eye and did a double take as he realized what he was looking at. He flung his arm around Cilia's shoulder again, putting his back toward the approaching person. He hissed, "It's the goddamn pillar! She's coming this way."

Cilia's eyes widened in a panicked grimace. "What? She's after us? What do we do?"

Frantically, Chase let the emotions pour through him, focusing on what they'd done. "Relax. We just keep walking. You've got the sketches hidden away. We've done nothing wrong. Just out taking in the sights, right?"

"Right," she said through gritted teeth. "Nice afternoon stroll." She exhaled. "We've got this."

Chase chuckled. Cilia really was not a fan of surprises. For himself, he'd done this dance too many times. He relaxed into his walk, letting his shoulders loosen, his gestures becoming more mellow as he moved, starting into a story about an innkeeper back in Isarn that Cilia had heard a dozen times before.

"Hey." The call rang out from behind them.

Chase ignored it at first. Reacting immediately showed that you were aware that people could call you out.

"You. Darkborn with the one hand. Halt."

So much for dissembling. Chase turned around with a questioning smile. He immediately focused on the Liberator striding toward them, the already thinned crowd parting further at her advance.

There was one thing he hadn't been able to tell about the pillar from a distance. It was obvious that she wasn't the charismatic type, and if she was a happy person, she hid it rather well. However, bearing down upon them, there was one thing that became extremely apparent. Her eyes *shone* with intelligence.

With an effort, Chase kept the dismay off his face. He *hated* the clever ones. They'd be the bane of his existence. Then he decided on his approach. That part, at least, was easy. If there was one thing clever people always expected from their surroundings, it was that they'd be dumber than themselves. That, Chase knew how to abuse. "Ah. Honored Pillar!" He bowed. "What can we do for you?"

"I could ask the same of you. Pillars have convocations at least three times a month. Yet you chose to come to mine. Unless I'm mistaken, your companion here took some very detailed notes while I spoke."

Crap. Crap. Crap. They'd been spotted. Somehow, that stupid—no, not stupid. Not stupid at all. That all-too-bright Liberator had spotted them amidst thousands and focused on them, enough to follow them. All right. Dissembling it was, but with a grain of truth. "Ah. You're entirely right. I'm sorry if we seemed overly curious. We're new to Salvation, and we're—" He waved out at the city. "Taking everything in. Learning. Trying not to make too big fools of ourselves, you know?"

"Aha," she said, her face not giving anything away. "How do you think you are doing at that?"

Chase frowned at the barely veiled accusation. She didn't *seem* belligerent. But then, why? He shrugged. "I guess, as well as you could expect from anybody coming from the outside who has no clue about the written and unwritten rules in this place? In fact, if you could come up with any advice to help us get better adjusted, we'd very much appreciate it."

Cilia added, "That was my reason for taking notes. There is *no* literature on Liberty out there in the Lightborn lands, as you might imagine. We need any help we can get."

She snorted. Then, still staring at Chase, her eyebrows shot skyward. "You actually mean that." Her eyes glanced ever so slightly upward at the facade of a house behind them. "I will grant you one piece of advice. One that should have been your initial introduction to Liberty. There is one rule, when it comes to survival in the blissful lands. *Do not cause a stir.* Do not be the cause of attention, especially public attention. The public eye is supposed to be focused on one person and one person alone."

"The Savior." Chase nodded in understanding.

"Exactly." She nodded, her strict demeanor wavering for a moment. "Even me chasing you down right now is outside of the norm. I wouldn't have done it either, but the city is abuzz with stories about you. Trying to steal from the palace. Taking down a rebel army, and Guardians by the scores. It is all such a horrible idea for you, but it is also a breath of fresh air."

"People...talk about us?" Cilia spoke up.

The pillar's eyebrow rose slowly. An extremely uncharacteristic look on the somber woman. "Of course they do. You have caused such a stir. That poor Elemental, Emily or whatever her name is, won't stop talking about you. She doesn't get it."

"Get *what*?" Chase asked, exasperated.

That look again. She was looking sideways at a house. A...Keeper? Of course, that was it. The scrawny Keeper wasn't looking in their direction, but it was less than ten feet away.

She seemed to come to a decision and shook her head. "Listen. Life as a pillar can be complicated. I noticed you in the crowd. I wanted to reassure myself that you weren't plotting anything involving me. I am happy to realize that wasn't the case. With that, our interactions are concluded. Best of luck for the future."

She turned on her heels and started to march away.

To Chase, little of their interchange had seemed *normal*, or even the sort of normal they'd approached here in Liberty lands. He turned toward Cilia, only to realize that she was also moving forward, catching up to the Liberator at a brisk pace. "What the Pits?" he murmured, then started moving himself.

The women were facing off right ahead, having a silent stare-down.

Chase hurried to catch up. The last thing he needed was Cilia going off on one of the most powerful people of the entire damn place! He only realized what was going on, as he burst through the effect of Cilia's Heart card and the conversation came to life mid-word.

"...thing. Now, you have the chance. Nobody can listen in on us right here and now. Just tell us." Cilia spread her hands in a beseeching gesture.

The pillar shook her head violently, eyes open in shock. "No! I didn't have anything to tell you. Also, disengage that *right now!*"

"Or what? Are you going to attack us? For talking to you? Or is it just because somebody might suspect you of some conspiracy? What is going on?" Cilia pushed.

Her nostrils flared as her eyes shot to either side.

To Chase, she looked like a deer who might balk and sprint away at any given second.

Blinking, she gulped in deep. "Okay. *Okay.* We'll talk. Not here, though. Two streets up, turn left in the alley at the second house belonging to a hand. Don't follow me for at least five minutes!" With that, she shook her head in exasperation, turned on her heels and left.

Chase and Cilia were left staring at each other. Then they slowly walked the other way, trying to act naturally—like somebody who *wasn't* about to follow a Pillar of Liberty into a dark alley.

"So, what was that about?" Chase said.

The five minutes had passed in tense silence, as they tried to think of all the implications of what had just happened. The street was nearly empty by now, as the hour approached the evening meal, and Cilia had activated her Heart card again.

"You acted rashly."

Cilia winced as though she'd been slapped. "I know."

"You showed her—somebody who should, by all rights, be our enemy—your Heart card. What do you think is going to happen to us, if they realize we're plotting in secret?"

"I *know*! All right? I know!" she huffed, avoiding his gaze. "I'm sorry. It's just—that woman. There was something. I could..."

"Cil, you're scaring the crap out of me. You're supposed to be the cool, collected one. I make drastic decisions, and Kith does dumb stuff. You can't just steal all our habits for yourself!"

Cilia laughed. Her voice was just a bit too high-pitched. "Earth smother your annoying tongue. I do love you sometimes."

Chase's eyebrows rose even further.

Cilia scoffed. "Like you didn't already know it. Here's the deal. You remember back on the Waves. I was alone there. Even with you boys. I never had anybody I could share with—my interest for books, for knowledge. How it was to be a mongrel, hated by everybody."

"Of *course* you could share that with us. We're your damn family!"

She shook her head sadly. "It's not the same, though. And that's my point. That woman, back there? She wanted to share something, but she was afraid. Deadly afraid." Cilia took a deep breath and nodded. "So, yes, I took a chance."

Chase's eyes narrowed. Then he burst out into laughter. "You know Kith is going to *love* this."

"You are never telling him." Cilia's voice was calm as the grave. "We are going to have a chat with the pillar, and then we are not going to go into details about this...*ever*."

"Yeah, I'm not seeing that. If we avoid getting ourselves into a serious mess, I see two options before me. Either Kith and I get to berate you for all the times you've been on our backs...or I'm getting your desserts *and* your komainey, forever."

"Two weeks."

"Done. Aaand I think this is our alley."

The alley in question looked like any of a thousand others in Salvation. Clean, wide enough to not be oppressive even walking two at a side, going straight through to the opposite side.

The pillar was waiting two-thirds down the alley. Miraculously, they weren't ambushed by anybody.

The Liberator spoke without preamble. "Is that silent card of yours activated?"

Cilia nodded.

"Good. To my knowledge, this is a dead spot. That is what we call a spot where we can talk without getting overheard by the Keepers. You should still keep your eyes open. Some of them do move around, if slowly."

"We will. And we'll try not to take too much of your time," Cilia said. "But there was clearly something you wanted to tell us before you left."

She didn't say anything, gaze shooting every which way. After a deep breath, the Liberator spoke up in a murmur, "It's too late anyway."

"What was that?"

"It's too late anyway," she said, louder. "You've caused enough of a ruckus. You're bound to be raised to heart any day now. Then, with all the attention on you, you'll see action all the damn time, until, eventually, you're dead."

Chase looked at Cilia. "This feels like those math puzzles Sera favors. You know, the one where you get the solution, and then you're supposed to figure out the rest, like magic."

"For once, I agree." Cilia turned toward the woman. "I will admit we've managed to...draw some eyes on us. Not all of it by design, mind you. But how does that amount to us being in danger? How do you know?"

"Liberty free your glacial mind. Because that's how it works!" she snapped. "You think you're doing good. That you're protecting your brethren. Yet, slowly you realize a number of things are off. That, even as it becomes harder to improve, the pressure is increased. That the fights you face are harder, you gain less support. That the numbers don't add up."

"Oh." Cilia sounded forlorn. "I suspected something of the sort. Do you know what happens?"

"I'm so lost here," Chase said.

"Nobody knows the exact details. Most don't even realize anything. But once you learn more, have access to the numbers...it starts becoming clearer. We should have more pillars. People at Tier six, or seven, even. We should be stronger. Instead, we fade. We die. As *heroes*." She snarled that last word.

Chase hissed as he finally caught the implications. "Are you close to Tier six?"

She nodded. As she responded, her voice cracked. "Close enough. I figured...heh. Even if they learn I talked to you, it won't make a difference. But somebody like you—young, coming from the outside—you still have the chance to find an alternative. Flee. Escape. Do something, before you're as caught up in it as I am!"

"Thank you for telling us," Cilia said. "But why not *do* something about it instead?"

She started to laugh. Loud, sobbing peals of laughter with an edge of hysterics. "Do *what*, exactly? Anybody who has risen up against the Savior dies. The very few who hit Tier six dies soon thereafter. Anybody who speaks out dies." She bowed her head sadly. "I'm too old to make a run for it. I'll enjoy what I can of my life until there is no more. And maybe, just maybe, I'll find a spark of joy in having found the courage to warn you and your friends. I hope you find a pleasant life, outside of Liberty."

She turned on her heels and walked away, her head held high, stiffly, unwavering. Even so, the cracks were showing.

CHAPTER 27

Honor be. Our lives are His. Honor be. Our hearts are His. Honor be. His life for us. This is one of a series of children's books we obtained. All professionally made. All revolving around the topic of the Savior and his relationship with the Liberators. However it works, there is a definite trade-off. Life, toil, and sacrifice in exchange for his protection and care. The process is rather nebulous. I suppose that is little surprise. The Savior would start the schooling and indoctrination at an early age to ensure their belief. (Page 47.)

Cilia and Chase returned from their outing and shared everything with the others. What followed was a long, loud debate about whether they should run for the hills right at that moment. Eventually, the response was, just like it had been before: "No. We are not in imminent danger at the moment." Also, they agreed that knowing that they were living on borrowed time could work to their advantage, given that those in charge might be less likely to look too closely at their actions until they approached the end of Tier five.

Apart from the two, only Sera had any weighty news to bring. She, in her chats with Reen, had managed to come up with an initial peace deal with him. She promised that there was going to be no blowback from his actions, and that they would simply be working together for their mutual benefit.

Of course, following the explosive revelation of the pillar, that promise would soon to be put to the test.

"She said that? A pillar?" Reen's voice was calm and collected, too much so, as if he held himself from exploding.

"She did," Cilia answered.

The two of them, as well as Chase, strode along on the streets, taking care to look like they were busy. They'd asked a random member of the mass to fetch Reen from within his house, and he had come through.

"I am unsure if I can take in the impact of this."

"Let me try to help you. I've had a night of not-so-restful sleep to take it in. Now, not only does your wonderful *Savior*," Chase imbued the word with enough scorn to make no secret just how much he meant it, "pressure everybody into fighting for their country—even if they don't want to—he also pushes them to take cards that benefit himself as an individual, making him grow stronger without any action on his part. As if that weren't enough, he also ensures that anybody who looks like they might grow strong enough to eventually become a threat to him wind up dead."

Reen's breath came fast and hard, like he was close to hyperventilating. "How? Do we know how?"

"No. She said she didn't know the details. Too many dangerous battles with the odds skewed against you, possibly? Perhaps the Savior himself comes to visit if you're too stubborn to die. Does it really matter?"

"No," Reen whispered. "Yes. It means that every triumph I have ever prided myself on in my work—every person I have helped choose the right cards and grow to loftier heights...I was steering them straight toward the precipice."

"You couldn't have known, mate," Chase said softly.

"You think they care?" he hissed. "Rotting in their graves. I should have guided them toward rebellion instead! At least that way, they would have had clean deaths."

"Stop." Cilia grabbed his shoulder gently. "This is something I have had to do with Chase and Liam especially. Once they get emotionally invested, they tend to lose focus of what is important."

"What's important?" Reen's eyes gleamed with unshed tears. "Me having wasted my life and ruined the lives of countless others is not *important*?"

"Not when it comes to your current decisions. Would you like to spend time spiraling, engaging in self-destructive behavior—or would you rather learn how to properly hurt that so-called god of yours?"

He reeled as though she'd punched him in the guts. He turned away, walking in silence for a while, before asking hoarsely, "How? How would I hurt him? I'm nobody. A petty hand, who's only good at bribery, and talking people into going to their deaths."

"That's where you're wrong," Chase said. "You know what we're doing. We're no saviors or anything like that. We want a deck. That's it. But you tell me. Right this moment, everybody here in Liberty believes that your Savior is just that—an actual god looking out for them. If they knew everything we knew, a lot of them would want to do something about it. You might be able to get rid of the bastard and build something real for yourselves. Only, there is one thing missing—for you *and* for us."

Reen snorted, seeming to regain a bit of his normal cynical veneer. "The fact that nobody's ever gone up against the Savior and *won*?"

"No. Well, actually, yes. That's sort of it. The point is that, with everything we know, he should be powerful. Overwhelmingly so. Yet, that's not what facing him felt like." Chase frowned.

"You actually went up against him when you tried to steal from him? I thought... Never mind. Please continue." Reen massaged his brow.

"I think I will take over here," Cilia said, brushing off Chase. "Because this is your domain, Reen, and mine. You know cards. You know that there are rules to it. Logic. Limitations. I *enjoy* the puzzle of it. Figuring out shortcomings, opportunities, and combinations. Teasing out the underlying logic and abusing it. Yet, when we were up against the Savior...there was nothing."

"Nothing?" Reen repeated.

"Exactly. Nothing worked. Our cards did not take effect. Existing buffs tapered off and turned to nothing. Kith's summons were unsummoned, and he was unable to summon new ones."

Reen frowned and blinked a few times. "That sounds...like a lot."

"We haven't even started yet," Cilia said. "My droplets did not work. I flung them, and they did nothing. Might as well have chucked a stone."

Chase added, "One of my Tier four cards worked for a second, then it fizzled out. The normal buffs faded. The lower-Tier cards failed to even activate. But, get this: my card that allows me to keep switching cards *worked*. Also, Home Defender—Sera's permanent buff—worked as well. The rules for what worked and what didn't were all over the place."

"On top of that, he was able to erect a barrier in the palace. Stronger, wider, than anything else I've seen. Finally, he handled most of this before we could even *see* him." Cilia frowned.

"Huh." Reen lowered his head.

"You see it, don't you?" Cilia asked. "He should be a normal human. Everything speaks to that. *Everything*. Only, if he is just like us—except at some insanely high Tier..." She looked intently at Reen.

Frowning, he spoke up, hesitantly. "The rules would still apply. A number of his cards might end up at Legendary rarity—between two and four, most likely, depending on his Potential. Also, his every attribute could be as high as your Mental Power when crafting, Cilia. But he would not be able to just do *everything*."

"Exactly!" Cilia smiled. "The different classes can't just do everything. Cards like that simply do not exist. And despite cards getting stronger the higher the Tier, even the legends about the strongest of all time mention their cards having drawbacks, openings, limitations."

"Do we know that, though?" Reen's downcast expression faded as he focused fully on the mental exercise. "Even if we agree that he was, at one point, actually a normal human—what if, at a high enough Tier, the cards *are* simply that powerful?"

Cilia shook her head vehemently. "Just think of the effects. Canceling buffs. Restricting the *activation* of new cards. Nullifying the magic in crafted items. *Unsummoning summoned creatures and suppressing new summons?* Even if we argue that his cards are powerful, what are the odds of the Savior having cards with all these effects at the same time, perfectly ready to use? Think about it. Even if he's a Tier-ten, you *know* most Tier five cards, right? Do any of those cards enable somebody to do some of that?"

Reen's frown deepened even further. "Yes—no. Not in the way that you explain, cutting off possibilities entirely."

"*Exactly.* That only leaves the Savior five cards above Tier five that are supposed to do *all of that.*"

He nodded, acknowledging her point. "On top of that, if he were that powerful, a few cards escaping the effect...hmm. It is a conundrum."

"That's why we're here, man." Chase grinned. "We figured you'd help us think of the type of cards that he might have—say, if you know weaker versions that might evolve into something like what we were exposed to. That way, we'd also be able to make an educated guess about his class and possibly his attributes." He smirked and winked. "You know, all the sort of knowledge that would be useful for any Liberator who'd want to take the bastard down."

A tic grew under Reen's eye. He hid it under a hand. "I can't believe you're talking about that so calmly." Blinking, he cleared his throat. "But...I guess his class is as good a place to start as any. I could picture most Liberty classes to eventually be offered cards that could cancel or subdue enemy cards for a very short while. Buffs, at least. Perhaps not summoners."

"We were fleeing for five minutes, at least," Chase added.

Reen shook his head incredulously. "Fighters are out, as are ranged fighters. Entirely. The ability to affect either summons or crafted items...no. The same for crafters. As you very well know, Cilia, they rarely get cards to be used in battle. Healers could handle that barrier you saw, but not the rest. Casters affecting summons? Perish the thought. Rogues? No. Just no."

Chase felt the need to speak up for his class, but decided not to interrupt.

Reen was deep in thought now, caught in a world of his own. "A summoner could surely affect the summoned creatures of others. Yet, they very rarely have effects that range farther than line of sight. Also, affecting crafted items? That is the manipulation of *permanent* magic. Not the normal purview of summoners." He grimaced. "With what I know, there is no way that any of the classes should be able to handle everything you state that you saw."

Cilia blinked. Then she spoke up, softly, at first. "Reen? How often do you see the Savior outside of the palace?"

His face scrunched up in confusion. "Why?"

"Humor me, please."

"Erm. The Savior has toured the width and breadth of the blissful lands. We have stories about it, even."

"Within the last two decades? And have you ever seen him yourself?" Cilia asked.

Reen's confused frown grew deeper. "Seen him myself? Once. During a ceremony here in Salvation. He attends those, at times."

Cilia sighed. "So, he does move about within Salvation. But I am clearly asking this wrong. Do you know of current situations where the Savior is *known* to tour the lands? Where he is seen outside Salvation, with no hint of a doubt that it's him?"

He started to respond, but stopped again. "Maybe eight years ago. A particularly large group of rebels was moving toward the capital. He ranged forth with the pillars and a large army of soldiers and squashed them. Plenty saw him then."

"But otherwise, he stays inside the palace. Lets the lower Tiers govern the lands?"

"Following his ruleset, of course. That is how he rules. It's been like that since the start." Reen squinted at her. "Just tell me? I'm clearly not getting whatever you're hinting at."

She sighed and nodded. "He's a crafter."

Reen blinked. Then he snorted in derision. "No, he's not."

"He is."

"He destroyed you, in person. You said so yourself."

"In a place he himself has been creating for decades." Cilia rested a hand on Reen's shoulder. "Listen. It's the only explanation that makes sense. He can ignore most of the usual limitations on cards and classes—not because he is all-powerful, but because he has built up the palace from scratch, imbuing it with protective items."

"But...the legends?"

"Legends he himself has created. Legends which they are teaching, *according to his instructions*. Also, during the tour of the palace, they actually said it themselves. There were items in there, whose effects they don't know. But okay, if you have trouble believing it—consider this: the Prism."

Reen waited. When he realized there was no more forthcoming, he cocked his head. "The Prism what?"

"Everything. Consider it. The Prism is, undoubtedly, magic. It messes with your mind, defends Liberty lands, ensures that the defenders are able to ambush incoming Guardians and soldiers, often safely, as long as the attackers are weakened."

"That is known."

Cilia slapped her fist into her palm. "Good. Then *think*. Not as somebody who has grown up listening to the legends of the Savior, but as a man who knows about classes. If you were told that somebody was able to manipulate magic that covered the width of an empire, that stayed active regardless of time and distance, what would you think?"

Reen's gaze unfocused. His eyes darted every which way. "Yet, our teachings clearly state that the Savior uses the Ænima sent his way to keep him safe." He was quiet for nearly a minute. Then he hissed, "I am going to see him *dead*!"

"Whoa. You pivoted kinda hard there, man," Chase said.

"It makes sense. *It makes sense!* If you accept that he's a regular human, restricted to a certain class, this is the only logical explanation. He would have to know how to craft permanent creations—"

"I've done that, and I'm only a Tier-four."

Reen spat on the ground, drawing the eye of a hand walking on the far side of the street. He closed his eyes. "Okay. I will try to calm down. It's just...if he's using all that Ænima, not for our defenses, but simply to grow stronger—Fire burn his rot-infested carcass!"

Chase nodded. "We get it, man. We're outsiders, like everybody loves to remind us. That means we barely know anything. But it also means we suspect everybody of being underhanded bastards. Sometimes, we're more right than we'd like."

For a while, they walked in silence. Reen's features went through a series of expressions, outrage, fury, and dismay being prominent among them.

His voice, when he spoke up again, was deadly intent. "How do we kill him?"

"Whoa. Reen." Chase laughed in shock. "I did not see that one coming."

"I am not joking. That bastard is killing people left and right, forcing the rest of us into battle, feeding on our Ænima and throwing those few of us who dare to dissent into work camps. *I want him dead!*"

"I—" Chase started and stopped himself. "We aren't god killers, man. We're thieves. Pretty sure we told you that already."

"Why are you even telling me this, then?" Reen hissed, his face a picture of pain and frustration.

Chase smiled intently. "Because this—what we're talking about right now—can be what you all need in order to get rid of the bastard. What we need to sneak past him is the exact same thing you will need to clean your house. Effective counters and strategies to what he's got. You help us come up with crafted items and card combinations we can use against him, and you will know what works for yourself. Pits, we can even craft extras! But we need help, because we don't know the specifics of Liberty cards."

"Where will that leave us then?"

Chase shrugged. "Better off than before. If you share this knowledge far and wide, there's no putting the lid back on. Everybody will know. Your vaunted Savior's not a god, but human. Also, he's a crafter, whose only contribution to your existence has been walling you off from the rest of the world and feeding you lies, while he grows fat off your Ænima. Do you really picture that just blowing over?"

Reen hesitated, but eventually shook his head. "No. This kind of secret, when it gets out, is going to spread everywhere. It is also going to result in a lot of blood being spilled."

"I don't disagree," Chase said somberly. "So, I guess that's the question. Do you think it'll be worth it, ridding Liberty of this so-called god?"

Reen didn't hesitate. He merely nodded. Something new was growing in his eyes. Some inner fire—of hope, of persistence and deep-seated hatred. "I will do what it takes. Now, shut up and let me think."

A few hundred feet along, they waited at the side of the road for a group of hopefuls to march past, led by a scarred hand. Their eyes gleamed with pride and determination, though some of them looked more guarded, like they had some forewarning of what they were going into.

Once they had marched past, Reen nodded. "That is what we're up against. An entire system, built to break down our people, spill our blood to strengthen one single person. To create unthinking fanatics and punish any who dissent."

Chase nodded. "Sounds a bit overwhelming, when you put it like that. Except, like Liam says, no meal is too big. You've just gotta take one bite at a time."

"That has got to be the worst comparison I've ever heard. I can't believe you guys have survived this far."

Walking up to wrap his arm around the shoulders of the smaller Liberator, Chase beamed with joy. "Neither can I, my friend. Neither can I."

They continued their walk in silence for a while. Eventually, Reen said, "I believe we will find the secret to defeating him in the card limitations set out by the palace itself."

"Ooh," Cilia said. "I like that line of thought. I was thinking something like that as well. Whatever he decides is off-limits is likely to be something that could be a threat to him and his rule. For instance, the limitations on anything revolving around shields."

"Exactly," Reen agreed. "The official reasoning that they're afraid anything might interact badly with the Prism has also sounded rather speculative. If, instead, it's because he's afraid someone will be able to raise shields to fend him off, or bring down the barriers he can erect inside the palace?"

"*Much* more plausible." Cilia nodded. "Also, those stupid restrictions on anybody building their attributes higher and higher—"

"And on stealing 'em from others," Chase added.

"Exactly. Those are clearly created to keep anybody from building a set of cards that could, theoretically, drain the Savior of his own powers."

Reen rubbed his hands together. "This...I am going to need to work on this. There are so many possibilities here, but also so many risks. Possible false starts. When do you plan to act?"

"As soon as possible," Chase said. "I mean, we don't *think* that we're about to get caught out, but in this place there's always a risk of us getting spotted doing something we're not allowed to. The thought that we can keep up our facade forever is not bloody likely."

Reen nodded, his entire being businesslike and to the point. "Understandable. If you are likely to be raised to hearts soon, would you pick your cards in order to succeed with your theft?"

Chase snorted. "That's the entire bloody point, man. If we can pick a set of cards—without getting ourselves executed, of course—that will help us against the bastard, we'll do it. Of course we will."

"Excuse me if not everybody can afford to pick their cards on a whim like that. Some of us only get a single set of cards."

"Well...then that's what we need to change." Chase smirked.

"What?"

"Well. There might be a tiny detail we haven't exactly told you yet. Hold out your hand!"

It took Reen awhile to get over the shock of realizing that, not only did they have other cards than the Elemental ones they'd told him about, but now, *so did he!* He walked like a drunk, lost in the notifications inside his mind.

"We need to find a way to set up a method for us granting cards to people who believe as we do, in secret. How do you think that is going to change things? Everybody you know will earn Light, Elemental, Fury, and Dark cards. If we share enough cards, we will even earn another Deck of Darkness that could stay with you."

"Buh." Reen looked confused, as though his brain refused to engage.

"What? It makes sense, doesn't it?" Chase turned to Cilia.

She rolled her eyes. "You are offering to upset the power balance in this place as a quick aside. I believe Reen is very justified in needing a few moments to take it in." Turning to Reen, she patted his arm. "Take your time. Sudden or not, I agree with the offer. It would make for a decent long-term solution, I believe. Even if we're gone, having all the cards we've shared and a Deck of Darkness might very well be what you need to turn the tide."

"What do you want in return?" Reen eventually asked.

"You're already giving it to us. Items for crafting, and the information we need. Contacts." Chase shrugged. "This will be helping us as well."

"Yes. The answer is yes," Reen hurried to say. "As to the rest: I need time. This is all very overwhelming and a lot to take in. I will think it over, and return to you as soon as I can." He hesitated before adding, "I have to admit, when I first met you? I believed you were going to stab me in the face. Now, I think you might just hold the key to our salvation."

"This, Reen...this is why we can't have nice things. You're still planning to depose one Savior. Don't go setting up the next one already!"

CHAPTER 28

We had to pay a good deal for these. A short bunch of written lists, enumerating soldiers and their positions, titles and schedules near a specific post. Although it gives an indicator of their military ranking systems, the real takeaway from this would be the numbers. There are more than three thousand soldiers posted here. Either this post at "A4" is a central military stronghold, or the Liberty military is numerous enough to rival at least the Furyborn. Rival the Furyborn? I doubt it.

But that's mostly because the Furyborn will all fight, if pressed. Still, there is no underestimating the numbers of Liberty. (Page 50.)

"This is overwhelming!" Kith spread the sheets of paper on the table in front of him. "Picking cards is supposed to be *fun*—not about memorizing all this crap!"

"Heh. Who's going to bet on Cilia's next comment?" Liam squinted at a page as if it were written upside down.

"Something, something, 'memorizing *is* fun'?" Chase hazarded.

"Behave," Sera said. "Also, speaking as a representative of those who have actually been forced to memorize endless lists of nobles, troop strength, trade goods, and worse, I have to say it. Memorizing isn't fun. But memorizing *this* is fun! We are not merely trying to remember which cards we are not supposed to use. We are also trying to cheat the system and evade their restrictions by means of creative thinking. Basically, this is just like you cheating nobles back in Isarn."

Kith frowned at her, then turned toward Chase. "Chaaase!" he whined. "Your girlfriend is trying to make learning fun!"

"Ah. In that case, I will do what any strong, independent man should. Accede to her whims." He bowed his head to the sound of Kith and Liam jeering. "Jokes aside...the scope of the information Reen's gathered or written himself is pretty excessive. Do you even think he's slept the last two days?"

"Definitely not. Or, well, judging from the look of his handwriting here, he might've fallen asleep halfway through a sentence." Cilia frowned. "Regardless, he's done an insane job. Not only does he come up with a ton of theories on how it should be possible to cheat the different rules, he also hypothesizes about all the known rules and why they have them. This is excellent stuff. Listen. 'Estimating an incremental amount of Ænima needed for each additional Step past the very first, we should expect the Savior to be anywhere between Tiers ten and twelve.' Assuming that the Savior is at least at Tier eleven, and also assuming that he will have crafted implements to boost his own stats, we should reckon that he has at least crossed a hundred in each attribute except Potential."

"A hundred!" Liam mouthed.

Kith shrugged in response.

Cilia ignored them, continuing. "This would explain one of the rules. Any card with fixed increases or decreases to an attribute will generally be acceptable across the board. Because Liberators are required to use their Tier increases to increase the rarity of their Devotion to Liberty card, we rarely earn cards higher than Uncommon rarity. Hence, any cards tend to boost or reduce an attribute, at most, about six points. Even finding a full group of six people with these types of cards would not be able to majorly impact any confrontation. However, cards with percentile or even multiplicative effects could wind up with major effects. Five people, each with a card granting a twenty-five percent reduction, will see a Toughness of a hundred reduced to twenty-four."

"But we don't really have any of those?" Liam said.

Chase snorted. "Not the point. We have Sera's Blessing of the Night that more than doubles any buffs. That's what we're talking about. Liam, your Strength's already at thirty-two. Take that, coupled with Blessing of the Night, Spark of Divinity, and your own Earthen Might that doubles your Strength for a short while. That leaves you *well* above a hundred with your Strength."

"I...didn't think of it like that," Liam admitted.

"That's the point, though. If we manage to pick some of the right choices in combination, and get away with it, we'll be able to actually be a match or more for the Savior."

Kith coughed. "Kind of downplaying the whole 'get away with it' part if we'd have to fight the bastard, aren't we? I like the idea, though. If we manage to somehow cheat their systems, we'd be able to custom-build something to work directly against the bastard and all his crafted crap."

"That's the spirit." Chase grinned.

"Sooo...I hate to be the one to say this, because Cil's the professional downer here." Kith leaned back on his chair, evading Cilia's punch. "But how *do* we get away with it? Sera managed to cheat that Heidel guy and make sure that we—well, she—has the cards to create some shields that are more powerful than average. I doubt we're going to be able to pull that one off twice, though. So...how?"

"I believe I have an idea for that," Sera said.

They all fell silent.

Sera smiled. "Sorry. This is no stroke of genius. I simply recommend that we repeat one of our old schemes."

"I'll have to vote against that," Chase said. "Those servant robes you wore sneaking into the cathedral in Isarn were *really* unbecoming on you. Also, they didn't help at all. Even though you were basically wearing a burlap sack, the guards still harassed you. Serves you right for being so damn stunning!"

"You are *so* funny." Sera rolled her eyes. "Not that scheme. I am talking about Cilia's armbands. You likely noticed that the illusions did pass muster? Until the Savior came out swinging, their illusions were still active."

Cilia frowned. "So, what, you want something to hide the new choice we make? That could be a possibility."

"Exactly. We will need illustrations showing what the cards look like, but I am certain Reen will be able to get those. Then, if we have the descriptions memorized, we can convince them we're going with a 'safe' choice, as long as we can recite the card description from memory."

"But what if he asks us to show the effect by activating the card? He did that twice last time."

"We just pick something we can fake. I have...Spark of Divinity, for instance. That can double as any Liberty buff!"

"Ooh. I have...Race of Life. That gives me a fixed Agility boost. I'm sure there's a Liberty equivalent," Chase exclaimed.

"That is my point exactly. Chase chooses his new card. Puts on an illusionary bracelet or something, making it look like a Liberty Agility boost. Then he fakes the effect with Race of Life. These are all things we can prepare beforehand."

"Most importantly, it should work—and it would allow us to pull a fast one on that damn Heidel. That would totally make my day." Chase showed his teeth. He turned toward Sera, who raised an eyebrow, her hands firmly placed on her hips. "Yes, dear. This is not about cheating tiny tyrants. It's about making it possible for us to complete a heist against a Tier ten asshole. But I need my small wins!"

They continued their work, with few distractions. Reen earned every ounce of praise they could lavish upon him, showing just how he'd managed to make it this far without getting busted. Not only did he have a huge number of friends, servants, and helpers who he could call upon to hide the fact that they were working together, he also delivered everything they asked for, no questions asked.

For two more days, a veritable stream of messengers moved back and forth between the two houses. The only time they left the house was for time to—quoting Liam—"punch something so he wouldn't go insane."

Once they fixated on the exact choices, they got the illustrations from Reen, along with a generous serving of leather items, and Cilia got to work crafting the illusion items. This time, instead of large, obvious bracelets, she went with small tooled and braided leather rings you could easily slip over a finger when you needed it. It would deliver the same effect, but for a shorter period. This was no issue, given that they just needed to fool Heidel for a brief time.

With that done, they spent their energy diving into the options available for them. The scope of that was an entirely different beast. They'd thought there were maybe a hundred Tier three options available to each of them. Turned out, the answer was closer to five hundred, with the caveat that third-Tier cards were less well-documented than first-Tier cards—hence, they might actually stumble on some unknown cards. If that happened, they had to be certain which options they were aiming for, and when they would be better or worse than the known options.

Chase was forced to spend some time touring the city. That was Reen's solution for sharing cards. They couldn't just have people knocking on their door at all hours. In no time, that would lead to investigations and added attention. Instead, they arranged circuits around the city, each about two hours long and changing every three days, which he'd try to walk at roughly the same time every day. This allowed people to approach him, say the agreed-upon code word, and touch his hand or shoulder in short order.

In theory, of course, this should let people get their cards and walk away without arousing any suspicion. In practice...well, there was a reason that they decided to change the routes every three days. At first, they'd thought changing it each week would be sufficient. Only, they'd forgotten to account for humanity. The people of Liberty had, for their entire lives, been taught that they had to move, choose, and act in a very specific way, select some very specific cards that would define them forever. Now, they were faced with something they'd never expected to see. Actual freedom.

Their reactions differed. Yet, the one common denominator among them was that there usually *was* a visible, audible reaction. People choked up, coughed, laughed out loud, sometimes burst into tears in the open street. For a people as controlled as the Liberators, those did not go off unnoticed.

This translated directly into danger. Yet, watching a kindly old grandfather drop his walking stick, and stare into oblivion with a blissful smile and a trail of tears running down his cheek, Chase knew one thing for sure. They were not going to stop. They had no intentions of committing suicide against some overpowered self-created faux god exploiting his own people. But they could still leave them with the means to rise up against the bastard.

Emilia came through for them. It took longer than she'd expected, but she came through. One day at the breakfast table, they were interrupted by a knock on the door. Minutes later, they were walking toward the palace, all caught up in their own heads, trying to remember the best choices, as they reassured themselves that, yes, they remembered the illusion rings.

Heidel was the exact same as last time. A facade of politeness, badly hiding the focused scrutiny underneath. As he congratulated them on their swift rise to approval and their impressive results in taming the stampede, none of them failed to read the suspicion right underneath the surface.

They were led to the same room, heard the same speech, and were nudged to read the same tome as last time. Of course, these were pages they'd already studied to death back at home. Still, they faked it, studiously investigating each of the banned cards, asking inquisitive follow-up questions to make it seem like they actually were interested.

The rings worked like a charm. The moment they chose their new cards, they slipped on their illusion rings, which depicted cards they were certain would pass Heidel's muster. Then they showed him, reciting the memorized texts of the card in question. Liam flubbed parts of the text, once, but Heidel didn't seem to notice.

Sera got to show off hers, faking a Liberty Toughness boost for their entire group by engaging Spark of Divinity.

This seemed to be the final touch needed to lay Heidel's suspicions to rest. Last time, it seemed like they'd constantly teetered on the edge of disapproval. Now, with them having chosen something that was well within the scope of what the Savior favored, the veneer of faked acceptance eased somewhat, and Heidel even finished their session with a few horrible jokes.

Somehow, they managed to make it all the way home without anybody spouting in public about their new cards. They didn't last more than a dozen feet past the entrance door until Kith howled in laughter.

"Can I...*thank* you, Cil!" He rubbed his hands together, chuckling darkly. "This was the *best*. We walked straight in there, looked the smarmy bastard right in the face and lied about everything! And he bought it!"

Sera smiled. "I will say, that was satisfying. Though, I am bursting at the seams to hear which cards you earned."

"You should be." Kith smirked. "I did what Cil always says, this time around. Thought about what card would be good *and* thought about combinations with my other cards—and considered what cards you guys have as well."

"I'm getting more and more suspicious the more he speaks." Cilia frowned.

"Usually, that's a great choice." Kith laughed. "Today, though, I'll be waiting for your apology. Check out...this!"

[**Enforced Entropy**
Uncommon, Liberty summoner
Tier three
Active, medium duration
This card, when active, grants each of your other summons an additional ability. As long as they are physically touching any hostile being, they will be exempt from any buffs or beneficial card effects otherwise affecting them. Already active effects will be canceled.
Long cooldown
"Nothing can touch you? Ah, but entropy is nothing, with a twist."]

Cilia glared at him for a long while. Then she sighed. "I am sorry, Kith. That is an amazing choice."

"Sorry. I don't get it. Not fully." Liam shrugged. "Let's ignore how you couldn't even summon any cards last time we were in the palace. Let's say he activates this on his Tainted Earth. It'll be able to remove any active buffs or active effects from anything it touches. That'd be able to level the playing field a bit between us and anybody who was boosted a lot. But if it's somebody like the Savior, they won't just stay still."

Kith's eyebrows waggled and he raised two fingers. "Apian God and Twice the Fun. If I get the chance, I'll be able to *fill* the damn palace with summons. Nobody will be outside of their reach."

"Okay, fine, I get it." Liam waved him off. "We still need to get to the point where you *can* actually summon the damn critters."

Cilia took a deep breath and sighed. "That was my main consideration for a card this time around. When we enter the palace, we need something that ensures that we are not kept down by the myriad effects of the Savior." She grimaced and elaborated. "In short, above all, we need something that ensures our freedom from the influence of his crafted items, in order to be able to make it past their security with all our cards and buffs intact. I think I got exactly that."

[Dab of Freedom
Uncommon, Liberty crafter
Tier three
Passive
One constant on Ordei lies in the ever-present existence of people trying to limit the freedom of others. When wielded, this card greatly strengthens the crafting of any items aiming to counter debuffs, negative effects, and especially movement-impairing effects.
"Do you like it? A collar of freedom? I relish the irony." A Liberty crafter loses his job.]

Sera had her eyes closed and wore a deep frown. "Countering debuffs and negative effects does sound like the exact result we would like. Yet...do you...do you believe that you would be able to create items that can overpower those of a Tier eleven powerhouse?"

Cilia gave a slight smile. "Without cheating? No. I think, however, that I know how to do it. With you granting me buffs and a number of our other tactics? Yes."

Sera burst into a wide smile. "In that case, I will do anything in my power to help you." Her warm laugh lit the room. "As if that were ever in question."

"And you? What did you get?" Chase asked.

"A solution to another problem," Sera said. "Cilia's creations on top of my Shimmering Sanctuary card might be enough to ward off all debuffs and effects canceling out our powers. That still leaves us with one major issue. The barriers."

"Oh," Liam said.

"Yes. Oh. Maintaining our powers has no point, if we cannot make it past those darned shields that kept us trapped last time. I hoped that I would earn a straight cancelation card that would work on shields. Only, my choices were questionable. Hence, I opted for this."

[Shield of Cancellation
Uncommon, Liberty healer
Tier three
Passive, medium duration
This creates a shimmering barrier, which, when in physical touch against hostile magic, will work to break down said magic. If the affected person already is subject to a shield effect, the canceling effect will be more effective.

"What do you mean how did I get in here? I'm a healer." The court cleric saves the treasurer's life, but fails to save her own.]

"Ohohoh." Liam chuckled. "I can see it. You got that other shield thing last time!"

"I did indeed. Bubbles of Blue strengthens any shield I create. Shimmering Sanctuary fends off hostile debuffs and effects. Shield of Cancellation on top *should* add up to create a much stronger effect that will burn through any barriers."

Liam clapped slowly. "I like it. You have all three combined to create something that should, hopefully, allow us to evade all those effects waiting for us, and get away safely." He nodded softly. "I decided that I'd need to go for something to help us if we *failed* to get away." He shrugged.

"We've talked about this a few times. The Savior's bound to be just as fast, strong, and tough as any of us, with all our buffs activated. How do we catch up? How do we counter that?" He shook his head. "The last Liberty card I got was awful. Useless, basically. Canceling out the momentum of an attack I parry? What good will that do if he's three times faster than me? No. I needed something that would help us even the odds."

[**Finger on the Scales**
Rare, Liberty fighter
Tier three
Passive, long duration
A constant in this life is the existence of imbalance. There will always be those who tilt the scale in their favor. This card attempts to counter that. Each hostile effect either boosting an enemy or debuffing you or your group members will grant you a +3 to all attributes except Potential. The effect activates, even if the hostile effect is suppressed or canceled.

"No, please, continue. Add a few additional cards to the mix. They tickle so nicely."]

Cilia made a sound deep in her throat. Hoarsely, she said, "Whatever I've said about you in the past, I take it back. You're a genius! Isn't that ridiculously powerful, though?"

"Eh." Liam wrinkled his nose. "Not really. Think about it. We've fought most against Guardians, right? How many Guardians would even activate this? And when you think of most Tier-twos and -threes, they tend to have direct abilities—a single attack or two, maybe a good defense. Buffs and debuffs are rare. So, nine times out of ten, this would be a wasted card." His grin was outright devilish. "That tenth time, though. How many crafted items do you think affected us when we were running through the palace? Five? Ten?"

Sera tapped her nose. "Also, Blessing of the Night will double any gains."

Chase blinked. "I second what Cilia said. You're a genius. If you ever need to stand up to the bastard, this should help you get there." He waited a few seconds for theatrical effect, then added, "And if it doesn't, my card should help. A bit." He grimaced.

[Double Dip
Rare, Liberty rogue
Tier three
Passive
Why limit yourself to just a single taste, when you can have more? Wielding this card, any debuffs applied on an enemy, by anybody, will take effect twice, if possible.
"I know what you're thinking. 'Did he use three cards, or six?' Well, to tell you the truth, in all this excitement, I kinda lost track myself."]

"Wait. So, every point of Agility removed by my Draining Ward would be doubled?" Liam asked.

"As would the Toughness drain from Kith's Tainted Earth," Chase agreed. "Or any other card we gain that debuffs an enemy. But I really chose it for Sticky Fingers." He shrugged and scratched his neck. "If Liam's card could raise his attributes to where he might actually keep the bastard back, this card, in combination with Draining Ward, Sticky Fingers, and Free of Perdition might actually grind him down to where we're both stronger *and* faster. That's the idea, at least."

Sera's hand clasped his. "I think it could work. Obviously, the plan is to never actually learn whether it *would* work. Yet, having it and not having to use it is better than the reverse." She squinted and mused, "Now, the question is whether or not we will be able to get ready to steal a deck before we are sent on our next mission or not. Are you all ready to work hard?"

"For the chance at building a legendary Wellspring with a power that hasn't been seen in hundreds of years?" Chase tilted his head left, then right. "Eh. Can I at least have a nap first?"

CHAPTER 29

The following is supposedly stolen information from a fac-tion called the Keepers in Liberty lands. Again, the language is cryptic, and we do not know who they are. Still—if true—it at-tests to a fractured society, with a large section of them work-ing undercover. Their purpose in society is, as of yet, uncon-firmed. Again, I am going to be *so* famous in researcher circles when I return to the Elemental library next. I see how they could misinterpret the situation here, though. The fact that a state spies on its own people...it's disgusting. (Page 52.)

Being raised to hearts came with another unsurprising change of housing. From the outside, there was little difference, even if the size of the house doubled from their pre-vious location. On the inside, however, the difference was im-mense. Every single piece of furniture was of better quality, every room larger, more ornate and elaborate.

The help was improved as well. They now had servants in the house at all times, except at night, and even had a hand around twice a week whose only job was to make the servants as invisible as possible, making them work around their sched-ules as smoothly as could be. This part did prove counter-pro-ductive at first, given that they had to take care not to be caught plotting out in the open. Shortly, they got more comfortable with the new servants and their habits, and learned how to work around them.

They bent to their tasks with a will. Kith and Liam spent an inordinate amount of time, for them, planning how best to handle themselves inside the wide hallways of the palace, which summons to combine if needed, how to best move through the place at speed and avoid any unnecessary conflicts.

Sera and Cilia teamed up to handle the crafting—Sera han-dling and coordinating all materials and tools needed, as well as the communication with Reen, while Cilia worked at all hours, trying to reach the result she was looking for.

Chase toured the city, continually giving out cards. By now, he'd given out hundreds of cards and was eagerly waiting to see the creation of another Deck of Darkness. He also visited a few of the public arrangements in Salvation hosted by some of the pillars or minds of the city. He didn't talk to any of them, the only interaction being a meeting of eyes with the pillar they'd previously spoken to. This served him fine, however, because the only thing he really wanted was to see the higher-ups inter-act with those lower in society, absorb their manners and way of speaking and moving.

They saw progress on all fronts.

Cilia created several dozen bracelets that should, theoret-ically, and in combination with Sera's cards, be able to cancel the influence of any crafted items in the palace. She insisted that she still was far from where she wanted to be, with perfection lurking just out of reach. The illusionary mask created to dis-guise one of them as the pillar was still acting up. She asserted she'd get there eventually, but the progress would be a question of trial and error for her.

Reen had arranged for a hideout for them. It wasn't much—merely the "misplaced" home of a member of the mass, that he'd managed to get lost in paperwork—but it was perfect for them to store all the goods they were preparing for their heist as well as their own armaments, in case they were needed. He also made sure to have Spike moved there, in order to reu-nite him with Kith. From that moment on, Kith was a lot happier, with several daily visits to his adoring Guardian.

Sera was taking careful stock of their goods, making sure they had a clear idea of how many items they'd need. She took charge of handling the purview of building their clandestine set of storage with long-lasting foodstuffs for the return journey, and started thinking about how to make it home. To arrange this properly, she talked to Nordon, who, by now was getting down-right antsy about how long they were staying. His experiments were becoming weirder, but the results were rather impressive. The boosts from some of his drinks actually outpaced regular buff cards.

In short, what started as entirely unrealistic was slowly starting to appear more doable, like an expected mirage on the horizon turning out to be real.

Chase was touring the city, yet again. He'd been noticing something strange lately and was deep in thought, considering whether it was something he should be reacting to. Perhaps he and Reen should adjust their methods on how to share cards?

All told, it might be a silly thought. Yet, Chase felt rather weird about it. Over the past couple of days, the people ap-proaching him in the streets were less shocked about their cards. Oh, their faces still lit up in joy and celebration. But that shock he'd seen during the first few days—the slack-jawed dis-belief of somebody who'd had their entire world turned upside down? That was gone. What could the reason be?

Maybe the first people to get new cards had been the least fortunate ones. People on the verge of giving up, who'd never expected that something would come along that could make their lives easier. Or maybe it was a case of the cards slowly spreading out far enough that word of their existence was becoming more of an open secret. If that were the case, they'd have to keep their eyes open, and likely he'd have to talk to Reen about who he told about everything. After all, it would only take a single person telling on them before they would be on the run, and have to go undercover in their hideout.

"Liberty free me."

It was a simple phrase. One uttered tons of times here—in prayer, in public speechcraft, and the like. It was not, normally, used as a greeting.

Chase forced down a smile. Carefully kept secret or not, this would never get old. With a mental nudge, he accessed that carefully kept space next to his heart, nudged the energy moving. Moments later, he felt the touch, as somebody wearing the bright-blue getup of a member of the mass "accidentally" touched his hand, and kept moving with just a tiny hitch in his steps. He couldn't help a grin from building. This guy was better than the average in hiding his emotions.

The person kept walking at a brisk pace. Then, suddenly, he stopped dead, just twenty feet ahead of Chase. He stood stock-still, looking down at the pavement.

Chase fought down a chuckle. That had happened to him as well, more than once, when he got a card that was better than he'd hoped for. Thinking back, he might have also thrown a tiny tantrum when Sticky Fingers underwent an unexpected change, going from Rare to Epic. He raised his hand to give the man a supportive pat on the shoulder when he passed him by again. Before that happened, however, the man turned around and faced Chase head-on.

The middle-aged man was a mixed-race. Half Liberator, half Furyborn. His hair was dark and short, but his eyes burned with a deep fire. It was the look on his face that captivated Chase, though. There was guilt there, mixed with determination, and a dozen other warring emotions.

"A warning," he said. "Reen has been taken in."

"Taken in by who?"

"By the guards. They came earlier in the day. I...you should probably hide."

For a moment, Chase just looked at him, as his world came tumbling down. He'd acknowledged the possibility. He'd known it could happen. But now that it *was* coming true, he blanked out as his mind refused to take it in.

Seconds later, he was walking home, sprinting when he reached stretches without Keepers.

"Oh, well. We had a nice run of it. Learned a lot. Got some nice cards. Time to get on the road and start running." Kith's voice was strained, but forcibly light. "Princess, you were about done with our escape plan, right?" He was stuffing a backpack with things, including his hand axes.

"Yes." Sera drew out the word. "We will be short on provisions, but we should be able to make do. Only…is that really the right decision?"

Kith snorted. "What do you mean? Of course it is. They got Reen. That means either they already got Nordon and all the other outlaws hiding out in his building, or they'll get him soon. Once they do that? They'll know everything. Who we are. What we were planning. Pits, there's bound to be a hunt in the weeks and months to come, to track down all of those who managed to get themselves some new shiny cards."

Sera looked aghast. "So, we are going to leave him to fend for himself?"

Kith snorted. "Listen, princess. This isn't a matter of giving up on him. It's a matter of what's humanly possible. We don't know where they'll be taking him. We don't know what they're going to be doing to him, but I'm sure it won't be nice—and the end result's bound to mean bad news for us, if they catch us. Do you truly want us to go digging in the palace? Especially knowing that, the moment I activate my shadows instead of that damn Devotion to Liberty card, they'll be aware that we're up to something?"

"I—no." Sera hung her head, curls hiding her face. "Trying to delve aimlessly through the palace would get us all killed. Is there truly nothing we can do?"

They shared glances across the cluttered kitchen table. Liam was awkwardly looking down, drawing doodles in the thin layer of dust on the table. Then he looked up, blinking. "Radine. Perhaps, if Nordon and the others haven't been caught yet, we can—"

Kith interrupted, nodding glumly with lidded eyes. "Way ahead of you. She's been hunting and is returning right now. She…no. The door to Reen's house is open and it's swarming with guards, moving in and out. No signs of any prisoners, but…damn. Those are some of Nordon's brewing implements they're carrying out. They've found the hidden rooms."

A pained silence filled the room. Chase's fist struck the table, again and again, until Sera grabbed his hand.

"We should go." Cilia's voice was a hoarse whisper. Louder, she repeated, "We should go. The more time we spend here, the larger the risk that our hideout is compromised."

"She's right," Liam said. "We need to be out of the city, the moment it's revealed that we've been part of it. Hiding from all those damn Keepers out in the country is going to be tough enough, even before they start looking specifically for us."

"No." Kith breathed.

"No?" Liam looked confused.

"I wasn't talking to you. Something's happening. I've got Radine circling the city, and it's chaos. A procession is coming from the palace. It's...the damn Savior! A ton of guards. And...they're bringing Reen out too."

"Where are they going?" Chase asked, in a voice that said he knew the answer already.

"Execution Plaza. They are going to kill him."

CHAPTER 30

"Mass Eivar Tolles, Mass Lina Movel, Hand Denna Wilek. No suspicious activity, all working within bounds. However, they have been spotted in shelters in A3 and subsequently A4, all three close apart. Continued observances should lead to in-terrogation." Pits. This is worse than I imagined. They're even keeping dossiers on who talks with whom? Then it truly is every Liberator for themselves here. (Page 53.)

The crowd was dead silent. A thousand citizens, more, surrounded the ornate wooden platform at the center of Execution Plaza. Yet nobody spoke. Even so, there were undercurrents, like in every crowd. An unspoken language that spoke louder than any noise. Body language was a huge part of it. One elderly woman watched, arms folded, a tiny sneer on her face. Next to her, a father hugged two girls close to him, turning their heads. A young man stood with his fist raised, fire in his eyes.

Overall, the mood of the crowd was mixed between that of exultation, relief that they weren't the ones up there, and inevitability.

On the platform itself, Reen's demeanor stood in stark contrast to the crowd. He moved softly, his movements limited, yet controlled. But he held his head high, letting the proceedings flow around him with a sad expression and downturned lips. His arms were bound behind his back.

The large wooden stage was covered in dark-blue cloth. At the center, where Reen stood, the blue was even darker, with reddish-brown stains, hinting at what was to come. It was surrounded by guards, a blend of hands and mass, all wearing helmets and weapons, yet no armor. They looked more ceremonial than martial.

"We truly live in a blessed time." The Savior's voice rang out—loud, clear, and inhuman. He faced the crowd directly, his perfect visage emotionless and deific. "Where, before, the blissful lands were ravaged by strife and constant turmoil, war between factions and the dishonesty of man, we have secured peace. Where we had the uncertainty and constant threat of invasion, we have ensured peace and safe borders. With our heads held high and sharp blades, we have removed infestations, cut by cut, to the point where, now, any defender of Liberty, from the lowest of the hopeful to the vital Pillars of Liberty, may travel our lands, east to west, without meeting a single hostile beast."

Again, reactions in the crowd were mixed. A few nodded along fervently. Others were also nodding, yet with lidded eyes that hid their true emotions. A few barely managed to hide their dislike of what was going on.

The Savior continued, his voice growing louder, even as it retained its near-emotionless pitch. "Yet, even today, we find those who would work against us. Who hate the peace we have wrought, who harbor no desires but to tear down that which we have built with generations of toil under my visage."

Chase spat, ignoring the nervous glance from a hand right ahead of him. This was familiar territory. The rhetoric was rather similar to the preachers back in Isarn, when they wanted to rile up a crowd against some poor bastard.

"Our Hands of Motion are supposed to be those who guide the labor of our blessed society—*your* labor! This is a sacred task, one vital to our society, to ensure that our hard work does not go to waste; that we move, think, and act as one, with the sacred, shared purpose of keeping us all safe and happy. You are doing amazingly, building toward paradise on Ordei. Yet, all our hard work can so easily be led to ruin."

"Nobody likes to hear their work's been wasted. Now, it's time to point out the culprit," Kith muttered under his breath with a sneer.

"This man. This *traitor* has not only shirked his responsibilities. He has abused his sacred station, using the resources allocated to him to help others of like minds avoid their duties. Under our very noses, he has built a clandestine network aiming to attack the state, to tear down the palace, and to *set himself up as a false god*!"

Now the crowd reacted. Loud jeers met rage-filled roars and demands for Reen's head.

Sera made a noise at the back of her throat...part distress, part outrage.

"Yet, as always, our Keepers work endlessly to keep us all safe from the undermining of treacherous thoughts. They exposed, not only this man, but a network of more than a hundred people, including collaborators from the outside!"

That got the crowd riled up even worse. One young woman on Chase's right hurled insults at the stage.

"That's right. They were bringing in all manner of illicit items from the outside. Weapons. Drugs. Anything to undermine our righteous seat of government." The Savior let the comment hang for a moment, the dark brilliance of his clothes an overpowering presence on the platform. "Yet, we are always watching for insurgents like these. Always vigilant! And together, with your help, we can keep protecting our lands against this scum, these infiltrators and traitors!"

The kettle was working to a boil. People were slowly getting properly riled up. Chase had to give it to the bastard. He knew how to work a crowd.

"People. *My* people. The champions of Liberty. You know the value of true freedom, of justice. You came here to support me, knowing what you were bound to see. Yet, you also come, because we, at the core, do not shy from the truth. We are not afraid to hear the dissenting voices, to accept the challenges. So, Hand of Motion, Reen Mattheren, what have you to say in your defense?"

Chase hadn't expected that. But he saw the point immediately. What could Reen do, really? He could, of course, attack the Savior, accusing him of every possible crime under the sun. Yet, even if it was all true, being the one accused would only see him shot down, the ideas ridiculed. He could try defending himself, explaining what he'd done. Except, with the mix of lies and truth set against him, and the few seconds he'd have available to himself for speaking, he'd never be able to make a credible effort of it. This could only really end up as a win for the Savior.

The others edged closer to Chase. "Are we really going to just stand here and watch this?" Liam murmured. "I'd rather just leave than see more of this."

"If we walk away now, we're going to stand out," Kith snarled. "Just...bear with it. It'll be over soon."

"But he's right here. That means the palace is empty right now." Liam protested. "We could..."

They all froze.

Reen took a step forward on the stage above. He looked, of all things, at peace. Serene. His voice rang out, loud, clear, without a hint at his usual surly disposition. "I should like to confess my sins. Knowingly, I have worked against the Savior, aimed for his downfall."

A hush went through the crowd.

Chase didn't get it. *Why the Pits would Reen act like that? Talk like that? What had they done to him?*

"It is true," Reen continued. "I have erred. I craved power for power's sake. Plotted the downfall of the Savior, in order to earn a slice of power for myself, regardless of cost." He wiped a tear away. "This is far from my only sin—but it is my worst one, thinking that I would be able to challenge the might of the Savior, when my own thinking is based on sin."

"Oh." Cilia squinted ahead, then turned back to the others, pulling them into a close circle. "Somebody needs to provide a distraction."

"I can do that. What is happening?" Sera asked.

"Just do what I say. Anybody have anything worth throwing?"

Chase snorted and pulled a handful of small rocks out of his pocket. "Like I'd walk anywhere without ammunition for my sling."

"Okay. This is what is going to happen…"

Half a minute later, Reen was still mid-speech, going on about his errors, and how he was too far gone to deserve mercy.

Cilia concentrated and looked at the others, then nodded.

Far off to the right, pain-filled screams rang out. People pushed against one another in a surge to get away.

Chase didn't turn. He already knew that there was nothing lethal going on. Rather, they were simply Sera's thorn bushes, created by the Nature's Blessing card, sprouting and spreading. Painful, but not dangerous.

On stage, the eyes of the Savior veered to see what was happening. Reen did the same, confused, even as he tried to continue his speech.

Now, Chase leapt into action. With two rapid motions, he tossed two rocks at the stage. They flew straight and true, and for a moment, it seemed like the world settled into a frozen tableau, before the Savior and his newfound penitent sinner could properly react to the screams off to the side.

The first stone hit Reen right in the midriff, hard enough to bruise. Completely unprepared for the attack, the middle-aged Liberator doubled over. Yet, his facial expression never changed beyond his former expression of confusion. No hint of pain.

The other stone hit the Savior. Right at the center of his forehead. Without even a hint at resistance, it passed through and emerged on the other side, and a person in the crowd beyond cried out in pain.

At first, nothing happened. Then a guard shouted something inaudible over the growing din. The Savior yelled a command, and the guards formed ranks, presenting arms against the crowd.

In seconds, chaos unfurled.

"Do you think we were spotted?"

They were back at the hideout, less than half an hour later. Their flight had been as part of the crowd, thousands fleeing at the threat of violence from the armed guards.

Spike was pacing back and forth between them all, sensing the agitation in the air.

"Spotted, yes. Recognized? I doubt it," Cilia said.

"So, are you going to let us all in on just what happened? Why did we just break our cover instead of toughing it out and running for the hills?" Kith's voice dripped with scorn. In a much sweeter tone, he continued, "Come here, Spike. We'll protect you. Yes, we will."

Cilia wiped a spot of sweat off her brow. "That wasn't Reen."

"Pits do you mean? I'd recognize that ugly face anywhere. I'll grant you, he didn't act his usual self," Liam said.

"He also didn't react when he was hit by that rock. That's not normal," Chase said.

Cilia nodded. "You know I've been working on my illusions. That, right there on the stage, was the next thing I was going to try. Pre-arranged illusions, allowing you to control which emotions you are going to show. That wasn't Reen. It was somebody wearing an *illusion* of Reen's face."

Liam groaned. "What?"

"But if that was just an illusion? And that second stone went right through the Savior's head as if he wasn't there. Fire torch me, it was all a setup! They wanted to see if they could draw somebody out to save Reen." Chase hammered a fist onto the table.

"That's part of it," Cilia agreed. "On top of that, they were playing to the crowd. They probably had some sort of public spectacle all planned. Reen would admit his crimes, then he'd be pardoned to go work off his sins at the front lines or some crap like that. Meanwhile, in real life, Reen is probably back at the palace *right* now, being tortured."

"I don't get it. Okay, I get it. But that doesn't change anything for us, does it?" Liam said. "We'll still need to get the Pits out of here, won't we?" He snorted with dark laughter. "Which is likely going to get even harder now that we got them all riled up."

"That's what we'll need to talk about. Because this could change everything...or nothing." She pointed at the wall, in the general direction of the palace. "We agreed that we were going to help Reen. Which, of course, is what we've been doing. We've been giving cards to everybody, helping Reen help the poor bastards find new lives. Only, now that he's been discovered, all his plans will turn to mud. Once he talks—and he will talk; I don't doubt it for a moment—those who've fled will be brought right back in, sent to camps. Those who've learned the secret about the Savior will be caught and killed. It will be as if we were never here."

"You don't know that they'll get all of them," Kith said with a deep frown.

"Of course I don't," Cilia snapped. "But you've seen this place. They're doing everything they can to ensure it's every man for himself. And now we've learned that the only place where the Savior *should* be exposed, away from his crafted safe haven, is a lie as well."

"What are you saying, Cil? Be clear about this, please," Liam said.

Her eyes wavered, and she couldn't quite meet his gaze. "Urg. Darkness hide me, I can't believe I'm saying this. I'm saying, they won't ever be able to end him. Should we try to do the hero thing here? Try to save them all?"

They reacted all at once. Kith scoffed. Liam sat back, blinking. Chase did a double take.

"We should," Sera said softly. "I know. You are all in this for yourselves, in order to create a good home. You have said so since the very start. Mind my words, though. If you walk away from this, knowing that you are condemning all of Liberty to remain under the reign of this tyrant, you are going to regret it for the rest of your lives."

"It's not *our* fault their fake god's got them all in a vise!" Kith cried out.

"No. But we have the power to try to change it."

"For the rest of your lives," Chase repeated softly, eyes fixed on the ground. "That could prove to be a very short time, if we challenge the bastard."

"I agree. And I am not saying that it is the clever choice. I am still going to try," Sera said.

Nobody said anything for a few seconds. Then Kith stood up and tipped his backpack over, screaming in frustration. Panting, he pointed at Sera. "You goddamn nobles. I always knew you were going to be the death of me!"

"Me too." Chase laughed. "Of course, I expected a hanging after getting caught crawling into a noble daughter's boudoir, not some heroic endeavors."

"You are actually considering it?" Sera's eyes widened in surprise.

Chase's laughter grew louder. "Considering it? It's already decided. Look at the morons. We've known for ages that we were going to help here. We just didn't expect we'd have to put our lives on the line. Now, shush. Let me come up with a dumb-ass plan that Cil can tear to pieces so we don't all get ourselves killed."

CHAPTER 31

Productivity of Heart's Succor is down for the third trimester in a row. Keepers report nothing extraordinary around the town. This means that the issue is likely internal. Please send an investigator—preferably a heart or stronger—to look into the matter. Again. This could be a benign situation; somebody looking to aid a town that is struggling. Yet, the way they handle it is nothing short of villainous. I hate this place. (Page 54.)

In the end, they opted for speed. They could try to improve their odds, craft items to aid their chances at success. However, with Reen gone, their easy access to crafting materials had also disappeared. On top of that, they knew that their hideout could very well be among the many secrets that Reen would end up disclosing.

In the late afternoon, Chase sprinted full tilt at a door of an unassuming house somewhere in the western part of Salvation. On all sides, shadows responded to his call, spreading around him to hide his existence. He flung the door open.

Beyond the door, a steam-filled, half-hidden world of fog emerged, threatening to drown him in vapor and turn him around in confusion. Cries of bewilderment arose around him from within the laundry. He ignored it all and moved ahead as fast as he could, grasping, discarding, snatching what he needed. He dodged worker after sweat-covered worker, until he reached the far end. There, his right leg slammed into a large, wooden chest kept closed by a massive iron padlock several times in succession.

The padlock didn't look like it would budge any day soon. However, the wood gave after just a few kicks, and he tore out a few boards, before being awarded with his prize: a row of long, exquisitely soft shirts, the dark blue of a moon-lit night, matching pants underneath. Seconds later, he was out the front door again, letting the shadows fade as he aimed for the nearest alley.

He joined up with the others, tossing the bundle of clothes at Cilia.

"We're on!"

They switched clothes in an alley. Then moved on, at a slow pace that belied their tension.

Screams arose before they even reached the gate. Not from their chosen gate, but the next one over, just a few hundred feet farther down the wall of the palace.

At this point, they'd been embroiled in enough life-and-death situations to be familiar with the different cadences of screams. These were screams of shock, yet not of pain. Everything was going according to plan, so far.

"What are you standing around for?" Cilia strode up ahead of the others, challenging the guards at the gate. "We are being attacked! Move!" She pointed at the next gate over, but didn't stop walking for even a moment.

Cilia was never going to have an intimidating physical presence. She was too small, too scrawny. Over the course of her life, however, she had worked hard to ensure that her force of will made up for that lack.

Up against a rapidly escalating situation, Cilia's demanding presence, the dark-blue outfit of a pillar, and the illusion of the still-unnamed pillar shrouding her real features, the guard did the only thing his station had prepared him for. He obeyed, and started to shout orders at the other guards to investigate the commotion.

Cilia didn't slow down for a second. She passed the guard, followed closely by the others, all dressed in the slightly brighter clothes of the Pristine Minds.

With swift steps, they moved straight for the center of the palace. Every inch of their composure was controlled and hardened, closed-off to show anybody that the mere thought of bothering them would end badly.

For a few minutes, it actually worked. They left the gate guards behind them, moving fast under the guise of importance.

When they found themselves at a crossing corridor blessedly free of people, Cilia paused. "Your vipers?"

"Dead and gone." Kith shrugged.

"Okay. Time to fade from their tracking. Everybody, switch away from Devotion to Liberty. Also...we are not going to reach the center unless we have further distractions."

Kith grinned a savage grin and faced her. He reached his hands out and asked, "I'm saving the insects for our main showdown. Will you let me do the honors?"

She reached into her pockets and extracted two droplets emblazoned with tiny images of flames. "Go right ahead, Kith. Let's give them something more to think of."

Within seconds, flames tore at both corridors, left and right.

Now they sped up, jogging through the palace. They put distance between themselves to not make it obvious that they were a full group. When they met with others, they yelled orders at them, anything to add to the chaos. About the fire, about attacks, about needing to reinforce their gates.

The notoriety of station helped them along. Most people inside the palace were servants, people of the mass, or hands, there to obey and serve—and definitely not ask questions of anybody as lofty as minds, let alone pillars.

On top of that, they nearly emptied Cilia's stores of fire droplets. On their way in, they set more than a dozen small fires, spreading smoke and panic throughout the palace.

Once, they spotted another mind in the distance, but they moved on fast enough that they weren't forced to talk to them.

The minutes pressed on, at once in a hurry and at a pace that felt too slow to be true. A pair of hearts in an otherwise empty corridor tried to challenge Liam. He slowed down to talk to them, and abruptly sucker punched one of them into oblivion, kicked the leg out from under the other one and punched him in the head on the ground. They left them lying unconscious in the corridors.

Soon, they recognized things from their tour: The large map room, showing the entire glory of the Liberty lands. The fantastic murals, explaining the made-up history of the Liberators and the villainous outsiders. A few details were different, though—among these, the large number of servants and guards running around mid-panic, almost like somebody had loosed hostile summons on the palace and was setting fires left and right.

It couldn't go on forever. They managed to make it farther in than they'd deemed possible, with maybe ten minutes to go. Yet, from one moment to the next, the corridors ahead of them rang with the sounds of weapons and yelled commands.

Cilia dropped back from where she'd been leading their advance. "A large group. Front and center," she yelled.

Chase raced ahead, putting himself at the head of their group. "We know what to do. First Sera, then Cil, then me. Go!"

Seconds later, they encountered the first concerted effort to stop them. A dozen guards, at least. They nearly filled the corridor. The front rank of fighters knelt with large shields, while archers and crossbowmen stood behind them, ranged weapons slowly rising to face them. At the far back, a person sporting the dark-blue color of a mind had his hands raised.

Possibly in supplication. More likely in the process of guiding the activation of some card. They never learned.

Sera shouted, "Now!"

Nature's Shield activated, and long vines bearing ten-inch-long barbs spilled out in the right side of the corridor. The vines thickened, turning and twisting, and solidified into long, rope-like tendrils, filling a third of the wide corridor in seconds.

The guards shouted, but didn't move, seeing as how even the nearest roots were feet away from them.

Then Cilia activated Touch Grass, and the roots started to move. Seconds later, the first screams started.

They tried to stand tall against the twisting vines. They really did. The mind at the back unleashed some shining globe that carved out a huge chunk of the growths, as well as anything else that moved into its territory.

Only, according to the Furyborn elders, Nature's Shield with a Mental Power of *twenty* was an effective deterrent against most humans. At the moment, Sera's Mental Power was at forty-nine.

Sera alone would have forged the vines into an impenetrable barrier, enough for a proper nuisance. But the vines now moved according to Cilia's will, and her will was steel. Combined, their creation was a menace. The guards cried out in pain and fear, as the tendrils snaked overwhelmingly and crushed the shining globe struggling against their growth, forcibly pushing it left, into the mass of soldiers, pushing them back against the opposite wall. The grating noise of thorns against steel armor mixed with screams as the thorns located exposed areas, impaled the flesh, and drew the full attention of anybody present.

Some of the ranged fighters still had the presence of mind to train their weapons on them. Only, Chase acted now, activating Circle of Darkness. With a mental nudge, he layered the darkness right on top of the soldiers, even as he laced a path of lighter shadows along the right side. From one second to the next, the beleaguered defenders were firing blind.

A few projectiles hit the wall. Yet, seconds later, they were past, and the screams of the soldiers behind them were the only signs that they'd even been there.

A few minutes later, they were beset once more, this time by a full group of ranged fighters who'd entrenched themselves inside a large, circular room containing dozens of immaculate art pieces. The archers and crossbowmen were divided throughout the room, using the art for defense.

This time, they didn't even attack. Liam leapt ahead with Helping Hand, activated Become the Clay, and hid behind his shield, allowing the defenders to turn him into a veritable porcupine. Following the initial volley, Chase used Circle of Darkness again, and they trailed after him through the room and into the far corridor, before Sera entirely blocked the opening with another serving of Nature's Shield.

"We're getting closer," Kith panted. By now, they were running in a group. The time for subterfuge was long past, and anybody they met either fled them, huddled down in fear and confusion, or tried to kill them. "Two more corridors."

Cilia was the hardest put-upon by their fast pace. Sweat ran down her face in rivulets, but she kept up without complaints. She slowed down slightly, extracted an intricately braided and carved leather ring from her right pocket, bent it in two, and placed it in her left pocket before continuing to lope ahead. "We..." She panted. "We don't know if these can protect us from the influence of his items, but they should. I have enough for an hour, at most. Make it count!"

"Damn straight we will!" Liam grinned. He raised his trusty truncheon in a salute.

Kith slammed his hand axes against each other, producing a ringing sound. "Time to carve up a god!"

Chase laughed, raising his short sword high. "This is insane. I love it. Please don't die!"

Sera shook her head in dismay at their antics, hefting her small bucklers. "We are about to challenge somebody stronger than anybody, anywhere in the world—and you still crack horrible jokes? I do love you all."

They entered the final corridor. Beyond that, they would reach right into the very center of the palace, reach the tower holding all the decks, the home of the Savior himself, their very target.

Only, the huge doorway leading into the floor level of the tower was not to be seen. In its place lay a shimmering, dizzying display of magic. An opaque shield, covering the entire passage in magic, blocked them off from entering.

Liam rolled his shoulders. "Well. That answers one question. Guess he's home! Who's knocking?"

Sera strode ahead. "You already know this is my task, silly. Now, remember the deal. From here on out, this is what I can do. Please keep distractions off my back and keep me alive." She activated four cards in short succession. Blessing of the Night would serve them as it had always done, more than doubling any buffs to their attributes. Bubbles of Blue would enhance their defense—especially that of Liam's Become the Clay—as well as the strength of her shields. Meanwhile, Shield of Cancellation would add a canceling effect to any shields she activated, and Shimmering Sanctuary provided them *all* with shields to defend against enemy hostile effects.

As they watched the miniature sun grow into existence above Sera's head and bathe them in a comfortable warmth, they all shot hopeful glances at the barrier ahead. This was the linchpin of their current plan. If it didn't work, they'd be stuck behind the shield, with nowhere to go but back.

Sera stepped ahead, head held high, gaze fixed on the swimming, shimmering barrier in front of them. "Whatever happens, know that I have cherished my time with you."

Kith snorted. "Stop that. Nobody likes that kind of talk. It's for losers." He watched the barrier intently, hungrily, as if waiting for it to fall. "You're not a loser, are you, princess?"

She moved right up in front of the barrier, holding her hands out. The small sun above her head bathed the shield in a vibrant, warm glow. "I told you before. We have no way of knowing if this will work, or if I am even strong enough to influence anything. Your goading has no sway on the effect here."

The shield burst apart in a shining spray of mist.

"Or does it?" Kith smirked. "I'd better keep it up. Just in case. You think you can keep up, little girl?"

CHAPTER 32

Productivity of camps F-H have improved by nearly twenty percent over the past year. We believe a multitude of reasons apply, yet our main theory lies in attributes. Lately, we have seen a larger percentage of mass and even hands being entered into the camps. Whatever the reason for this change, clearly the added attributes make up for the increased diffi-culty in ensuring their compliance. We recommend increasing the influx of higher-caste persons. Of course they would keep statistics on this. Yet, the coldness, the lack of humanity—it's hard to bear. I hope we live to see those camps torched. (Page 57.)

They walked straight into an onslaught. Two seconds after the shield dropped, a flurry of missiles welcomed them. Liam barely managed to leap ahead, interposing himself and his shield between the missiles and Sera. He kept the position, staying ahead of them, but not moving forward. "No Savior. *Packed* with guards!" he shouted. "Soon-to-be-blind guards," he added. Tribune of Retribution, Blindness was already activated, deteriorating the attackers' eyesight for each of their arrows.

"I'll flush 'em!" Chase shouted in return.

"I'll distract." Kith grinned. "This is going to *suck!*" A series of cards flashed, as they activated. First, his Apian God, summoning a huge, buzzing mass of insects into being. Next, Enforced Entropy, making sure that anybody his summons touched would be exempt from all beneficial buffs and effects. This, he followed up with his Heart card, doubling his attributes even as it leeched his life's blood. Building into a roar, he finished with Ties Airbound, twin tornadoes emerging to cover his feet. He kept roaring and flung himself into the bottom space of the huge tower with inhumanly rapid movement. Hundreds of insects buzzed past him to charge the defenders.

Cries rang out in response—orders, panic, and questions mixing into an incomprehensible babble.

Chase didn't listen. He moved forward slightly, glancing past Liam and then ducking back down behind the wide warrior. He had so many options available to him right now. With his Tier-three Winds of Change card active, he'd even be able to continue switching cards around, finding the perfect combination. For now, however, he settled on a specific combination. Then he nodded to himself as he agreed with Kith.

This was indeed going to suck.

He burst into the room at a dead sprint. Kith had moved right, so he ran left. As he sprinted, the bright platforms from Steps of Brilliance burst into being ahead of him, allowing him to leave the ground behind and race right into the open air of the room. He activated Among the Raindrops at the center of the room, starting a slow buildup of acidic raindrops capable of burning through even the best-treated leather armor. Then he focused on keeping up the creation of invisible platforms, taking in the situation and, well, not dying.

"Light!" Cilia yelled. Then she flung two droplets of light into the room, which erupted immediately, taking a large part of the defenders by surprise and blinding them entirely.

In those first, chaotic moments of racing through the air, blinking away light spots, attempting to evade arrows, card effects, and Kith, who was roaming the room like a drunken wind Elemental, Chase managed to gather a few things.

First, the massive entourage of guards and other people in the bottom layer of the Savior's tower attested to the fact that this was clearly some sort of fallback position. They'd trained for whatever was going on. The guards here were arranged in formation, just like the defenders they'd met in the hallways, prepared to throw extreme prejudice at any invaders. That organization dissolved within seconds, as they had to deal with being blinded, and also keep up with two insane people basically hurtling themselves through the air in circles around their formation.

Next, there were *many*. The place was crowded! The last time they'd been here, with the decks calmly floating in the air and a few officials tranquilly puttering about, the space had seemed one of peace and contemplation. With more than fifty well-armed guards taking up the center of the floor, there was no peace. There were also no decks hovering in the air. Every single deck was gone, removed to some safe space.

Also, whoever decided that everything inside the Liberty lands should be color-coordinated had clearly not been thinking about tactics. The higher-Tiered personnel with their darker shirts stood out, presenting themselves like they *wanted* to be targeted.

Finally, the paranoia of the Savior was front and center. The pillar had as much as confirmed it. He was deadly afraid that anybody would rise to the challenge and grow strong, to the point where he kept stronger Liberators apart, kept them from grouping up. This had never been as obvious as right now, when Chase let his gaze slide over the enemies arrayed before them and realized that there was but a single Tier-four there. Certainly, there'd be more of them inbound at any moment—but, at this point, the guards shouting, shooting, and defending below his hasty steps would, with a rare few exceptions, only have a single card available to them that wasn't Devotion to Liberty.

It was a curious design flaw—and Chase was going to make the most of it.

Mentally grasping the reins, he activated his A Friendly Wave card, reaching out for the liquid slowly building into puddles from his Among the Raindrops.

When first he'd used A Friendly Wave, it had been difficult. The liquid at his command had moved only languidly, and it took great concentration to move larger quantities.

Now, through tons of practice and a Mental Power at twenty-nine, the puddles arose at his merest mental touch. Below him, at the center of the Liberty formation, a wave grew into being, growing taller and taller, before cresting and starting into a circular pattern.

Where the wave touched, screams arose—and they never stopped.

It had been the card improvement from when Among the Raindrops increased to Epic. From then on, not only did the droplets have a caustic effect and were oily enough to make enemies slip and fall, they also became viscous, clinging to enemies and constantly eating away at exposed surfaces.

At first, the enemies were professional enough to ignore the effects of the acidic liquid. Yet, Among the Raindrops *kept* creating more liquid, which A Friendly Wave kept churning around in ever-widening circles to strike at any enemies still fighting. And Sera's sun lit up the open space, stopping any enemy hostile effects from coming into being, even as Kith's insects stopped any *beneficial* effects from working on them, while Liam and the droplets blinded them. Granted, the insects were slowly dying. The magical effects had no effect on friendly summons, but liquid still washed the insects away, drowning them in a mundane fashion. Yet, Kith kept them rushing in, keeping them covered, and unable to use any healing or canceling effects.

The result was horrific. Blinded and kept from using any proper defenses, the guards were unable to muster any effective defense, even as the caustic water ate into their flesh. Yet, where any regular people would have thrown down their weapons and cried out in surrender, they never wavered. Instead, they exploded into action, ranging out to attack and evade the range of the damaging wave.

They died slowly. With huge, open sores and barely able to see, the soldiers were easy targets for Liam, Kith, and Chase. Liam even activated Draining Ward, using the few flailing attacks that did land on his shield to boost his Agility. But they did die, all of them throwing down their lives in the defense of their deity.

Liam's arms fell as the final defender succumbed with a gurgling cry. He panted heavily. The clay of his arms and lower legs were heavily studded with missiles and he looked almost like Spike. Yet, there was nothing funny about his mien, as he let his truncheon slide down his extremities, snapping off the shafts of the arrows and bolts, ignoring the heads stuck inside the layer of clay. "Everybody okay? I am—" He grunted, as one of the arrowheads clearly bit into the flesh underneath. "Mostly unharmed."

They called back with confirmation. Chase blinked in surprise to see that he had actually been struck by something and was bleeding softly from his ankle. Unimportant.

"We are not safe. We are *far* from safe, actually. You can hear more incoming, right now," Cilia snapped. "We continue. We have no idea what is waiting for us. Be prepared. And remember—stick to the plan. He's a human. Not a god."

The wide stairway leading into the tower was still as impressive as the last time they'd been here. Circling the huge chamber without any obvious support, it let them stride into the air high above with plenty of space to walk in formation.

Without even talking, they dropped into the arrangement they'd practiced so many times before: Liam in front, shield at the ready. Kith just behind on his left, Chase on the right. Cilia, farther back, dead center, hands holding two different droplets. Finally, Sera, holding her bucklers, gaze flitting every which way...watching, assessing.

At any other time, they would have commented on everything. In hushed tones, likely. The majesty of the open, beautifully crafted space didn't invite loud voices. Yet, everything about the tower, the decorations, the sheer grandeur of the place, would at the very least have caused Kith to shoot a comment off about somebody compensating.

Now, however, they were silent, moving with military efficiency, focused only on what lay ahead. They jogged ahead and up, not too fast, conserving their energy for what was to come.

The throne room was exactly what one might have expected. The second floor was dedicated entirely to a massive, circular room. The floor was one huge mosaic, color-graded with the colors of Liberty. The entrance, at the southern side of the room, started in shades of the lightest blue, slowly shifting toward darker tones, drawing the gaze inevitably toward the far end, and the throne. The throne. A hugely intimidating construction of what looked like the night itself, replete with shimmering stars. It looked like one massive slab of stone, built to raise its holder three feet above any supplicant. On all sides, huge, tinted windows added to the kaleidoscopic effect of the room.

With the Savior on his throne, the place would've been intimidating, the gaze drawn automatically toward the far end. Even abandoned, the eyes reflexively went there, as if expecting something—somebody—to materialize at any moment.

"Subtle." Kith snorted.

"Quiet," Cilia scolded. "Be alert for anything. Traps. Ambushes. Invisibility."

Liam rolled his eyes as he advanced. "Invisibility? How the Pits am I supposed to look out for *invisibility*? Oh look! There's nothing there! Must be—"

"Focus," Chase snapped. His gaze shot upward, at the ceiling above them. It was tall, maybe fifty feet above their heads. Yet, it was still low enough there was no way that they were at the top of the building. "Stairs gotta be behind the throne, right?"

"Gotta be." Liam nodded.

Deadly traps failed to appear; they reached the throne, their surroundings dimming with every step.

Chase couldn't help but imagine the effect it would have, when the inhumanly tall, perfect man was actually seated, waiting for you to slink closer. Yet, right now, the threat was implicit, though everything persistently failed to appear.

A pair of large vertical banners hung behind the throne, brushing the upper edge of the throne's back.

When they reached it, they noticed that the wide banners helped obscure the fact that the space between the throne and the wall was hollow. There was a doorway, and another large opening in the wall with a handle.

With the shield firmly in place in front of his face, Liam used the truncheon to manipulate the handle. It slid up, revealing...

"That's a weird place for storage," Kith said. "Hey, look. Dirty plates. Guess god-king-wannabes get peckish too."

"Not storage. It's a lift. Look. There's a rope to operate it there," Cilia said.

"So, he's got to be up there, right?" Chase asked.

"I guess. That is a large number of plates for one person, right?" Kith shrugged. "Though, I guess, if I were a god-king, I'd want a harem or two as well."

"Silence, dammit," Cilia said. "I know you're nervous, but...let's *please* try to survive this."

They inched the door open. Overwhelming ambushes still failed to appear. Liam continued walking first, as Cilia cracked yet another of the leather rings.

The next stairway was...something different. Not only was it not ostentatious, it was also cramped, and placed *within* the walls. There were no lights, and the rough stone steps going up to the next level looked crafted to be more like something leading down into a city's dungeon than to the ruler's chambers.

The moment they reached the next floor, they froze. There were no traps, no attacks—in fact, no single hostile act. They simply crowded into the narrow doorway, gazing in disbelief at the sight beyond.

Nobody spoke. Kith walked with his eyes half-closed.

Eventually, Cilia held up a hand to Kith. "Don't!"

"Don't what?" he asked.

"You were working your way up to a joke about harems. I could tell."

"Normally, I would. But not for something like this, Cil. What the Pits is going *on* here?" He sounded seriously hurt.

The entire level of the tower was filled with cots. Side by side, they lay, in their hundreds, all the way across the width of the tower, except for a small space at the center of the floor. People, most of them middle-aged or older, all naked, all wielders, Tiers two and above.

"They are all chained to the floor! What *is* this?" Sera exclaimed in horror.

It was true. Every single person had a chain going from their leg to a ring forged into the floor. Also, they wore numerous rings on all fingers. On top of that, the single possession each of them had was a set of quills, ink, and paper on the floor at the foot of each cot. Next to each of the cots stood a bucket. Judging from the rank stench inside the room, they could guess what those were for.

"What's wrong with them? Are they drugged?" Liam asked.

Most of the people did indeed look like they weren't mentally there. Some lay back, gazing at the ceiling with open eyes. Others sat up, staring into infinity. A few slept. In the distance, one woman looked like she was jotting down a note. It didn't seem as if they were physically mistreated, as such—no bruises, no signs of violence. Yet, something was entirely wrong.

In between the rows of cots, though, there was movement. One young man, also naked, also chained, slowly shuffled among the rows. He bent down along the way, picked up a few notes and returned to a long table placed centrally in the tower. There, he placed the notes in two different piles, before sitting down calmly on a chair and gazing placidly into the distance.

They ambled out among the rows of cots, hands feverishly clenched on their weapons, ready for anything. At first, nobody noticed their presence, entirely caught up in their own worlds. A third along the way, one of the wielders sat up, grabbed for the quill at her feet, and spotted them.

She froze. Her hand slowly rose, pointing straight at them. A thin, keening voice came from her.

That caught the attention of a few others, including the young man walking between the rows. He nearly fell off his chair, then he prostrated himself before them.

Sera rushed forward, reaching a hand out toward the young man, but he curled up into a ball on the floor, trembling, producing a deep, guttural sound, over and over again. She tried to get in contact with him, but he refused to move even in the slightest. "What is going on here?" Sera repeated.

Cilia looked up from the table and held a scrap of paper up. "Productivity in F6 is up by three percent the past month. Exceptions: Honor's Crest, Dry Brook, Greater Fortitude. Recommendations: Monitor all three for issues." She grimaced and looked out over the naked prisoners around the room. "These, I'm afraid, are the ones who keep track of all the Keepers."

"That makes no sense," Chase protested. "There's got to be thousands of those damn snooping Keepers throughout the lands. There's, what, a few hundred people in here?"

Cilia shook her head and pointed. "Remember back in Furyborn lands? They had armbands of a sort, letting summoners swap Guardians around for different tasks. Check out those rings on their fingers. This has to be some of the same."

Kith let his hand rest on her shoulder. "I agree. Look at their cards. Those are definitely summoner cards, even if I don't recognize any of them." He shuddered. "Poor bastards. That could've been me."

Sera eventually managed to coax up the head of the young man. She gasped, whispering at him. "Oh. You poor thing."

The man looked up, tears in his eyes, still trembling all over. His mouth was open, and they could all see the stump of a tongue inside.

Liam snarled. "I was already going to kill the bastard. But now? Now, I believe I'm going to enjoy it."

They moved on, promising they'd be back to help the summoners as soon as possible. The next stairs were just like the last pair, simplistic and narrow, with another lift next to the doors. No embellishments. No traps. No ambushes.

"This was more akin to what I was expecting." Sera nodded.

The next floor was a huge workspace. Cilia slowly, hesitantly entered the room. "This is amazing. Leatherworking. Smithing. Pottery. Glassblowing. Alchemy. Carpentry. That…I don't even know what that thing with the cubes is."

"Does it matter?" Kith shrugged. "It's just more proof we were right."

"Yes. Yes, I agree." Cilia huffed and cocked her head back. "There can't be more than a single floor left, maybe two."

There was only a single floor. The door swung open, and they looked into a large, windowless room, lit by a series of crystals embedded in the walls that gave off a bright, joyless light. At the side of the room lay a large burlap sack filled with decks, carelessly tossed.

"You deceived me." The voice came from the far end of the room.

At long last, they spotted the Savior. Larger than life, clad in the dark vestures of his station, with the hood of his robe up, he slouched on a chair next to a bed at the far end of the room. A regular-sized bed, unmade, bedding bundled up, and a normal chair next to a drawer and mirror—furniture that'd be at home in any regular setting. The image of him stood out against the normal backdrop, creating a strange dichotomy.

"I believed you, Darkborn. I thought you were here to escape them, just like me. That is why I took pity on you. Yet, they sent you, did they not?" His voice pressed in on them, growing louder every second.

Cilia snapped another leather ring. "This is powerful. We won't have an hour," she murmured.

"We don't know what in the blistering Pits you're on about, man," Chase said. "We came here to find a deck, so we could create a safe home somewhere. Instead, we find some weird-ass psycho calling himself a god, lying to his people, spying on them, and enslaving them for his own profit."

"You are not with them? Truly?" The magnitude of the voice was less, took on an entirely different tone. The voice shook with barely constrained laughter. "And you're merely here for a deck?"

"Well, that's how it started," Liam said. "Now that we've seen what you're up to… Just like with White Wings back on the Waves, when some tough turns feral, somebody'll need to take them down."

A cold laughter emerged from the robed figure, as he slowly rose from the chair. "You. You are going to take me down? A handful of piddling Tier-fours? Let me show you just what I intend to do about it—" He raised a hand and…nothing happened.

"Sorry, man. I'd say it's nothing personal, but your personality's clearly awful. We'll be doing the world a favor by taking you out." Chase cracked his neck.

An amused snort was their answer. "All right, then. Do try. I am easily bored, but there is one thing that never gets old. Showing traitors like you that, after a certain point, there is no difference between having the strength of a god and *being* a god."

The Savior of the blissful lands leapt forward to kill them all.

Liam nearly died in that first attack.

The Savior's punch was straightforward, telegraphed clearly enough that they could all see it—yet, it came with a speed and enough power that stopping it would be as easy as stopping a stampede with your face.

Liam's skin was barely visible, covered in magical clay boosting his defense. Meanwhile, his Draining Ward improved his defense even further, and Finger on the Scales hit them all as a slap in the face, as it took the magic from all surrounding effects, canceled or not, and improved their attributes accordingly—doubled by Blessing of the Night. His parry was perfect, diverting most of the force.

Yet even with all of that, he barely held onto his shield. The wood caved in, and splinters filled the air as the Savior effortlessly continued his attack with a kick at Liam.

Again, Liam managed to get his shield up in time, a bit faster this time, compared to his attacker. Still, it wasn't enough, and the kick sent him flying back nearly twenty feet, skidding across the floor. His head slammed into the ground, and he coughed, spitting blood.

"Hey, freak." Kith floated forward softly, bounding unnaturally on the air swirling around his feet. "You seem to enjoy beating up smaller guys. Why don't you try me on for size? That should be even *more* fun for you." His blades rang as he clashed them together. He started to shine with a bright, ghostly light, as Divine Mentor came to life within his own body, guiding his movements. Around him, the light shone even stronger, as a swarm of spirits emerged. Their number doubled by Twice the Fun, Sacrificial Saints trailed all around his body, ready to lay down their spirit to protect him. Finally, he activated his heart card once more, granting him an almost otherworldly intensity.

The Savior halted for a second, allowing Liam to slowly get to his feet. He stared at the glow enveloping Kith. "Light? Are you assassins from the Light? What are you? I told them I would kill them all!" With an unhinged scream, he tore forward at Kith.

Chase tore himself free from his second of inactivity and activated his own cards. He hesitantly exchanged Winds of Change for Double Dip. Being able to switch between all his cards was less likely to be as effective as draining twice the number of attributes from their enemy. That said, he activated Sticky Fingers, grinning as he felt it activate twice, stealing a point of both Strength and Agility from the Savior. Next, he activated Nights of Criffhaven, starting the timer for the slowly building Agility buff. He could have gone with Race of Life for the instant boost, but doubted that this fight would be over quickly. Finally, he activated Clothed in Living Light, grinning as a shimmering hand emerged on his left forearm. Whatever happened to him today, he'd be able to flip off a god with either hand.

Kith lasted for nearly a minute. That, in itself, was incredible. It could only have been possible with the impressive boosts they'd already received, aided by his Heart card and Divine Mentor card, and added to the fact that Sera's cards were keeping any crafted items from aiding the Savior. The difference between the attributes of the two fighters was simply insane enough that it should have been over in seconds. Yet, Kith dipped and slid, flew and bounced, moved around like an insane, cackling ghost.

The Savior was entirely lost in his fury. He snarled, kicking and punching, throwing himself forward, attempting to grab hold of the slippery Furyborn. Yet, his inexperience in actual combat was evident; even though he was faster, stronger, and tougher than Kith, his movements were untrained and ineffective.

Slowly, the difference was starting to show, however. Regardless of Kith's control, he couldn't quite bridge the gap. Every so often, he would fail to dodge back fast enough, leap far enough to evade the grasping hands of the enraged Savior. Every time, one of the floating spirits would, with a keening cry, toss themselves in between the two, sacrificing themselves in Kith's stead.

Kith stumbled back. Only a few trailing spirits remained.

The Savior followed, snarling—only to reel back, as one of the two Divine Mentors inside Kith erupted into a blinding light.

He stumbled, blinking to regain his eyesight. Growling at them, he demanded, "Why do you persist? Can't you see that you're outmatched?"

Chase laughed. "That's not the sense I'm getting here. Can't you tell? You're losing. Surrender, and we will let you live." Surreptitiously, he fired off another Sticky Fingers, even as Nights of Criffhaven ticked upward. "We have no issues with you. Just the way you run things."

The Savior's eyes twitched between Chase and the others, as if calculating. Then he leapt for his dresser, tore a cupboard open, and dug inside. He grasped an item, grinned widely, and flung it at Liam.

Liam, back on his feet, with his shield raised, was nevertheless too slow to dodge the missile. His head rocked back; the bottle exploded into tiny shards and showered him with a clingy fluid. He grunted, took a step back, then steadied and wiped his head with his forearm, eyes still on the Savior.

The expressionless, perfect facade of the Savior remained unchanging. Yet, his voice betrayed his emotions. "What? How can you do that?"

"Talent. Good looks. Lots of exercise." Chase smirked, getting off another Sticky Fingers. "You should try it, man. Maybe some fresh air would help with a few of your issues."

"Yeah, man. Who throws bottles at people?" Kith jumped in. "That's just rude."

The man froze for a moment. Then, as if drawn toward her, his gaze fixed on Sera. "You. You are the one canceling my gifts!"

"Man—" Chase began, but didn't get any further before the Savior barreled toward Sera, arms outstretched.

Chase and Kith leapt to the rescue. However, the sheer speed was too much for any of them to overcome.

Liam got there first. His leg still flashed with the use of his Helping Step card, as he was transported right in front of Sera, half-ruined shield angled to rebuff the grasping hands of the irate attacker.

Then Chase and Kith joined in, one from either side, short sword and axes flashing out, attempting to reach the Savior's flesh.

He fell back, snarling.

Sticky Fingers, again. Agility and Mental Power.

This time, he spotted the flash on Chase's arm, and seemed to reach a conclusion. He went for Chase. Only, an axe from Kith slashed at him. He punched at him instead, and screamed in frustration as his hands found nothing but another spirit.

Something flickered over his face. Not fear, but some indeterminable decision. He reeled back toward the dresser again, arm dipping deep inside as he ignored them all. He found it, arm returning, grasping something, raising it to his lips—just in time for the fire droplet to strike his chest.

The roar of fire sounded bestial inside the closed bedchambers of the Savior. A ball of fire engulfed him, the dresser, and half the bed. When the fire faded, leaving a vivid afterimage of the explosion on their retinas, the dresser and bed were ablaze.

The Savior was not ablaze. Yet, the fire had not left him untouched. The bottle he'd grasped was ruined, smashed to shards inside his fist. Only, the real damage was to his clothes. Heretofore, nothing had seemed to be able to impact the integrity of the suit. Now, however, the chest of the robe was half-consumed, revealing...a pair of eyes.

"Gah. I knew I said you were a freak, but...Fury rend my mind. What the Pits are ya?" Kith gasped.

The Savior responded by truly losing his mind.

Before, his actions had been savage and untrained, but definitely calculated. His choices were deliberate, and he'd clearly aimed at something specific.

Now, he flung himself at Cilia relentlessly, with no hint at self-preservation.

Liam, Kith, and Chase reacted instantly. They threw themselves in his way, blocking his progress with their weapons and bodies.

He attempted to leap over the head of Liam, but Kith soared up to meet him halfway, tackling him off course.

They all worked together now, using everything they'd rehearsed through countless instances of life-threatening conflict to aid one another, take over and keep up the assault even when they were outmatched and underpowered compared to their adversary.

Every fifteen seconds, the Savior's attributes would dip a tiny bit more, even as Chase's improved. Every full minute, Chase's Agility would increase even further. Inch by bloody inch, they were bridging the gap.

Finally, it happened. The Savior leaned in with both hands, trying to tear the shield out of Liam's grasp, when Kith's left axe managed to hit him across the neck. It tore right into the back of the robe, and the blade receded...with a bright drop of blood adorning the edge.

The Savior chuckled. The eyes on his chest blinked. With a noise that started out high-pitched, it slowly built into a deep laughter. "This is what I've feared? This can barely be called pain. Why am I even holding back?" Still laughing, he flung himself right at Liam.

Liam's truncheon hit his arm with a resounding crack. His eyes shot open wide, as the Savior just pressed on, ignoring the damage. He fell back, with the Savior on top of him.

Kith leapt in, chopping with his full strength. Only, the attacks that landed seemed not to do the damage they should. Only thin lines of blood emerged. And all the while, the Savior let his fists pummel down onto Liam.

Chase leapt onto his right arm, using his own, glowing hand as well as his left, to keep him from savaging Liam any further.

The Savior laughed cruelly, pulled his head down, and tried to toss Chase forward.

Only...nothing happened.

Chase had both feet solidly planted on the ground, both arms fixed on the Savior's right wrist.

For a split second, the Savior froze, astonished by what was happening.

Chase, meanwhile, just used his shock to his advantage, pulling for all he was worth. And, as he'd found, there was one thing that Clothed in Living Light granted him above all: sheer grip strength. Another Sticky Fingers gave him another two points to Strength and two to Toughness, while taking from the Savior made the balance slip infinitesimally further in his direction.

Then Kith struck. He used the split second of full distraction to drop one hand axe, grasp the other in a two-handed grip and raise it above his head, before using his full body weight to bring it down. Right at his back.

The Savior moved, at the last second realizing his position. Yet, Chase still held onto him from one side, and Liam, battered and bruised, managed to grab onto him from below.

The axe descended.

The god of all Liberators. The dictator of the blissful lands. The strongest known person in all Ordei...screamed.

They stumbled back from the shrilly screaming man. Chase grasped onto Liam with his shining hand and pulled him away.

The Savior didn't even seem to notice.

His face was still serene. Perfect. Yet, the eyes below were wide and bloodshot, pain-filled screams reverberating between the walls.

A hellish vision appeared before them, unclear within the smoke and haze from the bed, which was now entirely in flames. The head and shoulders of the Savior seemed to roil and melt, as if the heat caused it to deform. The hand axe still stuck out from between the shoulder blades.

They pulled back slowly, Kith fumbling after and picking up his other axe as they retreated a few feet.

Liam's arm flashed weakly, as he switched Draining Ward for Cleansing Fire. He sighed softly as the weak healing ability slowly caused parts of his bloody face to rearrange themselves.

Cilia had a droplet in either hand, one raised to let go.

Sera looked everywhere, alert for any trick.

Eventually, the Savior's shape reformed. The robes were now slightly different, shorter. They revealed...something else. A different person, middle-aged, just about as tall as Chase, pockmarked, with a fading hairline.

The blade of Kith's hand axe was embedded halfway into his neck. Right where the shoulders of the tall, inhuman deity had seemed to be.

The Savior looked up at them, blood dripping from his lips, breath wheezing. He looked into Chase's eyes, brows furrowing, as if in deep confusion. Then, without a further word, he died.

CHAPTER 33

This is the first part of the autobiography of Baltasar Embertongue. Formerly a traveling tradesman between Liberty and Earth's Ward. Now, through a grueling series of drawn-out negotiations, a leader in the Council of Liberators. Wow. I can actually call myself a leader. That feels weird. Unreal. Maybe it will settle in time. This! This was the Savior? A traveling tradesman? And I rescued his diaries from the fires? Well, most of them. The historians of Ordei are going to crown me their queen when this is done! (Book 1, Page 1.)

Sometimes, when you've managed something you've planned for a long time, you can find yourself aimless, clueless as to what you're supposed to do next. That might have happened here. However, their situation and state conspired to guide them through the motions, at least to begin with.

First, they put out the fire and stopped the smoke from spreading throughout the room, causing them all to cough and choke.

Cilia took to investigating the Savior, ensuring that he really *was* dead. She found out that the Savior's entire set of robes had been a crafted item, somehow making his entire body and face look taller and more impressive than he really was, and powerful enough to overcome the effect of all of Cilia's crafted items. The face in his chest had been his actual face, while everything above that had been a carefully crafted illusion.

Next, they started arguing, obviously, while Sera switched cards to Warmth of the Circle to start healing Liam and Spark of Divinity to raise his Toughness and avoid any lingering issues. Only, before they got any further, shouts arose from the far end of the room. That turned out to be a small hand mirror, formerly suppressed, that transmitted both sound and vision of what was happening in the throne room. Where a large group of guards was debating whether they could trespass in the Savior's private rooms if it were for the purpose of his aid.

Fortunately, the momentary panic spawned by that development faded away before the soldiers made up their minds. Also, Kith's idea that he should put on the Savior's robes and see whether he couldn't fake being him was summarily downvoted.

The chaos as they started to release the summoners chained to their beds and descended among the former captives did not fade. It only spread.

First came the panic.

Then the anger, the loud debates of whether they should be killed. Also, the less loud debates with plenty of fingers pointing at the room below, questioning whether they *could* be killed.

Yet, slowly, eventually, rare voices started to ask questions. Questions which granted hard answers. About the naked summoners. About the corpse clearly dressed in the Savior's robes *not being the Savior at all*. And with every question they were able to answer—or at least, where the answer didn't strictly point in the direction of "These are cold-blooded killers who murdered our lord without reason"—opinion shifted subtly in their favor.

Things truly changed a few hours in, when a familiar, shell-shocked Pillar of Liberty walked in, slowly blinking as she took in the scenery and their presence at the center of everything. She immediately took point and barked out a number of orders. The last of these included secluding their group in a small sitting chamber and calling in the other pillars, while she figured out what was going to happen.

The look on the pillar's face, as the ornate door slammed shut behind her, was exquisite. Disbelief was front and center, but there was a core of relief, of burgeoning, unbridled joy that lay entirely at odds with the weary, cynical woman Chase and Cilia had last met. "You did it. You actually did it. We are free! Please tell me it's not a trick!"

"It's not a trick," Liam rumbled. "Also...who are you again?"

She ignored him and flung herself forward, grasping Chase in a deep, long hug.

Chase's arms moved to defend himself, until he realized what was going on. Then he slowly relaxed, and patted her back, as she started to sob into his chest.

Eventually, she backed up a bit, wiping at her eyes. "Lucille. My name is Lucille. I'd say, anybody who saves me from inevitable death can call me by my first name."

"Oh, that's *her!*" Liam smacked his forehead. "Say. Would you mind answering a quick question? It's not like we actually thought this far ahead, but I'd honestly have expected people to be a lot more doubtful that your big and mighty Savior was truly dead. Only, that's the one thing nobody's challenged us on. How come?"

She looked at them, then at the short sleeves on their shirts, displaying a wide range of cards that were definitely not Devotion to Liberty. She barked a laugh. Then, with a flourish,

Lucille showed them the Tier-one Liberty card, like that of everybody else in Liberty, visible to the world through the short sleeve of her shirt.

It was the same as always. The Savior of Liberty, painted in the darkest of blues, front and center. From all sides, flowing whirls of energy streamed toward him, in a color palette that started light blue and got consistently darker. It was megalomaniacal, intimidating, and memorable.

It was also, quite clearly, inert. The energy that always moved along the frame of cards had stilled, and there was no shimmer, no life.

"Oh. Okay. That answers that." Liam shrugged.

"No, it doesn't!" Cilia said. "Why would only *that* card cease functioning? Has everything about it stopped? What is the *logic*?"

"All good questions," Lucille agreed. "Possibly ones we should wait to answer, until we reassure ourselves that the lands of Liberty are not going to tear themselves apart, following your deed." Her eyes were red, but shone with inner fire.

Cilia blinked and coughed.

The pillar continued, starting to pace, filled with restless energy. "What you've managed is going to change...everything. I—" She laughed softly. "Nobody even knows your names. If you faded away right now, with the Keepers resting, nobody would ever find you. Is that what you want?" She nodded, self-assurance visibly reasserting itself. "That is a good starting point. I expect that the other two pillars will arrive within the hour, though Trevor may ensconce himself in his house indefinitely. He was ever timid. The Pristine Minds are already out in force. So, before you are expected to stand up before all and sundry, I ask you to be very clear in advance. *What do you want?*"

They shared glances for a while. Then both Kith and Sera burst out in laughter, while Cilia looked like a thunderstorm.

Sera ventured, "We should likely have given this some additional thought beforehand."

Liam snorted. "It's not like any of us really thought we'd be able to pull through and succeed." He held up his hand, stopping any complaints. "What? I'm just saying what we all have thought. Anyway, what we want is easy. Some friends of ours and their friends have been imprisoned within the past day. Reen, Nordon, a lot we don't know the names of. We want them out, and free, as unharmed as possible."

Lucille strode immediately to the door, slammed it open, and barked an order outside, before closing the door behind her again. "Done. What else?"

Liam blinked. "We want a deck. Also, we want for the people of Liberty to be free of tyrants like that insane Savior up there."

She nodded brusquely. "What else? I remind you, we likely have little time before the actual negotiations start."

Liam looked at the others uncertainly. "Erm. I think that's it?"

Lucille did a double take. Then she furrowed her brow. "Come now. Unless you're hiding something truly nefarious, I fully intend to be on your side."

"That *is* all." Sera rounded on her, her visage open and earnest. "We came into Liberty lands with one goal in mind. We wanted a Liberty deck, because that would enable us to create a Wellspring with all five decks and create a proper home, a safe home, for all."

"She's making it sound so warm and fuzzy, isn't she?" Kith smirked. "We were gonna steal the deck, Lucille. Not heroes."

Sera brushed him off before acknowledging the point with a grudging nod. "He is not wrong. We were also planning to help our imprisoned friend be in a position to eventually help you all stand up against the Savior."

"True. That's when we met you. Trying to figure out a way to sneak into the palace." Chase tapped his lips. "Okay, I have a thought. Lucille, you are clearly trying to look for the catch here. Like, what's going to be the hidden cost? What are our hidden motives? When are we going to take over as the new overlords?" He snorted. "Thing is, we don't care about any of that. We're simple people. Especially Liam."

Lucille's wide eyes, confused, taking everything in, slid toward Liam, who nodded happily in agreement.

"But," Chase said, drawing her eyes back on him. "Nobody's going to believe that. Who kills a ruler, only to walk off into the sunset? Nobody, that's who. So, I say we're going to come up with a short list of entirely fair demands, that aren't going to bankrupt Liberty. That way, we get to walk off with our pockets filled, and nobody in Liberty will need to be afraid that we're going to come back and take over, because we've already gotten what we want."

"I *love* this plan!" Kith burst out.

"What are we talking about here?"

Chase shrugged. "A cart or two filled with...quality crafted items? Food? Books...for Cilia, obviously."

"I also want to peruse the Savior's crafting stations. I'm dead sure he took all the best crafting material for himself, and I *want* some," Cilia said.

"I want a fancy helmet." Liam beamed. "Something with a feather."

Their gaze turned to Sera.

"I do not need anything. I also do not like the idea of extorting them, but...the logic is sound. If this is what it takes for Liberty society to start over with a clean break, then so be it. Honestly, I would just want to know that things are off to a good start before we leave. Knowing that your society will not devolve into squabbles and warfare would be a boon to me."

Lucille shook her head, her voice hoarse. "Let me be entirely clear about this. Nobody—*nobody* expected the Savior to die. For him to be replaced...the initial expectation would be that you step into his place. If you have no intentions of doing that? It will be a confusing period." She hesitated, then pressed on. "To be honest, having you here, in the background, while we figure out where to go from here, is likely going to be the best deterrent to anybody tempted to grasp for the reins of power in the interim."

They talked for a while, before Lucille was proved right. One other pillar had arrived, along with dozens of minds, and soon, everybody was clamoring to learn what was going to happen.

They decided to move the setting. Or, rather, Lucille did. Following their chat, she was like a transformed person. Lit with an inner fire, she took charge and corralled everybody to the room holding the huge, magical map over the Liberty areas.

There, she explained what had happened, reiterating all she knew, as well as what their group wanted. Following that speech, everything devolved into utter chaos again.

Everybody was waiting for somebody to take the lead and explain what was going to happen. When Lucille said that whatever happened, *she* would push for a society where no one leader would set the course for their lives, the weight of what was happening seemed to coalesce into clarity for a lot of them. People started to speak up, most coming up with issues, but a few offering ideas, propositions for reform.

The evening passed. Night fell. Still people argued, asked questions, *demanded* answers, reassurance, guidance. There were constant explanations about what had happened.

At some point, somebody brought news that Reen and Nordon had been located and released. They had not been treated well, but were resting and recuperating, while healers attended to them.

Their group didn't talk much. They explained their situation and reasoning once, then stepped into the background, letting the locals do the talking.

The next day dawned. Not much had been decided, though the numbers of people present grew as the news of what was happening spread like wildfire in Salvation.

Eventually, Kith yawned loudly enough to be heard even over the ever-present chatter of a hundred constant ongoing conversations. "Listen, Lucille, I don't know about you all, but I'm beat. I need a bed, and the chance to sleep. Besides, it doesn't feel like there's going to be a lot decided tonight."

She nodded. "You may be right. I'm still not taking the chance to miss any of what is going on." She held a hand in front of her mouth, hiding a yawn of her own. "We might end up retiring for a few hours, soon. I think we will need to decide on a few vital things first, however. Do you need a place to stay?"

"No," Cilia announced with finality. "I believe it's best that we stay in a place where anybody with a grudge won't be able to find us. We'll just slink off into the darkness."

"Yep. Just doing one thing before we take off." Chase grinned, wide enough you barely noticed the bags under his eyes. "I'm nipping off to grab a deck for us. Imagine that we came through all of this, only for some bloody thief to steal 'em all before we did!"

CHAPTER 34

"I thought, once I finally became a leader, I could help end corruption. Especially in a place as insular as Liberty, where you only have to take into account the demands of a single people. Except, even here, a thousand hands pull in a thousand different directions. How can this be changed? How can people improve?" Whoo boy. Those aren't red flags. They're city-sized red banners. Even knowing where this led to, my stomach's clenching up. (Book 1, Page 7.)

"**I** feel *amazing!*" Liam groaned and stretched. "You'd never think we've slept on the damn floor again."

They were back in the hideout. After leaving the palace, Chase activated Circle of Darkness, and, along with the guidance of Kith's shadows (and a whole lot of over-tired nonsense about how much Kith missed the shades) they'd walked straight home and collapsed. Now, at least six hours later, they were alone, slowly waking and trying to come to terms with the new world.

"What's happening today, then? We've killed a *god*! How do you top that?" Kith flung himself down on a chair, cursing as it almost tipped to deposit him on the floor.

"You don't!" Cilia said drily from where she sipped a cup of water at the table. "We are not topping anything. Ever. This is it. We've officially peaked, and I am *more* than happy with it. I am going to find a place to become a hermit for at least a decade or two!"

"Not before we have helped Liberty transition into a peaceful society that is *not* at the beck and call of a murderous madman!" Sera scolded with a smile.

A series of groans arose in response, along with Liam's whiny, "Do we have to?"

"I think you're forgetting a few tiny details." Chase smiled. He held up a burlap sack and extracted a softly glowing set of cards for all to see. "I mean, we're not building a Wellspring yet, but that doesn't mean that we can't celebrate."

Liam slowly got up and walked closer to the set of cards lighting up the small living room. "Celebrating by gaining Tier four cards?" He snorted. "That even beats cake. *Nothing* beats cake!"

"Are you all ready for this?" Chase leapt to his feet. "I am going to absorb this shiny little tidbit, and we will be the first people in living history to have absorbed decks from all five factions."

"Wait!" Cilia opened a small journal and set up quill and ink. "*Now*, I'm ready! I want all the sordid details."

Chase, chuckling, took a deep breath, and concentrated.

[You have located a Deck of Liberty. As the holder of a Deck of Darkness, you have the option to accept cards from it or bond with the deck, absorbing it. Which do you choose?]

Absorb. Finally. They had come such a long way for this: traversed what felt like the entirety of Ordei; been backstabbed—literally and figuratively; had done some backstabbing themselves; robbed, cheated, lied, and impersonated others. Now, they were finally getting what they'd earned.

The deck seemed to fall *into* Chase's body. A sea of stars settled on him, simultaneously hitting him with the impact of a butterfly's touch and a mental tidal wave, threatening to overwhelm him with sensations.

[You have bonded with a Deck of Liberty. From now on, through you, anybody may share in the gifts of Liberty. In addition, any Wellspring you create will be strengthened, carrying attributes and granting bonuses born of Dark, Light, the Elements, Fury, and Liberty.]

He sighed in relief. It had worked. Even though he knew it would, deep inside, he'd been waiting for something to arrive and ruin the moment. Wait—!

[You have continued working to restore the balance. Absorbing additional decks from other aspects and adding them to the wielders of the Deck of Darkness further tips the scale in the right direction. As a reward, the first ten card wielders of Darkness are granted an additional bonus to their Title based on their class.

You have received +2 to Agility per Tier from the rogue class.

From the secondary Deck absorbed, Light, you have received a boost to your health. Detrimental effects to your attributes and mentality last only half as long, and you are much less likely to fall ill.

From the third Deck added, Elemental, you have received a bonus of +1 to all attributes.

From the fourth Deck added, Fury, you have received the power of the soil. Whenever you are in the vicinity of soil blessed with the strength of a Wellspring with which you are aspected, you will gain an additional temporary +5 boost to all attributes.

From the final Deck added, Liberty, and by gathering the entire range of aspects, you have received the freedom of a better range of choices. For the purpose of determining the rarity of a card, the Potential of any wielder granted cards from your decks will be calculated at a fifty percent increase.]

Chase sank to his knees.

"Chase! What's the matter?"

A golden light fell over him, along with a weird, tinkling sensation, as Sera hit him with the healing wave of Warmth of the Circle. He blinked and stared off into the distance. "I am ascending. Becoming light. Evolving into the next Savior."

Kith rolled his eyes. "Okay, forget it. He's just being an ass."

"Not *just*!" Chase protested. "Seriously. This is insane!" He went on to explain the new change.

"Hold on. Let me just get this straight," Liam said. "You're telling me, that even somebody like me, who's never spent a *single* point in Potential, is going to have a seventeen in Potential, which is likely to nearly always net me Uncommon cards or better?"

"No." Chase laughed. "You're forgetting the Fury bonus. Whenever we're near a Wellspring, it'll *always* be a Wellspring we're aspected with from here on out! That means twenty-two."

"Between twenty-one and twenty-four, depending on whether the Fury bonus is calculated first or last, and whether it is rounded down or up," Sera adjusted.

"What about me?" Chase asked softly. "I'm at...thirty-four. What would that have me at?"

"Fifty-six," she whispered. "At least."

"I...don't even know what that means in practice." Chase rubbed his face.

"It means that when you're choosing your new Tier five card, you're pretty much guaranteed only Rares and better. Possibly Epic and better."

"That's ridiculous. Utterly, utterly ridiculous!" Chase muttered.

"Speaking of ridiculous." Kith smirked. "You haven't even offered any of us any cards. Even though there's something..." He trailed off. "Fury drain my veins."

"Now what?" Cilia asked.

"I was so tired yesterday, I didn't notice. I was the one who killed the Savior," Kith said.

"Yeah? Oh. Oooh! Tell us!" he whispered. "How many Steps did you gain?"

"Five!" His hand reached up to grasp the lock of hair that had started going grey. The hand shook slightly.

"Tier five!" Chase flung himself over and hugged the stunned man. "You made it! You absolute nutcase!" He laughed uproariously. "Nearly Tier six, even! If Instructor Brookwatch was right—"

"She is. She was the best instructor ever, outside of Master Benneth," Cilia said with finality.

Ignoring her, Chase pressed on. "Then this means that you've just gained at least another fifty years to live! And now, with everything that's happened, we'll be strong enough to face down whatever we need to *without* that ridiculous Heart card of yours."

"I...It's not ridiculous." Kith sounded entirely out of it.

"I don't *care* what it is," Chase barked. "All I care about is that now, we have forever to tease you about going grey this young!"

With a sound somewhere between a sob and a laugh, Kith shook his head. "You would, wouldn't you?" He cleared his throat and turned to Cilia, furiously wiping at his eyes. "Cil. Let's talk about something else, *please*! How do we choose this time around? What's the strategy?"

Cilia ignored his attempt at distraction. She got up from her chair, walked over and hugged Kith. Then she beamed a smile at all of them that was so unlike her, she seemed like an entirely different person. "I don't know. I also don't care. This is the best day of my life."

Kith clung onto her and started to sob.

Deciding that he'd best save Kith from the onslaught of emotions, Chase asked, "Ah. So, you agree that my idea of killing a god was excellent, and you were wrong to doubt me, Cil?"

From over Kith's shoulder, she glared. "That is *not* what happened!" Cilia said.

"Well, from here on out, that's how I'm telling the story, and you can't stop me." Chase waited for a moment. "And there's the frown back. Now I know you again."

Sera slapped his shoulder. "Moron." She beamed at Kith. "I am truly grateful you made it, Kith. As for your obvious diversion—might I come with a suggestion?"

He croaked. "Please! Save me, princess! All this talking about emotions is making me feel, and I don't like it."

She rolled her eyes. "Honestly, at this point, we have what we need for any fight that might come our way. I suggest that, whatever we choose today, we choose with an eye for the future!" She pointed at Cilia. "That might mean choosing a card that helps you being more comfortable when crafting, or even learning new techniques, if that's even possible." She tapped her own breastbone. "It could also be like my own Home Defender card, where we get to improve the attributes of wherever we call home. Choices that aid us wherever we decide to settle down." Smiling, she shrugged. "I truly believe, at this point, we should simply go with whichever route feels more comfortable to us. We have all the time we need ahead of us, and we have the luxury of being able to focus on whatever we want."

"Do whatever you want..." Liam cracked his knuckles. "I doubt I can actually mess that up!"

"Want to go first?" Chase asked.

Liam beamed. "You know what? Sure. I'm up for it."

Chase leaned forward and tapped the big guy on the bicep.

Immediately, Liam faded into a world of his own. He grunted, smiled, and even gave a long, low chuckle. Eventually, he clenched his fists tightly, as shudders rippled through him. Then he opened his eyes and smiled.

[**End to Strife**
Rare, Liberty fighter
Tier four
Passive, permanent
A good fighter knows that he can't win all fights. A *great* fighter is one who ensures that he only needs to fight when he wants to. When wielded, this card grants the fighter a mile-wide aura which works as a deterrent against otherwise naturally hostile wildlife and Guardians. The strength and efficacy of the aura is based on the combination of his Strength and Toughness.

"All those fangs, and such nasty claws. Yet, still, you didn't have the wisdom to turn around when you had the choice." The Penitent reflects over his life.]

"I love it," Kith said. "Picture using that on those carved plains? You'd have had half of them running right the other way. Maybe even that stupid behemoth would've thought twice before trying to eat us."

"It didn't really seem the type to think even once," Cilia drawled. "I still agree. This is wonderful. And it's permanent, meaning, when we find a place to settle down, you can wield it and forget all about it. It will still work to protect our home, even when you're asleep."

"Only one other detail," Liam said. "I hit my twenty-fourth Step, too. Right on the cusp of Tier five. Judging from Chase there, it'll probably be a while before I reach it, though."

Sera went next. She was, as usual, more stoic as she selected. Once she was done, however, she relaxed into a satisfied sigh. "Now, I truly cannot wait to find a place to settle down."

[**Free from the Sickness**
Rare, Liberty healer
Tier four
Passive, permanent
Most healers live their lives moving from one sickness to the next, dedicating most of their time and energy to fighting smaller battles. Wielding this card, the healer is able to safeguard their energy for the true life-and-death situations. Within a radius of five hundred feet of the healer, any smaller ills will automatically be reduced or outright cured, depending on the severity and the period of time spent within the area.

"Ah, yes. You pay to live here. But think of it. Guaranteed health. Is that not worth the price?"]

"Huh." Liam scratched his head. "Is that...good? It seems kind of weak!"

Sera shook her head fondly. "I sometimes forget that none of you really know the life of a healer. How about this? Back in Cemano, this card would likely have saved me about half to two-thirds of my work every single day."

"I think she'd be able to cure hangovers too," Chase whispered.

"Really?" Liam gawked. "Okay. I take it back. That's wonderful!"

She ignored them both. "Picture this. With the wording of the card, as long as I actually move about our home, I would be able to cure any smaller ills *before* they turn into anything serious. Curing a cough before it turns into pneumonia. Catching an infection that, left untreated, could have cost somebody a toe, or at least a fever. The vast majority of illnesses do not start out severe."

"Oh. In that case...well done?" Liam grinned.

"Thank you. That was all from me. Now. Chase. We are definitely saving you for last. A Tier four card with over fifty Potential...that is something to savor. Cilia?"

Cilia smiled and reached out a hand across the table toward Chase. Mere seconds later, she sighed and leaned back in the chair with a blissful smile.

"This isn't like yours. It isn't going to change anything large-scale. But I love it."

[**Personal Resonance: Leather**
Uncommon, Liberty crafter
Tier four

Passive, permanent

Only one Personal Resonance card can ever be chosen. It offers you a choice of generic materials. From here on, you will find that this material is able to absorb and hold thirty percent more magic, allowing you to create more powerful items across the board.

The effect of the card will remain active, regardless whether you switch to another Tier four card.

"Supposedly, this creation should be impossible. But they don't know me. And they don't know how much I love winning bets." Master Crafter Hermionous on his defining masterpiece.]

Cilia smiled softly. "That should help me overcome some of the difficult limits when crafting. More and more, I have found that the issue isn't having the mental or physical fortitude to craft what I want. Rather, it's that the materials are unable to bear as much power as I would prefer to put into it."

Liam smiled. "So, your normal droplets will be thirty percent more powerful."

"Liam...*anything* I craft from here on will be thirty percent more powerful, as long as I have the fortitude to keep going."

"Which she does." Sera added, "Also, she is mistaken. This is very much going to change something large-scale." She gave Cilia a fond smile. "Wherever we settle down, we all know you are not just going to craft for us. Think of it, Cilia. You have the rest of your life to craft, learn and improve. The difference that your creations will be able to make in a new-founded settlement is immense. Better protective gear. Your droplets. Items to boost attributes, to shield, to improve *anything*!"

"Anything?" Cilia smirked.

Sera coughed. "That may have gotten away from me a bit at the end."

"Still, I appreciate the sentiment," Cilia said. "And you're likely right. It's not like we've ever stayed in one place long enough to get settled. But the idea of building a place from nothing, with strong, crafted items to improve all manner of things? I can't say I dislike it. Also, if I ever hit Tier five, this is going to be my choice for upgrading. I can only imagine that the percentage will increase!"

From the fire in her eyes, her not disliking the idea was a hefty understatement.

Kith chuckled. "I, for one, look forward to having my very own personal craftswoman. You can make leather underpants, right?"

"I can. I'm not sure if I can craft something that can make its contents shrink, though. Let's call it a test."

"On second thought, I'm a huge fan of cotton." Kith snorted, then waved off the laughter. "Speaking of tests, it would appear that I'm next?"

"Normally, I would say something about how this *would* test my patience." Cilia frowned, but couldn't maintain the negative facade. "But I'm in an excellent mood right now. Do your worst, Kith!"

He laughed, the sound slightly unhinged. "I am about to gain *six* cards. Five of them will be Tier five, and my Potential is at twenty-six even before any boosts. I'm not sure we all appreciate just how bad my worst could be!"

Chase got up and walked over to him. "Brother. You *are* the worst." He paused, smiling at the shorter Furyborn. His hand shot out and clasped Kith's. "But you're also the best. You've kept it a secret just how much you've sacrificed to keep us all safe over the years. Even if you choose all six cards simply to summon nubile personal servants to fawn over you and feed you grapes, I say you've earned it."

"Oh, come *on*," Kith said hoarsely. "Now you're basically guilting me into picking something unselfish."

"Is it working?" Chase beamed.

Kith rolled his eyes and sat down again, getting comfortable with his back against the wall. His eyes flung wide open. "I forgot. I have five free points. I could throw them all into Potential if I wanted. That would give me...*tons* of Potential! What do I *do*?"

Name: Kith
Title: Dark/Light/Elemental/Fury/Liberty summoner
Step: 29 (Tier 5)
Strength: 19 (+1 Tier bonus) (+5) = 25
Agility: 24 (+1 Tier bonus) (+5) = 30
Toughness: 19 (+1 Tier bonus) (+5) = 25
Mental Power: 24 (+1 Tier bonus) (+5) = 30
Potential: 11 (+15 Tier bonus) (+5) = 31
Points available: 5

Sera nodded, with a no-nonsense attitude. "That depends entirely on what you want. Throwing everything into Potential will net you seven or eight additional points when it comes to calculating the rarity of your new cards. That could mean increasing the rarity of your offered cards by one across the board—possibly a bit less. However, that is a gamble. Whether that is what you want, or you would rather improve some of your other attributes? People rarely get a chance like this."

Kith gritted his teeth, looking around for support. Eventually, he sighed. "No. I'll leave the gambling to Chase this time around. I haven't spoken about this much, but the more summons I get, the harder they are to control properly. Five summons are no problem. But with Twice the Fun, I can end up with dozens of summoned creatures, with different physiques and minds. It's...taxing. I am going to do what Cilia talked about all that time ago, and increase my Mental Power so I can keep up. That said? I'm ready." He closed his eyes.

"Anybody want tea?" Liam said. "This could take awhile."

It did take awhile. At least twenty minutes later, they watched as Kith's head repeatedly hit the wall behind him. The uncontrolled spasming stopped after about ten seconds, leaving Kith panting as though he'd just run a sprint.

Sera was right in front of him, reaching out, when he opened his eyes and waved her away.

"Wow. That was special. Strongest one yet." He shivered.

"Carrrds," Liam groaned. "Now!"

"Okay, okay." Kith cleared his throat. "First was the Tier five upgrade. I went with Twice the Fun for obvious reasons. It's at Legendary now. And it was entirely the right choice!"

[...**Twice the Fun**
Legendary, Elemental summoner
Tier two
Passive, permanent
Sometimes, you crave something new and interesting. Sometimes, the best choice is simply more of what you already have. This card, when chosen, will double the number of summoned creatures for every card outside of Tier two.
"You think my summoned squirrels underwhelming? Wait 'till I show you...more squirrels!"]

"That is *so* ridiculous!" Sera burst out. "Well done, Kith."

"Thanks, princess." He laughed. "It'll put my improved Mental Power to the test. I'd have been quite fine with it working on four cards, but Legendary just makes a difference, it seems."

Chase snorted. "Sticky Fingers agrees with you! Now. Go on—tell us what else you got."

[**Burst of Disruption**
Rare, Liberty summoner
Tier four
Active, instant
This card summons an intangible spirit that, once summoned, will slowly seek out and meld with any nearby hostile with an active card effect. Once melded, the card will unravel

the energy in said effect into an explosion, with its power dependent on the effect canceled, and continue to the next target. The spirit will keep searching for targets until its power has been spent.

Medium cooldown

"Proper planning prevents poor—aargh!" A cleric blows up.]

"That's ridiculous and I love it!" Liam laughed.

"Could be truly powerful." Sera nodded.

"Mmm-hm," Cilia agreed. "The fact that it's moving slowly is a weakness. Even though it's intangible, magic can likely slay it before it impacts. Even so? Wonderful card. Self-targeting, weakening, disrupting, *and* damaging in one!"

"Next!" Chase burst, as he slapped the table. "Show us those sexy Tier five cards already!"

Rolling his eyes, Kith moved on.

[**Light of Day, Day of Darkness**

Rare, Light/Dark summoner

Tier five

Passive, long duration

This card summons a dozen sturdy humanoid beings of magic. The beings themselves are unremarkable. Yet, when summoned, they create a vast field between them in which magic is created. At night, they bring light. In the day, they bring darkness. Never again will this summoner be left to the vagaries of nature.

Medium cooldown

"Night divide day, day erase night. Light of day, day of darkness." The Green Carnation brings beauty.]

Liam whistled. "Damn. Never let it be said that Tier five cards aren't powerful. That can turn a battlefield totally on its head. Drown an army in darkness during the day. Or blind them with light at night, making them easier to hit in an ambush."

"The applications outside of battle should also be immense." Sera frowned. "With a long duration and just medium cooldowns in between, you could have people working on important projects all throughout the night, with just short breaks."

"Or you could get a good night's sleep, even if your blinds are broken and there's a crowd with torches *right* outside your window." Chase nodded. "What? It could happen."

"Ignore him, please," Sera said. "That is what I do."

Kith smiled. "You don't have to tell me. Now, the next one might be the weakest of my choices. I am so looking forward to seeing what it does, though."

[**Internal Spark**
Epic, Elemental summoner
Tier five
Permanent, passive
Summoned creatures are, by and large, only as effective as their summoner. Even the most powerful summoned beings will be diminished in effectiveness if their summoner is slow to give them the right commands. This card will aid with that, imbuing every creature summoned by this wielder with an inner fire, granting them limited mental faculties and independence. They will still follow every command, but will be able to understand more detailed commands.

The effect of the card will remain active, regardless whether you switch to another Tier five card.

"Creations, they call you. Pfah. My children. That is what you are. Now be seated and listen, my dears."]

"Get it over with, please," Kith droned. "Everything about how my summons can finally act like somebody's intelligent around here. Get it out of your system, so we can move on."

"We were planning *nothing* of the sort!" Liam protested.

"Definitely not!" Chase added.

"They might, but I would not," Sera said earnestly.

"I mean," Chase mused after a few seconds, "if the card text explicitly talks about our summoner being slow..." He trailed off, failing to hide even the slightest of his enjoyment.

"Any. One. Of you. Mocks Kith for this choice, and I'm giving you defective droplets next time," Cilia scolded. "This is the perfect choice. Having even slightly autonomous summons will grant you an insane edge over everybody else. The fact that it's always active, even when you don't have it equipped, is insane!"

"Right?" Kith burst out eagerly. "I can give them more general commands, have them act for themselves. It'll allow me to focus less on the details, and more on the overall plan, so I can fight better for myself." He paused before adding, "Of course, them earning more personality means I will have to come up with names for *all* of them."

They groaned as one.

"This one, for instance, I call the Slayer!"

[**Chariot of the Land**
Epic, Fury summoner
Tier five
Active, very long duration

The land provides. That is a well-known fact for any Furyborn. With this card, the land even provides transportation. When activated, it summons a grand chariot, drawn by four powerful summoned steeds, to do the summoner's bidding.

Long cooldown

"An army lives on its stomach—but it marches on its feet. Those poor plebeians." Summoner General Otensis knows his worth.]

"Kith!" Cilia sputtered. "That has got to be the most luxurious, lazy choice you have ever made."

Kith smirked. "So, what you're saying is that you still prefer to walk?"

"I—"

"I love it!" Chase interrupted. "That's going to make everything so much easier—not to mention efficient! We'll be able to outrun almost everything, cut down on travel time. Pits. If it says 'grand' chariot, we might even be able to sleep on it. There's no way any chasing Lightborn can catch us now! And with your Twice the Fun card we can even have two!"

Liam groaned. "The Slayer. A sleigh. I get it now. You're the worst!"

They burst into laughter.

Kith wiped his eyes. "Aah. I needed that." He blinked. "So, who's been keeping count?"

"One more. Have you been saving the best for last?" Cilia asked.

He nodded, suddenly doubtful. "I...think so?" Shrugging, he looked at the floor. "You know I'm not the best at this large-picture stuff. It feels powerful, though."

[**Monument of Pride**
Rare, Liberty summoner
Tier five
Permanent, passive
Few people reach the heights where they can see beyond their own horizons to consider the plights of their brethren. Yet, those who do are revered and praised above all else. This card, when activated, crystalizes into a permanent, large statue, exuding a powerful aura. The aura will increase the rarity of all new cards for all friendly summoners, except the wielder, within a five-mile radius by one.

The effect of the card will remain active, regardless whether you switch to another Tier five card. However, if the statue is razed, the card will remain permanently inactive.

"First among equals, you call me? Look at this monument and think again."]

Cilia sat at the table, unmoving. Tears slowly started to well up in her eyes. "Kith. I am so gods-damned proud of you!"

"Erm. Really? I wasn't sure, 'cause it's permanent, and it won't help any of us—"

"Kith, shut up, while I'm praising you," she scolded. "We are building a home. Not just a temporary settlement like Soil, or a village that can conveniently be moved like Cemano. A home. Like Earth's Ward, but with the potential for so much more. This single card not only raises the efficiency of all summoners already there—once its existence gets out, it's going to help ensure that people will want to move there. You, Kith, single-handedly just made sure that *all* summoners will want to become part of our town."

Kith looked on, open-mouthed.

Cilia didn't waver, though. She continued. "In fact, I believe that, whatever else happens, the most important choice you can possibly make, when you inevitably reach Tiers six and seven, will be increasing the rarity of this card. Imagine if it increases the rarity to *two*. You could have a home *filled* with wielders of legendary cards."

Kith scratched his neck. "Oh, I figured we could have that anyway. I mean, I'd want to use my Twice the Fun card on this one when I summon the statue. Two statues would be better than one, right? Hey, if I got two statues increasing two ranks each, would that give anybody earning cards instant Legendary cards? That'd be a sight!"

Cilia looked as though she were having an apoplectic fit. Her eyes blinked incessantly, and the corners of her mouth twitched uncontrollably.

Sera came to her rescue. "Listen, Kith. I very much doubt that is how they will work. However, if it is, I am sure they will erect additional statues to celebrate your statues. Only, it will be awhile before we will be in a position to activate it—so, maybe we should move on?"

"Be glad to," Kith said. "Time to focus on somebody else for a change." He winked at Chase. "No pressure."

"Yeah. None at all. Appreciate it." He cracked his neck. "Okay. Let's see what Liberty has to offer a man with above fifty in Potential."

The full-body shudder was harder than anything he'd ever tried before, like he imagined being constantly inside an active lightning storm, but at full power. Chase found himself looking *up* at Sera, whose eyes were wide open in shock. He gave a rattling laugh. "Whoa. Okay. New rule. Nobody picks new cards mid-combat. That could go *really* wrong."

"Are you okay?" she asked. "That looked like a seizure."

"Felt like it too." He smirked. "I have a hypothesis."

"Oh no. Is it contagious? Can Sera cure it?" Liam asked. Then he grinned. "Just kidding. You deserve that for trying to talk clever like Sera. It sounds fake when you do it!"

"Ignoring Liam now." Chase glowered at him. "I think that it's not just the Tier, but also the rarity of your card that affects how bad the sensation is."

"Are you saying what I think you're saying?" Cilia asked.

Chase nodded eagerly. "I was offered two Rares, two Epics...and one Legendary."

[Stealing is Giving, Too
Legendary, Liberty rogue
Tier four
Passive/active, extremely long duration
Rogues are often reviled—for rather good reasons, too. However, there are those among the class who operate in the morally grey areas, doing good as well as bad. This card adheres to that principle, taking and giving at the same time.

When activated, the wielder gets to borrow an attribute point of their choice from a friendly person in short range. He can continually maintain one borrow for each point of his Potential. Once the duration runs out, the point is automatically returned. However, there is a small chance that the attribute of the borrower in question is improved permanently by +1 upon return.

"So, it's in my own interest that you steal from me? Get out of here, woman!"]

Cilia rubbed her forehead. "Let me see if I understood this right. You can 'borrow' fifty-plus attribute points, at all times, from the same number of people near you."

"Only thirty-nine. The added fifty percent to Potential is for new cards alone," Sera said.

"That's how I understood it too, yeah." Chase nodded at Sera.

"*Only* thirty-nine points." Cilia's lip twitched. "The same as the combined attributes of a normal non-wielder! And you can keep getting new boosts from persons at any point, when one of these runs out."

"Yup. I think."

"And when they *do* run out, the person you're using it on has a chance to receive a permanent increase to their attribute?" Cilia continued.

"A 'small' chance, which translates to...Sera?" Chase asked.

"Likely five to ten percent," Sera responded.

Cilia leaned back in her chair and rubbed her eyes. "Okay. We need to find Nordon." Ignoring the reactions from the others, she continued. "With this, and Kith's monument card, we're going to see the largest influx of inhabitants any settlement in the history of Ordei has ever seen. *Free attributes!* Everybody's going to want to join us!"

Sera nodded somberly. "I believe you may be right. However, I am unsure as to what that has to do with Nordon."

Cilia snickered. "Oh, I just felt the overwhelming need to get myself very, very drunk."

CHAPTER 35

"I have been stuck, searching for the proper path forward. Always, what I saw would lead me straight back to repeating former self-destructive patterns. Were I to take power, others would eventually tear me down. But now I see it. I see the path. It will require a lot of sacrifices, but it may be doable. I have learned that, according to history, when you establish the very first Wellspring, you get to create the rules for the Wellspring yourself. Rules, which you can tailor to your desired utopia. Now, it is but a matter of planning." So, it was not only premeditated, he actively searched for a way to mold society into what he desired. With the best of intentions, of course. We should kill him all over again. (Book 1, Page 16.)

Not only was Nordon doing well, he was already hard at work dispersing drinks to the locals and making himself indispensable. It was rather easy to find him. They just had to return to where they'd left the locals in the palace, hard at work, attempting to build the future society of Liberty.

"I can't believe you did it," Nordon hissed under his breath. He looked wild-eyed, his usual calm demeanor far gone. "You know what I'm talking to them about right now? Opening trade with Earth's Ward and the Elementals!"

Kith raised an eyebrow. "But you're not in a position to talk on behalf of the Elementals."

"I know! But they don't know that! *Isn't it wonderful?*" Nordon huffed at Sera. "Oh, come now. Don't give me that look. You and I both know what's going to happen when I go back to Earth's Ward and tell them that I've got an exclusive trade agreement with Liberty, just ready for them to sign, and a bunch of Liberators tagging along to prove I'm not hallucinating."

Sera turned on him. "Nordon. We are staying here in Salvation for a while, *entirely* to ensure that the society that will emerge doesn't fall back to the predations of the old Savior. That *also* includes anybody trying to abuse them, trying to establish new trade channels!"

Nordon held a hand over his heart. "You hurt me! I would never—" Then he guffawed, interrupting himself. "Okay, I might. How about this: I promise that I won't try to eke any percentages out for myself. The only thing I'll try to attempt is to ingratiate myself with everybody and make myself entirely indispensable to all involved. That way, my contacts will increase, and I will have access to learning everything I could ever want." His eyes blazed with an eagerness that was near tangible.

Sera nodded. "That sounds decidedly fair. Try to help them as best you can."

With a brilliant smile, Nordon turned back to the Liberators, calling the name of one of the minds among them.

Kith smirked at his back. "What a two-faced bastard."

"What?" Sera asked. "Should we—?"

"Oh, I mean that in the very best way."

"That...is not how language works, Kith!"

"Shows what you know." He waved off her denial. "So. Anybody caught up with what's happening?"

Chase returned with a mug in his hand. He took a deep drag, blinked, and took another. "Nordon's had fun. Cold and spicy. That is *so* weird. Anyway, yes. Cil's been talking to them about those poor bastards upstairs."

"The summoners?" Kith asked.

"Yup. Turns out, there was a method to it. There were a number of cards which the officials recommended people to take if they had the chance. Only, if you did take them, what they earned you was the possibility to access the Keepers and a one-way trip upstairs. Oh, and the poor things *all* had their tongues removed." Chase grimaced. "Probably so they couldn't cry out and attract attention, stuff like that."

"But what about...everything. Food, waste, all that stuff?" Liam asked. "What if somebody *died*? I mean, you can't just ignore all that."

"He was a god to them." Chase shrugged. "He could likely have done it right in the open, and nobody would've complained. But he was all about keeping up an image, that lying piece of garbage! Anyway, some of the fresh arrivals among the summoners are less, erm, taxed, mentally. And the Liberators are working to get communications up and running again."

"What? No!" Sera burst out.

Chase laughed. "No. Don't worry. Not like that. They're saying that it'd be good to maintain the communication all through their lands, and remove all the surveillance. Just employ the summoners to communicate and coordinate. Make it a real job, honorable...not a prison sentence. Sounds like most of the old summoners like the idea of that. Being able to help." His grin grew even wider. "The summoners are also not hating that the first message they'll be sending *everywhere* is one where they explain what's happening, outlining the Savior's crimes."

Kith whistled. "They're doing that? Bold move."

"Yeah. There's bound to be a lot of chaos and kickback, once the message is sent out. But honestly, I think it's the right choice. If they tried to somehow hide it, soften the blow, it would lead to trouble down the road." Chase cracked up in a warm smile. "But what do I know? I'm just here to scare away anybody who tries to stab their new government."

"Me too, brother. Me too. Leave politics to filthy nobles and whatnot." Kith winked at Sera.

They looked at the myriad Liberators milling about. To their surprise, today, the crowd also contained hopefuls and others with rougher looks, clearly not the administrators the palace was used to.

"They're letting the mass and the hopefuls enter now?" Kith asked.

"Yes. I suggested it," Sera admitted unabashedly. "Building a new society by ignoring eighty percent of the populace or more seemed like an untenable choice. There are still many decisions to be made, and a lot of questions on how to unite them and work for a fair society, but...I approve of what they have done so far."

"Huh. Sounds like we'll be off before we know it, then." Kith managed to flag down a harried waiter and secure a mug for himself. "I'll have to admit, I look forward to it. All this *talk*! Liam's the only one who's made for that, I think!"

"What was that?" Liam smiled as he disentangled himself from a close discussion with a young woman and turned toward them.

"You like people, and talking, and it's weird." Kith rolled his eyes.

"Not that weird." Liam sent a coquettish wave and a wink at the woman. "It's not my fault if the girls like the Real Saviors!"

Cilia gaped at him. "I could *hear* the capitalization! Please tell me that's not a real thing."

Liam shrugged. "I mean, if they choose to repeat it, is it really wrong? We did save them—"

"I swear, Liam, if you set us up to be worshipped for the sake of tail, I will *geld* you," she hissed.

"Darkness hide me, Cil. Don't be like that. I won't do that—"

"Thank you, Liam."

"In the future." Liam finished awkwardly. "Maybe...I'd better go chat with a few girls again? Clear up a few misunderstandings?"

"Maybe," Cilia replied frostily.

"You know, Cil, don't be so hard on him. If they really, really like what we've done, who are we to fend off their gratitude?" Kith asked. "I'd better talk with a few, see if they're aware who *really* slew the Savior."

"Before you run off and earn Cilia's fury." Chase stopped him, ignoring the hissing sound emerging from Cilia. "What about the Furyborn elders? And the High Elementalist?"

"Oh, Cil helped me with a proper letter before we went to bed yesterday. Radine's already on her way. In a few days, they should learn what's going on. Then we can maybe even find a good spot to create our home." He grinned. "It'll be a number of days before we get a response, but I look forward to reading their reaction." He made a bad impression of Half-Swart's voice. "You did what? Explain yourselves! We asked you to get hold of a deck, not kill any heads of state!"

Chase laughed. "I mean, does it even count if we didn't originally set out trying to kill him?"

Sera was looking from one to the other with a horrified expression on her face when the shouting started.

Watching the effect of shouting on a crowd was always interesting. One detail to note was the marked difference between different societies. Lightborn were likely to grasp their purses first, then see whether the shouts affected them or not. Furyborn were likely to run to aid first, think about consequences next. Yet, the reactions also depended a lot on people's personalities. And Chase found it impressive how many people stepped up, eyes wide and alert, with the intention of *helping*.

It soon turned out that the half-panicked cries were caused by a message. A message that might be the precursor of more blood than an actual attack on the palace would have.

Pillar Lucille was the one who repeatedly cried for order and jumped up on a plinth with a statue of the Savior to catch everybody's attention. "*Thank* you. Now, let me repeat the news, so we can work up a response as soon as possible." She looked down, took a deep breath, and faced the crowd again. "It would appear that the Savior's death brought with it a number of unexpected consequences. As you all know, Devotion to Liberty is inactive, depriving us of the increased Title boost, but allowing us to retain all our Ænima."

"Get to the point," somebody in the crowd yelled.

"If you will let me?" she challenged. With a curt nod, she continued. "Most details of our society continuously function unimpeded. The same goes for crafted items in general. Only, a few of the more powerful crafted items in the palace have appeared to be made with certain...fail-safes in place, and have ceased to function. Some may be restored in time. Others seem to have been keyed to the Savior himself. Now that we are, ever so slowly, restoring contact with our Keepers out there, we are learning that the same applies to the rest of our lands. Most things continue unchanged." She shuddered, and spoke up. "Only, there is one notable outlier. The Prism is down."

That brought with it exactly the level of chaos anyone would have expected. For decades, the Prism had hid Liberty away from the rest of Ordei, while defending them and ensuring that any invaders would have to be severely weakened and disoriented, being whittled down as they approached, easy targets for their hopefuls. Now, they were going to return to a world where that was no longer the case.

Several hours later, Lucille drew them aside in the small sitting room again. While the death of the Savior had initially reinfused her with energy and a deeply felt desire to change her home, the past few hours looked as though they'd aged her a decade. "I am going to level with you. Everything—and I truly mean everything—is up in the air right now. This was too early. We were trying to build a sense of hope, but...I do not know if we can maintain it, knowing that our only defense might be gone and our hopefuls will be falling back, faced with Guardians and fighters too strong for them. I'm afraid that the first looters are going to start in the city within the next few days. Do you know anything that can help?"

Chase looked to the others. They didn't look less tense. "How do you define 'help'?"

"No." Cilia's gaze was murderous. "The answer is no. In fact, what we are going to tell you now is going to make things so much worse. Because, for the past month or more, right outside of your borders, you have had a large Lightborn army camped, waiting for an opening. And, inadvertently, we just gave them it."

CHAPTER 36

"I rejoiced too fast. I thought, with the Wellspring created, ensuring both the strength of my people, and for my own strength to grow, our world would be safe. Yet, the other nations are ever clamoring to affect our decisions, or to outright take over should we show an inkling of weakness. Perhaps it is time to leave them behind. Not for good—merely until our society has had a chance to find itself and settle." He actually meant it to be temporary? The more I read, the sadder and angrier I get. (Book 1, Page 28.)

"Whoo boy. She did *not* take that well." Kith leaned against the door he'd just shut after Lucille.

"Can't blame her," Liam mumbled. He'd seated himself on the floor with his head in his hands. "This is probably the worst mess we've ever caused."

Sera, pacing back and forth, slowed down. She started to laugh softly, with a tinge of hysteria. "We have removed the defenses of an entire nation at the same time that a large, hostile army is waiting right outside, and you say 'probably'?"

"Well. We've had a bit of experience causing messes lately." He shrugged.

Cilia had remained silent at the back of the room. "What do we want to do?" she asked earnestly. "Not what *can* we do. We'll figure that out. This is quite simple. What do we want to do? We have what we need to build our Wellspring and construct a permanent home somewhere. We have the Elementals and Furyborn waiting to aid us. But if we leave now, Liberty will be in a bad place."

Kith grimaced. "Let's not forget that the Lightborn lurking out there are after us in the first place. If we leave, can we make them chase after us, give the poor bastards here a reprieve and a chance to build up new defenses?"

A bronze statue to the Savior sat at the back of the room, in a cross-legged position of meditation. Chase, curled up in the lap of the statue, huffed. "That's like asking if you could keep a Waves cutpurse from robbing a fat merchant by parading another purse in front of him. Sure, they might get distracted for a while, but think about it. Liberty's an enigma, an unknown, and now, it's suddenly open to the Lightborn, ripe for the picking? There's no way they won't use this chance to invade."

With a grunt, Kith ceded the point. "So, we're back to that, are we? Flee or fight? Do we sacrifice ourselves for the good of people who've done nothing for us, or do we think of ourselves?"

"Feels like that *is* the real choice here," Liam admitted. "Also, we've faced off against Lightborn before. These won't be second-rate soldiers. These will be high-Tier crack troops—and they won't be crippled like the Liberty soldiers, who have crap first-Tier cards."

Kith groaned. "Yeah. Even if we wanted to help the poor Liberty sods, they'll always be handicapped by that. Sure, new wielders won't have to choose a useless card, but all veterans will be worth less than Lightborn at similar Tiers, because their first-Tier card is broken. Somebody should have a stern talk with the bastards who did that." He chuckled wryly. The smile didn't reach his eyes.

"Wait." Chase slowly got to his feet, throwing an arm around the neck of the over-dimensioned statue. "Cil. You've been reading the diaries of this madman. Would you be a dear and confirm again what we know about Wellsprings?"

She blinked, finger raised pensively to her lips. "Let's see. We've long known, and his writings confirm, that you get to make some general choices when you create your Wellspring. Arnault wrote some things in his unhinged annals, and both the Elementals and the Furyborn elders confirmed as much. We do not know what Arnault chose, though the wave of darkness rushing from his camp likely had something to do with it. As for the Lightborn, they have apparently focused on their city-building creations, such as the healing springs in the Waves, and the cards that the church offers to their inquisitors. The Furyborn, meanwhile, have their relationships with the Guardians, letting them co-exist alongside their population. Possibly, the Heart Halls have something to do with the Wellsprings as well, but that's speculation. The Elementals, we do not know. Yet, I would wager good money that it has to do with the towers." She waved in the direction of the Savior's tower. "As for Liberty, we all know what that was. That bloody Devotion to Liberty card."

"You don't think erecting the Prism was part of the Wellspring?" Chase looked downcast.

"No. I just got past that part of his diaries. The timeline doesn't match up. He created the Wellspring. Then, later on, he crafted the Prism. I believe, at least in part, that was actually one place where he did not dissemble. Either he somehow used some of the Ænima he received, or they were otherwise tied to his own self, or a card of his. I can't see how he could otherwise craft something that would work over such a long distance, in perpetuity."

"That would explain why they stopped working when he died. Urgh." Chase slapped his cheek softly. "Think, dammit. Think!"

"We're not inside your head, man." Liam smiled and leaned his head back against the wall. "What're you going on about?"

"Weighing the odds. Like Cil's taught us to do. But it all keeps coming back to what Kith said. Basically, our choice boils down to one of two options: either we jump ship and leave the bastards to fend for themselves, or we go all-in to aid them. We've got options for either of the two, but that's the bottom line. Agreed?"

"Let us see." Sera took a deep breath. "I shall try to keep my emotions out of this. If we leave, we will still be able to help. We could message the Elementals and the Furyborn, ask for their assistance against the Lightborn army—"

"We won't be able to for days, though." Kith interrupted. "Radine's off already, and I can't contact her from this far away. Also, it'll be weeks after that, possibly months, before any backup can arrive from the Furyborn lands or the Elemental towers."

"Yes." Sera ceded the point with a frown. "We could also, as Kith suggested, try to lead them off, or try to attack them, stall them, lead them the wrong way."

"I particularly like the one where we lead them the wrong way." Cilia nodded. "Yet, even if we succeeded in either of these, it would only delay the inevitable. With Liberty open, there will be more and more Lightborn amassing every day."

Sera nodded. "If, however, we throw in our lot with them, our options are...well, more or less the same. However, we will have a lot of people fighting along with us. The question, to put it frankly, is if it will be enough. This is a nation who is used to fighting dazed and confused enemies, who have been forced to pick useless and subpar cards, and who, with the Savior dead, might refuse to fight, rebel, or flee instead."

"Oof. Don't sugarcoat it on our behalf, princess," Kith said.

"I was not done. We will, theoretically, have huge numbers of people on our side—more than enough to beat this first army, I would say. Yet, with the future of Liberty thrown into question, the quality, commitment, and coherence of any troops to take our side will be a huge unknown. Meaning, we would be struggling to build a semblance of a governing body at the same time as we would be, quite literally, fighting for our lives. On top of that, *all* borders will be pressed, defending from Guardians, which will suddenly be much harder to kill than the hopefuls are used to."

They shared glances. For once, even Kith had no quips.

Chase pushed off the statue and asked Sera, "What would your choice be?"

"Please. Ask the do-gooder princess what she wants—"

"Stow it, Kith. You've said it yourself. Among us, we always get to say our piece. You get to argue that she's an idiot for whatever she chooses *afterward*."

"I want to run," Sera said.

"Wait. Really?" Kith's scrunched-up face made no secret of his confusion.

"Really." She nodded. Her eyes were wet, but she did not look away. "I want to help them as much as I can along the way. However, I also try to be realistic. Do we want to die trying to save a people we might not be able to save? Or do we try to create a long-term solution to everything, finally create a defense that will finish the onslaught of the Lightborn?"

"I— Wow. I guess I didn't see that coming." Kith scratched his head. "But it's hard to argue with that point. Looking at the larger picture, what's more important? Liberty, or the bloody world?" He took a deep breath. "On top of that, we've *done* what we could to help these poor bastards. Everything's not our responsibility. I say we leave, throw in an ambush, kick some Lightborn ass along the way, and then we find the Furyborn and start working on some serious long-term defenses. Who's with me?"

Liam started to nod slowly. His shoulders were tensed up, and his face closed.

Cilia looked uncomfortable and refused to say anything.

"I think...maybe we could have it all?" Chase said.

"Greed? I'm listening," Kith said eagerly.

"Not greed. Not this time." He took a deep breath. "You all know where we come from. What we've had to suffer through, what we've had to *risk,* simply in order to not die, to be allowed to grow stronger. Consider this, though. What if, at any point along this route, somebody had actually chosen to aid us. To give us a chance. Can you picture that?" He waited for a second. "Of course you can't. *Because it would change everything.* For all I know, if the bloody Church of the Circle had opened their doors to us, we could've been bloody inquisitors right this moment."

"That may be taking it a bit far," Liam rumbled. "But are you saying what I think?"

"I am. We could half-ass this. Leave the rest of the Liberty decks to them all, let 'em build a new Wellspring. Share enough Dark cards that we get another deck we could leave, for them to share. But none of us seriously thinks that would be enough to stop the Lightborn if they smell the chance for riches." He took a deep breath. "I say we take the damn chance—build the Wellspring, support them as best we can, and actually stand by them all the way. We want to build a new home where everybody's welcome? How about we start it *right* here, where tens of thousands of poor suckers have been cheated of their chances to choose proper cards?"

The others looked unconvinced.

"But Chase...we wanted a home where everybody is welcome. That's...not exactly how they think about outsiders here." Liam winced.

"Have they had the chance, Liam? They've never even *met* any outsiders, apart from on the battleground. Besides, saying we want everybody to join us and then leaving them all to fend for themselves...it requires a bit of mental gymnastics to accept, doesn't it?"

"It would be a major risk," Sera said. "We would be exposed as never before. Both to the Lightborn and any Liberators who would not agree with our approach."

"I'm not disagreeing there. Yet, we can either start from absolutely nothing somewhere else, or we can start with thousands of people who're bound to be on our side, because we give them access to a full gamut of cards. Also, here, we might be beset on all sides by friends and foes, but at the very least we *know* the situation. There's no risk that the High Elementalist tries to take our decks for herself—or that the elders change their minds and decide that we should all be placed within the Furyborn lands, under house arrest. This would be *our* choice."

Kith barked with laughter and pushed himself away from the door. "I hate it. Count me the Pits in!" Seeing the look on their faces, he grinned. "What? It's risky, gutsy, and is bound to end in horrible screaming. Of course I'm on board."

Cilia nodded and slammed her fist down on the table. Then she shook it, grimacing. "I'm in as well. I almost died, several times over, because nobody ever saw fit to give me a chance. Time to change it up."

Liam shrugged. "I guess somebody will need to protect all of you during this. Also, I do like the Liberty girls." The gradual unclenching of the muscles of his shoulders revealed his true emotions about the decision.

Sera looked from one to the next. Then she grasped her hair in frustration. "Have you no sense of self-preservation?"

Liam snorted. "With this face and these muscles? Please! They ran out of space for more wonders."

Chase gave her a crooked smile. "Sorry. You've spent so much time preaching how we should care, and it seems like you did a better job than you expected. Are you hanging around to keep us from getting killed?"

She hung her head, curls bouncing loosely in front of her eyes. When she raised her head again, her eyes shot fire. "Do I ever insult *you* like that?"

"Erm. Yes? Constantly."

"Huh. You must have earned it, then." She huffed, coloring slightly at the roars of laughter from the others. She strode over and embraced Chase gently. "Thank you for calling me out. I was wrong." Her eyes narrowed. "You best enjoy those words. I do not intend to ever repeat them."

"Said every woman ever." Chase waggled his eyebrows. Ducking from the inevitable slap, he raised his hand. "I have one request, though. One boon I would want granted before risking my life yet again." He smoothly slid onto his knees, facing Sera. "If we live through this mess—will you marry me?"

Her eyes widened. Then she fell into his arms.

The others cheered raucously as they kissed, lost in each other.

"That was a *solid* move, Chase." Liam nodded approvingly. "That mix of self-sacrifice and pressure. I think I'll use it myself."

"Not on me, you won't," Cilia snapped, resulting in a round of laughter.

After a while, Chase and Sera disentangled. Wiping a bit of moisture from his eyes, Chase didn't even try to obscure his blazing smile. "So. If we're staying, we'd better agree to an overall plan before we start talking to Lucille again. I build a Wellspring. Check. What else? Are we going to attack the Lightborn straightaway? Who's going to help build up a government here and make sure they're not overrun by rebels and whatnot? Finally, Lucille did have a point about the Prism. They're going to have trouble fending off Guardians for a bit, until they actually have enough power to stand tall against them on their own— their borders will be hard-pressed for a while. What do we do?"

Cilia stopped pacing. She emitted a soft sigh and rubbed her hands together. "We finally get to work on the real plans. Chase, hit us with your thoughts, so I can tear it apart."

CHAPTER 37

"They rebelled. Against me! I raised them into strength, granted them protection, and they spat in my eye! I will find the dissenters and tear them apart! They are hiding in clear sight, though. I will have to use guile to find them. Oh, this shall never happen again. I so swear!" Yep. He's definitely starting to show his true face now. (Book 2, Page 4.)

"You all know me. You have seen me in the city. I am the Pillar of Liberty Lucille. I am here to address you all in these trying times." Lucille looked out over the mass of people stretched out before her.

The crowd was never-ending. Execution Plaza was filled to bursting, with every single street leading into the plaza equally packed. Only a cordoned-off area in front of the raised platform was clear of people. Her voice, courtesy of the magical item she'd used last time Chase saw her, rang loud and clear, reaching everybody in the square. This time, however, it was different from last time. It held emotion. Energy. Hope.

"To make this clear—once we finish here today, we will have people traveling the lengths and breadths of Liberty to share the message. On top of that, any Keeper still functional will be contacted to let everybody know." She held a measured pause, looked down over the crowd. "The Savior is dead."

A hush fell over everybody, with a few alarmed cries ringing out. Most were silent, though, hard faces displaying they'd already known.

"Only, he *was* no savior. We have seen the proof. From today on, the palace will be open to everybody, and you will be able to see it for yourself. The one who styled himself our savior was a troubled man. Somebody who decided that no measure was too harsh to ensure that we were cut off from the outside, and that he would reign supreme. He has done a lot of good in his reign, yet I warn you...some of the truths you will learn will be hard to grasp. Let me tell you this, with no hint at doubt. *The Savior deserved to die.*"

The plaza was silent as the grave now. The pressure felt like a thunderstorm right before the first drop of rain.

Lucille continued, softer now. "We could lie to you. Make up a story about the Savior having ascended or something similar. Then we could act like nothing else happened, and let the minds and pillars rule the blissful lands from here on. Except, that is not what we want. We want this horrible experience to lead to something new. Something better. A Liberty nation, where we can stand tall and proud. For that, I want to introduce you to somebody."

Chase walked forward across the platform and picked up the tiny square clay item that Lucille held forward, still warm from her touch. He looked at the immense crowd in front of him, took a deep breath, and pressed on. His words rang out loud enough for the entire square to hear. "My name is Chase. You'll note that my clothes make me look like I'm a mind. Only, that's not really true. I was never raised properly beyond heart. Also, I am not from the blissful lands. Rather, I was raised in the worst slums of the Lightborn city of Isarn. And I helped kill the Savior."

A rising mutter rippled through the mass of humanity.

"We had no intentions of doing that. But when we came here, we discovered what he was doing. Learned about the camps where anybody unwilling to follow his plans were sent to work in slavery. Learned about all those slain, simply for wanting a different life. All in the name of unity and 'freedom.'" Chase shook his head sadly. "We could have left you all to fend for yourselves. But with the tyranny enforced upon you, you would never have been able to earn true freedom. Now…now you can."

He smirked. "I kind of insisted somebody else should speak instead of me. I don't know how to be diplomatic or nice about this stuff. But there is one thing I do know. You can talk all day and night. Unless you actually deliver, it's just that. Talk." He motioned with his hand, and Lucille and all the others moved forward, leaping softly off the edge of the platform.

Chase stayed up there for a while longer. "When I first learned that you actually *have* a place like this, I was furious. Execution Plaza? Where every presentation, every speech is delivered with this backdrop—with the unspoken threat that either you do as you're told, or you know what's coming for you? That is about as clear a threat as you can get. So, when Lucille here asked how we should properly frame the changes that we are going to bring, this came to mind immediately. From this day on, Execution Plaza will cease to be. Instead, it will the Freedom Plaza, a place of opportunities, given to you, with no requirements, no demands, no ridiculous limitations on your Ænima. In the future, all we ask is that you try to be a good person, and stand up for those you love."

He leapt forward, landing softly on the paving stones twenty feet below. Then he turned and grinned. "Like I just said, it's easy to talk and talk. Showing is much more efficient. Liam.

Would you mind showing them what we think about public executions and leaders trying to scare their people into obedience?"

Liam grinned widely and cracked his neck. Then he moved toward the end of the well-made wooden platform. He grinned right at the crowd and kissed his biceps, one after the other. Then he raised both arms, and three cards flashed on his body in short succession.

Intellectually, Chase was aware of the combinations. That Liam wasn't *this* much of a beast. He'd gotten a swig of a drink from Nordon that increased his Strength. Also, Sera had both Blessing of the Night and Spark of Divinity running, improving his Strength even further. Add to that the short-lived boosts from Liam's Optimal Offense, Earthen Might, and All Out, and you did end up with some massive increases.

Even so, as Liam grasped a wooden pillar as wide around as Chase himself, and *ripped it out of the damn ground*, Chase gasped right along with the crowd behind him. He gaped to see the handsome bastard moving forward, arms outstretched like a kid running through a corn field, wood splintering and exploding wherever he touched.

Less than half a minute later, Liam paused on the other side, tossing away a ragged piece of board taller and wider than himself as if it were a tiny twig. He paused and turned to look back, and brushed his hands off, grinning with self-satisfaction at the chaos of the torn-apart former platform.

Chase gawked. Then he picked up his jaw and grinned right along with him. This was exactly what they'd agreed to. They wanted to show to the world that they were done with the atrocities led by the Savior. However, they also had to show everybody that they were doing this out of benevolence, not weakness, and people wouldn't be able to take advantage of them. Liam had definitely nailed that part.

Engaging Steps of Brilliance, Chase walked through the air, until he found the highest part of the platform still standing. He stopped, balancing precariously on top of the dangerously leaning board and raised the crafted item again. "We don't just talk. We act. The time of public threats and Keepers looming over your every action is over. In the future? You will be free to become as strong as we are, should you so choose. And right now, I will make this possible for you, by creating a Wellspring right here, for the entirety of Liberty. Once that is done? You will all be able to get any cards you have the Steps to hold—from all five decks."

That woke them up. What had been shocked silence burst into an explosion of applause and chatter. The noise level grew and grew, right until he mentally located that single selection that he'd been harboring at the back of his mind since surviving the encounter with Arnault, ages ago.

[Do you wish to permanently place your Deck of Darkness and establish a Wellspring here? It will be influenced by the following:
 —Original Deck of Darkness
 —Deck of Light
 —Elemental Deck
 —Deck of Fury
 —Deck of Liberty
Hence, it will be established as a Legendary-rate Wellspring, tripling the rates of Dark Guardians being summoned, and the energy levels and effects bestowed upon them.
 Yes/No?]

He raced through the options, nodding to himself. Nothing changed here, but it clearly mentioned all the decks. No turning back now.

Yes!

Behind the burgeoning creation, he could see the crowd in front of him. His vision wasn't impaired or anything like that. Only, that would be like lying next to a naked Sera and deciding to stare at the bedsheets instead. Their presence was decidedly there—but it paled in comparison to what was slowly being born.

It was magic. At the same time, it was beyond understanding and the most natural thing in the world. Five kinds of magic came together, working to create something that was bigger than its separate parts, and, in this moment, everything seemed right.

Light shone down on the emerging creation. Yet, today, it felt thicker than usual, like a physical presence. In layers, it built up a shining foundation near the ground, almost too precious to look at.

Tiny roots and brambles crept up from underneath the paving stones, bursting through everything in their way, adding a tad of solidity and giving it a natural feeling, like the half-ephemeral presence of a waterfall in direct sunlight.

The elements crept in, little by little, in ways you would not have guessed. Dew dripped from a sharply defined edge. A thick layer of healthy soil sprang up around the base and was subsequently covered in a carpet of springy, healthy-looking grass. Wind arose, and Chase distantly felt it rushing through his hair. And the top of the emerging construction gained a hazy look, like a heat haze hanging over the plains on a warm day.

By now, it was clear to see what it was growing into. A plinth, exquisitely carved, waist-height, with a flattened square top. The ephemeral sensation slowly faded away as the presence became more solid, more *real*.

Then Liberty added its touch. The entire creation abruptly gained a *presence*. Where before, the details were impressive and extraordinary, but likely hard to see from afar, suddenly the plinth gleamed with presence, with promises of glory.

Finally, from everywhere, darkness crept in. In streaks and streams, they emerged from the flagstones, from the shadows behind people and the remnants of the platform, slithering like a thousand snakes to join the nest. They rushed into the plinth. When they were done, it solidified and earned an edge. A promise and a threat. The creation was, at the same time, mundane and utterly, undeniably not. A supernatural creation, yet familiar.

A notification erupted inside Chase's mind.

[Creating an original Wellspring grants you three choices. Three chances to influence the outpour of Dark magic, that may strengthen your people or Guardians; weaken your enemies; or build your home. Due to this being a Legendary-rate Wellspring, any choices will be improved from the baseline. Please select the order of improvement, from weakest (3) to strongest (1).]
[Cards] choose 1,2,3
[Guardians] choose 1,2,3
[Local effects] choose 1,2,3

Chase froze for a moment, reeling, trying to catch up with what was being said. First was the "original Wellspring" part. The Savior had clearly only had the single Wellspring inside his tower which faded with his death, meaning that had been an original Wellspring too.

Why had the Savior limited it to one Wellspring? Simplicity itself. He didn't want any easy access to cards. All should be controlled. Only, Liberty had tons of decks now, ready to be used. Not only would they be able to create a *new* "original Liberty Wellspring" and earn additional bonuses for that on top of what he was growing, they'd also be able to send out any additional decks to cities and towns farther out, which could *also* be strengthened. *So many possibilities!*

Chase frowned, taking in the word choices again. Okay. At a guess, any further Wellsprings would be weaker than the very first one. Meaning, they'd only get two or one selections they could boost, maybe even none at all if it was the hundredth Wellspring created in a nation. That could explain Isarn only having healing fountains while larger Lightborn cities produced those inquisitor cards or even stronger effects. Even so, they should, in time, be able to build to something impressive with Dark and Liberty Wellsprings operating side by side.

Weakest to strongest. He huffed. *What a world.* When he was growing up, his only choices were along the lines of: "Which mark is least likely to get me killed?" and "Can I brush off that mold and still eat it?" Now, he was supposed to make choices for an entire Fury-damned nation!

Still. Thinking about it, one choice was easily made. He mentally placed [Local effects] last. Though it would be nice to be able to focus entirely on Salvation, they had an army and other threats to focus on. If their enemies made it to Salvation in the first place, they'd be screwed. He'd rather make choices that improved their chances *beforehand*.

[Cards] or [Guardians]? What was the right approach? At a guess, Arnault had focused on [Guardians]—at least, that would explain the huge number of beasts he'd managed to amass. The Furyborn? [Guardians] as well. Their system with the Guardians granted them organization, messengers, and trusty helpers in their towns and cities, along with defenders when needed. Elementals? Absolutely [Local effects]. Their defenses were supernaturally strong, and it was surely owed in part to this choice. The Lightborn? That one was anybody's guess. Given that the border of defensive Guardians surrounding Lightborn cities was a universal thing, it could very well be [Guardians]—but the strength and efficiency of the border did waver a lot, depending on the place.

Chase shook his head like a dog coming out of the water. Irrelevant. This was all irrelevant. What did *they* need?

They needed defenders. That part stood crystal clear to Chase. With the Lightborn situation, they absolutely needed defenders to stand between them and their enemies, human or bestial. Yet, should those defenders be Guardians or humans?

Chase gave it some thought. Improving cards for the Liberators would strengthen them as a whole *right now*, while any strengthening of their Guardians would only take effect for new Guardians—and those would take time to spawn. Meanwhile, any improvement regarding their cards could wind up representing a huge advantage for Liberty as a whole.

Only...Liberty was *not* whole right now. They could not be expected to act as a united front in the near future. Also, they would need to adapt, to change their approach to defense that had stood unchallenged for four decades. On top of that, there was one detail they had already discussed back at the palace. They disagreed on many things. Yet, one decision was near-unanimous. For their entire lives, every single person, disregarding proclivities, desires, and physicality, had been forced to fight at the Prism until they earned their first card. That would change, and combat service would, from here on, be honored, but voluntary.

That all added up to one simple choice. Guardians would become the primary choice and defense. They would be thrown at their enemies, sacrificing their unnatural lives en masse to keep the Liberators from having to do the same. Chase couldn't find any fault with that. He looked at the order again.

[Guardians] 1
[Cards] 2
[Local effects] 3

That would do. He made his choice, and another notification appeared before him.

[Please specify tertiary choice: Local effects. Do you wish to: create imbued structures; enhance existing structures with magic; or create local imbued effects?]

Hrm. This choice, while seemingly overwhelming, did turn out a bit easier than expected. Salvation was, beyond a doubt, the largest city Chase had ever seen. If he decided to mess around with structures—defensive, offensive, or otherwise— there were bound to be huge parts of the city left untouched. So, basically, it boiled down to whether he wanted to tie any local effects to a structure, existing or not, or simply have them appear in some place. Usually, he'd want to hide some effect, hoping an eventual enemy would be unable to find and dismantle it. Yet, right this moment, he wanted to create a spectacle. He chose the enhancement option, and instantly, his gaze was transported out of his body, as he was granted a bird's-eye view of the city and prompted to select an existing structure to enhance.

Smiling, he focused, his vision coming closer, and closer again, until he saw himself still standing on top of the splintered remnants of the platform. He selected the plinth, and was guided through a number of selections, until he was eventually gifted with a notification.

[Tertiary selection decided. Anybody entering a five-mile radius of the Wellspring will be granted a +3 temporary boost to Potential.]

Dimly, just like back when somebody had blown out his eardrums (only, without the blood, pain, and dizziness), he noticed the amazed outcries of the crowd as the enhancement stepped into effect. Nice! That would be an amazing boon to anybody coming here to choose cards.

Chase focused and moved on. He was nowhere near done.

[Please specify secondary choice: Cards. Do you wish to create a custom card; add generic enhancements to the Wellspring as a whole or to specific classes; or create custom options?]

He eliminated two of those options straightaway. If he'd prepared with Cilia and Sera, he might have been able to create some truly useful custom cards. Even so, that would lock wielders into specific paths instead of choosing their own, and he *hated* that thought. The same applied to enhancing specific classes. They were going to create something for *everybody* here!

He toyed around with the options for adding generic enhancements, to see what was available, and found himself impressed. Even though it was "only" his secondary choice, the options were widespread, and would undoubtedly be effective. They would be able to add rank increases to random offered cards—always useful. They'd be able to grant added intake of Ænima within the radius, for faster growth. They could grant a boost of +1 to *all* attributes to anybody being granted cards here, or larger increases to specific attributes.

Chase almost selected the boost to Ænima intake, but decided to be thorough. He rummaged around the customized option and found it rather underwhelming. There were options to build specific choices here, mostly general boosts, but they had some weird outliers. For instance, they could grant increased affinity with specific aspects, better night sight and others. Improving Dark effects by fifteen percent did sound amazing—but again, it was just a single color. And most people would only have a single Dark card.

Then he saw a simple choice, buried among other generic choices: [Reset]. Confused, he selected the option to see what was meant by that.

He froze and felt himself nearly falling off the planks.

[Once in their life, any wielder may reset all their choices. They may select their class and cards anew. Every single one of their selections will be removed and reset, including any attribute increases from their Titles.]

Laughing with joy, he made the selection. It was just what he didn't know he'd been searching for! The perfect complement. Not only did it grant the people of Liberty the choice to rid themselves of the useless Devotion to Liberty card and get a Liberty card they could actually *use*, they could also choose afresh, going with any class and card they would want, not the ones foisted upon them by their dictator!

With a deep breath, he dove into the last one.

[Please specify primary choice: Guardians. Do you wish to create custom Guardians; add generic enhancements to your Guardians as a whole; or create custom enhancements?]

Oh. That was actually an easier choice than he had expected.

Custom Guardians might be nice if you were in the Elemental towers and could craft something for very specific situations. However, with a massive border, and faced with a prospective influx of various enemies, that would backfire on them.

The custom enhancements were amazing and so interesting. He could increase the chance that Guardians with magical abilities spawned, influence the *types* of Guardians—increased odds of fliers, tough beasts, or Guardians with ranged abilities, for instance. He could even, to a limited degree, then adapt and improve those abilities. In a perfect world, he could have paused the creation and asked the others for advice, but the process couldn't just be halted. Chase was left to his own lacking imagination.

Generic enhancements? He spent some time brushing through the options and groaned on the inside. So boring. But dammit if it wouldn't be powerful. It was easy to see the effect of Guardians being his primary choice. He would be able to grant every single Guardian a massive +5 to Toughness. FIVE! That would allow even the weakest Guardian to stand up to a non-wielder, and go toe-to-toe with enemies that were generally much stronger than themselves.

Then he found the resistance selection and froze. He moved back and forth between the custom enhancements and the generic ones, groaning.

[Resistance to Light. This selection will grant all Guardians a 50% resistance to Light cards, effects, and damage.]

[General Resistance. This selection will grant all Guardians a 25% resistance to all aspected cards, effects, and damage.]

He rubbed his face, frustrated beyond belief. How was this a fair choice? They were faced against an overwhelming Lightborn army. Light resistance would be *immensely* useful to aid them against their inevitable attacks. Only, that wasn't the *only* threat they were facing. Would it be worth it to make their Guardians permanently effective against one enemy, if they would be torn apart against enemies of other aspects?

Finally, Chase realized the obvious and slapped himself in the forehead. First, once they got the news to the elders and the towers, Furyborn and Elemental Guardians wouldn't be an issue anymore. That limited their problems to only Lightborn and unaspected. Second, and more importantly, this wouldn't be the only Wellspring here. If the Dark Guardians were attuned to dealing primarily with Lightborn threats, the Liberty Guardians could be more all-round or...whatever they decided.

He made the decision, and received a final choice.

[Please select ruleset for Guardians. Note: This can be changed at any time.]

Chase chose a generic ruleset, deciding to save this for later on. Finally, the notifications faded away, and he was treated to the sight of an entire people laughing at him. Blinking, confused, he turned around to understand what was going on.

Kith helped. He wiped tears from his eyes, pointing. "Your—your expressions! That was hilarious. Do it again. Especially slapping yourself!"

Chase was mortified, realizing he'd just made an ass of himself in front of the entire Light-blinded city. Then he snorted and shook his head...and promptly got distracted.

Below him, the plinth was undergoing its final transformation. Energies from all five aspects were drawn together, visibly contorting the air above. For a moment, it resembled a multicolored whirlpool, spanning several feet in height. Then, with a snap that was felt, rather than heard, it solidified, and a deck emerged, starting to softly spin right above the plinth.

Chase tried to collect himself, before speaking up. "I apologize for making you wait. I will only say that it was worth it. For anybody checking their attributes, you have already seen the *least* of its permanent effects."

The crowd was dead silent now. He had them more tightly in his hand than Scarlet doing her scarf dance back in the Filthy Sty. He smiled and waved invitingly at the deck. "From here on out, you may approach the deck and make your choice of any card of all five aspects. Yet, that is not all. For any of you who are not satisfied with the choices you have made to date, both with your class and your cards—you are allowed to remove all of it, and choose *everything* anew."

The ensuing clamor nearly burst another eardrum, as the people of Salvation went absolutely insane.

CHAPTER 38

"I have lain the groundwork for a wonderful invention. Honored summoners, being able to get in touch with Guardians placed at fixed locations throughout the blissful lands. With an organized schedule and intense footwork, we will be able to get constant reports from throughout my nation on a daily basis. We will also be able to direct the Guardians in case of emergencies. They will be my Keepers, always alert to danger!" This part, we are most definitely copying. The system still exists. We just need a breakdown of the Guardians and their positions. (Book 2, Page 17.)

<u>Lightborn camp, two miles south of Liberty lands</u>

Thomas Beforant was not a fan of hard work. That was something that happened to other people. Poor people, preferably. His attitude, he was aware, came as a surprise to most people who did not truly know him. He took that as proof of their limited mental capacities.

Why would you spend years working hard, sweating and panting, red-faced as a peasant, when you could skip straight past the preliminary work and earn the results straightaway? Finishing a handful of panting Guardians, properly fixed down by loyal minions, would net you the same Steps as would risking your lives to kill them yourself. Also, that would net you the attribute points needed, again, to skip said boring work. Of course, there were exceptions. Not everything could be handed off.

The whip cracked out with the sound of thunder. "Fifteen!" Beforant shouted, admiring the pattern on the soldier's back. He passed the whip to an underling and strode forward.

The soldier, bleeding and pale-faced, flinched as he saw his lord appear in his vision. He looked down at the ground, wavering on his feet.

Behind him, his fellow soldiers were lined up in perfect ranks, all affecting to be uncaring. Most failed.

Thomas Beforant knew power. There was power over death and life. Social power. The power of money. The raw power of cards and attributes. With each and every one of these, he towered over the soldier, a—his eyes flicked to check the soldier's arms—piddling Tier-two soldier. Like a giant before an ant, he was capable of crushing him even with the passing of his movement. Many of his peers used that power indiscriminately, caring not one whit for those they smashed underfoot. Many of his peers, admittedly, were morons.

"Rise, Awakened Callem." His voice rang out. Melodious. Powerful. Undeniably male, and attractive, to men and women both. He had trained it. "You were charged with conduct unbecoming an officer, is that not right?"

The soldier got to his feet, still refusing to meet his eyes. "Yes, sir." His voice emerged shaky, but getting stronger.

"Repeat your words, for all to hear." He could practically *feel* the tenseness wafting off the soldier.

"I said—I said that the lords back in the capital wouldn't know their pricks if they could find a mirror to spot the tiny things." He bowed his head.

A series of barely contained chuckles erupted around the grounds.

"You did." Lord Beforant let his voice ring out sternly. "My fellow nobles back in Stradeburg are proud and powerful. The backbone of our society and the fount of most of the riches and manpower that we, out in the fields, use to advance the power of the Lightborn throughout all of Ordei. Do you see the errors of your ways? Do you understand why you should not denigrate the nobility?"

"Yes, sir!" It was less an answer than an ingrained response bursting out, without any hesitation.

Lord Beforant reached out and raised the soldier's chin, looking him dead in the eye. He enjoyed the hint of shock and fear. "Good," he said. "Let us never hear you say anything like that again." He lowered his voice so only the awakened would hear and continued, mirth and cordiality intermingled. "Besides, most of them would need at least *two* mirrors, fat-bellied as the useless bastards are. We know how we feel about them, soldier. But we do not say it out loud."

That look. That look of shock, turning to realization before becoming awe, and utter worship…if he could bottle the essence of that look, he'd never have to buy any wine again.

As the soldier shouted his agreement and shot him the crispest possible salute, disregarding his back which had been torn to shreds, he knew. From here on out, that soldier was his. Body and soul. He would relive this incident until it had grown ten times larger in his mind. He would repeat it to his fellow soldiers until it grew to epic proportions.

He saluted back and strode away, keeping down the smile that wanted to affix itself on his face. This was what most of the—admittedly mostly fat and decadent—so-called lords in Stradeburg failed to understand. Power was always wonderful and you could never have enough. Yet, the mightiest power was the one you allowed others to instill in themselves.

"Archbishop Desahl." His voice rang out to the congregation. This was the same kind of power, applied with fear instead of love. He barely glanced at the dozens of inquisitors kneeling in front of their leader, knowing that this would show them somebody who was immune to their power. With the archbishop admitting that he could act as he wanted, whenever he wanted, he granted Beforant a higher rank and authority, ingraining it in their minds.

"My Lord Beforant." The archbishop inclined his head. His eyes didn't quite show his hatred, but it was very much there.

Beforant knew, and approved. This, as well, would have consequences, at least in the minds of the onlookers. It would spread, like circles in water. To think that he had come from a minor noble house. His father had always cared about what his peers thought, and had taken great pains to teach his son how to read the signs. How the doddering old fool had never taken those teachings to the inevitable conclusion that one should always be the one to *choose* what others thought was a mystery.

"Have you sent the messages?"

That brought a shadow of a scowl to the archbishop's features, quickly buried. "I have, my lord. I admit, I would have waited for confirmation myself. This will set a good deal of wheels into motion. Motion that we cannot easily reverse. As long as we do not know exactly what we're facing, it could become a very costly affair."

He almost laughed out loud. The archbishop *truly* didn't like his vaunted inquisitors being used as messengers. If it was that offensive to him, the church should really stop granting a number of them cards and attributes that were *perfect* for runners. "Ah, but that is where you are mistaken, dear Archbishop. We know exactly what we are faced with here. An opening." He put his hand on the smaller man's shoulder, right on top of some of his grisly scars. Just another unsubtle reminder.

With his other hand, he indicated the incline on their northernmost flank, dead grass leading up and up toward a rockier slope and a low wall. "Those are, beyond a doubt, Liberty soldiers. Your people have confirmed as much. Not only that, but they are *weak*. Non-wielders, Tier-ones and -twos, with a single Tier-three among them. And the fog that used to hide them? Has faded away, for miles and miles. Our three thousand would run them over in seconds."

"My lord, I do not disagree with your words. I merely mean to emphasize what I find to be the largest risk. To me, this absolutely looks like a trap. They have, purposely, deactivated their defenses right at the moment when we were present, to lure us into their lands. Taking the bait will be dangerous."

Lord Beforant laughed and clapped his shoulder. "I appreciate your considered thoughts—and your consideration for my well-being. However, you fail to remember one tiny detail. Our prey." As he watched the archbishop clearly struggle to keep up, it was hard to keep from sighing.

"The wielders of the Deck of Darkness? How would that be pertinent in this case?"

Now, he did sigh. "Think about it. These are hardened criminals, who have repeatedly proved that they are capable, that they can make their ways past security that should be closed to them, defeat schemes and..." He shrugged. "Admittedly, form a rather annoying pain in my behind. We have confirmation that they've made it into the fogs bordering the lands of Liberty. Can you really go so far as to attribute the defenses failing now to coincidence? Really?"

"No, my lord. Only, that doesn't really gainsay my argument. If they are as talented and insidious as you give them credit for—would there not be an increased risk that this is all a trap? That they have somehow infiltrated Liberty defenses and society to the point where they are able to turn off their defenses at will? Or that they have, somehow, managed to convince those in power that we, out here, are ripe for the taking?"

That...Lord Beforant had to admit that it was a well-constructed argument. If the archbishop were back in the capital, the weakling might actually be able to employ it to some efficiency in order to take some authority back. Good thing that he'd had the foresight to bring the scarred old man along—even if it had only been so he could present the image of a united front between him and the church to the public. Right now, right here, fortunately, he had him where he wanted him. "Ah. That is a very reasoned line of thought. Good thing that we aren't going to leap right in."

The archbishop actually looked relieved for a moment.

How had he ever risen as high as he did in the church's hierarchy? Possibly, his near-death and torture had ruined his command of the grand game.

His voice was solid, though, properly ministerial. "I appreciate your consideration. It goes well in hand with our thoughts. The Circle has always argued for this. A strong church married to a strong and well-founded military. This is the basis upon which our prosperity has been built."

Lord Beforant barely kept from laughing at the hypocrite. The church had tried, and failed, to take over the reins of power since time immemorial. When he decided to back Archbishop Desahl against the former archbishop, he honestly thought that Desahl was wise enough to realize that the proper place of the church was in serving him. Now, he was learning that this wasn't the case. Desahl was not strategically wise, simply weak and easily cowed. "Oh, I entirely agree. Alone, we are strong. Yet, together, using our separate strengths where they are demanded, we are unbeatable."

The archbishop caught it then. Finally. His eyebrows twitched, and eyes widened, ever so slightly. Too late, though.

Lord Beforant inclined his head. "My good Archbishop. Please lead the way into the unknown. Take your vaunted inquisitors and stride ahead, with the power of the Light in your able hands. Carve a path for the future of all Lightborn, that we may follow in your footsteps."

The archbishop complied.

As if he had a choice...

CHAPTER 39

"Layered defenses. Well-hidden permanent crafted items, attuned to specific gems, personally granted to commanders in secret. Upon their deaths, the gems are reclaimed and granted to new commanders. The perfect way to anticipate and ambush any would-be attackers." I believe I have an idea. A lot of what the Savior did is actually workable, if you remove the diabolical aspects of it. Take this. If we locate the activation gems and the crafted items, we would actually be able to reuse them for a concerted, layered defense that would be extremely effective against enemy high-Tier wielders. This will change how I read these blasted diaries. (Book 2, Page 23.)

"It worked." Lucille's voice was as tired as it was surprised. "It actually worked exactly as we wanted. Granted, we had to place guards to ensure that people didn't die in the rush to access the Wellspring and change their cards—but people are in awe, grateful...and quite a bit scared of your bald warrior here."

"Aw. Why? People shouldn't be afraid of *me*!" Liam said.

"You broke apart a well-made wooden platform weighing tons, like it was a castle made of twigs." Kith smirked. "I'd be surprised if they aren't saying that you're twelve feet tall, using a spear for a toothpick."

"He's not wrong," Lucille granted. "But, apologies, Liam, this is exactly what we wanted. Earning the gratitude of the people, along with a healthy show of power. It should give us a tiny bit of air to breathe and actually plan for the next stage. There *will* be some armed resistance, when people find out this is for real, but hopefully, we will have a vague idea of how we are going to build our society before then."

"How'd they take *my* surprise then?" Kith asked smugly.

Lucille rubbed her face. "It... They... Well, they appreciate the power. As to the lack of subtlety, I believe everybody knows about you by now."

"What I want to know is how to repeat it. Can you build another one for me?"

Not one to be upstaged, Kith had picked his moment—*right* after the Dark Wellspring came into place—to use his Monument of Liberty card. The shimmering ten-foot-tall statue that came into being right behind the Wellspring portrayed Kith, heroically placed alongside Spike, with Radine on his shoulders. Now, all summoners picking cards had all rarity ranks improved by one.

"Sorry." Kith smirked. "One time only. I guess I'll just have to deal with being the face of Liberty for all eternity."

Chase snorted. "Or until somebody's had enough and chops it down. Now. Moving on—where does all this leave us, though?"

"In deep trouble." Lucille sighed. "The news arrived less than five minutes ago, which is why I asked you in here. Parts of the Lightborn army have started advancing into our lands, and our forces are pulling back, entirely outmatched. Liberty is officially under invasion."

Kith cursed. Nobody else said a word.

Eventually, Chase spoke up again. "Do we have any numbers? Anything more solid? Has Radine returned, Kith?"

Kith shook his head. "She won't, for at least four or five days. It's a massive flight for her. Besides, her route wouldn't take her past their army, so I'd have to send her out to scout again."

Lucille bowed her head in dismay. "As you may have learned for yourself, the Savior did not like people taking cards that would help with scouting or far sight—no doubt, in order to avoid being spied upon. As such, we are near blind when it comes to details. But we do have their numbers. About three thousand. Two to three hundred of those are mounted."

"Three thousand," Chase repeated, frowning. "Okay, like you said yourself, people are lining up to change their cards to something they like. Can we actually present an army that would be able to fend that off straightaway?"

"Yes." She looked far less happy than that response should have warranted. "The real question is: can we fend them off *and* be sure that our forces here in Salvation can actually keep the peace and aid to make sure that we do not fall apart? To that, the answer is a resounding 'no.' We are already getting reports of hostile Guardians taking heavy tolls on the hopefuls all across the border."

"But that's no good," Kith complained. "We can't just send forces out there to aid all those poor bastards stuck at the borders, knowing they're facing Guardians that might be too tough for them. *Especially* when those forces are better used elsewhere."

"*I know!*" she admitted through gritted teeth. "But what would you have me do? If we pull back everybody, every tiny village between Salvation and all outlying borders will be left fending for themselves. It will be a slaughter. On top of that, I can't get anybody here to agree to any single action. It's like trying to herd cats! So, help me, damn you. If you agree to my plans, I believe I will be able to convince a large number of the others. Then, maybe, we will be able to come up with something useful and *act* instead of just reacting! We can weather this, I know—but we need our defenders to be able to circle back here and earn *proper* cards. Then, with time, and better strategies, we will be able to defend ourselves and build up a defense that will last in the long run. And...” In a tiny voice, she finished, “I just don't know anymore. I'm so tired.”

Sera sighed. “It is as I feared.” She faced the others. “The coming weeks are not going to be easy—for any of us.”

“You're saying that in a weird way. Why is that?” Chase asked suspiciously.

“Because you will be leaving me behind.”

Chase snorted. “Yeah. That's not happening.”

Sera grasped his hand. “It is. Let us face the facts. We have three fronts in this war—because it is a war, make no doubt of that. The border, with the hopefuls and their leaders. Underpowered, wielding poor cards, reeling. The Lightborn army, who we can expect to put everything and everyone they meet to the torch or enslave them. And finally, Salvation, where the battle for the future of a Liberator society will be fought.” She smiled ruefully. “Given a choice of these three battlefronts—where do you believe I would be able to do the most good? Fighting, or attempting to carve out something good within this web of diplomacy and bickering?”

“I will be staying, too,” Cilia said. The tone of her voice brooked no argument. “I entirely agree with Sera. Somebody needs to stay here and build up a new Salvation. I will be able to help with that. I can craft what needs to be crafted—items that we can send to aid the borders, or to build up a proper defense against the Lightborn. If it's just me, you know I'll run out of droplets within a few hours, and then I'm basically useless. Here? I think we could manage something good.”

Kith's demeanor was stuck somewhere between disbelief and dark humor. “Oh yeah. No worries. We'll take on three thousand Lightborn. There's a full three of us. That'll be easy.”

“You would not have to go alone,” Lucille offered. “We do not have the numbers to face their army without leaving Salvation defenseless—that is beyond discussion. Yet, I do believe that, with all the people choosing new cards right now, we would be able to find a decent number of volunteers who would be willing to aid you, knowing what you intend to do. Maybe a few hundred to harass and strike at their army.”

“I'm not even sure *what* we intend to do,” Kith said. “Die? Because without Sera on board, that's what's going to happen.”

Sera cocked her head. “Aw. That is almost sweet of you.”

Liam snorted. "No, it isn't. He's just wheedling. It's what he does, when he thinks he can avoid hard work." He lunged at Kith and grabbed him in a headlock.

"Gah. Get *off* me, you damn brute!" Kith struggled, but eventually relented, red face aimed at Sera. "See what you'd leave me to, princess?"

Lucille's wide eyes ranged from one to the other. "I prayed for a way out. For years, I asked the Savior for a way to live. This was...not what I expected."

Liam chuckled and mussed Kith's hair before releasing him. "We've heard that one before. I mean, not the praying part." Turning to Kith, he shrugged. "I'll say, it's pretty damn obvious what we're trying to do, isn't it? We're slowing them. Stalling. Drawing them in the wrong directions and making sure they're running themselves ragged. It's not like we need to kill them. We just have to make sure that they waste their time and energy chasing after us."

"Oh. Wait." Kith frowned. "We can do this!" He pushed off Liam and started to pace. "I tried out my Chariot of the Land this morning. It's bloody *massive*. It can easily hold a dozen, maybe fifteen people. But that's not the best part. It's fast, too." He snapped his fingers. "Lucille! If you get us ten, no, twelve people with good cards for continuous ranged combat, and...probably a good healer too. Then, we can stay ahead of them and slowly wear them down! If they ever make it as far as Salvation, they'll be too exhausted to even consider anything but surrendering."

"I can do that," Lucille said haltingly. "But...are you sure? Fifteen against several thousand? It sounds like suicide!"

"Also, why only twelve?" Cilia asked. "You can summon two, if you have Twice the Fun activated."

Kith grimaced. "Yes... but really no. I don't know if it's because I have to command four felines at the same time, or because it's a Tier-five card, but... I nearly passed out when I tried this morning. It may be possible in the future, but not as it is. I'll need to focus on Mental Power."

"It's plenty good as it is, mate." Chase patted Kith's back, then gave Lucille a lopsided grin. "It'd only be suicide if we intended to stand up to them directly. Kith's totally right. We have plenty of cards that can hurt them from a distance. With hundreds of miles for them to cross, and some helpers, we'll be able to hurt them badly. Besides, I do have a few ideas we can try first, and we'll have Cilia take a stab at the plans before we leave. Finally, I intend to use *diplomacy!*"

Liam frowned. "That doesn't sound like you."

"Lie." Kith grinned. "He's going to lie a lot is what he's trying to say."

Chase spread his arms and beamed. "You do know me."

Half a day passed, as they plotted and prepared. The palace started to look more like a beehive, with the constant coming and going of thousands of people—those who wanted to help forming a new society, guards, craftsmen, and the idly curious. Chase, Liam, and Kith were intentionally ignoring all the goings-on, in favor of properly planning for their own task. Sera and Lucille somehow managed to rustle up enough volunteers that Chase could use his Stealing is Giving, Too card, amplifying his attributes by a full thirty-nine points.

They'd been reunited with their old gear as well. They had located it all, safely stashed away in a storage room, along with what little they were able to salvage from Nordon's brews.

They also located the attribute-boosting leather armbands Cilia had managed to craft. Somebody had stolen a bunch along the way, but they still had enough that they were able to find two for each person joining their raid.

Finally, they all converged in the open area outside the palace. They had dropped the Liberty outfits and were back in their own clothes and armaments. Kith summoned his chariot, and they all stood back for a moment, taking it in.

"Those kitties pulling the thing are intimidating. The rest looks a bit...rough, doesn't it?" Liam asked.

"Like somebody decided to take a thorn bush and make a theme out of it," Cilia agreed. "At least they're only on the outside. Imagine sitting for hours with spikes up your behind."

"Actually—" Chase started.

"Hey! Anybody who thinks my glorious ride is ugly is more than welcome to get out and walk!" Kith snapped.

"Rough isn't necessarily a bad thing, is it?" Liam said. Then he burst into laughter. "Man, it could be bright pink, and I'd still ride the damn thing, if it means I get to nap along the way."

Sera stepped forward and dragged Chase into a hard hug. "I know telling you to stay safe would be ridiculous. So, I have only two things to say. Do not die. And return to me. We will have the largest, most ostentatious wedding ever."

He smiled. "I have no intentions of doing otherwise. We'll make those Lightborn nobles back in Isarn look like paupers. Now, any final good advice? That goes for all of you!"

Lucille shook her head ruefully. "We owe you all. I will make sure that everybody here knows what you are doing for us."

"Please, no!" Chase groaned. "They're already being plenty weird about things. This morning, somebody wanted me to hold a baby. *Why?* I wasn't buying!"

"We have already planned plenty," Cilia said, ignoring his antics. "You know which route to lead them down, if possible. You know the pass which would be a good ambushing spot. And Gelly there—" She pointed at a middle-aged, short-haired Liberator in a leather surcoat who'd look right at home wielding a cleaver at a butcher's block. "Got lucky and got a summoned steed as her first-Tier card. This will be your *one* possibility to send a fast messenger to us, if you need to."

"Until Radine returns," Kith mumbled. "Stupid bird."

"Yes. Of course, we've indicated on the map where there are Keepers, and at which times of day we intend to have somebody listening and watching for any updates. But we are still severely understaffed in that department, and you'll likely be on the move at most hours, so there may be delays." Cilia took a deep breath. "I do not like sending you off without us. Yet, it is the logical choice. And, as long as you manage to protect yourselves from the mounted troops, as we have talked about, you should be able to stay ahead of them and do some real damage."

"Real damage? That's our job," a gruff voice announced. An elderly mixed-blood man—half Liberator, half Furyborn—walked up. The burnished color of his skin and his pointed ears made no secret of his heritage, while his looks—corded muscles and a wiry, stark-white shock of hair—led the mind to think of old leather and steel. "I'm Banes. I reckon I don't know much about this mess. All this about the Savior being a lyin' bastard wouldn't surprise me none—but that's not why I'm here."

His upper lip rose in a half-snarl that looked about as close as he'd ever come to a smile. "You!" He pointed at Chase. "Made sure that I could get cards. Real cards, whatever I'd like. And you!" His finger continued to stab accusingly at Kith. "Made sure that all us summoners could be *powerful*. I used to have two cards apart from my Devotion card, one Common, one Uncommon. Now, I have *fifteen*. Two of 'em Rare! And those bloody outsiders think they can come striding in and take over? I'll feed 'em a good showing of Liberty. Right up their bloody bums!"

"And we appreciate it." Chase nodded at him, then at the large group behind him, each wielding their own backpack bristling with armaments. "I know that none of you are weaklings, or unused to conflict. What we are going into, however, will be different from what you're used to. There will be no Prism to disorient and slow our enemies. There will be nobody for us to call upon, if their powers turn out to be greater than we expected. We will only have ourselves to count on." He shot a savage grin at them. "But once you've seen Liam in battle, you'll find that those odds aren't the worst!"

CHAPTER 40

"Portable enhancement stones. They have worked a lot better than envisioned. Anything above six stones works to define an area, though the increase diminishes past twelve stones and outright stops around sixteen. I can grant them to specific wielders, let them increase their attributes to defeat strong Guardians or enemies breaking past the Prism, and demand them back afterward. Extraordinarily low-risk, and it makes our higher-Tier wielders look more impressive than they are." Beautiful. Again, remove the paranoia and desire to keep his underlings down, and you have a wonderful, workable idea. I think I could craft these. With the increasing effect, I might even be able to make them permanent. (Book 2, Page 25.)

This was their third time leaving Salvation. Everything was like it had always been, and entirely different at the same time.

They were traveling via one of the main arteries south from the city and one main thing stood out: the thousands of citizens lined up in the streets. Somehow, the news of what they were doing had made it to the general public, and they left, buoyed by a wave of support. There were few cheers or people rejoicing—that was not the Liberty way—but people bowed their heads as they passed, put their hands over their heart, and a few even flung quiet, defiant fists into the air to show their support.

On top of that, they also passed a few Dark Guardians along the way. That, to Chase, was absolutely mind-blowing. He'd known that, back in Isarn, it took the newly spawned Guardians days, maybe even a week, to gather enough solidity to start moving into the streets. Here, it had been about a full day, and already, they were starting to accumulate within the city, in packs or solo. That was apparently the difference from using a third-rate deck and using an original Legendary-rate deck to create your Wellspring.

He'd visited the Wellspring again to make sure that the selections regarding Guardian behavior were spot-on, and had been quite surprised at the degree of fine-tuning they'd been allowed to enter into the situation. In the future, it would be possible for them to steer the Guardians any way they wanted, decide specific areas that needed a higher density of Guardians than others, and even choose sections that would be entirely bereft of Guardian intervention. For now, he'd kept it simple, following a long discussion. All Guardians would stay in Salvation until further notice, where their numbers would accumulate until there were enough that they could make a real difference. Sending them off now, in smaller packs or groups, would just get them all slaughtered. The Guardians here would only act to defend themselves, except if they were faced with Lightborn Guardians and Lightborn soldiers, who would automatically be treated as hostiles.

The Guardians did get some dark looks. Dark monsters openly walking the streets would have that effect. Because they were clearly moving about peacefully, and they'd been *very* open in their declaration about them being created solely to defend them from the invaders, nobody acted against them.

Unfortunately, there were still no Liberty Guardians joining their ranks. Back in the palace, they were still debating exactly how to use their decks and why, which choices to go with in the creation of their new Wellspring. Lucille and Sera did insist that they were getting closer to reaching a conclusion.

Once they left Salvation and hit the road, everything seemed unchanged for a while. There were few people traveling the road these days, however. No hopefuls rushing out to do their duty for the Savior. Trade had dried up, because of the uncertainty. Even half the shelters they passed looked untended, compared to the immaculately kept places they were used to.

On the road, they spent a lot of time talking about tactics and approaches. They had already spent a good deal of time with Lucille doing this prior to agreeing on who would join them, so they wouldn't be saddled with a dozen people who were unfit for the task they embarked on. But now they planned their practical approaches, talked working card combinations and the like, and got prepared for the eventual confrontation.

They'd decided on eight summoners, three casters, and a single healer. The healer was the strongest of the lot, at his twenty-third Step. All twelve, however, had been carefully chosen because of their strength, damage output, powerful summons, and above all, for being able to maintain combat for a long time.

As they traveled, Gelly kept shooting off on short trips. Her first-Tier Elemental card was a gorgeous fire steed that was useless for anything but personal transportation, but managed wonderfully at that. Every single time the road coincided with an offshoot to nearby towns and villages, she'd hurry off to inform them what was happening in Salvation, to confirm the truth of the situation and to lure them out of hiding and reestablish connections with the capital.

A lot of the deterioration of the Keeper network, they learned, was simply due to fear. The messengers who took care of the Keepers and the shelters and ran messages and news from them to the local towns were not high up in the hierarchy. Hence, when they were called upon to deliver potentially life-changing news, it hadn't gone off well. Sometimes, they had not been believed, sometimes they'd been outright punished for lying and, a few times, they'd simply avoided performing their duties in the first place. Seeing Gelly bring the news, carried alongside officially sealed messages from the capital, however, made the truth of the situation sink in. This wasn't going to change anything when it came to the Lightborn army, but it did help to begin reestablishing communications behind them, without sacrificing any speed.

Every evening, they spent a few hours practicing. This was mostly to get an idea of the capabilities of the different Liberators and their cards, and how to best apply them to the mix. Considering they would all—except for Kith, Liam, and Chase—be working from a distance, efficiency was more important than proper teamwork. Also, their goal was to get to the Lightborn army as fast as possible, instead of sacrificing a lot of time on practice.

The large felines pulling the chariot were clearly Furyborn. Their skin was rough and clay-like, and they moved with an unnatural energy and endless stamina that was just impressive. Of course, because Chase realized this could become a point of pride, he decided to name the thing "Kith's kitty cart," to Kith's unbridled fury.

No matter the teasing, they moved *fast*. What would've at least been a week's travel on foot faded away—and in the late afternoon on the third day, they halted the chariot on a large hill, looking down on the advancing army.

Kith knelt at the edge of the hill, looking down. "Fury rend me, that's a shiny vision."

Liam leaned on his shield, open-mouthed. "I want to look as good as them. Why doesn't Cilia make us stuff this fancy?"

Chase snorted. "Because, when we're in a fight, we prefer to *not* be all shiny and attention-grabbing?"

"Oh yeah. That's the bird!" Liam nodded.

"Are you always like this?" Gelly glared at them, sitting on top of her flaming steed. "We are about to march into battle, and you act like a group of hopefuls who have just been admired by their first cadre of village girls."

"We have admirers?" Kith asked.

Chase rolled his eyes. "Just relieving stress, Gelly. Don't you worry. We've been in plenty of tight situations. As long as you and the others take care of your end, we'll handle ours.

Speaking of which." He spat over the edge. "The rightmost incline here looks smooth and easy to climb. Do you all think that this is a good spot to arrange our ambush?"

"What? You would go down there directly?" Gelly pointed at the massing forces below. "No preparation? No tactics?"

Chase shrugged. "We already know what to do. Once our ambush is over and done with, we jump on the kitty kart—"

"The Slayer!" Kith shot back.

"And roll away. Hopefully, we'll have done enough damage that their mounted forces are unable to keep up with us."

"That's a tall order." Banes's face scrunched up. "I'm counting two hundred and eighty riders, 'n some of those beasts look mighty tough."

"You're not wrong," Chase admitted. He glanced down at the moving forces below.

The mounted forces led the formation, arranged in two loose rows that formed a wedge across the entire front. Most of them were also armored; shining metal reflecting the bright sun that shone down on them.

Behind them followed the main forces, infantry marching in tight ranks. They were clearly arranged into formations based on their classes. The edges of a marching song reached earshot, even from this far away.

"Are you spotting any surprises waiting for us, Kith?"

Kith grunted with closed eyes, held up a hand, gesturing for him to hold. Still with his eyes closed, he grimaced, mouth moving slowly as if he were talking with somebody. "Yes. Most of them ugly. I've been talking to Raudt and Svart—"

Liam snorted. "I still preferred Blackie!"

"*Raudt and Svart!* And it's a good thing the Lightborn are as weird about wearing proper clothing as Liberty. Judging from their robes, each of those formations has a healer attached to them. On top of that, we've got a smaller group of casters farther back, attached to the command group. Maybe three dozen total."

"Nice. Nobody notice you yet?" Liam asked.

"Nah. I'm having them move close to the ground, and there's so much dust and motion, it'll be hard to see anything. We've—oh, crap!"

On the plain below them, an eruption of light faded, and shouts emerged.

"Okay, yeah, we're spotted. Poor Svart." Kith winced. "First, a bit of good news. Those at the back, breathing in the dust of the entire formation? Workers and indebted, all of them. At least three hundred indebted, and twice that who are workers and aides of all sorts. Obviously, that means they might have crafted items to throw at us...but that's nearly a third of their number who aren't high-Tier fighters. Bad news? I think I spotted the general or whatever he is. He's a Tier-six."

Chase exhaled softly. "Whew. And now they know we're coming. That...isn't going to make our lives easier." He cracked his neck and beamed them all a devilish grin. "Good thing we believe so hard that diplomacy is going to work, right?"

Five minutes later, they strolled down the hill—Chase, Liam, and Kith, all geared up and armed for war, but with their weapons sheathed for the moment. They only walked down to the bottom of the hill, and there, they readied themselves, sharing a waterskin, while the Lightborn forces slowly advanced toward them.

Before long, a single mount loped toward them. Chase admired the beast—one of the antlered beasts, faith deer, often employed in Lightborn armies. They were hardy creatures, known more for their endurance than their speed or maneuverability. This one didn't wear any barding or armor, and the light leather armor of the Lightborn on the mount indicated that he was a scout.

Said scout shouted in greeting, "Throw down your weapons and surrender! The forces of Light demand it!"

Kith snorted in response. "Yeah. I don't think that's happening."

The young man looked at them in astonishment. "Are you *blind*, man? Do you want to die?"

Chase smirked and slowly rolled up his pants leg, letting the scout catch a glimpse at the card on his leg. "This is *slightly* outside of your league, friend. Kindly rush back to your commander and ask him to come over for a polite chat. Oh, and don't try to surround us. You won't like the outcome."

The scout took one disbelieving look at his audacity. Then he—wisely—determined this was for his superiors to decide, turned his mount and rushed back to the oncoming army.

It seemed to take forever. An army in motion, it would seem, was not something you just stop from one moment to the next. A short while later, however, the army was arrayed before them—not prepared for hostilities, merely paused while they handled whatever was in their way.

Eventually, two persons sauntered into view, flanked by a guard of ten mounted troops. Or rather, one person sauntered, and the other walked slowly and, it would appear, rather painfully. The limping person was a Lightborn, maybe middle-aged, his bald head crisscrossed by scars too methodical to derive from battles. His eyes gleamed with fury. He was elaborately dressed in the garb of the Church of the Circle. The other was the prettiest man Chase had ever seen. Tall, handsome, with just the right balance between pretty and masculine. His jawline was practically begging for statues to be carved in its honor.

As they drew closer, the pair paused, and the taller man reached out, slapping the priest on the shoulder, laughing uproariously. "I told you!"

The priest inclined his head slightly, submissively, and said something in a low voice.

Chase looked at the oncoming pair, scratching his neck. "I wasn't sure what to expect from meeting my first bunch of real invaders. Backslapping and guffawing was *not* my first guess...or my tenth."

"Oh, worry not." The well-clothed Lightborn picked up the pace, leaving the priest to falter behind him. Somehow, he'd heard Chase's whispered voice from fifty feet away. "I am simply merry, because I was right. I do so love being right."

"Nice. That means we do have something in common." Chase spoke up. "I was not expecting that either. How about invaders? Do we also agree on how those should be treated?"

"Oh, I am sure we do. Fire. Swords. Leave no survivors, etcetera." He waved it off and shot an annoyed look behind him. "Would you *keep up*, Archbishop?"

"Archbishop? I...was not expecting to meet the archbishop today. Or, ever, really." Kith's gaze looked panicked. "Shouldn't there be, like processions? Kids with flowers?"

The Lightborn finally stopped, ten feet in front of them, and bowed. "Oh, I only stand on formalities when they are to my advantage. Still. Let us do this right. You are speaking to Lord Thomas de Beforant, Lord Commander of Stradeburg and Archbishop Desahl, leader of the united Church of the Circle." He waited expectantly.

"That sounded impressive. You think we should, what's that thing, prostrate ourselves before them?" Liam asked Chase.

Chase squinted. "Probably. Anyway. I've heard about the archbishop before. He had another name back then, though. But I've never heard about you. *Lord Commander.* Are you some sort of city guard?"

Beforant laughed, a loud, melodious sound, seemingly carefree and joyful. "You could say that. My noble house guards Stradeburg. And by extension, the rest of the lands of Light."

The archbishop caught up to him, stubbornly striding forward with a determined gaze.

Thomas slapped him on the shoulder, ignoring the wince. "The archbishop here is a new version, as you noted. The old one proved troublesome. Now," His eyes, though glinting with barely restrained mirth, held darker depths. "my former outburst was predicated on the fact that I guessed that I would find you again."

"Again?" Chase frowned. He was keeping up with the banter, if barely, but he was dead sure a third of the conversation was hanging right out of his reach, mocking him with context, missed pointers, and things that might actually make a difference. If only Sera were here...*no*. "Did I rob you at some point? You nobles tend to look the same. After the first fifty or so, you kind of blend into each other in the mind."

"Did you rob me?"

The mirth died down slightly. For a second, it felt like there was real pressure roiling down on Chase. Then it faded, and he wondered whether he'd imagined it.

"I guess you could say that you did. The missing hand and dark skin would make you Chase. Which means that the blindingly handsome young man here is Liam, and the recalcitrant rascal behind you both would be Kith. I would ask about your female friends, but that is not important now. What is important, nay, *crucial*, is that you understand that I know who you are. I also *know what you did*."

"You mean...run from the people trying to enslave us?" Kith raised an eyebrow.

"Kill an inquisitor?" Chase asked. "Because you can only prove we did that once. No. Twice."

"*You made me look bad*," Beforant snapped. "Like I care about the lives of any inquisitors. They are cheaper to buy than good boots."

"*My lord!*" The archbishop gasped audibly.

"Shut it, you sniveling cretin. There is nobody here to hear, and you know it to be true." He ignored the cavalry behind them both, pointing at Chase. "You. Ruined my plans. I momentarily lost face because of you. You could have had it all. A luxurious life back in Stradeburg, all the pleasures street slum like you could ask for, with few responsibilities. Yet, you decided to trick them all and run away. And you ran *right* here, with the clear intentions of snatching yet another deck for yourselves."

Chase drew back slightly before he realized he was giving away his shock. Catching the hint of satisfaction in the lord's gaze, he had to admit that the game was up. He nodded. "How did you even know?"

"It is the only logical deduction. Your stunt back in Isarn reverberated throughout the lands of Light, you must understand. The realization that the Deck of Darkness was real, and that its wielders were *hostile*. Oh, the lamentation of the clergy. Oh, the fearmongering." He snickered. "I must admit, for a while, I listened to their cries and found them almost realistic. Especially when you exposed the scheme of the church to steal decks in the Elemental towers. I did fear a greater conspiracy at that point, though it made little sense to me at the time. Why would you spend so much time there, only to end exposing yourself to counter the church? Was it because you were plotting a theft yourselves, or because you wanted to expunge their influence?"

"They are clearly heretics. Why you would even entertain this talk, Lord Beforant, I fail to—"

"Shush now." Thomas raised a finger, stilling the archbishop. "I'd say that the grownups are talking, but then I realize just how young you three are." He tapped his lip slowly. "No. My fellow nobles were fearmongering, but you are not moved by something as dark as that, are you?"

Chase considered the situation, then figured he had nothing to lose. The more they talked, the better the chance that they would be able to take the Lightborn by surprise or even talk them into not attacking. Not that he had high hopes of that. This Thomas person seemed like somebody who was used to getting what he wanted. He sighed. "We simply wanted a home."

"Chase!" Kith scolded.

Chase shrugged. "We're not gaining anything from holding back at this moment. It's all we ever wanted. A home for all of us, where we wouldn't have to fear being attacked while we slept. Where we wouldn't have to fear getting targeted by preachers foaming at the mouth."

The lord chuckled. "Oh yes. I see it now! You attacked the instigators in the towers, simply because you realized they would ruin your future home." He clicked his tongue. "Of course, dear Tatiana Skysworn realized that, even though you had saved *her* home, you could not stay—and so she cast you out, did she not? So cold-hearted."

Chase nodded softly. He glanced down to not let the relief show that he hadn't guessed that they were collaborating with the High Elementalist. "We gave her cards, and got some help. But she still ordered us to leave."

"You were being hunted, by then. Inquisitors everywhere. So, you turned to the only professed enemies of our empire, the Furyborn. And somehow, you convinced them to take you in."

Chase shook his head and lied. "Yes and no. We paid them off, gave them a secondary Deck of Darkness, too."

"You never allied with them? My!"

"No." Chase searched for something that would sound feasible. "While they did not doubt that we were running from you, we were not *of the blood*. We weren't born in Furyborn lands. So, the best we could get was an agreement that they'd distract

you all and let us slip away, at the cost of earning Dark cards."
He grimaced. "How *did* you find us, by the way?"

"Scouts." He smiled. "You were distracted, fighting some
Guardians, as you were traveling toward the border of Liberty
lands and they spotted you."

"Radine! I'll skin that bird!" Kith fumed. "She was sure nobody was watching."

The lord smiled. "Liberty, then. Why go to Liberty?"

Chase could see the opening now. It was a gamble, but
then, everything about this confrontation and the conversation
had been a gamble. At best, he could likely earn a ceasefire, a
temporary reprieve. It would still be worth it. He smiled mirth-
lessly. "Same as it's always been. We want a home. Just a place
where we can stay, among people, and not have to worry about
being killed every moment of every day. At that point, it seemed
like the safest choice was to see if we could make it into Liberty
lands."

"Then why did you not accept the invitation from the
Lightborn?" Lord Beforant seemed honestly perplexed.

"Really, man?" Kith snorted. "Invitation? That armsmaster, what'shisface—?"

"Armsmaster Rillek." Liam spat on the ground.

"Yeah. He held us up at swordpoint, and said we'd be
slaves, guarantees for Chase's good behavior, while hinting that
Sera and Cilia would be...used. Meanwhile, that Inquisitor Vor-
bis promised us death and torture. You call that an invitation?"

Beforant rubbed his forehead. "Can you see how hard it is
to get competent help? They are all stuck in their preconditioned
ideas of their own power and position in the world, and refuse
to change, even when presented with new information." He
shook his head. "I am not the same. I was...miffed with you over
my loss of face. However, now I see that you could not be blamed
for that. My apologies for the misunderstanding. Blaming you
would be senseless—and trying to do what others have done before me, even worse. Hence, I offer you exactly what you
wanted. I offer you a home. Free of responsibilities. Free of fear.
The only thing you need to grant us in return is what you have
already given the other nations. Cards." He pointed in the direction they'd been traveling.

Kith sneered. "You're not even going to *pretend* you're doing this for the sake of Light or something?"

"Come now. Why put on an act, when we all know this
would be something done in my own interest? This is why I
brought Archbishop Desahl in the first place. In order for you to
learn that I have the church solidly under my thumb."

The archbishop's gaze was fixed with subdued hatred, but
he didn't say anything.

Lord Beforant continued. "You come from the lands of Light. It has been a long, arduous journey. But you need not suffer any longer. Come home. To a *real* home, that you can choose and create for yourself. You won't have to worry about anything except enjoying your life."

Chase considered the offer. Truly considered it. What surprised him the most was the fact that he didn't even find it tempting. He wondered why that was. It wasn't that he thought the pompous bastard couldn't deliver. He was clearly rich and powerful enough that he could order just what he offered. Rather, it was the unspoken fact present behind the noble's words: "We are going to keep doing what we've always done and keep down anybody else while we take over the world."

A year ago, he'd have leapt at the chance. Guaranteed safety and luxury? Yes please. Now, he only considered the offer in order to see how he'd be able to manipulate the situation to their advantage and give Liberty a break, to solidify their strength and be able to stand up to the Lightborn.

"I like the idea, Lord Beforant," Chase began. "Which assurances can you give us?"

"Thomas, please. Anybody important enough that I desire to haggle with them in person can call me by my first name. Also...which assurances would you *like*? I have most of the Lightborn lands at my beck and call, own entire brothels, hundreds of businesses, command thousands of soldiers. I am at your disposal." He bowed.

How to frame this, then? They'd have to seem amenable to the idea, but could not afford to give away too much. "Okay. Thomas. If you are as rich as you claim, that part won't be an issue. We honestly won't require that much."

"Chase. What are you doing?" Kith hissed, alarmed.

"Taking care of us all. The way we'd *all* want to be taken care of, including Sera. You think she wouldn't want to get back in touch with some in her family?" Her family who had betrayed her at the tip of a hat. He couldn't say it any more clearly to Kith in front of the noble.

Fortunately, Kith subsided gracelessly. Liam took it better, simply accepting that these kinds of talks were not his forte and waiting for a decision.

Chase continued, gaze directly on the nobleman. He seemed so at ease, so in control, it unnerved him. "The single thing we want above all is safety. And, because you've been honest with us, I'll grant you the same courtesy. We have been promised a safe haven within Liberty. We intended to take it, but...didn't expect the fog of their defenses to be deactivated in the process. This is why we were here today. To see if we could meet your forces and handle the situation before war ensued."

"Ah. And have you found your answer?"

"The answer just became a bit more complicated than I expected." Chase grimaced. "I thought we'd have to run back to our defensive position with you on our heels. Only, it truly feels like you're giving us the best offer here. So, how would you go about letting us do that, without putting ourselves fully in your power, Thomas?"

"That does present a conundrum," he admitted.

"How about this?" Chase squinted, tapping his leg. "Unless I misread you completely, you're not the type who makes rushed decisions."

Thomas dipped his head, conceding the point.

"You don't *have* to invade right this moment. Further, I mean. First off, I doubt you'd be able to actually win, and second, this does not feel like a situation where you are pushed on all sides to solve it instantly." Chase raised an eyebrow, saw the infinitesimally small nod, and continued. "So, the real issue here is trust."

He pointed at the ground at their feet. "Set up camp. Right here. Reinforce, do whatever it takes for you to feel safe. We will go back to the Liberators and tell them we are negotiating on their behalf. A year from now, we will know that you are the type to stick to their word, that you won't use violence, coercion, and the like to get what you want, when all it takes is patience. Then, we will defect to your side and hand you Liberty on a golden platter."

Thomas paused for a moment, considering the offer. "Truth be told, that does not sound like a bad arrangement. I would have to promise my peers that the offer was made in good faith, of course. Also, I could not show up empty-handed. Do you have any decks you could give me?"

"Not right this moment," Chase said honestly. "Also, that would very much tip the agreement in your favor again. Why would you even suggest it?"

Innocently, Thomas smiled. "I was just trying to decipher just how much you were keeping back. Then I would, at the very least, require that I, as well as a handful of chosen people, were granted Dark cards. That way, we would be able to show our peers that the offer is real."

A drop of cold sweat ran down Chase's spine. Of course he could've done that. Only, the deck was back in Salvation. "We will have to think about that. I rather do like the rest of your deal. Give us a few days, and we will debate it, see if we cannot come to an agreement."

From one second to the next, the magnanimous facade cracked. "No." The word rang with finality, a death sentence. "This farce has gone on long enough."

"I told you, Lord Beforant. You cannot trust the spawn of Dark!" the archbishop spat.

He smiled wryly. "Spare me your gospel. This has nothing to do with the Dark, and you know it. This is simple dissembling." He sneered at the trio. "If you let amateurs talk for long enough, they will let things drop, that they would rather have kept secret. Such as the fact that they have already established a Wellspring." He shook his head dismissively. "Trying to buy me off with empty promises, while you establish yourself and spawn further Guardians and decks. It is a rather opaque stratagem. The only thing I still want to know: did you actually tell the truth about your time with the Furyborn and Elementals? I know you have access to Elemental cards."

Chase smiled a self-ironic smile at the noble. "Eh. Bits and pieces were true. Did you actually tell the truth, when you promised us the world?"

Thomas tilted back his head and barked with laughter. "Oh, that is rich. Chase. Chase. Chase. Such a ridiculous moniker. I would have loved to have known you earlier, so I could have established proper control over you. You are the most wonderful package of insouciance, street smarts, and a sharp tongue, all wrapped with a bow of raw power! The answer, of course, is no. Had I a way to truly control you? Most definitely. Yet, allowing you to live freely would be an ever-present dagger hovering near my back. Five Tier threes and fours, who might, with enough incentives, switch sides at any moment? Too powerful."

"I knew it. I knew he was a backstabbing bastard the moment I laid eyes upon him," Kith spat. He slowly drew his hand axes.

Ignoring him, Chase asked, "So, what happens now? We go back to Liberty and see you on the battlefield?"

With a puzzled smile, Thomas answered. A light burst into the air above him. "Why would I ever do that? What happens now is, I take by force that which should rightfully be mine."

CHAPTER 41

"At the core of Liberty lies the element of potential. This, obviously, can be used as potential for building something. Yet, Liberty is always stronger when it has something against which to struggle. This explains why a crafted Liberty item draining enemy boosts will always be more efficient than one building its own boosts from nothing." Dammit. How come he had to be such a bastard? Judging from his writings, he was a crafting prodigy. I would have loved to talk crafting theory with him for...a year! (Book 2, Page 43.)

Having risked his life too many times over the past months, Chase sometimes wondered whether he was getting inured to the sensation. If he was growing too accustomed to the rush, the joy of racing across the dagger's edge of oblivion.

It never left him, though. That throbbing thrill, the wave of throwing himself into something that could easily see him dead. Only, there was one emotion he had not expected to sense, comparing himself directly with a Tier-six enemy. The burgeoning sense of it being too *easy*.

Oh, Thomas most definitely tried to kill them all, right at the start, or at least hurt them badly. Three cards flashed on his body in succession, and light started to shine, as if he were a summoned Light Elemental. One card had no visible effect. One produced a swirling wave flashing around him in a constant circle, ebbing and flowing, while the final saw a flood of light emerge from his chest and burst outward ahead of the noble, as if he were going to drown the land in light.

Yet, to Chase, it felt like the powerful noble was moving within a layer of mud. He could *feel* the massive boost from Stealing is Giving, Too. That, on top of the handful of different attribute-increasing brews from Nordon, the two attribute-increasing bracelets from Cilia, and the bonus from their enchanted boar sleeping furs saw him at a level of power he usually associated with the end of a long, grueling fight.

Name: Chase
Title: Dark/Light/Elemental/Fury/Liberty rogue
Step: 24 (Tier 4)
Strength: 20 (+1 Tier bonus) (+13) = 34
Agility: 24 (+13 Tier bonus) (+16) = 53

Toughness: 23 (+1 Tier bonus) (+17) = 41
Mental Power: 28 (+1 Tier bonus) (+14) = 43
Potential: 33 (+1 Tier bonus) = 34

They'd agreed upon the tactics beforehand, of course. Chase had Winds of Change on, ready to switch cards at a moment's notice. On top of that, the moment Thomas attacked, he used Fight Another Day, increasing the running speed for Kith and Liam. Then he activated Circle of Darkness, allowing them all to run away under cover of darkness, without any overwhelming risk of a direct hit.

Kith had Sacrificial Saints applied on top of that, fending off any lethal attacks, while Ties Airbound had him sprinting back up the slope at a supernatural pace. The rest, he saved for the surprise.

Liam, although slower, was fully on the defensive as he hurtled backward, Become the Clay and Draining Ward joined by the magic-draining effects of Ravenous Shadows. He was ready to take any hit and keep going.

He might have had to, as well. The flood of light rushing from Thomas started as a blinding, fiery presence, and grew in both damage and intensity, with no sign of tapering out.

Only, Chase was running the opposite way. Toward Thomas. With his natural speed nearly tripled, his Steps of Brilliance took him above the brunt of the onslaught of the light, and within seconds, his sword flashed out several times in a row.

The first several strikes were deflected, clashing with the swirling force and gently pushed away, like a set of reproving hands nudging him off course. Yet, after the fourth strike, with Thomas slowly, ever so slowly, edging the beam of his attack upward, he felt the force diminish and fade. And his following strike hit flesh.

The attack didn't go off unnoticed *or* unpunished. From all sides, cards started to go off. So far, nobody had been fast or prepared enough to actually use anything against him. Another slash curved down and hit bone. Chase's next hit bounced off a gleaming barrier.

Chase groaned, as he saw the card flashing on the archbishop next to him. Yet another barrier was active on the healer himself. Too late. He flung himself sideways and down, continually using his Steps of Brilliance to shift altitude as he veered back and up the hill.

Now, the enemy was truly reacting. Arrows whizzed through the air, and yells and commands rang out in a chaotic mess.

Chase didn't care. They were getting away. They were in place for the next part, and Thomas, having taken a nasty wound, was unlikely to go after them personally. At least, so he hoped.

Within moments, the enemy unleashed their cavalry. The ordered ranks of the Lightborn exploded into a ragged advance.

When Chase made it up the hill, Kith was waiting. He wasn't even breathing hard. Instead, he stood right in front of his chariot, while shapes solidified around him.

He'd overtaken Liam, who was doggedly running on, halfway up. Smoke arose from one shoulder of his armor, but apart from that, he was suffering from no visible damage.

"Get ready! They're *all* coming! Hundreds of them! This will need to work!" Chase yelled. Then he placed himself right at the back of the group of bestial, bright, dark, and even demonic-looking beings appearing left and right, crowding the small hilltop. Right at their back, Spike bounced about, clearly uneasy at being out in the open for all to see.

Seeing Liam drawing closer to the lip of the hill, Chase ran a few dozen feet off to the side and switched away from Fight Another Day to Among the Raindrops. Keeping Circle of Darkness large enough to hide both himself and the ever-increasing group of summoned creatures, he sensed more than saw the drops building up a burgeoning mass of liquid all around him.

Nobody kept the cavalry back. Nobody countermanded the order to charge. They had to have spotted them on top of the hill by now—but they probably didn't believe that this small a group could have any effect on an army the size of theirs.

Obviously, they ought to be right in their presumption. The Lightborn were charging in several uneven lines hundreds of feet wide. The mounted troops were clearly aiming for a pincer maneuver—something particularly effective when they had as much space available as they did here. They might get bogged down at the center, but would be able to sweep around on either side and engulf them at will, overwhelming them from the sides and behind.

Chase readied his short sword, taking great care not to nervously finger the blade.

The first cavalry riders burst over the edge of the hill and barreled straight into the summoned defenders. Kith's Tainted Earth grasped at the legs of the armored faith deer. An Earth-aspected thing, looking more like a rolling hill than anything else, opened tree trunk-wide arms. Two dozen beings, chosen for toughness and defense, stood ready to grasp, to hold and slow.

Chase felt the first couple of enemy effects tearing at the edges of his Circle of Darkness card, but so far, his Mental Power reigned supreme. The darkness stayed active.

The first clash was loud: bestial screams and the battle cries of Lightborn charging in stark contrast with the absolute silence of the defending summoned beings. Then, the edges of the first wave started swinging inward to overwhelm them from either side.

Chase activated his surprise, switching from Circle of Darkness to A Friendly Wave. He flung his arms wide with a mental effort. Following the motion, the amassed acidic droplets from Among the Raindrops rose and traveled outward in growing waves, hitting the cavalry nearest their position first.

Where the wave struck, mounts and riders fell, pain-filled cries filling the air, as the acid started to burn and constrict their movement.

Unfortunately, he had not had enough time to truly build the wave, and it crested too early, leaving at least two-thirds untouched on either side.

Seeing their targets emerge from the darkness, they circled well around their impeded brethren, initiating a charge meant to overwhelm and kill.

In response, two things happened. First, a massive buzzing arose, as Kith's Apian God flung itself at the incoming cavalry, each of the tiny insects imbued with a spark of Enforced Entropy, removing any positive buffs or effects on the faith deer and their riders. Second, all other summoned beings on Chase's side flung themselves forward at the nearby enemies in a suicidal attack.

The central group of Lightborn cried in joy, as their opposition threw themselves at them. Even with most of their buffs and effects disabled, strong arms, well-trained mounts, and well-crafted weapons would carve the summons up in little time.

For any other force on Ordei, this would have been the end. All their summons defeated, they would be bereft of any weapons, forced to attempt a questionable surrender. However, this force had access to not just one, but five decks, granting them an unprecedented range of choice. Seconds after their first summons died, replacements emerged in front of them. They were still incredibly outnumbered, but it would take more than just a single round of extermination to cull the numbers of these summoners.

Also, strangely, the oncoming wave of riders was floundering. Some of the riders were slowing their advance. Others cried out in alarm. A few tumbled to the ground. One mount missed a pothole, crushing its rider underneath its armored bulk.

Chase cried out, "It's working! Now!" Then he flung himself forward to take the battle to the enemy.

This was what they'd based their entire plan upon. Liam's Tribune of Retribution, Blindness was truly useless against a force with healers on board, or in a life-and-death situation where everything would be decided in seconds. Yet, in a situation like this, they had been able to throw all their summoned beings at the enemy, absorbing enough damage to rapidly amass dangerous levels of retributing blindness on the enemy. From one minute to the next, the incoming cavalry, mounts and all, were effectively blinded.

Now, the defenders burst into a dozen different directions. Where the first batch of summons had been chosen due to their resilience, these were selected based on other criteria: speed, evasion, and, above all, damage output. A dozen blade-limbed foxlike creatures threw themselves at the legs of the faith deer with no sense of self-preservation. A living torch flung bursts of flame. One ponderous stick-thin, tall being with scythe arms seemed to carve chunks out of reality along with the antlered beasts.

On the left side of the hilltop, Chase sprinted among the enemy, short sword stabbing and biting with preternatural agility. He had no problems killing the Lightborn. They'd joined the invading forces and knew what they were going into. Sera might go into a long-winded philosophical debate on what constituted a real choice, but for Chase, it was easy. They could've run. They didn't. This made them fair game—blindness or no.

Attacking the blinded mounts cost him more. The poor beasts had no similar choice, and they were proud, powerful creatures. But he did not hold back—in fact, he targeted the mounts before the riders. A rider without a mount was just another body. A mount without a rider would still be able to challenge them for speed and be ridden by another. Also, their sense of smell and general instincts might make them more formidable opponents than the riders, when blinded.

On the right side, Kith did the same. Hand axes rising and falling in a lethal, unstoppable pattern, he dipped and weaved, flinging himself into openings, punishing them mercilessly. With his Heart card active, his movements were lithe and his attacks deadly. Even with his attention fixed on the enemies before him, his control over the insects—which kept any buffs on enemies from kicking in—was absolute.

The cavalry wavered. Little by little, they were realizing that this was not a fight that could be won. The rare few riders who had higher Mental Power and were less affected by Tribune of Retribution, Blindness could see the larger image and notice that the numbers were turning against them.

A trio of riders who seemed less affected by the blinding effect than others wheeled around the attacking creatures and aimed straight for the group of summoners controlling their summons from up on the chariot.

Liam stepped in their way. Like a defending wall, he placed himself right between them and their target and did not flinch or waver.

The first lance hit like an arrow striking a point, carrying the full momentum of both mount and rider, several hundred pounds of weight, with the added weight of a last-second burst of speed on top.

For the first time in actual combat, Liam used Canceling Strike. His shield slammed outward, striking the lance. By all rights, the lance strike should have continued and Liam bowled over by the incoming beast. Instead, the lance tip *stopped*, as if it had hit an invisible wall.

If he had been quick enough to react, the rider might have dropped the lance. But he was entirely dedicated to the strike, with the lance thoroughly couched under the arm. When the lance stopped, the shock slammed the rider backward, with a horrible tearing sound from the arm. The momentum of the mount tried to carry it forward, creating conflicting forces, tearing the rider off its back and slamming it to the ground.

Liam met the deer with the descending full force of his truncheon. The ring of the weapon against the helmeted skull of the faith deer sounded like a gong. The beast hit the ground and did not get back up.

The two other riders had to swerve to avoid their fallen comrade. One veered left, the other right. The one on the right yelled, panicking as he hauled at his mount's reins to avoid crashing. When he looked up again, Liam was sprinting right at them, truncheon raised.

The one on the left spotted his opening. Right this moment, nothing stood between him and the defenseless summoners on the chariot. His mount leapt, narrowly avoiding the steel obstacle of the downed rider, and he barely stayed in the saddle as it landed, loping onward. He couched his lance, readying for a bloody impact—and looked dead into the eyes of a Liberty caster.

Flame lanced out in a twenty-foot-long stream, engulfing the beast and rider both.

That was the sign for the three casters to finally let loose. They had been given firm orders: Wait for the enemy to become fully entrenched in their charge before attacking. Then, before they realize just how badly they are caught, strike with everything you have.

The casters, as all the defenders to join their group, had volunteered. They had been chosen for one specific quality: the ability to cause large-scale damage.

Seconds after the charging rider was torched, three cards activated. Two of them were Tier three, and the final actually Tier four. And, just like that, the battlefield changed.

A fiery formation blossomed at the back of the rightmost wing of the cavalry. Starting as a swirling core, it swiftly spread outward like an ever-expanding whirlpool of fire. And the fire *consumed*.

On the left, several smaller fields came into being. These were smaller, person-sized bursts of lightning that emerged and left again within seconds, leaving behind lingering images of lightning cages. They did not kill outright, but they stunned and left enemies drained, sometimes to the point where they dropped to the ground, unable to control their shivering limbs.

Between the cavalry and the rest of the Lightborn army emerged a larger presence. At first, it was barely perceptible: a slight fog, easily ignored amidst the multitudes of effects, fighters and cards clamoring for attention. Within seconds, it thickened, though, leaving a low-hanging carpet of greenish-grey fog covering the entire escape vector. Slowly, the fog traveled closer to the embattled cavalry force.

Now, cries arose among the cavalry. Even near-blinded, the Lightborn fighters were wreaking havoc on the fresh summons. Chosen for offense and damage, these summoned beasts and creatures were not hardy and rarely armored. Yet, with the new damaging effects emerging amidst their ranks from the casters, and Chase and Kith tearing through them like nightmarish monsters, the Lightborn were dropping faster than they were able to work their way through the summons standing in their way.

Cries of retreat started to erupt throughout their ranks. It started with one, then a smaller group, and finally an entire wave of confused and scattered riders struggled to remove themselves from the conflict. Some who were still able to see a bit grabbed the reins of friends too blinded to find their way.

The Liberators made the riders pay. With nobody defending themselves properly, the summoned creatures flung themselves suicidally at the fleeing riders. Kith and Chase followed their example, harrying their flanks, carving into the hind legs of any mounts attempting to put distance between themselves and the pursuit. When they reached the outskirts of the, by now, nearly impenetrable fog cloud, Chase and Kith stopped their pursuit, even as the summoned creatures kept on, charging into the obscuring mist with abandon.

The casters, Liam, Chase, and Kith focused on the enemies and mounts still present on their side of the fog. There were many—more than sixty left. Some were near paralyzed from the shocking experience of being unable to see; some turned on themselves in circles, striking or slashing out at any sound with claw, lance, and sword. Others were wounded, or slowly crawling away, hoping to last until reinforcements arrived.

They were easy pickings for the experienced trio and the casters who could pick their targets with ease. Mounts and riders fell from lethal card effects, carved or beaten to death, to the backdrop of the overhanging poison cloud.

From within the cloud, little could be seen. Yet, there was plenty to be heard. Too much. Harsh, bubbling cries. Wet, phlegmy sounds. Above all rang the thunder of the incoming army.

From one moment to the next, the poison cloud lifted. Dispersed like it had never existed, it revealed the situation of those left within.

Chase nearly gagged at the sight.

Summoned creatures, mounts and riders alike lay inside the cloud. Some still moved, struggling or dying. Slowly. Some foamed at the mouth. Others crawled across the ground, coughing through blood-tinged lips as they sought the salvation of clear air.

On the other side, bright lights emerged, lighting up the Lightborn as fighters with helping buffs reached them. Kith's insects had long since died inside the fog, and the Lightborn effects stepped in right away. Yet, many were too far gone for simple buffs to aid them, and the healers did not arrive with the front ranks.

Even so, the numbers were telling. Once the Lightborn ranks passed the downed cavalry, they'd be able to move straight past them and emerge on the other side, bearing down on Chase and the others.

Chase yelled, "Thirty seconds. Then we flee!" He stabbed into the throat of a downed deer and sprinted for a blinded rider on foot, who was circling around himself, stabbing at intervals at imagined foes. Three quick slashes saw him down, and then he ran back toward the chariot. Before long, the chariot was rolling, creating distance between themselves and the pursuit.

Inside the chariot, they allowed themselves to relax and drop to the floor, covered in sweat and worse. Their scheme had worked. They'd managed to end the fastest of their enemies and gotten away unscathed.

The battle might just have started. But they'd won the fight.

CHAPTER 42

"At times, I would love to open the borders slightly. There are so many creations I miss from Earth's Ward. Crafted items that would improve our lives. Not to speak of the food. Fire burn me, the food! Only, they would not be able to understand what I have wrought here. Their lack of vision would inevitably lead to conflict." Yes. Lack of vision. That's definitely it. At times, I actually think that he understood just how monstruous the society he built had become, but then he writes something like this. (Book 2, Page 51.)

"I figured we were dead meat." Gelly was back on her summoned steed. She'd taken to the role of outriding scout with ease, looping back and forth to ensure their pursuit wasn't catching up and that they didn't have any unforeseen surprises waiting for them ahead. Right now, she was riding alongside the chariot, delivering the summary of the army's proceedings. "They tried catching up to us for a while, but they finally relented. Their healers tried to save those they could from our fight." She spat to the side. "Ugly sight, that. But it's good news, for us. Barely any mounts made it."

"That is logical," an elderly summoner said. Gavin, an older mind, the only Tier-four to join them apart from the healer. Even though his body was frail and he looked like he would fall over at any moment, his mind was sharp and his reactions impeccable. He'd already stated that he would not mind giving his life to defend his brethren. "I have tested my card as often as possible in what little time we had—without targets, obviously. My fog hangs closer near the ground, hence, the mounts would have been the most exposed to the fumes."

"Not the worst outcome." Kith frowned as he made the chariot change directions to avoid an outcropping of rocks. "It was an ugly end, but it's done."

"I would do it again. Besides, left unchallenged, the horrors they would inflict on our people would be worse."

"Nobody's disagreeing with you there, Gavin." Chase patted his back gently. "For now, though, it's time to rest and apply any increases you've managed. It's a sad thing that having the Wellspring back in Salvation means I won't be able to grant anybody cards out here, but we can't have it both ways." He shrugged and grinned. "As for me, I've got increases waiting.

One Step! I finally made it! The moment we make it back to Salvation, I'm joining Kith in the Tier five club!"

"Another clash like this, and I might join you both," Gavin said. "Do you have any suggestions on where to apply my attributes? I will not spend them on Toughness, but I do not wish to fall behind in effectiveness."

"No Toughness? Why?" Kith frowned.

"My life is forfeit. That, I have adjusted to. I will not waste any points that might have helped me slay further enemies on prolonging my own lifespan." The gleam in his eyes was nothing short of fanatical.

"I—" Chase started over. "Not sure I follow your logic, man. The tougher you are, the more likely you are to live to see another fight."

He didn't answer, merely shook his head.

Shrugging, Kith took over. "If that's the way you want to do it, there's two paths available to you. As long as we manage to keep the chariot with us, we'll have the advantage of speed, and you won't need Agility or Strength. Meaning, either you double down even further on Mental Power for efficiency and control, or you go with Potential, hoping to get even better cards when we're back in Salvation."

He looked to the others, who were mostly paying attention, though a few looked about ready to keel over from exhaustion. "That goes for all of you, really. Toughness for staying power, Mental Power for efficiency, or Potential if you're aiming for better cards at higher Tiers. Agility and Strength are wonderful, if you want to get up close and personal. But right now, we have our work cut out for us. We need to be ready for the next part."

"What's that, then? You've been mighty tight-lipped, so far." Banes glowered.

Chase nodded, looking the gruff summoner in the eye. "We have. First, we needed to know what we were dealing with and how we'd do. Now, we're in a different position. I'm sure they'll have scouts and the like, rogues or summoners with cards that help them see or hear what's going on. Kith?"

He shook his head. "Nothing airborne. Been looking for my bloody bird for ages, and there's nothing up there."

"All right. We'll have to chance it. Without Cilia around, we'll just have to hope that nobody's listening in. The odds of somebody having cards that can let them listen in invisibly at this range are likely remote." Chase scratched his neck. "We'll have to time this. Kith's kitty cart—"

"I hate you so much," Kith snarled.

"Has a nasty downtime, and if we're caught with our pants down, we won't have any way of making it away safely. Also, we did manage to end most of their faster fighters...but we had to reveal a good deal of our cards to do it. Meaning, they'll be ready for us. At best, we get *one* shot to truly surprise them. We're taking it tonight. One overwhelming ambush. We go in, throw everything at them, cause as much damage as we possibly can, then we run off. Best-case scenario, they try to follow, and we can grind them down slowly from a distance."

Banes's mouth looked like he was chewing on hay. Eventually, though, his lips split in a grim smile. "Sounds like my kinda party. Best lie down for a while, then. I'm guessing we're hitting them at night?"

"You're guessing right. They're likely expecting it, but...I think we can still get the drop on them." Chase smiled.

About an hour before sunset, they were striding across the vibrant grasslands, taking the chance to enjoy the sounds of the wildlife. Once the Lightborn army entrenched themselves for the evening, they'd erected their own camp to rest and get what sleep they could. Their rest had been tense, with Gelly skipping her own sleep in order to patrol in the direction of the Lightborn and hopefully catch any raiding parties aimed their way.

Fortunately, the only Lightborn to leave the defensive confines were a large mass of scouts, likely rogues, indebted, and Lightborn summons roaming the ground in front of the barricades. Behind them, the camp stood, well-erected and lit up, as a monument, shouting for the challengers to do their worst.

The summoned creatures were actually a help—or, rather, they answered a few important questions for their group. First, of course, was the number of summoners hidden within the ranks of the army. Judging from the number of different types of summons, and allowing for at least half of the summoners to be sleeping, that had their number quite low...maybe around fifty summoners total. The second, even more important question, centered around the kinds of cards that the army had access to. Based on visuals alone, there was a decent chance that the majority of the army, very characteristically for the Lightborn, had *no* cards except for Light cards. This would make their job a whole lot easier—especially with Kith's Antithesis of Light summon being able to specifically debuff Light effects.

All told, the combined forces arranged outside of the swiftly arrayed defensive embankments were not unimpressive. There were perhaps a full three hundred indebted standing around with bad armaments and little to no armor. These indebted were likely to have little training, and their lack of any sort of formation attested to their situation being just like when Chase and his friends had been indebted.

The Lightborn rogues and archers, meanwhile, were spread out among their numbers. Most likely, they were chosen for their attention, and meant to spot any potential issues before the unprofessional indebted.

The rest of the defenses were rather more indefinable. A wide trench had been dug, and the soil used to erect a rough embankment—little more than a steep two-foot incline, but enough that they wouldn't simply be able to drive the chariot right into the camp.

At the moment, they were walking at a snail's pace, a few miles off from the sides of the camp, in near silence. Chase maintained his Circle of Darkness, keeping them all enfolded in a layer of shadows that allowed them to proceed, hopefully, unseen. Every ten minutes, they stopped, sharing a word or two with a summoner, before they found a place to hide.

Kith walked over to whisper to Chase. "You see that? Those formations are bloody *tight*! That's not promising! Also, they've got firepits set up well *behind* the defenders, so the people manning the defenses won't be night blinded, while any attackers will be looking into the light. Shows they're thinkers! I don't like it!"

Chase nodded. "I don't disagree. But you see that? They're also helping us along. Look at all those nicely arrayed formations."

"That's helping us?" Even in near complete darkness, there was no hiding the sarcasm in his voice. "Maybe they could launch a few arrow volleys at us, help even further."

"Sometimes, I think Cilia has the right of it, when she yells at you for existing," Chase said. "I mean, they're sleeping the way they're arranged on the battlefield. Companies along with their healers. Archers for themselves. Casters and summoners in separate camps. Easy to find your targets."

"Oh. Well, why didn't you just say that was your point?"

Chase decided not to engage, instead scowling at the contrary bastard, a gesture which was lost to the shadows. Shaking his head, he moved on to offer Gavin a pat on the back and a few whispered encouraging words as the surly caster searched for a proper hiding place. Then they left him behind as well.

Soon, Chase, Kith, and Liam were the only ones still marching. They picked up the pace, eventually reaching the far side of the army and set down to wait, about a mile back. They located a slight dip in the lands that would hide their presence once the sun emerged over the horizon.

Gathering in a huddle, they held a short, whispered conversation.

"What do you think Cilia would think of all this?" Kith asked gleefully.

Liam snorted. "Oh, she'd hate it. We know nothing about their powers and just finished the plan an hour ago. In fact, I can almost hear her shouting from here."

"I miss them." Chase nodded.

"Sure. Cilia's who you miss." Kith snorted. "Let's just get this over with, and you can return to your snooty noble. Speaking of which—are you sure going off by yourself is such a good idea?"

"Pits no. She'd use words like 'convoluted,' 'harebrained,' and worse." Chase shook his head. "In fact, I think it's a horrible idea. But it's the best I could come up with. If we want to surprise them after today, we need to be able to hit them entirely unawares and distract them from what's happening. That also means taking out their eyes. And I should be able to outrun any of them—I hope."

"Sounds pretty bloodthirsty. That Gavin guy would approve." Liam shuddered.

"Yeah. That one's damaged goods. But he's still out here risking his life with us. So, we give him some leeway, right?" Chase asked.

"Yup. Even if he's nuts," Kith said. "Now git. You'll want to be in position before sunup."

"Good plan." Liam added, "Also, I want to see if I can get an hour's sleep."

Chase shook his head in amazement and took off, loping softly across the grounds, until he was at the opposite side of the camp from where they'd dropped off the first of the summoners. There, he found himself his own spot to hide in, before he finally let the Circle of Darkness fade and started to pick out future targets. When this went off, he was not going to hold back.

CHAPTER 43

*"Thirty years. That is how long it should take me to se-
cure Salvation. Slowly expanding, adding defensive items
where necessary, maintaining a principle of carefully screened
secrecy that allows defenders to control some items, leaving
me with the bare minimum of necessary supervision. Then, I
will finally be able to end the sham of my illusionary doubles
and reign my capital supreme."* Pits. That is insane! It also
proves we were right to act. But...this means there are defenses in the palace that should still operate at the hands of
specific guards? We will have to find those! (Book 3, Page 2.)

Chase stretched inside the tiny dip of the land. He
cracked his neck, slowly unsheathed his short sword
and clucked over a nick in the blade from their latest fight. Then,
he sat back down and waited for Kith to ruin the day for a certain
Tier-six.

Inside the camp, the early hours of the morning carried
little activity with it at first. A few workers were preparing
meals, mending clothes and the like, but most of the camp was
still asleep. As they had learned for themselves on the Waves,
you learned to ignore constant movement and noise, tuning out
anything that wasn't likely to go for your own throat. As such,
the working day had clearly started for a good number of the
servants, but not for the fancy Lightborn.

On their way from Salvation, Kith had toyed around with
his new Tier five cards as much as he could. It hadn't been nearly
as much as he'd wanted to, given that his summoned chariot was
necessary most of the day to ensure their speed. Yet, he'd tested
each and every one, to see which of the other cards might be the
more efficient in any given situation.

Internal Spark, he'd already tested in the battle just past.
The passive card was wonderful—especially combined with
Twice the Fun, doubling the number of his summoned creatures.
Not only did it help the summons understand and interpret his
commands better, it also granted them a slightly improved sense
of self, helping them to fight wiser and less mechanically. On top
of that, it worked, even when he switched to other cards. He said
it produced better results all around: better survivability, more

damage, faster reaction times. In result, Kith was able to manage more summons at the same time, to better effect, with less micromanagement.

Monument of Liberty, obviously, was a thing of joy back in Salvation, but not something he could truly test out, except for hearing about the impressive average rarity of cards that the other summoners had gained back in the city.

Light of Day, Day of Darkness, though...that one had taken some getting used to. At first, the summon seemed hard to use. Not due to a lack of efficiency, truly. Rather, it was that what should have been a subtle instrument arrived as a beacon in the night, or a swathe of night during the day, shouting out its arrival for the heavens to hear. That was the cause for many cusswords from Kith at first. Summoning a dozen very obvious humanoids, which immediately turned everything between them into the polar opposite of the current hour of day, wasn't as much a tool as it was asking to have your card canceled outright. Also, commanding a dozen humanoids at once was an instant ticket to migraine city. The very first time he activated it, Liam actually had to step in and heal him.

After a dozen tries, however, he got it. It was all about mental space and focus. Not only did the summoned beings not have to engage their effect straightaway—you could also ensure that they themselves neither shone, nor emitted darkness. On top of that, Kith learned that he could actually command the beings one, two, or four at the time instead of handling them all at once. Finally, he had realized that there was no true upper limit for distance—the only difference being that the effect was gradual—and the larger the area they had to cover, the less severe an effect they were able to bring to bear.

Kith had spent the last couple of hours preparing. The humanoids surrounded the army at a safe distance, prepared to act.

Chase smiled as he spotted the first sign of movement. One of the humanoids moved slowly past him, just a few hundred feet away. It was a dull shape, like a lump of clay given a vaguely human outline and then a semblance of life.

Had it only been the one, nothing would have happened. However, right this moment, eleven other identical beings started to move from their spots and went inward, straight for the Lightborn camp. And in between them, darkness brewed.

It started off nearly imperceptible. Nothing more than the shade of a cloud crossing the sky following the break of dawn. However, once the effect truly started, it built and grew, as the humanoids moved closer to one another. The truly notable detail was that the effect was active *everywhere* between the dozen summons. Meaning, at this point, darkness sprouted over an area more than three miles wide.

Chase waited for his cue, coiled up like a spring, ready to leap into motion. When, at long last, the first shouts arose, he froze for a split second. Then he was off, cards flashing. His first Sticky Fingers took hold against an indebted woman freezing from the surprise, granting him a point to Mental Power, even as Nights of Criffhaven activated, starting a slow upward Agility tick. Furthermore, One with the Soil came alive, letting him feel perfectly in control of his steps, an unwavering balance granting him the sensation he'd be able to fling himself headfirst to the ground and still land upright.

The first person to spot him was another indebted. He cried out, raising a trembling hand at Chase, without even going so far as to raise the long sword he'd been granted.

Chase shot him a grin and a wink, before utterly ignoring the man and racing straight for a Lightborn about three hundred feet from where he'd been hiding—a man with a short bow and enough focus to keep trained on the outskirts even after hours of inaction.

The Lightborn reacted within seconds. His bow rose in impeccable motion, aimed solidly at Chase; he aimed and released, while a card flashed on his arm. The arrow gained a warm glow, pulsing with deadly promise.

The arrow flew true. For most people, that would have been the end of their lives, the plan extinguished just as it started. Yet, Chase was not most people. At this point—Sera had done the calculations—he had as many attributes as about five non-wielders combined. When the arrow whooshed at him, he barely had to engage his brain to take a single dip, bend his neck just so, and allow the arrow to pass at a safe distance.

The archer was shocked enough from the miss that he simply stood and gawked for several seconds. He managed to loosen another arrow when Chase came within twenty feet, only, this time, the card effect was on cooldown.

Chase contemptuously deflected the arrow. Seconds later, his blade sliced across the man's jugular. All around him, cries of shock arose. Chase took them in, then continued, on the hunt for his next victim.

Meanwhile, behind him, the web of darkness gathered and tightened around the Lightborn camp.

For the next few minutes, Chase hunted. He raced around the enemy camp, keeping well out of arrowshot from the embankments, as he located and felled the Lightborn rogues and ranged attackers arrayed outside of the defensive structures. Every fifteen seconds, he used Sticky Fingers, which, along with Nights of Criffhaven, sent his attributes exploding upward.

The Lightborn soldiers outside of their defenses were professionals, no doubt about it. They were alert, well-armed and armored, and well-used to ordering the indebted around to use as meat shields instead of the Lightborn. Only, they were not used to somebody like Chase.

He ignored any indebted, racing among them, waving merrily where he could, winking as he aimed straight at the Lightborn before shooting off into the distance again. Yet, any Lightborn in his path died, quickly and efficiently.

The people inside the camp noticed him. Of course they did. But he was outside their range—and they had other things to worry about. He knew that, right this moment, they'd be fending off summoned creatures pressing in on them from the summoners on all sides of the camp.

The Liberators had all the same instructions—all summoned creatures should press straight for the Lightborn army, and not engage with any of the indebted. They'd complained of the inefficiency, but eventually relented.

The effect was a Lightborn army finding itself waking up a few hours before they were supposed to get up, promptly dipped into a growing darkness, before finding out that they were being attacked on all sides by an unknown number of enemies.

Predictably, chaos ensued.

Of course, it couldn't go on forever. The darkness kept thickening inside the camp as Kith's summoned beings moved closer and closer together—meaning, the summons themselves were approaching the confines of the camp, moving into clear sight of the indebted and, soon, the defenders of the camps themselves.

Mere minutes after darkness started to assault the camp, it gradually brightened again, and, seconds later, yet again as people started to take out the humanoids bringing the darkness with them. Soon, the unnatural shadows were entirely gone, leaving only a Lightborn army finding itself beset by an underwhelmingly small number of summoned creatures and...something else.

Chase reached two-thirds of a full circuit of the camp, when the horns announced a shift in the game. Within seconds, he noticed the armored shapes leaping over the battlements, followed by a massive spear of light rushing across the sky in his direction. He promptly switched Nights of Criffhaven for Fight Another Day, sacrificing Agility for sheer speed, and turned to flee, in the opposite direction of Kith and the rest. He'd nearly done his part. Now, he needed to draw them away. Only time would tell whether their real aim had been successful.

He loped off into the growing light of day. The warmth of the sun rivaled the growing hope in his heart.

***

"Get up, slowpoke. We've been waiting since forever." In contrast to his smart-ass comment, Kith lowered a hand to Chase and patted him on the back when he leapt up into the chariot and promptly collapsed.

Panting, Chase didn't say anything straightaway. He rested his head against the floorboards of the chariot. They felt kind of tingly. Had to be the magic inside them. Eventually, he shuddered and said, "Light scourge me, that was rough. I led them on a merry chase, and easily managed to keep away from them, but they just *kept* following somehow. I think one of them had a card that let them find me. Then the boosts from Sticky Fingers ran out along with most of my energy. Almost fainted. From then on, it was a long, long grind. I..."

"You're rambling," Liam said, not unkindly.

"Probably am." Chase rubbed his eyelids and yawned mightily. With an effort, he sat up. "I think my part was a success. How about—wait. We're missing somebody."

Kith nodded with a distant gaze. "Gelly. And that summoner with the Light summon that fired beams from the eyes."

"Betan," Liam added.

"Right. I saw Betan fall to arrows, right when I was riding the chariot back to pick them up. Gelly just never showed up." Kith grimaced.

"Damn." Chase fell silent for a while.

"We made it, though," Kith said. "All those distractions worked exactly like they were supposed to do. My Coils of Shadow had already made it into the camp safely and undetected, and were lurking in a supply tent. When we attacked, they were given free rein to attack the company of casters and summoners. It was...it was ugly. But it worked. They're all done for!"

"It wasn't worth it." Banes shook his head grimly. "You'll need to do better, kid. We've lost two hearts, and for what? For a shot at their casters that we would've had anyway. You're tossing—"

"Stow it, Banes." The elderly Gavin cut him off. "The sacrifice was worth it. We lost two of our number, yes. But they knew the risks and joined us regardless. And for that, we have managed to take out the majority of the wielders who were truly able to cause damage against us from a distance. Now, we will be able to harry them from afar, attack from the shadows, with little risk of reprisal. Two lives, for a chance at actual success? I'd pay thrice that and consider it a fair cost."

Chase grimaced at the cold assessment. Even so, he didn't disagree about that part. He spoke up softly over the rumbling of the chariot's wheels slowly distancing them from any pursuit.

"We might have succeeded regardless of the rest of us stepping up, yes. I agree. It's a possibility. But I doubt it. You all know they have healers divided throughout the army. Kith's vipers are killers, but they are not fast killers. It would just take a single healer with a card against poison, or a single alert squad noticing their presence to take them out. Our distraction worked, and the poison of the vipers wiped them out. Also, I managed to end the majority of all scouts they had out in front of the army. It is as Gavin says. They'll be much less capable of striking back at us now—and they'll also be less likely to spot us in the first place."

Banes's face scrunched up in displeasure, but he eventually assented. "I don't like it none, but okay. Better make sure it's worth it!"

"That's the plan." Chase nodded. "Speaking of plans. Those Lightborn being able to follow me? It's got me kind of spooked. Especially with Gelly gone and unable to scout. I think that maybe we should put extra distance between us and the army until we strike next time and keep watch."

Kith groaned. "I can already guess what you're about to say. I'm on shade duty while you all rest?"

Chase shrugged. "Sera could likely sell this one better, tell you how talented you are until you think it's your own idea." He grasped Kith's shoulder. "We need you to keep us all safe, Kith. And yes, that includes sacrificing some sleep. Can you do that?"

"You know...I think I'd actually prefer it if you tell Raudt and Svart how wonderful they are," Kith grumbled.

"Yeah, that's not happening."

CHAPTER 44

"I keep believing that there is more I should be able to do with the Keepers. Watching and listening is all well and good. But what if my Keepers or their wards were to collectively rebel? What if they decide to aim them all at me, one after the other? Maybe I should find additional ways of keeping my chosen ones in check?" He had them chained up and their tongues cut out. That is keeping them in check? I am so glad we killed him! (Book 3, Page 6.) *Bit harsh, eh Cil?*

Salvation—Serafine

"No. I do not see how we can wait any longer. We have already listened to the reports. You have all had the chance to estimate for yourself how well they are handling the influx. The hopefuls are not doing well and they need help." Serafine's voice was calm, collected, and reasoned, just like she had been taught. Inside, however, she wanted to rail and curse.

"But we've got the Keepers—I mean, Guardians—arriving soon, don't we? That should be able to reinforce them. There's no need for our defenders to risk their lives for something that is already well in hand." The voice from among the gathered crowd was loud, reasonable, and so very recognizable. Dante was a local mind, quite extraordinarily handsome, and likely the loudest proponent for the higher-Tier wielders to take over and rule Liberty "for the good of all."

Sera wanted to punch him.

She walked among all those gathered, sharing a smile here, a touch on the shoulder there. She'd been surprised that they had actually chosen the floor of the Savior's tower as the place to agree on their future government. Everybody, old and new, saw reasons to keep their discussions there, even if they were mostly symbolic.

They were down to about a hundred participants now. The huge crowds of the first days had somewhat dissipated, now that people understood how much work was involved in actually steering the country. There was no way it would work in the long run, but at least for now, those present were solidifying into a group that would be able to get work done, and not stall in eternal squabbling and bickering over details.

She reached the center of the large, open tower, where she was able to clearly see Dante and his hangers-on. A group of about fifteen, all clustered up to one side, making no secrets of their affiliations. There were two more of them than the day before. Not a good sign.

She took a spot where most people in the room would be able to see her and shook her head gently. "No, Dante. The new Guardians will most definitely not be able to reinforce them. You have all heard the messages from the Keepers we have been able to contact out near the borders. We have updated the map room with the actual changes, so you can see what it means for yourself in a moment. For now, let me just tell you this: in the long run, the new Liberty Guardians may prove sufficient. They will aid your defenders and be able to help them survive and grow against hostile Guardians and beasts. But for now, they are getting pushed back on all sides. If we ignore our defenders, we risk the Liberty lands being *completely* overrun."

At least they *had* finally erected the original Liberty Wellspring. They still hadn't agreed on how the rest of the decks should be shared out—or even *if* they should—but the Liberty Wellspring stood proud, right next to the Dark Wellspring, flanked by Kith's horribly ostentatious statue. She couldn't fault their choices in erecting it, either. The improved overall strength to their Guardians, along with its minor boost to Toughness for all inside the radius of the Wellspring in Salvation would make life easier. Eventually.

"Well, that is all well and good. Easy for you to say. You are safely ensconced here in Salvation, and will not have to risk your life. Meanwhile, it will be Liberty lives on the line." Dante snorted. "Typical outsider attitude."

A low murmur rang through the gathering. Most disapproving, though. This would have worked better for him during the first couple of days. Now, most present had heard about her and the others.

How to tackle him, though? Sarcasm? No. The people of Liberty were not accustomed to sarcasm. Also, they were starting to develop an intense resentment against any high-handed behavior and authoritarian behavior. Simple honesty, then. "Were I not ready to invest everything in Liberty, I would be long gone. My husband-to-be is currently risking his life against the Lightborn army, and we have invested all the decks we have earned over time here in Salvation. I have *one* thing in mind, and one alone: the growth and well-being of Liberty."

Sera noticed his grimace and met his eyes. Damn. He was aware he had misstepped. Unfortunately, he wasn't stupid—merely untrained at public debate. He might become a dangerous opponent in the long run. For now, though, she grasped onto the murmurs of agreement and tiny nods throughout the tower and ran with the momentum. "I believe everybody here who has not had the chance already, should move to the map room and see the situation for themselves, where the hopeful and outmost villages are falling back as one. Then, we should reconvene here in an hour to vote on what to do about that."

"Agreed." Lucille spoke up quickly. "I will lead anybody there straightaway. For all those who have already seen the evidence for themselves, we have the latest news from our Keepers right here for reading." She waved people over.

Sera nodded and added, with a polite smile, "Anybody who requires any sort of clarification about this news or additional information, do come to me. I would love to share the situation as we know it." Competence and momentum. They were hard to defend against. Unless he actually had any evidence she was making mistakes, Dante wouldn't be able to counter any of it, and they should be able to enact their plan.

Because the hopefuls on the borders *were* failing. It was hard to dispute. It wasn't because they were untrained, unprofessional, or were failing to defend Liberty because their Savior had died. They were simply unable to stand against the pressure without the Prism to defend them.

The power games among Lightborn nobility were not like these. There was, typically, a person like the lord of Isarn who had the ultimate authority over the city, whose decisions were, by all rights, law. However, that didn't mean he could just do what he wanted. Any decision that seemed unwise or unfair would weaken his position to the point where he might eventually be sidelined or punished by public opinion or, in extreme cases, even ousted by those in charge in Stradeburg. Hence, there were always discussions, debates, and struggles going on regarding any edge cases.

Sera had spent enough time looking pretty at the noble court in Isarn to understand how to get what you want. Competence, momentum, and a good plan. It didn't need to be a perfect plan. You would ask for input along the way and thank anybody who could improve on the general outline. That would make any helpers seem like they were on your team, and any outright detractors would have to present a markedly better plan to be able to compete.

To be entirely frank? Sera did not believe they would be able to manage that. Not in the limited time she was allowing them.

She knew very well that she was manipulating them. Twisting the situation in order to obtain the results she preferred. Yet, at her core, she believed she was doing the right thing. The more she talked to Liberators, the more she found herself liking them.

Most held an ingrained sense of community, a deep-set willingness to do their part, even at personal cost, and an impressive tolerance for change. Yet, they were far from perfect. The long years under the Savior's rule had made them passive—too passive—and unless prodded in the right direction, they could spend ages debating back and forth instead of acting. She would not let them do that against their own people.

"What do you think we should do, Pristine Mind?" The question came from somebody she barely recognized. A young woman, a member of the mass, and, unless she'd missed her among the crowd, not somebody who had been here before yesterday.

"Sera. Just Sera, please. My mind feels far from pristine." She smiled softly to take any sting from her rebuke. "What I believe would be the wisest course? I believe that, even though it is going to be a lot of work, and costly to those involved, we should pull back everybody in the most outlying villages and towns at least a hundred miles. Then, with the added influx of defenders and capable hands, we would be able to fortify and reinforce a band of towns and cities farther toward the heart of Liberty. Also, we would be able to cycle any wielders inside those fortified villages back a little at a time, in order to grant them all cards from all five decks. With them returning back to the villages and cities, their increased strength should be able to fend off any hostile Guardians."

The woman opened her mouth in shock.

Sera had her arguments prepared. Yes, it was a far-reaching decision and a logistical nightmare. But the numbers and threats justified the move. Yes, a *lot* of people's lives would be affected. But if it was that or death? Yes, the new fortified border would also be at risk, but the border would be shorter, easier to defend.

Only, when the Liberator open her mouth, what emerged wasn't a protest. "If we want to fortify these towns, shouldn't we reroute the builders straightaway?"

"I—what?"

"The builders. The blissful lands are constantly under construction. Salvation itself and…everywhere else." She shrugged. "My husband is a builder. They're used to working according to very, very specific plans, but that's no reason why they wouldn't be able to work on defensive walls and the like, as long as they know what is needed. Besides, they travel the lands constantly, for when towns and villages need larger work done to a proper standard. *I* would think that, as long as the need is strong enough, it would make a lot more sense to have them working on our defenses out in the lands, than continuing the current expansion of Salvation."

Sera gawked, then picked up her jaw. A moment later, she found herself smiling, nodding along, as she prompted the young woman to continue elaborating on her thoughts. She was *really* starting to like these people. They were no shirkers.

***

"How are we doing?" Lucille's question made Sera realize she had been lost to her own thoughts for several minutes.

The vote was over. The message was reaching out across the lands through means of all the summoners who had agreed to come back and work—properly—with the Keepers, in order for them to reestablish communication throughout the lands. Shortly, hopefuls would be pulling back, building up defenses in select villages, towns and cities, and preparing themselves to strike back.

"Acceptably." Sera nodded curtly.

Over the past few days, the two had built up a good rapport. Sera had tested her on various occasions, and by now she believed without reservations that the former pillar wanted nothing else than to build a wonderful home for her kin. They did not quite work in lockstep, but it was close.

Lucille, more often than not, provided the know-how, local solutions or contacts that were needed to handle some of their issues, or avoid any blunders, while Sera provided the political savvy, the personal touch and, she grudgingly had to admit, the pretty face.

"I still believe that there is a risk Dante will end up causing trouble—yet, he is too overt in his reach for power, and continually makes mistakes. At this rate, he will either sideline himself with his own actions or wind up doing something drastic to try to make himself the next Savior."

Lucille nodded. "Then we simply avoid making any errors. Easy." She smiled wearily, letting Sera know that she was joking. "We will have our work cut out for us, handling the logistics for our plan for pulling back the border, but for now we've done all we can. Is there anything else we should focus on? I don't think we're making any *obvious* mistakes."

Sera grimaced. "There will be some explosions at some point. How could there not? Only...I have heard nothing obvious hinting at future threats. Our choice to open the rooms of the Savior and those of the Keepers to the public, for all to see, is paying off. Any truly outspoken religious opposition is guided to read a bit from the Savior's diaries and...that is usually the last we hear of that."

"Is that Cilia girl of yours still monopolizing those diaries?" Lucille asked drily. She was less enamored of Cilia than of Sera, for some reason.

"Yes. Any waking moment that she is not crafting or working with your local crafters. She still believes there are secrets waiting to be exploited from within his writings." Sera smiled. "Mind you, if anybody is able to wring secrets from a dead man's writings, it *will* be her."

"As long as she gives them back afterward. I am not sure she understands the sense of understanding, of belonging, my people will derive from those."

"I am sure she will. Oh. Two details. First, as you know, all public kitchens should be up and operating again soon. We do have some issues with some hearts and minds who believe they are still entitled to their servants, special treatment, food and the like—"

"Give me names, and I'll handle them." Lucille's half-sneer said she was going to enjoy it, too.

"I appreciate it. Also, a few of the guards spoke up yesterday, about people being attacked in the streets. No solid facts, but I believe them. What appeared like random attacks, but always when anybody was, through action or word, denigrating the Savior. Nobody has been killed, but…"

Lucille frowned and nodded. "Disturbing, nonetheless. I'll ask a helper to make the rounds and ask all guards. If we have anybody still loyal to the Savior, this could very well lead to deaths in the street. We need to look into that." She turned and wavered on her feet.

Sera immediately leapt forward and caught her arm. Her arm flashed and a Warmth of the Circle engulfed the older woman. "Are you all right?"

Lucille sent a wry smile at her. "I appreciate the sentiment. I'm not injured, though. Just tired. And ancient—at least, so it feels. I will enjoy the small boost to Toughness for as long as it lasts, though."

Sera shook her head. "Please look after yourself. What's going to happen to us all if you drop dead from overworking yourself?"

Lucille snorted. "Oh, I am *far* too busy to die. I have work to do. Anybody standing between me and a better tomorrow had better bring several armies."

CHAPTER 45

That last quote from the Savior stuck with me, rummaging around in the back of my head. I couldn't quite tell what I was looking for. Then I realized it. Depending on what he came up with, a way to control all the old Keepers still in Salvation could be an insanely effective defense. I will have to dedicate more time to reading. Two more books to go.

"Any comments before I get to work?" Chase looked at the others.

They all looked at him in return, with varying degrees of confidence—except for Kith, who had that faraway look that clearly meant he was deep within his mind, controlling his shades.

Liam shook his head. "Nah. I like it. If it works, it should be a real loss to the bright bastards. If it doesn't, you should still be able to run away and we simply won't engage. Just don't get yourself caught."

Gavin sneered. "I still think it the height of folly. In a fight, they are worth little compared to properly armed, trained combatants. Besides, they are outsiders."

Chase rolled his eyes. "So are we, man. That doesn't change how we're still here, fighting, right next to you. Anyway, the *real* question is: will you defend us?"

"Of course I will. Even if I think your plan is ridiculous, it will leave the rest of us in a fairly safe position and able to strike at the Lightborn."

"Good enough for me." Chase smirked and sent a jaunty salute at them all. As he strolled away, he saw them slowly climbing onto the chariot again.

Kith was actually becoming a fairly proficient charioteer. It had been almost a day since somebody fell out of the chariot last, and he was learning how to spot and evade the worst surprises in the landscape. Not that Chase intended to tell him that. Especially considering Kith himself had been the last one to drop off, from a particularly nasty pothole.

The look on his face had been... Chase put a promising jibe to the back of his mind and focused on the present. It was night, just past midnight, though the cloudless cover allowed for the light of the moon to illuminate the landscape with an ephemeral sensation. Chase didn't mind the hour, at all. He had always worked best with alternating hours, and sometimes, nighttime jobs were the most rewarding—especially because it often allowed you to catch a mark with their pants down.

This time, he hoped they'd be able to do the same—less literally than usual, though. There was little doubt that their last stunt should have the army on high alert. Only, he doubted they'd be prepared against what he was bringing to the table. Mostly, because he only intended to take a little stroll and have a chat or two.

Circle of Darkness worked as impeccably as ever. In fact, the more he used it, the better he got accustomed to manipulating the powers of the card. Today, instead of creating a massive blanket of darkness around himself, he wrapped himself in a circle of fog-like shadows. There would be less coverage, but it would also stand out less from the distance. Besides, it wasn't like he intended to keep himself entirely hidden today.

From the looks of things, little had changed in the Lightborn army since their last entrenched camp. Chase didn't believe that for a moment. The Lightborn were many things— but they were not incompetent. Within a few minutes of scouting, he noticed subtle differences.

The indebted were, again, lined up surrounding the army. They stood, just like Chase himself had stood back when they had been forcibly enrolled in their ranks, alone, or in smaller groups, less according to any form of discipline than due to who they knew and slept with. This time around, however, any scouts were farther back, within arrowshot of the frontmost defenders on the embankments.

Regarding the embankments, things had also changed there. He spotted more bows and arrows than last time, and even a few robes, demarcating some of the few surviving casters and summoners lined up with the other defenders. Clearly, they'd learned that clumping up was not a clever survival strategy.

It all suited Chase *just* fine. Today, he had no intentions of aiming for the scouts, or infiltrating the army. There were too few casters left for them to create any issues. He had to admit, though, that it was nice of them to bunch up his targets like this, all out in the open.

The pebble hit the ground, right next to the indebted. She was his first truly good choice. She was a middle-aged Lightborn, with the looks of someone who'd raised kids, worked hard, and was absolutely *done* with everything life tried to toss at her. More importantly to Chase, she looked like somebody who wasn't about to pee herself and wouldn't attack at the drop of a hat.

Chase marveled for a second at his own idiocy. Then he continued, because, whatever else happened tonight, he was going to give it his best. She jumped slightly, then squinted into the darkness. Not straight at Chase, but close.

"Please don't shout! I'm a friend." Chase pitched his voice low. Not at a whisper. Those traveled farther. Just talking normally, but lower. "I'm not going to harm you. I just want to talk." Slowly, he edged closer to her.

She adjusted her grip on her weapon—a long spear, in good quality.

The way she handled it, it looked like she knew what she was doing. Also, knowing how indebted received weapons, that had to put her at the more powerful end of the scale for the indebted. Promising.

She tensed up, then relaxed slightly. Her gaze softened, even as she continued staring out into the night. When she spotted him, she froze for a moment, before looking onward, acting like nothing had happened.

He was less than twenty feet away now and decided this was as far as he could move. She stood a few dozen feet from the nearest indebted, and he was already pushing it.

"Just listen. Don't say anything. Please." Spotting her tiny nod, he relaxed minutely. "If I could give you the chance to escape the army and find a new life, would you take it?"

A brief hesitation. No movement. No nod or any answer. Damn.

"I intend to give you all—every indebted—a chance to run. This night. We'll distract the army. We have a place for you all. When everything explodes, just run. You can be free. *Do you want it?*"

He couldn't fully see her expression in the darkness. She took her time digesting what he'd said. Maybe she hadn't heard him? Should he repeat himself?

Her eyes fixed fully on him now, intent. Her words were equally soft, yet he heard them, almost as clearly as if he stood next to her. "Are you the cripple from yesterday?"

He nearly laughed out loud. Never before had he been so relieved to be recognized like that. Slowly, he eased off the cover of darkness near the center of his circle and raised his left arm.

One more question. A simple one, candid. "Why?"

Now, Chase smiled softly into the darkness. There were many answers here. To deprive the enemy of a weapon. To hit them in a way they didn't expect. Because they couldn't defend properly against it. Because they did not want the slaughter if they could avoid it. There was only one *true* answer, though. "Because I was an indebted myself, once. Please. Alert those near you. Then I'll move on, tell more indebted. The signal will be easy to spot."

Those words struck home. She took a deep, shuddering breath, then nodded. Before he was able to sneak off for his next target, though, she spoke up again. "No. You stay. I will tell everybody."

For a moment, he almost told her to stop. Then, he paused and thought about it again. What were the odds that all indebted back near Isarn would've listened to an outsider telling them to flee? Horrible, of course. But somebody who knew others, knew who was trustworthy and most likely to rebel against their masters? Maybe this could work. Only, how would she even go about it? It wasn't like they were allowed to just walk around.

He observed her for the next five minutes. In those minutes, she didn't march anywhere. Instead, she, ever so slowly, sidled closer to somebody else. Then she stayed there for a while, before the other person started to move on, while she inched closer to another indebted.

In awe, Chase looked on, as the message spread throughout the amassed indebted, without him having to do anything at all. Honestly, he already had Squall Sling and a stone prepared, ready to knock out anybody trying to call an alarm. Deep within, he had expected them to start yelling for help instead of listening.

Instead, like rings in the water, the indebted moved about, just like they already did during the long night, sharing the information. Blessedly, not a single person seemed to take the chance to bring it to the notice of their masters.

Minutes passed, excruciatingly slowly. An hour. Two. In the blue-black darkness of the moon-covered landscape, it almost seemed like a dream to Chase, like something he was imagining.

Then, the night lit up, and he was fighting for his life.

It started as a wave in the night. A rush of sound, of burgeoning screams. Just like he'd always known it would. At his core, Chase had known that this would end in screams—one way or the other. If he'd miraculously managed to clear the entire round, he would've raised a hand, clad in light, as a signal to Kith. This? This was the signal they'd actually expected. Some Fury-rent Lightborn awakening to the fact that something was going on.

Kith acted in an instant.

Last time they'd attacked, they had carefully surrounded the Lightborn army, letting him slowly put the summoned beings from Light of Day, Day of Darkness in position to blind, confuse, and trick the Lightborn. This time, knowing that the soldiers were expecting them to attack, they dispensed with the formalities and attacked in one massive group.

They were only fifteen people to begin with. Thirteen after their last encounter. Except, nearly all of them were summoners with at least three cards at their disposal. With ample preparation, their numbers multiplied several times over—especially taking Kith and his Twice the Fun card into consideration.

The buzzing of Apian God could be heard even from the other side of the camp. That was one of the details from the card that they rarely got to use. Apian God would actually attract any local insects as well, adding to the number and variety of the buzzing, stinging mass of flying distraction. Kith had promised he'd keep the summoned creatures nearby, slowly building until they were ready to be unleashed...and damn, did he deliver.

For a moment, the cloud of insects blotted out the light of the moon. Then it was followed by other shapes, bestial and humanoid. The fires and explosions started just seconds later.

Chase readied himself as he saw the beginnings of movement among the loose ranks of the indebted. This was the pivotal moment. He'd need to do everything he could to defend them, as they ran away. Hopefully, the Lightborn would be so confused by what was happening that they didn't send armies after the runaways straightaway. He grasped onto his short sword, smiling softly at how ridiculous it felt to brandish a tiny bloody sword against an entire army.

From inside the army's embankments, a large group emerged. They leapt the trench and raced outward, every single one on foot, but running faster than any of them had a right to. All wore shining armor or brilliantly white cloth that shone in the darkness. As one, they ignored the running ranks of indebted, aiming straight for Chase.

Chase blinked once. He subconsciously stopped counting once their number passed thirty. Every single one an inquisitor. All of them sprinting right for where he was hiding. He bit back a curse, turned on his heels, and ran in the opposite direction.

Something was wrong. He could tell instantly. Even with Fight Another Day activated, his footsteps were sluggish and slow. On top of that, his pursuers ran faster than they should really be able to. Damn. Even despite his Circle of Darkness, they'd clearly thrown some sort of debuff on him, and were boosting themselves on top of that.

He leapt a small stream in the grasslands, landing softly and easily on the far side. No stumbling, no clumsiness. His gait was supernaturally smooth. His Agility was not afflicted. Hence, it had to be his running speed only. Chase considered the situation, even as he pumped his arms, trying to put distance between him and the pursuit. Even without Fight Another Day, his Agility should really be enough to outpace any of the inquisitors—especially the armored ones. *Conclusion. Conclusion...* He growled in frustration, dipping his shoulder per instinct, feeling a light breeze as something flashed past him.

Conclusion! Some debuff slowed his running speed, to the point where the slowpokes could keep up. Fight Another Day...he glanced down frantically, watching the greyed-out card on his arm. Damn. It was inactive. Meaning, *another* card was keeping his buff out of the game, and it would be a question of him making it until either the debuff ran out...or he got rid of the wielder or wielders *using* any of the debuffs against him. Damn. This was going to be a slugging match—and with all those inquisitors on his ass, he might as well not use his Dark cards, because they'd have counters for that.

Even with the odds stacked against him, and the dozens of fanatical killers at his heel, Chase felt a grin erupt into being. This! This was life. Running from pursuit and the threat of death. You just couldn't beat it. His grin turned mean, as cards flashed on his arms and legs. Winds of Change, for rapid card changes. One with the Soil, for added balance and maneuverability. Steps of Brilliance, to *really* confuse the bastards, run through the air and turn on a whim. Last, but not least, Among the Raindrops, to ruin the day for his pursuers. He grinned as none of the new cards were blocked or greyed out. They didn't have counters for everything. He could do this. This was just like running through the streets of Isarn—only without backup, and with trained killers instead of fat guards.

Within the first thirty seconds, he realized another few added difficulties. There were no crowds here, no stalls or buildings, nothing to hide behind or use for obstructions. Behind them all, the indebted were in full panic mode, running off into the unknown. Running straight at the main Lightborn army that was, by now, rousing itself to move out in force, sounded like a poor idea in the same way that Kith was slightly bad with women. In other words, he'd have to deal with the inquisitors, or find himself caught up by them regardless. Only...did he really?

For a few seconds, he broke one of his main rules for being under pursuit: don't look back. He figured, with them inevitably catching up on him, he'd have to think of something. *One. Two. Three.* He counted again. Not enemies, this time. Ranged weapons. Just three of them that he could see. One, an unwieldy crossbow, held by a panting struggler in heavy armor at the back of their numbers. The other two were short bows, carried by pursuers in leather armor who were slowly catching up on him.

His grin changed into a devil-may-care burst of laughter. If Cilia learned about this stunt, she'd have his *neck*. With a rapid application of Steps of Brilliance, he placed three shimmering platforms in succession in a steep turn, and two seconds later, without slowing down for a moment, he was running straight *at* his enemies.

At the sight of finally getting to close with him, the chasing inquisitors behaved in widely different ways. The ones in leather armor or robes swerved to the side. Meanwhile, the tougher, slower ones wearing chainmail or even, for two of them, plate armor, slowed down, hefting their weapons and shields, checking their distance to their comrades to ensure they'd be ready for a battle and moved to the front.

An arrow whizzed at Chase, swiftly followed by another. One barely missed, and he dipped to the left to avoid the other. With a low-pitched cackle, he yelled, "You want me? Then catch me, you short-armed losers!" He raced straight at them before activating Steps of Brilliance and leaping into the air.

Steps of Brilliance was a funny card. He'd heard stories about lucky bastards being granted the power of flight. Supernaturally fast, being able to whizz through the air at the speed of thought. His card was not that amazing. But it *was* a Light card, meaning, these fanatics were unlikely to be able to block it. Also, the platforms were invisible to anybody but himself, and his enemies couldn't see where he was aiming to go. Finally, it *did* allow him to go up into the air. About thirty feet. He'd learned that by painful accident. Enough to clear most walls and buildings. But if he was already, say, dropping from the Elemental towers, he could only move down or straight ahead.

But they didn't know that.

Hefting his short sword, Chase took one step after the other, dedicating a good deal of attention to continually placing the platforms ahead of him. He ran in a twisted pattern so as to not present a perfect target for the archers and the crossbowman.

At first, the responses were simple, professional. Short, barked orders as they followed his movements, spreading out, ready to engulf him when he came back down.

As he kept running in the air, those orders grew more confused and questioning. The archers worked on overtime, unleashing arrow after arrow up at Chase.

As a kid, Chase had always undervalued Mental Power. He'd seen it as something exclusively for casters or summoners, useless for normal people. Now, confronted with the need to continually create small, palm-sized platforms midair, step on those platforms, not drop down into the crowd of bloodthirsty fighters below, *and* avoid getting hit by arrows, his Mental Power was the only thing keeping him alive. That, and One with the Soil, granting him perfect balance and the ability to dodge, weave, and swerve with barely an effort.

Below him, the inquisitors were confused. A few of them even laughed out loud as he kept running about above their heads. Their mirth died quickly when, first one, then another, was hit by the caustic liquid Among the Raindrops continually rained down on them. Then, they started to see it.

"This stuff's not coming off. It's...gah. Burning into my skin!" one of them cried harshly.

"It's slippery, too. Avoid the puddles!" a female voice cried, after a short scream of surprise.

"He's stalling for time," a more collected voice rang out over the others. "Trying to wear us down with that slimy acid!"

"Took you this long, did it?" Chase called down at them, then took two rapid steps sideways in a drastic dance onto two swiftly created platforms, avoiding two arrows and a crossbow bolt, fired in impressive synchronization. "Doesn't have to be like this. You can just leave. No harm, no foul. All—" He grunted as a beam of light sizzled right past his shoulder. "All friends here!" He ran down an invisible patch of stairs until he was right above their heads, fouling the line of sight for the crossbowman. Then he started to rise again.

For a moment stretching into infinity, he danced a lethal dance, always on the verge of serious injury. One inquisitor revealed a card that sent a brilliant line of searing light tearing into the sky to follow him, damaging where it went. However, the effect turned out to be bearable, and the near-blinding effect of the beam was actually more dangerous than the real damage.

For every single second he survived, he knew, liquid would be building up below him, impeding and damaging his enemies, ruining their footing and tilting the battlefield in his favor. Another minute, perhaps two, and he'd be able to—

The gruff voice rang out, this time with a decisive order easily heard: "All. Throw weapons on my command."

Oh, crap. That...would not end well.

"Ready. Aim. Throw!" The command rang out, followed by a lethal storm of close combat weapons, tearing up into the sky.

Chase panicked. There could be no other explanation. He knew damn well that neither excellent balance nor fast reactions would help him here. Exchanging One with the Soil for Clothed in Living Light, he summoned a shield, shining dazzlingly bright in the darkness. He doubled the thickness, then doubled it again, layering the density and weight of the creation until it nearly tore from his grasp. Then, moments before the impending blizzard of deadly implements struck him from below, he leapt, and placed the shield right underneath him.

For a split second, Chase felt weightless. Then the shield pulled him downward—and the storm hit. He was flung, first in one direction, then another, pummeled by dozens of direct hits in swift succession. Tumbling end over end, he flung out three platforms in quick order, trying to grasp onto them to steer his fall. Clothed in Living Light fizzled out between his fingers, too damaged to keep active.

He managed to grab the third platform. Just for a few seconds, before it faded away in his hands, but it was enough for him to right himself and hang the right way up. Then he had to drop to evade the arrow aimed at his head.

He landed in the soft grass, surrounded by enemies, his entire body feeling like it had been hit by a strike from a gaborn. With a detached sensation, he noticed an arrow hanging from the meat of his left arm.

A few months ago, any part of this was likely to have killed him. The pursuit. The onslaught. Pits, half a year ago, dropping to the ground from this height might have done the trick. But Chase was not the same anymore. He got up and blocked the pain from his mind as unimportant.

For a second, two, the tableau froze. He stood at the center of a group of trained killers. Killers, who, at this moment, were either in shock that he'd survived, or scrambling to find dropped weapons, replacement weapons, *any* weapons. Then their leader barked an order again, to attack immediately.

In response, Chase called for the water.

A Friendly Wave responded to his call, as ever with the bubbling, insistent sensation that this was not just a card. This was an entirely natural state of being, and all was as it should be. The powers of nature at his disposal? All was right in the world.

This time, he didn't build the liquid around him into a single, overpowering wave. He didn't need to. He merely gave it the order to move—a hundred smaller waves, all swirling into glorious, joyful motion all around him. With a furious yell, Chase hefted his short sword and launched into their midst.

The first few heavily armored inquisitors didn't understand what had just happened. They flung themselves against him, their cards activating to boost, to parry, damage, whatever. The relief from finally being able to close with him was palpable. The poor suckers never stood a chance. With the first strides forward, they stepped into the softly swirling waves. Their feet shot right from under them and they slipped to the ground, where the caustic water from Among the Raindrops welcomed them, grasped them, and held tight.

The sounds coming from a young inquisitor pawing at a thick layer of liquid slowly burrowing itself into the back of her drenched head would likely stay with Chase for a while. Right this moment, he didn't allow himself the luxury of thought. He dipped right into their midst, sword bobbing and weaving, stabbing into any downed enemy, circling away from anybody who looked like they were ready for him. And always, he kept moving, kept the water in motion, even as the cries of the damned and dying arose around him.

It was a few seconds. A minute. A damn eternity. Chase lost all sense of time and the greater picture as his entire world reduced to the inquisitors in sight, carving everything into simple monickers, instructions for himself: Avoid. Engage. Drown. Stab. Slice. Leap. Kill.

What made him return to himself wasn't a conscious decision, or any outside event. Rather, it was the sensation that the thick blanket slowing his running speed down finally lifted. Life coursed into his legs again. He blinked, realizing what had happened. Then, he blinked again as he saw what the battlefield had turned into. A charnel house. All around him lay dead and dying inquisitors. A few in the distance were hobbling away, carefully, so as not to slip from the thick layer of caustic liquid burning into their legs. Yet, from the dozens of hostiles, only a trio still faced him, and one had to cling onto a comrade to stay on his feet.

Beyond, the Lightborn army was finally reacting, the first squads emerging in his direction.

Chase took one halting step away from them, and not one tried to follow. That first step turned into a quick sprint, then a steady jog. Then, with a long, soft exhale, he let his grasp of the water go and switched to Circle of Darkness and Fight Another Day.

Shadows covered him as he raced off into the night.

CHAPTER 46

"I believed it impossible. Guardians are, on the whole, beyond general reach. Of course they are. Otherwise, anybody would be able to influence them, turn them to their use. Yet, I might have found a focal point. A fulcrum, able to grant me control, should my Keepers or their wards act up." Well, then bloody *tell* me! What is it? Who censors their own diaries? I'll dig him up and slap what's left of his brains out of him. (Book 3, Page 51.)

"Chase! There you are, you bastard. I don't mind admitting, mate, that was a close call." Kith lay on his back in the soft grass, with an arm flung over his head. All around him, the others were similarly resting, with the only person moving being their healer, who was inspecting a deep cut on Gavin's arm.

Chase didn't answer for a moment. He stumbled past him and into the camp to find their goods, all stacked up like they'd been on the chariot before it was unsummoned. He grasped a waterskin and drank, in deep, greedy gulps before he poured the rest over his head. Shaking himself like a dog, he finally regained a semblance of his normal self. "What happened? I didn't really have the chance to see what was going on with you."

Liam snorted. "No wonder. They really went for you, didn't they? You'll have to tell us how you escaped." He paused, then nodded at Kith. "Kith was the one who saved us. We did as we planned. The moment things turned bad, we sent everything we had—summons, hostile cards, everything—at their flanks in one massive group, to burrow inward and keep them busy while those poor indebted got away."

"Oh yeah." Chase realized he'd forgotten all about their plight in his own fight for survival. "How did they fare?"

Liam grinned. "Not bad. I'd say two-thirds of them ran. There'll always be some who're too afraid of the unknown, or where the Lightborn are threatening families back in their lands or the like. The Lightborn were too shocked, it seemed, to send forces out to catch them at first. Also, they were too busy to try to enact their own plan to react quickly. A few might've died fleeing, but not many."

"Yeah," Chase mused. His mind was beginning to work again, as he thought back to the initial moments of the struggle. "Those inquisitors went *straight* for me. I...think that whatever they had that allowed them to trail me that first day was still active. Some card effect that let them trace me."

Liam nodded solemnly. "That would make sense. They could follow you all the damn time, feel you rummaging around just outside their reach. Probably had an elaborate trap ready for you. Then, at some point, when you failed to step into the trap, they decided to go for you instead."

Banes barked a deep, booming laugh. "And you still escaped, leaving those inquisitors trailing in your wake. Are they still following, do you think?"

Kith sat half up with a shudder. "Urgh. Yes. I'm sure they are. Raudt and Svart, to the rescue. I'll get to it."

"No need for that, mate," Chase said softly. "They're dead. Only a handful of them still alive."

For a while, nobody said anything.

Then Kith smiled and sank back on the grass. "Oh, thank the Light. I'm so tired!"

"What happened with you, then?" Chase asked.

Liam shrugged. "Well, they exploded after you. Probably half the inquisitors they had. Or, at least, once we attacked, the other half went after us. At least sixty."

Chase hissed, "That's more than half."

"Well, they were prepared, this time. They'd caught onto the trick with the chariot. Because the inquisitors ignored all our summons and went straight for the chariot. They probably figured that if they were able to destroy it, we would be easy to hunt down." Liam snorted. "They'd be right, too. But Kith insisted that we take a detour and let all summoned creatures move a bit farther along the edge of their encampment before attacking."

"Ooh. So, when they tore right past all your summons to find you?"

Liam grinned. "They found us standing five hundred feet farther away than they'd expected." He rubbed at a layer of dust on his arm. "I don't mind admitting, it was still close. They weren't even defending themselves, just trying to tear a wheel off, kill one of the summoned beasts pulling the chariot...anything to stop us."

Banes cracked his knuckles. "Stupid. Whatever else they might've done, that part was nuts. Liam there threw 'em back and we punished them bad. Spike simply placed himself right in their way, letting them impale themselves along the way. At least half their number ain't among the living no more, and I'm at Tier four now."

That led to a general discussion about advances. Most of them had managed a Step. Chase grimly acknowledged that the massive slaughter had granted him a single Step. What the stories said about higher Tiers being hard to reach was definitely true, and if the last Step to Tier five was hard to crest, the end of Tier six would likely be even harder. Yet, even as he considered that part, he couldn't help but marvel at the fact he and Kith both were, indeed, closing on Tier six now. That was the realm of legends, of those who made it into tales and history books. At some point, the story of Chase might be told in nurseries throughout the lands. He'd need a moniker. Chase the Champ? Nah. Chase the Chaste? Liberty fend. His brain was so scrambled!

Thankfully, his musings were interrupted by a loud avian scream.

Kith bolted upright before starting to shout abuse at the skies. "Now? *Now* you arrive? An hour after you could have saved us all from a nasty ambush is when you choose to return to me? *Radine, you worthless sack of feathers, come down here so I can pluck your hide!*"

The bird landed. It seemed to take his invectives as praise, because it waddled and hopped closer to him, making soft mewling sounds. The large hunting bird looked rough. Its outline was somehow fuzzy, and the normally gleaming brown and orange plumage was irregular and patchy.

Kith glowered, then subsided, and began to pet something in thin air. Clearly, he was touching the real Guardian, not the illusion. A few feet over, the image of Radine saw its feathers, disarrayed by its long travels, slowly smoothened. After a while, Kith reached in to grasp the leg and undo the tightly folded message scroll attached there. He squinted at the tiny letters, then slumped back to the ground. "Somebody! Take over! My energy is gone. If I have to read too, I may expire."

Gavin tromped over, looking down at him with disdain. "How you people ever managed to even get *near* the Savior is beyond me." He unfurled the scroll, extracted another, smaller scroll from within and squinted at the writing near the bottom. "High Elementalist Tatiana Skysworn. Please tell me this is a joke. That is a Title I have heard only in legends. Who *are* you people?"

Chase waved weakly. "That's...a really, really long story. Could we do with the words please?"

The older man shook his head softly and started to read. "Dear all. Whatever you are doing, it is working. The Lightborn forces have never been lighter on the ground surrounding Earth's Ward. The latest weeks have been a relief, to the point where we have been able to build a significant surplus. If you actually come through with what the elders state might be possible, we will be able to dedicate *substantial* resources to your cause. Regardless, you should know that the inner workings of the Lightborn empire are in turmoil. Currently, there are rumors flying everywhere, with little I can properly confirm. The only thing we know for certain is that the archbishop of the Church of the Circle has been replaced. The new one is less militant, more of a political creature. Let us know of any proceedings, and we will be able to act. High Elementalist Tatiana Skysworn."

Chase grimaced. "Meaning, she didn't even know that the Savior's dead yet. Nothing truly useful to us, is there?"

Kith snorted. "Not really. Feels like we know more than she did. Also, we've met the new damn archbishop, wet blanket that he is. Next, please."

With increasingly raised eyebrows, Gavin read the other, larger scroll aloud. "We never expected anything like this. Yet, one thing is for certain. Now that you have all five decks under your command, we will be able to restructure the power landscape of Ordei. When next you return to the bloodied grounds, the entirety of the Heart Halls will resonate with the thunderous echoes of our celebrations. Please, return to us as soon as possible, and you can decide which home you will want to erect for your future bastion."

Gavin paused. "What bastion would that be?"

Chase shook his head sadly. "It doesn't even matter. If we get bored over the next few days, we can tell you. We've made our choice, though, and are sticking with Liberty. Come what may."

"Good. I will continue." Gavin started to read aloud again. "You may read what the High Elementalist wrote, and we have, in the meantime, sent messengers, informing her about your success. We will forward any additional news with your flier, when next she returns."

"You hear that, you winged menace? Who's about to go on another trip? You are!" Kith said, with a singsong voice.

"Oh." Gavin stopped reading. His gaze flickered to the horizon. As he started to read again, his voice cracked and nearly broke. "Whenever you choose to return, please be aware—not only is there a Lightborn army stationed right outside the Liberty border, additional armies, numbering in the tens of thousands, have been drafted from other nobles, and will join the original army, likely within a few days of you receiving this message. Do take the necessary precautions when returning. We advise that you circle west of their forces when you return. Regards. The Furyborn council of elders."

Liam looked at Gavin. With a tiny voice, forlorn and lost, he said simply, "Oh."

Any idea of sending Radine back to the elders straightaway was tabled, and Kith sent her out to scout. Even though they were all exhausted, a good number of them still bearing freshly healed wounds along with the drain of resources that entailed, nobody was able to go to sleep. They went back and forth, rehashing their options, again and again.

Finally, several hours later, they watched as Kith, who'd been increasingly absent, staring into the far distance, rubbed his face. Without turning, he spoke up, with none of his usual emotion. "It's true. They're coming. In the thousands. We're so dead."

CHAPTER 47

"I tested it earlier today. It worked. Of course, I told no-body what was going on, and there will be a few adjustments needed. The deaths were few in number, though. Another iteration or two, and I will be safe from any treason from my Keepers." Stop! Bloody! Alluding to it! I...I will return to reading later. (Book 3, Page 58.)

The ensuing discussion was harsh, but short. Within a few minutes, they had to agree. Even though the timing was horrid, even if they'd made so much progress, and the Lightborn had few proper defenses left, there was no way they would be able to stand up to an army that was several times larger. They had been fortunate to be able to take out the casters, summoners, and even the inquisitors among their number the first time around. Now that the enemy was wise to their strategies, they would drown in numbers and be overwhelmed if they tried to repeat the success.

Instead, they considered what they *could* do. That took a while longer. The main issue they had was the lack of mobility. Everything needed to happen right now, and they would honestly be best off if they were able to be in three different places all at once.

Eventually, they agreed to dividing the workload. Chase would activate Fight Another Day and run as fast as he could to the nearest Keeper, where he'd inform those back in Salvation what was happening. Meanwhile, Kith would split his attention, having Radine scouting the incoming armies, at the same time that he would have the chariot circle the original army. That way, the others would be able to unleash everything they had, paring down enemy numbers before reinforcements arrived. They harbored few illusions that they would be able to finish off a lot of them or end some of the important figures in time. Still, it felt like the best of a number of bad options. They might get lucky and end that damn Thomas, or the archbishop.

Chase ran off. The others relaxed for a few hours, still trying to recuperate their energy before they would leap straight back into violence. Around them, the world seemed to move past whatever advantages they managed to carve out for themselves. Soon, the battles reengaged.

In the dead of night, Chase stumbled back into their camp. Panting and sweating, his legs kept moving, bringing him halfway past the huge circle of long grass trodden down underfoot. He stopped and nearly fell, before catching himself, swaying on his feet, looking off into the distance.

At the far side of the dark camp, Liam stared at him, truncheon raised threateningly before letting it fall. "Pits. Chase, you look rough! What happened?" He squinted, then added, "We weren't expecting you for at least six hours."

Chase blinked and rubbed his face. "I decided to make it back here six hours faster, that's what happened." He laughed softly, before indicating the rest of the large circle. They had their original number, all impressively still alive. Only, now, their number had been increased manyfold by a lot of sleeping figures. Primarily Lightborn, the newcomers looked like crap, and slept where they lay, most of them dead to the world. A few stared at Chase nervously, while others simply stared off into the night with dead eyes. He waved at those who looked coherent.

"Oh. Yeah. That's Kith's doing," Liam said.

"Again now?"

"Well." Liam cleared his throat. "I agreed with him. Turns out, once Radine started scouting, Kith found out that most of the indebted hadn't made it too far from the army." He shrugged. "Lost in a hostile land that's mostly a myth to you...what are you to do? So, Kith decided that he should send Raudt and Svart touring those closest to us, talk to them through the shades and convince them to join us."

Chase grimaced. It was the right thing to do. Of course it was. He'd told as much to the Keeper, informing those back in the capital that they were to keep an eye out for, and rescue, any stray Lightborn wandering the lands, lost. However, it also saddled them with new responsibilities—right this moment being about a hundred indebted, all recently escaped from slavery, likely suffering from malnourishment along with any number of other ills. Yeah. That wasn't likely to end well for anybody. "How did you do? With the fighting, I mean?"

"So-so. Our summons were able to do some damage to their regular troops. So were the casters. That horrible poison cloud was nasty enough that the archbishop had to step in." Liam looked into the distance, where the Lightborn army was likely to be resting. "It's a damn shame. Give us a week, and we'd have been able to grind them down, I'm sure. We could have ended them before they ever made it to Salvation."

Chase winced. "I know. I told the Keeper as much. There's nothing for it. We've done all we can. For now, we've got our orders. The three of us will be taking the chariot back with anybody who's made it to a higher Tier and can get new cards. Meanwhile, the rest will be guiding the poor indebted back to Salvation—with us out in front, they won't get attacked. Where's Radine right now?"

"She's off," Liam said. "Kith sent her with a message to the Furyborn elders before going to sleep. Don't worry. We had Gavin go through it, so it made sense. Yet, we figured they'd need to know immediately. Likely, they won't be able to reach us in time to do anything about the reinforcing armies—but at the very least, they should be able to intercept any further armies. Tatiana might be able to make some waves to make sure they don't start conscripting even more armies in the future."

Liam sighed, letting his gaze slide over the indebted sprawled everywhere. "I've been thinking, and I'll be joining the indebted here as well. The poor bastards right here need somebody who looks like them and knows what they've been through. Besides, I'm not a Tier-five yet." He smiled at Chase. "Don't worry. We'll make it back to fight with you before the army arrives."

"I don't like it. We're already split up. Now you want to split our numbers even further?"

"Oh, stop it." Liam shot him a lopsided grin. "Like anybody's going to be able to take me on. Besides, I can take the time to beat some spirit into all these people. Might be they'll even be some help. For now, though? Catch some winks. The chariot won't be available for at least a handful of hours anyway."

Chase grimaced, but acquiesced. He unfurled his own bedroll and fell asleep in minutes.

Their return travels were swift. The weather was lovely, and the journey easy. A few hours saw them to one of the main roads throughout Liberty lands, and from there on, they sped up a lot. Even so, the atmosphere was tense, and their conversations were stilted and testy.

The entire situation was a mess. There were no obvious solutions to their plight, and all their allies were far away. Now, all threads were starting to pull together, indicating a showdown in Salvation. But they weren't ready. A year—half a year, even—would've seen them strengthened and ready for an assault of this kind, with an operable government and a cohesive army of Liberators holding cards from all five decks. Now...they were being pushed back on all fronts. Something would have to give.

***

<u>Salvation. Crafting square. Cilia.</u>

"*Why* have you not invited me here before?" Nordon's boisterous voice cut across the chatter in the tent. "This place is *bustling.*"

"Nordon." Cilia nodded, her eyes not leaving the nervous man in front of her. "Listen, Baeric, I need this leather. As much of it as you can get. The natural resilience of the material bonds with Air in a manner I've never seen before!" She tapped the leather on the table.

"I will give you everything we have, Mind Cil—sorry. Cilia. It is not easy to get, though. Bruise-buck leather is typically only granted to hearts and above. They repel liquids, and..."

"Baeric. Let me make this *exquisitely* clear to you." She locked eyes with the Tier-three, and he looked like a rat freezing before the gaze of a snake. "If you get me a hundred pounds of this material, I might be able to create a knockback droplet that can save hundreds of lives when the Lightborn army comes rushing in. If it stays right where it is, it may save the couches of some high-Tier people from a handful of ugly spills. *Which do you think I care about most?*"

He bowed his head and coughed. "The lives, erm, Cilia. I will do what I can."

"Do more! Invoke my name, Sera's, Lucille's, or the name of the bloody Savior. I don't care. *Just get me that damn leather!*" She scowled at his retreating back, before expelling her breath in a rush. "Aaand he's gone." Turning to Nordon, who was going industriously through the mess of materials on the table before her, she complained, "Why? Why are people so difficult?"

"You do realize that you're asking that of a man who has dedicated their entire life to getting people drunk enough he doesn't have to deal with their normal, annoying personalities?" He chuckled. "I'm only kidding, of course. I love people. Even here in Liberty, where they are a bit more, let's say, understandably reticent."

Cilia snapped, "Well, I don't. I never thought I would miss being shunned for my ancestry back in Isarn." She shook her head and sighed. "Ah. Never mind me. I am just unused to spending so much time dealing with people. It's not my strongest suit. There are good people here. And so many interesting materials! Did you know that they have a beast here that has natural camouflage? Not a Guardian or anything. A regular, silly little beast that can go half invisible. And they use them for *pets*?"

Nordon frowned. "And you suggested gathering and skinning them?"

"Of course. Picture the possibilities!"

Nordon hid his mouth behind a hand. "I bet that went down well. *Anyway.* I actually came looking for you specifically."

"You did? Also, what *have* you been up to? It's been a while now!"

"Well, that's what I wanted to talk to you about. What with the Savior's people and turmoil, there really aren't the same security measures in place anymore, so I just went about, making friends, asking a few innocent questions."

"Yes...?" Cilia asked hesitantly.

"Remember how we wondered about the uniformity of their lower-grade crafts? I got to the bottom of it. I located their crafting centrals!" Nordon beamed.

"Wait, what? I thought these were the crafting centrals. No. That's not entirely right," Cilia corrected herself, frowning.

"Exactly." Nordon leaned forward over the table, beaming with energy. "*This* place is for those who craft, but decide not to make it their profession. The others—those who craft for a living? They are sealed off in specific locations otherwise closed to the public, depending on their crafts. Places where they have access to specific machinery that helps them produce a lot of lower-grade materiel very fast. Places I now have access to."

Cilia stood up. Her hand shook slightly. "I...have been using the Savior's own crafting stations. I have been able to construct a handful of truly effective items in the time I've had. But the numbers are not enough. They won't be able to make a difference in the grand scheme of things. Are you telling me that you can take some of my successes and...multiply them?"

Nordon grimaced. "Likely not. Cilia, I don't think you understand entirely how strong you've gotten. I don't think you understand how much theory you have internalized in that head of yours. An uneducated Tier two crafter with no education could not hope to match you, machinery or not. But!" He held up a finger. "If we're lucky, we'll be able to take some of the simpler items you've made, pare them down a lot in efficiency and duration...and create a hundred of them in two days. How does that sound?"

She gawked at him. She cleared her throat. "Sounds like I have some thinking to do."

"You do that. We have maybe a week and a half before the army arrives. I'll be back later today, for samples and a list. Then, we'll see if the locals can't create a few miracles of their own." With a large smile, he turned and walked away. Over his shoulder, he shot, "I've been working on material lists, too. I'll bring some for you. I know you like lists."

Cilia sat down heavily on her chair, staring off into space. The burgeoning smile on her face was competing with the frown. "Was he...coming on to me?" she murmured.

A few minutes later, Cilia was hard at work, writing at the table, when another shadow loomed over her. "I'm busy. Leave it on the table, or tell Mattheus, if it's important."

The shade moved. Her table rocked and nearly tipped, spilling her off her chair and onto the ground with a shocked expression, while scrolls and ingredients hit the ground everywhere.

"Oh, I think you will find time for this, *Honored Mind.*"

That voice. Cilia's gaze rose from the floor, over the spilled mess of lists and materials, ignoring the shocked looks of the surrounding crafters in the background. "Emilia!"

Emilia was there. The heart who had joined them on their travels and helped them come to terms with their new situation. Who had, after a rocky start, become friendly, and might in time have become an actual friend. Only, right now, she was looking anything *but* friendly. One hand rested on the pommel of a studded club, sheathed at her side. The other was raised to hold back two bulky men at her side, both armed and armored, both waving weapons at anybody nearby. "Yes. Me. The one you lied to. Abused. Cheated, in order to *slay our Savior*!"

Cilia frowned before nodding slowly. "That is…exactly correct."

"See?" She raised her voice to a shout, projected to reach the entire tent. "She doesn't even protest. They would have performed *any* crime in order to kill the single person trying to protect us all."

Cilia looked at Emilia. Truly looked at her. The creases and massed dirt on her clothes. The hints of blood spatters on the club at her side. Slowly, she got to her feet, as she put two and two together. "That, however, was all wrong. Wait. You're the ones. The ones who've been going around the city, roughing up people for badmouthing the Savior."

"Of course we have," Emilia spat. "It's the least they deserve for the sacrilege. They—"

Cilia spoke over her. "Except, I haven't just said bad things about him. *I helped kill him, Emilia.*"

She reeled back as though she had been struck. "Exactly—"

"Only, you have decided to not face the truth." Cilia spoke intently, her gaze boring into Emilia's, daring her to look away. "You have decided to ignore the evidence against your precious Savior. Blind yourself to what he did. Who he killed. Instead, you act out, trying to force people to act like nothing happened and that the truth is what you *say* it is."

"Lies!" Emilia shouted. Spittle flew from her lips, as she brandished the club, pointing it at Cilia. "Filth and lies. You would say anything, invent anything to make it seem like you were in the right! Only, we faithful will not let it stand. We will show *everybody* what happens when you defy the will of the Savior."

Cilia's voice lowered. "Oh, that is what you're going to do then, is it?" She slowly unbuttoned her jacket, revealing the crisscrossed belts underneath. Belts bristling with droplets, arranged by type and power. "Ordinarily, I might have tried to talk you down." Her eyes never wavered, even as she picked out items from the belts, one by one. "But I've spent days talking to people, and earlier, somebody might have been *flirting* with me. In fact, I'm rather *happy* you came here. Because, Emilia, I am frustrated, and I truly need somebody I can take my frustrations out on."

Ten minutes later, the crafters were helping right some of the overturned tables, cleaning spills and sorting scattered materials. Cilia sat at one of the few intact tables, quill in hand, when a guard arrived, helmet in hand. "Honored Mind—"

"Just Cilia, please." She kept writing.

"Cilia. They are all three healed and out of mortal danger. What would you have us do with them?"

She tapped her lip, leaving an ink splotch and grimacing at the taste. "I...want you to show them. This entire mess came about because they *refused* to face facts. I want you to take all three on a tour of the Savior's premises. Show them all the ugly truths. Then, I want you to let them all sit in on a full reading of his diaries, start to finish. There should be copies made of all of them by now and I know they're arranging these things. When that is done? I don't know. Probably have Sera deal with it. I'm busy. Or at least, I will be, once Baeric returns with that blasted leather."

CHAPTER 48

"It is done. I shall keep it handy. Hidden, yet, in the open. Ready for anything, should they try to rebel. Yet another brick in the wall of my eternal palace. At long last, another worry laid to rest. It has been worth every cost." That's it. The last hint to whichever item it is, maybe eight years back. I've gone over all the books twice now, with no proper clues. I'm dropping it. I would rather spend my time on something actionable. (Book 3, Page 81.)

"It will be *easy*. The progress has already begun and the hopefuls have pulled back from the Prism. We merely expand what we have already done once. Our trusted defenders are already trickling back to Salvation to gain their cards. We merely keep them here, and bring the rest in. Soon, we will have enough people to defend ourselves from the Lightborn. We can always fix the rest of Liberty later, once we are safe."

The voice was strong, reasonable. The speaker looked like the epitome of Liberty. Tall, handsome, bordering on pretty, with the ever-present pointed ears and the gravitas of a man moving from youthful exuberance into well-earned wisdom. His position with his earnest, serious supporters as a backdrop at the bottom floor of the Savior's tower added to his impressive looks.

"It would *not* be easy. We are receiving constant reports from most towns and villages within the blissful lands." Sera's voice, in contrast, was poignant, appealing to reason. "They are struggling. Fighting. Dying. Yet, they are *holding*. Holding the ground against an onslaught of Guardians that nobody within Liberty would have been able to foresee. Some of the more intelligent Guardians from outside must have realized that they have an opening, because they are pushing through in large numbers. How do the hopefuls hold? By ingenuity, improved defenses, and *sacrifice*. Unless they are reinforced soon, however, they *will* break, and they will break bad. Ordering them to pull back, nation-wide, in the middle of an attack of Guardians will see a slaughter unseen since the cleansing of the Church of Darkness. Would you be responsible for that, Dante?"

The tall Liberator sneered. "If the alternative is letting Salvation fall? Of course I would. Letting the Lightborn take over would mean the entire downfall of our nation. Letting the villages and towns drop would be much less harmful."

"Have you ever faced a Guardian, Dante?" a voice called out from among the crowd. The voice was cheerful, laced with irony and challenge.

The Liberator faced the newcomer. "Of course I have. I am—was—a Pristine Mind. Like every hopeful, hand and heart before me, I have done my duty, taking multiple turns against the enemies of our lands. Now, could we—"

"Those look like caster cards to me." The voice came again. "Meaning, you've taken on Guardians and other enemies weakened and confused by the Prism, using your cards to end them from a safe distance. Yet, you stand there, all self-righteous, asking people who never asked to be put in their position, to face Guardians head-on at their strongest, defending their kin while they flee, across hundreds of miles."

"Of course I do. I would sacrifice the same for them, were the roles reversed," Dante crowed. "Show yourself and tell us all why we should even listen to *you*! What have you done that lets you say what is and isn't possible?"

The voice grew lower, but more intent. "I have been in an army overrun by Guardians. I have faced a gaborn with nothing but a dagger. I have fought against beasts and Guardians of every aspect there is and lived to tell the tale." He stepped out from within the crowd, a shit-eating grin on his face as he waved his hand and an amputated stump at everybody. "I'm also absolute trash on a lute. My name is Chase. You may have heard of me."

The crowd parted as the awed whispers spread everywhere.

Dante grimaced and backed down.

***

"Chase! You ass!" Sera slammed the door to the sitting room behind her and turned around, flinging herself at the dust-covered Darkborn. She hugged him until he groaned, then grasped his ears and pulled him in to kiss him thoroughly.

When they parted for air, Chase grinned. "Is this how you greet anybody coming back with reports?"

"Only those who interrupt my carefully planned monologues!" she growled.

"Oh, crap. I didn't even realize. Did I ruin anything? I just arrived and noticed him being an absolute ass."

She waved away his apology and hugged him again, resting her head against him. "Honestly? No. Most people realize that this is not about Dante wanting what is best for Liberty, of course, but just about him saving his own behind. The real issue here is that he is making *some* sense. Our numbers, when looking at the incoming Lightborn, simply do not match up. The difference is that we do not wish to sacrifice ninety percent of Liberty to save ourselves."

The door opened and closed again. Lucille entered, nodding carefully to Chase before addressing Sera. "All right. That's them kept busy for the time being. Catching everybody up on the larger plans being enacted right now should give us an hour, at least."

"Perhaps I should be out there myself?" Chase asked. "I'm in dire need of learning what's going on, and that way, I won't waste your time."

"Please. It's simple, as long as you don't care about the numbers." Lucille snorted. "It's just what you saw in there. We're scrambling for answers. The capital, as you'd likely expect, is where people go when they're *done* fighting. Not when they're ready to fight. We have plenty of people, but far from enough actual fighters to face off against the tens of thousands that the Lightborn are bringing."

"Do we know more about their armies by now?" Chase asked.

"Yes. We heard back from a village they will be passing soon, just this morning." Sera grimaced. "Based on your initial success, a group of veteran fighters marched out to repeat some of your feats—targeting the healers and casters of the groups. They were eradicated to the man." Shaking her head softly, she continued. "They did well, carved deep into the Lightborn mass. But they simply enfolded our attackers and buried them in numbers. They have taken to keeping all their vulnerable classes well dispersed. There was...there was no way."

Chase grimaced. "Any actual estimates? Numbers and Tiers?"

Lucille cleared her throat. "Well, that's where we do have a bit of good news. Judging from the message from the Furyborn elders, and some of the knowledge Sera here has about Lightborn nobility, we are not faced with the ultimate military powers of the Lightborn empire. Rather, they are weaker nobles, easily bullied by somebody like that Lord Beforant."

Chase frowned. "Plenty of indebted too, then?"

Lucille nodded.

"Okay. That's an opening. Something we can use. We..." Chase snapped his fingers. "That loud-speaking cube you borrowed for us when we were addressing the crowd. We can have somebody fast trail their army, tell them all we're ready to take in all indebted. Anybody who decides to join us instead of fighting will be welcome."

"Will they?" Lucille looked to Sera for confirmation. "Be welcome, I mean?"

"Most definitely." She nodded. "There will be actual criminals and troublemakers among their number. Yet, having them run away and join us instead of being part of the attackers would be a wonderful move—if it can be done."

"But it won't be enough," Chase half-asked, half-said.

"No. We have sent messages throughout the blissful lands, asking for any defenders who can be spared to return, to join our ranks. We have told them about the new decks, the advantages currently waiting for them in Salvation. Yet, at our last estimates, even with every single indebted joining our side, our fighters will form about one in four, compared to their numbers."

Chase cursed. "Really? I thought we were like a hundred thousand here in Salvation?"

"Yes. But not many are ready to fight. Besides, a great many disagree with us, blame us for everything, or prefer to wait and see what will happen. Most will flee. Some may join us in time." Lucille shrugged. "Some may stab us in the back."

"Okay. One in four," Chase mused. "Those are bad odds, obviously, but...we've faced worse and lived. Also, didn't you once tell us that the odds are always in favor of the defenders in large conflicts, Sera?"

"You do listen!" She smiled. "They are. Unfortunately, the usual reasons for this are mostly unapplicable to Salvation." She counted on her fingers. "Usually, there are local advantages, such as knowing secret hiding places, being able to arrange ambushes, hide traps and the like. Then we have natural defensive positions—defensive walls, gates and other chokepoints, any geographical or constructed advantages that can be prepared and abused against an attacker. Finally, we have the advantage of storage. Any invading army will be living on what they can carry and have limited equipment, while the locals will have the chance to stockpile anything necessary." She shot him a sad smile. "Of all these, only the stockpiling truly applies to us—and with the Lightborn armies having recently arrived, they are not likely to run out of provisions any time soon."

Chase opened his mouth and closed it again. He groaned. "Of course. The city is so wide open, and even the alleys are wide and inviting. It's perfect for invaders."

"Just so," Sera said drily. "I would bring a map, but you already know exactly what it will look like. Everything is straight, open, with large squares and crossing roads or alleys every few hundred feet, for convenience. We are experiencing the same issues out in the villages and towns right now, only on a much smaller scale. At least, out there, the enemies are Guardians, unthinking and likely to fall for obvious traps or being funneled into ambushes. Here, even if we were to build up roadblocks, defensive positions in the squares or the like, they could simply shrug and take the next road over. Even if we were to call all builders back to Salvation right this moment, we would not be able to erect proper defenses in time."

"Then, what do we do?" Chase asked earnestly.

"We prepare as best we can. Call out for all to help us and join our ranks, to craft items to aid us. Have our fighters practice incessantly with their new cards—because that's one place where we *will* have an advantage," Lucille said. "Apart from that? Pray for a miracle. Because we'll need it."

Chase laughed out loud. Eyes gleaming, he shook his head.

"What? What am I missing?" she said, for the first time genuinely confused.

"Lucille. At this point, we've killed clerics of both Light *and* Dark. Add to that, taking down the Savior, who was supposed to be a living god...I think the only answer if we start praying is going to come in the shape of lightning and rocks falling from the sky."

***

"I call to order this meeting of the greatest minds of Salvation. That's minds as in brains, Liam, not as in those weak-ass Tier-fours they have prancing about the place." Kith stood proudly, looking down the others over his upturned nose. "As the supreme and foremost power of this place—"

"As a representative of 'those weak-ass Tier-fours,' I'm telling you, you'd better shut up, or I'll do it for you. Besides, you don't even know what we're doing here." Cilia sat with her arms around her knees, glowering up at him.

The others were arrayed on thick blankets on the grass, except Nordon, who was solemnly lowering a clinking basket down onto one blanket well apart from the others.

"Panicking?" Kith raised an eyebrow. "I thought we were panicking, and planning to abscond with as much stuff as we could before the army hits us. Or just planning to fully enjoy one of the last days of our lives." He gestured at the open, sunny park surrounding them.

"Well. That first part's not wrong." Chase chuckled. "I recommended the absconding part too, and my shoulder's still hurting from getting hit."

"What we *are* doing is taking stock and trying to come up with some last-minute ideas that'll help us survive the days to come. I know we've all been working hard the past days—even Kith—but things will be coming to a head in the next few days, and it's not looking good," Cilia admitted.

Chase nodded. "Okay. Where do we start? With where we're at? I mean, the people of Salvation are definitely starting to panic. But what's our situation actually looking like?"

"That is a logical place to start." Sera nodded, sitting up straighter. "From the status discussion last evening, we are, numbers-wise, above theirs. Except, of course, if we start counting actual fighters. The vast majority of our numbers consist of regular citizens, with the minimum experience of having fought near the Prism. And the citizens of Salvation are not going to fight. Too much has happened in too little time. They might not have loved their old lives, but they knew that they had at least earned safety. Now, they feel that everything is at risk. In practice, we are likely looking at numbers of around one in four, compared to the Lightborn army—and of those, many will be lower-Tiered than the aggressors."

"When is the army coming?" Chase asked.

"Two days from now. We do have a few volunteers out, probing, attacking from afar, but they are unlikely to keep them back for long enough to earn us another day of reprieve." Sera smoothed her robe. "We expect them to show no mercy and aim straight for the Wellspring in order to take our decks for themselves."

"That's a whole lot of reasons to not stick around," Kith murmured. "What've we got going for us? Anything?"

Sera smiled. "We have not been idle. First and foremost is the fact that we have come to an agreement about the Liberty decks already present in the city. Apparently, you cannot establish Wellsprings within the reach of another active Wellspring of the same kind—yet, we have been able to erect Wellsprings all around the city, on the outskirts in the four cardinal directions."

"Both Liberty and Dark Wellsprings, that is," Chase added. "People haven't been idle in visiting our new Dark Wellspring to gain cards, and I've had *four* new decks pop up since creating the damn thing in the first place."

"Thank you, Chase." Sera smiled. "Yes. Also, we have established the Wellsprings with the army's approach in mind. The Wellsprings facing south boost Toughness and Agility respectively, in anticipation of the fighting starting there. On top of that, I decided to re-activate my own Home Defender card down there, granting +3 to all attributes except Potential and making sure the southern area is truly prepared for the fight. Meanwhile, the Wellsprings of the other directions boost the rarity of cards for each of their class."

"Wait. You didn't—" Kith started.

"We absolutely did." Sera beamed. "At the center, Kith's statue will improve the rarity of cards for summoners and the Wellspring boosts Potential for anybody. West, we have crafters and fighters. North is ranged fighters and rogues, with east being healers and casters."

"Whoa." Liam blinked. "No, wait. I don't get it. Anybody trying to get cards from those Wellsprings aren't going to get anything but Dark and Liberty cards. Of course, they can go to the plaza later, for the other decks, but then those will be a lower rarity. Or what?"

Sera smiled. "We did not expect this, but it is a wonderful boon. The boosts? All of them? They linger. Meaning, as long as a prospective fighter walks out to gain the buff from the western Wellspring, and hurries up, the boost will still be active when they reach the plaza. On top of that, they will gain the boost to Potential from the central Wellspring, and Kith's statue for summoners."

"Oh. Ho-ho. That is amazing! I'm guessing almost everybody gets better cards than we did? Excepting Chase, of course, that freak." Liam grinned.

"Not a Common card in sight. Uncommons are the most, well, common ones. However, there are plenty of Rares and even the occasional Epic. In time, they will absolutely outmatch us."

Chase grimaced. "If they survive that long."

"There is that," Sera agreed. "To make it that far, we have been working on a lot of different plans. I have primarily toiled to ensure that Liberty as a whole actually has some sort of cohesion instead of imploding. What little energy remained outside of that has been used to carve out some sort of plan we can use for the invasion. I would like your eyes on it later—but for now, let us focus on what you have all managed."

Liam started. "I've been taking care of the indebted. They are, like you'd imagine, pretty shaken by the whole thing. But most of them are starting to come around, and I'd say the rest will join in once I introduce them to the Wellspring and show them what they'll have. We've located most of those who managed to run away in the first place, and...well, I like them. Most are going to help us fight. A lot of those who don't, because they're hurt or messed up or just plain afraid, are still hoping to help others among the indebted to get away."

Kith snorted. "Looks like, if we manage this, Liberty's gonna have a new Lightborn ghetto."

"If we do survive, I intend to have the survivors installed in palaces for their aid!" Sera smiled. "What about you, Cilia?"

"Droplets," Cilia said simply. "I started investigating all sorts of new, miraculous crafted items, but then I changed my mind. It took too long! Instead of spending my time hoping for a miracle, I went with what I know. I know how to create efficient droplets, and I know how to make them well. With the high-quality material I've been able to scrounge, the effects will be beyond anything I've managed before. Now, I'm not going to be able to outfit a full army or anything—I think my arms would fall off first—but I can deliver a full complement of droplets to at least ten veteran groups."

Kith whistled. "We're still far behind them on numbers. But those ten groups, if they're high Tier to begin with, could likely do some *real* damage with fire, shadow, and blinding droplets in their hands. *Well* done, Cil!"

She grimaced, then spoke up rapidly, words falling over each other to get out. "I've also been talking to Emilia. I didn't like what happened, at all, and she's been through a *lot* of crap."

Liam snorted. "She also attacked you."

"Yeah. But she was brainwashed. And...I beat her and her friends pretty horribly, I'll admit. But I actually managed to get through to her. She'll be helping defend the city. And...she helped me with another thing. I'm not sure it works, though, so...yeah. Nordon?"

Nordon spoke up, eyes still lingering on his basket. "I'll start by saying that this very much is *not* what I signed up for." His glower devolved into a tiny smirk. "But since I've already visited the plaza and have a full set of cards, I'm very much not complaining. On top of that, I've learned *so* much in here, both concerning crafting and Liberty in general." He beamed before noticing the glances aimed at him. With a soft chuckle, he continued. "Of course, you're likely more interested in what I've done for the war. For that, I can only say one thing: The Savior was a *genius*. He might not have been any fun at parties, but his work to expand on crafting to make it more of a communal task than something single crafters have to take on...it's impressive!"

"Impending invasion, man. Get to the point, *please*!" Kith groaned.

"Oh. Well. I've sort of helped open the entire stores for crafters throughout Salvation and taken over the official crafting channels."

Cilia was the only one who didn't look surprised. Chase just said, "What?"

"Well, with the Savior out of the picture, nobody was really giving them any work. So, when I started pulling some strings, most were pleased to get back to doing something useful." He shrugged. "It took a bit of work to hunt down the people loitering in their homes, but we're at around seventy percent normal capacity, and I've got it all geared at the war effort. Anybody who's ready to lift a finger to defend us will be outfitted in time." He leaned forward, pointing at Liam's armor. "Of course, it's not going to be at the level of Cilia's craftsmanship, but...it's not bad. I'm pretty sure we'll be, on the whole, better equipped than the Lightborn."

"Very well done," Cilia said. "How did you manage on your other experiments?" For the benefit of the others, she added, "He was planning to mass-produce some of our droplets with local materials."

Nordon drew a leather item from the basket next to him. It was oval, unornamented, and reeked of recently treated leather. It was also, quite clearly, a copy of the droplets on Cilia's belts. "Good news and bad. We did manage to create a low-quality version of those shadow droplets of yours. By the day after tomorrow, almost every frontline fighter will have one of those."

"That's...okay, that's actually really impressive. If we're able to, at any time, drown their forces in darkness, we can do a lot to shape the battlefield as we want it," Chase mused. "Of course, with their numbers and the bastards all having Light cards, they'll have a lot of counters. Still. Well done, man. What was the bad news?"

"I failed at everything else. Whether it's due to Cilia having a ridiculously high Mental Power or some specific process or mindset, we've been unable to recreate any of your other creations. Also, I have spent *way* too long on another project which, I'm sad to say, is looking like an abject failure." He softly reached into the basket, extracting a wine bottle filled with a murky liquid. "This is a local byproduct of their soap. Shaper oil, they call it. It's usually used for deeper cleaning or for, ahem, blowing up rocks, unsafe buildings, and the like."

Very carefully, Kith spoke. "You're telling me that the bottle you're fumbling with right there could blow us all to the Pits?"

"Oh yes. Definitely. If I were clumsy. Which I'm not." Nordon rolled his eyes as he put down the bottle again. He ignored their shocked stares. "I was hoping to be able to reduce the volatility of the oil before mass-producing it for the army, grant them a few hundred gallons of an explosive substance they could toss at the enemy from the rooftops. Alas, I have failed. I should've spent my time on something better."

Sera stood up. She stared wide-eyed at the seated brewer. "Please be *very* precise here, Nordon. Are you telling me that you have a hundred gallons of an explosive liquid that you intend to ignore because it is too volatile?"

He shook his head. "Oh, no."

Sera deflated with a grimace.

"It's more like a thousand gallons."

She perked up again, blinking. Then she took a deep breath. "Nordon. Dear Nordon. Let me ask you something. Our one main issue with the upcoming battle is the fact that the city is wide open and we cannot rearrange our streets in time to form even impromptu defenses and blockades. Are you truly telling me that this is powerful enough to, say, demolish a two-story building and make it block a street?"

"Oh. *Oh.*" Nordon rubbed his face. "I...guess that would be a possibility. As long as you took care in transporting it there and placing it properly. Do you intend to use it in the city?"

"If need be." Sera's voice was cold and dangerous. She strode over to where she sat and rummaged around a backpack, before emerging with a large vellum map, which she unfolded on top of the blanket. "I was going to use this time to try to come up with some sort of cohesive plan we could use for our defense. I was expecting that we would have to pick some streets to secure, or maybe cordon off parts of the inner city. Only, with this shaper oil, we have options. Look!" She waved them all over, then leapt to a nearby gravel path and picked up a handful of gravel.

Shooting glances at her, they slowly gathered around the map. There was nothing new to see, except for the fact that a bunch of new structures—the Wellsprings—had been painted onto the map. The rest of the map still portrayed the streets of Salvation going in a pattern that, to Chase, was unnaturally regular and straight. There were no unexpected cul-de-sacs, no weird expansions or small pockets of architectural insanity. Everything was straightforward, easily approachable, with equidistant streets running both north to south and east to west.

"This?" Sera's eyes gleamed with excitement as she knelt next to the map. "Is a tactical nightmare for a defender." She took her handful of gravel and started to pour small piles of it onto a smattering of the streets, seemingly at random. However, before long, the straight and open streets turned into something else. "This, on the other hand, is an *opportunity.*"

"It's a maze!" Chase breathed.

"That is exactly what it is. If this oil can produce the needed effects, with some proper planning, we can block entire streets and turn Salvation into a maze where we can slowly grind the Lightborn army into the soil as they follow the course *we* set."

Liam cleared his throat. "Just checking here. Because to me, it sounds a lot like you're planning to blow half of Salvation up."

"Not in the least." She shook her head, not letting her eyes leave the map for a moment. "At most five percent. But you should not worry. When the Lightborn do enter the city, anybody within the houses will be long gone. They have already been warned, and know what is coming. Those who do not intend to stay and fight are already starting to leave the city."

They spent a few hours coming up with plans on how to turn Salvation into a hellish nightmare for the invaders. Then they split up, each going their own way. They didn't expect to see one another until the day of the battle.

CHAPTER 49

"This is it. With the camps active and running independently, I no longer have to worry about rebels. With the policies for cards properly embedded, there are no risks of anybody outgrowing the expected limits to pose a direct threat to me. The Keepers will catch any brewing unrest in the blissful lands. The second-to-last phase is done. Now, I merely have to properly expand my direct influence within Salvation, and then, the rest of Liberty. At long last, everything will be entirely secure, for everybody." This was dated a few weeks ago. Even if I die in the next few days and the Lightborn take over the world, this paragraph is everything I need to read, in order to know that I've done something good with my life. (Book 4, Page 57.)

What is going *on?*" Chase shouted. "I ran all the way out here as soon as I heard the horns!"

Liam shrugged. "I was on my way out here to welcome a group of indebted who managed to sneak away from the army. Now, those horns started blowing. It can't be the army yet, can it?"

"Nope. Sera insists they'll arrive tomorrow around noon."

"Then who the hell *are* they? They're looking mighty pointy-eared for indebted Lightborn, and they're dusty enough that they've clearly been on the road for a long time." Liam squinted at the incoming swarm of people in search of answers.

"No clue. Whoever they are, there's a lot of them. And a good number of them are armed. That's either a really good or really bad sign." Chase tried to count the unwashed horde slowly making their way down the incline snaking its way down toward Salvation and failed. There were too many, without any sort of organization whatsoever.

They stood in silence for a while as the people slowly ambled closer. Now, they started to spot some weird incongruencies in them.

"You know, that's kind of weird. First you think something's strange. Then you slowly get used to seeing it everywhere—and you don't even notice it until it's not there anymore." Chase scratched his neck.

"What's that?"

"The clothes, mate. The clothes. There's almost nobody in those groups wearing that bloody Savior's getup, but they're nearly all Liberators."

Liam gawked. "Oooh. Yeah, that is bloody weird. Maybe—"

"Now, ain't that a sight for sore eyes. I had my hopes up, but I sure wasn't expecting a welcoming committee." The coarse voice shouting from within the crowd of people sounded like it would break right over into a coughing fit.

"I know that voice." Chase blinked, eyes searching the marching, dust-covered people. "No gods-damned way. Toran! *What the Pits are you doing here?*" The last sentence was half shout, half laugh.

The large Liberator waved with his half-ruined right hand and spoke a few words to the people walking on either side of him. The huge procession slowed and, little by little, halted entirely, while Toran strode forward toward them. If possible, the strong man looked even more tired than the first time they'd seen him and strong-armed him into torching his own village. But there was something else in his eyes now, something vibrant. He looked Chase up and down, taking in his bare arms and the cards lining them. With a wide grin, he said, "I heard you folks have cards to spare?"

Fifteen minutes later, the soldiers rushing toward the gates had halted, and Liam and Chase strode toward the center of the city, while local citizens rushed out with food, water, and a helping hand for those following on their heels.

"About nine hundred of us in total. We're actually doing better now than when we started out. We managed to snag ourselves some good provisions. I never thought it'd be possible to actually heal while on the march, but you should have seen some of them before. It was ugly."

Liam looked back at some of the people following them and grimaced. They didn't exactly look fighting fit, so picturing them worse off was nauseating. "There were only about a hundred of you before. What happened, Toran? And how the Pits did you make it here unseen?"

He barked a laugh that sounded almost bear-like. "Long story. But...you know how I told you we have some contacts in the villages? A couple weeks ago, our contacts started spouting some *weird* nonsense about the Savior dying. Killed by a group with a rather *specific* getup. We didn't believe it at first, but then we got to thinking and a daredevil activated Devotion to Liberty, saw that it was inactive. And...well, then I got an idea."

"This is where Cilia usually starts ragging on me, sounds like." Chase smirked. *"You know that you're not supposed to think!"* he scolded in a horrible imitation of her voice.

Raising an eyebrow, Toran shook with laughter. "Well, I figured, if this is actually true, what happens to the camps?"

"The camps?" Liam repeated, then his eyes widened. "Oh!"

"Exactly." Toran grunted. "The camps where they send all the rebels and those who misbehave. What would they do with the Savior gone? So, we decided to send people to all the camps."

"To *all* the camps?" Liam perked up.

"Yeah. We went to the camp closest to Salvation first. The guards at the camps were still there, but confused and aimless. The moment they realized how many we were, they surrendered and let us free everybody. Then, I volunteered to take people here to check that this wasn't some weird trap, while the others are moving for the rest of the camps. Now that we know, we'll have people coming in over the next weeks. We'll all be free. And it's all your fault. You'll have to tell us how you managed it!" Slowly, his face fell, as he watched Chase and Liam exchange glances. "What?"

"I...damn." Liam gulped. "Well, it's all true. And we're glad you guys made it, and freed all those poor bastards. But you haven't exactly arrived at the safest of times."

"What do you mean by that?"

Liam looked at Chase before shaking his head softly. "I'll tell you guys. Then, we're letting you choose your new cards, before we're finding a place for you to rest. And *then*...we need a bloody drink."

The next day went by in a haze of last-minute preparations. Suddenly, everything was urgent and should truly have been handled way earlier. They, along with the rest of the damn city, ran around—super busy, afraid, and confused, all at the same time. The return of the Liberators from the camps didn't help the confusion either.

As word spread, however, they did send a bolt of energy into the people of Liberty. These were actual sons and daughters of Liberty, many of which had been thought lost or dead long since, now returned to Salvation. There were tearful reunions, families reunited, and old wounds torn back open, right in the middle of an already tense situation.

During those last twenty-four hours, the city saw hundreds of situations it had never before experienced: People in the southern district refusing to leave their homes, even if they were smack in the middle of where the Lightborn army were likely to invade. Looters. Single people and groups fleeing the city north in an ever-growing stream, forcing massive blockades on the otherwise wide paved roads.

Chase and the others did their part, but were all too aware that they were just a tiny part of a huge crowd of people with far from enough control to do much about the overall direction of these thousands and thousands.

In the late hours of the evening, Chase took in the series of lingering notifications with a contemplative smile playing on his face. He would've preferred to go over everything, celebrate his new cards with his family. Only, they were all rushing around, too busy to make time for something like this. What should've been a celebration for the ages was reduced to just another task to check off on his mental checklist in preparation for the day after.

That being said, he wasn't complaining about the results. He brought up his new cards again, one by one.

[**Among the Raindrops**
Legendary, Elemental rogue
Tier two
Active, medium duration
Upon activation, this card will start summoning large quantities of puddles for the duration of the effect in a thirty-foot radius around the wearer. The puddles of water have a triple effect, all working only against enemies. First, they have an oily, slippery effect and will make it hard to keep your equilibrium. Second, they have an acidic effect, causing ongoing damage against any exposed skin or equipment. Third, the puddles have a viscous quality, clinging to anything and anybody unlucky enough to enter. Finally, the wielder may direct exactly where the puddles appear.
Long cooldown
"Your fancy power is to make me stand in a puddle of water? Hah. Wait. Why are you laughing?"]

His choice of Tier five upgrade had been easy. Among the Raindrops had saved his life several times over now, and the upgrade was *solid*. More water, placed exactly where he wanted it? Yes please!

[**Sticky Shadows**
Rare, Dark rogue
Tier five
Active, medium duration
Upon activation, the wielder may continually summon sticky patches of cobwebs to be sent flying at targets within a distance of fifty feet. The cobwebs are extremely clingy and resilient, and enfold the target in a thin layer of blinding shadows.

Long cooldown
"What do you mean 'you finally caught me'? The real fun starts now!" The Spinner of Shadows escapes again.]

Sticky Shadows should allow him to completely tie up smaller groups of enemies, blinding and restraining them. It might not be all-powerful, but for sheer distraction and disruption, it would likely be wonderful.

[**Warmth of Touch**
Epic, Light rogue
Tier five
Active, short/medium duration
When activated, the wielder has exactly thirty seconds. Any friend or ally touched within that time will have a powerful buff applied to them which boosts all their attributes except Potential for a medium duration.
Long cooldown
"You get a boost. You get a boost. Everybody gets a boost!"]

Warmth of Touch should be amazing. Combined with his already high Agility and Fight Another Day, he estimated that he'd be able to buff at least fifty allies within those thirty seconds. More, if they lined up properly.

[**Sudden Breeze**
Legendary, Elemental rogue
Tier five
Active, very short duration
The wielder calls an extremely powerful gust of wind into being. For a very short while, he may direct a sustained force of air anywhere he chooses within close range.
Short cooldown
"Blow me? Funny you should say that."]

Sudden Breeze was one of those choices that just *felt* right. He'd be able to switch to it, throw a powerful gust at his enemies, and swap back to another card again. Also, the short cooldown would allow him to use it often—and at Legendary rarity, he had high hopes for the efficiency.

[**Temper Tantrum**
Epic, Furyborn rogue
Tier five
Active, short duration
Emotions are a powerful tool. When properly manipulated, they can take the reins entirely, superseding the mind and logic

for brief bursts. This card multiplies and enhances the existing emotions of people in a fifty-foot radius around the wielder several times over. The higher the difference between the wielder's Mental Power and that of the targets, the more pronounced the effect. With a high enough difference in Mental Power, the wielder may choose which emotion to instill to override the existing ones.

Medium cooldown

"Come, feeble minds. Show me what you truly feel. Let the world know!" Ghurstown, before the riots.]

Chase wasn't fully sure what to make of Temper Tantrum. But he had an idea. Emotions on a battlefield already ran high. Amplified several times over? That would make for some *very* angry or afraid enemies.

[**Mine Now!**
Epic, Liberty rogue
Tier five
Active, instant
Most often, proper preparation decides the outcome of a conflict. At times, those very preparations may turn against you. When activated, this card steals every positive buff from hostile wielders within a fifty-foot radius and applies them to the wielder, with their original effects and durations intact.

Long cooldown

"Yoink!"]

This last one, Chase thought would be a good game changer, if he ever found himself surrounded. Not only would it strip his enemies of their advantages, but it could also, with enough buffs, make him virtually undefeatable for a while.

He smiled to himself. He had done what he could. Now, they would see this through.

That night, few people slept. In the morning, as an evil omen, above the rise overlooking Salvation, dust clouds indicated what was to come.

The Lightborn army had arrived.

Sera stood in the Freedom Plaza, surrounded by people. Closest to her were Liam, Cilia, and the others. Then came the rest of what would likely become the new Liberty government in time. Nearly as one, they looked to her. Over the last few days, almost all detractors had either joined her side, or jumped ship entirely. Dante fled the city a day or two earlier.

You would think with the incoming army, that the people still remaining in the city were either die-hard in denial, refusing to see the danger, hoping to weather the invasion in safety somewhere, or ready to fight. Yet, there was still a sensation of incredulity in the air, of indecision.

The open area was filled to the brim, crowd standing shoulder to shoulder, all of them looking toward the Wellsprings, looking for words, for hope or guidance.

Sera stepped up. With a step as light as a feather, she leapt onto the knee, then the shoulder of Kith's statue. There, she stood, as securely as if she were on the ground, looking over the crowd ahead of her while the burgeoning wave of sound slowly died down.

Her voice arrived clearly through the loudspeaker cube, sincere and firm. "There are times in our lives, where we are tested. Where we—deservedly or not—wind up in situations where we will have to prove our worth, to ourselves and to the world at large. Some of us are tested more than once. Yet, everybody here today is, through no fault of their own, faced with the same test." She pointed straight south. "Within hours, the Lightborn army will be right outside Salvation. They are going to do their very best to do what the Lightborn nobility does best: subdue those they think below them and take anything they want for personal gain."

She shook her head. "I was a Lightborn noble myself. I had to fight, had to run in order to evade that fate. I thought I had escaped it already. Yet now, they are back. And this time, I am not going to run!"

A mutter ran through the crowd.

"We came to Liberty with ill intentions—for personal gain. I readily admit as much. We decided to stay and tie our lot to that of Salvation when it became fully clear that there is so much worth fighting for here. A nation of people who are willing to toil and sacrifice for others before themselves. Selfless, strong fighters, who will aid even without being asked. Salvation…you are beautiful, and I wish I would have had the chance to meet you in better times!"

She shook her head sadly and her voice ditched the wistfulness and grew in intensity. "Yet, we are not allowed to choose when we are tested. Today, we will all face the ultimate test. Some of us will run. Some will not. Yet, where I should be afraid, I instead find myself optimistic, looking to the future with open eyes."

Her arm shot out, steady, pointing at Chase and the others. Kith froze mid-movement as he was scratching his head, a ridiculous caricature as he leaned up against his own statue. "These four. They were hard-boiled criminals, ready to rob you for coin, for a scrap of food, living in the worst slums of the Lightborn empire. Yet, now, they are here, putting themselves on the front line, standing between you and the invaders."

She moved her arm, indicating a group of Lightborn, decked out in armor and weaponry, standing in an uneasy group in the square. "Indebted. Those are supposed to be among the worst criminals among the Lightborn, enslaved, forced to fight in an attempt to redeem their crimes. Yet, now that they have been freed, have they run back home? No, they are right here, next to us, fighting your fight!"

That got more than just a low mutter. Scattered applause even broke out here and there.

Sera ignored them all. Her arm moved again. "Liberty rebels! A mixed group of those fleeing from regular Liberty society, those trying to work against rules they saw as unfair, and those trying to gather up in arms. Many of them have toiled in horrible camps for years, thought lost to us all. Only weeks ago, the Savior talked about them, naming them all criminals. Now, we can see that they were the ones who were brave enough to stand up for what they believed in." She paused her impassioned speech and huffed. "My opinion doesn't really matter here, though. I'm an outsider, and I have neither the experience nor the right to judge them. What I *do* know is that, even with everything life has flung at them, they are still here, ready to stand up, in order to protect all of you. To protect the freedom for each and every one of us.

"We have managed to secure a lot of things that would not have been possible just weeks ago. Right behind me, we have the united crafters of Salvation, ready to hand out their combined works, armor and weapons for anybody willing to fight. We even have crafted one-time-use items from Cilia, the Tier four crafter who helped slay the Savior."

Her voice grew somber, even as she smiled. "For those of you who are still undecided: I cannot make the decision for you. I can only say, with absolute certainty, that this is the moment where you are being tested, like you have never been before. We have the tools needed to defend us all. We need willing hands to take us there. So, I need to ask—no, beg you all." She paused, letting her earnest gaze slide over the entire convocation, before asking softly, "Salvation...will you face your test head-on? *Will you fight for Liberty?*"

The roar that answered her rang to the heavens.

***

Liam and Chase stood side by side, facing the invading army. The Lightborn had taken their time, advancing slowly, scouts carefully moving first, looking for ambushes and traps.

Truth be told, they'd planned a good many different traps, especially for the path down the hillside. However, they'd eventually judged the decline to be too soft to create any truly effi-cient traps. If a trap failed, the army would be able to just go off the paved road and choose any way across the open ground down to Salvation.

Now, the Lightborn army was in place, and they looked the part. They might have arrived as part of different noble contin-gencies. Yet, Beforant had clearly imposed his own view of for-mations on them, because they were lined up outside the city in tight, impressive formations, armors shining and pennants wav-ing.

There had been some changes from their marching order. Each and every large unit held both close combat fighters and ranged fighters at the back and, somewhere at their center, oth-ers who might be summoners, casters, or clerics. It looked like there were about twenty of these units in total, each of them sporting nearly a thousand soldiers.

There were no indebted.

They'd had rogues with movement powers surrounding the army for the past number of days with loud-speaking items, shouting to anybody with ears that all indebted would be wel-comed in Liberty society if they jumped ship. Once they started getting the indebted sorted out in Salvation, they added names to the list, as proof that they were indeed accepting them and getting to know them. Chase had spent a good while fine-tuning the Guardian settings on the Wellspring to ensure they wouldn't attack the indebted in the city.

It had been a costly decision for the Lightborn, but at some point, the army had simply left a few hundred soldiers along with the thousands of indebted that the nobles had brought along, to ensure they wouldn't rebel or be instantly freed. They debated sending soldiers out to release them, but decided against it when they realized they wouldn't make it back in time to influ-ence the result.

The inquisitors had arrived as well. In a brilliantly white unit, their loose formation stood out among the razor-straight ranks of the soldiers. Thankfully, their numbers had *not* been inflated from the original group. Whatever relationship allowed Lord Beforant to treat the archbishop as his personal valet ap-parently did not extend to the nobles, and only a few additional white-clad fanatics were now shooting hateful glances at Liam and Chase from afar.

Now, the ranks shuffled aside, allowing two persons to walk forward. Two very familiar faces.

"You ever wonder where it went wrong?" Liam asked. "I mean, one day, I was flirting with the staff on Kevsan's raft, help-ing you escape from the city guard. The next, we've got entire Fire-scoured empires wanting to chase us down. It feels like I blinked and missed a few connections."

Chase chuckled. "Honestly, I'd say it means we're doing something right. I mean, you don't get the higher-ups all riled up unless you're succeeding in whatever you're doing!" He grimaced. "It does feel like we're succeeding a bit *too* hard, though. I swear, if we make it through this, we're taking a break for a *year*!"

"I'm with you there. It feels like it's been ages since I had a break. Also, there's a Tier-three potter who says she really wants my input on her technique."

Chase blinked, looking away from the arriving Lightborn. "A potter? Like, somebody who makes pots and jars? Just how are you able to help her?"

Liam's gaze softened. "That was what I asked, too. She said that her technique was very hands-on and she would have to show me in person. Then she winked. *She winked, Chase!*"

Chase couldn't help it. He doubled over with laughter. "I guess we have a reason to survive today, then. We can't have you growing old without an education, can we?"

For a few seconds, the two were silent. Then Chase said softly, "Honestly. It's been a good run. Thank you for everything."

"Don't make me all maudlin. We need our wits about us. Especially with...this." He indicated the backpack placed on the ground between the two.

"I agree. I can't believe Cil actually spoke in *favor* of this. She must be truly desperate."

"Her and me both." Liam eyed the backpack, frowning. "If things do go sideways, you know the drill. I'll keep us both safe."

"As you have ever done, brother." Chase reached out and clasped him around the neck.

"Am I interrupting? That looks like a truly touching moment." Thomas Beforant had dressed for the occasion. His uniform was white and gold, pristine except for the long ranks of medals, ribbons, and badges on the left breast. His shoulders carried golden epaulettes, polished to a near-blinding shine. It was all outdone by his glorious smile, though, self-satisfaction mixed with sheer joy of living. Beside him, the archbishop limped, shooting hateful glances at them, using a large, ornate staff with golden runes to carry him forward.

"The more the merrier, we usually say," Chase shot back. "I think, just this once, we could do without adding to the company, though."

Thomas slapped a hand over his heart, making his decorations jump. "I am hurt. Am I not wanted here? How sad." His voice shifted in a split second. "Honestly, I couldn't believe it, when I recognized you. I was dead sure you'd run away. I nearly had you last time."

"That's not how I remember it." Chase grinned.

He washed away Chase's comment with a wave of his hand. "Okay. Daylight is wasting, and I'm sure that you've got your Wellspring producing Dark Guardians—"

"Abominations," the archbishop barked.

"Yes, yes, Archbishop. Now, do be silent for a while. I'll let you know if you're allowed to speak." Beforant's voice was playful, but held a dangerous edge.

"Why do you just take his abuse?" Liam asked. "Okay, I get that this guy's somebody important and we're supposed to be, like, the epic tome of evil—"

Thomas burst into laughter. He managed in a strained voice, "Epic. Tome?"

"Sure. Saw it on one of your wanted scrolls back in lands of Light. Epic tome of evil. Means we're supposed to be the worst, I think."

The noble's eyes glinted. "Yes. Of course. Please continue. This is wonderful."

"What I mean is, you're supposed to be the leader of the church. That makes you important, too. If I had so-called friends who treated me like that, I'd do something about it. Why don't you leave?"

"Oh, do answer that. This should be fun," Thomas said.

The archbishop spoke, his voice sounding every bit as tired as he looked. "It is not as simple as you would make it. You are, basically, kids and cannot be expected to understand. Sometimes, you are forced to deal with forces you would rather avoid, in order to obtain the results you desire."

"Oh. Cilia's talked about that. It's like how you guys talk about how the Church of the Dark was consorting with demons and sacrifices to get what they wanted." Liam nodded.

"What? No. That is not what this is like at all, you simpleton!" the archbishop erupted.

"No? Ah. I guess not. I mean, that was a lie the church made up back then as an excuse to attack them and steal their cards." Liam blinked. "Wait. Wouldn't that make this *twice* as similar to back then?"

The archbishop's face contorted as he tried to follow Liam's logic.

Thomas's giggling laughter interrupted their stilted discussion. "As much as I am enjoying this titillating back-and-forth, we should likely get moving. Now. This is an official parley between the Lightborn and Liberty. You are, apparently, the chosen representatives for Liberty. Hence, it falls to you to provide the stance of the wonderful city spread out before us. Are we in agreement so far?"

"A bit more highbrow than I'm used to, but unless I misunderstand you, the answer is yes. We're speaking for Liberty right now," Chase said.

"Wonderful. Wonderful." He rubbed his hands together. "In that case, I request the instant and abject surrender of the entirety of Liberty. Would you be so kind as to agree? It would allow me to skip all this *tedious* slaughter and go straight to my well-deserved payout. I do so look forward to seeing what I can do with Elemental cards. I have a feeling I would have a natural aptitude for Fire. What do you think?"

"I think you're a lunatic, and the worst possible thing that could happen to *any* nation." Chase met the eye of the archbishop, who'd caught himself nodding along with the assessment. "But no. We do not agree."

"Ah. How very sad." Beforant clapped his hands together, smiling brightly. "In that case—"

"Wait. Wait just a damned moment." Chase held up his hand. "There is one thing that we need to discuss before you start attacking us. Well, two things really. We'll start with the most pressing. Last time we met, you tried attacking us. There is one good reason why you shouldn't do that."

Thomas laughed, a dangerous light in his eyes. "In my defense, you were *right* there in front of me. Just like this time, except I have prepared for any surprises. But do go ahead. Why should I not try to kill you right away?"

"Except for this being a parley? Aren't we supposed to all be nice about these things?" Liam shot back.

"Please." Chase snorted. "People like him only care about rules when they work in their favor."

Lord Beforant smiled brilliantly, not gainsaying him in the least.

"The reason you should not attack us is that the backpack right here at our feet contains a large container of very, very volatile materials. Materials that, if jostled, are going to leave us all pasted across a large area of these so-very-well-made paving stones. And I swear, in the name of my mother, whoever she may be, if you attack us, the last thing I'll do is kick that container *right* in your pretty face." Chase snarled that last part, eyes locked with the noble.

Thomas's smile did not waver in the least. "Where have you been all my life? Usually, enemies are so *dull*!" He tapped his lip. "Desahl. You would be able to shield me from some large explosion, would you not?"

The archbishop looked at Liam, then gulped. "I...cannot be sure, without knowing what the substance is, my lord. My shield works best against aspected damage."

"Shame. Okay then, *Chase*. You have earned another few moments. What is your other reason we should not attack?"

"Honestly? Because it's not going to end well for you." Chase shrugged and pointed south. "What I didn't tell you last time? We've long been in talks with both the Furyborn elders and the High Elementalist about building a safe place for all. They know what's going on right now, and are sending forces in this direction. Even if you succeed today, they're going to find and end you. It's going to end in tears for you."

Thomas's eyes widened. Then he flung back his head and laughed. "Oh, that is just *wonderful*. You all surprise me at every turn. Again, I am so sorry I will have to slaughter you."

"But not sorry enough to stop." Liam frowned.

"Now you're catching up, young man." Thomas shook his head, eyes filled with mirth. "I *am* impressed. Unless you are lying, you managing to make deals with the two powers on Ordei who have been able to challenge the might of the Lightborn empire? It's laudable. However, there is something you are not seeing. First off, you just made this reward even more tantalizing. Your Wellspring will have all five decks waiting for me? How could I *not*?"

Halting, he considered something, then pressed on. "Ah, but I forget myself. The odds are good that this is just a bluff and a diversionary tactic. A *good* bluff, and a believable one, but I cannot know. Regardless, it truly doesn't matter. I think I'll be pressing on ahead regardless."

"*Why?*" Chase growled. "Why the Pits would you go ahead with something as costly as an invasion, if you actually believe that I'm right?"

"Ah. It's simple. Once I've won and have my decks, I don't need to win. I simply need to make it back home. Even if you aren't lying. Why would I need to stay with the army? My dear archbishop and I should have no trouble escaping an army who has no clue where we are, am I right? Once I'm home, having Fury and Elemental armies marching about in Liberty lands, far away from home, would just make my life easier for me." He beamed with the satisfaction of a child who just got a difficult question right.

Chase looked at Liam and then at the archbishop. Both returned his stare with their own, both showing nothing but abject terror. This insane bastard would not balk at sacrificing thousands of lives, as long as he got what he wanted.

CHAPTER 50

To anybody who might find and read this or any of the other diaries. If I am no longer alive to ensure that it reaches safe hands, please help them along the way. I don't care if you're Lightborn, Furyborn, or a damn gaborn. If you care the least bit about the truth, please make sure the books make it to a real historian. If I am dead, I still want the true story about Liberty to come out. *Don't be like that. The real Cil isn't that dramatic.*

The army advanced. To the sound of trumpets and marching feet, the Lightborn began their advance to extinguish the nascent spark of independence for Liberty.

The few flying summons among the Lightborn had torn across the sky over Salvation for at least an hour, taking in the lay of the land as well as any visible troops on the streets, before they finally committed to a plan.

Now, the Lightborn battalions stretched across the land-scape, five of them marching side by side in an unstoppable tide. They each aimed for a different street, with some distance between each of them. Their advance had a clear agenda. They were going to enter the streets far enough apart that any defenders would have no choice but to face each battalion separately. On top of that, they would be able to switch side streets on their march inward, leaving defenders scrambling to catch up and adjust their defenses.

Chase stood at the center of the street. From his vantage point, standing alone out front, it was easy to see the gleaming armors of one of the battalions, as it bore down on his position at the central street. So far, so good. According to Sera, this was among the optimal approaches they could hope for. Now, to make them pay.

As the soldiers slowly advanced toward them in tight ranks, Chase struggled to keep down the roiling nerves. He told himself it was natural, that anybody in his position should be dead scared at what was happening, that he would be able to do his job without any issues.

"Are you peeing?" a voice whispered right near his ear.

Chase jumped, shouting, his arm shooting out to grasp at...nothing. A dark shade receded slightly.

Dozens of surprised faces looked out at him from within the windows of nearby houses. He waved them off, cursing. "Kith, you bloody asshole! If I hadn't already wet myself, I sure as spit did there! What the Pits are you up to?"

"Oh, just being a friend. Checking up on you guys. Liam's ready and waiting, in position."

"You can stop being helpful now. I'm all out of liquids. Also, talking to a shade is really weird."

The shadow somehow managed to look affronted. "That's a really hurtful thing to say to Raudt. Oh, and we're all in position. All's ready to go. Give 'em a good run for their money. Also...don't die, moron."

The shade flew straight through the nearest wall, aiming for the next street over. Chase chuckled at it. That was so Kith. Even though he and Sera were in charge of giving orders to the entire army, even with the pressure of handling four damn shades at the same time, somehow he found the time and surplus to fly by and give Chase lip. Even with the adrenaline of the shock still running through him, it made him feel better about everything. Some things never changed.

The foremost ranks of the Lightborn were entering the city proper now. The front lines carried heavy shields and were advancing mercilessly. The shields looked like they could be interlocked at a moment's notice, granting them extraordinary defense on top of the heavy armor glinting behind the shields. Behind them, a row of long spears waved into the air, likely to be raised over the shield bearers to stab between the ranks and into any enemies from behind.

Chase sidestepped smoothly, avoiding a stray arrow that might actually have hit him. He'd have to hand it to whichever archer took that shot. At this distance, they had to be talented to hit that well. He drew his short sword and gave it a whirl, feeling the solid, comforting heft of it. "One last time, yeah?" he said to himself. Then he set himself in the streets and prepared to run.

They didn't even bother to stop and send a volley after him. Whoever led the battalion likely knew that it would be a waste for just a single enemy. Instead, their archers were allowed to take potshots as they advanced.

Chase danced between the arrows. Once, he had to deflect an arrow with the blade, when it came buzzing at twice the speed of a regular arrow. Yet, at an Agility of fifty-three, he should be ashamed if he let any regular archers hit him, cards or not!

Finally, the Lightborn came close enough that the arrows ceased to fall. The foremost line hefted swords, as short as Chase's to be effective in the brutal close ranks of a shield wall. Eyes closed on him, and cards flashed, brief bursts of light that faded as they prepared to tear him down and run past to conquer a city.

In response, the city exploded.

Like a giant drum, four loud booming noises erupted, two west and two east of Chase, followed by a cacophony of screams, shouts, and falling stone.

In front of Chase, the ranks closed, more cards flashing; a bright shield shimmered into effect around the entire battalion, as they prepared for anything to hit them.

Nothing else happened on their street.

Chase finally engaged his own card. His entire body glimmered as a wave of light rushed over him. The light slowly transformed, coalesced into a full-arm sleeve that built into a long-sleeved glove of stars and living light. He took a deep breath as he raised the middle finger on the newly formed glove high in the direction of the incoming enemies. He yelled, at the top of his lungs, "Want some of that? *Come catch me, you needle-pricked assholes!*" Then he turned and ran.

The Lightborn battalion followed on his heels down the streets of Salvation. It should have felt stressful as anything. Yet, Chase was relieved that the wait was finally over. If anything, he actually felt the familiar excitement of being hunted bubbling right beneath the surface. Sure, this wasn't an irate shopkeeper, but a thousand armed professionals. Nevertheless, his heart reacted in the same way, telling him that, as long as he kept his focus and kept running, nobody was going to catch him, ever.

The Lightborn were starting to get annoyed by his presence. There was no discussing that. He dodged a couple of additional arrows propelled by cards—one that veered to catch him, and another infused with a pulsating inner light. Another card hit him, a debuff, robbing him of a few points of Agility, and a salvo of bright light shot in his direction, a near-dozen glowing missiles trying to ventilate him.

Nobody got truly close. And now, he was approaching the next point of the plan. At the next intersection, he kept running straight and passed the containers left at either side of the street. He pushed down the brief flash of tension, and ran past without any overt reaction. Once he was past, and felt that he was at a safe distance, he slowed down, ensuring that he wouldn't be too far away, when their surprise struck.

Chase nearly lost his head when the explosion went off.

Even with his Agility and the Mental Power high enough to see and process things a lot faster than regular uncarded people, he could not keep up. One moment, he was jogging along merrily, twisting and dodging occasionally to evade the few arrows trying to strike him. The next, the street behind him erupted into massive explosions, sending paving stones flying every which way, making the two-story houses of former hearts on both sides of the street collapse into the thoroughfare.

One wayward paving stone whizzed right past his head at a speed where Chase felt like he could *feel* the superheated rock passing by. He hit the ground, covering his head for any other wayward missiles. Then, with the houses still collapsing, dust covering everything, he burst into motion.

With cards flashing all over, he charged right back in the direction he had been coming from. He activated cards, feet pounding, taking him into the thick of it as fast as he could. Circle of Darkness hid his presence in a lovely cover of shadows, as dense as he could build them. Steps of Brilliance took him—still hidden—into the air, above the loose ranks of the reeling enemies.

He ran on top of the platforms, right above their heads, sword slashing down at helmets and exposed heads, abusing the confusion and panic while they still hadn't realized what was happening. Every step took him closer into their midst, every leap rife with the risk that somebody was going to dispel his card or understand what was happening. He pushed it as far, as fast as he believed he could. Then, with a brief prayer at whoever might listen, he activated Temper Tantrum.

Chase had no idea exactly what the activation of the card would bring him. The card description was delightfully vague. "Enhances the existing emotions..." What would that even mean in practice? Truthfully, he was more interested in the second part of the effects, where it said that he'd be able to override their current emotions. So, constantly thinking that they should rage at anybody in the nearest vicinity, he hoped for the best.

Never...*never* in his life could he have imagined as explosive an effect as the one he got. In a split second, the cohesion remaining in the shell-shocked unit burst, replaced by a dozen different reactions. Some soldiers flung themselves to the ground, wailing. Others ran away, lost to panic. Still others shouted or yelled at their fellow soldiers. Some either managed to ignore the effects, or what was enhanced was them being stalwart and resolute, because they kept their temper and stayed in place, ready to react despite the darkness. Yet, their level-headedness meant nothing, as a full third of those affected at the center of the battalion lashed out at anything in their vicinity.

Chase watched through the darkness as a grizzled archer, blinded by the darkness, reached out in front of him. With fumbling hands, he dropped his bow and reached out to the soldier ahead of him. Then, with a bloodthirsty cry, he grabbed onto the soldier's neck and stabbed the man with his arrow in a mindless frenzy.

He continued running ahead on top of his platforms, even as the bright ranks fell apart below him, until he hit the collapsed wreckage blocking the entirety of the street. Climbing farther up to reach the apex of the wreckage, he shot a look back at the ranks emerging from the Circle of Darkness, able to see once the darkness passed.

It was utter chaos. Lightborn fought Lightborn, while others fled, cried, yelled, or had gone utterly catatonic. And behind them, shapes came into view along the street. The second part of their plan was swiftly unfolding.

Hundreds of shapes materialized on the flat rooftops. Already, arrows darkened the skies, and flashes seemed to appear everywhere, as they unleashed everything they had down into the chaotic brawl that had, moments earlier, been an orderly Lightborn battalion.

Chase kept running. Even if he wanted to help finish them, he had to keep moving. The rest of the army was sure to be inbound soon, and they needed to get to it. He'd have to trust their ability to down them quickly and efficiently.

"Slowpoke!"

The voice nearly made him miss his next platform. Chase growled, started to teeter sideways, and managed to create a new platform to adjust his descent. Seconds later, he hit the ground and ran for the southern exit of the city.

"Don't be like that." The shade floated backward in front of him, effortlessly, as though it cost him nothing.

"You're an asshole, Kith. How are we doing?" Chase asked through gritted teeth.

"First five battalions are handled. For one of them, the Lightborn managed to escape relatively unscathed. The explosions went off wrong and didn't block the street, so they were able to retreat with limited losses. Three ambushes went off perfectly. Beautiful explosions taking out a third of them or worse from the start, followed by shadow droplets keeping them in the dark while they were slaughtered. Oh. The last explosion was good, but we had to send in Liam with a veteran squad, since they were annoyingly quick to adapt to the ranged attacks."

"He crushed them?"

"He crushed them." Kith's satisfaction was audible. "Sera says good job on making them chase you. She's betting on them trying to follow the central street for their next attack. I agree with her. You're damn good at being annoying."

Chase released a sigh of relief, even as he flipped off the shadow. That was a good start. It had taken them ages to come up with the concept, but eventually, they'd agreed on how it would have to be. All ranged fighters, casters, and summoners would be arranged into smaller teams with mobile ladders and hide in houses until Kith could tell them to swarm out, climb to the roofs, and attack. Meanwhile, all fighters, rogues, and healers, along with the few high-Tier veterans, would be combined into larger forces to move about the city to handle any problems. With Sera managing their forces through a lot of aides, good maps, and Kith's shades, they were able to respond and shift their forces swiftly. With the shaper oil, they were able to rearrange the shape of the city itself and trap incoming forces at a moment's notice.

They'd managed to finish somewhere between four and five of the twenty battalions in one fell swoop. Now, things were bound to become harder—especially if that damn Thomas was anywhere near as clever as he seemed to think.

The shade was still roaming next to him. Chase decided that was a good sign, or Kith would have moved it elsewhere. "What are they doing?"

"Floundering, looks like. Remember? We hid a bunch of archers and summoners with flying summons near the city edge. They've been taking out their eyes ever since the attack. They might've caught what happened this time around, but from here on out? They're blind! The next battalions have stopped, waiting for orders most likely. Waaait. Be right back."

Chase kept running, with the shade floating peacefully alongside. If he didn't know better, he'd swear the damn thing was smiling at him.

On either side, the ranged wielders Kith just mentioned were climbing off the rooftops, starting to move farther back. They whooped and hollered with joy as they ran.

Moments later, he left the buildings on either side behind. In front of him, he saw the Lightborn forces milling about. They seemed to be in disarray, but if Chase had to guess, this was the whole military thing where there was supposed to be a method to the madness.

He had to fight himself not to do something stupid—like hiding himself in darkness and rushing into their midst for another unleashed Temper Tantrum. If it worked, sure, it'd likely mess up their operations badly, but the odds that some healer had a card with a counter waiting for him were just too ugly. Getting caught by Thomas would *not* end pretty. He just itched to *do* something, to *act*!

Yet, he pulled himself under control. Sera had seen it coming right from the start. If this, their first move, worked, everything would hinge upon how the Lightborn reacted.

If they decided to take a slower approach, it would be a boon to their own forces. Anybody who'd managed to earn a higher Tier in that first clash would be able to rush back to the

Wellspring and gain new and better cards. Their forces would only improve with time.

Nobody thought that was likely to happen, though. Thomas knew as well as anybody that the clock was against him here. Everything, from the size of the population to the eventual arrival of Furyborn and Elementals, spoke to him needing to move fast.

After a lot of discussions, they eventually settled on two major directions they were likely to take. Either they'd decide to split up their forces even further, make it harder for the defenders of Salvation to react to their routes and overwhelm them with numerous different angles of attack at the same time. Or, and this was Sera's favorite approach, gather their forces and rush into the city as a cohesive whole, try to simply power through anything the defenders might push at them.

In the end, they went with neither of those choices.

"What *is* that?" Chase asked himself.

"They're...repeating the last attack?" Kith's voice arrived from the shadow, filled with incredulity.

"Sure looks like it." Chase watched a battalion slowly starting to move in his direction. "But what was up with all the rearranging of troops? And why the Pits are they aiming for the same damn streets as last time?"

"I..." Kith's voice faded away and reappeared about half a minute later. "Sera says she thinks they'll be stress testing our traps. Trying to break through without putting everything at risk. Are they that stupid? They aren't that stupid, are they?"

"We can only hope. I...had probably better start to move." Chase looked at the incoming soldiers and jumped up and down, waving at them and grinning. It was time to prepare a warm, warm welcome!

All streets leading into the city had been booby-trapped. Making sure that they were able to hit *any* section right where the Lightborn tried to enter accounted for about half of their entire stock of the shaper oil. Right this moment, a trio of very stressed summoners would be working their asses off, all because they had the fortune of earning summoned creatures that were, through one method or the other, able to move the shaper oil without any risk of blowing up. They were the sole people in charge of moving the remaining containers about as the battle proceeded, ensuring that any street the Lightborn chose could be rigged against them.

So many moving pieces. So many things that could go wrong. And one Lightborn noble who looked like he might come up with something truly unforeseeable. Chase just hoped that they'd be able to prepare in time.

He reached the intersection with the former trap. Ahead, the street was entirely ruined, with the houses on either side having caved in to create a dangerously unstable pile of broken stone and wood. The streets on either side were calm and wide open, though. From here, the Lightborn could choose to go both left and right, moving a street over to continue for the center uninterrupted. Both sides had already been rigged farther back, though.

Pulling down his pants, he bent over in front of the army, granting the Lightborn a blindingly white target. One rushed arrow made him leap awkwardly to avoid well-earned retribution. Then he pulled the pants back up, shouted derision at their ability to aim, their manhood and their ancestors, and ran for the rightmost street. Arrows followed his retreating form, and he had to summon his light hand in order to close the buckle while running.

"You were supposed to get 'em to run *after* you, not drive 'em off! Hey. Did you get another card on your ass? Because I feel blinded!" Kith was apparently feeling damn good about the situation, because he stayed with Chase all the way.

"And *I* thought you were supposed to help. This isn't—oh, crap!" Chase turned, as he realized that the Lightborn weren't following him anymore. Except, they weren't moving left either. Instead, they carefully and meticulously climbed across the broken wreckage of the houses, even as archers enfolded their ranks on either side, preparing to fire on Chase or...well, anybody coming too close.

Kith didn't answer. He was clearly already busy reporting what was happening.

Chase considered the situation. This wasn't great. As the Lightborn forces advanced, the poor Liberty summoners would be running themselves ragged placing shaper oil, ready to greet any deviation of the five battalions. Only, now they'd have to adjust to them actually following their original directions. That...wasn't insurmountable. But it *would* require some last-minute adjustments that they just didn't have time for right now.

"We need to delay them." He spoke the words, even as he came to the realization. "*I* need to delay them. Damn." His feet were already in motion, carrying him where he needed to be. Not toward the waiting archers, though. No, he was climbing platforms, carrying him to the top of the nearest roof.

Yells followed his approach, but they were unable to stop him. Once he was up there, it was an easy task to move to the far side of the flat rooftop, leaving him out of view of the Lightborn ground troops. Then he took a deep breath and started to run across the rooftops.

For a brief moment, this was just like back in Isarn. They'd used those rooftops as another shortcut to evade pursuit, to hide, and sometimes, even just to cross from one street to the other at speed. If anything, the roofs of Salvation were even easier to navigate. The alleys between some houses were wider than the shadowy, ambush-worthy backstreets back in Isarn, but the distance was no issue to somebody with fifty-three Agility. He didn't even have to activate Steps of Brilliance to cross.

He reached the end of the final rooftop. Beyond lay the blown-up street, filled with Lightborn troops slowly working their way in the direction of and up the mountain of bricks, dirt, and wreckage. Before he even thought about his plan, Chase was airborne. Cries arose below him as a series of platforms let him run across the open air to reach the top of the piled-up ruins.

A giant of a Lightborn was leading their ranks in climbing the wreckage. The no-necked, thick, frontline fighter moved like a golem, like somebody incapable of losing his balance or even stopping. He'd almost reached the apex of the climb and was turning to see the progression of his fellows.

Chase's sword took him at the nape of the neck and bit deep. The giant tumbled to the ground with a massive roar, even as Chase took his position at the top of the pile. *"You want to get up here? You'd better fight me for it, then."* Not the most epic of taunts, he had to admit—but it worked. The closest Lightborn sped up in their attempt to reach him, even as those farther down activated cards and reached for bows in order to take him down.

Chase activated One with the Soil, granting him perfect balance, breathed a silent prayer, and activated Sudden Breeze.

There was a reason that people of Tiers five and above were generally the wielders people talked about, the ones who became Names, people of import. Regardless who you talked to, people agreed on the one thing: Tier five was where you started to reach epic levels of power.

In one regard, it had to do with being granted cards with scopes or possibilities that simply weren't available at lower ranks. Like Kith's Light of Day, Day of Darkness, which was able to influence an entire damn battlefield. Or his chariot, which enabled an entirely changed modus of travel, freed from the confines of walking or having to deal with living creatures.

Sometimes, however, it was simply a matter of sheer power. Nothing about Sudden Breeze sounded inhumanly powerful. Yet, the gale force-like wind that gushed into existence at his back, tearing down toward the Lightborn, was incomparable to anything else he had at his disposal. The sole exception might be A Friendly Wave, at its utter maximum capacity.

In a split second, enemy archers became entirely useless. Even activating their cards, any arrows became more of a hazard to themselves than him. Half the front line imploded, fighters tumbling down the pile of wreckage, flung around like dry sticks in a storm. Casters and others farther down slid around and hid behind other soldiers, trying to find shelter.

For a full ten, fifteen seconds, nobody even considered striking back at Chase. Meanwhile, he abused One with the Soil, racing around to strike at any nearby frontline fighter managing to stay up. At times, it felt like his upper body wanted to lift off from the ground, but his feet felt glued to the ground, the sensation as natural as if he were running through a soft summer breeze.

When the card abated, Chase grinned down at the enemy soldiers, winked, and switched to Circle of Darkness. "Come get me, losers!" Then he faded into the shadows.

The next five minutes weren't fun. The few healers among the enemy managed to ladle a good number of debuffs onto him, to the point where his feet and arms started to feel heavy. They also kept trying to dispel all cards of his, especially Circle of Darkness. Yet, Chase's Mental Power and the card being Tier four meant that they failed to do anything beyond lightening the darkness slightly. The casters and archers kept flinging everything they had at the darkness, trying to fill the air with enough missiles that he'd eventually be hit through sheer volume.

Compared to the Lightborn frontline fighters, though, Chase was having a blast. The poor bastards kept climbing the broken wreckage with a downpour of arrows and cards impacting right over their heads. The last part of the climb was wrapped in shadows, too, forcing them to fumble their way in near-blindness. And when they reached the top, without fail, Chase re-activated Sudden Breeze to force them all back again.

He would not be able to keep it up. There were simply too many of them. At some point, one of them would be lucky and land a direct hit, their cards would dispel Circle of Darkness, or they'd overwhelm him with numbers. His left leg was already slowly dripping blood into his boot from a light burst tearing a funnel across the outside of his calf, and a huge bruise was spreading on his cheek where he'd hit a wall face-first in an evasive maneuver. Yet, he *was* keeping them back, and the frontline fighters were starting to show an outright aversion to climbing the wreckage.

Chase considered taking a risk. He'd seen how effective Temper Tantrum could be. He felt that, if he got into their midst, he'd be able to take out the pesky healers and casters who truly threatened his life. Only, to do that, he'd have to get there unscathed first, and, well, they were very much aware of his movements.

"Show-off!"

Chase yelped at the voice appearing at his side. Then he flung himself downhill, hiding behind the half-ruined remains of a kitchen. "You *ass!*"

Kith's laughter rang over even the furious sounds of the pursuit. "Just wanted to tell you, you can move back now, tough guy. We've got the street rigged. You've got them pissing their breeches badly, though. I can leave you alone to handle them yourself, no problem."

Chase expelled a stressed laugh. "I...think I could do with a break." His feet felt like they were floating as he ran down the far side of the wreckage on his platforms. He might be forced to pull back, but he'd put himself up against a thousand Lightborn and held. Fire burst his eyes, he'd *held*. He'd earned a breather. "How are the others doing?" he asked as he ran.

"Poorly." Kith's voice was strained. "You're the only one who managed to keep them back entirely. Also, not only did they trick us with this, once they were on the other side, the bastards actually brought their own ladders and climbed the houses."

"Oh." Chase tried to visualize that. It wasn't a pretty sight. The Liberators who'd climbed the houses last time to ambush the Lightborn would no longer be met with a shell-shocked battalion on the ground below them, but instead, with battle-ready archers on the same level as themselves. "What are we doing? What do *I* need to do?"

"You've done your part. We're taking care of things—we're throwing numbers at them now. We're hitting their battalions one at a time with everything we've got, and slowing down the others with collapses. Spike's helping. It's not pretty, but it works. As to them climbing to the roofs...well—"

A loud explosion rocked the city.

"*Nice* timing on that one. Well, the shaper oil does the same to them, whether they're on the ground or on the rooftop."

Chase spotted the signal indicating a trap had been laid. A few houses beyond that, a door opened, and a hand waved him into a crowded room that was filled with waiting archers, casters, and, blessedly, a healer. Head reeling, he found himself healed and downing a large mug of water, with people patting his back and nodding at him in respect.

The Lightborn, when they arrived a few minutes later, had regrouped and reestablished their formations. On top of that, they'd rearranged their ranged attackers to run along the rooftops on either side of the street, prepared against any surprises from above or the streets on the other side. They had long ladders, clearly equipped for siege battle, that allowed them to cross alleys and climb to the roofs, albeit clumsily. This time, they were ready.

He'd never really gotten to understand the exact method that went into setting off the shaper oil. Yet, he was watching them from within a Circle of Darkness on the rooftop of the next street over. Crouched down, wrapped within a gradated layer of thin shadows, with only his eyes emerging the slight overhang at the eaves of the roof, he saw everything.

The explosion went off perfectly. Right at the edge of the much-abused Lightborn battalion, the cloud of debris and dirt enveloped the hind third of their numbers immediately.

Chase was off instantly, stepping off the roof onto a floating platform, sprinting as fast as he could. He emerged less than ten seconds later to impact on a roof, where the ranged Lightborn were adjusting to their rear guard having fallen into the ruined mess behind them. He had to hand it to them, though. The Lightborn soldiers were consummate professionals. Where amateurs would be screaming for help, be deep in shock, or simply be stunned by the surprise, they were already adjusting, eyes searching, weapons veering in order to greet the ambush they expected was coming.

Their instincts were correct. The direction wasn't.

When Chase hit the roof, only a few of them were even glancing in his direction. He took one step, grinned, and activated Sudden Breeze, aimed directly at their exposed backs.

This time, with Circle of Darkness still active instead of One with the Soil, he was affected along with their number. He felt himself being forcibly pulled toward the edge and embraced it. He rushed ahead with the wind, and with a mighty whoop, he leapt into the open air, platforms emerging under his feet, even as the storm propelled him forward at top speed.

Chase ran straight across the street, even as bodies fell down into the street on either side of him.

Now came the most dangerous part of this gambit.

Right this moment, even enveloped in darkness, Chase was exposed, running out in the street, with nothing to hide behind. He veered, running sideways to evade the Lightborn on the opposite rooftop. He activated Fight Another Day, doubling his speed and rushing across the open air; the shadows around him hid his form, even as he roamed about.

Every single archer and caster on the opposite rooftop decided that he had to die. Card effects and arrows filled the air, trying to take him down.

Sudden Breeze saved his life. Even from across the wide street, the remnants of the card effect were massive enough that almost every arrow was thrown askew. Topped with his speed and the shadows hiding him, Chase managed to avoid getting aerated by a hair.

He didn't escape damage outright. A wave of light tore through his cloud, leaving him feeling burned alive. Twin miniature suns with some sort of searching essence managed to follow him, even at his speed, and erupted a few feet from him, nearly tossing him off his feet. Always—*always*—arrows and throwing weapons were everywhere in the air around him, making the skies feel nearly solid.

Bruised, burned, and reeling, Chase knew that he wouldn't be able to survive another minute of this. Fortunately, he only needed a third of that.

They emerged from within the homes and climbed up their own stairs. Silent and focused, they abused the ringing in the ears from the explosions and the loud noise of the enemies' cries to hide their own steps. As one, they climbed the back of the building where every single eye was currently trained on Chase and arrived in a swarm, hitting the backs of the exposed ranged fighters as a massive wave. Some had light weapons, others simply used lowered shoulders or fists. Whatever the method, the Liberators hit the Lightborn with the force of a Tier-six card.

Sometimes, Chase had learned, battlefields saw sudden breaks or silences. Weird standoffs, where an unexpected action or experience suddenly managed to throw everything off-kilter, earning a brief few seconds for everybody to readjust mentally, until fighting would inevitably resume.

This one lasted only for about five seconds, as the Lightborn down on the streets suddenly saw their comrades raining down from *both* sides of the street.

Following this, however, the ranged Liberators rushed up to the edges of the rooftops on both sides of the street. Then, they hefted their ranged weapons, activated their cards, and unleashed a rain of death on the scattered Lightborn. The silence broke right there. The Lightborn broke soon thereafter.

CHAPTER 51

I want you to know, Kith. I cut a deal with one of the Keeper wards. I arranged for one of them to move a Guardian here, to keep an eye on the diaries for a few days. To him, it's a break. For me, it's the final, undeniable proof that you're going through my stuff, like I specifically asked you not to. If you're reading this, I just want you to know. You're dead. Heart card or not. I will hunt you down and wear your face.
Sincerely, Cilia.

"**W**e're backing off. Back toward the center." Kith's voice was frazzled, sounding like he was unfocused.

"Why? I thought we were doing good?" He had to repeat himself twice before Kith was back.

"Huh? Oh. Yes. I guess. Just get back here. Give me a moment."

Chase stood up from where he'd been resting, knees cracking. "All right!" he shouted. "Everybody, back toward the center! Those who have Tiered up, remember to hit the Wellspring. This might be your last chance to grow stronger before everything comes to a head."

He crossed the street and told the people on the other side. Then he took a last look at the street. When he'd entered Salvation for the first time, he'd been amazed by how pretty everything was. The streets so orderly, everything with a fresh coat of paint, nobody dirty, hungry, or hurt. Now, there were corpses and wreckage everywhere, and one house teetered as if it were about to follow the example of its neighbors and keel right over.

Leaving people to find their own way inward, he tried to fend off the sudden influx of doubt and dark thoughts. This was going to be over soon. One way or the other. There'd be plenty of time for recriminations later, if he were still alive.

On all sides, he saw waves of motion. Locals, mostly, who were moving inward, rushing or marching. Once, he spotted a group of indebted who looked as though they'd walked through a hail of living steel, almost every one of them carrying somebody wounded along with them.

The farther he came, the more Chase realized that they weren't even the people who looked hit the worst. Many groups returning were absolutely mauled, with healers activating cards and trying to help the worst of them, even as they moved.

Gritting his teeth, Chase decided to take Kith's continued absence as a bad sign, threw caution aside, and engaged Fight Another Day as he ran. Speed would be of the essence now.

People milled everywhere in Freedom Plaza. There was an overt sense of panic in the air, people running everywhere with wild looks in their eyes. At the far end of the plaza, three northbound streets were blocked off by crowds of soldiers surrounding what looked like healer, crafter, and equipment stations respectively.

Crowds were always different. This was something Chase had thought a lot on in his life. Mostly as something running in the back of his mind. A certain mood. A feeling, of a crowd ready to turn ugly, an overhanging sense of danger, or maybe a careless, buoyant mood that would ease his theft.

Today was new. There was fear there, of course—plenty of it. Stress, and hope. The occasional barked laughter that cut off just a little too fast. The unexpected part, though, was what lay at the core. Because this crowd had a heart. He saw it in the brief glances, the way everybody circulated around a specific point of the plaza. This crowd had a heart. A beating heart, ensuring that everything circulated and kept working. Currently, everything here revolved around one specific spot.

Chase dropped from his last platform, hitting the ground next to Kith and Sera and sliding to a stop.

Sera stood, her back ramrod straight, next to Kith, who sat cross-legged, his eyes closed.

"What's happening?" he asked.

Sera held up a finger. "We will want redundancies on Eleventh and Thirteenth Streets. Both shaper oil and archers. All hidden, all ready to move in or fall back at any point. Are the last reserves moving yet?"

"Limping, more like," Kith muttered. "But yes." He grimaced. "Doubt they'll make it back before the Lightborn. Hey, slowpoke." He didn't even open his eyes, just subsided back into silence, eyelids twitching, making weird grimaces, fingers moving in elaborate gestures as he received, sent, and handled input from his shadows.

Sera exhaled softly and put her hand on Chase's arm. "I am glad you are here. Well done, so far."

"What's going on?"

"It is all coming to a head. The Lightborn are committing now. They have been readjusting their forces. Now, they are coming." Sera looked him deep in the eye.

"All of them?"

She nodded. "All of them, in one massive formation. We are busy readjusting the city to be ready, with shaper oil in place for every eventuality."

"How are we doing?" Even with the wounded he'd passed, they had not suffered any outright defeats so far, and, at a guess, the mood in the plaza was edging toward positive.

"We are…managing. We have more fighters out of commission than I would have liked. Their adjustments this last time took us by surprise, and their ranged attackers did a number on ours. Yet, the odds have adjusted slightly in our favor. As long as they have no further tricks to throw at us, we will be able to grind them down and beat them with shaper oil—and sheer numbers—when, and if, they make it to the plaza."

Chase groaned. "Which they absolutely will. That bloody noble—no offense—might be insane, but he's clever. What's our play here?"

She softly touched Kith's shoulder. "How far along are they?"

"Entering the city in a minute. That large a force moves *slow*."

"Okay. Chase. We are flooding attackers, ready to ambush them in every point along their route. We will be able to hit them from everywhere—alleyways, rooftops, from the rear even. On top of that, we will bog them down and cut them apart with the shaper oil at every chance. We need you out there, to aid where needed, and to ruin their plans. If they disrupt us entirely, we will pull back and rethink our approach. Also, we are keeping the new Guardians back. They will be the backup, for when Thomas unleashes his surprises."

Chase rolled his shoulders and cracked his neck. "You've got it. I'm off."

Her hand shot out and grasped his shoulder. "Chase." Her eyes met his. They said everything that needed to be said. Her mouth quirked up. "Stay alive. That is an order."

As Chase raced back into the city, he felt a weird sensation of peace. Everything was up in the air right now. Yet, he knew that he'd already given it his all, and there was no chance that he was going to let his friends, his family down.

It felt almost leisurely, being able to breeze through the city at full speed, not giving a second thought to flaunting his powers. Everywhere around him, armed people were marching, some in a semblance of order, while a lot of them looked like they'd only just been granted a weapon this morning for the first time. Still, there was a fire in their eyes. The citizens of Salvation were not going to break easily.

Chase took the notion of what would happen if they *did* break, and tamped it down hard. That would not—could not—happen.

He found his place on top of an untouched rooftop about a mile out from the southern edge of town. He wasn't the only one. He had to duck between a handful of taller persons in order to find a place from which to observe. Locals everywhere were climbing the roofs to see what they would be up against. When he finally saw the remnants of the Lightborn force, the sight took his breath away.

Light blind him. There were so many of them. This was not at all like the last time. He'd thought a thousand soldiers pushed into the narrow confines of the city streets looked overwhelming. He'd been wrong. Ten thousand soldiers moved as one cohesive force, a never-ending wave of soldiers, bristling with weaponry. They filled the entirety of the street as they moved, and the tail end of their force was nearly half a mile behind the front rank. Not only that—now that they were truly moving into the city proper, he started to see signs of cards and effects. Everywhere! They were truly holding nothing back now. Glowing bubbles and domes conjoined; gleaming, bright effects glowed and intermingled; eyes, armor, and weaponry glowed bright with the brilliant shine of magic.

Chase chuckled softly. "They do look pretty, don't they?" he said to the Liberators on the roof with him.

The tall man right behind him gulped. He looked like a blacksmith. Arms nearly as wide as Chase, with a beard that Raudt or Svart could've hidden behind. Yet, his unease was obvious, as he asked, his voice higher pitched than Chase expected, "How do we face something like that?"

He gave the question its due consideration. It *was* indeed hard to see where you'd even start. Then he smiled and shrugged. "Simple. We don't." He pointed at different spots along the length of their body. "They might look impressive right now. But picture them separated into eight, or ten different units, cut off, fallen houses intersecting their length. Then picture them being attacked from either side at the same time, and the roofs."

The blacksmith nodded slowly.

Chase continued, warming to the image. "They strike back hard? We run. Back into the city. We've got eyes everywhere. They don't. If they follow, we'll ambush them. If they don't, we'll loop around, find another place to hit them. This isn't a stand-up fight. This is us chopping them into smaller chunks, so we can deal with them, bit by bit."

They watched in companionable silence as the force advanced. Eventually, one of the wielders asked, "You're...him, right?"

Chase shot the young man a lopsided smile. "That's a pretty vague question. But I guess, in this situation, the odds are pretty damn good that you're right."

"Aren't you supposed to be, like, out there?" He pointed vaguely at the army.

"Yup. Only, we aren't hitting them just yet. If you watch, you'll see that there are no people roaming around that far out. We'll wait until they're at least a few hundred feet past the original ambush point, then—"

The last of his words were swallowed by an explosion.

His eyes veered for the front of the advancing army. *Had he been wrong about the spot? Should he—?*

In an area at least a hundred and fifty feet ahead of the army, wreckage slowly settled as a blinding light faded into a more tolerable spectrum. Yet, this had not touched the Lightborn army at all. In fact, it only affected the area in a wide cone *ahead* of the soldiers. Not only that, the army wasn't stopping. They still marched on, straight toward what was left of the ruined street.

Another bright light appeared. This one was less blinding, shimmering into view softly, growing, modulating itself until it settled down upon the ruined street.

The Lightborn army continued to march, right onto the shining area. They walked, climbing the hill of ruins that had, just a few seconds ago, been a regular street in Salvation. At no point did anybody look like they were about to fall. Rather, they moved like the brilliant surface was a paved road, allowing them to walk ahead as if nothing stopped their forward movement.

Their passing took only a single minute, while Chase and everybody else watched on in astonishment. Then, even as they were reaching the end of the safe surface that carried them securely across the wreckage, the blinding light erupted again.

This time, the card was punctuated by twin explosions, as the effect hit and set off the shaper oil that had been prepared to surprise the oncoming army. Yet, if there was a difference, it was only in how the effect of that first, devastatingly damaging light effect was amplified. Less than half a minute later, the army started to march again, moving onto the next platform.

"Please tell me you're seeing this," Chase whispered. "Kith. What the Pits are we supposed to do about *that*?"

For a full minute, there was nothing. Only increasing panic on the rooftop, as people started to realize that no imminent reaction was inbound against that overwhelming Light attack.

Chase sighed audibly as a shadow zoomed across the sky toward him.

"Hoo boy." Kith's voice was audibly stressed. "We're in so much trouble. We've gotten our closest ambushers moving back so they aren't in danger of getting blown the Pits up. But...what do we do? *What do we do?*"

Chase tried to ignore the despair that wanted to grow inside him. "I'm not sure, man. This is Thomas, right? Have you seen it? Him?"

"It is. The beam comes straight from him. Also, it being Tier six is the one explanation for how damn *powerful* it is. That other card they're walking across might be that damn priest. I can't tell for sure, because its origin is harder to spot."

"Doesn't matter, really. They're bound to be safely at the center of a ton of defenders, right? Hidden where we'd have to throw everything at them to end them."

"Yes. And I shudder to think of what would happen if any of our forces got caught in that effect."

Chase grimaced. "Yeah. We're not doing that. How long have we got?"

"How long? No clue. We— Wait a moment." Kith grew silent, then returned a moment later. "Sera says that, at this rate of progress, unless Lord Beforant grows tired or there are some cooldowns we're not seeing, we have about an hour and a half before they hit the plaza."

Chase groaned and massaged his temples. He saw, in the distance, as a group of archers climbed to a rooftop a street over from where the Lightborn army was advancing.

With no intact rooftops nearby, there'd be no easy way for their archers to aim and hit. Yet, with these numbers, they were pretty much sure to hit something. Arrows started flying and hitting among the Lightborn. Most were repelled by armor, effects, or shields, but a few soldiers went down. This might be a way to slowly grind them down.

The beam reappeared. Instead of hitting the street ahead of them, it swept over the far rooftop. When the blinding light faded, the rooftop, along with any archer on top, was simply gone.

A collective wave seemed to sweep across Chase's own rooftop. A few of the people standing around him started to take soft steps back, as if readying themselves to flee.

"I have an idea," Chase said. "I actually have an idea. Kith!"

"We're listening. Well. I am. But I'm repeating everything to Sera."

"Follow me, Kith!" Chase leapt off the rooftop, sprinting back toward the plaza. He forced out the words while he ran. "Okay. What we need to do is dangerous. It's stupid. And it's going to put us in a ton of danger."

"What else is new?" Kith chuckled.

"First. We're unleashing the Guardians. All of 'em. Straight at the army."

"That's why you're going back? Okay, but why? Even if we've got a good bunch of them by now, that beam is going to tear them apart."

"No, it won't. The thing is, we're going to put ourselves up as the juiciest targets in the world. Meanwhile, we'll have Sera directing everybody else to attack and dismember their force. Here's the plan…" Chase's words poured out as he sprinted, laying out the plan as he saw it.

Kith's only response was a chuckle and a strangled, "You're right, man. That's going to be dangerous. Cil's gonna hate it. Let me tell Sera, then get your ass back here."

***

Half an hour later, their group was approaching the Lightborn army. Even though they were jogging at a fast pace, Cilia talked constantly, berating Chase for his insanity and making changes on the fly, suggesting alternative cards for all of them.

Liam, running right next to her, reached out and squeezed her shoulder. "Cil. We're here. Settle down and settle in. We know what we're doing." He positioned his shield in place, then gave it a good whack with his truncheon for good measure, before grinning widely at them all and placing himself firmly at the center of the street, facing away.

Kith gave Cil a side hug, then passed her by, unsheathing his hand axes to take his place, behind and to the left of Liam. "Yeah, Cil. We know what we're doing. And when we don't, we'll just make it up."

Chase shrugged and grinned before taking his own spot to Liam's right. "We really are clueless. I'm so sorry."

Sera gave Cilia a full hug. Then she took her own place, right behind Liam. "I am sorry, too. Sorry that this is what we have to deal with." Then she extracted her two bucklers and shot Cilia a grin that was *entirely* out of character for her. "Still. If I have to go, I would rather it be like this. Among family."

Cilia sighed and shook her head. She ambled up to her own spot and checked over her belts without even looking down. "I do love you all. Don't die. Idiots."

The Lightborn army was coming into view properly now. It was truly an impressive sight. They shone like the sun, gold and white, regardless of the clouds of dust and the mile of demolished cityscape they left behind them. They packed the street from side to side, advancing at an even pace, like an unstoppable machine left to run unchecked.

"They do look pretty," Liam said. "I'm almost sad we have to mess them up."

"I'm not," Kith said. "I've always wanted to punch an arch-bishop."

"It's that damn noble for me. This is going to be like the spring festival in Isarn, only with violence instead of plum schnapps." Chase cracked his neck.

"Focus," Cilia snapped. "Does everybody have their boosts activated? This won't work if we don't come out prepared."

A chorus of confirmations rang out. Kith simply nodded behind himself, where a pair of bright birds hovered in midair. The summoned creatures from Antithesis of Light really looked flimsy, but the loud hum emanating from them promised power, and lots of it.

"Okay. In that case, you know what to do. Everybody, get back farther. For the first beam, we're hiding behind Liam, just in case."

They did just that, gathering in closer, kneeling behind the large Lightborn. He gave them all a dazzling smile. "I've kept you safe for this long. There's no way I'm letting you down *now*."

As if on cue, a blindingly bright beam of light burst into being from ahead. There was little reaction time. One second, the light appeared. The next, it washed over Liam, top-down. For one second, two, the beam persisted, then it faded away into nothingness.

Liam blinked, then looked down over himself. He shot a goofy grin at them all. "Still alive." His gaze went remote for a second. "And Ravenous Shadows ate up enough magic to give me an extra three to Strength. Not bad. How are—"

He was interrupted by another beam, raising his shield at the last second. This beam didn't stay trained on him, though. Rather, it flashed back and forth, washing over the houses on either side of the street.

The beam faded away, and their sights reappeared amidst colored spots in their visions.

Cilia looked them all over. "Damage?"

"Just a bit," Chase said. Where the beam had washed over him, the exposed skin was red, like a really bad sunburn. A quick Warmth of the Circle hit him, healing any damage done. "Thanks, Sera." Then he pointed at the walls, grinned, and let out a whoop of triumph. "It's still standing. *We're* still standing! Another triumph for my harebrained schemes!"

Even Cilia had been forced to admit it was the best approach they could come up with at short notice. She and Sera, of course, had been the ones to teach them about the concept to begin with. A powerful card was well and good. A powerful card that built on any *other* card of yours was even better. But neither of those had anything on a well-planned combination of cards across several different classes and builds.

Sera's Blessing of the Night, at Epic rarity, was already wonderfully efficient at repressing Light cards and effects. Combined with Kith's Antithesis of Light summons, however, they had calculated that the effect on any nearby Light cards was diminished by about *ninety percent*. What had been a city-breaker turned into a danger, but not imminently lethal. Add to that Liam's ability to absorb the magic and turn it into Strength for himself, and it was barely an inconvenience.

Kith's eyes were closed. "The fastest of our Guardians should be arriving in...two minutes at most. Better get our asses moving."

"Tell all nearby ambushing teams to ready themselves. The moment they lock into conflict with the Guardians is when we'll want to hit them. They will be scrambling to catch up, and realizing that Blessing of the Light completely ruins *all* Tier one and two Light cards," Sera instructed Kith, who nodded and went distant again.

Chase let out a wild laugh. "You think they're scrambling *now?* Just wait until they realize we can keep this up and they'll need to catch us to do something about it. *That's right, you bastards! We can do this all day!*" he yelled at the army.

They ambled back slowly to the nearest intersection. Once more, the beam struck them, only to fade away when it did no obvious damage.

Happily waving to the army, Chase was the last to leave the street. Sera quickly unfurled her map, then pointed in the direction they needed to go.

Behind them, the world turned bright again, as the beam reappeared, almost hopefully, as if checking whether it might work when they weren't in direct view. The answer, as expected, was a huge, resounding no.

For about ten seconds, the Lightborn army wavered, as they reconsidered their approach. Then, they went straight to the inevitable conclusion, realizing that they needed to down the group that managed to turn their most powerful attack into an overly ambitious night-light.

Thousands of armored boots accelerating into a run made their decision public.

They ran the streets of Salvation, playing hide-and-seek with a force ten thousand strong. It was, they soon realized, surprisingly easy.

First off, they ran with Kith's shades constantly keeping an eye on their surroundings, when they weren't off to give orders left and right.

Second, they were able to climb the low roofs with relative ease. Even Cilia, with the lowest Agility and Strength, could easily leap high enough to reach a waiting hand and be towed up.

Third, the Lightborn, at least at first, didn't waste time to actually check over the houses. Really, who would leave their front door unlocked during an invasion?

Finally, very soon, the army found itself in a constant state of distraction.

The Dark Guardians, along with a minority of newly fledged Liberty Guardians, were the first to hit. Roars and cries rocked the streets of Salvation as every Guardian birthed since the creation of the Dark Wellspring was unleashed at the invaders.

Having already been alerted this would be the signal, dozens of smaller groups ambushed the army from all sides within the minute. From then on out, the world went insane.

Kith kept up a running commentary on the fights as they moved about.

They had ambushers everywhere, climbing the roofs to unleash death on the Lightborn invaders. Whenever they'd struck, they ran, crossing rooftops to escape reprisal.

Even when the Lightborn managed to close with enemies, the experience had to be harrowing. The unknown powers of the Liberty Guardians were bad enough. But, often as not, what they clashed with was, for them, mythical Guardians, creatures from the most horrifying of nightmares, now made flesh.

A large group of indebted managed to come up with a new approach. They'd stripped the uniforms off fallen Lightborn and used the disguises to great effect. They'd rush in, yelling and screaming about enemies, before charging right at the frazzled invaders.

The former rebels fought alongside citizens of Salvation. They were lower in Tiers and experience, compared to the veteran Lightborn, and they paid for that deficit dearly. Yet, they refused to surrender, taking their toll in blood.

"And *stay* down." Liam pushed the dead Lightborn soldier away, then ran to catch up with the others. On his way, he nearly fell over another body.

Kith hadn't seen this group in time, and they'd actually managed a volley of arrows before their group was able to overrun them completely. Sudden Breeze had ended the threat of the arrows instantly.

"Things are getting chaotic here," Kith growled through gritted teeth as he ran, Sera holding his shoulder to ensure he was able to handle his summons while he moved. "There are soldiers everywhere. Can't keep track of it all."

"What's it been? Thirty minutes? An hour? This is *insane!*" Chase announced.

"It has been fifteen minutes, at most," Sera corrected. "How are we doing, Kith? Tell the three groups on the southeast to circle east and then lope around and climb a rooftop on Eighth. That should allow them to take care of the Lightborn pursuing our eastern groups."

"I'll tell them. We are *strained*. Okay, no. That one's just me. We're doing okay. Beforant's at a safe range, with a street between us. But we can't allow ourselves to get too far away from the main body of the army. When we're in range, their buffs are reduced as well and the main army is *much* less effective."

"I agree, Kith," Sera said. "But if we are forced to choose, we stick near Beforant. We may take additional losses, but I can still help them organize. If we let him slip through our hands, we are *bound* to lose."

Kith groaned. "Okay! But we can't keep running. We need to hit back, or we'll be forced into a corner."

"We're fighting more? Good!" Liam grinned. He was enjoying the action, and nothing so far had been able to force him off-kilter.

They moved out, into an intersection, allowing them to take a glance at the back of the Lightborn army from a few hundred feet's distance. The ranks were entirely divorced of their earlier coherence, and soldiers were yelling left and right, climbing up and down houses, smaller squads leaving and rejoining the larger army. A few of the soldiers pointed in their direction.

Chase grunted. "Hey. You think we have time to send these people A Friendly Wave?" He wiggled his eyebrows. "With these nice, straight lines, as long as I have a full minute to let the raindrops build up, I think we could wreak some *nice* havoc."

Liam flexed. "I think I can hold them for two. At least."

"I have plenty of droplets—something's wrong here." Cilia interrupted herself, her tone one of confusion and suspicion.

"The fun stops here."

With those words, the world shimmered, and the empty street suddenly changed. Less than thirty feet away, Thomas slowly edged into visibility, as if somebody pulled layer after layer of half-illusionary material away from over the man.

Behind him, a full platoon of heavily armored Lightborn appeared as well, including a deadly pale archbishop, wheezing with effort.

"You led me on a merry chase. I don't mind admitting that. But you forget a very important detail. Light is blinding, scouring, and burning. Yet, it is also dazzling. The good archbishop here is very talented at hiding in the shadows. Yet another reason he has survived this long, most likely."

"All right. You got us." Cilia stepped forward toward him.

Chase's head snapped toward her. *What the Pits was she up to?* She was cradling something in her hand, tensed up. This wasn't surrender. *What was it, though?*

The noble's eyes were firmly fixed on Cilia, clearly ready to unleash everything that he had at his disposal. At this distance, even severely reduced, his damaging cards were likely to hurt or kill her outright.

"I admit it, Lord Beforant. I underestimated you. *We* underestimated you. My apologies." She got down on her knees.

"You're surrendering?" The giggle emerging from him echoed the incredulity written on his features.

"I am reciprocating. You have done your utmost to strike against us and now you have us in your grasp. The Savior, former leader of Liberty, Light save his soul, prepared himself for just such an event. This device—" She pulled something from within her coat. It looked like a short, stubby vase. Well-made and pretty, it was nevertheless so unremarkable that it could be placed anywhere without drawing any eyes. "Activates every single Liberty Guardian hidden within the city and is locked into performing the wielder's desires. I got it from somebody who, eventually, regretted supporting the Savior."

Thomas looked absolutely hypnotized, both by her and the object.

Cilia moved slowly, like a mouse staring down a viper. Her voice was low, intent, and her eyes entirely focused on the vase. "Another detail you might not be privy to. The Savior was a singularly paranoid person. This effect includes every Guardian birthed throughout at least four decades."

That was a massive exaggeration, of course. A lot of those Guardians were out in the blissful lands, acting as Keepers. A good deal were bound to have died as well, one way or another...from simple lack of magic, old age, or good old violence.

Thomas Beforant did not know this. His eyes fixed on the vase as if it could bring his personal doom. He giggled again. "What a ridiculous notion. Yet, so believable. So in tune with everything else I've been told. I *adore* it! What is your play here, girl? I expect that you will be threatening me to withdraw my forces, or you will activate it?"

Cilia's smile was angelic, for once entirely free of any pessimism, criticism, or irony. She beamed at the most powerful man in the Lightborn empire and said, "No. I activated it the moment you appeared."

The sound of splintering wood merged with the cracking of old mortar as a grinding, crunching assault on the ear. All eyes were drawn to a wall right next to Thomas, where a *creature* peeled itself away from the wall.

The thing looked ridiculous. It was like a spider, if the spider had been painted over several times and had mortar slapped onto it on multiple occasions. A few of its limbs that weren't covered were half see-through. It must have weighed less than twenty pounds and should have been less intimidating than a pet cat. Except, it *oozed* intention and focus, as it slowly ambled closer to the Lightborn.

All around them, similar noises attested to other Guardians bursting out to join their comrade.

When Thomas acted, only two people were ready for it. He flung himself forward, rapier aiming straight for Cilia's throat.

One was Cilia herself. She'd been dead focused on him. The moment he started to move, she flung herself back, hands flying to throw a fire droplet at him.

He managed to tap the droplet midair, guiding it away from his midriff. It continued through the air, erupting amid the other Lightborn. His rapier, meanwhile, veered back toward its target.

Liam arrived first. His Helping Step activated, flinging him in front of Cilia in a split second. The shield rang from the impact, sending the rapier wide.

Thomas simply stared for a second.

"Why don't you pick on someone...well. Me?"

Liam's taunt made the Lightborn roll his eyes and throw himself forward. Just like that, the impasse broke entirely.

Within seconds, the entire intersection erupted into utter chaos. Forty Lightborn hurled themselves at five defenders, while Guardians burst from their hiding places all over the city, ignoring the entire war to race straight to this one fight.

It should have been over in seconds. A Tier-four against a Tier-six. An archbishop, the epitome of his art when it came to healing and shielding. Forty veteran soldiers. Against self-taught amateurs, despite all their cards.

Except, they had been educated in the school of desperate struggles for survival. Within seconds, Cilia was whipping droplets left and right, fire exploding alongside shadows blossoming into life.

On top of that, a burgeoning growth erupted from the ground right at the center of the Lightborn. Their panic emerged as Sera's Nature's Shield burst into being, and was instantly grasped by Cilia's Touch Grass, resulting in an explosive growth of thorny vines that stretched and enveloped, clutched and held. They couldn't pierce the heavy armor of the Lightborn, but went straight for faces and other visible soft spots. Even where they found no weaknesses, they slowed, constrained and held back.

Kith burst into motion. He was almost impossible to watch as his entire body seemed to flash and distort at once. His Heart card burst into action, doubling his stats. Apian God flared to life in a thousand buzzing voices, flinging themselves at the enemies. Everywhere they touched, Enforced Entropy stepped into effect, removing any positive effects from enemy cards and buffs. Meanwhile, the twin birds of Antithesis of Light hovered way up in the air, adding a tiny bit of damage while reducing enemy Light effects, and Internal Spark ensured that every single summon of his worked that bit smarter and smoother. It was enough to make you dizzy, even before you tried to catch up with the blur of his twin axes.

Sera barely moved. She held herself ready, eyes constantly moving, even as she stayed in place at the back of their formation. The Flame Within boosted her own attributes, even as she grew thorns and kept Blessing of the Night debilitating the Light effects. She layered that with Shimmering Sanctuary, shielding them all from enemy debuffs.

Liam held his own. The noble was an excellent fencer, and his strikes drew blood every other moment. However, Liam didn't care about blood. He had his task, and he would manage. Slashes stopped drawing blood as Become the Clay engaged, covering him in a protective layer of hardened magical clay. Draining Ward added to the efficiency of the defense, even as it slowly drained Thomas of his Agility.

Every so often, the noble would activate one of his cards. Damaging, dazzling, or blinding light erupted from him, tearing at Liam, trying to surprise and overwhelm him. However, with Ravenous Shadows engaged, the vastly reduced damage of his cards only made Liam grow stronger.

Thomas tried to move past Liam twice to strike at the others. Every time, he engaged Helping Step, emerging right where Thomas intended to go, punishing him.

The archbishop tried everything he was able. He engulfed Thomas in shields, healed the fighters, tried to help where he could. Yet, his strained expression showed the truth. He'd been struggling to keep up already. Now, he was near the edge.

Chase let loose. For so long, they'd been struggling through uphill battles, smashing through obstructions, only to realize that they were about to face off against somebody stronger, better, or more powerful. Now, he finally hit the top of the curve, and realized...he was the powerful one.

He eschewed any long-winded buildup. There'd be no powerful acidic waves for this. No drawn-out struggle where he'd sap the enemies of their attributes and wear them down. This was going to be fast, dizzying, and dirty. Steps of Brilliance and Fight Another Day worked together flawlessly at this point, barely affected by gravity as he raced at supernatural speeds through the air. Winds of Change, as always, was ready if he needed to switch, while One with the Soil gave him perfect balance.

Racing through the air at head height, he yelled at Kith, "Fiery End. Now!"

Kith didn't question him. The bugs crawling all over the enemies, subduing their buffs, froze for a second. Two. Then they erupted into a fiery conflagration, sacrificing their life's blood to damage the enemies.

The explosion was massive, rocking back their enemies. A dozen of them hit the ground, screaming or deadly quiet. The remainder wavered, blinded and hurting. Shortly, however, all their buffs would start having an effect, letting them get back to their feet.

Chase used Mine Now!

He experienced an overwhelming burst of energy as the combined buffs of the Lightborn, subdued until just a few seconds before, were canceled as one and layered onto himself. For a second, he was almost drunk with power, wondering whether this was what the Savior felt like all the time.

Then he attacked.

There was nothing pretty about this. He ran circles around the enemies, cutting down anybody standing. Tearing through shadows and fire alike, he moved around Kith, hit every Lightborn fighter struggling to move within the massive thorn bush. In a series of cuts and strikes, the intersection was covered in blood as he carved a bloody half-circle through the entire group.

His brain barely activated throughout the entire ordeal. Acting entirely on instinct, he rushed along, flinging himself sword-first at the greatest threat in reach. His speed, his momentum, the myriad buffs—all worked together to throw him forward at a velocity he'd never reached before.

He hit the ground, took one step—sword reaching, diving— and his momentum stopped from one second to the next.

Liam stumbled backward. He stared at the sword tip suddenly appearing out of nowhere. Then he froze, and his eyes met those of Thomas.

The Lightborn noble struggled to speak. One trembling hand reached downward, feeling the tip of the blade impaling him from behind, emerging through the archbishop's shield, through the leather armer, and emerging out the front of the armor. A bubble of blood emerged on his lips. "Pe-peace," he managed through the blood.

Chase held onto the hilt of the sword as if it were the only thing keeping him from flying toward the next enemies. His eyes were wild and the snarl feral, barely human. "Peace?" he repeated, as if tasting the words. "I don't think so." With a savage growl, he twisted the sword and pulled it back out.

Thomas Beforant fell to the ground. He was still feebly trying to form words as he bled out.

EPILOGUE

Apparently, a lot of people are eager to read my commentary along with the Savior's diaries. It would seem that the perspective of an outsider provides an angle that Liberty as a whole is not used to, but helps understand the entire transition. That thought is slightly intimidating. Yet, I will honor the request in the spirit it is intended. As such, I am not going to redact *anything* in my commentary. May history judge me fairly.

Cilia. Liberty/Darkborn crafter. Born and raised in poverty in the Lightborn empire.

Don't worry, Cil. We're always watching. Always judging. Smooches. Kith.

"Explain that one to me again, only slower, please. The agreement was to 'Sneak in and steal a deck. Then return to the bloodied grounds and form a proper home.' Right?"

A vein pulsed on Half-Swart's forehead as his fists clenched at his sides. With his dusty skin and gleaming, bald skull, it made him look like the epitome of fury.

The throne room in the palace didn't look anything like it used to. The throne was gone, for one. They were still in the process of planning the exact constellation of their future system of governance, hence there was no point in starting to craft anything fancy. For now, a simple wooden lectern was placed where the throne used to be, facing an open circle, ringed by a large number of chairs haphazardly fanning out. Toward the back of the room, several smaller tables with chairs were placed. Speakers would be able to swap places at the lectern quickly, walk back and forth to mingle or talk in peace at the back of the room, while the official decisions, votes, and proceedings took place at the front.

The trappings and decorations were almost unchanged. "Almost" meaning that any murals or wall hangings depicting the supposed history of Liberty were annotated with plaques on the walls describing both the actual history and any important places in the Savior's diaries that spelled out the truth. It was one of the rare few decisions everybody agreed on right away. They'd learn from history, not avoid it.

They stood in a half-circle near the back of the room.

Kith hemmed and hawed, scratching his cheek. "Really? Getting in and out without any issues? That doesn't really sound like us."

Chase smirked. "Let's just say, there were a few...what should we call them?"

Sera draped an arm over his shoulder. "Extenuating circumstances?"

"Yeah. That works." Chase nodded merrily.

Tatiana Skysworn laughed, a clear, brilliant sound. "Killing this Savior of theirs does sound like something beyond your everyday occurrence. Which Tier did you say he was again?"

Chase shrugged. "We have no way of knowing. Sera and Cilia tried to do some guessing—"

"Math," they said in unison.

"*Educated* guesswork, based on how much Ænima he was likely to receive, how much additional Ænima you need to Tier up, and a bunch of other dull stuff. Their best guess is ten to twelve."

"I don't *care* that you killed a god!" Half-Swart erupted. Then he blinked, taking in what he'd just said, before shaking his head. "You could have returned to us without the deck. Or as soon as you got the deck. This was *beyond* reckless."

Sera shook her head. "We could not. With all due respect, Half-Swart, that would have left Liberty to fend for themselves— in one scenario, bound in slavery to a tyrant, and in the other, with their fledgling independence crushed and usurped by the Lightborn empire. Neither of those were inducive to our long-term well-being."

"See? This is why I'm marrying her. All those brains *and* that figure?" Chase smirked, fending off the cuffs to his shoulder.

Tatiana smiled in disbelief. "Disregarding the late Savior for a minute, I cannot state just how strange this all feels to me. You insist that the Lightborn have stopped invading? My informants claim the same, both concerning Earth's Ward and the Furyborn borders. Yet, I keep expecting some ugly surprise to surface and threaten us all."

"It's the archbishop," Kith said. "I was going to run him through, just like Chase did to that nasty Lord Beforant. Liam stopped me, though, which turned out to be a good choice. We're working on returning him to the lands of Light, and we're milking it for *all* it's worth."

"What Kith means," Cilia added drily, "is that we're holding him, along with five lesser nobles and about five thousand surviving Lightborn soldiers, ransom. With that, we are pushing for hard assurances from the Church of the Circle that they will not move against us. If the rest of the Lightborn empire were united, they might simply push to elect a new archbishop and move on. Only, they've got other problems. Lord Beforant had a tight grasp on his power. With him gone, we have trouble even finding a representative who can speak for them all."

Her lopsided grin grew brighter. "Of course, it doesn't hurt that they're facing pressure on several fronts. With Gunnha hard at work, the Dark cards are spreading throughout their lands like wildfire, providing an alternative path to personal power. Also, we have you to thank for keeping them in check."

That sparked a ferocious smile on Half-Swart's face. "You best believe it. The past weeks have been the easiest the blood-ied grounds have had it for *decades*. The tree keepers of the Heart Halls are planting seeds right up to the very edge of the official borders. Give us a few years, and they'll never be able to root us out, even if they wanted to."

Tatiana inclined her head gratefully. "The same goes for us. As you are aware, our power is not as heavy in soldiers as other nations—but we are pushing the Lightborn hard diplomat-ically. Also, we will be expanding the walls, granting us added space for farming and...cooperating with powerful foreign forces."

Kith barked a laugh. "Is that what we are now? Powerful foreign forces?"

"You tell me," she countered. "The world, as we know it, has changed. You are the fulcrum of that change. We, along with the world, are at this moment waiting to hear what your wishes and desires for the future are."

Kith's eyes widened comically. He erupted into a wheez-ing, coughing laugh that left him unable to answer. Liam, nod-ding in understanding, patted his back.

Once the worst had abated, Cilia answered. "*Please* ignore him. We all do." Giving Tatiana a rare smile, she said, "High El-ementalist. Half-Swart. We set out on this insane journey with one simple desire. To find a home. Somehow, we actually man-aged." She indicated their surroundings. "However, we aren't planning to be kings and queens here. We only aim to help them get a new, better society built, protect them in case of trouble. Yet, one thing they have already agreed on is that the borders, from here on, will be open to *anybody* friendly to Liberty. That includes you and all of yours. Anybody who wants cards will al-ways be welcome here."

"But...our plans fell through. We don't have anything to give in return," Half-Swart said.

"Please." Chase snorted. "You helped us. You gave us a deck. You trained us and outfitted us—Furyborn and Elementals both. Are we supposed to forget about that, now where we've hit a stroke of luck?" He sneered. "Not happening. You'll have to argue the specifics with those back there, and they'll probably try to nudge you into some agreements on trade and defense and whatnot." He winked. "A little hint. If you think they're being bastards, they absolutely adore Sera and are likely to follow her example in anything. As well they should."

Half-Swart and Tatiana blinked and shared a glance. He bowed his head. "Thank you. I believe my kin out there discovering Salvation at the moment will be pleased learning that. We'll try to respond in the same spirit. What do we do about the Lightborn, then?"

"What about them?" Sera asked. "You *could* engage in all-out war while they are weak to punish them for past atrocities. You could make the most of this, steal back lands and power. Or, we could use this chance to build a lasting peace, build a balance that will endure regardless of one party."

"You really think that'll work?" Half-Swart asked incredulously. "They've been aiming to rule the world for hundreds of years now. Damn well nearly succeeded, too."

Liam flexed. "Now they've got us to deal with. Plus, they've never been weaker, and they're not just dealing with three separate powers, but *allies*. If they make too much noise, we can deal with it. The hard way."

"Then...what is the plan? How are your thoughts on how best to handle this going onward?" Tatiana asked.

Chase grinned. "I'm so glad you asked. We have talked this over *thoroughly* and have worked out an in-depth plan."

"We have?" Liam asked.

"Oh yes, we have. Kith here, for instance, is going to spend a lot of time sleeping."

"What?" Half-Swart frowned.

"Liam has ambitious plans, too. He intends to get to know at least ten percent of the unmarried young women of Salvation."

"Damn straight," Liam agreed.

"Cilia is a hard one. She's probably going to lose herself in crafting and emerge in a year or two, with enough new inventions to rock the entirety of Ordei."

"I resent that," Cilia said. "Not least how correct it is."

"Of course, all the actual *work* will go to my wonderful Serafine Valerian."

"Oh really?" Sera crossed her arms and raised an eyebrow. "Exactly what do *you* plan to do with all your time? I do not believe I agreed to getting married to a wastrel."

"I am going to be performing the most important task of them all. Being an inspiration." He tapped his forehead with a finger. "When I stroll around on the streets of Salvation, everybody will be asking, '*You?* You saved us?' That will teach them the most important lesson of all."

"That your upbringing doesn't matter as much as what you do with your life?" Tatiana hazarded, blinking.

"Please. No. The *obvious* lesson here is this: as long as you manage to secure yourself a woman with morals and a serious work ethic, you'll be able to laze about for the rest of your days while your wife and crew do the real work." He instantly dove to the side to evade the slap flying in his direction. Resurfacing, he beamed. "Ha! I—" He took an apple to the forehead.

Liam leapt on top of him straight afterward.

"This is what the future of Ordei looks like?" Half-Swart gaped. "We're doomed."

With a small smile playing on her lips, Tatiana replied, "Honestly, I find it reassuring. If you can go through an ordeal such as they have, and still emerge as a loving family, malfunctioning though it may be? There is hope for us all!"

"See? I'm an inspiration!" Chase managed, before Liam put him in a headlock.

"You're inspiring me to kick your ass!" Liam growled.

Half-Swart flung up his hands in disgust. "On your neck be it, then. When the bards want this discussion repeated for posterity, this is exactly what I will tell him. That the most important power struggle in the history of Ordei ended with butt jokes."

From within his headlock, Chase froze. Then he laughed. "I have never heard of anything more fitting."

The end of Theft of Decks 4, the final book in the Theft of Decks series.

CARD REFRESHER

This chapter consists solely of the overview of the main group's cards and abilities. You can skip it freely, if you do not care for a refresher.

Chase:

[**Nothing to See Here**
Heart card (amplified)
Active, medium duration
The attention span of the average person is a fickle thing. What will keep you interested one moment will seem dull and unimportant the next. Sometimes, to get from one to the other, all it takes is a nudge. For a limited time, become less interesting to anybody around you. Those with much higher Mental Power than yours may be less affected or unaffected.
Medium cooldown
"Now, to all those watching, I would love to extol upon you the forty-eight virtues of clean living. The first..."]

[**Sticky Fingers**
Legendary, Dark rogue
Tier one
Active, instant
Stealing is such a clumsy endeavor. Too easy. Anybody can steal a purse. This card allows you to go a step further, carefully manipulate strands of Darkness to grasp onto the key attributes of a mark, temporarily making them your own from a short distance.
There is a minuscule chance of the increase becoming permanent.
Short cooldown
"You lost what, ma'am? Your Agility? Oh. Perhaps I can help you find it near my virility and hairline?"]

[**Steps of Brilliance**
Rare, Light rogue
Tier one
Active, instant

This card grants you the option of creating three palm-sized platforms wherever you may choose. These platforms are visible and tangible only to yourself, unless faced up against an adversary with much higher Mental Power than yours. The platforms only last for a short duration, but you may constantly create up to three platforms.

"I saw him, once. His was not the power of flight. No, it was a lot more unnatural. He moved like he did not belong in this world." A bystander, about the Acrobat of Virn.]

[Squall Sling
Rare, Elemental rogue
Tier one
Active, instant
This card allows you to create a localized brief burst of concentrated air from your hand. This will allow you to add increased impetus to thrown items, deflect incoming strikes, or even change your direction midair.

Very short cooldown
"Out-throw Kargar the Giant? Kargar laugh! Kargar...HOW YOU DO THAT?"]

[Unending Decay
Epic, Fury rogue
Tier one
Instant, medium duration
A tree rarely topples from a single stroke with an axe. Animals are rarely taken down with one bite or swipe of a claw. With this card equipped, every single strike of your weapon following the first on the same enemy will result in fifteen percent additional damage, to a maximum of an additional one hundred and fifty percent damage. Striking other enemies will reset the count.

Medium cooldown
"I done told ya, didn't I? Mess with me, and regret it later." The hangman wins his duel, twenty minutes in.]

[Nights of Criffhaven
Uncommon, Dark rogue
Tier two
Active, medium duration
Some rogues go for the throat right away. Others like to drag out the fun, bleed their enemies and make them truly realize their defeat before they have even lost. This card, once tapped, grants you a slow build-up for as long as you remain engaged in hostilities. Every minute you remain engaged in hostilities grants you an additional temporary point to Agility, to a

maximum of +15. After fifteen minutes, you have five minutes at the maximum boost, following which the buff is deactivated.

Long cooldown

"Stop trying to hit me and hit me!"]

[Race of Life
Uncommon, Light rogue
Tier two
Active, medium duration
This card, once tapped, grants you a small boost to Agility. It can be used several times a day, making it perfect for those who often need to work in bursts.

Medium cooldown

"Some people say that life is a marathon, not a sprint. Some people are wrong. Life, the way I see it, is a marathon of sprints. And we should plan accordingly."]

[Among the Raindrops
Epic, Elemental rogue
Tier two
Active, medium duration
Upon activation, this card will start summoning puddles for the duration of the effect in a thirty-foot radius around the wearer. The puddles of water have a triple effect, all working only against enemies. First, they have an oily, slippery effect and will make it hard to keep your equilibrium. Second, they have an acidic effect, causing ongoing damage against any exposed skin or equipment. Third, the puddles have a viscous quality, clinging to anything and anybody unlucky enough to enter.

Long cooldown

"Your fancy power is to make me stand in a puddle of water? Hah. Wait. Why are you laughing?"]

[Fight Another Day
Rare, Fury rogue
Tier two
Instant, medium duration
Some wielders make history. Their approaches, tempers, and cards vary wildly. They all have one thing in common, however. They lived to grow strong. Reaching that point sometimes means a tactical retreat.

Upon activation of this card, you, and anybody grouped with you, receive a marked increase to running speed as long as you are running away from enemies.

Long cooldown

"Stand and fight? I mean, I could. But...I'm not going to."
The Lion of Tekarn has yet to earn his moniker.]

[**Free of Perdition**
Rare, Dark rogue
Tier three
Active, medium duration
Tapping this card allows you to forcibly swap one of your chosen attributes temporarily with that of another living creature in short range. For a brief while, become as strong as an indomitable rager, as swift as a sky hare. If the target does not resist the effect, they will also see their attribute score temporarily replaced with yours. The effect remains until the cooldown runs out.
Medium cooldown
"How did you do that? Those skinny arms? It cannot be. 'The Beast' Sinclair has been brought low!"]

[**Spoils of the Undeserving**
Rare, Light rogue
Tier three
Passive, permanent
In this life, all good comes to those who earn it. Some people, though, are able to adjust the tendrils of fate, carve off more for themselves than what they actually deserve. With this card, the wielder will improve their attributes through training at a triple pace compared to others.
"You can tell me, man. What potions are you on? I want some."]

[**Winds of Change**
Rare, Elemental rogue
Tier three
Passive, permanent
Versatility is a way of life. You understand that. Most don't. However, being able to surprise others with a vast array of abilities at hand may win you the day. This card is passive, remaining in effect whenever equipped. For as long as you have it equipped, you may switch freely between all other cards. There will be no limitation except a thirty-second cooldown after switching a card from each separate Tier.
"You hear that, you gods-forsaken bastard? It's the wind. It's blowing with the winds of change."]

[**Home Turf Advantage**
Epic, Fury rogue
Tier three
Permanent, passive

Any successful rogue is a distrustful rogue. They need to be alert, awake, perceptive and cautious, ready to catch any danger to themselves and their kin. Yet, nobody can live their life in constant alertness without losing their edge.

This card, when wielded, allows the rogue, and anybody in their group, added benefits while resting. They will recuperate easier, their wounds close faster, and they will need less sleep to stay sharp. Also, any food and drink consumed will be more nourishing.

"It's like I said. Food just doesn't taste the same when you're away from home."]

[Circle of Darkness
Uncommon, Dark rogue
Tier four
Active, short duration
Darkness is the friend of any rogue. That is a well-known fact. This card allows a rogue to bring the Darkness with them, even in broad daylight. Upon activation, a thirty-foot circle of absolute darkness surrounds the wielder, staying with them, even if they move. Meanwhile, the darkness will be fully see-through for the rogue. Even enemies with higher Mental Power than the wielder will have trouble gazing through this short-lived circle of shadows, allowing them to get in a cheap shot, get the goods, or get away.

Short cooldown
"An eclipse? No, my stupid, stupid friend. This is theft."]

[Clothed in Living Light
Rare, Light rogue
Tier four
Active, long duration
The one constant for rogues, ironically, is a need for versatility. They need to adjust to their surroundings, often on the fly and under unhealthy or threatening conditions. This card allows the wielder that versatility. Upon activation, the card bestows the wielder with a quantity of living material that he can move, fix, and adjust with a mental nudge. A weapon? A shield? A set of skis? Any of these can be created and adjusted with this card. Any damage to the material reduces the pool of material available to the wielder. The material can be every bit as sharp as the wielder's Mental Power allows.

Long cooldown
"It's my time to shine." The Thief of Valkeer makes his move.]

[A Friendly Wave
Rare, Elemental rogue
Tier four
Active, short duration
Rogues, more than any other class, are aware of their surroundings. They learn how to use the terrain to their advantage, always on the outlook for cover, for hiding places and terrain that will aid them and work against their enemies. This card allows the wielder to take a more direct hand in adjusting the surroundings to their advantage. For a short duration after activation, the wielder is able to command any water in their surroundings, making the water splash onto pursuers, soak clothes, ruin footing, and even drown an unlucky pursuer.
Medium cooldown
"Getting your hands dirty is part of being a criminal, they say. But...look at me. My hands have never been cleaner!" A crime scene is swept clean by a rogue wave.]

[One with the Soil
Epic, Fury rogue
Tier four
Instant, long duration
The stories all tell us about the massive fireballs, the summoned swarms of locusts, and ground-breaking attack cards. Yet, they neglect to remember one thing: that is not how most fights are won or lost. The slip of a foot. A patch of gravel or slippery mud. These are the small things that spell the end for a huge number of fighters. With this card, you and your group will retain perfect balance, regardless of footing and weather.
"Dear Lord Baluz. It takes more than a punch to the chin, a muddy slope, a dozen summoned simians, and an Agility debuff to throw me off my feet. Admittedly, not that much more. Call it a tie?"]

Kith:

[Cost of Life
Heart card (amplified)
Medium duration
At what cost, power? This is a question many ask themselves. You do not need to. You know the price. Whenever you need to, you have power, right at your fingertips. Upon activation of this card, your attributes are doubled for the full duration of the card, with no instant detrimental effects afterward. The only detraction? Every activation will cost you a year of your life force.

Cost of Life will now also increase the rarity of all your cards by one for the full duration.

Long cooldown

"It whispers, does it not? That pulse, that promise, of strength and power, right at your disposal. You need only reach out."]

[Shadow Master
Rare, Dark summoner
Tier one
Active summon, long duration
This card allows you to manipulate your own shadow, split them into two shadows and order them around at a distance like they were your own summons. The augmented shadows are magically strengthened and enemy eyes cannot pierce them. The summoner may at any time choose to see through the shadow's eyes and speak through the shadow's mouth as if it were his own body. They can only be destroyed by magic or Elemental damage. If destroyed, there is a 12-hour cooldown for the next summon.

"It flew, I tell you. His shadow burst from his body, walked right up to me and mocked me. Threatened me. I seen it!" Careem. Denizen of the slums of Veriten.]

[Divine Mentor
Rare, Light summoner
Tier one
Active, medium duration
This summon brings forth a divine entity from the heavens. Internalized, the being will aid the summoner, increasing all their attributes and improving their movement speed. It can also be expended, guiding the entity to a chosen position before making it burst in a blinding light.

Long cooldown

"Behold, oh mortal. I am you. Only better, bereft of this fragile shell of yours. Follow my guidance, if you can."]

[Apian God
Rare, Elemental summoner
Tier one
Active, medium duration
The queens are commonly recognized as the highest ranking in a beehive. However, with the use of this card, you summon something else: an apian god, controlling hundreds of tiny air-aspected summons. They are not as large as regular bees, but still cause tiny amounts of stinging air damage.

In addition to this, depending on the Mental Power of the summoner, nearby regular flying insects may recognize the natural hierarchy of the apian god and join in the attack.

"I. Summon you. Into. Beeing!" The Court summoner finally snaps.]

[Let Them Go
Epic, Fury summoner
Tier one
Active, medium duration
Any summoner worth their salt knows when to dig deep to protect a summon, and when to let it go. With this card, the summoner can actively sacrifice a summon or group of summoned creatures. The energy tied up in the creatures will be spread out as a passive temporary boost to all attributes except Potential to every other person or summoned creature in the group. Any bound Guardian sacrificed will grant triple the boost.

"Let them go, and we will rise like the break of dawn." The High Elementalist surrenders control for personal gain.]

[Tainted Earth
Rare, Dark summoner
Tier two
Active summon, medium duration
This card allows you to awaken the soil anywhere you choose. It cannot be used directly on rock or crafted surfaces. When you tap the card, the earth grows to life in a shallow puddle of tainted earth. The earth is extremely adhesive and hard to remove. It can move, but only slowly. When touching skin, the soil drains enemies of Toughness at a slow rate. If destroyed, there is a 4-hour cooldown for the next summon.

"What's that? Get it off. Get it off!"]

[Crescendo of Might
Rare, Light summoner
Tier two
Active, short duration
Most summons are brought into the world with the desire to keep them present and active for as long as possible, given that they are the tools with which the summoner interacts with Ordei. This summon is the exact opposite. It comes with a time limit and the express desire to create as much damage as possible while it can.

Medium cooldown

"I am reading its mind right now. 'Rend, tear, kill!' Are you sure this is a being of Light?"]

[...Twice the Fun

Epic, Elemental summoner
Tier two
Passive, permanent
Sometimes, you crave something new and interesting. Sometimes, the best choice is simply more of what you already have. This card, when chosen, will double the number of summoned creatures for up to three other cards.
"You think my summoned squirrels underwhelming? Wait 'till I show you...more squirrels!"]

[**Ties That Bind**
Rare, Fury summoner
Tier two
Passive, permanent
Most summons are temporary, restricted to when the card is active. Yet, with the right choices for a Wellspring, any summoner earning new cards may choose a card like this. With permission from the owner of the Wellspring, you will be able to bond with any resident Guardian. This Guardian will then be permanently attached to you like a regular summon, until the Ænima powering it runs out. The effect of this card will remain active, regardless whether you switch to another Tier two card.

In addition to the Guardian's own attributes, it will be awarded a permanent increase to its Agility, with one point for each three points of your own Agility.
"What do you mean, I cannot summon this again once I let it die? Go away, you ridiculous little man." The summoner of Naz has an ugly eye-opener.]

[**Coils of Shadow**
Rare, Dark summoner
Tier three
Active, long duration
This card, once tapped, summons a number of small, venomous dredge spitters, calculated as one viper per two Mental Power of the summoner. These vipers are hard to spot in the dark, but vulnerable to Light powers and effects.
"Who's a lovely danger noodle? You are, my beautiful hazard spaghetti." The Valniers head chef races toward disaster.]

[**Sacrificial Saints**
Uncommon, Light summoner
Tier three
Passive, long duration
Nearly all summoning cards are active cards, requiring a certain degree of manipulation on behalf of the summoner. The

bright saints summoned by this card do not. These are erstwhile heroes, souls so suffused with the power of self-sacrifice, that they feel the need to continue their deeds in the afterlife. Activating the card summons a random number of saints, between three and five. Each saint will attempt to block one attack against the summoner, be it magical or physical. Bear in mind that some attacks may be too powerful to be wholly blocked.

"You would not get this from any other. I will never give you up, nor let you down. We are no strangers. You know the rules, and so do I."]

[**Fiery End**
Uncommon, Elemental summoner
Tier three
Instant
Sometimes, in order to obtain your goal, you will have to make sacrifices. Summoned creatures are a means to an end. This card can ensure that the end in question will not be yours. Upon activation, any summoned creatures of yours explode in a violent conflagration, doing fire damage to anybody caught in their vicinity, proportional to their size and mass.
Long cooldown
"Outmaneuvered? Outmatched? One could see it that way. Only, why do you believe I have spread my summons this far out?" The last day of the city Acs Epilium.]

[**From Out of the Pits**
Rare, Fury summoner
Tier three
Active, instant
At the core of the Furyborn lies the concept of blood. Of being ready to sacrifice for your kin, should the path take you straight to the Pits themselves. Yet, if you are fast and crafty enough, you can extract enough to let you and your kin live another day.
Activating this card allows the summoner to sacrifice a third of their own health. Doing so will grant the same health to each and every person in their group, including their summons. There is no natural limiter to the usage of this card. The summoner may die from using this card.
Medium cooldown
"I would do anything for love. I would also do this." Rolat Polpettone dies for his beloved.]

[**Antithesis of Light**
Uncommon, Dark summoner
Tier four
Passive, long duration

Most summons are aspected, but still geared toward facing any sort of enemy. Not this summon. The Antithesis of Light is just that. A summoned entity that not only flings bolts of shadows when summoned, it also reduces the efficacy of nearby Light-aspected cards and effects by forty percent.

Long cooldown

"Come closer, morsel. I smell your terror. And I hunger."]

[Crystalline Guard
Rare, Light summoner
Tier four
Passive, long duration
Most summons are both offensive and defensive to a certain extent. Not this one. The Crystalline Guard is fully passive, brought into being purely to act as a shield between the summoner and their foes. Its crystalline skin deflects most ranged attacks and magical attacks, while the crystal shards of its body, when attacked, explode into deadly splinters, capable of piercing skin.

Long cooldown

"Listen. I...can't see you on the other side of this crystal thing. Ms. Summoner? Are you still there? I surrender. Please. I've been here for hours, and I'm wounded and tired."]

[Pillars of Air
Rare, Elemental summoner
Tier four
Active, medium duration
Usually, summoned entities are their own individuals, with a certain degree of autonomy. The Pillars of Air are not. For as long as the twin pillars are called into being, they meld with the legs of the wielder, forming a creation that responds entirely to the whims of the wielder's movements and thoughts. This allows them to use the power of the air in their movement, leaping long distances and run like the wind. A lapse in concentration can lead to the Pillars disappearing, however.

"Wheeeeeeeeeeeeeeeeeee." The self-titled Aerial Plague leaps to his death.]

[Ties Airbound
Rare, Fury summoner
Tier four
Passive, permanent
Most summons are temporary, restricted to when the card is active. Yet, with the right choices for a Wellspring, any sum-

moner earning new cards may choose a card like this. With permission from the owner of the Wellspring, you will be able to bond with any resident winged Guardian. This Guardian will then be permanently attached to you like a temporary summon, until the Ænima powering it runs out. The effect of the card will remain active, regardless whether you switch to another Tier four card.

In addition to the Guardian's own attributes, it will be awarded a permanent increase to its Agility and Toughness, with one point for each three points of your own Agility and Toughness.

"I know. You are kin. Do you like watching me soar?"]

Liam:

[Heart and Hearth
Heart card (amplified)
Long duration
From the heart comes that which we love. It provides life, love, and heat. For a while, you are able to control the heat around you, at short range. You may banish the cold for your loved ones, make your friends comfortable, and make annoyances overheat and leave.

Long cooldown
"Come close, love. Do you feel this? This, from my heart to yours."]

[One Heart, Opened
Uncommon, Dark fighter
Tier one
Active, instant
This card grants you a short-term Life Share ability. At your choice and direction, you may drain your own health and divide it among others, healing their wounds. Be warned that there is no upper limit here. If overused, you will drain your own heart's blood.

"I...did say I would give you my heart, did I not? Last C—"
Final words of Shadow Knight Georgius Micael.]

[Waterfall of Light
Uncommon, Light fighter
Tier one
Active, instant
There are those fighters who advocate for technique, know-how, and weapon control to save the day. They tend to ignore one detail: with enough power, everything else falls at the wayside.

Tapping this card causes your next attack to gain Trample. The attack will be very difficult to deflect or block, and has a medium chance to stun the enemy or knock them prone.

Short cooldown

"Rise, good sir. I was merely delivering a point. Get up...please." The chevalier earns his exile.]

[**Become the Clay**
Epic, Elemental fighter
Tier one
Active, medium duration
For a while after activation, the outermost layer of your skin is converted into a thick layer of magically thickened wet clay. The clay will make it much harder for any attacks to pierce and may cause weapons to get stuck. Also, the effect of the clay becomes malleable, tied to the will of the Wielder. The layer is heavy and may make it harder for you to move if you do not have the Strength to handle the weight.

Medium cooldown

"Give that back, you stupid, filthy weapon thief." A master duelist is defeated.]

[**Optimal Offense**
Uncommon, Fury fighter
Tier one
Active, medium duration
The best offense is a good defense. Or was it the other way around? Regardless which school of thought you adhere to, you now get to double down on your choices. Upon activation of this card, you get to increase the strength of your offense by a full thirty percent, at the cost of a twenty percent reduction in defense, or vice versa. Whichever choice you make lasts for the full duration of the card, and cannot be willfully canceled.

Short cooldown

"I am getting bored. Are you all getting bored? You have been trying to get through my armor for a while. Should we finish this?"]

[**Draining Ward**
Common, Dark fighter
Tier two
Passive, permanent
Many fighters believe that the pathway to victory means not getting hurt. Amateurs. Veterans know that the only thing that counts is being the last one standing on the bloody field of victory. This card works on your currently worn armor and

adapts it in two ways. First, it grants the armor a minor increase to its protection. Second, anybody who scores a hit against the wearer on the armor sees their Agility drained by a point.

"Hold on. A second. I've stabbed you. Three times. Why are you. Getting faster?" The death of Squire Ulrien.]

[Cleansing Fire
Uncommon, Light fighter
Tier two
Active, instant
When activated, this card sends a wave of purifying power through the body of the wielder. It cleanses the body of most diseases and hostile effects, while also granting the wielder a weak healing effect.
Medium cooldown
"Who's ready for the next round? I can keep this up forever."]

[Earthen Might
Common, Elemental fighter
Tier two
Active, very short duration
Sometimes, the best way to end a conflict is through instant, overwhelming force. How you decide to apply said force is up to you. For a brief window of time, the fighter's Strength is doubled.
Short cooldown
"Yeah, I guess I'm a bit scrawny. I 'unno. I think I can take you in arm wrestling. Care for a tiny bet?"]

[Escalating Defenses
Rare, Fury fighter
Tier two
Active, short duration
It can be so hard to truly let loose. To unleash the constant need for personal protection and focus on attacking. This card is for those who desire to leave the boring, self-restraining back-and-forth of regular combat behind and opt for something more...exhilarating. For every successful attack on an enemy, regardless of damage inflicted, you summon a single magical shield for you to control mentally, up to a maximum of three shields.
"Hey, wait. That's not fair." Arghan the Butcher faces five archers.]

[Ravenous Shadows
Uncommon, Dark fighter
Tier three

Active, very short duration

Some cards only need a single thought as you activate them, then you can forget about them. This card does not. Upon activation, it smothers the wearer in a layer of magical shadows that absorb a level of impacting magical attacks for a brief while. Once this duration has passed, any consumed energies are converted into a Strength boost with short duration for the fighter.

Medium cooldown

"You don't fight fair. But that's okay, see if I care. Hit me with your best shot!"]

[Convince the Unbeliever
Uncommon, Light fighter
Tier three
Passive

This card consists of a passive and an active element. The passive element is a weak, but constant self-heal. The active element engages at the start of any conflict, granting a +1 to the wearer's Agility for every minute, maxed at +5.

"I say to you again. My beliefs grant me the strength needed to persevere. Is that all you would send against me?"]

[Unleash the Elements
Common, Elemental fighter
Tier three
Active, long duration

Activating this card adds an Elemental aspect to your attacks. For every attack made, another Elemental aspect is added. When all four Elements are engaged, their power grows with each successive attack.

"My power is no match for yours, esteemed Protector Erfwen? Give it time."]

[All Out
Rare, Fury fighter
Tier three
Passive

Sometimes, simplicity is key. That principle is the foundation of this card as well. As long as the card is equipped, any offensive cards equipped by the wielder have their offensive effects increased by forty-five percent.

"I am too weak, you say? Allow me to slip into something more suitable." Grandstanding turns violent.]

[Tribune of Retribution, Blindness
Uncommon, Dark fighter

Tier four
Passive, medium duration
This card activates a punitive system, aiming to dispense karmic justice upon anybody attacking the fighter and his group. Any damage or damaging effect by an opposing force, regardless of whether the damage is nullified or not, results in an equivalent temporary reduction to their eyesight that lingers for the full duration of the card's effects. The more damage, the worse the blinding effect.
Long cooldown
"Crawl, maggots. You brought this on yourselves. Now, my friends and I will disperse justice." The Adjudicator of Dark at the Battle of Tempor.]

[Helping Step
Rare, Light fighter
Tier four
Active, very short duration
Being of the Light means being there for those in need. This card, when activated, lets you move to anybody in your group currently engaged in a fight in the blink of an eye. It will, at most, let you travel forty-five feet.
"Surrender, Darkspawn. There is no point on this battlefield I do not command."]

[Tempest of the Land
Uncommon, Fury/Elemental fighter
Tier four
Active, short duration
Natural disasters are not all bad. They roam and ravage, yet the energy unleashed in their passing can leave the soil revitalized, soon ready to easier grow to even further heights. In the same manner, sometimes, it is necessary for a fighter to unleash all their energy in one tempestuous assault. For the duration of the card, this will imbue all their attacks with a full gamut of Elemental aspects, and grant their body the strength and fury of the soil. However, once the card runs out, it will leave the fighter weakened for a short while, unable to use any cards. This is a dual card, working on more than one aspect.
"We surrender." The Tempest of the Land is not unleashed. This time.]

Cilia:

[Death of Distractions
Heart card (amplified)
Active, permanent

The Hand of Liberty keeps everything in check. Even distractions. Those pesky, tiny outside influences and sensual bombardments that constantly derail our thoughts, leading us to reduced productivity, minimal output, and any number of mental irrelevancies. This card can be activated at will, without cooldown. It will activate a small area of perfect control within fifty feet of the card holder, preventing anything auditory or olfactory from entering.

"Yeaaargh." The death of the scribe. He never heard the goblin sneaking up on him.]

[Manipulate Darkness
Uncommon, Dark crafter
Tier one
Permanent, passive
This card opens the gates, allowing you to manipulate the Dark aspect within you and, eventually, add them to your crafts in myriad ways. Manipulating your aspect will drain your stamina.

"From my soul to yours. A little shadow, a little mischief, to blanket the world and erase the tedium." Poet-crafter Erudian Nightstone.]

[Manipulate Light
Common, Light crafter
Tier one
Permanent, passive
This card opens the gates, allowing you to manipulate the Light aspect within you and, eventually, add them to your crafts in myriad ways. Manipulating your aspect will drain your stamina.

"Some people hack and slash to spread Light into this world. Not us. We, my dear, create." World-famous Light artist Everam Witteras.]

[Manipulate Fire
Common, Elemental crafter
Tier one
Permanent, passive
This card lights your inner furnace, allowing you to manipulate the fire aspect within you and, eventually, add them to your crafts in myriad ways. Manipulating your aspect will drain your stamina.

"Feel that? That rage, that wonderful heat. 'Tis yours, with but a thought. Feel it warm your soul."]

[**Manipulate Fury**
Common, Fury crafter
Tier one
Permanent, passive
This card lets you connect to the world around you, allowing you to manipulate the Fury aspect within you, in the soil and the air and, eventually, add them to your crafts. Manipulating your aspect will drain your stamina.

"Take a dash of home. Add a splash of family, of heat and hearth. Season with that rage you hold so dear. This concoction is an ember, just waiting to burn." Fury brewer Darintas addresses the crowd.]

[**A Hint of Permanence**
Uncommon, Dark crafter
Tier two
Passive, permanent
The quality of your creations is decided by the deftness of your fingers and the accumulated wealth of your expertise in your chosen trade.

The grade and power of the aspect you pour into your creation is defined by your Mental Power, your concentration and mental fortitude, and your expertise at applying it to your crafting process throughout the protracted creation period.

However, one thing holds true. The longer a crafted item lasts, the better it is. People remember the eternal, the items holding permanent effects. With this card, your Mental Power sees a medium increase when attempting to craft long-lasting items or items with permanent imbues.

"Might is right. Knowledge is power. Yet, permanence outlasts them all."]

[**Apex of Growth**
Uncommon, Light crafter
Tier two
Permanent, passive
There are few ultimate truths as a crafter. One of the rare exceptions is this: Aspects do not blend well. This card ameliorates some of the natural imbalances existing between the different aspects, making it easier to craft items merging powers from different aspects. Any difficulties from crafting items with conflicting abilities or powers still remain.

"Take the cold control of Liberty. Add a splash of unbridled Fury. Mix in the pure decadence of Darkness. Oh, my friends. This sinful concoction will be unforgettable."]

[**Ritual of Fire**
Rare, Elemental crafter

Tier two
Passive, activated
Crafting by itself can be draining, both on willpower and stamina. Now, however, you can decide whether you want to sacrifice your energy for improved results. Once activated, this card will continually siphon small traces of stamina from the crafter to remain working. While in effect, for the purposes of crafting, the crafter's Mental Power is increased by seventy-five percent.

"Donande-tak, donande'tek, eru menthala-ze...damn. Candle blew out. Lousy secondhand candle makers. Kill 'em all when I rule the world."]

[**From Farm to Table**
Uncommon, Fury crafter
Tier two
Permanent, passive
The vast majority of crafters prioritize. They outsource, purchase goods, ingredients and materials, purchase semi-finished products. It allows them to trade on the craftsmanship of others and craft a lot faster.

Yet, there is a joy in handling every part of the process, a certainty in knowing, intimately, every tiny item that you include. With this card, throughout the entire gathering and crafting process, you are able to imbue minute quantities of magic into the materials. Hence, the enhanced effects of the final product will be improved, based on how large a part of the process you have handled yourself, up to a maximum increase of sixty percent.

"Get yer filthy hands off me kill. That'll be a coat worthy of a king, it will!"]

[**A Dearth of Materials**
Uncommon, Dark crafter
Tier three
Passive, activated
Darkness is much associated with a lack, something missing. Hence, why should it surprise people so that it is a fantastic tool for filling out those missing links? This card allows the crafter to use their magic to fill in instead of regular materials. Depending on the materials at hand, the result may even become better for it.

"Ah. We are out of thread for the needle. Magic will suture that well and tight." A proper battle doctor improvises.]

[**A Testament to Light**

Uncommon, Light crafter
Tier three
Passive, activated
There are cards which help with given aspects of the crafting process. Some help shut out distractions. Others help with the stamina cost. This card, instead, holds a tiny collection of recollections, from Light masters of old. These assembled tidbits of brilliance aid with any single creation that involves the use of Light magic. The boost is lower overall, yet the card will aid with every part of the process, and may even aid with intuitive leaps in the creation processes.

"They say that having voices in your head is madness. Only, when those voices keep being right and result in better creations? People shut up."]

[**Chosen Focus: Fire**
Common, Elemental crafter
Tier three
Passive, activated
At third Tier, everybody gets this choice, for all of their decks. It can also be chosen at later Tiers, and you can only have a single focus. When activated, this will increase your control and output of Fire at any stage of the crafting process. It will allow your creations to hold more of the element, will grant you a better understanding of the bindings, and will drain you less during the crafting process.

"Hearken my words, knave! There is a purity to Fire, a clarity you do not see in other elements. It burns, but it also cleanses!" "Sire, art thou aware thou hath entered Wendie's domain?"]

[**A Familiar Tool**
Epic, Fury crafter
Tier three
Active, medium duration
No one knows the hammer like the smith himself. This old adage rings with truth. If you created an item, worked with it intimately, you will know it beyond somebody who simply bought it from a market stall. You will be aware of the imperfections beyond a simple look, the strength hidden in the grain of the fabric, the stress they can and cannot handle.

This card takes that strength of knowledge and cements it into being. Any item created by the crafter themselves will have seventy-five percent added to their magical effect in combat, be it offensive or defensive, as long as the crafter is the one to wield it.

"They said that poison could not defeat the tainted count. And I laughed. For did I not create this poison myself? Now, stab me and be done with it, you cretin, for you are already dead."]

[**Trail the Mirror's Edge**
Rare, Light/Dark crafter
Tier four
Active, long duration
Most cards focus on the effect, on improving the end result. This ignores the fact that most crafters focus not only on improving the end result, but also on finishing in a timely manner. With Trail the Mirror's Edge active, any Light or Dark enhancements will be completed forty percent faster. This is a dual card, working on more than one aspect.
Very long cooldown
"Any path traversed on the mirror, dark or bright side, can trail off endlessly. Trail the mirror's edge, though, and you will get there faster." The philosopher makes up vague crap to get his point across.]

[**Siphon the Source**
Rare, Elemental crafter
Tier four
Passive, permanent
The best crafters are those fully in touch with their aspects. Of course, a wind-aspected crafter performs better work when he is fully in tune with the wind itself. This card enables that connection, letting the crafter siphon connection, power, and inspiration from nearby pervasive presences of the aspect they are manipulating in their crafts. The stronger the presence, the greater the effect. The effect of the card will remain active, regardless whether you switch to another Tier four card.
"Sense it, boy. The rock around you. It steadies the hand, calms the mind. It sings, a tune to guide your mind." Elementalist-crafter Hibertus, explaining his craft.]

[**Touch Grass**
Uncommon, Fury crafter
Tier four
Active, medium duration
In many instances, the crafting itself isn't what matters, but the circumstances surrounding the crafting. An item crafted in wind and rain with a rotting tree stump for a table will inevitably be worse quality than one made in a warm house. This card allows you to sense, shape, and direct the soil and plants around you with a speed and efficacy depending on your Mental Power.

Long cooldown
"No crafting bench, dear? Ah, but nature provides. It always does."]

Sera:

[**Look Deeper**
Heart card (amplified)
Instant, short duration
With a mental activation, the card wielder can pit their Mental Power against anybody, disclosing information about them up to a maximum distance of twenty feet. The higher the difference in Mental Power, the more information is disclosed about a person's Step, class, current active effects and cards, even their attributes.
Medium cooldown
"Sire. I regret to inform you that this cad has used his Mental Nudge card to influence your decisions." A merchant loses his head.]

[**Blessing of the Night**
Epic, Dark healer
Tier one
Passive, long duration
Once tapped, any attribute increases on you and group members in range are further boosted. Any active Light card effects of nearby hostiles are reduced to a third, sometimes outright quelled.
Long cooldown
"You dare come into this, my domain, and challenge my superiority?" The king of Fury is brought low.]

[**Warmth of the Circle**
Rare, Light healer
Tier one
Active, instant
This healing card is not the most powerful of all heals, granting a medium effect heal. However, it has an exceedingly fast effect and leaves the recipient with a small boost to Toughness that has a medium duration.
Medium cooldown
"This sensation. There is a joy here, a lingering trace of something divine. I thank you, Priestess, for this gift."]

[**Tongues of Pride**
Uncommon, Elemental healer
Tier one

Active, long duration

Once tapped, this card grants two effects. A weak fiery layer comes into being, adding itself to your weapon, as well as any allies' weapons in range. You will have weak fire damage added to your attacks. Finally, it carries a minor cleanse ability, continually working against any lower-Tier poison or debuffs used on allies.

"You ask me to bring the heat? Really? That is ironic." A Plague Knight falters.]

[**Natural Decomposition**
Rare, Fury healer
Tier one
Active, variable duration

Over time, nature will break down anything. This card allows the wielder to target any enemy, who will see any active defensive effects up to Tier three break down. The time needed depends on the Tier of the effect and the Mental Power of the healer and the target. With matched Mental Power, Tier one is instant, Tier two takes fifteen seconds, while Tier three takes thirty seconds.

"Missed? My dear nemesis, I do not miss. Nature simply takes its time. Now, be kind enough to hurry and succumb."]

[**Cry for Blood**
Uncommon, Dark healer
Tier two
Active, short duration (effect instant)

Tap to place marker on a chosen enemy. If that enemy dies while under the influence of Cry for Blood, you drain his life force to be redirected to a place of your choosing as one of the following:
—One-person heal, instant.
—One-person physical shield, medium duration.
—One-person increase to Toughness, medium duration.

The effectiveness of any heals, shields, or increases is determined by the enemy's Toughness.

"Do not cry, love. You may die. But I will use your essence well."]

[**Spark of Divinity**
Uncommon, Light healer
Tier two
Passive, long duration

Sometimes, it is less about the power of the boost than the adaptability, being able to apply what you want and where. Tapping this card allows you to select an attribute. You can then select to either apply it to a single person for a medium increase to said attribute or your entire group for a small increase. Also, for the full duration of the boost, you may change your selection.

"Ah hah hah, Lord Agravon. You have grown stronger since last we met. Allow me a second to adjust. It would not do for me to fall behind."]

[**Unexpected Spillage**
Uncommon, Elemental healer
Tier two
Active, instant
A battlefield is like an ocean. The waves go low and high. Sometimes, they act exactly as expected. Sometimes, you find unexpected lulls and towering waves coming from out of nowhere. Upon activation of this card, the healer may transfer one hundred percent of the force of an incoming attack, magical or physical, made on the wielder or anybody grouped with the wielder, to another being within range of the card.
Short cooldown
"Stop hitting yourself. Oh, who am I kidding? By all means, keep it up!"]

[**Nature's Shield**
Uncommon, Fury healer
Tier two
Instant, medium duration
Part of a healer's job is taking care of damage. Yet, an even better approach is ensuring that the damage never happens in the first place. Some healers weaken enemies or shield their allies to ensure the damaging blows can never land. Yet, ensuring that the enemy never arrives in the first place is surely preferable to either approach. Upon activation of this card, the wielder calls upon nature to raise, shape, and place a few lengths of thorny underbrush. The height and toughness of the raised plants depend on the Mental Power of the healer.
"Oh, you're stuck? How sad. Maybe you shouldn't have tried to kill my friends!"]

[**Heart of Hearts**
Rare, Dark healer
Tier three
Passive, permanent
When equipped, this card takes that which your companions hold in their hearts and makes it stronger. Effects are dras-

tically increased, as are durations, while cooldowns may be reduced. Beware, however, that the card may also increase existing drawbacks to the use of Heart cards.

"You've always had the power, my dears; you just had to learn it for yourself. Also, I've nudged the power along a bit." Famous high priest of the Circle to his congregation.]

[**Mallet of the Ancients**
Uncommon, Light healer
Tier three
Passive, long duration
Activating this card summons the Mallet of the Ancients. A massive, magically enhanced, though not unbreakable, mallet that will circle the healer for the duration of the card, fending off attacks and striking against any enemies who come too close.
Long cooldown
"What do you mean, the whoppening? That is not a word. Now draw your weapon, you imbecile." Lord Actrus of Standale, seconds before the whoppening.]

[**The Flame Within**
Uncommon, Elemental healer
Tier three
Active, medium duration
This card will light a boosting fire within the healer. The benevolent flames of the fire will increase all attributes of the healer, growing in strength and effect for a full ten minutes before burning out.
Medium cooldown
"At the apex, there is a sensation of becoming...what I was supposed to be. Approaching the divine. As if I could reach out and touch it. Yet, you cannot touch this." Mareus Corex Hammer.]

[**Home Defender**
Rare, Fury healer
Tier three
Passive, permanent
Some people do not care about home. Others will take what they have and defend it to the last. This lets you designate an area with a one-mile radius for yourself, where you will always have the upper hand against any intruders. Inside that area, your attributes, except Potential, and the attributes of those allied with you, will be increased by +3.

The effect of the card will remain active, regardless whether you switch to another Tier three card. Once activated, you cannot establish a new home area for a full month.

"I was unaware the Wind-torn Healer lived here... Lads. I'm sorry. Put those weapons away. We're going home." A sergeant saves his men.]

<u>Reviews</u>

Anybody who's ever spent any time with me knows that I'm a simple creature. I prefer my beers liquid, my whiskey in a glass and my metal as extreme as humanly possible.

Yet, according to several police officers, I need to *pay* for my alcohol. The injustice!

You've already done your part to help me there, by buying my book or reading it on KU. I salute you. Now, if you're actually an angelic enough person that you're willing to help me more, (And of course you are, if you're reading the back matter, you absolute saint.) there is one thing.

Review mah book! Or somebody elses. Preferrably somebody amazing, like Rachel Ní Chuirc. Or Brian J. Nordon. Even Jez Cajiao's. Be sure to use long words – they confuse the hell out of him!

But seriously. That's the best piece of free aid you can give to writers like us. Review our books, tell the world exactly why you love them. We don't care about eloquence. But we do love you too!

Thank you so much.

-Lars

<u>Patreon!</u>

Okay then, now for those of you that don't know about Patreon, it's essentially a way to support your favorite Cheetos-smelling, sweatpants-wearing lunatics, otherwise known as writers. You can sign up for a day or a month or a year, and you get various benefits for it, ranging from my heartfelt thanks, to advance access to the books and art and more.

At the time of me writing this, the Patreon readers have access to the full final book of the World of Chains series, which is available nowhere else. Also, there will soon be entirely new series appearing. It will be... weird! Good weird!

<u>https://www.patreon.com/Moulder666</u>

Arise Alpha

By Jez Cajiao

When you steal a hundred grand from some very bad people, the best way to survive is to stay small and quiet...

Possibly its not to save a pair of drowning girls, not go 'viral' on social media and certainly not to let the local police take your passport, trapping you on a small 'party' island in the middle of the Mediterranean Sea.

But Steve isn't the average guy, he's ex-military, ex-enforcer and ex-human. He's a one-man nanite fueled nightmare for those that cross the line, and he's decided that it's time to clean up his act. He's going to make up for the things he's done, and save 'the little guys'.

It's a nice fantasy, but even he has to admit, it's really just a justification, because he's a very bad man, with horrifying abilities, and he's only just learning what he's capable of.

He needs a reason to not go to the dark, and if that's hunting down the creatures of the night and beating them to death with their own femurs?

Well, he's just the man for the job.

Stolen money. Greek Islands. Werewolves and Enforcers...
What could possibly go wrong?

https://mybook.to/AriseAlpha

Quest Academy

By Brian J. Nordon

A world infested by demons.
An Academy designed to train Heroes to save humanity from annihilation.
A new student's power could make all the difference.

Humans have been pushed to the brink of extinction by an ever-evolving demonic threat. Portals are opening faster than ever, Towers bursting into the skies and Dungeons being mined below the last safe havens of society. The demons are winning.

Quest Academy stands defiantly against them, as a place to train the next generation of Heroes. The Guild Association is holding the line, but are in dire need of new blood and the powerful abilities they could bring to the battlefront. To be the saviors that humanity needs, they need to surpass the limits of those that came before them.

In a war with everything on the line, every power matters. With an adaptive enemy, comes the need for a constant shift in tactics. A new age of strategy is emerging, with even the unlikeliest of Heroes making an impact.

Salvatore Argento has never seen a demon.
He has never aspired to become a Hero.
Yet his power might be the one to tip the odds in humanity's favor.

Buy on Amazon

<u>Wandering Warrior</u>

By Michael Head

***A divine quest to deliver justice.
One year to accomplish his mission.
After nineteen planets, there's something different about
this one.***

James Holden has reached the maximum level there is for a human. That's perfect, since he's the only one of his kind. A wandering warrior, without control of his destination, tossed between universes by gods who've failed to tell him why. James is the lone Judge on a new world in need of someone to balance the scales. He isn't afraid to do so with extreme prejudice. As the Chief Justice, he has to right the wrongs the innocent can't fix themselves.

As James quickly discovers, the roots of corruption run deep. Guilds choose to protect themselves rather than the people. Monsters roam the wilderness unchecked. Judgment is usually a decision between right and wrong, but nothing is ever that simple. This time, being the strongest human won't be enough to punish the guilty. James might have to recruit some new blood, even if he prefers to work alone.

On his twentieth world, he is going to win, no matter the cost. James will have to find a way to break past the limits of the system if he's going to have a chance at making a difference.

<u>Buy on Amazon</u>

<u>WELCOME TO THE DARK AGES</u>

Morgan and Merlins excellent Adventures
Book One
By
Malory

When Merlin needs a hero to save the world, he gets... well, me.

Fan-bloody-tastic.

I was supposed to be dead. Instead, I wake up face-down in Dark Age mud, possessing some poor bastard's body, while the ghost of history's most famous wizard rambles on about being murdered, cosmic energy and the end of all reality.

Just one tiny problem: I know about as much about cultivation as a pig knows about particle physics.

Now I'm fumbling with mystical energy that feels like juggling nitroglycerin, trying not to get shanked by everyone and their grandmother, and dealing with Merlin's constant "helpful" commentary.

Something dark is rising in Arthurian Britain.

Something that made even Merlin scared. They say fate has a sense of humour. Turns out it's the kind that laughs while setting your hair on fire.

Welcome to the Dark Ages, where cultivation meets chaos, and the only thing sharper than a sword is my questionable wit.

<u>Read Now!</u>

<u>Knights of Eternity</u>

By Rachel Ní Chuirc

When Zara awoke in chains she thought she'd gone mad.

She was Zara the Fury - mistress of flame and fear. Her name was whispered across the land, from ramshackle taverns to the royal court. Even the heroic Gilded Knights thought twice before crossing her path.
She was feared—*respected*.
Now she was curled up on a dirt floor on her fiancé's orders. Valerius, leader of the Gilded, mocks her cries for help. And the kingdom is on the brink of war over the missing Lady Eternity...
But that wasn't why Zara thought she had gone mad.
The reason why is that the last thing she remembered was blood, an arcade screen, and the gun that changed everything.

But no chains can hold the Fury, and when she gets out?
The world is going to *burn*.

<u>Buy on Amazon</u>

<u>Scarlet Citadel</u>

By Jack Fields

Gormon Hughes is 19, thin as a broom, and has—not for the first time in his life—been swept into the path of trouble. Poor, recently heartbroken, and indebted to the sort of people who file their teeth into needle points and devour wriggling bloated spiders for fun, Hughes sets his sights on salvation.

That salvation is the Scarlet Citadel, a wealthy organization of pageant fighters, monster hunters, and secret keepers. With the aid of strange oracles, rare good fortune, and a unique power that bubbles like champagne in the core of Hughes' being, he must join the Citadel and advance himself.

But the ladder of progression is harsh and dark. The rungs are slippery.

And falling means disaster...

<u>Buy on Amazon</u>

Facebook and Social Media

If you want to reach out, chat or just tell me my book was horrible, you can always find me on either my author page here:

https://www.facebook.com/groups/357145749698735/

OR

Legion recently set up a new Facebook group to spread the word about cool LitRPG books. It's dedicated to two very simple rules;

1: Let's spread the word about new and old brilliant LitRPG books.
2: Don't be a Dick!

They sound like really simple rules, but you'd be amazed...

Come join us!

https://www.facebook.com/groups/LITRPGLegion

I'm also on Discord here: **https://discord.gg/gyRkEgesH5**

In short, hit me up. I'd love to chat!

<u>Legion</u>

This is my first series with the Legion Publishers! It's run by Christine Cajiao and Geneva Agnos, who are also kind enough to let Jez Cajiao prance around in his underwear, where he can hurt nobody else.

It has, so far, been an absolutely enjoyable experience. You are welcome to reach out and ask if things have changed since I wrote this, of course. My safe word is **Jez is the nicest person in the world.**

They're taking on new authors, as we speak. So, don't be afraid to reach out.

Apart from being good people, I like that they have everything out in the open. Their contracts aren't hidden behind layers of legalese, you can find them here:

<u>https://www.legionpublishers.com/legioncontract</u>

If you want to reach out and ask any questions, get an idea of the support they offer, and possibly become part of the family? Just tap the link and fill in the form:

<u>https://www.legionpublishers.com/contact-and-sub-missions</u>

<u>Recommendations</u>

I'm often asked for personal recommendations, so if this book has whetted your appetite for more LitRPG, please have a look at the following, these are brilliant series by brilliant authors!

The Ten Realms by Michael Chatfield

Wandering Inn by Pirateaba

The Daily Grind by Argus

Quest Academy by Brian J. Nordon

Wandering Warrior by Michael Head

Calamity by Rachel Ni Chuirc

Codename: Freedom by Apollos Thorne

God of the Feast by Kevin Sinclair

Rise of Mankind by Jez Cajiao

LITRPG!

To learn more about LitRPG, talk to other authors including myself, and to just have an awesome time, please join the LitRPG Group

www.facebook.com/groups/LitRPGGroup

Facebook

There's also a few really active Facebook groups I'd recommend you join, as you'll get to hear about great new books, new releases and interact with all your (new) favorite authors! (I may also be there, skulking at the back and enjoying the memes...)

https://www.facebook.com/groups/LitRPGlegion/

https://www.facebook.com/groups/GamelitSociety

https://www.facebook.com/groups/LitRPG.books

https://www.facebook.com/groups/LitRPGforum/

www.ingramcontent.com/pod-product-compliance
Lightning Source LLC
Chambersburg PA
CBHW060754210726
48292CB00013B/107